INFINITE
STARS

ANTHOLOGIES AVAILABLE FROM TITAN BOOKS

INFINITE STARS

THE DEFINITIVE ANTHOLOGY OF SPACE OPERA AND MILITARY SF

Edited by
BRYAN THOMAS SCHMIDT

TITAN BOOKS

INFINITE STARS
Print edition ISBN: 9781785655937
Electronic edition ISBN: 9781785654596
Paperback ISBN: 9781785654589

Published by Titan Books
A division of Titan Publishing Group Ltd
144 Southwark Street, London SE1 0UP

First edition: October 2017
2 4 6 8 10 9 7 5 3 1

Did you enjoy this book?
We love to hear from our readers. Please email us at
readerfeedback@titanemail.com or write to us at
Reader Feedback at the above address.

TITAN BOOKS.COM

To Bob Tucker for coining the term, and E.E. Smith, Jack Williamson, and Edmond Hamilton for paving the way, and George Lucas for helping me and so many fall in love with space opera.

And to Bob Silverberg, whose Lord Valentine's Castle *made teenage me want to write novels, and whose friendship and support of adult me means so much.*

Lastly, for my cousin David Melson, who introduced me to Star Wars: A New Hope *and books like* Ender's Game *that led to genres that have been lifelong loves.*

CONTENTS

EDITOR'S NOTE AND ACKNOWLEDGEMENTS
BRYAN THOMAS SCHMIDT

In so many ways, space opera has been my entry gate into speculative fiction. From the *Star Trek* reruns and the original *Star Wars* movie, which made me want to be a storyteller, to my own first novels, a space opera series *The Saga of Davi Rhii*, I have probably read more in this subgenre of science fiction than any other. So assembling a definitive collection like this was a particular thrill.

It also allowed me to work with some of my writing heroes and favorites. Who thought I'd ever edit an original Ender story by Orson Scott Card, or a *Dune* story? Or publish Leigh Brackett and Edmond Hamilton, Larry Niven, and Jerry Pournelle, or Lois McMaster Bujold. All those dreams and more were realized with this volume, so I hope you enjoy reading it as much as I did putting it together.

There are fourteen new stories and ten reprints here. Most of them from popular space opera and military science fiction series spanning the decades from the 1950s to the present. These include Hugo and Nebula Award winners, *New York Times* bestsellers, and more. When Titan editor Steve Saffel and I met at the World Science Fiction Convention in Spokane, Washington, to discuss working on a project and he proposed this, I knew it was the chance of a lifetime.

And it has been, in every way, so here's hoping it's the read of a lifetime, too. Admittedly, there are gaps. James S.A. Corey's stories were tied up with SyFy Channel, for example. Others were hindered by availability, space, and budget, but hopefully will show up in future volumes. I also used a somewhat broad definition of space opera which includes a few stories from closely related subgenres such as "sword and planet." The crossover is obvious, and the genres have influenced one another such that many stories cross over, and authors frequently slide between them.

For many readers, military science fiction and space opera are indistinguishable, but I tend to define the latter as being more focused on military infrastructure, rank and file, strategy, and war-related activites than space opera often is. Regardless of such distinctions, the two are intimately intertwined, and the intent here is to represent definitive stories that influenced these subgenres—and science fiction as a whole—both then and now. I hope most readers will agree with the significance of my choices.

This book wouldn't have been possible without a lot of support, and here are a few to whom I must express my gratitude: fellow editors Gardner Dozois, Rich Horton, Steven Silver, Alex Shvartsman, and Robin Wayne Bailey for story suggestions. Fellow fans Charley and Linda McCue, Ken Keller, Mia Kleve, Peter J. Wacks, and Todd McCaffrey for their suggestions. Eugene Johnson and Carol Hightshoe for retyping stories from old sources. And of course, Steve Saffel and all at Titan Books for the opportunity.

My cousin David Melson gets credit for taking me to *Star Wars*, a truly life-changing moment at age seven or eight. I've been addicted ever since. And for sharing so many wonderful books and stories, like introducing me to *Ender*, *Dune*, and more.

I thank my friend and writing hero, Robert Silverberg, for a great introduction essay, and all the writers for being so dedicated to writing memorable stuff that would enhance the canons and entertain the fans of each universe included here. Last but not least, thank you to the readers, collectors, and fans who will make this book—the first of a series, we hope—a success and enjoy it for years to come.

Without further ado, I am pleased to present *Infinite Stars*, a rich tapestry of space opera and adventure. May it inspire you to imagine, dream, and reach for the stars well into the future.

Bryan Thomas Schmidt
Ottawa, KS
January 2017

SPACE OPERA: AN INTRODUCTION
ROBERT SILVERBERG

"Birth, and copulation, and death," said T.S. Eliot. "That's all, that's all, that's all." The critic Damon Knight, in one of the finest of his incisive essays on science fiction, simplified Eliot's formula by eliminating copulation from the sequence and asserting that the only important themes of fiction are birth and death. Maybe so. I would not want to dispute these things with Messrs. Eliot and Knight, for whose critical acumen I have the highest respect.

As a science fiction reader and writer, though, I have worked from a different set of criteria: the two fundamental themes of science fiction, I think, are journeys in time and journeys in space. We have been dealing in matters of time travel since H.G. Wells set us on that path with *The Time Machine* more than a hundred years ago. And as for space, well, we have had fictional voyages into space at least since the time of Lucian of Samosata, who lived in the second century AD and who, in his satiric fantasy *The True History*, sent his party of travelers flying off to the Moon. Since then, many another fictional voyager has gone into space, of course, even Cyrano de Bergerac (in a wonderfully wacky seventeenth-century tale), but in the twentieth century there developed a special subgenre of the space-voyage theme that we know as *space opera*.

Space opera has been defined in a variety of ways. One good definition came from Jack Williamson, who as an early master of the genre knew whereof he spoke. Writing in *The New Encyclopedia of Science Fiction* in 1992, Williamson called it "romantic adventure set in space and told on a grand scale," emphasizing that it was concerned primarily with "the mythic thread of human expansion." For Williamson, born in Arizona in 1908 before Arizona had achieved statehood, and brought to New Mexico a few years later by covered wagon, it was an easy imaginative jump from the settlement of the American West to mankind's colonization of the galaxy.

Most other definitions of space opera have stressed the necessity of interstellar travel as an essential aspect of the form: starships, faster-than-light travel, galactic empires, the nearly god-like ability to move at will through the immeasurable vastnesses of the universe. A common feature, also, is violent conflict: the war of good against evil, the use of super-weapons, blasters, energy beams, disintegrators. There are some who would include fictions of a less cosmic sort in the genre: the novels of Edgar Rice Burroughs, for example, that tell of the adventures of John Carter on Mars among alien beings of various colors and shapes. Other students of the field dismiss these as "planetary romances," limiting space opera to galaxy-spanning tales that readily move beyond the confines of our solar system. Be that as it may, we can safely say that space opera is a subset of science fiction, romantic and colorful, that lays its main stress on the wonders and marvels of the distant realms of space. In its range it has included all manner of work from the most crude and juvenile of early science fiction to the complex and thought-provoking novels and stories of modern times.

The term itself was coined by Wilson ("Bob") Tucker, an early science fiction fan who was employed as a projectionist in Illinois movie theaters, though he later wrote some superb science fiction novels. In 1941 Tucker proposed "space opera," by analogy with "soap opera" (popular serialized radio shows, romantic and sentimental, most often sponsored by manufacturers of soap products), out of which had come "horse opera" (Hollywood jargon for low-budget Western movies), to mean what he called the "hacky, grinding, stinking, outworn spaceship yarn"—a phrase that has gone ringing down the decades.

The kinship between crude space opera of the sort churned out by hack writers for cheap pulp magazines and the formularized horse operas produced by the movie industry in such vast numbers in the 1930s and 1940s was never more clearly set forth than in an advertisement written by H.L. Gold, the brilliant, cantankerous editor of the superb science fiction magazine *Galaxy*, for the back cover of *Galaxy*'s first issue, which appeared in the fall of 1950. Under the heading "YOU'LL NEVER SEE IT IN GALAXY," Gold offered the opening paragraphs of two short stories, set side by side in parallel columns.

"Jets blasting, Bat Durston came screeching down through the atmosphere of Bblizznaj, a tiny planet seven billion light years from Sol," is the way the column on the left-hand side of the page began. "He cut out his super-hyper drive for the landing... and at that point, a tall, lean spaceman stepped out of the tail assembly, proton gun blaster in a space-tanned hand.

"'Get back from those controls, Bat Durston', the tall stranger lipped thinly. 'You don't know it, but this is your last space trip.'"

The right-hand paragraph offered this:

"Hoofs drumming, Bat Durston came galloping down through the narrow pass at Eagle Gulch, a tiny gold colony 400 miles north of Tombstone. He spurred hard for a low overhang of rock... and at that point a tall, lean wrangler stepped out from behind a high boulder, six-shooter in a sun-tanned hand.

"'Rear back and dismount, Bat Durston', the tall stranger lipped thinly. 'You don't know it, but this is your last saddle jaunt through these here parts.'"

Gold then went on to point out that the first story was simply a Western transplanted to an alien planet. "If this is your idea of science fiction," he said, "you're welcome to it. YOU'LL NEVER SEE IT IN *GALAXY*." And he kept his promise throughout his years as the magazine's editor, bringing his readers such sophisticated science fiction as Alfred Bester's *The Demolished Man*, Isaac Asimov's *The Stars Like Dust*, and the original version of Ray Bradbury's *Fahrenheit 451*.

But even in *Galaxy* the line between space opera and more sophisticated science fiction was hard to draw, as could be seen in such complex works as the Asimov novel, Alfred Bester's second book, *The Stars My Destination* (which can be viewed as a translation of *The Count of Monte Cristo* into science-fictional terms), and Robert A. Heinlein's furiously paced tale of alien invasion, *The Puppet Masters*, all of which Gold published. They could be considered space operas too. Obviously Wilson Tucker had intended the term "space opera" to be a pejorative one, describing the worst sort of science fiction, but most science fiction readers, Tucker included, quickly adopted a broader meaning for it, using it to represent not just the sort of dreary, clumsy pulp fiction typical of the host of cheaply produced pulp magazines that had sprung up just before World War II but also the wide-ranging, powerfully imaginative stories of galactic exploration, more carefully written, that had long held their place in the affections of science fiction readers.

Plenty of space operas both good and bad had been written by the time Tucker coined his immortal phrase, and the best of them have become classics of the field, antiquated in style and technique but ably depicting the scope and grandeur of the immense universe and still giving pleasure to readers nearly a century after they first appeared. E.E. Smith's *The Skylark of Space*, for example, written in 1915 but not published until 1928, tells a story that modern readers can only regard as preposterous, but tells it with such vigor and gusto that such readers, if they are willing to make allowances for the novel's adherence to the stylistic norms of magazine fiction of a century ago, can find it an enjoyable period piece. As one reviewer said of Smith's work in general when his novels were reissued in book form in the 1940s, it is marked by "incredible heroes, unbelievable weapons, insurmountable obstacles, inconceivable science, omnipotent villains, and unimaginable cataclysms." That is virtually the complete catalog of ingredients characteristic of the prototypical kind of space opera Tucker was writing about. Even so, despite having been forced into the Procrustean modes of old-time magazine entertainment, those ingredients retain a certain power to this day.

In *Skylark of Space*, we see Smith getting his story off to the sort of dynamic start that was *de rigueur* for the form from the beginning:

"Petrified with astonishment, Richard Seaton stared after the copper steam bath upon which, a moment before, he had been electrolyzing his solution of 'X', the unknown metal. For as soon as he had removed the beaker, with its precious contents, the heavy bath had jumped endwise from under his hand as though it were alive. It had flown with terrific speed over the table, smashing a dozen reagent bottles on its way, and was even now disappearing through the open window."

The intrepid Seaton learns how to employ X, the inadvertently discovered catalyst that releases the atomic energy of copper, not just to create a flying steam bath but to power a spaceship that will take him and an assortment of appropriate sidekicks on a cosmic odyssey across the galaxy, pursued, of course, by a villainous rival scientist in the pay of the evil Steel Trust that wants to steal Seaton's secrets. But Smith was just warming up. After three Skylark novels he produced the six-book Lensman series (1934–1950), portraying the cosmic struggle between the wise and benevolent race of Arisians and the wholly evil Eddorians for control of the universe. The Arisians have created a Galactic Patrol to wage war against the Eddorians. Members of the Patrol are provided with the Lens, a bracelet that gives them telepathy and other powers. The main protagonist of these books is the dynamic square-jawed Earthman Kimball Kinnison, who can be considered the sheriff of this group of space operas; but whereas the Western story was populated almost entirely by white men, Kinnison works in collaboration with three alien life-forms, Worsel of Velantia, Tregonsee of Rigel Four, and Nadreck of Palain. It is very much as though a sheriff were rounding up the bad guys with the aid of a Navaho, a Comanche, and, perhaps, a Chinese. Off they go from world to world, doing battle with the Eddorians and their puppets wherever they turn up. It is all gloriously silly, and Smith's prose style is something less than elegant, but the books still make irresistible reading after all this time.

Just about as popular a purveyor of space opera in the 1930s was Jack Williamson, who made his mark with the classic *The Legion of Space* in 1934. This novel, serialized in the appropriately named magazine *Astounding Stories*, involves the adventures of a quartet of heroes whose task it is to protect the guardian of a doomsday weapon known as AKKA and prevent it, and her, from falling into the hands of hostile alien beings, the Medusae, who will use it against us. Williamson's main man is lean, rangy John Ulnar, later known as John Star, whom we meet as a new member of the Legion of Space, the Solar System's peacekeeping force. When Aladoree Anthar, the young and beautiful guardian of AKKA, is abducted by the aliens, John Star must travel to far-off Barnard's Star to rescue her, accompanied by three fellow legionnaires, Jay Kalam, Hal Samdu, and the roguish, Falstaffian Giles Habibula, who is the only character anyone remembers after reading the book. ("'Dear life— not now!' gasped Giles Habibula. 'Not into that wicked thing they call the Belt of Peril!… Sweet life, not yet,' sobbed Giles Habibula. "Give us time, Jay, for a single sip of wine! You couldn't be so heartless, Jay—not to a poor old soldier of the Legion…'")

These four, after much anguish, fight their way grimly across the nightmarish jungle of the Medusae's home world, rescue the fair Aladoree and save the world from its alien enemies, but not without leaving room for two sequels. Along the way, John Star falls in love with the delectable Aladoree and marries her. Williamson, who lived on into the 21st century, produced many another space opera, and plenty of more complex science fiction as well, in the course of a distinguished 75-year career that saw him designated a Grand Master by the Science Fiction Writers of America.

The third of the great pioneering figures of space opera, and the most prolific, was Edmond Hamilton, who was writing epics of the Interstellar Patrol years before Williamson had brought us his Legion of Space and Smith the Galactic Patrol. Hamilton first staked his claim to eminence in the genre with *Crashing Suns*, serialized in *Weird Tales* in 1928. Though primarily dedicated to fantasy and tales of the supernatural (it was the primary magazine publisher of H.P. Lovecraft and Robert E. Howard) it ventured frequently into science fiction also in its earliest years, much of it the work of Hamilton. In *Crashing Suns* a star is on a collision course with our sun, threatening to create a "titanic holocaust" in which the planets of the Solar System will "perish like flowers in a furnace," and must be deflected somehow by the gallant men of the Interstellar Patrol. "As the control-levers flashed down under my hands our ship dived down through space with the swiftness of thought," is how Hamilton begins the first of his many space epics. "The next instant there came a jarring shock, and our craft spun over like a whirling top." And so it goes as our patrolmen—Hal Kur, Jan Tor, Hurus Hol, and the rest—zoom back and forth across the galaxy at hundreds of times the speed of light until the tentacled aliens who are causing the trouble have been overcome and the sun has been saved.

Having begun his series with such glorious melodrama, Hamilton had no choice but to keep upping the ante for the Interstellar Patrol in the next few years. The names of his novels tell the tale: *The Star Stealers, Within the Nebula, Outside the Universe, The Cosmic Cloud*, and, eventually, in the 1930s *The Universe Wreckers* (misnamed, actually, since it is only our solar system, once again, that is threatened by destruction.) Hamilton never created characters as memorable as E.E. Smith's four Lensmen or Williamson's Giles Habibula—it is hard to tell his monosyllabically named Jhul Dins and Dur Nals apart— but his novels go beyond theirs in their picture of the grandeur and color of the distant worlds he invents.

Some years after his Interstellar Patrol days, it was Hamilton who created the Captain Future series—a kind of comic book in prose that very likely was on Wilson Tucker's mind when he described space opera as "hacky, grinding, stinking, outworn." *Captain Future* was the name of a quarterly pulp magazine launched in 1940 that featured in each issue a novel by Hamilton telling of the adventures of the eponymous hero "Captain Future," Curt Newton, also known as "the Wizard of Science," who, of course, was supplied with the proper set of comic-book companions—Grag, a giant metal robot, Otho, a synthetic android, and Simon Wright, a disembodied brain housed within a plastic case. This quartet travels from world to world, dealing with crises far and wide in a manner similar to that of the team aboard the starship *Enterprise* of *Star Trek*, for which the Captain Future stories may well have served as a prototype. Hamilton, like Jack Williamson, lived on into the modern era of science fiction, and, like him, eventually moved away from the frenetic tropes of early space opera toward a quieter, more mature type of story that nevertheless demonstrated science fiction's ability to convey the wonder of galactic space that had been the hallmark of his storytelling skill since the days of *Crashing Suns*.

Such writers as Smith, Williamson, and Hamilton—and there were dozens of others in the olden days, Homer Eon Flint (*The Lord of Death*), J.U. Giesy (*Palos of the Dog Star Pack*), Ralph Milne Farley (*The Radio Man*), Garrett P. Serviss (*A Columbus of Space*) and many more, all but forgotten today—provided what we can regard today as guilty pleasures. As Brian W. Aldiss put it in an essay on space opera in 1974, "Its parameters are marked by a few mighty concepts standing like a watchtower along a lonely frontier. What goes on between them is essentially simple—a tale of love or hate, triumph or defeat—because it is the watchtowers that matter. We are already familiar with some of them, the question of reality, the limitations of knowledge, exile, the sheer immensity of the universe, the endlessness of time."

All through the 1930s and 1940s science fiction writers, particularly those who specialized in space opera, had been almost exclusively male. But along the way two conspicuous exceptions arose among all those men and between them brought about a revolution in the writing of this kind of science fiction.

The first was Catherine Lucille Moore, who, concealing herself behind the epicene byline of "C.L. Moore," gave no indication that she was female and left many readers with quite the opposite belief. Beginning with "Shambleau" for *Weird Tales* in 1933 and continuing on through the entire decade of the 1930s, she produced a series of stories that made use of the formulas of space opera but embedded them in a supple, elegant prose that pulp-magazine readers had never seen before. They were set on Mars or Venus, mainly. Her chief protagonist was an adventurer called Northwest Smith, who seemed to have wandered into those worlds out of the American West.

But it was not the Mars and Venus of astronomers where Northwest Smith roamed; they were exotic, mysterious worlds that owed something to the Orient of Somerset Maugham and Joseph Conrad, and much to Moore's own fervid imagination. ("Northwest Smith leant his head back against the warehouse wall and stared up into the black night sky of Venus. The waterfront street was very quiet tonight, very dangerous. He could hear no sound save the eternal slap-slap of water against the piles, but he knew how much of danger and sudden death dwelt here in the breathing dark, and he may have been a little homesick as he stared up into the clouds that masked a green star hanging lovely on the horizon— Earth and home.") No one had ever seen science fiction like that in 1934, and there has been little of its kind since. Eventually Moore abandoned Northwest Smith, but her later work, such as the 1943 novel *Judgment Night*, retained the vivid sensuality of the early stories while moving away from the more formulaic aspects of space-opera technique.

The year 1940 saw the debut of a second gifted female writer of space stories who, like Moore, made use of a gender-free byline in the pulp magazines whose readership, and authorship as well, had been nearly entirely male. This was Leigh Brackett, whose first story, "Martian Quest," immediately established her as one who paid as much heed to matters of style and mood and characterization as she did to the romance and exoticism of space opera. Though she spent much of her career in the movie industry (she and William Faulkner worked together on the screenplay for the 1946 Humphrey Bogart film *The Big Sleep*, and thirty years later she was one of the writers of the screenplay for the second Star Wars movie, *The Empire Strikes Back*), she remained loyal to the pulp magazines as well, most notably with a series of stories set on Mars and dealing with the exploits of an adventurer named Eric John Stark, a literary descendant, perhaps, of Moore's Northwest Smith. ("The ship moved slowly across the Red Sea, through the shrouding veils of mist, her sail barely filled by the languid thrust of the wind. Her hull, of a thin light metal, floated without sound, the surface of the strange ocean parting before her prow in silent rippling streamers of flame. Night deepened toward the ship, a river of indigo flowing out of the west. The man known as Stark stood alone by the afterrail and watched its coming. He was full of impatience and a gathering sense of danger, so that it seemed to him that even the hot wind smelled of it.") Brackett's prose, like Moore's, was sinuous and vivid, richly colored and appealing powerfully to all the senses. She employed it, like Moore also, in the service of the rugged themes that we regard as those of space opera. One of her last stories, written not long before her death in 1978, was a Stark tale written in collaboration with her husband, no less a space-opera titan than Edmond Hamilton, whom she had married in 1946.

Impelled by writers like Moore and Brackett, and by other newcomers like Ray Bradbury, A.E. van Vogt, James Blish, Jack Vance, Henry Kuttner (who married C.L. Moore in 1940 and collaborated fruitfully with her thereafter), Cordwainer Smith, and Poul Anderson, the space story, like science fiction in general, began to undergo an evolution in the late 1940s and 1950s. The infelicities of style, the scientific impossibilities, the melodramatic confrontations between noble heroism and black villainy, all the hallmarks of the pioneers of the genre, gave way to a subtler, more adult, kind of work. And so "space opera" ceased to be the pejorative term that Wilson Tucker had meant it to be. It was understood now to be something much more than the Captain Future stories: it became simply one subdivision of science fiction, one kind of story, as variable in quality as any other specialized type of story can be. And some years later space opera would move beyond the science fiction magazines into the mainstream of American entertainment, most notably with the television show *Star Trek* and then with the series of *Star Wars* motion pictures, both of which were solidly grounded in the concepts and manner of true space opera. And today space opera, with no Tuckeresque negative connotations attached, has become the province of some of the most creative and imaginative of science fiction writers.

That transformation was well illustrated by several modern collections, such as *The New Space Opera*, edited by Jonathan Strahan and Gardner Dozois, published in 2007 and including work by such modern notables of the field as Nancy Kress, Stephen Baxter, Peter F. Hamilton, and Alastair Reynolds. And in 2006, when David Hartwell and Kathryn Cramer produced a massive anthology called *The Space Opera Renaissance* that covered the entire span of the literature from its beginnings under Edmond Hamilton and Jack Williamson to such modern practitioners as Samuel R. Delany, Gregory Benford, and Ursula K. Le Guin, the editors were able to offer this redefinition, which stands as well as any as a summation of what the term "space opera" has meant and what it signifies today:

"Many readers and writers and nearly all academics and media fans who entered SF after 1975 have never understood the origin of 'space opera' as a pejorative and some may be surprised to learn of it. Thus the term 'space opera' reentered the serious discourse on contemporary SF in the 1980s with a completely altered meaning. Henceforth, 'space opera' meant, and still generally means, colorful, dramatic, large-scale adventure, competently and sometimes beautifully written, usually focused on a sympathetic, heroic central character and plot action... and usually set in the relatively distant future and in space or on other worlds, characteristically optimistic in tone."

The days of E.E. Smith and Edmond Hamilton are far behind us. But space opera lives on, however evolved and transformed it may now be, continuing to call forth the efforts of the best of our writers and to hold the attention of a multitude of readers who seek that wonder-laden view of the farthest galaxies and of the centuries to come that science fiction, and only science fiction, is capable of providing.

In 1977, Orson Scott Card burst onto the science fiction field with a novella in Analog Science Fiction and Fact that would launch an empire. "Ender's Game" later expanded into a novel which spawned a whole series of sequels, won the 1985 Nebula Award and 1986 Hugo Award for "Best Novel." It has been recommended reading by the US Marine Corp for soldiers at many ranks, and it was made into a film starring Harrison Ford in 2013. The latest spinoff series, Fleet School, debuts in 2017, and this story is the first appearance in print of its protagonist, Dabeet Ochoa. It also stars Ender and Valentine Wiggin, and is a bit of a murder mystery in colonial space written just for this book. Our adventure begins with...

RENEGAT

ORSON SCOTT CARD

Dabeet Ochoa was surprised that the speaker for the dead came so soon, but apparently he had already been en route to Catalunya, for reasons that were apparently none of Dabeet's business. Yet Dabeet was proconsul of Starways Congress here—in effect, governor—so everything on Catalunya was supposed to be his business.

He made the decision to meet the speaker at the shuttleport before he was aware that he was considering such a gesture of respect. He knew himself well enough to know that part of his motive had to be a bit of bureaucratic resentment and dread that there would now be, in this colony, a person who had secrets, a person who had protection from Congress or the Fleet that trumped his own. Dabeet put those feelings in the compartment of his mind where he kept his painful self-knowledge. He would be constantly aware of those feelings, so he could guard himself against acting upon them.

There were other reasons that did not need to be hidden from others, however. The obvious one was that it was Dabeet Ochoa himself who had summoned a speaker—*a* speaker, not this one, but that's how speaking for the dead worked. You called, and the nearest one came. No choosing. No doubt this speaker would not even realize what a mark of honor it was for him to come and greet a visitor in person.

Dabeet decided to come without an open bodyguard. No need to advertise the precariousness of lawful government in the colony of Tarragona. He would tell this speaker soon enough about the seething unrest that the speaker's coming was meant to help allay. Meanwhile, Dabeet had two I.F. marines in plain clothes hovering within ten meters, in case some kind of emergency arose.

At first, Dabeet did not realize that the unprepossessing young man with only one bag was the speaker—especially because he was accompanied by a woman of about the same age—maybe twenty-five?—who had not been mentioned in the dispatches Dabeet had received by ansible. A wife? It was hard for itinerant speakers to marry and raise a family; Dabeet had read up on this semi-monastic order before he called for a speaker to come to the planet Catalunya, and he knew that most speakers who married did so when they took themselves off the circuit and settled near a large urban area on a long-civilized world, where they would have plenty of work to do and yet their children could grow up in the same neighborhood through their entire education.

Once he realized that no one else could possibly be the speaker for the dead, Dabeet strode toward him, lifting his hand in the single-fist salute of the Exploratory Service. The young man saw him, smiled slightly, and nodded in recognition. He did *not* raise his own fist—showing that he understood the protocol. Speakers were, by definition, not part of the I.F. or the E.S. or MinCol or any other organization. No saluting, no bowing, no accommodation to local custom, unless it happened to coincide with their own personal custom. Which, in this case, appeared to be a handshake, since the speaker's hand came forward as Dabeet came near.

It was not until they were grasping hands that, with a dizzy rush of understanding, Dabeet realized that he actually knew this young man—though he had no business being so young.

"I know you," said Dabeet, not yet daring to say the name that had come into his mind, though he did not doubt his own memory—he had never had to doubt his own memory.

"Do you?" asked the speaker.

"We had a conversation by ansible once," said Dabeet.

"How remarkable. It must have been before you came to Catalunya, Governor Ochoa, because your request for a speaker was the first communication I had ever received from this planet."

Dabeet stored this information: The speaker had been coming to Catalunya, and yet he had never received any communication from here. Why, then, was he coming?

The young woman joined the conversation, also with a handshake. "My name is Valentine," she said. "I'm his older sister and, from time to time, his conscience."

"I rarely find that I need one," said the speaker, causing Valentine to chuckle.

"I'm a historian," said Valentine. "I have all the top clearances from MinCol and the I.F., and so I would appreciate being given access to all the documents of the Tarragona colony."

Dabeet smiled. "Oh, surely a historian has little interest in our tedious little colony. It's our predecessor, the rogue colony of Fancy, back in the days when this world was called Whydah, that most researchers are interested in."

"What you say is correct, but it doesn't apply to me. There are already a dozen reasonably good histories of Fancy. I'm here for Tarragona. I'm here for Kenneth Argon."

Again, Dabeet felt himself inwardly reeling with surprise. "Miss—Doctor? Professor?—Valentine, surely you know that Kenneth Argon is dead."

"Since it's Argon's death you invited me here to speak," said her brother, "that fact could not possibly have escaped her."

"Ken wrote very little," said Dabeet. "I'm surprised you would think him worth writing about. Because—forgive me if I presume too much—it seems to me that you were already coming here for Kenneth Argon *before* I asked for someone to speak his death."

Valentine smiled cheerfully. "Very good," she said. "Yes, I thought he might be worth a biography. So much easier to do when he was alive. And my brother consented, for once, to let *me* choose the itinerary, since Catalunya was isolated and strange and would doubtless have no shortage of dead people for him to study and speak for."

"Isolated enough that there has never been a speaker for the dead here," said Dabeet. "But let's stop entertaining the locals with our conversation. I have a hover waiting outside the terminal, which is the most comfortable transportation available in our rather spartan colony."

"You say 'spartan,'" said Valentine as they began walking, "but I hope you have plenty of retail establishments. I travel without luggage, because I prefer to buy my clothing locally, so I'm not so obviously a stranger on the streets."

"There are a few retail clothing stores, but they sell clothes for working people. You might think that's a good thing, but from your speech and your profession, Doctor Valentine, it will make you seem condescending and false. You have money and status, and should dress according to your station, here in Tarragona."

"Surely there's not a uniform," said the speaker, with an arched eyebrow.

"There are uniforms everywhere," said Dabeet, "at every level of society, and none are so rigorously required as those which pretend not to be uniforms."

The speaker laughed out loud. "Well observed, sir."

They took only a few moments to enter the hover, because Valentine had no luggage and the speaker would not let his single bag out of his possession. "It's a diplomatic pouch," the speaker explained, with some appearance of embarrassment. "I don't let it out of my personal possession."

Of course Dabeet was curious about why a speaker for the dead would be carrying diplomatic correspondence—and why his entire suitcase would be given the highest security Starways Congress had to offer. But then, if this speaker was the person that Dabeet believed him to be—and he was, he *certainly* was—it might make a kind of sense. If there was anyone to whom Starways Congress owed extraordinary privileges, it was this astonishingly young man.

"I remember you now," said the speaker, once the hover was sealed shut and began the journey. "We talked by ansible when we were both children."

Dabeet shook his head. "We were young and small, sir, but we were never children."

The speaker smiled. "Perhaps so, considering the responsibilities thrust upon us at such an early age. But we were also sequestered to such a degree that we were even younger than our ages, knowing little of human society outside of the military schools we attended."

"They shaped our reality however they wished," said Dabeet. "And we made all our decisions surrounded by their arcane mysteries."

"*We* shape reality now," said Valentine.

"Dabeet Ochoa," said the speaker. "I should have recognized your name. But Ochoa isn't a rare name, and I don't remember if 'Dabeet' was written anywhere."

"It wasn't," said Dabeet. "But I hope that you'll use that name, and dispense with the title of 'governor,' since my primary goal in life is to get rid of that title."

"I know the feeling," said the speaker. "When we spoke by ansible, I was on my way to my first stint as governor of a colony."

"I remember wondering whether being who you are would make that task easier or harder, considering your age at the time," said Dabeet.

"Isn't relativity wonderful?" asked Valentine. "We still look barely older than children, since we've spent most of the last five hundred years near lightspeed, skipping through the years without letting them leave many tracks on us."

"Apparently I've spent more of my years in realtime on a planet's surface than either of you," said Dabeet. "The tracks are plain enough on my face."

"I would guess your absolute age to be about thirty-five," said Valentine. "If you're older, the years rest lightly on you."

"No, your guess is about right," said Dabeet. "I have a reputation as some kind of troubleshooter, so I get sent to problem colonies."

"But it takes you longer to shoot the trouble than it takes me to speak a death, I imagine."

"I hope so," said Dabeet. "Because I sent for a speaker in order to help me deal with the Kenneth Argon problem."

"Dead, and still causing problems?"

"When he was alive, my job was to keep him from provoking the colonists, since it was by his actions alone that Tarragona was kept from achieving continuing status, let alone independence."

"And his death was a mark that your efforts had failed?" asked the speaker.

"Even that is still unknown," said Dabeet. "There may have been dangers I could not have anticipated."

"Cause of death?"

"Abrupt cessation of life," said Dabeet. "You'll have to speak to the E.S. medical officer, who also serves as coroner here."

"Where are his loyalties?" asked the speaker.

"The exact question," said Dabeet, "that bends all my attempts to assess information I'm given."

"Everything is tentative," said the speaker.

"Everything that comes from other people," said Dabeet. "I have to trust my own observations and memories."

Valentine cocked her head. "You regard yourself as infallible?"

Dabeet grinned. "My observations and memories are, or I have to treat them as such, because they're all I've got. But the conclusions

I base on those observations and memories are far from infallible. I know that I have limitations like any other person. And, like every other person, I don't know where those limitations are."

"But you have to act as if you did know," said the speaker.

"What should I call you, sir?" asked Dabeet. "Neither you nor Doctor Valentine has bothered to provide me with any guidance."

"All my work is published pseudonymously," said Valentine. "My pseudonyms have been awarded quite a number of honorary degrees from many planets. Personally, I've never received any college degree or teaching position. So perhaps you'd be kind enough to call me Valentine, and introduce me to people as Valentine Wiggin."

"Never married?" asked Dabeet.

"Tactfully phrased," said Valentine, "but I'm married to my work, and for now, at least, it's a comfortable arrangement."

"And you, sir?" Dabeet asked the speaker.

"Andrew Wiggin," said the speaker. "Some people call us 'speaker' as if that were a title, but it isn't. I'm simply Andrew Wiggin, though if you need to explain who I am, there's no problem with your calling me 'Andrew Wiggin, a speaker for the dead.'"

"But not Ender," said Dabeet.

"Not in public, and not in private, if you'd be so kind," said Andrew. "It's a name that raises too many eyebrows."

"After the war, millions of children were named 'Ender,'" said Dabeet. "Because you had saved the human race."

"And when *The Hive Queen* appeared," said Valentine, "all those children had their names legally changed—either by their parents or on their own, as soon as they were old enough to do it. Because Ender Wiggin was now notorious for having wiped out a beautiful sentient species that was *not* planning to attack us again."

Andrew grinned at Valentine, and she smiled sadly back.

"How ironic that you now practice the profession that was named for the anonymous author of *The Hive Queen*," said Dabeet.

"Irony is in the eye of the beholder," said Andrew. "That book took away my name. It seems appropriate that it gave me a new one. Now let's move on to housekeeping issues. Where will we be staying?"

They went back and forth about whether they should stay in the fully protected E.S. compound, the I.F. barracks, or the MinCol guest quarters. Valentine argued for staying in a local hotel, which Dabeet had to veto for the simplest of reasons.

"Tarragona has not been granted continuing status," he said, "so this remains the only city. It's rather a large one, and we have a significant footprint on the land, but people visiting the city from outlying agricultural settlements stay in the homes of friends and family, in rooming houses, or in taverns."

"Then one of those," said Valentine.

"Why don't you make a decision after you've had a chance to get a feel for the public mood?" said Dabeet. "Once it becomes known that you have *any* interest in Kenneth Argon, you'll find yourself very uncomfortable in any of those unofficial dwellings. Mostly because I don't think any of them will allow you to stay."

"What if we simply buy a house?" asked Andrew.

"People don't buy houses here," said Dabeet, "because people don't sell them. If you want a house, your friends help you build one. You don't have any friends, and you won't get any."

"You said that in such a kindly way," said Valentine, "that it almost sounded hopeful."

"I hope you'll come to regard me as a friend, but if you succeed in your work, then I'll succeed in mine, and we'll all be off-planet as quickly as possible."

"Unless everyone loves the outcome of our work," said Andrew. "Then they might insist we stay."

"No one will love *any* conceivable outcome of your work or mine," said Dabeet, "and the only permanent residence you'll be offered is to enter the ecosystem as a heap of protein being digested by the local fauna."

"Now, wait a moment," said Valentine. "What if our work results in a recommendation for continuing status and independence for Tarragona? Or for the whole of Catalunya?"

"You mean, what if we discover that Ken Argon was a loon, and we overturn all his recommendations?" asked Dabeet. "That's what I personally believe we'll find, and no, they won't love us for it. They want independence so they can get rid of us. They want my title to be Legate or Ambassador—but they would be happier if my title were Ex-governor and Former Resident."

"So your charms haven't won their hearts," said Andrew.

"I believe you remember perfectly well that from my childhood on forward, I am famously charmless," said Dabeet.

"You're thirty-five. You're brilliantly intelligent. Surely you've learned how to fake being a regular guy."

"I have," said Dabeet. "A charmless regular guy. But here we are.

Tonight, at least, stay in a couple of the rooms at the E.S. compound. I'll be within easy reach, since I live there, too, and perhaps we can plan how we'll all go about our various investigations." To Valentine, he added, "Our library and archive, such as they are, reside on the E.S. computers. For safety."

"Backed up where?" asked Valentine.

"Everywhere," said Dabeet. "By ansible. The E.S. takes no chances with records of exploration and colonization. No disaster is allowed to erase the knowledge gleaned from any planet."

"So I could have done my research from any library, on any planet?"

"With your security clearances, from any E.S. outpost or office. Public libraries don't get any of this until the information is old and therefore safe."

"And when it comes to Catalunya..." said Andrew.

"None of the E.S. information is old yet," said Dabeet.

"Which explains the paucity of information about Kenneth Argon and his work with the llops," said Andrew.

Dabeet nodded slightly. "The llops. Everything comes down to them."

"The early reports compared them to hyenas," said Valentine.

"Not really a fair comparison," said Dabeet.

Valentine grinned. "Which is it unfair to? The llops or the hyenas?"

"It depends on what you favor," said Dabeet. "Hyenas are pure predators. The llops—they're omnivores, but in winter they hunt. Not in packs, but fairly effectively. From the vids of hyenas that I've seen, they'll take down an animal and eat its bowels while the victim is still alive and alert. That's hard to do unless you hunt in a pack, so your companions can hold the victim immobilized."

"How do llops do it, then?" asked Valentine.

"They have serious jaws."

"Hyenas are only joking?"

"Long jaws," said Dabeet, "and massive muscles at the fulcrum of the levers. The lower jaw is solidly anchored to the shoulders and breastbone, so it's the upper jaw that does the clamping."

"Where's the brain?" asked Andrew.

"Directly behind the jaw assembly. Part of it is in the upper jaw, part in the lower. The upper jaw clamps down, then slides forward. Clamp, slide, slide back, and the head or limb plops to the ground."

"Gruesome," said Andrew.

"Effective," said Valentine. "Andrew's a little squeamish. He just didn't torture enough animals as a child."

"Why didn't Kenneth Argon certify these killing machines as non-sentient and let things move forward?"

"He felt sorry for them," said Dabeet. "I don't know if that was his reason, because he didn't explain himself. But he did say that he was sorry for them."

"Because they never got to eat prey with its head attached?" asked Valentine.

"The story here isn't the llop, that's what everybody misses— including, I think, Ken, though he certainly *knew* about it."

"What's the story, Dabeet?" asked Valentine.

"It's the cats," said Dabeet.

"Oh, yes. The pets they kept on the pirate ships."

"Cats are never pets," said Dabeet. "They're sport killers, and they're out-hunting the llop."

"Housecats taking down the same prey as the llop?" asked Andrew skeptically.

"They've gotten bigger, but no, they go after much smaller prey. All the smaller predators are starving—the E.S. operates four sanctuaries, and half our work is keeping housecats out of them. We have no idea how many species we've lost. We're preserving thirty or so that we know of."

"I read that the colony pays a bounty on cats," said Valentine.

"Cats reproduce faster than the Tarragonans can kill them," said Dabeet. "Besides, for everyone bringing us cat heads for the bounty, there's somebody feeding cats at the back door. If we catch them, they say they're luring them so they can collect the bounty. How can we disprove the claim?"

"The cats are wiping out smaller predators," said Andrew. "But you're saying that they outcompete the llop."

"They harry the herds of the llops' natural prey. They leap on their backs and ride them, claws dug in. They keep working the claw in, in, in between the vertebrae. About a quarter of the time, their sharp little probes sever the spinal cord and the animal drops. Far more often, the prey animal collapses from blood loss or exhaustion or both."

"So they do hunt the big prey animals," said Andrew.

"Hunt them, but they don't *eat* them. They walk away from the corpse."

"Why aren't the llop following the cats around, eating what they leave?"

"They won't eat any prey that cats have touched," said Dabeet.

"Have to kill their own?" asked Valentine.

"No," said Dabeet. "They have no problem with scavenging. Except when a cat made the kill."

"So the cats eat the smaller prey animals, starving out their small and midsize competitors," said Valentine. "Then they kill the large prey animals and leave the bodies to rot, and the llop won't touch the carcasses."

"Kenneth Argon didn't have a theory?"

"About this? It wasn't a theory; it was a fact. Because they won't eat cat kills, the llop are about the only major land species in the wild that isn't affected, one way or another, by *Toxoplasma gondii*."

"The psychoactive protozoan that can only reach adulthood in the gut of a cat," said Valentine.

"She's coaching me," said Andrew. "She thinks I don't remember."

"I think you never knew," said Valentine. "You weren't on Earth long enough."

"Incurable, yes?" asked Andrew.

Dabeet shook his head. "We have several cures that work on some people some of the time. Prevention is the best policy, though. I can assure you that the human population of Tarragona is toxoplasma-free. Because we don't keep cats indoors, so we don't share breathing space with cat poo, and the only meat we eat comes from flocks and herds kept in complete cat-free isolation."

"So the cats have *Toxoplasma gondii*," said Andrew.

"*T. gondii* doesn't kill or damage the cats," said Dabeet. "It does make them reproduce frantically and hunt incessantly, but since that's pretty much what cats do even if they don't have *T. gondii*, I don't think the cats are suffering. The toms just get lucky when they're dating at a higher than normal rate."

"What does it do to other animals?" asked Andrew.

"Despair, more or less," said Dabeet. "Infected animals lose all fear of cats, or at least they don't try very hard to get away. With Earth-source animals like mice and rats, it keeps them from going to the effort of trying to run away."

Andrew shook his head. "I've never seen alien species where Earth-source infections have the same effects."

"*T. gondii* tries all kinds of things, but what works is behavior modification that helps cats succeed as hunters, so they can eat infected meat and get infected, so the protozoa can get into their gut and become mature and reproduce."

"The effect on humans?" asked Andrew.

"It generally raises suicide and depression rates in its human victims," said Dabeet, "especially women, especially pregnant women and new mothers."

"I don't see how that helps them," said Andrew.

"It doesn't," said Valentine. "But they don't know that. They just do what they do. If we left suicide victims out for the cats to eat, then it *would* help *T. gondii*. But we don't, so it doesn't."

Andrew and Valentine then fell silent, and Andrew's eyes closed. Dabeet knew that he was thinking. So he didn't barge in with the answer.

"Who told the llops not to eat cat kills?" asked Andrew.

"Exactly," said Dabeet. "I think that's why Ken wouldn't certify that the llops aren't sentient. Because *not* eating cat kills is starving them to death, even as it keeps them from getting infected. How did they know? They have no microscopes, they can't read our lab reports, they don't understand spoken English. Or, uh, Starways Common Speech."

"All three of us grew up in America," said Valentine. "It's English."

"And you don't know if Ken had a theory about this," said Andrew.

"I'm certain that he did," said Dabeet. "He just didn't tell *me*."

"So you hope that Valentine and I will find out his theory," said Andrew.

"I hope you'll find out that he was a loon," said Dabeet, "so I can regard his decisions as insane and let this colony of completely uninfected people become self-governing."

"What if we find the one llop that speaks fluent Starways Common and he explains that the llop really have a very high civilization, they just don't make tools or weapons or buildings because it's so inconvenient to do so without fingers. They construct all their monuments in the shared memory of the tribe."

Andrew seemed completely serious. Dabeet didn't know how to answer such an impossible proposition. He wanted to say: If nobody can see it, and they can't say it, then the tree fell noiselessly in the forest. They are only sentient, for E.S. purposes, if the E.S. can tell that they say things or make things or remember things.

The Hive Queens couldn't talk to humans either—but there was never any doubt they were sentient, because they made machines. That essay by the original Speaker for the Dead had made them out to be beautiful, and sorry about the millions of humans who died as a kind of typographical error. But Dabeet had to make judgments in the real world.

He had been reasonably good at making such judgments, which is why he had been sent here to deal with *this* nightmare. But the matter was beyond him, so far at least, which is why he had called for a speaker for the dead, to be another pair of eyes, to be someone who was not official, yet could ask questions. But if he was going to bring up hypothetical nonsense…

"The E.S. has been studying the llop for a century," said Dabeet, "since before we allowed colonists to come here."

"And the E.S. always catches everything?" asked Andrew. With that same unexpressive expression. Yet the question was clearly ironic, so perhaps a completely blank face was Ender Wiggin's irony face.

"I'm as skeptical of bureaucracy and bureaucratic science as you are. Maybe more," said Dabeet. "But there are a lot of very good, rigorous scientists in the E.S., and Ken Argon was one of them. I've duplicated and checked their work myself, and had offworld surrogates check it too. Somehow the llop keep themselves uninfected, *and they always have.*"

"This cat-kill avoidance began while the pirates still ran things?" asked Valentine.

"They weren't scientists, but you don't survive in a generation ship if you don't have really good, observant, careful technicians," said Dabeet. "That's who first noticed what the llop weren't eating— anything killed by a cat."

"So who killed Ken Argon?" asked Andrew. "Not the cats, not the llop, and not any of the Tarragonans, or your report would have said so."

"My report said we had no conclusive proof," said Dabeet, "but I didn't absolve *anybody.* The likeliest thing is that he came in contact with some as-yet-unknown native venomous creature, and the toxin was so lethal it overwhelmed his body. But 'unknown native venomous creature' isn't a report that the E.S. wants to see. Nor do *I* want that to be my report."

"None of the colonists are good with chemicals?"

"Not *that* good," said Dabeet. "Nobody in the whole E.S. recognizes the venom as being from any known species. Nobody can figure out how it's made or how it works. But Ken had a lot of it in his system when he died. In excruciating agony, after demonstrating that no known anti-venom had any effect."

"So a guy that the whole colony wants dead, *gets* dead, but he's killed by a venom that nobody in the colony could possibly make. Or find." Valentine had *her* blank face on. Maybe it was her historian face. Or maybe it was her "Is everybody really this stupid?" face.

Her observation hung in the air, because Dabeet couldn't dispute what she had said, or even respond to the implication that Ken's death had been murder.

"I'm glad you brought *us* here," said Andrew. "Because we're super smart."

"So am I," said Dabeet.

"I know," said Andrew. "We all have the test scores to prove it."

Dabeet shook his head. He had meant, "*So am I glad I brought you,*" not, "*So am I super smart.*" But he'd roll with the misunderstanding. "Now you're making fun of me," said Dabeet, "because back when we first met, I was still proud of my test scores."

"Now you're not?" asked Andrew.

"I had a friend who told me that being good on tests means nothing, because with a test, you always know that there's a desired answer. Even if it's a supposedly no-win test, *that's* the desired answer: 'This can't be done.' With real-world problems, the ones that matter, you can't be sure whether there's an answer or not, because nobody made up the problem and gave it to you in order for you to show how quickly you can find the expected answer, if ever."

"So we can't guess what the testmakers meant, because there were no testmakers," said Valentine.

"Well, except," said Dabeet with a sigh.

"Except what?" asked Valentine.

"Except God," said Dabeet. And then, at Valentine's raised eyebrow: "I was being facetious."

"Let's just suppose that this *is* a test question given to us by God," said Valentine. "Does he want us to find an answer, or to *not* find an answer?"

"Or does he want us to find an answer if we do, or not find one if we don't," said Dabeet. How quickly theological speculation became an angels-dancing-on-pinheads discussion. "I bring up God because that's what I keep hearing from Tarragonans. 'What does God mean by this?' A lot of true believers here."

"Catholic?"

"No religion is given official recognition on an outpost that doesn't have continuing status," said Dabeet, "but yes, of course, Catalunya was part of Spain during the Inquisition. Any non-Catholic genes were eliminated in the sixteenth century."

They laughed at his little joke, which he appreciated, because it showed that they didn't think he *meant* it.

"What I'm wondering," said Andrew, "is whether there's anything to be gained by letting us go out and hunt with the llops."

"They mostly ignore us," said Dabeet. "It's safe enough, unless you try to interfere. Then you get nipped a little."

"Those neck-slicing jaws can 'nip'?" asked Valentine.

"They bite off smaller pieces," said Dabeet.

This time no laugh.

"A joke," said Dabeet.

"Can't wait till we think it's funny," said Valentine.

✦ ✦ ✦

Dabeet did not want to go with Andrew Wiggin to "hunt with the llop," since he wasn't sure the llop understood the difference between eco-tourist and prey. Whatever happened to the speaker for the dead among the llop would be recorded by the system of ambient cameras that one of Ken Argon's predecessors had set up all through the woodland where the nearest troop of llop gave birth and took care of their young. Ken had called it their homeland, which was one of the signs that he was going native—or crazy. But there were thousands of hours of video showing Ken walking among the llop, talking to them, touching them, and it was certainly true that none of it showed any of the llop acting in a hostile manner toward him. But much of the video had been deleted before Dabeet arrived—a clear breach of protocol, reason enough to sack Ken if that had been Dabeet's purpose in coming to Catalunya.

Ken had never admitted that he deleted the video, but he had also never denied it. He said things like, "Isn't it possible there was an intermittent short in the wiring? Or some kind of periodic atmospheric interference with the radio frequencies?" Yes, of course both things were possible. But Dabeet had technicians look into both issues, and, more important, Dabeet had also examined the deletions. There was no way to tell for sure. But no deletion began or ended while Ken was present with the llop on camera.

Since Ken spent so much time with the llop, it was not likely that *none* of the breaks would come when he was there. To Dabeet, there was no chance that Ken was not responsible for the deletions. And to cement this likelihood into certainty was the fact that any intermittent short or atmospheric interference ceased completely when Dabeet arrived.

Mine was such a healing presence, thought Dabeet more than once. All kinds of strange things stopped happening.

Dabeet still thought that he *should* offer to go with Andrew. But then there was always the chance that Andrew would accept the offer. For all Dabeet knew, that might have been Andrew's entire purpose in going to the llop immediately—so that Dabeet would come with him. This would free Valentine to do what was almost certainly the real purpose of their coming to Catalunya—talking to the people of Tarragona about Ken Argon's death. Dabeet needed to be with her to cut off any line of questioning that would stir up trouble.

"Of course you can't come with me," said Valentine cheerfully. "That would defeat the purpose."

"Provoking a new wave of agitation and unrest would defeat *my* purpose."

"I'm so glad you told me. Now I will carefully refrain from provoking agitation and unrest, whether in the form of a wave or surge or tsunami."

Dabeet knew she was toying with him. She was acting out the part of the clever rebel who disarms the unimaginative bureaucratic clod who stands in the way of her noble purpose. He had watched many popular or highly esteemed vids during his voyages between worlds—enough to recognize the cliches.

But I'm not an unimaginative bureaucratic clod.

No, I'm a somewhat imaginative one. But imaginative enough to keep control of this situation?

Dabeet almost laughed aloud—but didn't, because the two office workers who were within earshot in the E.S. building would have been curious, and the less curiosity people directed toward Dabeet, the better. It was precisely the image of bureaucratic clod that Dabeet had cultivated in Tarragona, so that the people wouldn't feel threatened by him. There was no chance that they'd like him, because he represented the authority that was keeping them from full participation in Starways Congress. But on the extremely likely chance that Ken Argon had been murdered by one of the

Tarragonans, Dabeet thought it was prudent to avoid provoking unnecessary levels of hostility, or creating any sense of urgency about his removal from authority.

That was why Dabeet had been sent here, wasn't it? To remove himself from authority. His orders had mentioned—which meant that they *insisted*—that the E.S.'s only goal was to get Catalunya off their books. "We are not in the business of administering colonies beyond the earliest stages, but MinCol doesn't want Catalunya either, not as long as the sentience issue is unresolved. We hope that you will quickly resolve that issue and that your recommendation will allow us to put Tarragona into continuing status followed as quickly as possible by independent membership in Congress."

There was nothing in those orders about solving the mystery of the death of Ken Argon. But until Ken's death was explained, and the perpetrators, if any, brought to justice, this colony would *not* be ready to take its place among the civilized worlds.

This is still a pirate colony, Dabeet often told himself. Even though the last pirates had abandoned the colony of Fancy decades before the E.S. arrived, there was enough lore that appealed to the Catalan settlers that they had adopted the pirate mystique. Such tourists as came here usually did so in order to see the ruins of Fancy, and the locals made sure there were plenty of "artifacts" available to sell to the piraticles, as these tourists were called in Tarragona—whenever the piraticles were not present to hear them.

Valentine also refused to wear any kind of recording device— or at least, any such device that could be read or copied by Dabeet's people. Since Valentine was a serious historian—though it bothered Dabeet that she would not tell him any of her titles, or the name or names under which she had published them— she would need to have recordings in order to cite them as independently verifiable sources. Everything she did would be on record—but Dabeet had already ascertained that despite his absolutely top clearance in the E.S., he did *not* have any access to electronic data belonging to either Andrew or Valentine Wiggin. Whatever authority protected them, it was far above Dabeet's pay grade even to ask for an exemption.

After all, he had invited them here, hadn't he? Why would he think he could control or even observe the actions of a speaker for the dead? Or, for that matter, his "just another tourist" sister?

"I won't attempt to force my company on you," said Dabeet.

"I'm sure you believe that my presence would keep anyone from talking freely to you."

She smiled benignly and said nothing.

"But these streets and roads are not safe for you," said Dabeet.

"Your crime reports show an unusually high number of barroom brawls, but crimes against tourists are right at zero. Is that datum incorrect?"

"Crimes against tourists don't happen, because the Tarragonans aren't idiots. They know that the piraticles bring in a significant percentage of our off-planet income."

"Eighty percent is firmly within the 'significant' range," said Valentine.

"But the moment you start asking about Ken Argon—"

"I move out of the tourist category," said Valentine, completing his sentence.

"So I will send along two bodyguards," said Dabeet. "I'm not asking you, so don't bother telling me why you absolutely do not need them. They'll be there, and one of them will be just outside the door of any house you enter. He'll have the tools necessary for immediate entrance if he, in his sole discretion, believes you are in danger. There is no lock on Catalunya that will delay him, let alone stop him."

"And while he's waiting at the door, eager to huff and puff and blow the house down, what will the other bodyguard be doing?"

"Engaging in quiet prayer and meditation, of course," said Dabeet.

"None of my business, then," said Valentine. "I appreciate your telling me I have no choice. It saves us so much arguing time. I assume that my bodyguards will have listening devices that will allow them to record every word that's said?"

"I believe that in their mission to keep you safe, they will not be underequipped to assess the level of threat to you."

"So you'll be listening in, too," said Valentine.

"I would not presume to violate your right to privacy."

"But in a colony without continuing status, the *colonists* have no right to privacy, isn't that so?"

"If we need to listen to a colonist's conversations, we have the legal right to do so without any kind of warrant. Well, no—I'm the one with the authority to issue such a warrant."

"You know, Andrew never told me about his ansible

conversation with you. It must have been a doozy."

"I was a supplicant then, and I needed ethical and practical guidance. I asked for it from MinCol, and I was redirected to an ansible conversation with the most famous expatriate in human history."

"You didn't ask to speak to Ender?"

"I wanted Graff to guarantee my mother's safety so I didn't have to make decisions based on my enemies' threat to kill her if I didn't obey them."

"And Graff, no doubt guessing what you wanted, decided it would be good for you to handle things without his intervention, so he sent you to Ender to figure out that when Graff decided you were on your own, there was no way to change his mind."

"That was never said, in so many words."

"But you got that message."

"I knew that from the fact that MinCol wouldn't see me. Now I know that you and Andrew are playing your own game, here, and all you want from me is to continue to pretend that I don't know that you have the potential to foment an active revolt."

"And how would I do that?" asked Valentine.

"By asking about Ken Argon."

"They loved him so much?"

"I think some of them, maybe many of them, know who killed Ken. Even if *nobody* knows, they *think* he was probably poisoned by a fellow colonist."

"So if they cooperate with me at all," said Valentine, "they're ratting out a Tarragonan."

"Not really. You'll be able to assess whether somebody's lying to you or concealing information. What foments rebellion is not what *you* might find, because they all know you'll find nothing. It's simply the fact that you are inquiring that will give them a sense of urgency. Because they'll assume that you represent government authority."

"Your having bodyguards accompany me will certainly lend credence to that notion."

"Since you *do* represent government authority," said Dabeet, "having been given a landing permit precisely because I need your help in resolving how Ken Argon died, they will correctly assume that the E.S. is much closer to making a final decision about the future of Tarragona."

"Which might well be that Catalunya should be an independent world."

"Or that it should have continuing status as a colony. Or that it should be disbanded and all colonists evacuated immediately, by force if necessary."

"And they *assume* you want that last outcome?"

"They know Ken Argon wanted it."

"How do they know that?"

"Because he told everybody. All the time. The llop had a civilization before humans came and wrecked it."

"Civilization? The llop?" Valentine's disbelief was exactly right. She had done her reading.

"Fingerless bone-crushing predators are what pass for civilization on Catalunya," said Dabeet.

"They don't even have language."

"Neither did the Hive Queens."

Valentine sighed. "I really will tell you everything important that I find out."

"I'm sure you will," said Dabeet.

"You're sure that your recordings will give you everything," said Valentine. "But they won't give you what I conclude from the things I learn."

"Which is why I so look forward to our conversation." Dabeet smiled, rose to his feet, and ended the briefing. Not that he had *called* it a briefing. But Valentine certainly behaved as if she understood perfectly well what their meeting had been about.

+ + +

This is not a competition, Dabeet told himself. I invited a speaker for the dead so that he might see what I have not been able to see. This means that his success is *my* success.

It's Ender Wiggin, the honest part of his mind murmured.

Yes, I *am* competing with him. I have mastered my competitive instinct, I have subdued it, except this is *Ender Wiggin*. The idiotic world can revile him because of that stupid book, *The Hive Queen*, which was based on *what*, after all? Supposition about a wiped-out alien species whose arrival was the worst disaster in human history, and it destroys the reputation of a child who was the best of us, the best of the human race.

I hate him for being the best.

All right, I've faced it, I've allowed myself to think it. But now think again, because I also love him and admire him and yearn to someday be the kind of hero that he was, a savior of a lost cause.

And maybe this is it. Resolving the problems of the planet Catalunya, the city of Tarragona, or, at the very least, Kenneth Argon, who became a friend before he died. There is an answer here somewhere, and I have been entrusted by the E.S. to find it and allow this colony to move forward—into continuing status, perhaps, or into exile. Somewhere.

Watching the feed from the cameras observing Andrew Wiggin would tax anyone's patience—the man was just sitting there, staring off into space, while the llops move around him, occasionally sniffing him and even nosing him a little. But such a deep nothing was going on that it shunted away Dabeet's attention.

And listening to the audiofeed from Valentine's interviews was almost as boring. She was learning what Dabeet already knew. If something surprising came up, one of his assistants would tell him.

If Dabeet was to contribute to this project, he couldn't just delegate it to the speaker for the dead and his sister, or to Dabeet's own staff of trained observers, scientists, and government functionaries. He had to *do* something or he'd drive himself crazy with trying *not* to watch or listen to the others.

Good thing he had never attempted cooking in any serious way. He was the ultimate watcher of not-yet-boiling pots.

Ken Argon. It all comes down to him. Those maddening gaps in the recordings of his work. What was he doing?

Dabeet got into the directories that contained the posthumous Argon archive that his staff had assembled. All the files were labeled by time and place. There was also a document—a long one—listing all the gaps, along with information from Ken's appointment book and research notes to fill in at least some of the times he hadn't been observed.

And finally it dawned on Dabeet how strange it was that there was a gap right at the end of Argon's life. He had always regarded it as suspicious that this sequence was missing, but he had regarded it as evidence that Argon was murdered—his killer would have searched for and erased the relevant surveillance records. That implied that the killer was part of the E.S., because he would have had to be able to get into the surveillance files—and to do that, he'd have to know that such records existed in the first place.

But that line of thought had led nowhere. Now Dabeet realized that he was not doing enough lateral reasoning. Was there some other way that surveillance records of Ken's activities leading up to his death might have been deleted?

No, even that is another assumption. What if there never *had* been any surveillance of Ken Argon during those gaps? What if he had persuaded the automatic recording systems to ignore him at certain times?

Instead of looking at the recorded surveillance, Dabeet began searching in the software that governed the surveillance systems, trying to determine how it worked. Naturally, the system resented his intrusion, and he kept getting pop-ups warning him that he was not authorized to make any copies of or alterations in the software. Finally, he logged himself in again as administrator, only this time he asserted his position as commander of this field office and claimed emergency powers. The security algorithm demanded to know what the emergency was, because it was going to make an automatic report by ansible. So Dabeet wrote: Ken Argon died without surveillance. I want to know why. The pop-ups stopped.

Soon Dabeet identified the changes Ken had made. First, he had turned off the automatic warning system, so that after the first time, the security system would not notify headquarters when Ken signed on to alter the software. Then he made a few simple changes that allowed him to switch off or destructively erase any recording he wished to eliminate.

Much later, there was one final change. Ken had permanently blocked all surveillance in one lab in the ALR—the Alien Life Repository.

Ken's body had been found in that building. But not in that lab.

Dabeet called up a visual sequence that he and everybody else who had investigated Ken's death had looked at repeatedly: Ken's actual death. He staggered out of his office into the common area, empty because it was about three in the morning. He fell to the ground as if his legs had turned to liquid, and lay there whimpering in agony and murmuring something that no amount of analysis of either sound or lip movements could turn into any discernible language.

He came out of his office. Dabeet checked, and whatever happened in the office had been deleted.

That was Ken's last action: the deletion of surveillance records. He had deleted the recording of himself deleting the recording.

Too recursive. Analysis of the toxin had revealed that Ken Argon died in unimaginable pain, but there would have been no impairment of mental function. Ken might have been frantic and distracted by the pain, but he wasn't crazy. So he would not have gone into his office just to delete a record of himself going into his office.

What was he trying to hide?

Dabeet used his deep-diagnostic software—the analytic programs he had access to only because he asserted an emergency—to search for the automatic backups of file allocation tables. He wanted to verify *when* the surveillance footage had been deleted, and then to see what else had been deleted around the same time.

But one of the deletions had been the very allocation table backup that he had been looking for.

How could Ken have deleted *that*? The diagnostics Dabeet was using did not give him the power to delete the diagnostic backups. *Nothing* gave that power.

Except that obviously something *did*, because it had happened.

Dabeet wrote a quick message to the head of the ITDS—Info Tech Diagnostic Service—asking how that particular backup allocation table came to be deleted. Because Dabeet had asserted emergency mode, his question would be given urgent priority—the head of ITDS would be called out of any meeting, or wakened out of a sound sleep. And Dabeet wasn't afraid of any resentment over this, because the disappearance of a backup diagnostic file would cause even more consternation at ITDS than it was causing Dabeet here.

Meanwhile, though, Dabeet still had his best diagnostic tool—his brain, with its ability to remember pretty much everything, even things that he had not paid attention to. He put himself into what he called "calendar mode," thinking through events during the last few days before Ken died. It had been a tricky time for both Dabeet and Ken, because they both knew that even though Ken was still nominally in charge of the local E.S., which meant the whole human presence on Catalunya, Dabeet had been sent there to investigate him, and Dabeet could countermand any order or action by Ken.

Why hadn't Dabeet been notified that Ken took the system into emergency mode?

Because that's not what Ken had done. However he got the power to alter and delete files, Ken had accomplished it in a way that left no marks behind, a way that notified nobody.

What was Ken so determined to hide?

His tracks, that's for sure. Whatever he was hiding, he also went to some effort to hide the fact that he had hidden it. He might even have hoped that it would look like a system malfunction, and not a deliberate action at all. For all Dabeet knew, that's the answer the ITDS would return to him: system malfunction, cause unknown.

Dabeet felt a kind of excitement grow inside him. It wasn't the excitement of knowing that the solution was within his grasp. Rather it was the deep satisfaction of knowing that he had found a new question, one that might lead him to find out what was, after all, one of the most important questions facing him: How and when did that toxin enter Ken Argon's body?

And now his mind put together two newly acquired facts and brought them to the forefront of Dabeet's attention: Ken was hiding the activity that killed him, and kept hiding it even when it must have been obvious that he was dying.

Ken had fairly recently blanked out all recording in Lab 3 of the ALR.

Dabeet thought about these two facts. Because nothing was recorded in Lab 3, there would have been nothing for Ken to erase, if that had some significance in the last hours of his life.

Ah, but there would have been video of Ken *emerging* from Lab 3, perhaps in visible distress from the toxin, if he acquired it there. Lab 3 was important to Ken—and it was important to him that no one see what he did in there. Was it even more important than that? *So* important that when Ken got envenomated, instead of seeking any kind of treatment he staggered to his office and spent his last minutes of life erasing his trail so that no one would be led back to that lab?

Somebody must have seen this already. After Ken's death, some offworld investigator would have uploaded all the surveillance records and tried, at least, to track Ken's movements. It was impossible that nobody had attempted this, so they must surely have noticed the gaps.

Dabeet brought up the raw data from the coroner's investigation and, yes, there it was, a report on surveillance of Ken Argon's movements in the hours prior to his death. Leaving his rooms. Then "missing record." Then his appearance in the common room, dying.

And that's where they had left it. Nobody—including Dabeet, he had to admit—had thought to figure out *why* those records were missing. Dabeet left that kind of thing to the offworld investigators, because they had diagnostic tools that he could only access by calling for emergency powers. Now that he was thinking about it, he remembered wondering when they would inform him of what happened to the missing records.

In fact, he'd assumed that the records would have been backed up offworld, the way everything was supposed to be from a world still officially in the exploratory phase. But it had slipped away from his attention. He had deceived himself by looking elsewhere with too much concentration.

Staying out of the way of the speaker for the dead and his historian sister had, perhaps, freed up Dabeet's attention so he could look elsewhere.

Ken could not have imagined that nobody would ever notice his deletions. The missing records were noticed in the first ten minutes after E.S. headquarters was notified of Ken's troubling death. Before any analysis of the toxins in his system—before it was known that there *were* toxins—those missing surveillance records should have been the primary focus of the investigation, because if Ken had been murdered, the assumption would be that the killer or killers had pulled off the computational coup of hiding their tracks so thoroughly.

Another realization: I no longer believe that Ken was murdered.

From the moment Dabeet had discovered how thoroughly the surveillance of Ken's last minutes had been erased, it never crossed his mind that someone other than Ken had done the deletion.

That didn't mean that Dabeet was *right*—he knew perfectly well that just because he had unconsciously excluded murder as a possibility did not mean that Ken wasn't murdered. But Dabeet had learned in early childhood to trust the "intuitions" that arose from his unconscious mind. For the time being, Dabeet would continue to act on the assumption that Ken Argon died from something other than a human attack on his body.

Whatever killed Ken, he wanted to hide it from those who would inevitably investigate his death.

No. Get rid of the abstraction. Ken spent his last moments hiding the manner of his death *from me.*

And because of my inattention, he has succeeded for months. It could easily have been forever. I conspired with him to hide this from myself.

The report on the missing files was there, much later in the investigation. And, as Dabeet had guessed, there was no cause assigned. Suspected: local system malfunction, perhaps caused by human action of unknown nature.

That was the lazy initial report, but there was no other. No doubt whoever made this report expected to be ordered to follow up and identify the system malfunction. He probably didn't have the authority to initiate a deeper investigation without orders. And the orders had never come.

I could have given exactly those orders. But I paid no attention.

What am I paying no attention to now?

Even as he was forming this question, he noticed that there was a second page to this minimal report. Since the first page had only three lines of text, and there was no reference to further material, Dabeet might have looked at this report a dozen times without noticing the existence of another page.

He flipped to that page. It was full. Not of the data the investigator had been assigned to look for, but rather a complete description of what he had *not* found.

You were better than I was, Dabeet said silently to this unknown investigator. Without orders, you documented all the gaps in all the surveillance systems.

We couldn't track when the *deletions* took place, but this investigator had tracked all the times and places that had been blanked out of the record.

It was a kind of path. The start and end times of the deletions were identical, rounded to the exact half-hour on the start time, and to a sequence of end times that moved forward minute by minute until the last one, completed just seconds before Ken staggered out of his office.

And now we know when the deletions took place. Ken couldn't delete surveillance footage that didn't yet exist. So every deletion had been marked from the same start time until "now"—the exact moment Ken performed the deletion.

He could have grouped all the deletions into a single operation, so they would all have the same end time. Why didn't Ken— obviously, because he didn't know when he would die. He didn't know if he could finish the deletions. If he started marking all the deletions in a group, but died before he finished, then *none* of the deletions would have taken place, and he would have been found with the group definition still on the screen. The files would exist, *and* Ken's actions would have called particular attention to the very surveillance records he wanted to eliminate.

So Ken had deleted them one at a time.

Most important ones first. That's how he would have done it. So which was the oldest deletion?

The corridor outside Labs 3 and 4. Then the catalog room in the ALR. Then the entrance foyer. Then...

Obviously, Ken had erased his trail from Lab 3.

The last two deletions were unrelated to the path between Lab 3 and Ken's office. Dabeet spent a while wondering what possible connection they had to anything else that Ken was doing, but then it occurred to him that Ken probably realized that his deletions also marked his path, so he was going on to delete other surveillance zones as red herrings. But then the pain got so bad, he was so close to death, that he gave up. He had done all that was possible. He blanked his computer, staggered out of his office, and then—was he trying to get help? No. He could have gotten help much faster by calling someone from his office. He just wanted his body to be found.

He wanted his body to be found because he wanted the toxins to be found, before they broke down. He wasn't trying to hide the manner of his death—just the manner of his acquisition of the venom that killed him.

It was time to find out what was in Lab 3.

The answer was simple.

Nothing.

The samples of alien life had been scanned in every way possible, with the data uploaded to many offworld sites. Scientists and students all over the Hundred Worlds were studying them, printing 3D and 2D models, analyzing the chemistry, and then writing detailed reports. And as each sample was scanned and uploaded, the physical sample was incinerated, unless it was flagged for another option, like "release into wild"—that was only for living samples—or "return to natural environment."

Dabeet saw that most samples had been tagged for return to natural environment. In other words, they were taken outside the compound and buried. Early on, some living samples were released into the wild—including a couple of scanned and recorded llops. Dabeet tried to imagine how that was handled, back in the earliest days of the E.S. survey. How did they know, before scanning, what tranquilizers, and in what doses, would be appropriate for the llop? And how did they get the other llops to let them *take* the tranquilized llops?

Dabeet would have to look that up sometime. The fact remained that the llops were returned to the wild, presumably no worse for wear.

What had this experience meant to the llop—the fact that humans had kidnapped a couple of them, taken them away, and then returned them? What sense had they made of this?

Maybe they learned the only lesson that mattered: Humans can immobilize you whenever they want, but they don't kill if you don't force them to.

Dabeet doubted that the earlier pirate colony had been so tender-hearted. They didn't have the equipment anyway. Maybe the first lesson the llops learned was the bloody one: don't fight the humans. You can tear human bodies to pieces, but only if you get close enough, which you never will. Dabeet thought back to his orientation as he approached Catalunya. Yes, the pirates had even called it The War of Dogs.

The Catalan settlers had found their own names for everything. "Llop" just meant "lobo"—wolf. But the pirates would never have called the llops "wolf," because among the names that their victims used for pirates were *wolves*, *blood wolves*, and *void wolves*. No doubt the pirates took pride in these vulpine names, so they couldn't call their only enemy in their new colony by the same name. If the pirates were wolves, then these alien bone-splitters had to be called *dogs*.

So by the time the E.S. arrived, the llops must have learned to regard human beings as bitter enemies—if not as prey. This meant that tranquilizing, studying, and returning llop specimens might have signaled a new relationship with humans. *This* group of humans isn't interested in killing you.

And that's why Andrew Wiggin could be sitting out there among the llop, unmolested. So far. It's why Ken Argon was able to live with the llop for days at a time, and, on two occasions, for several weeks at a stretch.

Lab 3. Lab 3 was empty. All the remaining samples had been preserved using various methods, and were kept in Lab 2, the largest of the labs, where most of them were kept in refrigerated cases. Lab 1 was used for ongoing research, of which there was very little—only one full-time xenologist and a couple of techs remained at this installation to study any new samples that might pop up in the course of planetary exploration. Lab 3 was used for nothing.

Was it possible that Lab 3 would still yield information about what Ken had been doing there?

Dabeet almost got up and went directly to Lab 3 to satisfy his curiosity. But no, that would be a mistake. In all likelihood, whatever killed Ken Argon had been inside Lab 3. Perhaps someone had set a trap. Perhaps an alien sample released a toxin, or had toxins embedded in its surface, or on spines. Perhaps something had been put into the air.

Surely someone was cleaning the lab regularly. It must be on the schedule, and if it wasn't safe, we'd have a high attrition rate among the custodial staff.

Except that the lab was listed as closed. Which meant that the door was locked, the space was not heated or cooled, and nobody ever went inside to clean.

No, that's what was *supposed* to happen to a closed lab. But a quick check revealed that not only was Lab 3 still connected to atmospherics and given a stable temperature, but it also had water connections that showed a steady slow use of water.

Yes, Dabeet needed to go there, but *not* alone, because whatever Ken had been doing in there might still be going on. He would need witnesses, in case entering Lab 3 killed him.

And, perhaps most important, he knew he had to play fair with Andrew and Valentine. They would share what they had learned today, all three of them, and then make a plan of action. They would do this together. If there was one thing Dabeet had learned in Fleet School, it was the fact that smart people worked together and pooled their resources—including their knowledge.

They could talk during supper.

✦ ✦ ✦

To Dabeet's surprise, they didn't seem all that eager to talk about anything substantive. Valentine spent a while telling Andrew about how Tarragonan fashions were a kind of living archaeology, the styles of the previous century still being sold to customers for current use. And Andrew answered with his llopological observations— how they were like many baboons in that their social hierarchy was entirely maintained among the females, while the males remained in many ways like useful children, sent out to bring home meat, but otherwise just tolerated until they went away.

How fascinating, Dabeet wanted to say. But he knew that despite Valentine's comedy monologue and Andrew's amateur naturalist disquisition, they would be alert to any hint of mockery from Dabeet. If Dabeet ended up making a difficult or controversial decision about

Catalunya, he could use the full support of two people with the kind of security clearances these two had. *Somebody* took them very, very seriously at the highest levels of government—probably above the level of anybody in the entire E.S. So if they backed him, this adventure might not ruin his career.

Sourly he thought, I'm the careerist now that I always used to despise. But it's not about ambition. I already have the job I want—troubleshooting the trickiest problems facing the Exploratory Service on the newest or most exotic worlds. If they took that away from me because they lost trust in my judgment after Catalunya and Ken Argon, then what would the rest of my life even mean? Yes, maybe I could find some woman who imagined she could put up with me, and we could raise a passel of children, while I figured out how to be the thing I never had—a father. *That* would be an exotic new world to explore.

"We lost him," said Andrew.

"No we didn't," said Valentine. "He's awake."

"But not listening to us," said Andrew.

"I am," said Dabeet, "but I'm not remotely interested in anything you're saying, because I need your help, and you're withholding it by talking about... about—"

"About the things that are a pleasure to talk about while eating," said Valentine. "Serious conversations can give you indigestion. You're older than we are now, surely you've discovered this."

"I have indigestion from *not* talking about anything," said Dabeet. "I'm glad you find the provincials interesting. I'm glad you find similarities between hierarchical behavior among baboons and llops. I rejoice at your ability to amuse yourself in this sad little lump of a city, on this overstudied and underutilized planet."

"Well," said Valentine, "it looks like somebody wanted a meeting instead of a meal."

"What do you want to know?" asked Andrew.

"Since all outward appearances suggest you accomplished nothing—" Dabeet began.

"Well, we weren't trying to *accomplish* anything yet," said Valentine. "I was just trying to discover how murderous the people are. If they killed one administrator, they might kill another. So for what it's worth, they don't hate you, Dabeet. They also didn't really hate Ken Argon. They feared what he would do and they thought he was crazy, but he was a likable guy. No, I didn't meet any murderers, and I didn't meet anybody who was trying to cover up for a particular murderer. But I *did* find quite a few people who believed that *someone* in Tarragona murdered Kenneth Argon, and therefore they were apprehensive about what a speaker for the dead would uncover. They've never actually seen a speaking, but they've read about some of the more outlandish ones, including a couple of Andrew's, though they didn't know that. They're afraid that Andrew's speaking will reveal something that leads *you*, Dabeet, to evacuate the colony."

"Do they really love their lives here so much?" asked Andrew.

"It's the only world any of them have known. Their grandparents and great grandparents came from other worlds—mostly from Earth, in fact—but it's all just stories to the people now. This is home, and they're afraid to leave it. Especially because that crazy dangerous animal somehow might qualify in some idiot's mind as 'intelligent.'"

"Smart as can be," said Andrew. "But the question isn't about 'intelligence.'"

Dabeet laughed grimly. "What *is* your definition of 'intelligent.' Or 'sentient.'"

"Oh, *we* don't have to have one," said Andrew, smiling. "That's *your* decision."

Dabeet grimaced. "The E.S. has about six different definitions, all of them mutually contradictory and most of them *self-contradicting*."

"Yet somehow the E.S. makes decisions about the presence or absence of sentient species on every world we've settled," said Valentine.

"Because we've never found any," said Dabeet.

"Are you hinting that there might be a bias against declaring another species sentient?" asked Valentine.

"Of course there is," said Dabeet. "We're in the colonization business now. I was openly told before I came here that my job was to clear things up well enough to give Tarragona continuing status. Which means I'm supposed to find that no matter how clever the llop are, they are *not* as smart as *H. sapiens* and his friends."

"Well then," said Andrew. "What did you call for *us* for?"

"Officially, to help resolve Ken Argon's cause of death."

"Come on," said Valentine. "You have the chemical formulae of several different toxins found in his body."

Dabeet rolled his eyes.

"He can still roll his eyes," said Andrew. "He's not completely a grownup yet."

"Dabeet Ochoa," said Valentine, "what I have found out is this: the people of Tarragona had nothing to do with the death of Ken Argon, but they fear that someone among them *might* have done it, and because of that, they're circling the wagons to protect each other from the evil bureaucrats who will never, never understand them and their lives. I'm also reasonably sure that this is what you already believed."

Dabeet nodded. "I'm glad to know we've reached the same conclusion."

Valentine turned to her brother. "Andrew, what did you learn from the llop?"

"They once knew how to do things they no longer know how to do," said Andrew. "But they remember that they did them. They remember being smarter and more capable than they are."

Dabeet raised his eyebrows.

"You're such a relentless interrogator," said Andrew. "But you've broken me down, I'll tell you what I think. I think that the llop once knew how to speak."

Dabeet could not hear this in silence. "How can you tell that a creature *once* knew how to talk?"

"By the way they listen. The females, not the males. And only the older ones. They attend to my speech and I think they understand me, even though I was speaking Common instead of Catalá."

"Ken would have spoken Common," said Dabeet.

"So would the pirates," said Andrew. "But let's stay with Ken. Let's say he was the *only* human whose speech they learned. I watched as much footage as you had on my way in, and I have to say, whenever Ken was with the llop, he never stopped talking. This was not a case of sentimentalizing or anthropomorphizing the alien smash-beast. It looked to me as if Ken were carrying on sustained conversations, so I did the same."

"You mean they answered you?"

"They never answered Ken, either," said Andrew. "It's not about getting answered, it's about being understood. I asked them all kinds of questions and strung out all kinds of stories. They listened with some attention—the adult females, I mean, because the males and children grew bored quickly enough and left us alone."

"They never showed *threat* to you?"

"Let me tell it in order, please," said Andrew, smiling. "I saw that they understood complex narratives, and, like you, they sometimes disbelieved me."

"How did they show comprehension?" asked Dabeet.

"They didn't blink once for yes and twice for no, if that's what you're thinking. I'm not offering you scientifically verifiable information, Dabeet. I'm offering you my perceptions and conclusions."

"Sorry," said Dabeet. "That's what I need from you."

"We're missing something huge, still," said Andrew. "About Ken, about the llop, and mostly about what Ken thought he had discovered about the llop. If he believed they were sentient, or had the potential to be sentient—that's the standard, isn't it?"

Dabeet nodded.

"If he declared them sentient, then the question of continuing status is moot. But think. He worked with them for *years* and certainly knew everything that I learned about them plus a lot more. Yet he *never* made a finding of sentience, did he?"

Dabeet could only agree.

"So even if he went native to some degree, he didn't go so far as to impair his ability to assess intelligence. He did *not* think the llop, as they presently are, make very good candidates for the first sentient species since the Formics."

"As they presently are," Dabeet prompted him.

"I think that what Ken couldn't get over were those tantalizing letters from some of the pirate colonists. That the dogs told them things. Where to find game. Where to plant crops. Just a couple of things, and by 'told' they might have meant 'showed.'"

"Or, as the consensus had it, *must* have meant 'showed,'" said Dabeet.

"What did *Ken Argon* believe?" asked Andrew. "I think it was those pirate-colony letters that made it so he couldn't leave the llop alone, had to find out what those letters *meant*. But generally speaking, the llop neither tell us nor show us anything. They behave like a troop of hyenas or a pack of wolves—the constantly shifting game of king of the hill that the males play, and the quiet leadership of the females as they forage, feed the pups, and carefully observe whatever human has come along to bother them."

Valentine chuckled. "You observe them for one day, Andrew, and you're already annoying them? They *are* sentient."

Dabeet didn't appreciate the humor, mostly because hearing the sentence "they *are* sentient" gave him a shiver of excitement. Even though his assignment here was to certify continuing status for the colony of Tarragona as soon as possible, he was like everyone else in the E.S. He wanted to find a sentient species, especially a non-technological one that couldn't come to Earth and attempt to destroy the human race.

"So I've reached a couple of tentative conclusions," said Andrew, "and then I invite you to prove me wrong, because I think the conclusions are, like Ken Argon, borderline insane."

"That implies that somebody knows where that borderline is," said Dabeet sourly. "I've been probing for it my whole life."

"Oh, I think you crossed over and back again several times," said Andrew with a smile. "That's what your father thought, anyway."

Dabeet looked at him sharply. "If you're pretending that you know who my father was, then you've lost all credibility with me."

"Just because you haven't found out a thing doesn't mean that nobody else knows it," said Valentine. "That's what I keep learning over and over, usually under embarrassing circumstances. But I think Ender dropped that little morsel into the conversation in order to fluster you and distract you and make it possible for him to get us to take his proposal seriously."

"What proposal?" asked Dabeet. He noticed that Valentine had used the name "Ender" for her brother; perhaps the name she used whenever *she* wanted to irritate *him*.

"I want to see Lab 3," said Andrew, "but I want to bring along the top female from this local troop of llop."

"Let's see, a savage predator with the ability to remove any appendage, from toe to head, without our being capable of defending ourselves," said Dabeet. "What could go wrong?"

"She won't do that," said Andrew.

"Did she sign a contract to that effect?" asked Dabeet. "Or was the agreement oral? One yip means yes…"

"I drew her a picture," said Andrew, "and she drew one back to me."

"Art class," said Valentine.

"In the dirt," said Andrew. "My guess is that the cameras are at a bad angle to see what we were doing. It's remarkable how small and fine her drawings are. It's not the first time she's communicated this way."

"You took pictures?" asked Valentine.

Andrew touched the jewel attached to his earlobe. "I'm sure pictures must have been taken. Jane is pretty efficient about recording things."

"Can she show us?"

"I don't want her to," said Andrew.

"Because we'll see that it isn't really a picture?" asked Valentine.

Dabeet appreciated the way that Valentine did his job for him.

"Because you won't agree with me about what it means," said Andrew, "and I'm right anyway."

"What will we think it means?" asked Dabeet.

"You'll think it means nothing," said Andrew. "But I think she drew it for Ken. I have to see what's in Lab 3, but I need to have her with me."

"Have you named her?" asked Valentine. "When you bring home a pet and want Mommy to let you keep it, it's much more convincing if you've already named it."

"She has a name," said Andrew. Then he made two high-pitched hips, a low growl, and two panting noises.

"How do you spell that," said Dabeet, making a show of preparing to write it down.

"She answers to it, and nobody else does," said Andrew. "So I called her that fairly early this morning, and she came and talked to me."

"Because you called her by name," said Dabeet.

"Nobody else has," said Andrew. "At least since Ken Argon died."

"What did she draw?" asked Dabeet. "Whether you think we'll agree with you or not doesn't matter. If you want access to Lab 3, with or without the llop, you have to tell me—or show me—what she drew."

"Back when humans first came here," said Andrew, "at least some of the llops engaged in conversation with at least some of the colonists. I think it terrified the pirates that llops could understand and reproduce human speech."

"But they can't," said Dabeet.

"But they did," said Andrew.

"How can you tell?" asked Dabeet. "Oral conversation doesn't leave much of an archaeological record."

"The letters again," said Valentine.

"Not the letters," said Andrew. "The fact that she understood me."

"Because you know how to read llop body language," said Valentine.

"I studied the exploratory teams' reports about the llop on the way here," said Andrew. "I knew what to look for."

"I've read them many times," said Dabeet, "and *I* don't know."

"Because the reports were written by people from E.S. who explained away all evidence of sentience as 'simple animal communication,'" said Andrew. "But it was there. The llop understood human speech."

"Because they left when somebody said the word 'specimen,'" said Valentine.

"Yes," said Andrew.

"What are you talking about?" asked Dabeet.

"Show him, please, Jane," said Andrew.

Dabeet's holodisplay turned on and in a moment, there were a couple of members of the exploratory team, conversing, with two llop peacefully lying on the ground nearby. Nothing was audible until the woman who was in charge said, "Protocol is that we study some specimens and report."

Instantly, the two llop bounded to their feet and left the holofield.

"Coincidence," said Dabeet.

"If they had said anything about vivisection," said Andrew, "I wonder who would have vivisected whom."

"Did your friend Yip-yip-grrr understand you?"

"I tried writing letters on the ground," said Andrew.

"She corrected your spelling?" Valentine turned to Dabeet. "Andrew makes the silliest spelling errors sometimes."

"Yes," said Andrew. "But not the way you think. She stopped me from writing by wiping her foreclaw across the letters, and then pushing away my stick when I tried again."

"So, art criticism?" asked Valentine. "Or literary criticism?"

"Then she drew something on the same patch of dirt."

"Show me," said Dabeet.

"Go ahead, Jane." Andrew paused for a moment. "No enhancements. The clearest raw picture."

The holofield showed the patch of dirt, horizontally. Both Dabeet and Valentine stood to get a clearer view.

The llop had apparently drawn with a single claw, because the lines were sharp and clear. But it looked like nothing at all to Dabeet.

"What are we supposed to be seeing here?" asked Dabeet.

"I think those are the wheels," said Valentine. "It's a mail delivery truck. She's complaining that they haven't had any letters for a while."

"OK, Jane, *now* enhance it."

Immediately some of the lines in the dirt grew light. Now it was a weird drawing of a four-legged creature with alligator jaws. But without perspective, absolutely flat as if the four legs all came straight down from the trunk of the body, and the jaws came out of a ball on one end.

"I wonder what other pictures you can find in that, by selecting the right lines," said Valentine.

"Jane and I showed the enhanced version to her. She agreed."

Dabeet was more impressed than he wanted to let on. "The lines *are* there," he said. "But there are a lot of other lines."

"I think some of them represent the fact that she didn't think to lift her claw when moving from one part of the drawing to another," said Andrew.

"Stray marks, then," said Dabeet. "And she did this after stopping you from writing."

"Let me show you the reason I want to get into Lab 3," said Andrew.

At once, in yellowish light, the round head was highlighted, along with about a dozen stray lines coming out of it. Not the jaws of the llop, though. That remained the original color.

"I thought that was the head," said Valentine.

"I still think it is," said Dabeet.

"It may be," said Andrew. "I don't know. But I always intended to show you this before we went to Lab 3."

"Why?" asked Dabeet.

"Because I asked her why this round thing didn't look like her head."

"What did she say?" asked Valentine facetiously.

"She trotted toward the E.S. compound," said Andrew.

"Well, that's clear," said Dabeet.

"Everything she did looked to me like comprehension and an attempt to converse."

"And trotting toward the compound meant…"

Valentine supplied the answer. "Andrew thinks it means the

round thing is inside the E.S. compound."

"The round thing," said Dabeet, "is either a childish representation of the llop head, or it's the sun with those yellow rays coming out."

"Color choice, Jane," said Andrew.

The yellow circle and its appendages turned pink.

"Well, that's nauseating now," said Valentine. "It looks like an extruded stomach."

"A heart with veins and arteries coming out," said Dabeet.

"If the free-association game is over," said Andrew, "will you let me call her and bring her inside?"

"We've never let an alien creature inside an E.S. laboratory under its own power, without sedation or some kind of restraint system," said Dabeet.

"It is forbidden?"

"Of course it is," said Valentine.

"Not explicitly," said Dabeet. "We're told the protocols for sedation and restraint, but we're not told *explicitly…*"

Valentine laughed. "You want to do this, don't you, Dabeet?"

Dabeet didn't know why she was laughing. "Yes," said Dabeet. "It could end my career. It could end our lives, if the llop goes crazy on us. But I think Andrew's interpretation of that drawing is… the *existence* of that drawing…"

"Changes everything?" asked Valentine.

"Invites some unusual responses." Dabeet turned again to Andrew. "Do you think she *wants* to get inside?"

"She kept trotting toward the compound," said Andrew. "She's waiting outside. But none of the others followed her."

"Is that unusual?"

"She's the matriarch," said Andrew. "A parade of females and their young follow her wherever she goes."

Valentine asked, with obvious curiosity, "I've never thought to ask. Do the llop nurse their young?"

"No mammary glands, no paps," said Andrew. "But they do swallow some of their prey nearly whole, and then come back to the campsite and vomit it up for the young to eat. Several species on Earth do that."

"Birds," said Valentine.

"No, mammals too. Some dogs, for instance."

"I didn't know that was a mammalian thing," said Valentine.

"As so many human males fail to understand," said Andrew, "mammary glands are not the beginning and end of mammalian happiness."

"Yes," said Dabeet. "I'm going to chance it. But you can't bring her in through the front. Come around the south side, and I'll open the lab complex through the cargo door."

"Any cameras pointed that way?" asked Valentine.

"Why don't you want cameras?" asked Dabeet.

"I'm a historian," said Valentine. "I want them everywhere. What if this is a complete failure? What if we end up chopped to bits lying around the lab, except for whatever parts of us Yip-yip-grrr swallows so she can disengorge it for the babies back at camp? Somebody needs to know the magnitude of our stupidity."

"If Ken hadn't erased everything," said Andrew, "wouldn't our lives be simpler?"

"Maybe Ken wanted to prevent us from doing exactly what we're doing."

"He didn't bring in a dog," said Valentine. "To use the pirate term for them."

"How do you know?" asked Andrew.

"Because he didn't let one out. Nobody fiddled with the door record, and during the time when he erased everything, no door opened. Yet there was no llop inside. Ergo."

"Sum," said Andrew.

"Always you forget to cogito first," said Valentine.

Their life was one long in-joke, Dabeet thought. Though at least he recognized this one—Descartes' famous a priori statement, *Cogito ergo sum*. "I think, therefore I am."

"Go get the llop, Andrew," said Dabeet.

"Want company?" asked Valentine.

"No," said Andrew.

"Want a collar and leash?" asked Valentine.

"I'll just say 'heel' and she'll come along," said Andrew.

"Let's go open the door for the boy and his dog," said Valentine to Dabeet.

+ + +

Dabeet *had* been around the llop many times, back when Ken Argon insisted on it, but it always made him uneasy. It especially made him tense this time, because the llop matriarch was not acting llop-like. She was more like a trained dog, staring intently at the door.

"It looks like she thinks this is the right place," said Valentine.

"Maybe she smells something we can't smell," said Andrew.

"I'm about to open the door," said Dabeet. "For the first time, I think, since Ken visited here right before he died."

"We *should* be in hazmat suits," said Andrew, "but I worry that might lose us some trust with our four-legged companion."

"I think that whatever killed Ken wasn't loose in the atmosphere," said Dabeet, "because then he would have given us a warning. Ken was a decent guy. He wouldn't have left things set like a trap for anyone who happened to come in."

"Because people who have just absorbed a killing dose of alien venom are always thinking of the welfare of others," said Valentine.

"People behaved pretty decently back in the First Formic War, when the aliens were on Earth," said Andrew, "killing people and animals and plants with their defoliation spray."

"Aren't humans wonderful," said Valentine.

Andrew grinned. "They kind of are," he said. "Present company excepted, of course."

Dabeet palmed the door code.

Nothing happened.

"Oh, this is anticlimactic, isn't it," said Valentine.

"Ken didn't have the clearances to block me out," said Dabeet. "When I came here, everything was rekeyed to my control by the E.S."

"Ken Argon did a lot of things he didn't have the power to do," said Andrew.

Then Andrew reached out his hand, palmed the doorpad, and it opened.

Dabeet might have made some caustic comment about Andrew Wiggin having higher clearances than God, but the door was open, and the llop matriarch was padding slowly in.

Dabeet followed her. Andrew deferred to him, perhaps because he was embarrassed that he could open a door in Dabeet's own bailiwick that Dabeet himself could not control.

The room showed no sign that a man had been envenomated here. Was Dabeet's conclusion wrong? Was it possible that this wasn't where Ken was working when he was attacked?

"Doesn't smell awful or anything," said Valentine. They were inside the room, now, too.

"Nothing knocked over," said Andrew. "Nothing spilled, nothing broken."

"Ken Argon died so tidily," said Valentine.

"When he left here, he might not have been feeling the full effect of the venom, yet," said Dabeet. "He might not even have realized it was going to be fatal."

"Or this might not be where he was envenomated," said Andrew. "Looks like he was cleaning up. That sponge."

"That sponge is round and beige with tendrils coming out," said Valentine.

Dabeet understood at once. "The picture."

The llop was already heading directly toward it, not eagerly, but with complete certainty. Dabeet was quite certain that *this* was what she had come for, what she had asked the speaker for the dead to do for her. Now he saw the picture as a depiction of a llop with a round parasite perched on its head, or perhaps covering it.

The llop's head was at about the same level as the countertop. She picked up the sponge between her jaws with surprising gentleness, tipped her head back, and swallowed it.

"This was all about lunch?" asked Valentine softly.

The llop's eyes went black.

Then a viscous liquid the same color as the sponge began to flow slowly out of the llop's ears and nostrils. Defying gravity, the liquid flowed upward until it covered the crown of the llop's head. In a very short time, it formed a globe from which the llop's jaws protruded, along with holes for her eyes.

The llop turned to face Andrew. "Thank you," she said.

The voice wasn't human—far from it, and not machine-like, either. And not doglike. Too smooth for an animal, too high for a human, high enough that the effect was almost funny. Like having a dog speak with the voice of a very young child.

"Thank you," she said to Dabeet. But not a word to Valentine. She knew who had been making the decisions, apparently.

"Am I talking to—" Andrew made the sound of the llop's name.

"You're talking to me," said the llop. "Great Mother. But now I've found my voice again."

"You've had this… companion before?" asked Andrew.

"I'm very old," she said. "From a time when every woman had a voice."

"No males, then?" asked Dabeet.

Great Mother ignored him. "My companion is dying," she said. "Ah. Ah ah ah. We are too late."

"We're just in time," said Andrew. "Say what you can."

"For ten thousand generations we lived in this companionship. We kept our history then in songs. I barely remember them now, and have no time to sing them, not in this language. So hard to translate."

"Why is your companion dying?" asked Andrew.

"They all died. All. But she is so sorry. So sorry to learn that Ken Argon is dead. She didn't mean to."

Dabeet could only assume that since connecting with—since extruding herself from—Great Mother, the parasite had been informed of Ken's death. Or perhaps of every single thing in the llop's mind.

"What did she do?"

"She thought Ken Argon was poisoning her. So she poisoned him back."

"She's venomous?" asked Andrew.

"Only at need. He had her in a jar. He sprayed her with something that made her feel very sick."

Dabeet shook his head. "He was working on a cure for feline toxoplasmosis."

"I know," said Great Mother. "He told me. I knew he had this one here. He understood that if I joined with this one, I would also become infected and die, and in all likelihood I would spread the cat sickness to the others. The whole family."

"So he was trying to cure it before you joined with it," said Andrew.

Dabeet looked for anything written. There was a notebook. There were several vials with dry stains and dried-up residue in the bottom. Maybe the notebook had some information about what Ken was trying. The formula he had devised for curing the parasite of toxoplasmosis.

But the pages were blank. Knowing Ken, Dabeet realized that he would write things down only if the treatment worked.

"It was painful, what Ken sprayed onto your companion?" asked Dabeet.

"It felt like an agonizing death," said Great Mother, answering Dabeet at last.

"Is she still in pain?" asked Dabeet. "Obviously she didn't die."

"The pain is gone," said Great Mother. "She was starving and drying out. She tried to guess which would kill her first. The nutrient solution was very rich at first, but for the past seventeen days it has been nothing but water, and not enough of that."

"Nobody knew that the nutrient solution was exhausted," said Dabeet. "Nobody knew there was anything alive in here."

"Did Ken's formula work?" asked Andrew. "Did it cure her toxoplasmosis?"

"No," said Great Mother. "She isn't actively sick; she doesn't have symptoms. But the disease forms cysts inside the body, and those are wakening now and spreading throughout my body. I will soon die."

Only then did Dabeet realize that the llop had come here, if not expecting to die, then... then hoping to reconnect with the parasite that gave her a voice, even if it killed her.

"Do you have a way to record my song?" asked Great Mother. "I would like to sing it in our native language. I will start by telling you the meanings of a few words, and then you can learn the rest of my language from the songs I sing before I die."

"Can't you tell us if—" Andrew began.

"This is the last of her kind," said Great Mother. "We will never have voices again. O Speaker for the Dead, please let me sing my own death, the death of my people."

"We'll leave now," said Dabeet. "All humans will withdraw from—"

"Too late," said Great Mother. "Now we're no longer wise. If you want to leave, go. But not until you have killed all the cats. Don't leave this world of ours to the cats."

"Sing," said Valentine, setting down her recorder. "This can hear you and record you for twenty hours."

"I will be dead long before that," said Great Mother.

"Do you want us to stay?" asked Valentine. "So you have someone to sing to?"

"No," said Great Mother. "I will sing to my people. Take this recording and play it to them. Play it every day. Maybe some of them will understand even without companions. Maybe some of them will learn our language."

"Let's go," said Andrew.

Immediately Valentine headed for the door.

Dabeet knew he should go. Yet this had been so fleeting, so impossible, so sudden. He wanted to know everything, yet he knew that she didn't have time to answer his questions. She had a hope, still—the hope that her songs would waken something in the minds of her... of her people. How dare he even think of interfering.

She began to sing in a language made of highly articulated yips and growls, sighs and whispers, with rhythm and pitch in patterns that bespoke a kind of music, though nothing like anything Dabeet had ever heard.

Andrew took him by the arm and led him from the room.

Andrew palmed the door closed.

"With all the cameras off," said Dabeet, "how will we know when she is through?"

"Don't you know how quickly toxoplasmosis works on living creatures on this world?" asked Andrew. "It was in the reports."

"Yes, I know," said Dabeet. "She has only a few hours."

"And then what?" asked Valentine. "Do they have a death ritual of some kind? A funeral? A burial?"

"Not for those that die of the cat disease," said Andrew. "It's in the reports. They shun the bodies, for fear of picking up the cysts from the corpse. They eat nothing that dies of cat disease."

"We really should have found a solution to the toxoplasmosis problem centuries ago," said Valentine.

"We did," said Dabeet. "We made it a high crime to bring any cat into space."

"So a colony of criminals arrived with their cats," said Valentine.

"Such a terrible chance that this is where they came," said Dabeet.

"I think we need to find a virus that seeks out and kills the *Toxoplasma gondii*," said Valentine.

"Or a virus that kills only cats," said Dabeet. "That's the one we need. Because even without toxoplasmosis, the cats have killed off dozens of species of small animals just for the fun of it."

"How many of the people here have caught the parasite?" asked Andrew.

"We check everybody every three months," said Dabeet. "Nobody has it."

Andrew and Valentine said nothing.

"I'll use my authority to compel everybody to be tested here, by E.S. personnel, instead of by local medical technicians," said Dabeet.

"Would they really conceal infections?" asked Valentine.

"Toxoplasmosis isn't usually dangerous to humans," said Dabeet. "But it does predispose us to be kind to cats."

"Are people still bringing in cat skins for the bounty?" asked Andrew.

"As many as ever," said Dabeet.

"But nowhere near fast enough to keep up with feline population growth?" asked Andrew.

"Nothing can keep up with feline population growth," said Valentine.

"How will the people react to the decision to deny the colony continuing status?" asked Andrew.

Dabeet didn't want to answer. But he owed the truth to this speaker for the dead. "They will have their continuing status," he said. "We will also continue our efforts to exterminate the cats and perhaps *Toxoplasma gondii*. And the llop will have a vast reserve of choice habitat that will be theirs forever."

"Until Catalunya becomes an independent world and makes their own laws," said Valentine.

"That's possible," said Dabeet, "though I'll recommend that Starways Congress never grant independence without a firm guarantee—"

"Firm guarantees will become worthless as soon as the side with all the power decides that the llop are dangerous wild animals," said Valentine.

"She drew the picture," said Andrew. "She came here to find her companion. She gave her life for her people. How can you say that the llop aren't sentient?"

"Because they aren't," said Dabeet. "Not with all the companions dead. We'll search for more. On an island somewhere, perhaps. It's not impossible. Or a genetically related species that we might be able to alter for them. We'll try. But I was sent here with clear instructions."

"To discover that the llop are not sentient and Ken Argon was a loon," said Valentine.

"Yes," said Dabeet.

"I think you don't want me to speak the death of Ken Argon," said Andrew.

"Yes, I do," said Dabeet. "For me. For my staff. Some of them, anyway. But not for the people of Tarragona."

"Some of them might change their minds," said Valentine. "If they knew the truth."

"No," said Dabeet. "They'll blame the pirates and the cats and say, 'Why should *we* pay for their crimes? The damage was already done before we got here. A tragic disease, not of our causing, not of our bringing. Tragedy is no reason we should give up this beautiful world,' they'll say. Ken Argon was a renegat, a traitor, the enemy."

Andrew and Valentine nodded as if the same puppeteer were moving their heads.

"I'm glad you came," said Dabeet. "I had to know. Even though I also knew what the E.S. wanted the outcome to be. Soon they would have replaced me and sent someone more obedient. Perhaps my replacement is already on his way."

"He is," said Andrew.

Dabeet smiled ruefully. "Andrew, do you really know who my father was?"

Andrew shook his head. Though whether that meant "No, I don't know" or "No, I won't answer you," Dabeet had no way of knowing.

"Andrew," said Dabeet. "Don't speakers for the dead fearlessly say what no one wants to hear, as long as it's true?"

"We do," said Andrew. "But Dabeet, my friend, you are not dead."

Our next story is the latest entry in the long running Dune saga. It takes us back to Frank Herbert's Dune, *the novel that launched the series. Authors Brian Herbert—Frank's son—and Kevin J. Anderson offer us a tale that takes place during the two-year gap where Gurney Halleck is off on his own, and Paul Atreides is becoming the Fremen leader. For decades readers have asked, "What was Gurney doing?" This is his story.*

THE WATERS OF KANLY

FROM THE LOST YEARS OF GURNEY HALLECK

BRIAN HERBERT AND KEVIN J. ANDERSON

I

"Blood is thicker than water.
Water is more precious than spice.
Revenge is most precious of all."
—songs of Gurney Halleck

The baliset strings thrummed and the flywheel spun, producing a sad song… as it always did.

Gurney Halleck used the multipick, focused on the music that came from his beloved instrument, immersed in the mood, the sorrow, the anger. With the music, he didn't need to think about the crackling dry air, the rock-walled caves of the smugglers' hideout, the grief that had set deeply into his bones, still undiminished even after a full year.

Harkonnen forces had swept into the Atreides stronghold in Arrakeen as soon as the household shields were dropped, thanks to an as-yet unidentified traitor, no doubt someone trusted… and deadly. Gurney was convinced that person was the she-witch Jessica, and because of her Duke Leto was dead. Young Master Paul was dead, too, and so was the loyal Duncan Idaho, a Swordmaster like Gurney.

And so, if reports were to be believed, was Jessica herself.

After the Harkonnens had once again taken over Arrakis, the planet commonly known as Dune, Gurney Halleck was the only surviving Atreides lieutenant, he and 73 other men. The Atreides Mentat, Thufir Hawat, had been captured alive, now forced to serve the vile Baron Harkonnen. Only Gurney and his men remained free, and they spoke often of seeking revenge.

But it was difficult and long delayed.

He let the emotions flow as he sang a sad refrain…

"A man of his people, not of himself,
Duke Leto betrayed, oh how can it be?
Of all the nobles, why our gallant Duke?
I shall never forget, shall never forgive…"

Gurney looked up as a shadow fell over him, cast by the light of the glowglobes suspended near the rock ceiling. A burly man stood a head taller than Gurney with blocky features that looked as if they had been carved from lava rock by an inexpert sculptor who had imbibed too much spice beer. Orbo was one of the reliable smugglers who had served their leader Staban Tuek reliably for years, a muscular man who excelled in physical endurance and strength, but was never called upon to do much thinking.

Gurney kept playing absently, though his singing faltered into silence as he saw the angry expression on Orbo's face. The large group sat inside the rock-walled assembly hall of the smugglers' hideout, their improvised sietch in the deep desert. The natural caves had been cut deeper with heavy equipment, the living chambers outfitted to look like the cabins and piloting deck of a spice freighter.

Many of Gurney's men were in the assembly room playing gambling games, talking about their long-lost homes on Caladan, describing their prowess with women from bygone days. Few discussed business, because Staban Tuek was the one who determined the time and the place of their raids, and his smugglers followed.

Gurney's fingers stilled on the baliset strings. Orbo's face rippled with uneasiness and anger, as he seemed to be having difficultly articulating what was upsetting him.

"Don't you have a fondness for music, man?" Gurney asked. He realized that the big muscular man had often shown discomfort whenever he played and sang.

"Oh, I like music all right," Orbo said in a voice thick from a lifetime of breathing and speaking dust. "I just don't like your music. I want happy music, joyful music." He scowled. "Your songs have too much anger, too much revenge."

Gurney's eyes narrowed. This man was treading on dangerous ground and could get hurt for doing so, no matter his size. "Perhaps vengeance is the most important thing I have to sing about... after what House Harkonnen did."

Orbo shook his head. "We are smugglers and have no time for politics. You are dangerous."

With the palm of his hand Gurney stopped the flywheel spinning. "When my men and I joined you, I swore to Staban I would delay my revenge and find an appropriate way, but I never promised to forget about it entirely." His voice hitched, but he clamped down on his emotions. "Thinking about revenge keeps me going."

Orbo seized the baliset, snatching it right out of his hands. Gurney grabbed for it, but the big man swung it and drove it hard against the heat-smoothed stone wall. He smashed the instrument, causing it to make a discordant jangle, like ghosts of the saddest songs ever sung. With an angry grunt, he tossed the string-tangled splinters in a heap at Gurney's feet. "Now you don't have music either, and we can finally have peace."

At another time, Gurney would have murdered him on the spot. He tightened his jaw, making the inkvine scar there ripple and dance like a purplish dying snake. Several of the other Atreides survivors rose to their feet, casting deadly glances toward Orbo as he stalked off. Gurney raised a hand, stopping them. He quelled his own anger, walling it off into a safe internal compartment, as he'd been doing since that terrible night.

Staban Tuek emerged from a small side chamber he used as an office, his expression dark. First looking at the departing Orbo and then at the wrecked instrument on the floor, he asked, "What have you done now, Gurney Halleck?"

Gurney struggled to control himself. *Everything in its time, and there is a time for everything.* "As I sit here with my prized possession ruined, your first thought is to ask me what *I've* done?"

"Yes, I do." He glanced at the tunnel where Orbo had vanished. "That man doesn't have the imagination to be cruel. You must have done something to irritate him. *Seriously* irritate him."

Gurney twitched his fingers as if he could still play an imaginary baliset. "Apparently some of your men don't like sad songs."

The smuggler leader snorted. "None of us do. And we're growing pretty tired of you." His expression softened and he gave a hint of a smile to mitigate his words. "You obsess on the defeat of your House Atreides rather than victories to come. You and your men are smugglers now and should be thinking of raiding spice, developing black markets, and stealing equipment from the Harkonnens to sell back to them at exorbitant prices." Staban shook his head. "The past is the past. And remember what I told you when you first came to me after the fall of Arrakeen, when you were burned and dirty, weak and starving."

"The same night your own father was murdered by the Harkonnen monsters," Gurney said.

Staban twitched, but narrowed his gaze and focused his words. "I gave you a home but I warned you not to seek revenge too soon, bringing down the anger of our new planetary masters, House Harkonnen. As my father said, 'A stone is heavy and the sand is weighty; but a fool's wrath is heavier than both.'"

"I remember the quote," Gurney muttered, "but I prefer another from Esmar Tuek." He smiled, softening the features on his lumpy face. "'There's more than one way to destroy a foe.'" He kicked the jangling wires and debris of his baliset as if it meant nothing to him. Compared to his plans, the lost instrument was indeed a trivial thing. Revenge against the Harkonnens, against the loathsome acting governor Beast Rabban was paramount. "I've been pondering something in the Orange Catholic Bible: 'A thinking man has infinite options, but a reactive man is doomed to only one path.'"

"You always have a quote. One for every occasion, it seems. Now what the hell does that one mean?"

"It means I have an idea about how to hurt Rabban, one that should also prove profitable for us."

Tuek was intrigued. "I much prefer this line of thinking. Tell me."

Gurney brushed himself off and walked with the smuggler leader back to his office, speaking in a low voice. "Regular shipments of supplies and equipment come from offworld to Rabban's garrison city of Carthag. The Beast should not be entitled to all of them." He paused, letting the idea sink in. He could see the thoughts churning on Staban's face.

"First," Gurney continued, "we have to arrange a meeting with the Emperor's unofficial ambassador to the smugglers."

II

As far as Gurney was concerned, this was not a man to be trusted.

Count Hasimir Fenring was a weasel-faced, dithering imperialist who held a great deal of power. Apparently, Fenring had been a childhood friend of the Padishah Emperor Shaddam IV. They had shared many schemes and violent adventures, and according to rumor had even assassinated Shaddam's father, placing the Crown Prince on the throne. On the surface, Fenring had the ability to seem innocuous and foppish, with a meandering conversational style, yet he had a gaze like a pair of surgical needles. This was a deadly killer and the Emperor's proxy on Arrakis. Gurney knew well, he was not a man to be underestimated, and might even have been involved in the plot to destroy House Atreides.

Fenring had come to Carthag on official business, to meet with Glossu Rabban and ensure that after a full year the Harkonnen spice-harvesting operations were producing the expected amounts of the valuable geriatric substance melange, found only in the deep deserts of this planet. Count Fenring had countless unofficial dealings on the Emperor's behalf, of which neither the Harkonnens nor the Landsraad nobles knew anything. Because of his illicit interactions with smuggler bands such as Staban Tuek's, he held the whispered, unofficial title of "Ambassador to the Smugglers."

Carthag, a brassy and blustery new city thrown together with prefabricated buildings and no finesse, was a place of dark alleys and sharp corners where Harkonnen troops held as much power over the populace as they could grab, a city where happiness was a rare and expensive commodity.

Through his connections among the merchants and military quartermasters in Carthag, Staban had slipped him a message, and Count Fenring had arranged this meeting in an airlocked bar down a side alley, where the price of water was more expensive than any exotic or extravagant alcoholic drink. The proprietor had paid substantial bribes to Harkonnen guards and officials to ensure that this unofficial drinking establishment remained unharassed, the patrons allowed a small measure of privacy.

Gurney and Staban wore dusty desert robes, and Gurney kept a stillsuit mask across his face and a cowl around his head, while Staban was more brash, confident that no one would recognize him... or at least no one would care. Eerie warbling semuta music played in the background. Incense wafted pinkish clouds of aroma into the stuffy air. All manner of dusty, dirty patrons filled the bar, many of whom were engaged in whispered conversations, as if they were plotting something illegal.

A man entered through the door seal, and Gurney recognized

Fenring, the Imperial representative, a man with secrets and goals of his own. He wore traditional local garb without Harkonnen military markings: drab and dusty folds of cloth, a breathing mask across his face, but he didn't seem to belong here. At first Gurney thought that Fenring—with his fine upbringing and noble ways—was just uncomfortable in a seedy place like this, but realized as Fenring's close-set eyes flashed that this wasn't the case at all. No, the part of Fenring that didn't belong was an act. At any moment he could glide into the shadows with a dagger or other weapon and do exactly what needed to be done, without flinching or the slightest remorse.

Staban signaled him with a subtle hand gesture, and Fenring glided over with a jouncey step. He sat on a hard chair, removed his head covering. Gurney and Staban already had their drinks; diluted spice beers.

Fenring lifted a finger as the surly, wrung-out waitress came up to him. "Ah, I would like water please. Purified water of course, but with a splash of citrus flavoring. Let's make it special tonight for this meeting, hmmm?"

"Water," she said. "I'll see if I can find something to add taste."

Though Staban had requested the meeting, Fenring took charge, leaning over the table, glancing at Gurney without recognition but focusing his piercing gaze on the smuggler leader. "I have come to oversee Governor Rabban's activities here. I fear he will not do well, hmmm."

"We hope that is the case," Gurney muttered.

Fenring suddenly paid attention to him. They had met previously, a brief occasion when Gurney was with Duke Leto, but the Count still showed no indication of knowing this. Still, something seemed to be nagging at him, tickling his memory. "Interesting... hmmm."

Staban sucked in a breath and interrupted. "We don't care who the planetary governor is, so long as we are able to perform our own work, unmolested."

"And that is why I do business with you, my dear Staban, ahhh," Fenring said. "For all the good intentions—or bad— of the new Harkonnen overlords, the Padishah Emperor does not like a bottleneck in the flow of spice, nor does he care for a single disreputable source of melange. Imperial governors are so notoriously... ummm... unreliable. After all, look what happened to poor Duke Atreides, hmmm?"

Gurney felt a flush of angry heat through his skin, took a deep breath for courage. He reached up and removed the nostril plugs, the covering over his mouth, slid down the cowl to expose the prominent inkvine scar on his cheek, the scar that Rabban himself had inflicted upon him after the horrible rape and beating he had committed against Gurney's sister, right before his very eyes… "Yes, look what happened to the Atreides. Look what happened to my Duke." He waited a beat as Fenring studied him, worked through his thoughts and memories, tried to recognize who Gurney was.

"You are one of the Duke's men. A well-known one, hmmm." He pursed his lips. "Ah yes, Halleck, isn't it?"

"Gurney Halleck."

"Most unfortunate what happened to your Duke, yes, most unfortunate, indeed. And I'm not surprised some of the Duke's men survived, though I am surprised that you would fall in among the smugglers."

"I had few choices," Gurney answered in a growl. He sipped his diluted spice beer, and the waitress shuffled over with Fenring's water. It looked murky from some oily additive. Fenring sipped, grimaced, but thanked the waitress anyway.

"The Atreides fell, and it was not entirely due to the Harkonnens. There was treachery." Gurney leaned over the table. "Was it treachery from the Emperor?"

Fenring looked astonished by the suggestion. Staban reacted with alarm. "He didn't mean that, sir—"

The Count glared at Gurney. "I assure you, hmmm, that the Emperor takes no part in the petty squabbles of Landsraad nobles."

The Swordmaster rested his elbows on the table. "Then we must have been imagining things when we fought enemies in Harkonnen livery who were quite clearly trained as Sardaukar."

Fenring paused for a moment too long before saying, "Then the Baron must have hired some mercenaries with excellent training."

Gurney didn't believe him for a moment, but let the matter drop. Fenring knew something, though he probably was not involved in the planning. As a minimum, he and the Emperor looked the other way and let the Harkonnens commit their treachery. He took a deep calming breath. That assessment wasn't his focus right now. "Politics and politics," he said, "and damn it all to the Seven Hells. I know who the traitor was—Jessica, the concubine of my beloved Duke, the woman who shared his bed, the mother of—" His voiced hitched. "The mother of Paul Atreides, dear Paul. All of them gone now." He drew a deep breath, felt his face flush. "There must be an accounting against the Harkonnens, sir." His voice was hard and determined, and just across the table from him Fenring's eyes bored into his, like a laser cutter. "Even before House Atreides moved to this damned desert planet, we knew there was a plot. We knew the Duke's enemies had gathered against him. Duke Leto Atreides formally declared Kanly on the Baron Vladimir Harkonnen. There are rules and expectations to that ancient blood feud." Gurney waited a beat. "And now I insist on my right. Sir, on behalf of my fallen House and my noble Duke, I demand satisfaction."

Fenring's eyes lit up, and a sardonic smile curled at the edges of his mouth. He sat back, took another unconscious sip of the murky water. "Yes, rules, hmmm. Rules."

"I demand that the forms be obeyed."

"But, ahhh, Duke Leto is dead now," Fenring pointed out. "As is his son and heir Paul."

"I know. And when all the lights go out, darkness only wins until another flame lights the shadows. I am the Duke's last remaining lieutenant. I claim the right of Kanly. I will finish this battle against House Harkonnen—in my own way."

Fenring let out a long and weary sigh and drained half of his water in one gulp. "Hmmm, vows of revenge are so tedious, so boring to me. Is that why you brought me here?"

Staban Tuek quickly broke in, looking uneasy. "My companion focuses too much on revenge and forgets the more relevant part of this discussion. He has developed a plan of action—a fascinating one, I think you'll agree.

"The Harkonnens supply Rabban's military outpost in Carthag with offworld water, shipped from their homeworld, Giedi Prime. The water costs little, although the transportation is expensive. A supply tanker of water, enough to fulfill the extravagant needs of the Harkonnen troops, arrives each month. To the people on Giedi Prime, it is mere water, practically free. To the people of Arrakis, it is a treasure worth more than spice. For some it is worth more than life itself."

"We intend to hijack the tanker and take the water," Gurney interrupted, catching Fenring's attention again. "We need to enlist your assistance, your connections, Count Fenring. We require access to the Guild Heighliner. When it arrives, we need to know the crew and defenses aboard the Harkonnen tanker when it's still up in orbit. Once we get aboard, we'll handle the rest."

Staban interjected, "Stealing that tanker will be a great embarrassment for Rabban—and thus Gurney gets his revenge and can declare Kanly complete. And we smugglers receive a water prize worth a huge number of solaris here on Arrakis."

Fenring sounded dubious. "And why would I assist you in this? What possible reason would I have?"

Gurney chose to state the matter flat out. "Because we will pay you an enormous bribe."

Staban looked as if he had just swallowed sand and choked on it.

Fenring did not laugh, nor dismiss the suggestion. "And the Guild itself will require tremendous payments, hmmmm." He tapped his fingers on the tabletop. "I admit there is a measure of amusement in placing Rabban in an awkward position. It is never good to have a planetary governor who grows too complacent. Giving him a black eye could be very beneficial."

Gurney knotted and unknotted his fists on the table. "We will pay the inducement. We will round up additional spice, and you will have the funds you need."

"I haven't even quoted the price yet, hmmm. You may find it overwhelming."

"We will pay it," Gurney said, and Staban glared at him. Fenring's eyes narrowed, flicking back and forth as he performed calculations in his mind. Gurney was reminded of how Thufir Hawat had concentrated with remarkable focus and intensely, when he performed Mentat projections.

Then Fenring quoted an amount so astronomical that Staban gasped and looked at him in disbelief. Gurney had made calculations of his own, knowing the smugglers and the Atreides fighters would find ways to gather extra spice in their raids, perhaps with the cooperation of desert villagers, maybe even the Fremen.

"We will pay it," the Atreides man said again.

III

It was not difficult to rally the desert villagers and the Fremen against the Harkonnens. Gurney had known it wouldn't be. He knew Beast Rabban.

Less than a week after their secret meeting with Fenring, smuggler scouts and spice hunters on the edge of the desert plateau spotted a black flag of smoke curling up from the elbow of a canyon, the site of one of the hardscrabble graben villages. A squalid town that collected droplets of moisture from the air with huge skimmers and condensers, people who coaxed useful minerals and metals from the rocks and scavenged just enough spice from the open desert to trade in the cities for supplies and medicines they needed, and no luxuries. The smoke had wafted up, dissipating for hours before a spotter reported it.

After checking the weather report and verifying there were no sandstorms or turbulent cyclones on the flight path, Gurney flew the low-altitude ornithopter. Beside him, a concerned-looking Orbo rode, along with Staban and ten other armed smugglers in seats at the back, all clad in desert gear. Even after being stranded here for a year in the smuggler crew, Gurney still found it awkward to prepare for combat without a personal shield, but no one on Arrakis wore a shield. Not only did the sand and dust make the devices malfunction, the pulsing field-effect invariably attracted and maddened a giant sandworm.

No amount of personal protection was worth the risk of facing a monster like that.

Gruff Orbo looked through the 'thopter's scratched and pitted plaz window as Gurney flew in toward the smoke.

Once or twice he had considered challenging the bigger man to a duel, to slay him in front of the other smugglers for the insult of smashing the baliset. The smuggler caves were without music now, and Gurney found them a much sadder, lonelier place. But he knew that if he challenged Orbo, who had many friends among the smugglers, he would damage his own position among them. Even if he won the duel, he would have to leave. Gurney didn't want that, couldn't afford it. He needed these hardened smugglers, especially now that he was so close to achieving what he wanted so badly. He had not forgiven Orbo, but gave the matter no further thought now, blocking it away like putting it inside a walled fortress. He did not allow the incident to fester within him the way the thought of Rabban did.

The way the traitor Jessica festered within him.

"I know what *that* is," Orbo said, pointing down at the surface. The rattling hum of the engine and flutter of the articulated wings nearly drowned out his voice.

Gurney looked to the side, through the window past Orbo. "What is it? What's out there?"

Orbo simply stared out the window.

Just behind Gurney, Staban leaned close. "His village is out there. He came from the desert people and joined us. Sometimes we bring water and supplies to that settlement."

As Gurney flew in, he realized with a sinking sensation what the curling smoke meant. "Looks like someone else found it, too."

Orbo just stared gloomily. He'd already figured this out himself.

The smugglers were greatly uneasy as Gurney brought the 'thopter around the high cliffs and into the elbow canyon. Black starbursts of explosions marked the desert floor and cliff walls. The once huddled buildings of the small outpost had been smashed and burned. Bodies lay sprawled in the streets, their skin blackened, some of their desert stillsuits smoldering as slow-burning fires ate through the sandwiched fabric and cooked the dead flesh underneath.

Gurney had barely landed the 'thopter when Orbo cracked open the door and burst out, his boots sinking into the stirred gravel and sand. He didn't even affix his nose plugs or breathing mask. He bounded forward, letting out primal sounds as the other smugglers followed.

Gurney shut down the rotors, racked the articulated wings into their resting position, then joined Staban outside. While Orbo and the smugglers searched the mangled remnants of huts, the low dwellings built into cliff walls, the supply sheds that had been leveled with explosives, frantically looking for survivors, Gurney knew they would find none. Rabban would not have left any.

Orbo came back, his face distraught. Soot smeared his cheeks and desert cloak. Other smugglers had dragged out the bodies of dead villagers, laying them out on the bleak canyon floor.

"Who did this?" Orbo sobbed. "Why?"

"You know who did it," Gurney said. "Perhaps your people didn't pay Rabban the tithes he demanded, or maybe his men were just bored."

"No survivors?" Staban asked.

"They're all dead. He wanted to burn everything so no one would find this village at all. A single sandstorm can wipe out the rest of the evidence."

"Rabban doesn't care about any evidence he leaves behind," Gurney said. "He's perfectly happy to let you find it. Dozens of other villages in the pan and graben have suffered the same fate in the past year. Rabban needs to make everyone fear him." He clenched his jaw.

"Any fool would know this is wasteful, not leadership."

When he glanced up, he caught a flicker of movement in the cliffs, in the shadows of rock, while a figure, a human figure, darted into a cleft. As Gurney watched, a camouflage cloak swirled up and he could no longer see the person.

"Fremen," Staban muttered.

Gurney was intrigued. "An eyewitness, maybe?"

"More likely just drawn to the smoke to investigate—and to scavenge what he can."

Gurney looked down at the bodies lined up outside the village, recalling a rumor he'd heard that Fremen took corpses and extracted the water from their flesh. Yes, water was indeed a precious commodity here. If Gurney and the smugglers hadn't flown in, maybe the Fremen would have stolen the bodies so that no one knew what happened to them. He looked around at the cliffs, saw no further movement, could no longer see a hint of where the furtive Fremen had vanished. He suspected others were also watching, camouflaged as well. They would be listening.

Gurney looked at Orbo, then at the smuggler leader, and spoke loudly. "Staban, this is the time for revenge. You have made me wait too long. Now Orbo's village is destroyed, his entire family. Staban, your father is also dead—because of the Harkonnens." He raised his voice to a shout, "And all you Fremen, I know you're listening. Spread the word among your sietches. Tell the desert people in the graben villages and those hidden in the deepest wilds that we need a huge amount of spice... not for our own profit, but to make the proper bribes. Tell them we have a way to hurt the Beast who did this."

Gurney knew if his words resonated here, the message would spread. The survivors and bereaved from other villages Rabban had preyed upon... those people would help him. He wasn't the only one with justification for a vendetta. So much blood had been spilled that the cost in spice was not even worth measuring.

They had three weeks to raise the enormous amount of melange before Count Fenring returned.

They would get more than they needed in two.

IV

Twelve men, all loyal, tried-and-true Atreides veterans for the mission.

Gurney selected them himself and disappointed others back

in the smugglers' hideout, because every one of his men who had survived Arrakeen still served the memory of their beloved Duke Leto and his family and wanted to share in Gurney Halleck's quest to meet the requirements of Kanly. They all wanted to shed Harkonnen blood, but he could only take a small number on the mission up to the Guild Heighliner, where they would steal Rabban's water tanker. A dozen men following him… and Gurney didn't promise they would survive. He merely told them they might, and might not die. Brave and dedicated men, that was good enough for them.

"For House Atreides!" they called out in a cheer, joined by the other Atreides men who had failed to make the cut.

Staban Tuek then insisted that Gurney also take six of his original smugglers to ensure his own profit as well as Gurney's vengeance. Orbo led this smaller group, but they would follow Gurney's orders, to complete his plan.

The squad traveled surreptitiously to the battle-damaged spaceport at Arrakeen, much smaller than the large industrial platforms in Rabban's city of Carthag. Following the attack a year ago, using modern weapons and old-style artillery, the Harkonnen invaders had damaged much of the Arrakeen spaceport, and although it had been patched and repaired to make it serviceable, no one had bothered to clean up all the battle debris, not thinking it mattered.

That's how the Harkonnens were, and Carthag was their capital here, while Arrakeen was just a sad and painful memory of the all-too-brief Atreides rule. Gurney wanted to depart from the Arrakeen spaceport for a purpose, though. He despised Carthag and the pigsty stink of Harkonnens there. The frontier town of Arrakeen was more familiar to him, and more appropriate for the purpose of Kanly.

The forms must be obeyed, he thought.

By his reaction, Count Fenring had obviously been surprised to receive the enormous spice bribe he'd demanded. The amount was so exorbitant he'd never imagined that even the largest smuggling crew could achieve it, but he accepted the shipment with good grace and no questions. In return, he provided the vital information Gurney had requested, Guild access cards, stolen uniforms, codes and schedules… basics that the raid required.

Gurney had led his own men into battle many times. They were well versed in Atreides code language, and would follow his orders instantly and efficiently. They understood his tactics instinctively, and never questioned an order in the slightest degree. He spent more of his time discussing the plan with Orbo and Staban's men, all of whom gruffly acknowledged his instructions. They could smell profit and the adrenaline-rush of adventure. The thought of seizing an entire Harkonnen tanker filled with water destined for Rabban's troops filled them with excitement and anticipation.

Back on Caladan, Gurney had often listened to half-drunk men in dockside taverns sharing preposterous stories about great fish they had nearly caught out on the sea, but had gotten away. The water tanker would be like that in Gurney's secret plan, unrevealed to them, or to anyone else. His plan within a plan.

This big fish would get away… or it would seem to do so.

The men were silent, huddled with excitement and wrapped in desert clothes like refugees as they rode together in the rumbling liner that lifted off from the Arrakeen spaceport. The Guild pilot asked no questions of his passengers, merely acknowledged that their documents were correct and their passage was paid for, along with the additional bribe Gurney had paid to him, to ensure the man's best work. Few workers were able to buy their way off the desert planet, particularly now that Rabban had clamped down on veteran spice crews in order to increase production, but Gurney had found a way to circumvent the system.

The Duke's man knew that all necessary details were in order; Staban Tuek had enough connections to make it so. The only questionable part about their disguises, he realized, was that these men were intent and grim—and any workers truly escaping from Arrakis would be celebrating. But none of his team could find it within their hearts to fake that part, even though it had been suggested.

The lighter was an old-model ship with few amenities. Gurney gripped the armrests of his worn seat, holding himself against violent tremors as the craft heaved itself out of the planet's gravity well, like an old man rising roughly to his feet. Through thick plaz portholes he could see the cracked scab of the desert dwindling below, smeared and softened by a haze of high, orangish dust. He turned his gaze upward to where the sky darkened and the atmosphere thinned toward space, and the huge Guild Heighliner waited for them.

His pulse raced. Plans and memories collided in his mind, and his fingers twitched involuntarily, as if playing the strings of an imaginary baliset.

His men muttered to one another, pretending to make idle

conversation but listening to few of the words. An island in their midst, Gurney focused his thoughts forward, reviewing each step they would take once they reached the huge ship.

The Heighliner's enormous hold carried countless separated vessels on docking cradles. A Guild navigator would fold space and transport the immense spacefolder from star system to star system, stopping along the way so that smaller ships could disembark and fly to their destinations. But first, he had something to do…

The lighter rising from Arrakeen reached orbit less than an hour after the huge Heighliner arrived. Gurney had complete confidence in Fenring's information, but he also had every reason not to trust the man. *Visionaries and fools feed themselves on optimism, not bread.* Even so, Gurney thought he could rely on Fenring to get them inside the big vessel. After that, he would count on nothing but the skill, dedication, and courage of his best men.

The lighter came aboard the huge ship, maneuvered into the central hold as the great bay doors opened and the administration work took place, with Guild officials accounting for all arriving craft, assigning docking cradles, finishing documentation so that the outbound vessels could depart for Arrakis.

According to Fenring, the bribe to the Guild was enough for them to bureaucratically stall the release of Rabban's water tanker.

"We won't have much time," Gurney said to his men, repeating what he'd told them earlier.

Orbo held his hands out in front of himself, palms facing and fingers curled, as if he were thinking of strangling a succession of enemies. He had been murderously gloomy ever since seeing the massacre of his village by Rabban's troops.

The lighter docked, its slender form clicking into the clamp, and the egress tube deployed from the Heighliner wall, connecting to the main hatch of the lighter. Gurney motioned to his men that it was time. When the hatch opened he led his team through the connecting tube, shucking their dusty and tattered desert cloaks along the way because they would not need them again. Beneath their traditional clothes, they wore the Guild uniforms Fenring had obtained. Gurney had used makeup over the inkvine scar on his face, but his lumpy features and characteristic rolling gait could never be concealed from anyone familiar with him.

Gurney intended to kill any Harkonnen who showed the slightest inkling of recognizing him. And if they didn't show any such sign, he would still kill them, though perhaps not so quickly. Fortunately for him, many Guildsmen also had imperfect features. He felt comfortable on their ship; he was fitting in well.

Once away from the lighter, Gurney consulted the detailed schematic of the vessel that Fenring and the Guild had provided. His men had to work their way through the inner hull decks of the Heighliner to find the Harkonnen water tanker, a trivial ship among the thousands of vessels carried by this enormous transport.

Inside the sandwiched hull decks they rode tube transports, sitting alongside silent Guildsmen who showed no interest in their presence. Gurney's squad traveled along the hull, rising up the curve, counting decks until they reached the appropriate sector that contained the docking clamp holding the water tanker.

Gurney and the uniformed men carried packs, tool kits, diagnostics, and false documents showing that they had been sent to inspect the manifest of the Harkonnen transport. All perfectly routine. Gurney knew none of the Harkonnen crew would be suspicious because they were arrogant. His men also carried packs with hidden weapons, knives, and maula pistols as well as personal shields—which were never used down in the desert, but Gurney insisted on them here. This would be his kind of fight, and on his terms, his own retaliatory sneak attack.

Gurney also had a special surprise inside his pack, something required by the Kanly he intended to administer.

His men were subdued and intense, their eyes shining and deep blue from frequent consumption of the spice melange. This distinctive tint might have been problematic, except Guildsmen also imbibed heavily in spice. In all likelihood no one would question the coloration... at least not before his team had their chance.

Gurney felt a rush of relief as they came upon the access ramp assigned to the Harkonnen water tanker. Gurney used his access cards, having no choice except to hope Fenring and his Guild allies had deflected the previously assigned Guild inspection teams, leaving the way open for him and his crew. As a matter of practice, the Spacing Guild did not involve themselves in petty family feuds, especially not something so small as a single water tanker... and certainly not an outburst from the last remnants of a fallen noble house of the Landsraad. House Atreides was irrelevant to them, but it was not irrelevant to Gurney or to any of his men.

Staban's six smugglers were efficient enough, and businesslike, but the Atreides men were on a higher level, more intense. Orbo almost had that, impressing Gurney a bit, but not causing him to let down his guard. He recalled something the assassinated Duke Leto had said to him once, that "an enemy can be anywhere, declared or undeclared."

At the end of the ramp, the hatch opened to the tanker, and they boarded through the lower deck. Inside, a surly-looking engineer stood with arms crossed over his wide chest, a frown on his face. The griffin symbol and the colors of House Harkonnen drove a knot into Gurney's stomach, but he maintained a neutral expression.

"About damn time," the engineer said. "We need to depart within the hour. Do your inspections and sign off on the paperwork."

"We'll be faster if you leave us to our own work," Gurney said.

"All right, go about it, then," said the Harkonnen engineer. "I have enough of my own damn work trying to take this load down to Carthag. The captain says there's been a security alert on the Heighliner, and we've all had to do nonsense drills. I don't have time to show you around anyway."

Gurney felt a chill, and his men flicked glances at one another. One twitched toward his pack and the weapons hidden there, but Gurney made a subtle gesture to calm him.

"We'll be efficient," he said. "I just need to see your cargo hold, and these men will verify your atmospheric engines."

Showing impatience, the engineer pointed them in various directions for the inspections.

"Security alert, Gurney?" muttered one of his men, as soon as the engineer was out of earshot. "Do you think we've been betrayed?"

"There's always a chance of that, but I've heard that security alerts are commonplace on Heighliners. This is a fresh crew. Did you see the water fat on his face? He's never been to Arrakis before."

The other man grumbled, "No appreciation for water, that's for sure."

Gurney nodded. "All to our advantage. Now go."

The men split up, going about their "Guild inspection" duties. Their uniforms made them invisible to the Harkonnen crew. Gurney hoped they didn't have to begin killing before it was time, or that could alert others. Fenring had instructed Gurney not to make any move until the water tanker dropped out of the Heighliner's hold and was free of Guild jurisdiction—he had made the importance of that eminently clear.

Acting his part as "Chief Cargo Inspector," Gurney made his way to the lower bulkhead that sealed the bulbous compartment holding a large bubble of water—water from Giedi Prime, a place where such a substance was as unremarkable as air, a shipment that cost the Baron Harkonnen almost nothing, yet was worth an incredible treasure here on Arrakis. It was worth a great deal to the man.

Plaz observation ports providing them with views into the cargo hold showed only murky liquid, but Gurney knew its potential, its worth. This water represented *revenge* to him. Kanly. It represented hope, and death. A smile twitched across his face.

He found an access port for drawing samples and testing the water, but from the look of things Gurney doubted if the tanker captain had ever bothered to do this himself. These Harkonnens did not yet have an appreciation for the value of water on the driest, most desolate planet in the universe.

He unshouldered his pack and got to work, doing his secret thing, the thing that even his most trusted followers did not know about.

When it was done, Gurney stared at the precious cargo behind the plaz observation window, but he thirsted for something else.

V

It was easy enough to fool the tanker's systems. Playing their role as Guild functionaries, Gurney and his men verified the tanker's engines, acknowledged the cargo of water, signed off on the tanker's departure from the Heighliner. An hour later, after most of the other Arrakis-bound ships had already dropped from their docking cradles and descended to the desert planet, the water tanker was at last cleared. The Guild inspectors departed through the access tube into the main ship again—at least that was what the records showed—and the tanker captain received authorization to depart.

But after Gurney and his team supposedly left the access tube, two of his men remained behind, hidden on the engineering deck, where they could divert the sensors on the sealed door. When clear, they let the fighters back in, and they rushed to take hiding places among the engine blocks and cooling racks. Gurney knew it was an inelegant hiding place, but they needed only ten minutes before the tanker dropped out of the Heighliner and began its spiral toward the desert planet on course to Carthag.

Huddled in the dark and noisy lower decks, they heard the

thump and felt the jarring vibration through the hull as the tanker drifted free. Slow suspensor engines guided it carefully among the other stowed vessels within the Guild ship's hold, then the tanker dropped out into open space over the desert planet. The more powerful engines ignited, driving it down toward Arrakis.

Gurney's heart raced as if he had taken a heavy dose of stimulants. Revenge was his stimulant. All of his men felt the same. Orbo's hooded brow shaded his gleaming eyes, and he continued to strangle imaginary foes.

Concealing himself among the conduits and cooling tubes, Gurney held his breath, counting silently as the tanker dropped away from the Heighliner. When he knew it was safe, Gurney gestured silently to his team. They attached their shield belts, clipping them into place but not activating them yet. After he closed his eyes and breathed a prayer, he raised a hand, and his men surged out of their places of concealment.

They boiled out of the hidden compartments, knowing their one goal was to reach the piloting deck and seize control of the tanker. According to Fenring, only seven Harkonnen crew would be on the piloting deck, four more down in engineering, and two more in other duties around the tanker. Gurney had enough fighters to overrun them, and he had the element of surprise.

The impatient engineer was the first man they encountered. "You're not supposed to be—"

One of the smugglers fired a maula pistol, and the projectile ripped through the engineer's chest. The boom of the spring-wound weapon was loud, but mostly drowned out by engine noise. Another engineer shouted, calling for help. Gurney ran straight at him, holding his knife in one hand. He preferred to use the more personal touch of death, because this was a very personal matter. He bounded ahead as the astonished second Harkonnen engineer turned to flee, grabbed the man by the collar of his overalls, yanked him backward, and swiftly drew the blade across his throat, spilling blood across the deck.

Gurney realized he had lived on Arrakis for a long time, because his first thought was not to savor victory, but to frown at the waste of viable water gurgling out of the man's severed arteries.

The attacking squad rolled forward, independent but efficient, focused on the same goal. They easily found two other workers on the engineering deck and slew them without fanfare. Gurney motioned for the team to follow him to the piloting deck.

They hammered up metal staircases, passed through bulkhead doors. One sleepy man emerged from cramped crew quarters, calling out a question more than an alarm. His mouth was still open when Orbo grabbed him by the hair, yanked his head back hard enough to snap his neck, and threw him with disgust down onto the deck.

"One level up," Orbo said. "That's where we'll find the controls."

Gurney and his men ran and burst through the hatch, charging onto the piloting deck, with him and two Atreides fighters in the lead. The bulkhead door created a bottleneck, and only three could pass through at a time, but he saw instantly what he had feared.

Instead of the tiny crew Fenring had said there would be on the piloting deck, twenty armed Harkonnen soldiers faced them. Alarms had begun to ring throughout the tanker, despite their attempts at swiftness and caution.

As Orbo and two more fighters crowded through the bulkhead doorway one of the smugglers called out, "We've been betrayed! This is too many."

"Not too many for us to fight." Gurney activated his personal shield. The other men did the same.

With a roar, Orbo pushed past them, lumbering across the deck and throwing Harkonnen fighters from side to side.

"Use your shield, man!" Gurney said.

"Don't need a shield," Orbo replied and crashed into two armed Harkonnen guards, grabbing them and smashing their heads together. He turned to fight two more, but they opened fire, cutting him to pieces. Lurching forward, the big smuggler managed to collapse on top of them, knocking the Harkonnens down as more Atreides fighters rushed onto the piloting deck.

The Harkonnens had advanced weapons, but Gurney's team fought like madmen. The pilot continued to work the controls, hunched over the console and glancing nervously from side to side as the battle continued around him.

"We're outnumbered, Gurney!" one of his men shouted. "But we'll fight to the death. For House Atreides!"

The others picked up the defiant cheer. "For House Atreides!"

Gurney slashed the throat of another man and glanced around the deck, looking for any additional threats. Fenring had provided a schematic of the tanker so he could see the water hold and the engineering deck. He had also noted a large escape pod on the starboard side of the piloting deck. He had his own plan, one his men didn't know about.

The Atreides men fought furiously. They had already lost so much with the assassination of their Duke, and now they were willing to pay with their lives for Kanly, for Gurney's revenge… but it belonged to them as well. They had no need for regrets. So far they had killed five of the Harkonnens, losing Orbo, one other original smuggler, and two of his Atreides men.

Then the secondary door to the piloting deck opened and ten more armed Harkonnen soldiers appeared. A cry of despair rippled through his team, particularly Staban's smugglers. "This is not what we were promised!"

"We were not *promised* anything," Gurney said, "just given information we hoped would be reliable. Will you whine and snivel, or will you fight?"

"For House Atreides!" his men shouted, and their fierce response drove the Harkonnen guards back, but at the loss of more of Gurney's men. Shot in the chest, one of his men still managed to get to the pilot, shooting him through the head with a maula pistol. The pilot slumped and fell aside while the injured Atreides man shoved the bleeding body aside to work the controls. The tanker lurched as Gurney's man changed course, heading down through the rough atmosphere. Thin winds and veils of dust screeched and buffeted against the hull.

Another Harkonnen guard killed the Atreides at the piloting controls, and the tanker careened out of control. The Harkonnens had managed to transmit a distress signal, calling for assistance, and Gurney had no doubt that Harkonnen fighters were already streaking upward from the military base in Carthag.

He didn't have enough time, and was losing too many men. They had put up enough of a fight; no one would doubt their intent. Yet the full measure of his revenge required the next step, his secret plan. "We cannot win, and I will not let us all die. To the escape pod!"

Fighting furiously, the team reacted with dismay. "I die for House Atreides!" one of his men vowed.

"It is not necessary." Gurney ran to the starboard side of the piloting deck. "Come all of you—to the escape pod. Join me!"

A Harkonnen guard lunged at him, and Gurney blocked him with his activated, shimmering body shield. His foe moved slowly, trying to penetrate the intangible barrier, but Gurney brought his knife into the man's gut, driving it deep, twisting, finding the abdominal artery and severing it. The man bled out within seconds, but Gurney held onto the body like another shield, backing toward the pod's hatch. He activated it with a backhanded swat of his hand. "With me! You'll die if you stay here. Harkonnen ships are coming."

"But we can't just leave!" one of his men yelled.

"We will; I command it. We've shaken them, and we'll fight elsewhere." Gurney dragged the dead Harkonnen guard, who was limp in his arms. Letting go, he fell backward into the large escape pod, and his reluctant men tumbled in after him, crowding into the interior chamber. The last ones continued to fight, and three more of Gurney's men fell... three more he would have to add to the verses of his sad victory song.

The water tanker roared and rattled through the atmosphere, dropping through the sky as Gurney took the controls, even from the pod, trying to stabilize the flight. Just before the escape pod disengaged, Gurney could feel the ship under control again. The tanker would indeed fly into Carthag as planned, its decimated, surviving crew shaken.

Rabban would declare it a victory.

"Now!" Gurney yelled, releasing his control over the water tanker. The escape pod released, bursting out into the winds and flying to a dangerously low altitude. The clunky vessel had minimal guidance, but he hoped the Harkonnen pursuit 'thopters racing up from the industrial military city below would be more interested in saving the tanker and its valuable cargo.

Gurney controlled the pod as best he could, sending out a coded signal to Staban Tuek, asking the smugglers to intercept them wherever they crashed out in the desert. He prayed he could guide the pod close enough to the rocks to avoid being devoured by a sand-dwelling worm before they could be saved. The five surviving men with him were injured, and needed medical attention.

He sat hunched over his knees. The makeup covering his inkvine scar had flaked away under beads of perspiration. He thought of his sister raped and murdered by Beast Rabban, thought of Duke Leto, and dear Master Paul.

He had done this for them, and would remember that when he counted his loyal dead.

VI

In the smugglers' sietch hidden in the deep desert, the mood was a stew of somberness mixed with anger.

As the Harkonnen air defenses swooped in to intercept and escort the battered tanker, Gurney's escape pod tumbled off into the desert. Well away from the tanker, smuggler ships retrieved Gurney's pod just in time by darting into the canyons and hiding in the rock shadows as a ruthless desert storm built in the atmosphere. The Harkonnens had found the crashed escape pod, but none of the smugglers, and then the storm had driven them back to Carthag.

In the tunnels, Staban Tuek's glare was like a fusillade of weapons fire directed at Gurney. But Gurney held on to hope as if it were a lifeline. The dead had been counted after the raid, and the smugglers were dismayed at the loss of thirteen fighters, their bodies left behind in the clutches of the Harkonnen animals. Gurney was sickened by that. Of the twelve, nine loyal Atreides men had been slain and four of the original smugglers, but they'd known full well what they were fighting for; none of them would have any regrets.

He felt sadness for Orbo, even though the man had been surly and smashed Gurney's baliset, stealing music from the smuggler hideout just as smugglers stole spice from the Harkonnens. In his life, Gurney had held numerous grudges, but this was not one of them. He understood Orbo, and appreciated him now for his courage. The big man had fought Harkonnens, and he'd exacted his own vengeance.

Gurney only wished he could have seen the rest of the plan…

"I shall write a song for them," Gurney said aloud, lost in his thoughts. "One verse for Orbo and his men, and another for the Duke's brave men. All will be remembered."

Staban's face reddened, his eyes narrowed. The smuggler leader lurched out of his alcove-cave office. "*Remembered*, Gurney Halleck? Not a one among us would forget! The raid was a failure. The Harkonnens fought better than expected." He came forward and thrust a finger in front of Gurney's face. "What I did not expect was for you to be such a coward."

"We were outnumbered and getting killed," Gurney said. "We couldn't have survived, and it took skill and courage to bring the survivors home."

"You should have fought harder, should have fought longer. We lost good men, some of my best. Thanks to you and your foolish plan, we spent half a year of profits on the spice bribe for Count Fenring and the Guild…" He drew a deep breath, as if he could barely phrase his own disgust. "And you lost the water! Everything! I never believed you would give up so easily. The great Gurney Halleck. I thought all your fury and passion were wrapped up in this scheme. You retreated too soon. I've heard the reports on you."

Gurney thought of the battle, of the armed Harkonnen guards on the piloting deck. "No man among us is ashamed at how he fought. We killed many. Man for man, their losses were twice ours."

"But our losses count more," Staban said. "Now I have to find more men to replace the ones we lost." The smuggler leader sounded exhausted. He shook his head as he reiterated, "And you lost all the water."

Gurney's anger boiled. He had held it inside for too long, not just about how the raid ended, but the long-simmering poison of everything that had gone wrong, the treachery since the moment that fighting first broke out on the terrible night in Arrakeen a year ago.

"I didn't want the water," he confessed in a husky voice. "I wanted revenge. I wanted Kanly."

He departed, leaving Staban looking confused. Back in the escape pod he found the uniform from the last Harkonnen guard he had killed; it lay folded and cleaned as he had instructed, the knife tear in the belly repaired. He shook out the fabric, inspected it. Now he had everything he needed.

He had to get back to Carthag—and he had to hurry.

VII

The uniform fit well enough, though he despised the markings and the fact that others might look at him and consider him a Harkonnen. But the disguise was necessary. Thanks to the repressive mood that Rabban engendered among his loyal troops as well as the downtrodden people who worked the new garrison city, few people would ask questions. Gurney would use their own suspicions and fears against them. He would use Rabban against himself.

Carthag was on high alert after the attempted hijacking of the water tanker. The fact that some of the men had called out the name of House Atreides during the raid had set the Harkonnens on even more of an edge, but because the Harkonnens had won, defeating the raiders, they were giddy. Rabban had declared a day of celebration.

The water tanker had been brought in under heavy guard, and Rabban made bold announcements about how the smugglers had been thwarted, the last remnants of Atreides fighters shamefully defeated. He had mutilated the bodies of the fallen smugglers, including Gurney's men, for a macabre public spectacle. And when the people of Carthag did not cheer sufficiently, he gave orders for them to do so—and they obeyed.

The increased security bound the Harkonnen troops more tightly together in their crackdown on the city people in Carthag, and they never thought to look carefully at one another. Gurney had spent many horrible years on Giedi Prime under the Harkonnen boot heel, and he could speak convincingly to the troops, so that they easily accepted him. The Harkonnen blind spots were evident to him.

Gurney adjusted his uniform, but had removed the insignia of the tanker ship so that no one would ask questions. He couldn't stomach the other soldiers congratulating him, and none of the surviving tanker crew members were visible, even on this day of celebration.

Yes, Rabban had declared victory and publicly acknowledged the surviving crew members for their bravery in driving off the attempt. But Gurney had made quiet inquiries and was not surprised to learn that Rabban had quietly killed them, imposing punishment because they had allowed the dire situation to occur in the first place.

Gurney had known Rabban would never remain quiet about the victory, about the Atreides loyalists who had been defeated. It pleased him to hear a rumor that the escape pod had crashed and all the remaining smugglers had been killed. It didn't matter how many of the people of Carthag actually believed it. Gurney was perfectly content to let Rabban think that any renegades involved were dead.

Gurney savored the anticipation as he walked confidently into the barracks, acknowledging the troops who bothered to look at him. He moved as if he had important orders from Rabban himself, and no one would challenge him. A desert hood covered his hair and the side of his face, and his stolen uniform was dust stained, some of the markings strategically obscured.

Now that the tanker was safely arrived, Rabban wanted to demonstrate largess, to show his appreciation for his troops who had been assigned to this blasted awful planet. In the main barracks assembly hall, he had gathered his men for the event. Gurney had to see this with his own eyes. Someone had to witness his revenge, in the name of his beloved Duke Leto Atreides and all of his men who had died at the hands of the Harkonnens.

Gurney slipped from one point to another as if he had a destination, but he just wanted to keep moving, keep watching. The soldiers talked in a low buzz as they sat looking down at their trays of food. Most of the men had removed their nose plugs and face masks inside the barracks, but they still wore their desert gear. At a glance he could tell which of these soldiers had been on Arrakis for the past year and which were new arrivals.

Gurney wanted to see them all dead. They were all Harkonnens. Even the freshest arrivals were not innocent.

Rabban's very existence was like abrasive powder in Gurney's arteries, making the center of his chest hurt. The husky man sat at a table raised above the troops so he could look out upon the lines of tables. Rabban had a feast set before him, far more extravagant than the rations of his troops—but the new governor of Arrakis had his own point to make. He did not stand as he raised a crystal goblet in his left hand. "We have water, and on Arrakis water is life. Our tanker arrived safely, but it was a very close thing, a near disaster. This planet is dangerous, and there are those who wish to harm our rule."

With his other hand he picked up a pitcher of water and poured it into the crystal goblet. "Those who tried to steal that tanker would steal our lives, but we stopped them." He slammed the goblet down onto the tabletop, breaking the crystal and spilling water... a stupid, wasteful thing to do on Arrakis. "*We stopped them!*" The men cheered. "This water is from the tanker we saved. Extra rations for you on this meal, so you know your worth to House Harkonnen."

Servants rushed in carrying pitchers, and the soldiers muttered, but this time the buzz seemed less dour, more curious than appreciative. "One cup apiece from the newly arrived supplies. Those of you who have been with us know the very high value of the reward I give you, the supreme value of water on Arrakis."

The soldiers grunted and cheered, and Rabban held up his crystal goblet, waiting as the servants went through the room pouring water. Someone put another goblet on the table next to Rabban, but he put a hand over the top, and shook his head. The servant looked astonished. "But, sir, it's... you don't want any water?" Rabban again refused, and the servant surreptitiously poured a goblet for himself and gulped it down.

Into his own goblet Rabban poured a pale vintage from a green bottle. "I will celebrate with my own reward. Caladan wine. Drink up!" He drank deeply from the goblet, while the others consumed their water.

Gurney hadn't expected this, but he didn't show any emotion, and kept moving by the table as if he had a seat to claim or a place to go. He stood off to one side, watching them all. Waiting.

Over the next hour Rabban consumed two bottles of Caladan wine and demanded that the servants open a third. He got sloppy drunk, and Gurney grew impatient, nervous. Why wasn't he drinking any of the water?

It took nearly ninety minutes for the neurotoxin in the water to take effect on the others. Gurney had known it would take this long, but still felt time dilating, dragging out. He feared his presence would be discovered, and knew he needed to leave. Some of the people were noticing him, remarking on how he stood aside and was not drinking the water, not celebrating with them.

Now Rabban noticed him from his high table. His wine-bleared gaze locked onto Gurney's angry glare and seemed to see something there, to recognize an ancient memory of pain. Did Rabban even remember what he had done to Gurney's sister so long ago, the rape and murder? And what he had done to Gurney, the scarring with a whip? The inkvine scar burned on his cheek and he was sure the makeup was sloughing off. Rabban hesitated.

Suddenly, one of the soldiers groaned loudly and slumped to the table. Others twisted and spasmed, sliding off their benches onto the dusty stone floor. One after another. The Harkonnen troops inside the barracks were beset with paroxysms of pain, vomiting, twitching with their eyes rolled back in their heads. As alarms sounded, medics rushed in, but there was nothing they could do. They had all drunk the water from the tanker that Gurney had poisoned, and he knew there was no antidote. Those with a smaller body mass were affected first, while the heavier ones could only watch in horror, terrified of what was to come within the next few minutes... and it always came.

Rabban roused himself enough to bellow for his guards to find the perpetrator, but his protectors, too, were debilitated. Gurney watched them die, one by one and in clusters of screaming pain.

By the end of the night, hundreds of Harkonnen troops lay dead, all poisoned from the deadly nerve toxin he had poured through the sample access hatch into the tanker's cargo hold during the supposed Guild inspection. Only one taste of a droplet was a fatal dose, and Gurney had added more than a liter to the supply… enough to kill every man, woman and child in Carthag.

But Beast Rabban would not share the water with civilians, with servants, with merchants or tradesmen. He had only given it to his troops, and they were the ones condemned for death.

"Kanly?" he said in a quizzical tone as his men died around him.

Gurney slipped out of the barracks before anyone could ask the wrong questions. He remembered how the Harkonnens had conquered Arrakeen, not just because he remembered how the Harkonnens had conquered Arrakeen, not just because they'd enlisted a traitor, or because they'd been in possession of superior weapons, but also because they used archaic and unorthodox weapons, a method of attack that even Thufir Hawat had not anticipated. For the sneak attack on House Atreides, their archenemies had brought in artillery, old-fashioned projectile weapons that were normally useless due to the prevalence of shields. Many Atreides soldiers had died that night in Arrakeen and in the defensive battery caves in the Shield Wall, bombarded by artillery projectiles.

Duke Leto had said in despair, "Their simple minds came up with a simple trick. We didn't count on simple tricks."

Now Gurney had come up with a simple retaliation of his own.

Staban Tuek, Count Fenring, and the Guild representatives had all believed that Gurney's true goal was to steal the water tanker— and that would have achieved a certain measure of revenge. The loss of that water would have placed great hardship on the Arrakis garrison and caused extreme embarrassment for Rabban.

But for Gurney, stealing the tanker—or attempting to do so— was merely a diversion. He had never intended to escape with the water because he had poisoned it while aboard the tanker. Because they'd fought so hard and lost men, the Harkonnens would never doubt that the raid was sincere. They simply had not had the imagination to figure out what Gurney had really been doing.

And he had known from Rabban's past behavior that he would probably attempt to buy the loyalty of his troops with a few sips of water, without knowing it was deadly poison.

All those deaths... Rabban would cover it up. He would make excuses to his domineering uncle, and the Baron Vladimir Harkonnen would certainly not believe them.

Gurney heaved a deep, satisfied breath, and felt a shudder—not of relief or satisfaction, but of acceptance. He had achieved *Kanly*. If only Rabban himself had imbibed the poison water, his revenge would have been sweeter, but this would do for now. For Duke Leto. For young Master Paul. It was not enough, but Gurney Halleck had sent a powerful message.

Still wearing his Harkonnen disguise, Gurney slipped out of the Carthag barracks, leaving behind the moans of the dying, along with the alarms and shouting medics. Gurney struggled to conceal the satisfied smile on his face. After this massacre, he would leave Carthag and return to the smugglers.

But he couldn't depart from the city just yet. He wanted to go into the town, find a merchant and spend some of the money he had brought with him. He needed to buy a new baliset, one that made sweet music to keep the smugglers company in their hideout.

Now Gurney had a new song to compose.

From William C. Dietz comes an entry in his popular Legion of the Damned series, featuring societal misfits and outcasts transformed into more-than-human warriors. These unlikely heroes turn out to be the last best hope for human salvation. This story takes place after volume nine of the original Legion series, A Fighting Chance, *giving us a moving story wherein a soldier makes sacrifices to aid and save a girl in need, acting as...*

THE GOOD SHEPHERD
WILLIAM C. DIETZ

I am the good shepherd. The good shepherd lays down his life for the sheep.
John 10:11

THE PLANET SAA-NA, THE CONFEDERACY OF SENTIENT BEINGS

Tara was a Class III "drop city," meaning a prefab community which could be dropped into a wide variety of planetary environments and brought online in ninety standard days. And that was the kind of efficiency a company like Madsen Mining required to keep costs low and profits high.

But just because drop cities made financial sense didn't mean they were pretty to look at. And Tara wasn't. "Form should follow function." That was one of the many guiding principles Madsen Mining administrators were expected to follow. And that explained why the plex looked like a stack of randomly placed blocks sitting on top of a "scalped" hill. An antenna farm had replaced the feather trees and the globular water tank sat next to a cluster of three landing pads.

And that's where Corporal Mike Murphy stood as a yellow dwarf called Pylo II did its best to melt the fused dirt under the Trooper 5's blocky feet. But, because Murphy was equipped to handle just about anything, the cyborg barely noticed.

The other legionnaires weren't so fortunate. They were bio bods, meaning flesh and blood human beings, who were sweating into their shimmery light-bending camos. Did Murphy feel sorry for them? Hell, no. Because they could eat food, drink beer, and have sex. Not virtual sex... *Real* sex. Something that Murphy and his electro-mechanical comrades were no longer capable of. Murphy's thoughts were interrupted when Sergeant Omar spoke. "Atten-hut!"

The six legionnaires came to attention as a door opened and a teenaged girl appeared. Did she rate such a courtesy? No, but Governor Reginald Smith did, even though her father was nowhere to be seen. Why was that? Murphy wondered. Supposedly, according to what Sergeant Omar had been told, the governor was taking his daughter to school in Ubba. A Class II drop city located 500 standard miles to the east.

Caitlin Smith looked to be about sixteen or seventeen. She had lime-green hair, and was sporting a pair of sunglasses so large that they hid half her face. A skimpy blouse and some short-shorts completed the ensemble. Caitlin paused as two contract workers arrived, each lugging two shiny suitcases. "Be careful," Caitlin chided. "Each one of those bags costs more than you make in a week."

Murphy reckoned that was probably true, since contract workers weren't paid very well. A reality that was everything to do with the partial work-stoppage currently underway. Two-thousand miners had walked off their jobs three months earlier, shutting down three of Saa-Na's five mines. And that mattered because gadolinite, a mineral composed of cerium and yttrium, was critical to certain high-tech products the Confederacy's military-industrial complex produced. One of which was Murphy's war form.

That's why a detachment of legionnaires had been sent to Saa-Na. Their job was to protect the company's personnel and property from the rebellious workers who wanted more pay and better healthcare. Murphy "felt" the sudden downdraft via his sensors as the fly form's engines fired up and the VTOL's rotors began to turn.

Like the Trooper 5 the boxy aircraft was controlled by a human brain which served as the aircraft's sole pilot. The ramp was down and Caitlin's platform shoes made a clomping noise as she walked up into the yawning cargo bay. The workers, suitcases in hand, followed along behind. "At ease," Omar said over the tactical frequency. "You know the drill... Follow me, sit aft, and keep your yaps shut."

The last part of the order was unusual, and Murphy figured that Omar was concerned that his legionnaires might swear in front of the girl. Or, worse yet, tell each other about sexual exploits both real and imagined.

Murphy followed the bio bods up the ramp to the point where

the Titan's crew chief stood waiting. He nodded. "Good morning, Corporal... Did you safe your weapons? Good. Please step over to the port side."

Murphy had been through the process countless times before. The fly form had seats for the bio bods but not for seven-and-a-half-foot tall Trooper 5s. Murphy stopped in front of slot number seven, performed a perfect about face, and backed into the waiting recess. Connections were made as two arm-like clamps emerged from the bulkhead to hug Murphy's chest. Others captured his legs.

The contract workers were gone by then. The ramp produced a whining noise as it came up and was locked into place. *Still no governor*, Murphy thought. *Not that I give a shit.*

The outer world faded to black as Murphy shut his video pickups down. He "heard" the fly form's pilot make the usual announcements, and "felt" the VTOL lift off before he drifted off to sleep. There were dreams. Dreams of Ellie's smiling face. The two of them were standing on a beach, and about to share a kiss, when the bomb exploded. The fly form jerked violently and began to shake.

Murphy's video inputs snapped on in time for him to watch the crew chief get sucked out through a hole in the fuselage. The VTOL shuddered and began to lose altitude. "This is the pilot," the fly form said, "we have an onboard emergency and..."

That was the moment when a *second* explosion blew the Titan in half. The aft section of the aircraft performed a series of cartwheels as it fell. Murphy felt the impact as the wreckage hit the top layer of the triple canopy jungle. The trees gave, and by doing so, they served as shock absorbers. Then the aft section of the VTOL fell to the point where a *second* layer of foliage waited to slow the wreck even more before it hit the ground. Murphy felt the violent impact as a host of alarms sounded.

The Titan had multiple backup systems. One of them did its job by releasing the cyborg from slot seven. As that occurred Murphy's onboard computer was burping status reports. One of his watertight seals had been damaged... And a message was scrolling across the bottom of his vision. "Your war form has been involved in a traumatic incident. Notify a tech at the earliest opportunity." *No shit*, Murphy thought. *I'll get right on that.* What about the others? The normally voluble Sergeant Omar was silent.

The wreckage was tilted at an angle. A shipping module had broken free and was sitting in front of the cyborg. Murphy circled the obstruction to discover that the other legionnaires were dead. Judging from the blood and gore splattered on the walls the bio bods had been killed by shrapnel encased in the second bomb. Murphy felt a surge of sorrow. Six lives all snuffed out. Six friends gone. He would grieve when he could.

The girl... Had Caitlin survived? Murphy turned to the left. A section of the Titan's alloy skin had collapsed down during the crash. The metal groaned as Murphy placed a massive shoulder against the obstruction and pushed. There was a screeching sound as the barrier gave way, and that was when Murphy saw Caitlin. She was alive, but clutching a bloodied arm, and rocking back and forth. When she turned to look at him Murphy could see the tears running down her cheeks. "I'm hurt," she said. "Don't just stand there... Help me!"

Murphy extended both of his arms for her to see. One was an air cooled .50 caliber machine gun, and the other was a fast recovery laser cannon. "I don't have hands," Murphy told her. "So you'll have to perform first aid on yourself. But I'll tell you what to do. Release your harness and maintain pressure on the wound as you do so."

"*No!*" Caitlin said emphatically. "I want a *real* person... Not a machine."

"I'm all you have," Murphy told her. "The real people are dead. So, would you like my help? Or would you prefer to fend for yourself?"

Murphy watched Caitlin take it in. "All of them are dead? You're sure?"

"I'm sure," Murphy replied. "Like I said... Release your harness and keep the pressure on. Then you need to stand. See the first-aid kit clamped to the bulkhead? You need it. Reaching for it will force you to take the pressure off the wound. But, if you elevate your left arm, that will slow the bleeding while you release the clamps. Then we'll go outside and patch you up."

Caitlin stared at him. Her eyes were huge. "I can't do it."

Murphy shrugged. "Roger that... Good luck." And with that he turned to go.

"Wait!" Caitlin said. "Don't go... I'm getting up."

Murphy turned back. "Good. Grab that first-aid kit and let's get out of here. I haven't seen any smoke, but you never know. This thing could blow."

That seemed to get through to Caitlin who stood, made her way over to the first-aid kit, and fumbled with the latches. The plastic case came free.

"Well done," Murphy said. "Tuck it under your left arm, put the pressure on again, and look to your right."

Caitlin obeyed, and was about to ask why, when Murphy fired the cannon. More than a dozen energy bolts were required to outline a new door. But a powerful kick was sufficient to open it up. Murphy stepped out onto solid ground and turned to face the ship. "Now it's your turn."

"I feel dizzy," Caitlin said.

"Step through the opening and grab my arm."

Caitlin obeyed. Murphy could barely feel the pressure she put on the machine gun. "Come on," he said. "Let's go over there... We'll sit under that tree."

Very little sunlight was able to penetrate the layers of foliage above. So there was hardly any undergrowth. That made it easy for Caitlin to cross a small clearing to the point where she could sit on a fallen tree. Murphy paused to check his readouts for indications of electro-mechanical activity, incoming heat signatures, or radio chatter. There were none. And that wasn't surprising. No more than fifteen minutes had passed since the crash.

But it pays to be careful so Murphy activated his personal drone. It was about the size of a hummingbird, equally agile, and generated a soft buzzing sound as it emerged from a recess near Murphy's left shoulder. The device hovered in front of Murphy as the cyborg eyed a menu of standard commands and chose three of them. Then the tiny device took off. That meant Murphy could "see" what the drone saw, and react accordingly.

Caitlin had opened the first-aid kit by then and was staring at the tightly packed contents. "First you need to clean and disinfect the wound," Murphy told her. "I don't know if Saa-Na is home to microbes that can hurt us. But if it is, you can bet that the right bug killers are in that kit. Once the cut is clean we'll decide what to do next."

"It hurts," Caitlin complained.

"Roger that," Murphy replied. "So let's get this over with."

Caitlin managed to open a packet, remove a moistened towelette, and wipe most of the blood away. Murphy swore silently. The cut on Caitlin's left forearm was about three inches long and oozing blood. Not gushing, thank God... But oozing.

"Okay," Murphy said. "You could pull the margins together

with butterfly closures, or you could close it with sutures. That's what I would do. Sutures will hold up better while you're running through the jungle."

"*Or*," Caitlin said pointedly, "I can wait for the medics to get here. How soon will they arrive?"

"I don't know," Murphy replied. "It could be minutes or days."

Caitlin frowned. "But you have a radio, and you called for help, right?"

"No, I didn't call for help," Murphy replied. "Because I don't know who might respond. Would it be your father? And the people who work for him? Or the folks who placed the bombs in your luggage?"

Caitlin looked alarmed. "*Bombs*? In *my* luggage?"

"Yes," Murphy responded. "*Two* of them. I figure they were trying to assassinate your father. Someone had access to your luggage. Servants perhaps."

Caitlin was holding a fresh bandage against the wound. Her face was pale. "He wanted to come... But he didn't show up."

Murphy nodded. "I get that. But, until we have more information, I don't think it's a good idea to let people know where we are. It's safe to assume that the Titan's emergency beacon is on— and broadcasting its location. But where *is* it? At the front of the aircraft? Which could have crashed miles away... Or is it here with us? If that's the case, we could be in deep doo-doo."

"But *why*?" Caitlin wanted to know. "If you're correct it's my father they want."

"And you would make an excellent hostage," Murphy countered. "A way to bait him. So, what's it going to be? Butterfly closures? Or stiches?"

Caitlin frowned. "Sutures I guess. Will it hurt?"

"Yes. Like getting your ears pierced."

It took Murphy half an hour to coach Caitlin through the process of stitching herself up. Murphy had never performed the procedure himself. But all sorts of information was stored in his on-board computer—including a video that showed how to do it. And to Caitlin's credit she managed to put four sutures in while tears streamed down her cheeks.

Once the process was over, the bleeding stopped. A fresh dressing went on over the cut.

"Good work," Murphy said. "Now gather up all of the trash and bury it over there... Like I said earlier, we don't know who may show up here. Meet me at the wreck. You're going to need supplies, and that's where they are."

+ + +

THE LUCKY STRIKE MINE

The Lucky Strike Mine had been discovered by a sixty-nine-year-old prospector named Three-Fingered Jack when a mechanical problem forced him to land his ship right on top of a huge deposit of yttrium. A once in a lifetime discovery that he immediately filed a claim on and subsequently sold to Madsen Mining. Except that Madsen's workers had taken possession of the mine, and had no intention of giving it back until their demands were met. Their so-called "command center" consisted of a cavern located more than two hundred feet under the planet's surface where it was safe from bombs. Cables snaked across the uncomfortably low ceiling, water was seeping through the walls, and gear was piled all around.

George Reeger felt a growing sense of anger as he listened to the report. Rather than abort the assassination attempt the moment it became clear that Governor Smith wasn't going to accompany his daughter onto the fly form, the idiot in charge of the Tara cell had allowed his people to move forward, with disastrous results. Both he *and* his co-conspirators had been arrested. But Marci, the woman he was talking to via a locked beam wasn't to blame, which meant Reeger couldn't express his frustration. "I see," he said. "That's very unfortunate. Thank you for letting me know. So the governor's daughter was killed?"

"Quite possibly," Marci allowed. "But we can't be sure until they find the wreckage. There could be survivors."

Reeger's mind was churning. It was a long shot... But what if the little bitch was alive? And what if the Worker's Army could find her? The governor would be forced to accept the workers' demands or watch a video of his daughter being executed! *Yes*, Reeger decided, *it's worth a try.*

+ + +

CRASH SITE TWO

In order to gather the items that Caitlin might need, they had to return to the wreck and enter the area where the Legionnaires' badly mangled bodies were. Caitlin took one look, gagged, and turned away. "I'm sorry," Murphy said. "But it has to be done. I would do it for you if I could. But that isn't possible. Not without hands."

Caitlin bent over and threw up. Then, after wiping her chin, she turned back. Her eyes were focused on him instead of the gore. "Do I have to?"

"Yes, and quickly too... We need to put some distance in between ourselves and the crash site. Then I'll try to contact the Legion."

Caitlin was careful to avert her eyes as she took a carbine from one legionnaire, a pistol from another, and ammo from both. Private Corci's boots were the most difficult part of the process. They looked like they would fit, and Caitlin was going to need them.

But that meant stripping them off Corsi's mangled body... Something Caitlin hesitated to do. But Murphy refused to let up.

Caitlin sobbed as she pulled the boots free. "Get her pack too," Murphy instructed. "There will be some rations inside, plus a set of camos. Maybe they'll fit. Come on, bring the boots, and let's get out of here."

Once outside Murphy told Caitlin to climb up on his back. "Hang the pack on the hooks and attach the boots," he said. "We'll sort things out later."

Murphy turned and Caitlin saw that steps were built into the back of his legs. With a pistol belt cinched around her waist and the carbine dangling from a shoulder, Caitlin climbed up to the point where the hooks were waiting. The pack fit perfectly. And after tying the boot laces together Caitlin secured them as well. A headset was waiting in a recess and she put it on. "Can you hear me?"

"Five by five," Murphy replied. "Bend your knees, and grab onto the bar in front of you."

Murphy took off at a ground-eating jog. Thanks to the video feed provided by the drone circling above Murphy could see where he was going. They needed a place to hole up. A spot near water, but one that they could defend, and that suggested a hill. There were plenty to choose from. A dozen vegetation-clad mini-volcanoes dotted the otherwise flat jungle. Had they served as vents at some point in the distant past? Murphy thought so.

It took an hour and a half of relentless running to close with the nearest hill. And that was a long time for an inexperienced rider to spend on a T-5. Caitlin made no secret of her discomfort. "My knees hurt!" she complained. "A branch hit my face!" "I need to pee!"

But Murphy refused to stop until they reached the hill. Then he let Caitlin climb down and take a bio break. After she returned Murphy led her to the top of the hill where a deep depression kept them off the skyline.

The drone needed charging so Murphy brought it in. Then he cranked his vision up to 10X and peered out over the verdant jungle. A pair of contrails clawed the lavender sky, a flock of white birds skimmed the treetops, and a ribbon of water sparkled in the distance. It was getting late and Pylo II had sunk low in the sky. *So far, so good*, Murphy thought. *It's time to call for the cavalry.* Murphy selected a high-priority emergency channel and announced himself. "Bravo-Five-Four to Overwatch-Six… Do you read me? Over."

There was a long pause followed by a female voice. "This is Overwatch-Six… What's your mother's maiden name? Over."

"Owens."

"Where were you born?"

"The city of Los Angeles on Earth."

"What's the legion's motto?"

"*Legio Patria Nostra.* (The Legion is our Country.) Over."

"Roger that, Four. We're very happy to hear from you. What's the status on the rest of your squad? Over."

"They're dead," Murphy replied flatly. "But I have the package we were supposed to deliver and it's intact. Over."

Murphy knew his transmissions were encrypted. But if the WA could place bombs in Caitlin's luggage, what else were they capable of? It was better to be safe than sorry.

There was another long pause, as if the woman was discussing the situation with someone else. Then she was back. "Good work, Four… What happened to the Titan?"

Murphy told Overwatch about the bombs, the way the fly form broke in two, and the subsequent crash. "Got it," Overwatch said. "The beacon was in the front half of the Titan so we found that right away. We're searching for the rest of it. Are you at the crash site? Over."

"No," Murphy replied. "We didn't know who would come looking first, so it seemed appropriate to clear the area. Over."

"And you were correct." Overwatch assured him. "All right, here's the situation. We're stretched thin. WA terrorists attacked most of Saa-Na's major cities during the last six hours. So most of our resources are committed. Your orders are to travel cross-country to the town of Keebler's Gap. Check your nav system. The community is small, but you'll see it. We should be able to dispatch a Search and Rescueunit by the time you arrive. We'll pull you out earlier if we can. Report every six hours. Do you have any questions? Over."

"No. Over."

"Watch your six," the woman cautioned. "Overwatch out."

✦ ✦ ✦

THE LUCKY STRIKE MINE

Reeger was monitoring the steady flow of reports from WA cells in cities all around the world as he spooned lukewarm nutra-blend into his mouth. Things were going well, very well indeed. The company's drop cities had been paralyzed by a series of perfectly coordinated suicide bombings. And the Legion didn't have a tenth of the troops required to lock everything down. "Hey, boss," a voice said. "We have a fix on them."

Reeger turned to find a com tech named Foley standing behind him. "You have a fix on *who*?" he demanded.

Judging from the expression on Foley's face he thought his task should be top of mind for everyone—Reeger included. "On the legion guys… The ones who were on the VTOL. We got a cross fix on them when they called in."

Reeger was surprised. Even though Foley and his techs had been ordered to try, Reeger hadn't expected them to succeed. "You're sure it's them?"

"Hell, yes, I'm sure," Foley replied. "The transmission originated from a hill about three miles from the crash site."

"Well done," Reeger said. "Was the transmission in the clear?"

"No, it was encrypted."

Reeger shrugged. "That figures, but I had to ask. Send for Gilman… I've got a job for him."

✦ ✦ ✦

NORTH OF KEEBLER'S GAP

Murphy's conversation with Overwatch had been somewhat depressing. The fact that the legion couldn't spare a SAR team to rescue the governor's daughter spoke volumes. It didn't take a general to realize that the brigade was up to its ass in trouble. But Murphy didn't want to worry Caitlin any more than necessary, so he gave her the facts minus any editorial comments. "So," he concluded. "We'll have to hoof it. And, according to the map stored in my nav system, Keebler's Gap is forty-six miles away."

Caitlin looked at him. There was something different about it. Like most teenagers, Caitlin had a disturbing way of switching back and forth between child and adult. Now Murph found himself face to face with a young woman. A woman who reminded him of Ellie. Steady. Intelligent. Serious. "It says 'Murphy' on your chest," Caitlin said. "Is that it? No first name?"

"It's Mike. But my friends call me Murph."

"Okay, Murph… I'm not a friend, but I hope to become one. Tell me the truth, Murph… It's bad isn't it?"

"Yeah," Murphy answered reluctantly. "It's bad. We have roughly 3,000 legionnaires on Saa-Na and we're struggling to cope. But we'll win. We always do."

Caitlin's eyes narrowed. "Was there any mention of my father?"

"No," Murphy replied. "There wasn't." And that seemed strange. If Caitlin was *his* daughter, and *he* was governor, Murphy would be throwing his weight around. But Murphy couldn't say that, and didn't. A change of subject was in order.

"Open the pack," Murphy suggested. "Let's see what you have while we still have some daylight." The answer was a set of camos which, as it turned out, were one size too large. But anything was better than the absurd outfit Caitlin was wearing. There were two MREs as well, plus some candy bars, and a water bottle that was half full.

Then Caitlin came across the zipped bag that contained some earrings, some clear nail polish, and a photo of a young man. She burst into tears.

Murphy wanted to comfort her, to place an arm around her shoulders, but was painfully aware of what that arm would be: Either a machine gun or an energy cannon. "Don't cry," he said awkwardly. "Corci was a legionnaire. She chose to be a soldier."

"What about you?" Caitlin demanded, as she wiped her nose with a sleeve. "Did *you* choose to be a legionnaire?"

That was a painful subject. One that Murphy didn't like to discuss. But, if it would take Caitlin's mind off Corci, then he would. "I was a bio bod before I became a cyborg," he told her. "And I was married to a girl named Ellie. She was better than I was in every way. But somehow, for reasons I never understood, she loved me. And I loved her.

"I was working the nightshift at a factory. So she was alone the night a man named Orson Warky broke into our apartment. He raped Ellie. Then he killed her. And left his wallet behind."

It was dark by then. But both moons were rising, and Murphy could see the way Caitlin was staring at him. He looked away. "They tried Warky," Murphy said. "And I thought the jury would find the bastard guilty. But his attorney pointed out that Warky had been in our home the day before the murder to repair the toilet. That, he said, was when Warky lost his wallet. And, with no DNA or other physical evidence connecting Warky to the crime, he got off."

Caitlin frowned. "So you joined the legion?"

"No," Murphy replied. "I killed Warky, and they gave me a choice. The state of California was going to execute me no matter what. But, if I chose to, I could live on as a cyborg. A brain in a box. I said 'yes.' So they killed me the way I killed Warky. With three blows from an axe. Then they brought me back. And here I am."

Caitlin stood and came over to sit next to him. Murphy was too big to hug, so all she could do was pat his energy cannon. Tears rolled down her cheeks. "I'm sorry, Murph… But I'm glad too. Glad that you're alive."

They sat that way, side by side, as the moons arced across the sky—and the night creatures came out to eat and be eaten. Caitlin fell asleep after a while. But Murphy was awake. *I should have chosen death*, he thought. *Next time I will.*

✦ ✦ ✦

Murphy awoke to a persistent beeping sound. The drone! After launching it around 0300 Murphy had allowed himself a nap. And now, as the machine circled above, it was trying to warn him. Murphy switched from his sensors to the drone feed. And sure enough, there they were, *three* incoming heat signatures. All hot enough to suggest electro-mechanical activity. The green blobs were a mile out and traveling single file.

Murphy stood. "Caitlin… Wake up. Company is on the way."

Caitlin was curled up in the fetal position. She stirred. "*Company*? What kind of company?"

"The bad kind," Murphy replied. "The legion would have

notified me if it was sending a team in. Put your pack on, eat a candy bar, and drink some water."

"*Why*? What are we going to do?"

"We're going to do the thing they least expect us to do," Murphy answered. "We're going to attack."

Caitlin was on her feet by then. She grabbed the carbine. "Will I have to shoot people?"

"No," Murphy replied. "Not until you have some training. Mount up… We're leaving."

Once Caitlin was on his back Murphy scrambled up over the rim and began the trip down. By putting the hill between him and the enemy Murphy hoped to conceal his movements. Did the enemy have a drone of their own? No, not according to *his* drone, which was equipped to detect such devices. That meant he could circle around and surprise the bastards.

What are they? Murphy wondered, as he skidded down the slope. Had the WA dispatched a team of robots to do their dirty work? That would account for the heat and the speed with which they were approaching the hill.

The moons had set by then. But thanks to Murphy's night vision and thermal imaging capability he could "see" quite well. Small blobs of heat fled in every direction as Murphy forced his way through the jungle. And the normally raucous creatures that lived up in the trees fell momentarily silent as the man-machine closed in on his prey.

The would-be attackers were following a meandering game trail. So thanks to guidance from above Murphy was able to establish an ambush at the point where the path crossed a clearing. And just in time too because the first enemy unit arrived moments later.

Rather than a robot Murphy found himself looking at a twelve-foot-tall industrial exoskeleton—which was equipped with two light machine guns, one mounted on each side of the operator's protective cage. Had the machines been "liberated" from Madsen Mining? Of course they had.

Wait for it, Murphy told himself. *Wait for the third mech to enter the clearing.* Murphy fired the fifty as the last exo appeared. Tracers drew a straight line between him and the machine. The operator turned the exo, or tried to, but was killed in a matter of seconds. And when his hands left the controls the mech collapsed.

So far so good. But the clock was running. Could Murphy nail the number two machine? And do it *before* the third exo could take a crack at him? He had to try.

Murphy fired the fifty *and* the energy cannon. They were a deadly combination. The outgoing fire converged on the mech, found an ammo bin, and triggered an explosion. A bright flash strobed the jungle and thunder rolled across the land.

But there was no time in which to celebrate as the third operator opened fire with a cage-mounted rotary grenade launcher. The first bomblet struck the ground fifteen feet in front of Murphy, exploded, and peppered him with shrapnel.

Murphy staggered, caught his balance, and fired both weapons. His antagonist turned, ducked, and fired again.

The second grenade was closer and Murphy realized that he'd been wrong. Attacking the mechs was a stupid idea. But what was, was. So Murphy did the only thing he *could* do, and that was to charge the miner, hoping to get so close that his opponent's grenade launcher would be useless.

Murphy uttered an incoherent roar as he collided with the exo, knocked the machine off its feet, and stomped it. He was still dancing on the twisted wreckage when Caitlin spoke to him over the intercom. "He's dead, Murph... You can stop."

Murphy remembered the axe, the way the first blow split Warky's skull in two, and his need to whack the bastard again. He stopped. "Yeah... Asshole down. Are you okay?"

"Sure," Caitlin replied. "I've never been better." Then she threw up.

+ + +

THE LUCKY STRIKE MINE

Reeger was lying on a filthy cot deep inside the Lucky Strike Mine as legion aerospace fighters bombed the facilities on the surface. Would they resort to bunker busters? Hell, no. Madsen Mining wouldn't allow that. The corpies wanted to kill the rebels, import *new* workers, and resume production as quickly as possible. Collapsed tunnels would interfere with that.

Reeger heard a muted thump as a 2,000-pound bomb exploded hundreds of feet above him and the cot trembled. Particles of dirt fell onto his face and he brushed them away. Reeger wanted to sleep, he *needed* to sleep, but sleep wouldn't come.

A headlamp emerged from the surrounding murk. It bobbed slightly. "Boss? Are you awake?"

"Yeah, I'm awake," Reeger replied. "What's up?"

"It's the mechs," Foley said, as he came closer. "The ones you sent to find the legionnaires. And the girl."

Reeger raised a hand up to shield his eyes from the light. "What about them?"

"Our guys were close, *real* close, when they were ambushed. Gilman got a message out. They were up against a Trooper 5, maybe *two* Trooper 5s, and he caught a glimpse of the girl. She was riding a cyborg. Then Gilman went off the air. We haven't been able to raise him since."

"What about the transponders on the exos?" Reeger wanted to know.

"We've been pinging them," Foley replied. "But there's no response."

Reeger swung his boots over onto the dirt floor. "Shit."

"Yeah."

"All right… If we can't grab the bitch then we'll kill her… And send a video of it to her father. Let's get to work."

✦ ✦ ✦

NORTH OF KEEBLER'S GAP

Pylo II was rising. As it did the day dwellers came out to screech, howl, and make strange clicking sounds. The clearing was two miles behind them by then, and even though Murphy could have continued, he knew his charge needed a break.

So Murphy stopped under a thick canopy of trees where it would be difficult to spot them from above. He coached Caitlin through the process of heating an MRE. And she must have been hungry, because no one eats ham and limas unless they are.

Once the meal was finished Murphy put Caitlin through an accelerated firearms course. It began with a safety lecture, followed by a brief introduction to Caitlin's weapons, and a half hour of target practice. The girl had a good eye… And both weapons were equipped with laser sights. So by the time the session was over Caitlin could hit a man-sized target with some regularity.

Next it was time to load up and move out. The latest conversation with Overwatch had been no better than the first. The legion was still stretched thin—and still unable to pull them out. Or were they unwilling? That was Murphy's guess. It was, he supposed, a matter of priorities. As for why Governor Smith wasn't in the mix, *that* remained a mystery.

A straight line is always the shortest route between two points. But that didn't mean it was the fastest. Not in the jungle. So Murphy was forced to follow a series of meandering trails, switching as necessary, to stay on course. A practice the drone made possible by scouting ahead.

After two hours of walking they emerged from the forest onto a U-shaped trough. It was about a hundred feet wide, about fifteen feet deep, and ran straight as an arrow toward the south. It was as if a giant had passed that way, dragging his staff along behind him.

Though covered with low-lying plants, only a few widely separated trees were growing in the trough. That made for easy walking, and Murphy decided to follow it. But Pylo II was near its zenith by then… And the combined heat from the sun and Murphy's war form would make things miserable for Caitlin. She hadn't complained though… And the cyborg's opinion of her continued to climb. That's what he was thinking when she spoke over the intercom. "Murphy… Look up! I see a wing!"

Murphy looked up expecting to see some sort of aircraft. But what he actually saw was something different. The "wing" Caitlin had referred to was a bird that was shaped like an Earthly manta ray. Except that it was flying through air instead of water.

"Run!" Caitlin said, as the creature circled above them. "Find a place to make a stand… The varmin watch the wings, and when they circle above potential prey, the varmin attack. *Hundreds* of them… After they feed the wing will land and eat whatever remains."

The information had a familiar ring to it. As if the information was buried in the planetary orientation crap that Murphy had been ordered to download upon arrival.

But, based on the urgency in Caitlin's voice, Murphy was willing to take her word for how dangerous the situation was. So he ran. And the obvious destination was the manmade something up ahead. A ship? Which was large enough, and heavy enough, to carve a furrow in the ground? Maybe.

Murphy could run at a speed of 50mph on open ground. The knee-high foliage slowed his pace. But even at 40mph Murphy was making progress. And a good thing too, because varmin had begun to appear on both sides of the U-shaped trough.

They were small feathered bipedal animals, with long, narrow skulls. Big eyes stared down on the humans as they ran past. That was when Murphy heard a blood-curdling chitter and sensed that the creatures were going to attack.

Murphy swore and Caitlin struggled to hold on as the cyborg drew level with the ship's stern. He saw a jagged hole and had to duck to pass through it. The compartment beyond was home to some incomprehensible equipment. A hatch opened into the ship's belly but, when Murphy attempted to close the door, it wouldn't budge. That meant there were *two* ways for the critters to enter.

"Get down," Murphy ordered. "Your job is to guard that hatch. Don't let any of those things get inside. Understood?"

Caitlin said, "Yes," and hurried to get in position. And not a moment too soon as the varmin rushed the ship. Even though the feathered creatures were small, they had a lot of teeth and claw-equipped tails. That made them deadly in large numbers.

Murphy stood in the gap and fired the fifty. He soon discovered that while the big slugs killed three or four varmin at a time— it wasn't going to stop the mob. So he slaved the energy cannon to the drone above, and allowed the machine to select targets. It felt weird to have an external force control his arm but there were definite benefits.

The laser had to recharge in between each shot. But, thanks to the drone's computer, each bolt hit a target. That meant the energy cannon was killing twenty animals a minute. And the combined kill rate was much higher.

Meanwhile Murphy could hear the systematic crack, crack, crack of the carbine. Caitlin was doing her job. But what would happen when she ran out of ammo? The answer was obvious. The carnivores would take her down. Rather than allow that to happen Murphy stepped outside.

His plan was simple: Pull the varmin away from Caitlin, force the animals to bunch up, and slaughter them. And it worked. Sort of. *Rivers* of chittering varmin poured in to surround the cyborg. So many that he couldn't kill them quickly enough. And it wasn't long until they were gnawing on his armor. Murphy kicked the creatures, stomped some into a bloody pulp, and continued to blast the rest. All to no avail. Then, as if a signal had been sounded, the attack stopped. The animals disappeared into the surrounding foliage.

A shadow passed over Murphy. And, when he looked up, Murphy saw the manta-shaped wing. Not only would the scavenger lead the varmin to their prey, it would feast on *them* if they were killed. Murphy turned to find that Caitlin was exiting the ship. "You did a good job," Murphy told her. "A *very* good job. Come on... Let's haul butt before every scavenger in the jungle shows up for a free meal."

Caitlin didn't flinch as she surveyed the sea of dead bodies. Nor did she throw up. "We kicked their asses, Murph... We kicked 'em good."

It was the kind of thing that one of Murphy's fellow legionnaires might have said, and he smiled. Except that Murphy didn't have a face to smile with.

Once Caitlin was strapped in they left. It was possible to walk next to the ship most of the time. But when the walls of the trough began to close in on them Murphy had to climb up into the steadily encroaching jungle. They put the wreck behind them after a quarter mile or so. The canopy was lower, which meant the undergrowth was thicker, and difficult to push through. In fact, the vegetation was so thick that the cyborg had to use his energy cannon like a machete at times.

Eventually they arrived at a river which though not especially fast, was quite deep, and very wide. Murphy could have walked across the bottom but Caitlin couldn't. So the cyborg cut some trees down and Caitlin used vines to bind them together. The process consumed two hours. By the time they crossed, Pylo II was hanging low in the western sky.

Once the march resumed Murphy was on the lookout for a place where they could hole up for the night. The drone spotted a possibility fifty yards east of the game trail they were on and Murphy went to investigate. The jumble of rocks didn't qualify as a hill. But it was home to a clearing that was protected on three sides. And that was pretty good.

They settled in as the sun set. And it wasn't long before they had a fire going—and Caitlin was eating her last MRE. The entrée was pork and beans this time... And a lot better. "We should arrive in Keebler's Gap tomorrow," Murphy told her.

"Yeah," Caitlin replied. "That's good."

"You don't sound very excited. Your father might be there."

The fire crackled and shadows danced on the rocks around them. "Maybe he will," Caitlin allowed, "and maybe he won't. There's been no sign of him so far."

So there it was. Caitlin had doubts about her father. "He has a planet to run," Murphy reminded her. "And things aren't going well."

"That's what I tell myself," Caitlin said. "But I don't know if that's the problem. Mom and Dad split up about a year ago. Dad wanted to take the position on Saa-Na and Mom refused to go. I lived with her for six months, and we fought all the time. So I came here. But Dad's so busy that I rarely see him. Maybe I should go back."

Caitlin looked away, and Murphy knew she was crying. "I think you should talk to him," Murphy said. "Tell him how you feel. Give him a chance."

Deep down Murphy wasn't sure that Governor Smith deserved another chance. But it seemed like the right thing to say. Caitlin wiped her face with a sleeve before turning back. "That makes sense, Murph... We'll see how things go."

The moons rose and arced across the starry sky as animals, birds, and insects battled to survive in the surrounding jungle. At one point Murphy heard a boom as one of the legion's fly forms broke the sound barrier. Caitlin slept through it. She was a good girl.

What would Ellie and I have had? Murphy wondered. *A boy, or a girl? I would want either one to be like Caitlin. Are you out there, Ellie? Among those stars? I miss you.* There was no answer.

Hours passed. And Caitlin was awake and hungry by the time Pylo II rose. "Your breakfast is waiting in Keebler's Gap," Murphy told her. "Mount up. Let's go."

The freshly charged drone was up and scouting ahead as the pair continued south. Murphy had just waded across a river when the alarm came in.

As Murphy switched to the video feed provided by the drone, he saw a machine the size of an apartment house, which was traveling on massive wheels. The leviathan *ate* the jungle as it ground forward. Rotating blades fed trees, bushes, and rocks into the construct's gigantic maw where they were converted into mulch prior to being spewed out of side-mounted chutes. And the monster was headed their way.

Murphy paused to tell Caitlin about what he was watching. "That's a Madsen Company scalper," she responded. "The company uses them to clear land before they open a strip mine."

Murphy considered that. Was the company preparing to open a new mine even as it fought a war with its employees? No, that was absurd. So what were they up to?

Then it occurred to him. What if the Worker's Army had control of the machine? Yes, that made sense. Murphy's first impulse was to run. But, from what he could see, the scalper could travel just as fast as he could. And it was surprisingly agile. "How do those things work?" Murphy inquired. "Are there people aboard?"

"No, not normally," Caitlin replied. "The scalper should be accompanied by a drone similar to yours only a lot larger. The operator would use it to scout ahead, and relay control signals to the machine."

"That makes sense," Murphy replied. "I think they intend to run over us. So I'm going to get their attention. In the meantime, I want you to head east, and circle around. Then, once the scalper is committed, I'll head west."

"*No*," Caitlin said. "I'm staying with you."

"I'm in charge here," Murphy replied sternly. "Get down."

Caitlin dropped to the ground. "*Please*, Murph… Let me come."

"Thanks," Murphy said. "But no thanks. Don't worry, I'll be fine. I'll see you in Keebler's Gap."

Caitlin stood and stared as Murphy left her. He was jogging now, running west. The juggernaut turned to intercept him. And it did so quickly. Then, when Murphy veered to the east, the scalper changed direction again.

Murphy's suspicions were confirmed. After selecting the most intense heat source the drone was locked onto it. *I need a hill*, Murphy thought. *A slope so steep that the scalper won't be able to climb it. Then I'll fire at one of its tracks. Who knows? Maybe I'll get lucky.*"

But when Murphy ordered the drone to show him a 360 there were no hills to be seen. None close enough to use anyway. Meanwhile the distance between Murphy and the scalper had begun to narrow. And as the cyborg topped a rise he could see the gigantic machine without any assistance. *You need to buy time*, Murphy thought. *So Caitlin can circle around.*

The scalper was *huge* by then. The machine's engines roared, its rotors clattered, and the ground shook as it continued to advance. Murphy fired both of his weapons to no effect.

As the scalper's shadow fell across him Murphy knew he was going to die. He could run, but *why*? Ellie was waiting for him. He hoped so anyway. So Murphy cut all of the incoming video feeds and replaced them with an image of Ellie's smiling face. *I'm coming, hon. I love you.*

The noise grew even louder and Murphy felt a wave of heat embrace him as the scalper bore down on him. Then Murphy heard three shots fired in quick succession. As video was restored Murphy saw that the three-story-tall machine was looming over him! The scalper's engines continued to run, but the rotors were motionless, as were the behemoth's massive treads. "Murph? Are you okay?" Caitlin had to shout in order to be heard.

Murphy turned to discover that Caitlin was standing behind him. The assault rifle was cradled in her arms. Then Murphy understood. "You shot their drone down! The one they use to control the scalper!"

Caitlin grinned. "Lead the target. That's what you taught me… And I was lucky."

"You were supposed to circle around."

"I'm a teenager… And a disobedient one at that. Ask my mother."

Murphy couldn't help but laugh. "Come on… Let's get out of here."

They followed the path the scalper had left for a while, veered south, and arrived in Keebler's Gap two hours later. A squad of legionnaires was waiting to receive them as was a middle-aged civilian. A bandage was wound around his head and his left leg was in a cast. He came forward on crutches. "Caitlin! Thank God, you're all right."

Murphy watch Caitlin hug him. "Your head… Your leg… What happened?"

"A suicide bomber blew herself up sixty feet away from me," Governor Smith answered. "Two pieces of shrapnel hit me… One of them knocked me out. My chief of staff thought it was best to keep my condition secret for a while. And, by the time I came to, you were hiking out."

Murphy felt a sense of relief. Caitlin's father *did* care.

"There's someone I want you meet," Caitlin said. "Corporal Murphy saved my life."

"And your daughter saved *mine*," Murphy said. "She's a remarkable young woman. You have every reason to be proud of her."

The governor started to say something, but Murphy turned and walked away. He didn't want to linger… He didn't want to see Caitlin with her father… Or to think about the daughter he would never have. Murphy's mission was complete—and the legion was waiting. That would have to do.

A truly legendary story by a legendary author, "The Game of Rat and A
A truly legendary story by a legendary author, "The Game of Rat and
Dragon" first appeared in the October 1955 issue of Galaxy *magazine and*
went on to win the Best Short Story Hugo in 1956. It has made many
appearances since because it still holds up as great writing, and great space
opera. It's a personal favorite of many, including this editor.

THE GAME OF RAT AND DRAGON

CORDWAINER SMITH

I. THE TABLE

Pinlighting is a hell of a way to earn a living. Underhill was furious as he closed the door behind himself. It didn't make much sense to wear a uniform and look like a soldier if people didn't appreciate what you did.

He sat down in his chair, laid his head back in the headrest, and pulled the helmet down over his forehead.

As he waited for the pin-set to warm up, he remembered the girl in the outer corridor. She had looked at it, then looked at him scornfully.

"Meow." That was all she had said. Yet it had cut him like a knife.

What did she think he was—a fool, a loafer, a uniformed nonentity? Didn't she know that for every half-hour of pinlighting, he got a minimum of two months' recuperation in the hospital?

By now the set was warm. He felt the squares of space around him, sensed himself at the middle of an immense grid, a cubic grid, full of nothing. Out in that nothingness, he could sense the hollow aching horror of space itself and could feel the terrible anxiety which his mind encountered whenever it met the faintest trace of inert dust.

As he relaxed, the comforting solidity of the sun, the clockwork of the familiar planets and the moon rang in on him. Our own solar system was as charming and as simple as an ancient cuckoo clock filled with familiar ticking and with reassuring noises. The odd little moons of Mars swung around their planet like frantic mice, yet their regularity was itself an assurance that all was well. Far above the plane of the ecliptic, he could feel half a ton of dust more or less drifting outside the lanes of human travel.

Here there was nothing to fight, nothing to challenge the mind, to tear the living soul out of a body with its roots dripping in effluvium as tangible as blood.

Nothing ever moved in on the solar system. He could wear the pin-set forever and be nothing more than a sort of telepathic astronomer, a man who could feel the hot, warm protection of the sun throbbing and burning against his living mind.

Woodley came in.

"Same old ticking world," said Underhill. "Nothing to report. No wonder they didn't develop the pin-set until they began to planoform. Down here with the hot sun around us, it feels so good and so quiet. You can feel everything spinning and turning. It's nice and sharp and compact. It's sort of like sitting around home."

Woodley grunted. He was not much given to flights of fantasy.

Undeterred, Underhill went on, "It must have been pretty good to have been an ancient man. I wonder why they burned up their world with war. They didn't have to planoform. They didn't have to go out to earn their livings among the stars. They didn't have to dodge the rats or play the game. They couldn't have invented pinlighting because they didn't have any need of it, did they, Woodley?"

Woodley grunted, "Uh-huh." Woodley was twenty-six years old and due to retire in one more year. He already had a farm picked out. He had gotten through ten years of hard work pinlighting with the best of them. He had kept his sanity by not thinking very much about his job, meeting the strains of the task whenever he had to meet them and thinking nothing more about his duties until the next emergency arose.

Woodley never made a point of getting popular among the partners. None of the partners liked him very much. Some of them even resented him. He was suspected of thinking ugly thoughts of the partners on occasion, but since none of the partners ever thought a complaint in articulate form, the other pinlighters and the chiefs of the Instrumentality left him alone.

Underhill was still full of the wonder of their job. Happily he babbled on, "What does happen to us when we planoform? Do you think it's sort of like dying? Did you ever see anybody who had his soul pulled out?"

"Pulling souls is just a way of talking about it," said Woodley. "After all these years, nobody knows whether we have souls or not."

"But I saw one once. I saw what Dogwood looked like when he came apart. There was something funny. It looked wet and sort of sticky as if it were bleeding and it went out of him—and you know what they did to Dogwood? They took him away, up in that part of the hospital where you and I never go—way up at the top part where the others are, where the others always have to go if they are alive after the rats of the up-and-out have gotten them."

Woodley sat down and lit an ancient pipe. He was burning something called tobacco in it. It was a dirty sort of habit, but it made him look very dashing and adventurous.

"Look here, youngster. You don't have to worry about that stuff. Pinlighting is getting better all the time. The partners are getting better. I've seen them pinlight two rats forty-six million miles apart in one and a half milliseconds. As long as people had to try to work the pin-sets themselves, there was always the chance that with a minimum of four-hundred milliseconds for the human mind to set a pinlight, we wouldn't light the rats up fast enough to protect our planoforming ships. The partners have changed all that. Once they get going, they're faster than rats. And they always will be. I know it's not easy, letting a partner share your mind—"

"It's not easy for them, either," said Underhill.

"Don't worry about them. They're not human. Let them take care of themselves. I've seen more pinlighters go crazy from monkeying around with partners than I have ever seen caught by the rats. How many of them do you actually know of that got grabbed by rats?"

Underhill looked down at his fingers, which shone green and purple in the vivid light thrown by the tuned-in pin-set, and counted ships. The thumb for the Andromeda, lost with crew and passengers, the index finger and the middle finger for Release Ships 43 and 56, found with their pin-sets burned out and every man, woman, and child on board dead or insane. The ring finger, the little finger, and the thumb of the other hand were the first three battleships to be lost to the rats—lost as people realized that there was something out there *underneath space itself* which was alive, capricious, and malevolent.

Planoforming was sort of funny. It felt like—

Like nothing much.

Like the twinge of a mild electric shock.

Like the ache of a sore tooth bitten on for the first time.

Like a slightly painful flash of light against the eyes. Yet in that time, a forty-thousand-ton ship lifting free above Earth disappeared somehow or other into two dimensions and appeared half a light-year or fifty light-years off.

At one moment, he would be sitting in the Fighting Room, the pin-set ready and the familiar solar system ticking around inside his head. For a second or a year (he could never tell how long it really was, subjectively), the funny little flash went through him and then he was loose in the up-and-out, the terrible open spaces between the stars, where the stars themselves felt like pimples on his telepathic mind and the planets were too far away to be sensed or read.

Somewhere in this outer space, a gruesome death awaited, death and horror of a kind which man had never encountered until he reached out for interstellar space itself. Apparently the light of the suns kept the dragons away.

Dragons. That was what people called them. To ordinary people, there was nothing, nothing except the shiver of planoforming and the hammer blow of sudden death or the dark spastic note of lunacy descending into their minds.

But to the telepaths, they were dragons.

In the fraction of a second between the telepaths' awareness of a hostile something. Out in the black, hollow nothingness of space and the impact of a ferocious, ruinous psychic blow against all living things within the ship, the telepaths had sensed entities something like the dragons of ancient human lore, beasts more clever than beasts, demons more tangible than demons, hungry vortices of aliveness and hate compounded by unknown means out of the thin, tenuous matter between the stars.

It took a surviving ship to bring back the news—a ship in which, by sheer chance, a telepath had a light-beam ready, turning it out at the innocent dust so that, within the panorama of his mind, the dragon dissolved into nothing at all and the other passengers, themselves non-telepathic, went about their way not realizing that their own immediate deaths had been averted.

From then on, it was easy—almost.

Planoforming ships always carried telepaths. Telepaths had their sensitiveness enlarged to an immense range by the pin-sets, which were telepathic amplifiers adapted to the mammal mind. The pin-sets in turn were electronically geared into small dirigible light bombs. Light did it.

Light broke up the dragons, allowed the ships to reform three-dimensionally, skip, skip, skip, as they moved from star to star.

The odds suddenly moved down from a hundred to one against mankind to sixty to forty in mankind's favor.

This was not enough. The telepaths were trained to become ultrasensitive, trained to become aware of the dragons in less than a millisecond.

But it was found that the dragons could move a million miles in just under two milliseconds and that this was not enough for the human mind to activate the light beams.

Attempts had been made to sheath the ships in light at all times. This defense wore out.

As mankind learned about the dragons, so too, apparently, the dragons learned about mankind. Somehow they flattened their own bulk and came in on extremely flat trajectories very quickly.

Intense light was needed, light of sunlike intensity. This could be provided only by light bombs. Pinlighting came into existence.

Pinlighting consisted of the detonation of ultra-vivid miniature photonuclear bombs, which converted a few ounces of a magnesium isotope into pure visible radiance.

The odds kept coming down in mankind's favor, yet ships were being lost.

It became so bad that people didn't even want to find the ships because the rescuers knew what they would see. It was sad to bring back to Earth three hundred bodies ready for burial and two hundred or three hundred lunatics, damaged beyond repair, to be wakened, and fed, and cleaned, and put to sleep, wakened and fed again until their lives were ended.

Telepaths tried to reach into the minds of the psychotics who had been damaged by the dragons, but they found nothing there beyond vivid spouting columns of fiery terror bursting from the primordial id itself, the volcanic source of life.

Then came the partners.

Man and partner could do together what man could not do alone. Men had the intellect. Partners had the speed.

The partners rode their tiny craft, no larger than footballs, outside the spaceships. They planoformed with the ships. They rode beside them in their six-pound craft ready to attack.

The tiny ships of the partners were swift. Each carried a dozen pin-lights, bombs no bigger than thimbles.

The pinlighters threw the partners—quite literally threw—by means of mind-to-firing relays directly at the dragons.

What seemed to be dragons to the human mind appeared in the form of gigantic rats in the minds of the partners.

Out in the pitiless nothingness of space, the partners' minds responded to an instinct as old as life. The partners attacked, striking with a speed faster than man's, going from attack to attack until the rats or themselves were destroyed. Almost all the time it was the partners who won.

With the safety of the interstellar skip, skip, skip of the ships, commerce increased immensely, the population of all the colonies went up, and the demand for trained partners increased.

Underhill and Woodley were a part of the third generation of pinlighters and yet, to them, it seemed as though their craft had endured forever.

Gearing space into minds by means of the pin-set, adding the partners to those minds, keying up the minds for the tension of a fight on which all depended—this was more than human synapses could stand for long. Underhill needed his two months' rest after half an hour of fighting. Woodley needed his retirement after ten years of service. They were young. They were good. But they had limitations.

So much depended on the choice of partners, so much on the sheer luck of who drew whom.

II. THE SHUFFLE

Father Moontree and the little girl named West entered the room. They were the other two pinlighters. The human complement of the Fighting Room was now complete.

Father Moontree was a red-faced man of forty-five who had lived the peaceful life of a farmer until he reached his fortieth year. Only then, belatedly, did the authorities find he was telepathic and agree to let him late in life enter upon the career of pinlighter. He did well at it, but he was fantastically old for this kind of business.

Father Moontree looked at the glum Woodley and the musing Underhill. "How're the youngsters today? Ready for a good fight?"

"Father always wants a fight," giggled the little girl named West. She was such a little little girl. Her giggle was high and childish. She looked like the last person in the world one would expect to find in the rough, sharp dueling of pinlighting.

Underhill had been amused one time when he found one of the most sluggish of the partners coming away happy from contact with the mind of the girl named West.

Usually the partners didn't care much about the human minds with which they were paired for the journey. The partners seemed to take the attitude that human minds were complex and fouled up beyond belief, anyhow. No partner ever questioned the superiority of the human mind, though very few of the partners were much impressed by that superiority.

The partners liked people. They were willing to fight with them. They were even willing to die for them. But when a partner liked an individual the way, for example, that Captain Wow or the Lady May liked Underhill, the liking had nothing to do with intellect. It was a matter of temperament, of feel.

Underhill knew perfectly well that Captain Wow regarded his, Underhill's, brain as silly. What Captain Wow liked was Underhill's friendly emotional structure, the cheerfulness and glint of wicked amusement that shot through Underhill's unconscious thought patterns, and the gaiety with which Underhill faced danger. The words, the history books, the ideas, the science—Underhill could sense all that in his own mind, reflected back from Captain Wow's mind, as so much rubbish.

Miss West looked at Underhill. "I bet you've put stickum on the stones."

"I did not!"

Underhill felt his ears grow red with embarrassment. During his novitiate, he had tried to cheat in the lottery because he got particularly fond of a special partner, a lovely young mother named Murr. It was so much easier to operate with Murr and she was so affectionate toward him that he forgot pinlighting was hard work and that he was not instructed to have a good time with his partner. They were both designed and prepared to go into deadly battle together.

One cheating had been enough. They had found him out and he had been laughed at for years.

Father Moontree picked up the imitation-leather cup and shook the stone dice which assigned them their partners for the trip. By senior rights he took first draw.

He grimaced. He had drawn a greedy old character, a tough old male whose mind was full of slobbering thoughts of food, veritable oceans full of half-spoiled fish. Father Moontree had once said that he burped cod liver oil for weeks after drawing that particular glutton, so strongly had the telepathic image of fish impressed itself upon his mind. Yet the glutton was a glutton for danger as well as for fish. He had killed sixty-three dragons, more than any other partner in the service, and was quite literally worth his weight in gold.

The little girl West came next. She drew Captain Wow. When she saw who it was, she smiled.

"I *like* him," she said. "He's such fun to fight with. He feels so nice and cuddly in my mind."

"Cuddly, hell," said Woodley. "I've been in his mind, too. It's the most leering mind in this ship, bar none."

"Nasty man," said the little girl. She said it declaratively, without reproach.

Underhill, looking at her, shivered.

He didn't see how she could take Captain Wow so calmly. Captain Wow's mind *did* leer. When Captain Wow got excited in the middle of a battle, confused images of dragons, deadly rats, luscious beds, the smell of fish, and the shock of space all scrambled together in his mind as he and Captain Wow, their consciousnesses linked together through the pin-set, became a fantastic composite of human being and Persian cat.

That's the trouble with working with cats, thought Underhill. It's a pity that nothing else anywhere will serve as partner. Cats were all right once you got in touch with them telepathically. They were smart enough to meet the needs of the fight, but their motives and desires were certainly different from those of humans.

They were companionable enough as long as you thought tangible images at them, but their minds just closed up and went to sleep when you recited Shakespeare or Colegrove, or if you tried to tell them what space was.

It was sort of funny realizing that the partners who were so grim and mature out here in space were the same cute little animals that people had used as pets for thousands of years back on Earth. He had embarrassed himself more than once while on the ground saluting perfectly ordinary non-telepathic cats because he had forgotten for the moment that they were not partners.

He picked up the cup and shook out his stone dice.

He was lucky—he drew the Lady May.

The Lady May was the most thoughtful partner he had ever met.

In her, the finely bred pedigree mind of a Persian cat had reached one of its highest peaks of development. She was more complex than any human woman, but the complexity was all one of emotions, memory, hope, and discriminated experience—experience sorted through without benefit of words.

When he had first come into contact with her mind, he was astonished at its clarity. With her he remembered her kittenhood. He remembered every mating experience she had ever had. He saw in a half-recognizable gallery all the other pinlighters with whom she had been paired for the fight. And he saw himself radiant, cheerful, and desirable.

He even thought he caught the edge of a longing—

A very flattering and yearning thought: *What a pity he is not a cat.*

Woodley picked up the last stone. He drew what he deserved—a sullen, scarred old tomcat with none of the verve of Captain Wow. Woodley's partner was the most animal of all the cats on the ship, a low, brutish type with a dull mind. Even telepathy had not refined his character. His ears were half chewed off from the first fights in which he had engaged. He was a serviceable fighter, nothing more.

Woodley grunted.

Underhill glanced at him oddly. Didn't Woodley ever do anything but grunt?

Father Moontree looked at the other three. "You might as well get your partners now. I'll let the scanner know we're ready to go into the up-and-out."

III. THE DEAL

Underhill spun the combination lock on the Lady May's cage. He woke her gently and took her into his arms. She humped her back luxuriously, stretched her claws, started to purr, thought better of it, and licked him on the wrist instead. He did not have the pin-set on, so their minds were closed to each other, but in the angle of her mustache and in the movement of her ears, he caught some sense of the gratification she experienced in finding him as her partner.

He talked to her in human speech, even though speech meant nothing to a cat when the pin-set was not on.

"It's a damn shame, sending a sweet little thing like you whirling around in the coldness of nothing to hunt for rats that are bigger and deadlier than all of us put together. You didn't ask for this kind of fight, did you?"

For answer, she licked his hand, purred, tickled his cheek with her long fluffy tail, turned around and faced him, golden eyes shining.

For a moment, they stared at each other, man squatting, cat standing erect on her hind legs, front claws digging into his knee. Human eyes and cat eyes looked across an immensity which no words could meet, but which affection spanned in a single glance.

"Time to get in," he said.

She walked docilely to her spheroid carrier. She climbed in. He saw to it that her miniature pin-set rested firmly and comfortably against the base of her brain. He made sure that her claws were padded so that she could not tear herself in the excitement of battle.

Softly he said to her, "Ready?"

For answer, she preened her back as much as her harness would permit and purred softly within the confines of the frame that held her.

He slapped down the lid and watched the sealant ooze around the seam. For a few hours, she was welded into her projectile until a workman with a short cutting arc would remove her after she had done her duty.

He picked up the entire projectile and slipped it into the ejection tube. He closed the door of the tube, spun the lock, seated himself in his chair, and put his own pin-set on.

Once again he flung the switch.

He sat in a small room, *small, small, warm, warm,* the bodies of the other three people moving close around him, the tangible lights in the ceiling bright and heavy against his closed eyelids.

As the pin-set warmed, the room fell away. The other people ceased to be people and became small glowing heaps of fire, embers, dark red fire, with the consciousness of life burning like old red coals in a country fireplace.

As the pin-set warmed a little more, he felt Earth just below him, felt the ship slipping away, felt the turning moon as it swung on the far side of the world, felt the planets and the hot, clear goodness of the sun which kept the dragons so far from mankind's native ground.

Finally, he reached complete awareness.

He was telepathically alive to a range of millions of miles. He felt the dust which he had noticed earlier high above the ecliptic. With a thrill of warmth and tenderness, he felt the consciousness of the Lady May pouring over into his own. Her consciousness was as gentle and dear and yet sharp to the taste of his mind as if it were scented oil. It felt relaxing and reassuring. He could sense her welcome of him. It was scarcely a thought, just a raw emotion of greeting.

At last they were one again.

In a tiny remote corner of his mind, as tiny as the smallest toy he had ever seen in his childhood, he was still aware of the room and the ship, and of Father Moontree picking up a telephone and speaking to a Go-captain in charge of the ship.

His telepathic mind caught the idea long before his ears could frame the words. The actual sound followed the idea the way that thunder on an ocean beach follows the lightning inward from far out over the seas.

"The Fighting Room is ready. Clear to planoform, sir."

IV. THE PLAY

Underhill was always a little exasperated the way that Lady May experienced things before he did.

He was braced for the quick vinegar thrill of planoforming, but he caught her report of it before his own nerves could register what happened.

Earth had fallen so far away that he groped for several milliseconds before he found the sun in the upper rear right-hand corner of his telepathic mind.

That was a good jump, he thought. *This way we'll get there in four or five skips.*

A few hundred miles outside the ship, the Lady May thought back at him, "O warm, O generous, O gigantic man! O brave, O friendly, O tender and huge partner! O wonderful with you, with you so good, good, good, warm, warm, now to fight, now to go, good with you..."

He knew that she was not thinking words, that his mind took the dear amiable babble of her cat intellect and translated it into images which his own thinking could record and understand.

Neither one of them was absorbed in the game of mutual greetings. He reached out far beyond her range of perception to see if there was anything near the ship. It was funny how it was possible to do two things at once. He could scan space with his pin-set mind and yet at the same time catch a vagrant thought of hers, a lovely, affectionate thought about a son who had had a golden face and a chest covered with soft, incredibly downy white fur.

While he was still searching, he caught the warning from her.

We jump again!

And so they had. The ship had moved to a second planoform. The stars were different. The sun was immeasurably far behind. Even the nearest stars were barely in contact. This was good dragon country, this open, nasty, hollow kind of space. He reached farther, faster, sensing and looking for danger, ready to fling the Lady May at danger wherever he found it.

Terror blazed up in his mind, so sharp, so clear, that it came through as a physical wrench.

The little girl named West had found something—something immense, long, black, sharp, greedy, horrific. She flung Captain Wow at it.

Underhill tried to keep his own mind clear. "Watch out!" he shouted telepathically at the others, trying to move the Lady May around.

At one corner of the battle, he felt the lustful rage of Captain Wow as the big Persian tomcat detonated lights while he approached the streak of dust which threatened the ship and the people within.

The lights scored near misses.

The dust flattened itself, changing from the shape of a sting ray into the shape of a spear.

Not three milliseconds had elapsed.

Father Moontree was talking human words and was saying in a voice that moved like cold molasses out of a heavy jar, "C-a-p-t-a-i-n." Underhill knew that the sentence was going to be "Captain, move fast!"

The battle would be fought and finished before Father Moontree got through talking.

Now, fractions of a millisecond later, the Lady May was directly in line.

Here was where the skill and speed of the partners came in. She could react faster than he. She could see the threat as an immense rat coming directly at her.

She could fire the light-bombs with a discrimination which he might miss.

He was connected with her mind, but he could not follow it.

His consciousness absorbed the tearing wound inflicted by the alien enemy. It was like no wound on Earth—raw, crazy pain which started like a burn at his navel. He began to writhe in his chair.

Actually he had not yet had time to move a muscle when the Lady May struck back at their enemy.

Five evenly spaced photonuclear bombs blazed out across a hundred-thousand miles.

The pain in his mind and body vanished.

He felt a moment of fierce, terrible, feral elation running through the mind of the Lady May as she finished her kill. It was always disappointing to the cats to find out that their enemies disappeared at the moment of destruction.

Then he felt her hurt, the pain and the fear that swept over both of them as the battle, quicker than the movement of an eyelid, had come and gone. In the same instant there came the sharp and acid twinge of planoform.

Once more the ship went skip.

He could hear Woodley thinking at him. "You don't have to bother much. This old son-of-a-gun and I will take over for a while."

Twice again the twinge, the skip.

He had no idea where he was until the lights of the Caledonia space port shone below.

With a weariness that lay almost beyond the limits of thought, he threw his mind back into rapport with the pin-set, fixing the Lady May's projectile gently and neatly in its launching tube.

She was half dead with fatigue, but he could feel the beat of her heart, could listen to her panting, and he grasped the grateful edge of a "Thanks" reaching from her mind to his.

V. THE SCORE

They put him in the hospital at Caledonia.

The doctor was friendly but firm. "You actually got touched by that dragon. That's as close a shave as I've ever seen. It's all so quick that it'll be a long time before we know what happened scientifically, but I suppose you'd be ready for the insane asylum now if the contact had lasted several tenths of a millisecond longer. What kind of cat did you have out in front of you?"

Underhill felt the words coming out of him slowly. Words were such a lot of trouble compared with the speed and the joy of thinking, fast and sharp and clear, mind to mind! But words were all that could reach ordinary people like this doctor.

His mouth moved heavily as he articulated words. "Don't call our partners cats. The right thing to call them is partners. They fight for us in a team. You ought to know we call them partners, not cats. How is mine?"

"I don't know," said the doctor contritely. "We'll find out for you. Meanwhile, old man, you take it easy. There's nothing but rest that can help you. Can you make yourself sleep, or would you like us to give you some kind of sedative?"

"I can sleep," said Underhill. "I just want to know about the Lady May."

The nurse joined in. She was a little antagonistic. "Don't you want to know about the other people?"

"They're okay," said Underhill. "I knew that before I came in here."

He stretched his arms and sighed and grinned at them. He could see they were relaxing and were beginning to treat him as a person instead of a patient.

"I'm all right," he said. "Just let me know when I can go see my partner."

A new thought struck him. He looked wildly at the doctor. "They didn't send her off with the ship, did they?"

"I'll find out right away," said the doctor. He gave Underhill a reassuring squeeze of the shoulder and left the room.

The nurse took a napkin off a goblet of chilled fruit juice.

Underhill tried to smile at her. There seemed to be something wrong with the girl. He wished she would go away. First she had started to be friendly and now she was distant again. *It's a nuisance being telepathic,* he thought. *You keep trying to reach even when you are not making contact.*

Suddenly she swung around on him.

"You pinlighters! You and your damn cats!"

Just as she stamped out, he burst into her mind. He saw himself a radiant hero, clad in his smooth suede uniform, the pin-set crown shining like ancient royal jewels around his head. He saw his own face, handsome and masculine, shining out of her mind. He saw himself very far away and he saw himself as she hated him.

She hated him in the secrecy of her own mind. She hated him because he was—she thought—proud and strange and rich, better and more beautiful than people like her.

He cut off the sight of her mind and, as he buried his face in the pillow, he caught an image of the Lady May.

"She *is* a cat," he thought. "That's all she is—a *cat!*"

But that was not how his mind saw her—quick beyond all

dreams of speed, sharp, clever, unbelievably graceful, beautiful, wordless and undemanding.

Where would he ever find a woman who could compare with her?

Set just before the novel Brother In Arms, *our next story—about the namesake character of Lois McMaster Bujold's hit Miles Vorkosigan series— first appeared in 1987 and tells the story of Miles leading a snatch-and-grab raid to rescue a military genius from under the nose of the Cetagandans, so he can organize a new Marilacan resistance movement. One of the few full novellas in our book, this story well demonstrates both why Bujold's work has topped award nominations and critics' rankings throughout her career, and why Miles Vorkosigan has become one of the most beloved space opera characters of the last thirty years.*

THE BORDERS OF INFINITY
LOIS MCMASTER BUJOLD

How could I have died and gone to hell without noticing the transition?

The opalescent force dome capped a surreal and alien landscape, frozen for a moment by Miles's disorientation and dismay. The dome defined a perfect circle, half a kilometer in diameter. Miles stood just inside its edge, where the glowing concave surface dove into the hard-packed dirt and disappeared. His imagination followed the arc buried beneath his feet to the far side, where it erupted again to complete the sphere. It was like being trapped inside an eggshell. An unbreakable eggshell.

Within was a scene from an ancient limbo. Dispirited men and women sat, or stood, or mostly lay down, singly or in scattered irregular groups, across the breadth of the arena. Miles's eye searched anxiously for some remnant of order or military grouping, but the inhabitants seemed splashed randomly as a liquid across the ground.

Perhaps he had been killed just now, just entering this prison camp. Perhaps his captors had betrayed him to his death, like those ancient Earth soldiers who had lured their victims sheeplike into poisoned showers, diverting and soothing their suspicions with stone soap, until their final enlightenment burst upon them in a choking cloud. Perhaps the annihilation of his body had been so swift, his neurons had not had time to carry the information to his brain. Why else did so many antique myths agree that hell was a circular place?

Dagoola IV Top Security Prison Camp #3. This was it? This naked… dinner plate? Miles had vaguely visioned barracks, marching guards, daily head counts, secret tunnels, escape committees.

It was the dome that made it all so simple, Miles realized. What need for barracks to shelter prisoners from the elements? The dome did it. What need for guards? The dome was generated from without. Nothing inside could breach it. No need for guards, or head counts. Tunnels were a futility, escape committees an absurdity. The dome did it all.

The only structures were what appeared to be big gray plastic mushrooms evenly placed about every hundred meters around the perimeter of the dome. What little activity there was seemed clustered around them. Latrines, Miles recognized.

Miles and his three fellow prisoners had entered through a temporary portal, which had closed behind them before the brief bulge of force dome containing their entry vanished in front of them. The nearest inhabitant of the dome, a man, lay a few meters away upon a sleeping mat identical to the one Miles now clutched. He turned his head slightly to stare at the little party of newcomers, smiled sourly, and rolled over on his side with his back to them. Nobody else nearby even bothered to look up.

"Holy shit," muttered one of Miles's companions.

He and his two buddies drew together unconsciously. The three had been from the same unit once, they'd said. Miles had met them bare minutes ago, in their final stages of processing, where they had all been issued their total supply of worldly goods for life in Dagoola #3.

A single pair of loose gray trousers. A matching short-sleeved gray tunic. A rectangular sleeping mat, rolled up. A plastic cup. That was all. That, and the new numbers encoded upon their skins. It bothered Miles intensely that their captors had chosen to locate the numbers in the middle of their backs, where they couldn't see them. He resisted a futile urge to twist and crane his neck anyway, though his hand snaked up under his shirt to scratch a purely psychosomatic itch. You couldn't feel the encode, either.

Some motion appeared in the tableau. A group of four or five men approaching. The welcoming committee at last? Miles was desperate for information. Where among all these countless gray men and women—no, not countless, Miles told himself firmly. They were all accounted for here.

The battered remnants of the 3rd and 4th Armored All-Terrain Rangers. The ingenious and tenacious civilian defenders of Garson Transfer Station. Winoweh's 2nd Battalion had been captured almost intact. And the 14th Commandos, survivors of the high-tech fortress at Fallow Core. Particularly the survivors of Fallow Core. Ten thousand, two hundred fourteen exactly. The planet Marilac's finest. Ten thousand, two hundred fifteen, counting himself. Ought he to count himself?

The welcoming committee drew up in a ragged bunch a few meters away. They looked tough and tall and muscular and not noticeably friendly. Dull, sullen eyes, full of a deadly boredom that even their present calculation did not lighten.

The two groups, the five and the three, sized each other up. The three turned, and started walking stiffly and prudently away. Miles realized belatedly that he, not a part of either group, was thus left alone.

Alone and immensely conspicuous. Self-consciousness, body-consciousness, normally held at bay by the simple fact that he didn't have time to waste on it, returned to him with a rush. Too short, too odd-looking—his legs were even in length now, after the last operation, but surely not long enough to outrun these five. And where did one run to, in this place? He crossed off flight as an option.

Fight? Get serious.

This isn't going to work, he realized sadly, even as he started walking toward them. But it was more dignified than being chased down with the same result.

He tried to make his smile austere rather than foolish. No telling whether he succeeded. "Hi, there. Can you tell me where to find Colonel Guy Tremont's 14th Commando Division?"

One of the five snorted sardonically. Two moved behind Miles.

Well, a snort was almost speech. Expression, anyway. A start, a toehold. Miles focused on that one. "What's your name and rank and company, soldier?"

"No ranks in here, mutant. No companies. No soldiers. No nothing."

Miles glanced around. Surrounded, of course. Naturally. "You got some friends, anyway."

The talker almost smiled. "You don't."

Miles wondered if perhaps he had been premature in crossing off flight as an option. "I wouldn't count on that if I were—*unh!*" The kick to his kidneys, from behind, cut him off—he damn near bit his tongue—he fell, dropping bedroll and cup and landing in a tangle. A barefoot kick, no combat boots this time, thank God—by the rules of Newtonian physics, his attacker's foot ought to hurt just as much as his back. Fine. Jolly. Maybe they'd bruise their knuckles, punching him out…

One of the gang gathered up Miles's late wealth, cup and bedroll. "Want his clothes? They're too little for me."

"Naw."

"Yeah," said the talker. "Take 'em anyway. Maybe bribe one of the women."

The tunic was jerked off over Miles's head, the pants over his feet. Miles was too busy protecting his head from random kicks to fight much for his clothes, trying obliquely to take as many hits as possible on his belly or ribcage, not arms or legs or jaw. A cracked rib was surely the most injury he could afford right now, here, at the beginning. A broken jaw would be the worst.

His assailants desisted only a little before they discovered by experimentation the secret weakness of his bones.

"*That's* how it is in here, mutant," said the talker, slightly winded.

"I was born naked," Miles panted from the dirt. "Didn't stop me."

"Cocky little shit," said the talker.

"Slow learner," remarked another.

The second beating was worse than the first. Two cracked ribs at least—his jaw barely escaped being smashed, at the cost of something painfully wrong in his left wrist, flung up as a shield. This time Miles resisted the impulse to offer any verbal parting shots.

He lay in the dirt and wished he could pass out.

✦ ✦ ✦

He lay a long time, cradled in pain. He was not sure how long. The illumination from the force dome was even and shadowless, unchanging. Timeless, like eternity. Hell was eternal, was it not? This place had too damn many congruencies with hell, that was certain.

And here came another demon… Miles blinked the approaching figure into focus. A man, as bruised and naked as Miles himself, gaunt-ribbed, starveling, knelt in the dirt a few meters away. His face was bony, aged by stress; he might have been forty, or fifty—or twenty-five.

His eyes were unnaturally prominent, due to the shrinking of his flesh. Their whites seemed to gleam feverishly against the dirt darkening his skin. Dirt, not beard stubble—every prisoner in here, male and female, had their hair cut short and the hair follicles stunned to prevent regrowth. Perpetually clean-shaved and crew-cut. Miles had undergone the same process bare hours ago. But whoever had processed this fellow must have been in a hurry. The hair stunner had missed a line on his cheek, and a few dozen hairs grew there like a stripe on a badly mown lawn. Even curled as they were, Miles could see they were several centimeters long, draggling down past the man's jaw. If only he knew how fast hair grew, he could calculate how long this fellow had been here. *Too long, whatever the numbers,* Miles thought with an inward sigh.

The man had the broken-off bottom half of a plastic cup, which he pushed cautiously toward Miles. His breath whistled raggedly past his yellowish teeth, from exertion or excitement or disease— probably not disease, they were all well immunized here. Escape, even through death, was not that easy. Miles rolled over and propped himself stiffly on his elbow, regarding his visitor through the thinning haze of his aches and pains.

The man scrabbled back slightly, smiled nervously. He nodded toward the cup. "Water. Better drink. The cup's cracked, and it all leaks out if you wait too long."

"Thanks," croaked Miles. A week ago, or in a previous lifetime, depending on how you counted time, Miles had dawdled over a selection of wines, dissatisfied with this or that nuance of flavor. His lips cracked as he grinned in memory. He drank. It was perfectly ordinary water, lukewarm, faintly redolent of chlorine and sulfur. *A refined body, but the bouquet is a bit presumptuous...*

The man squatted in studied politeness until Miles finished drinking, then leaned forward on his knuckles in restrained urgency. "Are you the One?"

Miles blinked. "Am I the what?"

"The One. The *other* one, I should say. The scripture says there has to be two."

"Uh"—Miles hesitated in caution—"what exactly does the scripture say?"

The man's right hand wrapped over his knobby left wrist, around which was tied a rag screwed into a sort of rope. He closed his eyes; his lips moved a moment, and then he recited aloud, "...but the pilgrims went up that hill with ease, because they had these two men to lead them by the arms; also they had left their garments behind them, for though they went in with them, they came out without them." His eyes popped back open to stare hopefully at Miles.

So, now we begin to see why this guy seems to be all by himself... "Are you, perchance, the other One?" Miles shot at a venture.

The man nodded shyly.

"I see. Um..." How was it that he always attracted the nut cases? He licked the last drops of water from his lips. The fellow might have some screws loose, but he was certainly an improvement over the last lot, always presuming he didn't have another personality or two of the homicidal loonie variety tucked away in his head. No, in that case he'd be introducing himself as the Chosen Two, and not be looking for outside assistance. "Um... what's your name?"

"Suegar."

"Suegar. Right, all right. My name is Miles, by the way."

"Huh." Suegar grimaced in a sort of pleased irony. "Your name means 'soldier,' did you know?"

"Uh, yeah, so I've been told."

"But you're not a soldier...?"

No subtle expensive trick of clothing line or uniform style here to hide from himself, if no one else, the peculiarities of his body. Miles flushed. "They were taking anything, toward the end. They made me a recruiting clerk. I never did get to fire my gun. Listen, Suegar—how did you come to know you were the One, or at any rate one of the Ones? Is it something you've always known?"

"It came on me gradually," confessed Suegar, shifting to sit cross-legged. "I'm the only one in here with the words, y'see." He caressed his rag rope again. "I've hunted all up and down the camp, but they only mock me. It was a kind of process of elimination, y'see, when they all gave up but me."

"Ah." Miles too sat up, only gasping a little in pain. Those ribs were going to be murder for the next few days. He nodded toward the rope bracelet. "Is that where you keep your scripture? Can I see it?" And how the hell had Suegar ever smuggled a plastic flimsy, or loose piece of paper or whatever, in here?

Suegar clutched his arms protectively to his chest and shook his head. "They've been trying to take them from me for months, y'see. I can't be too careful. Until you prove you're the One. The devil can quote scripture, y'know."

Yes, that was rather what I had in mind... Who knew what opportunities Suegar's "scripture" might contain? Well, maybe later.

For now, keep dancing. "Are there any other signs?" asked Miles. "You see, I don't know that I'm your One, but on the other hand I don't know I'm not, either. I just got here, after all."

Suegar shook his head again. "It's only five or six sentences, y'see. You have to interpolate a lot."

I'll bet. Miles did not voice the comment aloud. "However did you come by it? Or get it in here?"

"It was at Port Lisma, y'see, just before we were captured," said Suegar. "House-to-house fighting. One of my boot heels had come a bit loose, and it clicked when I walked. Funny, with all that barrage coming down around our ears, how a little thing like that can get under your skin. There was this bookcase with a glass front, real antique books made of paper—I smashed it open with my gun butt and tore out part of a page from one, and folded it up to stick in my boot heel, to make a sort of shim, y'see, and stop the clicking. Didn't look at the book. Didn't even know it was scripture till later. At least, I think it's scripture. It sounds like scripture, anyway. It must be scripture."

Suegar twisted his beard hairs nervously around his finger. "When we were waiting to be processed, I'd pulled it out of my boot, just idle-like, y'know. I had it in my hand—the processing guard saw it, but he just didn't take it away from me. Probably thought it was just a harmless piece of paper. Didn't know it was scripture. I still had it in my hand when we were dumped in here. D'you know, it's the only piece of writing in this whole camp?" he added rather proudly. "It must be scripture."

"Well... you take good care of it, then," advised Miles kindly. "If you've preserved it this long, it was obviously meant to be your job."

"Yeah..." Suegar blinked. Tears? "I'm the only one in here with a job, aren't I? So I must be one of the Ones."

"Sounds good to me," said Miles agreeably. "Say, ah"—he glanced around the vast featureless dome—"how do you find your way around in here, anyway?" The place was decidedly undersupplied with landmarks. It reminded Miles of nothing so much as a penguin rookery. Yet penguins seemed able to find their rocky nests. He was going to have to start thinking like a penguin—or get a penguin to direct him. He studied his guide bird, who had gone absent and was doodling in the dirt. Circles, naturally.

"Where's the mess hall?" Miles asked more loudly. "Where did you get that water?"

"Water taps are on the outside of the latrines," said Suegar, "but they only work part of the time. No mess hall. We just get rat bars. Sometimes."

"Sometimes?" said Miles angrily. He could count Suegar's ribs. "Dammit, the Cetagandans are claiming loudly to be treating their POW's by Interstellar Judiciary Commission rules. So many square meters of space per person, three thousand calories a day, at least fifty grams of protein, two liters of drinking water—you should be getting at least two IJC standard ration bars a day. Are they starving you?"

"After a while," Suegar sighed, "you don't really care if you get yours or not." The animation that his interest in Miles as a new and hopeful object in his world had lent Suegar seemed to be falling away. His breathing had slowed, his posture slumped. He seemed about to lie down in the dirt. Miles wondered if Suegar's sleeping mat had suffered the same fate as his own. Quite some time ago, probably.

"Look, Suegar—I think I may have a relative in this camp somewhere. A cousin of my mother's. D'you think you could help me find him?"

"It might be good for you, to have a relative," Suegar agreed. "It's not good to be by yourself, here."

"Yeah, I found that out. But how can you find anyone? It doesn't look too organized."

"Oh, there's—there's groups and groups. Everyone pretty much stays in the same place after a while."

"He was in the Fourteenth Commandos. Where are they?"

"None of the *old* groups are left, much."

"He was Colonel Tremont. Colonel Guy Tremont."

"Oh, an officer." Suegar's forehead wrinkled in worry. "That makes it harder. You weren't an officer, were you? Better not let on, if you were—"

"I was a clerk," repeated Miles.

"—because there's groups here who don't like officers. A clerk. You're probably OK, then."

"Were you an officer, Suegar?" asked Miles curiously.

Suegar frowned at him, twisted his beard hairs. "Marilac Army's gone. If there's no army, it can't have officers, can it?"

Miles wondered briefly if he might get farther faster by just walking away from Suegar and trying to strike up a conversation with the next random prisoner he came across. Groups and groups. And, presumably, groups, like the five burly surly brothers. He decided to stick with Suegar for a while longer. For one thing, he wouldn't feel quite so naked if he wasn't naked by himself.

"Can you take me to anybody who used to be in the Fourteenth?" Miles urged Suegar anew. "Anybody, who might know Tremont by sight."

"You don't know him?"

"We'd never met in person. I've seen vids of him. But I'm afraid his appearance may be… changed, by now."

Pensively, Suegar touched his own face. "Yeah, probably."

Miles clambered painfully to his feet. The temperature in the dome was just a little cool, without clothes. A voiceless draft raised the hairs on his arms. If he could just get one garment back, would he prefer his pants, to cover his genitals, or his shirt, to disguise his crooked back? Screw it. No time. He held out a hand to help Suegar rise. "Come on."

Suegar glanced up at him. "You can always tell a newcomer. You're still in a hurry. In here, you slow down. Your brain slows down…"

"Your scripture got anything to say on that?" inquired Miles impatiently.

" '…they therefore went up here with much agility and speed, through the foundation of the city…' " Twin verticals appeared between Suegar's eyebrows, as he frowned in speculation at Miles.

Thank you, thought Miles. *I'll take it*. He pulled Suegar up. "Come on, then."

Neither agility nor speed, but at least progress. Suegar led him on a shambling walk across a quarter of the camp, through some groups, in wide arcs around others. Miles saw the surly brothers again at a distance, sitting on their collection of mats. Miles upped his estimation of the size of the tribe from five to about fifteen. Some men sat in twos or threes or sixes, a few sat alone, as far as possible from any others, which still wasn't very far.

The largest group by far consisted entirely of women. Miles studied them with electric interest as soon as his eye picked up the size of their unmarked boundary. There were several hundred of them at least. None were matless, although some shared. Their perimeter was actually patrolled, by groups of half a dozen or so strolling slowly about. They apparently defended two latrines for their exclusive use.

"Tell me about the girls, Suegar," Miles urged his companion, with a nod toward their group.

"Forget the girls." Suegar's grin actually had a sardonic edge. "They do not put out."

"What, not at all? None of them? I mean, here we all are, with nothing to do but entertain each other. I'd think at least some of them would be interested." Miles's reason raced ahead of Suegar's answer, mired in unpleasantness. How unpleasant did it get in here?

For answer, Suegar pointed upward to the dome. "You know we're all monitored in here. They can see everything, pick up every word if they want. That is, if there's still anybody out there. They may have all gone away, and just forgotten to turn the dome off. I have dreams about that, sometimes. I dream that I'm here, in this dome, forever. Then I wake up, and I'm here, in this dome… Sometimes I'm not sure if I'm awake or asleep. Except that the food is still coming, and once in while—not so often, anymore— somebody new, like you. The food could be automated, though, I suppose. You could be a dream…"

"They're still out there," said Miles grimly.

Suegar sighed. "You know, in a way, I'm almost glad."

Monitored, yes. Miles knew all about the monitoring. He put down an urge to wave and call *Hi, Mom!* Monitoring must be a stultifying job for the goons out there. He wished they might be bored to death. "But what's that got to do with the girls, Suegar?"

"Well, at first everybody was pretty inhibited by that—" He pointed skywards again. "Then after a while we discovered that they didn't interfere with anything we did. At all. There were some rapes… Since then things have been—deteriorating."

"Hm. Then I suppose the idea of starting a riot, and breaching the dome when they bring troops inside to restore order, is a no-go?"

"That was tried once, a long time ago. Don't know how long." Suegar twisted his hairs. "They don't have to come inside to stop a riot. They can reduce the dome's diameter—they reduced it to about a hundred meters, that time. Nothing to stop them reducing it down to one meter, with all of us still inside, if they choose. It stopped the riot, anyway. Or they can reduce the gas permeability of the dome to zilch and just let us breathe ourselves into a coma. That's happened twice."

"I see," said Miles. It made his neck crawl.

A bare hundred or so meters away, the side of the dome began to bulge inward like an aneurysm. Miles touched Suegar's arm. "What's happening there? More new prisoners being delivered?"

Suegar glanced around. "Uh oh. We're not in a real good position, here." He hovered a moment, as if uncertain whether to go forward or back.

A wave of movement rippled through the camp from the bulge outward, of people getting to their feet. Faces turned magnetically toward the side of the dome. Little knots of men came together; a few sprinters began running. Some people didn't get up at all. Miles glanced back toward the women's group. About half of them were forming rapidly into a sort of phalanx.

"We're so close—what the hell, maybe we've got a chance," said Suegar. "Come on!" He started toward the bulge at his most rapid pace, a jog. Miles perforce jogged too, trying to jar his ribs as little as possible. But he was quickly winded, and his rapid breathing added an excruciating torque to his torso.

"What are we doing?" Miles started to pant to Suegar, before the dome's extruding bulge dissolved with a fading twinkle, and he saw what they were doing, saw it all.

Before the force dome's shimmering barrier now sat a dark brown pile, roughly a meter high, two meters deep, three meters wide. IJC standard ration bars, Miles recognized. Rat bars, apocryphally named after their supposed principal ingredient. Fifteen hundred calories each. Twenty-five grams of protein, fifty percent of the human MDR for vitamins A, B, C, and the rest of the alphabet—tasted like a shingle sprinkled with sugar and would sustain life and health forever or for as long as you could stand to keep eating them.

Shall we have a contest, children, to guess how many rat bars are in that pile? Miles thought. *No contest. I don't even have to measure the height and divide by three centimeters. It has to be 10,215 exactly. How ingenious.*

The Cetagandan Psych Ops corps must contain some remarkable minds. If they ever fell into his hands, Miles wondered, should he recruit them—or exterminate them? This brief fantasy was overwhelmed by the need to keep to his feet in the present reality, as ten thousand or so people, minus the wholly despairing and those too weak to move, all tried to descend on the same six square meters of the camp at once.

The first sprinters reached the pile, grabbed up armloads of rat bars, and started to sprint off. Some made it to the protection of friends, divided their spoils, and started to move away from the center of the growing human maelstrom. Others failed to dodge clots of operators like the burly surly brothers, and were violently relieved of their prizes. The second wave of sprinters, who didn't get away in time, were pinned up against the side of the dome by the incoming bodies.

Miles and Suegar, unfortunately, were in this second category. Miles's view was reduced to a sweating, heaving, stinking, swearing mass of elbows and chests and backs.

"Eat, eat!" Suegar urged around stuffed cheeks as he and Miles were separated by the pack. But the bar Miles had grabbed was twisted out of his hands before he had gathered his wits enough to follow Suegar's advice. Anyway, his hunger was nothing to his terror of being crushed, or worse, falling underfoot. His own feet pummeled over something soft, but he was unable to push back with enough strength to give the person—man, woman, who knew?—a chance to get up again.

In time the press lessened, and Miles found the edge of the crowd and broke free again. He staggered a little way off and fell to the dirt to sit, shaken and shaking, pale and cold. His breath rasped unevenly in his throat. It took him a long time to get hold of himself again.

Sheer chance, that this had hit his rawest nerve, his darkest fears, threatened his most dangerous weakness. *I could die here,* he realized, *without ever seeing the enemy's face.* But there seemed to be no new bones broken, except possibly in his left foot. He was not too sure about his left foot. The elephant who had trod on it was surely getting more than his fair share of rat bars.

✦ ✦ ✦

All right, Miles thought at last. *That's enough time spent on R&R. On your feet, soldier.* It was time to go find Colonel Tremont.

Guy Tremont. The real hero of the siege of Fallow Core. The defiant one, the one who'd held, and held, and held, after General Xian fled, after Baneri was killed.

Xian had sworn to return, but then Xian had run into that meat grinder at Vassily Station. HQ had promised resupply, but then HQ and its vital shuttleport had been taken by the Cetagandans.

But by this time Tremont and his troops had lost communication. So they held, waiting, and hoping. Eventually resources were reduced to hope and rocks. Rocks were versatile; they could either be boiled for soup or thrown at the enemy. At last Fallow Core was taken. Not surrendered. Taken.

Guy Tremont. Miles wanted very much to meet Guy Tremont.

On his feet and looking around, Miles spotted a distant shambling scarecrow being pelted off from a group with clods of dirt. Suegar paused out of range of their missiles, still pointing to the rag on his wrist and talking. The three or four men he was haranguing turned their backs to him by way of a broad hint.

Miles sighed and started trudging toward him. "Hey, Suegar!" he called and waved when he got closer.

"Oh, there you are." Suegar turned and brightened, and joined him. "I lost you." Suegar rubbed dirt out of his eyebrows. "Nobody wants to listen, y'know?"

"Yeah, well, most of them have heard you at least once by now, right?"

"Pro'bly twenty times. I keep thinking I might have missed one, y'see. Maybe the very One, the other One."

"Well, I'd be glad to listen to you, but I've really got to find Colonel Tremont first. You said you knew somebody...?"

"Oh, right. This way." Suegar led off again.

"Thanks. Say, is every chow call like that last one?"

"Pretty much."

"What's to keep some—group—from just taking over that arc of the dome?"

"It's never issued at the same place twice. They move it all around the perimeter. There was a lot of strategy debated at one time, as to whether it was better to be at the center, so's you're never more than half a diameter away, or near the edge, so's to be up front at least part of the time. Some guys had even worked out the mathematics of it, probabilities and all that."

"Which do you favor?"

"Oh, I don't have a spot, I move around and take my chances." His right hand touched his rag. "It's not the most important thing, anyway. Still, it was good to eat—today. Whatever day this is."

"Today is November second, 'Ninety-seven, Earth Common Era."

"Oh? Is that all?" Suegar pulled his beard strands out straight and rolled his eyes, attempting to look across his face at them. "Thought I'd been here longer than that. Why, it hasn't even been three years. Huh." He added apologetically, "In here it's always today."

"Mm," said Miles. "So the rat bars are always delivered in a pile like that, eh?"

"Yeah."

"Damned ingenious."

"Yeah," Suegar sighed. Rage, barely breathed, was camouflaged in that sigh, in the twitch of Suegar's hands. *So, my madman is not so simple...*

"Here we are," Suegar added. They paused before a group defined by half a dozen sleeping mats in a rough circle. One man looked up and glowered.

"Go away, Suegar. I ain't in the mood for a sermon."

"That the colonel?" whispered Miles.

"Naw, his name's Oliver. I knew him—a long time ago. He was at Fallow Core, though," Suegar whispered back. "He can take you to him."

Suegar bundled Miles forward. "This is Miles. He's new. Wants to talk to you." Suegar himself backed away. Helpfully, Miles realized. Suegar was aware of his unpopularity, it seemed.

Miles studied the next link in his chain. Oliver had managed to retain his gray pajamas, sleeping mat, and cup intact, which reminded Miles again of his own nakedness. On the other hand, Oliver did not seem to be in possession of any ill-gotten duplicates. Oliver might be as burly as the surly brothers, but was not otherwise related. That was good. Not that Miles in his present state need have any more worries about thievery.

Oliver stared at Miles without favor, then seemed to relent. "What d'you want?" he growled.

Miles opened his hands. "I'm looking for Colonel Guy Tremont."

"Ain't no colonels in here, boy."

"He was a cousin of my mother's. Nobody in the family— nobody in the outside world—has heard anything from or about him since Fallow Core fell. I—I'm not from any of the other units or pieces of units that are in here. Colonel Tremont is the only person I know anything about at all." Miles clasped his hands together and tried to look waif-like. Real doubt shook him, drew down his brows. "Is he still alive, even?"

Oliver frowned. "Relative, eh?" He scratched the side of his nose with a thick finger. "I suppose you got a right. But it won't do you any good, boy, if that's what you're thinking."

"I..." Miles shook his head. "At this point, I just want to *know*."

"Come on, then." Oliver levered himself to his feet with a grunt and lumbered off without looking over his shoulder.

Miles limped in his wake. "Are you taking me to him?"

Oliver made no answer until they'd finished their journey, only a few dozen meters, among and between sleeping mats. One man swore, one spat; most ignored them.

One mat lay at the edge of a group, almost far enough away to look alone. A figure lay curled up on his side with his back to them. Oliver stood silent, big fists on hips, and regarded it.

"Is that the colonel?" Miles whispered urgently.

"No, boy." Oliver sucked on his lower lip. "Only his remains."

Miles, alarmed, knelt down. Oliver was speaking poetically, Miles realized with relief. The man breathed. "Colonel Tremont? Sir?"

Miles's heart sank again, as he saw that breathing was about all that Tremont did. He lay inert, his eyes open but fixed on nothing. They did not even flick toward Miles and dismiss him with contempt. He was thin, thinner than Suegar even. Miles traced the angle of his jaw, the shape of his ear, from the holovids he'd studied. The remains of a face, like the ruined fortress of Fallow Core. It took nearly an archeologist's insight to recognize the connections between past and present.

He was dressed, his cup sat upright by his head, but the dirt around his mat was churned to acrid, stinking mud. From urine, Miles realized. Tremont's elbows were marked with lesions, the beginning of decubiti, bedsores. A damp patch on the gray fabric of his trousers over his bony hips hinted at more advanced and horrible sores beneath.

Yet somebody must be tending him, Miles thought, *or he wouldn't be looking even this good.*

Oliver knelt beside Miles, bare toes squishing in the mud, and pulled a hunk of rat bar from beneath the elastic waistband of his trousers. He crumbled a bit between his thick fingers and pushed it between Tremont's lips. "Eat," he whispered. The lips almost moved; the crumbs dribbled to the mat. Oliver tried again, seemed to become conscious of Miles's eyes upon him, and stuffed the rest of the rat bar back into his pants with an unintelligible grumble.

"Was—was he injured when Fallow Core was overrun?" asked Miles. "Head injury?"

Oliver shook his head. "Fallow Core wasn't stormed, boy."

"But it fell on October sixth, it was reported, and—"

"It fell on October fifth. Fallow Core was betrayed." Oliver turned and walked away before his stiffened face could betray any emotion.

Miles knelt in the mud and let his breath trickle out slowly.

So. And so.

Was this the end of his quest, then?

+ + +

He wanted to pace and think, but walking still hurt too much. He hobbled a little way off, trying not to accidentally infringe upon the territory of any sizeable group, and sat, then lay in the dirt with his hands behind his head, staring up at the pearly glow of the dome sealed like a lid over them all.

He considered his options, one, two, three. He considered them carefully. It didn't take long.

I thought you didn't believe in good guys and bad guys? He had cauterized his emotions, he'd thought, coming in here, for his own protection, but he could feel his carefully cultivated impartiality slipping. He was beginning to hate that dome in a really intimate, personal way. Aesthetically elegant, form united with function as perfectly as an eggshell, a marvel of physics—perverted into an instrument of torture.

Subtle torture… Miles reviewed the Interstellar Judiciary Commission's rules for the treatment of POWs, to which Cetaganda was a signatory. So many square meters of space per person, yes, they were certainly supplied with that. No prisoner to be solitarily confined for a period exceeding twenty-four hours—right, no solitude in here except by withdrawal into madness. No dark periods longer than twelve hours, that was easy, no dark periods at all, the perpetual glare of noon instead. No beatings—indeed, the guards could say with truth that they never laid a hand on their prisoners. They just watched, while the prisoners beat each other up instead. Rapes, even more strictly forbidden, doubtless handled the same way.

Miles had seen what they could do with their issue of two IJC standard ration bars per person per day. The rat bar riot was a particularly neat touch, he thought. No one could fail to participate—he rubbed his growling stomach. The enemy might have seeded the initial breakdown by sending in a short pile. But maybe not—the first person who snatched two instead of one left another foodless. Maybe next time that one took three, to make up for it, and so it quickly snowballed. Breaking down any hope of order, pitting group against group, person against person in a scrambling dogfight, a twice-a-day reminder of their powerlessness and degradation. None could afford for long to hold themselves aloof unless they wished to embrace slow starvation.

No forced labor—hah, check. That would require the imposition of order. Access to medical personnel—right, the various units' own medics must be mixed in out there somewhere. He reran the wording of that paragraph through his memory again—by God, it *did* say 'personnel,' didn't it? No medicine, just medical personnel. Empty-handed, naked doctors and medtechs. His lips drew back in a mirthless grin. Accurate lists of prisoners taken had been duly dispatched, as required. But no other communication...

Communication. This lack of word from the outside world might drive even him crazy shortly. It was as bad as prayer, talking to a God who never talked back. No wonder they all seemed touched with a sort of solipsistic schizophrenia here. Their doubts infected him. *Was* anybody still out there? Could his voice be heard and understood?

Ah, blind faith. The leap of faith. His right hand clenched, as if crushing an eggshell. "This," he enunciated clearly, "calls for a major change of plans."

He drove himself to his feet to go find Suegar again.

✦ ✦ ✦

Miles found him not far off, hunkered in the dirt doodling. Suegar looked up with a brief smile. "Did Oliver take you to—to your cousin?"

"Yes, but I came too late. He's dying."

"Yeah... I was afraid that might be the case. Sorry."

"Me, too." Miles was momentarily distracted from his purpose by a practical curiosity. "Suegar, what do they do with dead bodies here?"

"There's a rubbish pile of sorts, over against one side of the dome. The dome sort of extrudes and laps it up every once in a while, same way as food and new prisoners are introduced. Usually by the time a body swells and starts to stink, somebody'll drag it over there. I take 'em sometimes."

"No chance of anybody sneaking out in the rubbish pile, I suppose?"

"They microwave-incinerate it all before the portal's opened."

"Ah." Miles took a deep breath, and launched himself. "Suegar, it's come to me. I *am* the other One."

Suegar nodded serenely, unsurprised. "I'd had it figured."

Miles paused, nonplussed. Was that all the response...? He had expected something more energetic, either pro or con. "It came to me in a vision," he declared dramatically, following his script anyway.

"Oh, yeah?" Suegar's attention sharpened gratifyingly. "I've never gotten a vision," he added with envy. "Had to figure it all out, y'know, from context. What's it like? A trance?"

Shit, and here I thought this guy talked with elves and angels... Miles backed down slightly. "No, it's like a thought, only more compelling. It storms your will—burns like lust, only not so easy to satisfy. Not like a trance, because it drives you outward, not inward." He hesitated, unsettled, having spoken more truth than he'd intended.

Suegar looked vastly encouraged. "Oh, good. I was afraid for a second you might be one of those guys who start talking to people nobody else can see."

Miles glanced upward involuntarily, returned his gaze straightly to Suegar.

"—so that's a vision. Why, I've felt like that." His eyes seemed to focus and intensify.

"Didn't you recognize it in yourself?" asked Miles blandly.

"Not by name... it's not a comfortable thing, to be chosen so. I tried to evade it for a long time, but God finds ways of dealing with draft dodgers."

"You're too modest, Suegar. You've believed in your scripture, but not in yourself. Don't you know that when you're given a task, you're given the power to accomplish it as well?"

Suegar sighed in joyous satisfaction. "I knew it was a job for two. It's just like the scripture said."

"Uh, right. So now we are two. But we must be more. I guess we'd better start with your friends."

"That won't take much time," said Suegar wryly. "You got a step two in mind, I hope?"

"Then we'll start with your enemies. Or your nodding acquaintances. We'll start with the first bleeding body that crosses our path. It doesn't matter where we start, because I mean to have them all, in the end. All, to the last and least." A particularly apt quote shot across his memory, and he declaimed vigorously, " 'Those who have ears, let them hear.' All." Miles sent a real prayer up from his heart with that one.

"All right"—Miles pulled Suegar to his feet—"let's go preach to the unconverted."

Suegar laughed suddenly. "I had a top kick once who used to say, 'Let's go kick some ass,' in just that tone of voice."

"That, too." Miles grimaced. "You understand, universal membership in this congregation won't come all voluntary. But you leave the recruiting to me, hear?"

Suegar stroked his beard hairs, regarded Miles from beneath raised brows. "A clerk, eh?"

"Right."

"Yes, sir."

✦ ✦ ✦

They started with Oliver.

Miles gestured. "May we step into your office?"

Oliver rubbed his nose with the back of his hand and sniffed. "Let me give you a piece of advice, boy. You ain't gonna make it in here as a stand-up comic. Every joke that can possibly be made has been run into the ground. Even the sick ones."

"Very well." Miles sat cross-legged, near Oliver's mat but not too near. Suegar hunkered down behind Miles's shoulder, not so welded to the ground, as if ready to skip backwards if necessary. "I'll lay it out straight, then. I don't like the way things are run around here."

Oliver's mouth twisted sardonically; he did not comment aloud. He didn't need to.

"I'm going to change them," Miles added.

"Shit," said Oliver, and rolled back over.

"Starting here and now."

After a moment's silence Oliver added, "Go away or I'll pound you."

Suegar started to get up; Miles irritably motioned him back down.

"He was a commando," Suegar whispered in worry. "He can break you in half."

"Nine-tenths of the people in this camp can break me in half, including the girls," Miles whispered back. "It's not a significant consideration."

Miles leaned forward, grasped Oliver's chin, and twisted his face back toward him. Suegar sucked his breath through his teeth with a whistle at this dangerous tactic.

"Now, there's this about cynicism, Sergeant. It's the universe's most supine moral position. Real comfortable. If nothing can be done, then you're not some kind of shit for not doing it, and you can lie there and stink to yourself in perfect peace."

Oliver batted Miles's hand down, but did not turn away again. Rage flared in his eyes. "Suegar tell you I was a sergeant?" he hissed.

"No, it's written on your forehead in letters of fire. Listen up, Oliver—"

Oliver rolled over and up as far as supporting his upper body with his knuckles on his sleeping mat. Suegar flinched, but did not flee.

"You listen up, mutant," Oliver snarled. "We've done it all already. We've done drill, and games, and clean living, exercise, and cold showers, except there ain't no cold showers. We've done group sings and floor shows. We've done it by the numbers, by the book, by candlelight. We've done it by force, and made real war on each other. After that we did sin and sex and sadism till we were ready to puke. We've done it all at least ten times. You think you're the first reformer to come through here?"

"No, Oliver." Miles leaned into his face, his eyes boring into Oliver's burning eyes unscorched. His voice fell to a whisper. "I think I'm the last."

Oliver was silent a moment, then barked a laugh. "By God, Suegar has found his soul-mate at last. Two loonies together, just like his scripture says."

Miles paused thoughtfully, sat up as straight as his spine would allow. "Read me your scripture again, Suegar. The full text." He closed his eyes for total concentration, also to discourage interruptions from Oliver.

Suegar rustled around and cleared his throat nervously. " 'For those that shall be the heirs of salvation,' " he began. " 'Thus they went along toward the gate. Now you must note that the city stood upon a mighty hill, but the pilgrims went up that hill with ease, because they had these two men to lead them by the arms; also they had left their mortal garments behind them in the river, for though they went in with them, they came out without them. They therefore went up here with much agility and speed, through the foundation upon which the city was framed higher than the clouds.

They therefore went up through the regions of the air...' " He added apologetically, "It breaks off there. That's where I tore the page. Not sure what that signifies."

"Probably means that after that you're supposed to improvise for yourself," Miles suggested, opening his eyes again. So, that was the raw material he was building on. He had to admit the last line in particular gave him a turn, a chill like a belly full of cold worms. *So be it. Forward.*

"There you are, Oliver. That's what I'm offering. The only hope worth breathing for. Salvation itself."

"Very uplifting," sneered Oliver.

" 'Uplifted' is just what I intend you all to be. You've got to understand, Oliver, I'm a fundamentalist. I take my scriptures *very* literally."

Oliver opened his mouth, then closed it with a snap. Miles had his utter attention.

Communication at last, Miles breathed inwardly. *We have connected.*

"It would take a miracle," said Oliver at last, "to uplift this whole place."

"Mine is not a theology of the elect. I intend to preach to the masses. Even"—he was definitely getting into the swing of this—"the sinners. Heaven is for everyone.

"But miracles, by their very nature, must break in from outside. We don't carry them in our pockets—"

"You don't, that's for sure," muttered Oliver with a glance at Miles's undress.

"—we can only pray, and prepare ourselves for a better world. But miracles come only to the prepared. Are you prepared, Oliver?" Miles leaned forward, his voice vibrating with energy.

"Sh..." Oliver's voice trailed off. He glanced for confirmation, oddly enough, at Suegar. "Is this guy for real?"

"He thinks he's faking it," said Suegar blandly, "but he's not. He's the One, all right and tight."

The cold worms writhed again. Dealing with Suegar, Miles decided, was like fencing in a hall of mirrors. Your target, though real, was never quite where it looked as though it should be.

Oliver inhaled. Hope and fear, belief and doubt, intermingled in his face. "How shall we be saved, Rev'rend?"

"Ah—call me Brother Miles, I think. Yes. Tell me—how

many converts can you deliver on your own naked, unsupported authority?"

Oliver looked extremely thoughtful. "Just let them see *that* light, and they'll follow it anywhere."

"Well… well… salvation is for all, to be sure, but there may be certain temporary practical advantages to maintaining a priesthood. I mean, blessed also are they who do not see, and yet believe."

"It's true," agreed Oliver, "that if your religion failed to deliver a miracle, that a human sacrifice would certainly follow."

"Ah… quite," Miles gulped. "You are a man of acute insight."

"That's not an insight," said Oliver. "That's a personal guarantee."

"Yes, well… to return to my question. How many followers can you raise? I'm talking bodies here, not souls."

Oliver frowned, cautious still. "Maybe twenty."

"Can any of them bring in others? Branch out, hook in more?"

"Maybe."

"Make them your corporals, then. I think we had better disregard any previous ranks here. Call it, ah, the Army of the Reborn. No. The Reformation Army. That scans better. We shall be re-formed. The body has disintegrated like the caterpillar in its chrysalis, into nasty green gook, but we shall re-form into the butterfly and fly away."

Oliver sniffed again. "Just what reforms you planning?"

"Just one, I think. The food."

Oliver gave him a disbelieving stare. "You sure this isn't just a scam to get yourself a free meal?"

"True, I *am* getting hungry…" Miles backed off from the joke as Oliver remained icily unimpressed. "But so are a lot of other people. By tomorrow, we can have them all eating out of our hands."

"When would you want these twenty guys?"

"By the next chow call." Good, he'd startled the man.

"That soon?"

"You understand, Oliver, the belief that you have all the time in the world is an illusion this place fosters on purpose. Resist it."

"You're sure in a hurry."

"So, you got a dental appointment? I think not. Besides, I'm only half your mass. I gotta move twice as fast just to keep up the momentum. Twenty, plus. By next chow call."

"What the hell do you think you're gonna be able to do with twenty guys?"

"We're going to take the food pile."

Oliver's lips tightened in disgust. "Not with twenty guys, you're not. No go. Besides, it's been done. I told you we'd made real war in here. It'd be a quick massacre."

"—and then, after we've taken it—we redistribute it. Fair and square, one rat bar per customer, all controlled and quartermasterly. To sinners and all. By the next chow call everybody who's ever been shorted will be coming over to us. And then we'll be in a position to deal with the hard cases."

"You're nuts. You can't do it. Not with twenty guys."

"Did I say we were only going to have twenty guys? Suegar, did I say that?"

Suegar, listening in rapt fascination, shook his head.

"Well, I ain't sticking my neck out to get pounded unless you can produce some visible means of support," said Oliver. "This could get us killed."

"Can do," Miles promised recklessly. One had to start lifting somewhere; his imaginary bootstraps would do well enough. "I will deliver five hundred troops to the sacred cause by chow call."

"You do that, and I'll walk the perimeter of this camp naked on my hands," retorted Oliver.

Miles grinned. "I may hold you to that, Sergeant. Twenty-plus. By chow call." Miles stood. "Come on, Suegar."

Oliver waved them off irritably. They retreated in good order. When Miles looked back over his shoulder, Oliver had arisen, and was walking toward a group of occupied mats tangential to his own, waving down an apparent acquaintance.

+ + +

"So where do we get five hundred troops before next chow call?" Suegar asked. "I better warn you, Oliver was the best thing I had. The next is bound to be tougher."

"What," said Miles, "is your faith wavering so soon?"

"I believe," said Suegar, "I just don't see. Maybe that makes me blessed, I dunno."

"I'm surprised. I thought it was pretty obvious. There." Miles pointed across the camp toward the unmarked border of the women's group.

"Oh." Suegar stopped short. "Oh, oh. I don't think so, Miles."

"Yes. Let's go."

"You won't get in there without a change-of-sex operation."

"What, as God-driven as you are, haven't you tried to preach your scripture to them?"

"I tried. Got pounded. Tried elsewhere after that."

Miles paused, and pursed his lips, studying Suegar. "It wasn't defeat, or you wouldn't have hung on long enough to meet me. Was it—ah, shame, that drained your usual resolve? You got something to work off in that quarter?"

Suegar shook his head. "Not personally. Except maybe, sins of omission. I just didn't have the heart to harass 'em anymore."

"This whole place is suffering from sins of omission." A relief, that Suegar wasn't some sort of self-confessed rapist. Miles's eyes swept the scene, teasing out the pattern from the limited cues of position, grouping, activity. "Yes… predator pressure produces herd behavior. Social fragmentation here being what it is, the pressure must be pretty high, to hold a group of that size together. But I hadn't noticed any incidents since I got here."

"It comes and goes," said Suegar. "Phases of the moon or something."

Phases of the moon, right. Miles sent up a prayer of thanks in his heart to whatever gods might be—to Whom it may concern—that the Cetagandans appeared to have implanted some standard time-release anovulant in all their female prisoners, along with their other immunizations. Bless the forgotten individual who'd put *that* clause in the IJC rules, forcing the Cetagandans into more subtle forms of legal torture. And yet, would the presence of pregnancies, infants, and children among the prisoners have been another destabilizing stress—or a stabilizing force deeper and stronger than all the previous loyalties the Cetagandans seemed to have so successfully broken down? From a purely logistical viewpoint, Miles was elated that the question was theoretical.

"Well…" Miles took a deep breath, and pulled an imaginary hat down over his eyes at an aggressive angle. "I'm new here, and so temporarily unembarrassed. Let he who is without sin cast the first lure. Besides, I have an advantage for this sort of negotiation. I'm clearly not a threat." He marched forward.

"I'll wait for you here," called Suegar helpfully, and hunkered down where he was.

Miles timed his forward march to intersect a patrol of six women strolling down their perimeter. He arranged himself in front of them and swept off his imaginary hat to hold strategically over his crotch. "Good afternoon, ladies. Allow me to apologize for m'beh—"

His opening line was interrupted by a mouthful of dirt abruptly acquired as his legs were swept backward and his shoulders forward by the four women who had parted around him, dumping him neatly on his face. He had not even managed to spit it out when he found himself plucked up and whirled dizzily through the air, still face-down, by hands grasping his arms and legs. A muttered count of three, and he was soaring in a short forlorn arc, to land in a heap not far from Suegar. The patrollers walked on without another word.

"See what I mean?" said Suegar.

Miles turned his head to look at him. "You had that trajectory calculated to the centimeter, didn't you?" he said smearily.

"Just about," agreed Suegar. "I figured they could heave you quite a bit farther than usual, on account of your size."

Miles scrambled back up to a sitting position, still trying to get his wind. Damn the ribs, which had grown almost bearable, but which now wrung his chest with electric agony at every breath. In a few minutes he got up and brushed himself off. As an afterthought, he picked up his invisible hat, too. Dizzied, he had to brace his hands on his knees a moment.

"All right," he muttered, "back we go."

"Miles—"

"It's gotta be done, Suegar. No other choice. Anyway, I can't quit, once I've started. I've been told I'm pathologically persistent. I *can't* quit."

Suegar opened his mouth to object, then swallowed his protest. "Right," he said. He settled down cross-legged, his right hand unconsciously caressing his rag rope library. "I'll wait till you call me in." He seemed to fall into a reverie, or meditation—or maybe a doze.

Miles's second foray ended precisely like the first, except that his trajectory was perhaps a little wider and a little higher. The third attempt went the same way, but his flight was much shorter.

"Good," he muttered to himself. "Must be tiring 'em out."

This time he skipped in parallel to the patrol, out of reach but well within hearing. "Look," he panted, "you don't have to do this piecemeal. Let me make it easy for you. I have this teratogenic bone disorder—I'm not a mutant, you understand, my genes are normal, it's just their expression got distorted, from my mother being exposed to a certain poison while she was pregnant—it was a one-shot thing, won't affect any children *I* might have—I always felt it was easier to get dates when that was clearly understood, *not* a mutant—anyway, my bones are brittle, in fact any one of you could probably break every one in my body. You may wonder why I'm telling you all this—in fact, I usually prefer not to advertise it—you have to stop and listen to me. I'm not a threat—do I look like a threat?—a challenge, maybe, not a threat—are you going to make me run all around this camp after you? Slow down, for God's sake—" He would be out of wind, and therefore verbal ammunition, very shortly at this rate. He hopped around in front of them and planted himself, arms outstretched.

"—so if you *are* planning to break every bone in my body, please do it now and get it over with, because I'm going to keep coming back here until you do."

At a brief hand signal from their leader the patrol stopped, facing him.

"Take him at his word," suggested a tall redhead. Her short brush of electric copper hair fascinated Miles to distraction; he pictured missing masses of it having fallen to the floor at the clippers of the ruthless Cetagandan prison processors. "I'll break the left arm if you'll break the right, Conr," she continued.

"If that's what it takes to get you to stop and listen to me for five minutes, so be it," Miles responded, not retreating. The redhead stepped forward and braced herself, locking his left elbow in an arm bar, putting on the pressure.

"Five minutes, right?" Miles added desperately as the pressure mounted. Her stare scorched his profile. He licked his lips, closed his eyes, held his breath, and waited. The pressure reached critical—he rose on his toes...

She released him abruptly, so that he staggered. "Men," she commented disgustedly. "Always gotta make everything a peeing contest."

"Biology is Destiny," gasped Miles, popping his eyes back open.

"—or are you some kind of pervert—do you get off on being beaten up by women?"

God, I hope not. He remained unbetrayed by unauthorized salutes from his nether parts, just barely. If he was going to be around that redhead much he was definitely going to have to get his pants back somehow. "If I said yes, would you refrain, just to punish me?" he offered.

"Shit, no."

"It was just a thought—"

"Cut the crap, Beatrice," said the patrol leader. At a jerk of her head the redhead stepped back into formation. "All right, runt, you've got your five minutes. Maybe."

"Thank you, ma'am." Miles took a breath, and reordered himself as best he could with no uniform to adjust. "First, let me apologize for intruding upon your privacy in this undress. Practically the first persons I met upon entering this camp were a self-help group— they helped themselves to my clothes, among other things—"

"I saw that," confirmed Beatrice-the-redhead unexpectedly. "Pitt's bunch."

Miles pulled off his hat and swept her a bow with it. "Yes, thank you."

"You moon people behind you when you do that," she commented dispassionately.

"That's their look-out," responded Miles. "For myself, I want to talk to your leader, or leaders. I have a serious plan for improving the tone of this place with which I wish to invite your group to collaborate. Bluntly, you are the largest remaining pocket of civilization, not to mention military order, in here. I'd like to see you expand your borders."

"It takes everything we've got to keep our borders from being overrun, son," replied the leader. "No can do. So take yourself off."

"Jack yourself off, too," suggested Beatrice. "You ain't gettin' any in here."

Miles sighed, and turned his hat around in his hands by its wide brim. He spun it for a moment on one finger, and locked eyes with the redhead. "Note my hat. It was the one garment I managed to keep from the ravages of the burly surly brothers—Pitt's bunch, you say."

She snorted at the turn of phrase. "Those jerks... why just a hat? Why not pants? Why not a full-dress uniform while you're at it?" she added sarcastically.

"A hat is a more useful object for communicating. You can make broad gestures"—he did so—"denote sincerity"—he held it over his heart—"or indicate embarrassment"—over his genitals, with a hang-dog crouch—"or rage"—he flung it to earth as if he might drive it into the ground, then picked it up and brushed it off carefully—"or determination"—he jammed it on his head and yanked the brim down over his eyes—"or make courtesies." He swept it off again in salute to her. "Do you see the hat?"

She was beginning to be amused. "Yes…"

"Do you see the feathers on the hat?"

"Yes…"

"Describe them."

"Oh—plumy things."

"How many?"

"Two. Bunched together."

"Do you see the color of the feathers?"

She drew back, suddenly self-conscious again, with a sidewise glance at her companions. "No."

"When you can see the color of the feathers," said Miles softly, "you'll also understand how you can expand your borders to infinity."

She was silent, her face closed and locked. But the patrol leader muttered, "Maybe this little runt better talk to Tris. Just this once."

✦ ✦ ✦

The woman in charge had clearly been a frontline trooper once, not a tech like the majority of the females. She had certainly not acquired the muscles that flowed like braided leather cords beneath her skin from crouching by the hour in front of a holovid display in some rear-echelon underground post. She had toted the real weapons that spat real death, and sometimes broke down; had rammed against the limits of what could really be done by flesh and bone and metal, and been marked by that deforming press. Illusion had been burned out of her like an infection, leaving a cauterized scar. Rage burned permanently in her eyes like a fire in a coal seam, underground and unquenchable. She might be thirty-five, or forty.

God, I'm in love, thought Miles. *Brother Miles wants YOU for the Reformation Army…* then got hold of his thoughts. Here, now, was the make-or-break point for his scheme, and all the persiflage, verbal misdirection, charm, chutzpah, and bullshit he could muster weren't going to be enough, not even tied up with a big blue bow.

The wounded want power, nothing else; they think it will keep them from being hurt again. This one will not be interested in Suegar's strange message—at least, not yet… Miles took a deep breath.

"Ma'am, I'm here to offer you command of this camp."

She stared at him as if he were something she'd found growing on the walls in a dark corner of the latrine. Her eyes raked over his nudity; Miles could feel the claw marks glowing from his chin to his toes.

"Which you store in your duffel bag, no doubt," she growled. "Command of this camp doesn't exist, mutant. So it's not yours to give. Deliver him to our perimeter in pieces, Beatrice."

He ducked the redhead. He would pursue correction of the mutant business later. "Command of this camp is mine to *create*," he asserted. "Note, please, that what I offer is power, not revenge. Revenge is too expensive a luxury. Commanders can't afford it."

Tris uncoiled from her sleeping mat to her full height, then had to bend her knees to bring her face level to his, hissing, "Too bad, little turd. You almost interest me. Because I *want* revenge. On every man in this camp."

"Then the Cetagandans have succeeded; you've forgotten who your real enemy is."

"Say, rather, that I've discovered who my real enemy is. Do you want to know the things they've done to us—our own guys—"

"The Cetagandans want you to believe this"—a wave of his hand embraced the camp—"is something you're doing to each other. So fighting each other, you become their puppets. They watch you all the time, you know, voyeurs of your humiliation."

Her glance flicked upward, infinitesimally; good. It was almost a disease among these people, that they would look in any direction at all in preference to up at the dome.

"Power is better than revenge," suggested Miles, not flinching before her snake-cold, set face, her hot coal eyes. "Power is a live thing, by which you reach out to grasp the future. Revenge is a dead thing, reaching out from the past to grasp you."

"—and you're a bullshit artist," she interrupted, "reaching out to grasp whatever's going down. I've got you pegged now. *This* is power." She flexed her arm under his nose, muscles coiling and loosing. "This is the only power that exists in here. You haven't got it, and you're looking for some to cover your ass. But you've come to the wrong store."

"No," Miles denied, and tapped his forehead. "*This* is power. And I own the store. This controls that"—he slapped his bunched fist. "Men may move mountains, but ideas move men. Minds can be reached through bodies—what else is the point of all this"—he waved at the camp—"but to reach your minds through your bodies. But that power flows both ways, and the outflow is the stronger tide.

"When you have allowed the Cetagandans to reduce your power to *that* alone"—he squeezed her bicep for emphasis—it was like squeezing a rock covered in velvet, and she tensed, enraged at the liberty—"then you have allowed them to reduce you to your weakest part. And they win."

"They win anyway," she snapped, shrugging him off. He breathed relief that she hadn't chosen to break his arm. "Nothing that we do within this circle will result in any net change. We're still prisoners, whatever we do. They can cut off the food, or the damned air, or squeeze us to mush. And time's on their side. If we spill our guts restoring order—if that's what you're trying to work up to—all they have to do is wait for it to break down again. We're *beaten*. We're *taken*. There's nobody left *out there*. We're here forever. And you'd better start getting used to the idea."

"I've heard that song before," said Miles. "Use your head. If they meant to keep you forever, they could have incinerated you at the start, and saved the considerable expense of operating this camp. No. It's your minds they want. You are all here because you were Marilac's best and brightest, the hardest fighters, the strongest, baddest, most dangerous. The ones any potential resisters to the occupation would look to for leadership. It's the Cetagandans' plan to break you, and then return you to your world like little inoculated infections, counseling surrender to your people.

"When this is killed"—he touched her forehead, oh so lightly—"then the Cetagandans have nothing more to fear from this"—one finger on her bicep—"and you will all go free. To a world whose horizon will encircle you just like this dome, and just as inescapably. The war's not over. You are *here* because the Cetagandans are still waiting for the surrender of Fallow Core."

He thought for a moment she might murder him, strangle him on the spot. She must certainly prefer ripping him apart to letting him see her weep.

She regained her protective bitter tension with a toss of her head, a gulp of air. "If that's true, then following you puts us farther from freedom, not closer."

Damn, a logician to boot. She didn't have to pound him, she could parse him to death if he didn't scramble. He scrambled.

"There is a subtle difference between being a prisoner and being a slave. I don't mistake either for being free. Neither do you."

She fell silent, staring at him through slitted eyes, pulling unconsciously on her lower lip. "You're an odd one," she said at last. "Why do you say 'you' and not 'we'?"

Miles shrugged casually. Blast—he rapidly reviewed his pitch—she was right, he had. A little too close to the edge, there. He might yet make an opportunity of the mistake, though. "Do I look like the flower of Marilac's military might? I'm an outsider, trapped in a world I never made. A traveler—a pilgrim—just passing through. Ask Suegar."

She snorted. "That loonie."

She'd missed the catch. Rats, as Elli would say. He missed Elli. Try again later. "Don't discount Suegar. He has a message for you. I found it fascinating."

"I've heard it. I find it irritating. So, what do you want out of this? And don't tell me 'nothing,' 'cause I won't believe you. Frankly, I think you're after command of the camp yourself, and I'm not volunteering to be your stepping stone in some empire-building scheme."

She was thinking at speed now, and constructively, actually following out trains of thought besides that of having him removed to her border in bits. He was getting warmer...

"I only wish to be your spiritual advisor. I do not want—indeed, can't use—command. Just an advisor."

It must have been something about the term "advisor" that clicked, some old association of hers. Her eyes flicked fully open suddenly. He was close enough to see her pupils dilate. She leaned forward, and her index finger traced the faint indentations on his face beside his nose caused by certain control leads in a space armor helmet. She straightened again, and her first two fingers in a V caressed the deeper marks permanently flanking her own nose. "What did you say you were, before?"

"A clerk. Recruiting office," Miles replied sturdily.

"I... see."

And if what she saw was the absurdity of someone claiming to be a rear-echelon clerk having worn combat armor often and long enough to have picked up its stigmata, he was in. Maybe.

She coiled herself back up on her sleeping mat, and gestured toward its other end. "Sit down, chaplain. And keep talking."

+ + +

Suegar was genuinely asleep when Miles found him again, sitting up cross-legged and snoring. Miles tapped him on the shoulder.

"Wake up, Suegar, we're home."

He snorted to consciousness. "God, I miss coffee. Huh?" He blinked at Miles. "You're still in one piece?"

"It was a near thing. Look, this garments-in-the-river bit—now that we've found each other, do we have to go *on* being naked? Or is the prophecy sufficiently fulfilled?"

"Huh?"

"Can we get dressed now?" Miles repeated patiently.

"Why—I don't know. I suppose, if we were meant to have clothes, they'd be given to us—"

Miles prodded and pointed. "There. They're given to us."

Beatrice stood a few meters away in a hip-shot pose of bored exasperation, a bundle of gray cloth under her arm. "You two loonies want this stuff or not? I'm going back."

"You got them to give you clothes?" Suegar whispered in amazement.

"Us, Suegar, us." Miles motioned to Beatrice. "I think it's all right."

She fired the bundle at him, sniffed, and stalked away.

"Thanks," Miles called. He shook out the fabric. Two sets of gray pajamas, one small, one large. Miles had only to turn up the bottoms of the pants legs one fold to keep them from catching under his heels. They were stained and stiff with old sweat and dirt, and had probably been peeled off a corpse, Miles reflected. Suegar crawled into his and stood fingering the gray fabric in wonder.

"They gave us clothes. *Gave* us," he muttered. "How'd you do that?"

"They gave us everything, Suegar. Come on, I've got to talk to Oliver again." Miles dragged Suegar off determinedly. "I wonder how much time we've actually got before the next chow call? Two in each twenty-four-hour cycle, to be sure, but I wouldn't be surprised if it's irregular, to increase your temporal disorientation—after all, it's the only clock in here…"

Movement caught Miles's eye, a man running. It wasn't the occasional flurry of someone outrunning a hostile group; this one just ran, head down, flat out, bare feet thumping the dirt in frantic rhythm. He followed the perimeter generally, except for a detour around the border of the women's group. As he ran, he wept.

"What's this?" Miles asked Suegar, with a nod at the approaching figure.

Suegar shrugged. "It takes you like that sometimes. When you can't stand sitting in here anymore. I saw a guy run till he died, once. Around and around and around..."

"Well," Miles decided, "this one's running to us."

"He's gonna be running away from us in a second."

"Then help me catch him."

Miles hit him low and Suegar high. Suegar sat on his chest. Miles sat on his right arm, halving his effective resistance. He must have been a very young soldier when he was captured—maybe he had lied about his age at induction—for even now he had a boy's face, ravaged by tears and his personal eternity inside this hollow pearl. He inhaled in sobbing gasps and exhaled in garbled obscenities. After a time he quieted.

Miles leaned into his face and grinned wolfishly. "You a party animal, boy?"

"Yeah..." His white-rimmed eyes rolled, right and left, but no rescue approached.

"How 'bout your friends? They party animals too?"

"The best," the boy asserted, perhaps secretly shaken by the suspicion that he'd fallen into the hands of someone even crazier than himself. "You better clear off me, mutant, or they'll take you apart."

"I want to invite you and your friends to a *major* party," Miles chanted. "We gonna have a party tonight that's an his-tor-i-cal event. You know where to find Sergeant Oliver, late of the 14th Commandos?"

"Yeah..." the boy admitted cautiously.

"Well, you go get your friends and report to him. You better reserve your seat aboard his ve-hic-le now, 'cause if you're not on it, you gonna be *under* it. The Reformation Army is moving out. You copy?"

"Copy," he gasped, as Suegar pressed his fist into the boy's solar plexus for emphasis.

"Tell him Brother Miles sent you," Miles called as the boy staggered off, glancing nervously over his shoulder. "You can't hide in here. If you don't show, I'll send the Cosmic Commandos to find you."

Suegar shook out his cramped limbs, his new used clothes. "Think he'll come?"

Miles grinned. "Fight or flight. That one'll be all right." He stretched himself, recaptured his original orientation. "Oliver."

✦ ✦ ✦

In the end they had not twenty, but two hundred. Oliver had picked up forty-six. The running boy brought in eighteen. The signs of order and activity in the area brought in the curious—a drifter at the edge of the group had only to ask, "What's going on?" to be inducted and promoted to corporal on the spot. Interest among the spectators was aroused to a fever when Oliver's troops marched up to the women's border—and were admitted within. They picked up another seventy-five volunteers instantly.

"Do you know what's going on?" Miles asked one such, as he fed them through a short gauntlet of inspection and sent them off to one of the fourteen command groups he had devised.

"No," the man admitted. He waved an arm eagerly toward the center of the women's group. "But I wanta go where *they're* going…"

Miles cut the admissions off at two hundred total in deference to Tris's growing nervousness at this infiltration of her borders, and promptly turned the courtesy into a card in his own hand in their still-continuing strategy debate. Tris wanted to divide her group in the usual way, half for the attack, half to maintain home base and keep the borders from collapsing. Miles was insisting on an all-out effort.

"If we win, you won't need guards anymore."

"What if we lose?"

Miles lowered his voice. "We don't dare lose. This is the only time we'll have surprise on our side. Yes, we can fall back—regroup—try again—I for one am prepared—no, compelled—to keep trying till it kills me. But after this, what we're trying to do will be fully apparent to any counter-group, and they'll have time to plan counter-strategies of their own. I have a particular aversion to stalemates. I prefer winning wars to prolonging them."

She sighed, momentarily drained, tired, old. "I've been at war a long time, y'know? After a while even losing a war can start to look preferable to prolonging it."

He could feel his own resolve slip, sucked into the vortex of that same black doubt. He pointed upwards, dropping his voice to a rasping whisper. "But not, surely, to *those* bastards."

She glanced upwards. Her shoulders straightened. "No. Not to those." She took a deep breath. "All right, chaplain. You'll get your all-out effort. Just once…"

Oliver returned from a circuit of the command groups and squatted beside them. "They've got their orders. How many's Tris contributing to each group?"

"Commandant Tris," Miles quickly corrected for her as her brows beetled. "It's gonna be an all-out shot. You'll get every walking body in here."

Oliver made a quick calculation in the dirt with his finger for a stylus. "That'll put about fifty in each group—ought to be enough… matter of fact, what say we set up twenty groups? It'll speed distribution when we get the lines set up. Could make the difference between bringing this off, and not."

"No," Miles cut in quickly as Tris began to nod agreement. "It has to be fourteen. Fourteen battle groups make fourteen lines for fourteen piles. Fourteen is—is a theologically significant number," he added as they stared doubtfully at him.

"Why?" asked Tris.

"For the fourteen apostles," Miles intoned, tenting his hands piously.

Tris shrugged. Suegar scratched his head, started to speak— Miles speared him with a baleful glance, and he stilled.

Oliver eyed him narrowly. "Huh." But he did not argue further.

+ + +

Then came the waiting. Miles stopped worrying about his uppermost fear—that their captors would introduce the next food pile early, before his plans were in place—and started worrying about his second greatest fear, that the food pile would come so late he'd lose control of his troops and they would start to wander off, bored and discouraged. Getting them all assembled had made Miles feel like a man pulling on a goat with a rope made of water. Never had the insubstantial nature of the Idea seemed more self-apparent.

Oliver tapped him on the shoulder and pointed. "Here we go."

A side of the dome about a third of the way around the edge from them began to bulge inward.

The timing was perfect. His troops were at the peak of readiness. Too perfect… the Cetagandans had been watching all this; surely they wouldn't miss an opportunity to make life more difficult for their prisoners. If the food pile wasn't early, it had to be late. Or…

Miles bounded to his feet, screaming, "Wait! Wait! Wait for my order!"

His sprint groups wavered, drawn toward the anticipated goal. But Oliver had chosen his group commanders well—they held, and held their groups, and looked to Oliver. They *had* been soldiers, once. Oliver looked to Tris, flanked by her lieutenant Beatrice, and Tris looked to Miles, angrily.

"What is it now? We're gonna lose our advantage…" she began, as the general stampede throughout the camp started toward the bulge.

"If I'm wrong," Miles moaned, "I'm going to kill myself—wait, dammit! On my order. I can't see—Suegar, give me a boost—" He clambered up on the thin man's shoulders and stared toward the bulge. The force wall had only half twinkled out when the first distant cries of disappointment met his straining ears. Miles's head swiveled frantically. How many wheels within wheels—if the Cetagandans knew, and he knew they knew, and they knew he knew they knew, and… He cut off his internal gibber as a second bulge began, on the opposite side of the camp from the first.

Miles's arm flung out, pointing toward it like a man rolling dice. "There! There! Go, go, go!"

Tris caught on then, whistling and shooting him a look of startled respect, before whirling and dashing off to double-time the main body of their troops after the sprint groups. Miles slithered off Suegar and started limping after.

He glanced back over his shoulder, as the rolling gray mass of humanity crashed up against the opposite side of the dome and reversed itself. He felt suddenly like a man trying to outrun a tidal wave. He indulged himself with one brief anticipatory whimper, and limped faster.

One more chance to be mortally wrong—no. His sprint groups had reached the pile, and the pile was really there. Already they were starting to break it down. The support troops surrounded them with a wall of bodies as they began to spread out along the perimeter of the dome. The Cetagandans had outfoxed themselves. This time.

Miles was reduced from the commander's eagle overview to the grunt's worm's-eye as the tidal wave overtook him. Someone shoved him from behind, and his face hit the dirt. He thought he recognized the back of the surly Pitt, vaulting over him, but he wasn't certain—surely Pitt would have stepped on, not over him. Suegar yanked him up by the left arm, and Miles bit back a scream of pain. There was enough howling already.

Miles recognized the running boy, squaring off with another tough. Miles shoved past him with a shouted reminder—"You're supposed to be yelling *Get in line!* NOT *Get fucked!*... The signal always gets degraded in combat," he muttered to himself. "Always..."

Beatrice materialized beside him. Miles clung to her instantly. Beatrice had personal space, her own private perimeter, maintained even as Miles watched by a casual elbow to somebody's jaw with a quite sickening crack. If he tried that, Miles reflected enviously, not only would he smash his own elbow, but his opponent's nipple would probably be quite undamaged. Speaking of nipples, he found himself face to—well, not face—confronting the redhead. He resisted the urge to cuddle into the soft gray fabric covering home base with a contented sigh on the grounds that it would certainly get both his arms broken. He uncrossed his eyes and looked up into her face.

"C'mon," she said, and dragged him off through the mob. Was the noise level dropping? The human wall of his own troops parted just enough to let them squeeze through.

They were near the exit point of the chow line. It was working, by God it was working. The fourteen command groups, still bunched rather too closely along the dome wall—but that could be improved next run—were admitting the hungry supplicants one at a time. The expediters kept the lines moving at top speed, and channeled the already-supplied along the perimeter behind the human shield wall in a steady stream, to flow back out into the larger camp at the edge of the mob. Oliver had put his toughest-looking bravos to work in pairs, patrolling the outflow and making sure no one's rat bar was taken by force.

It was a long time since anyone here had had a chance to be a hero. Not a few of the newly appointed policemen were approaching their work with great enthusiasm—maybe some personal grudges being worked off there—Miles recognized one of the burly surlys prone beneath a pair of patrollers, apparently getting his face beaten in. Miles, remembering what he was about, tried not to find music in the meaty thunks of fist on flesh.

Miles and Beatrice and Suegar bucked the stream of rat bar-clutching prisoners back toward the distribution piles. With a slightly regretful sigh, Miles sought out Oliver and dispatched him to the exit to restore order among his order-keepers.

Tris had the distribution piles and their immediate lines under tight control. Miles congratulated himself on having the women hand out the food. He had definitely tuned into a deep emotional resonance there. Not a few of the prisoners even muttered a sheepish "thank you" as their rat bars were shoved into their hands, and so did the ones in line behind them, when their turns came.

Nyah! Miles thought upward to the bland and silent dome. *You don't have the monopoly on psychological warfare anymore, you bastards. We're gonna reverse your peristalsis, and I hope you barf your bowels out—*

An altercation at one of the food piles interrupted his meditations. Miles's lip curled with annoyance as he saw Pitt in the middle. He limped hastily toward it.

Pitt, it appeared, had repaid his rat bar not with a "thank you" but with a leer, a jeer, and a filthy remark. At least three of the women within hearing were trying to rip him apart, without success; he was big and beefy and had no inhibitions about fighting back. One of the females, not much taller than Miles himself, was knocked back in a heap and didn't get up again. In the meantime, the line was jammed, and the smooth civilized flow of would-be diners totally disrupted. Miles cursed under his breath.

"You, you, you, and—you," Miles tapped shoulders, "grab that guy. Get him out of here—back to the dome wall—"

Miles's draftees were not terribly pleased with their assignment, but by this time Tris and Beatrice had run up and led the attack with rather more science. Pitt was seized and pulled away, behind the lines. Miles made sure the rat bar distribution pile was running again before turning his attention to the savage, foul-mouthed Pitt. Oliver and Suegar had joined him by this time.

"I'm gonna rip the bastard's balls off," Tris was saying. "I command—"

"A military command," Miles interrupted. "If this one is accused of disorderly conduct, you should court martial him."

"He is a rapist and a murderer," she replied icily. "Execution's too good for him. He's got to die *slowly*."

Miles pulled Suegar aside. "It's tempting, but I feel real uneasy about handing him over to her just now. And yet... real uneasy. Why is that?"

Suegar eyed him in respect. "I think you're right. You see, there's—there's too many guilty."

Pitt, now in a foaming fury, spotted Miles. "You! You little cunt-licking wimp—you think *they* can protect you?" He jerked his head toward Tris and Beatrice. "They ain't got the muscle. We've run 'em over before and we'll run 'em over again. We wouldn'ta lost the damn war if we'd had real soldiers—like the Barrayarans. They didn't fill their army with cunts and cunt-lickers. And they ran the Cetagandans right off their planet—"

"Somehow," Miles growled, drawn in, "I doubt you're an expert in the Barrayarans' defense of their homeworld in the First Cetagandan War. Or you might have learned something—"

"Did Tris make you an honorary girl, mutant?" jeered Pitt in return. "It wouldn't take much—"

Why am I standing here bandying words with this low-life crazy? Miles asked himself as Pitt raved on. *No time. Let's finish it.*

Miles stepped back and folded his arms. "Has it occurred to any of you yet that this man is clearly a Cetagandan agent?"

Even Pitt was shocked to silence.

"The evidence is plain," Miles went on forcefully, raising his voice so all bystanders could hear. "He is a ringleader in your disruption. By example and guile he has corrupted the honest soldiers around him, set them one against another. You were Marilac's best. The Cetagandans could not count on your fall. So they planted a seed of evil among you. Just to make sure. And it worked—wonderfully well. You never suspected—"

Oliver grabbed Miles's ear and muttered, "Brother Miles—I know this guy. He's no Cetagandan agent. He's just one of a whole lot of—"

"Oliver," Miles hissed back through clenched teeth, "*shut up.*" And continued in his clearest parade-ground bellow, "Of course he's a Cetagandan spy. A mole. And all this time you thought this was something you were doing to *yourselves.*"

And where the devil does not exist, Miles thought to himself, *it may become expedient to invent him.* His stomach churned, but he kept his face set in righteous rage. He glanced at the faces around him. Not a few were as white as his must be, though for a different reason. A low mutter rose among them, partly bewildered, partly ominous.

"Pull off his shirt," Miles ordered, "and lay him down on his face. Suegar, give me your cup."

Suegar's plastic cup had a jagged point along its broken edge. Miles sat on Pitt's buttocks, and using the point as a stylus scratched the words

CETA
SPY

across Pitt's back in large print. He dug deep and ruthlessly, and the blood welled. Pitt screamed and swore and bucked.

Miles scrambled to his feet, shaking and breathless from more than just the physical exertion.

"Now," he ordered, "give him his rat bar and escort him to the exit."

Tris's teeth opened in objection, clicked back down. Her eyes burned into Pitt's back as he was hustled off. Her gaze turned rather more doubtfully to Miles, as she stood on one side of him and Oliver on the other.

"Do you really think he was a Cetagandan?" she asked Miles lowly.

"No way," scoffed Oliver. "What the hell's the charade all about, Brother Miles?"

"I don't doubt Tris's accusation of his other crimes," said Miles tightly. "You must know. But he couldn't be punished for them without dividing the camp, and so undermining Tris's authority. This way, Tris and the women have their revenge without half the men being set against them. The commandant's hands are clean, yet justice is done on a criminal, and a hard case who would doubtless be stockade bait outside is removed from under our feet. Furthermore, any like-minded souls are handed a warning they can't ignore. It works on every level."

Oliver's face had grown expressionless. After a silent moment he remarked, "You fight dirty, Brother Miles."

"I can't afford to lose." Miles shot him a black look from beneath his own lowered brows. "Can you?"

Oliver's lips tightened. "No."

Tris made no comment at all.

+ + +

Miles personally oversaw the delivery of rat bars to all those prisoners too sick or weak or beaten to have attempted the chow line.

Colonel Tremont lay too still upon his mat, curled up, staring blankly. Oliver knelt and closed the drying, fixed eyes. The colonel might have died any time in the last few hours.

"I'm sorry," said Miles sincerely. "Sorry I came so late."

"Well..." said Oliver, "well..." He stood, chewing on his lip, shook his head, and said no more. Miles and Suegar, Tris and Beatrice, helped Oliver carry the body, mat, clothes, cup and all, to the rubbish pile. Oliver shoved the rat bar he had reserved under the dead man's arm. No one attempted to strip the corpse after they had turned away, although another one stiffening there had already been so robbed, lying naked and tumbled.

They stumbled across Pitt's body shortly thereafter. The cause of death was most probably strangulation, but the face was so battered that its empurpling was not a certain clue.

Tris, squatting beside it, looked up at Miles in slow re-estimation. "I think you may be right about power after all, little man."

"And revenge?"

"I thought I could never get my fill of it," she sighed, contemplating the thing beside her. "Yeah... that too."

"Thank you." Miles prodded the body with his toe. "Make no mistake, *that* is a loss for our side."

Miles made Suegar let somebody else drag it to the rubbish pile.

+ + +

Miles held a council of war immediately after chow call. Tremont's pallbearers, whom Miles had begun to think of as his general staff, and the fourteen group leaders gathered around him at a spot near the borders of the women's group. Miles paced back and forth before them, gesturing energetically.

"I commend the group leaders for an excellent job, and Sergeant Oliver for choosing them. By bringing this off, we have bought not only the allegiance of the greater part of the camp, but time as well. Each chow call after this should run a little easier, a little smoother, each become a real-life practice drill for the next.

"And make no mistake, this is a military exercise. We're at war again. We've already suckered the Cetagandans into breaking their carefully calculated routine and making a countermove. We acted. They reacted. Strange as it may all seem to you, *we* had the offensive advantage.

"Now we start planning our next strategies. I want your thinking on what the next Cetagandan challenge will be." *Actually, I want you thinking, period.* "So much for the sermon—Commandant Tris, take over." Miles forced himself to sit down cross-legged, yielding the floor to his chosen one whether she wanted it or not. He reminded himself that Tris had been a field officer, not a staff officer; she needed the practice more than he did.

"Of course, they can send in short piles again, like they did before," she began after clearing her throat. "It's been suggested that's how this mess got started in the first place." Her glance crossed Miles's, who nodded encouragingly. "This means we're going to have to start keeping head counts, and work out a strict rotation schedule in advance of people to divide their rations with the short-changed. Each group leader must choose a quartermaster and a couple of accountants to double-check his count."

"An equally disruptive move the Cetagandans may try," Miles couldn't help putting in, "is to send in an overstock, giving us the interesting problem of how to equitably divide the extras. I'd provide for that, too, if I were you." He smiled blandly up at Tris.

She raised an eyebrow at him, and continued. "They may also try dividing the chow pile, complicating our problem of capturing it so as to strictly control its redistribution. Are there any other really dirty tricks any of you can anticipate?" She couldn't help glancing at Miles.

One of the group leaders raised his hand hesitantly. "Ma'am— they're listening to all this. Aren't we doing their thinking for them?"

Miles rose to answer that one, loud and clear. "Of course they're listening. We've doubtless got their quivering attention." He made a rude gesture domewards. "Let them. Every move they make is a message from outside, a shadow marking their shape, information about them. We'll take it."

"Suppose," said another group leader even more hesitantly, "they cut off our air again? Permanently?"

"Then," said Miles smoothly, "they lose their hard-won position one-up on the IJC, which they've gone to enormous trouble to gain. It's a propaganda coup they've been making much of lately, particularly since our side, in the stress of the way things are going back home, hasn't been able to maintain its own troops in style, let alone any captured Cetagandans. The Cetagandans, whose published view is that they're sharing their Imperial government with us out of cultural generosity, are claiming this as a demonstration of their superior civilization and good manners—"

Some jeers and catcalls marked the prisoners' view of this assertion, and Miles smiled and went on. "The death rate reported for this camp is so extraordinary, it's caught the IJC's attention. The Cetagandans have managed to account for it so far, through three separate IJC inspections, but one-hundred-percent would be a bit extreme even for them to justify." A shiver of agreement, compressed rage, ran through his rapt listeners.

Miles sat again. Oliver leaned over to him to whisper, "How the hell did you come by all that information?"

Miles smirked. "Did it sound convincing? Good."

Oliver sat back, looking unnerved. "You don't have any inhibitions at all, do you?"

"Not in combat."

Tris and her group leaders spent the next two hours laying out chow call scenario flow charts, and their tactical responses at each branching. They broke up to let the group leaders pass it on to their chosen subordinates, and Oliver to his crew of supplementary Enforcers.

Tris paused before Miles, who had succumbed to gravity sometime during the second hour and now lay in the dirt staring somewhat blankly at the dome, blinking in an effort to keep his blurring eyes open. He had not slept in the day and a half before entering this place. He was not sure how much time had passed since then.

"I thought of one more scenario," Tris remarked. "What do we do if they do nothing at all? Do nothing, change nothing."

Miles smiled sleepily. "It seems most probable. That attempted double-cross on the last chow call was a slip on their part, I think."

"But in the absence of an enemy, how long can we go on pretending we're an army?" she persisted. "You scraped us up off the bottom for this. When it runs down at last, what then?"

Miles curled up on his side, drowning in weird and shapeless thoughts, and enticed by the hint of an erotic dream about a tall aggressive redhead. His yawn cracked his face. "Then we pray for a miracle. Remind me to discuss miracles with you... later..."

He half-woke once when somebody shoved a sleeping mat under him. He gave Beatrice a sleepy bedroom smile.

"Crazy mutant," she snarled at him, and rolled him roughly onto the pad. "Don't you go thinking this was my idea."

"Why, Suegar," Miles muttered, "I think she *likes* me." He cuddled back into the entwining limbs of the dream-Beatrice in fleeting peace.

+ + +

To Miles's secret dismay, his analysis proved right. The Cetagandans returned to their original rat bar routine, unresponsive again to their prisoners' internal permutations. Miles was not sure he liked that. True, it gave him ample opportunity to fine-tune his distribution scheme. But some harassment from the dome would have directed the prisoners' attention outward, given them a foe again, above all broken the paralyzing boredom of their lives. In the long run, Tris must prove right.

"I hate an enemy who doesn't make mistakes," Miles muttered irritably, and flung his efforts into events he could control.

He found a phlegmatic prisoner with a steady heartbeat to lie in the dirt and count his own pulse, and began timing distribution, and then working on reducing timing.

"It's a spiritual exercise," he announced when he had his fourteen quartermasters start issuing the rat bars two hundred at a time, with thirty-minute breaks between groups.

"It's a change of pace," he explained in an aside to Tris. "If we can't induce the Cetagandans to provide some variety, we'll just have to do it ourselves." He also finally made an accurate head count of the surviving prisoners. Miles was everywhere, exhorting, prodding, pushing, restraining.

"If you really want it to go faster, make more bleeding piles," Oliver protested.

"Don't blaspheme," said Miles, and went to work inducing his groups to cart their rat bars away to distribution piles spaced evenly around the perimeter.

At the end of the nineteenth chow call since he had entered the camp, Miles judged his distribution system complete and theologically correct. Calling every two chow calls a "day," he had been there nine days.

"I'm all done," he realized with a groan, "and it's *too early*."

"Weeping because you have no more worlds to conquer?" inquired Tris with a sarcastic grin.

By the thirty-second chow call, the system was still running smoothly, but Miles was getting frayed.

"Welcome to the long haul," said Beatrice dryly. "You better start pacing yourself, Brother Miles. If what Tris says is true, we're going to be in here even longer because of you. I must remember to thank you for that properly sometime." She treated him to a threatening smirk, and Miles prudently remembered an errand on the opposite side of the camp.

She was right, Miles thought, depressed. Most prisoners here counted their captivity not in days and weeks, but months and years. He himself was likely to be gibbering nuts in a space of time that most of them would regard as a mere breath. He wondered glumly what form his madness would take. Manic, inspired by the glittering delusion that he was—say—the Conqueror of Komarr? Or depressive, like Tremont, curling up in himself until he was no one at all, a sort of human black hole?

Miracles. There had been leaders throughout history who had been wrong in their timing for Armageddon, leading their shorn flocks up the mountain to await an apotheosis that never came. Their later lives were usually marked by obscurity and drinking problems. Nothing to drink in here. Miles wanted about six doubles, right now.

Now. Now. Now.

+ + +

Miles took to walking the dome perimeter after each chow call, partly to make or at least pretend to inspection, partly to burn off a little of his uncomfortably accumulating nervous energy. It was getting harder and harder to sleep. There had been a period of quiet in the camp after the chow calls were successfully regulated, as if their ordering had been a crystal dropped in a supersaturated solution. But in the last few days the number of fistfights broken up by the Enforcers had risen. The Enforcers themselves were getting quicker to violence, acquiring a potentially unsavory swagger. Phases of the moon. Who could outrace the moon?

"Slow down, Miles," complained Suegar, ambling along beside him.

"Sorry." Miles restrained his stride and broke his self-absorption to look around. The glowing dome rose on his left hand, seeming to pulse to an unsettling hum just out of the range of his hearing. Quiet spread out on his right, groups of people mostly sitting. Not that much visible change since his first day in here. Maybe a little less tension, maybe a little more concerted care being taken of the injured or ill. Phases of the moon. He shook off his unease and smiled cheerfully at Suegar.

"You getting any more positive responses to your sermons these days?" Miles asked.

"Well—nobody tries to beat me up anymore," said Suegar. "But then, I haven't been preaching so often, being busy with the chow calls and all. And then there are the Enforcers, now. It's hard to say."

"You going to keep trying?"

"Oh, yes." Suegar paused. "I've seen worse places than this, y'know. I was at a mining camp once, when I was scarcely more than a kid. A fire gem strike. For a change, instead of one big company or the government muscling in, it had gotten divided up into hundreds and hundreds of little claims, usually about two meters square. Guys dug out there by hand, with trowels and whisk brooms—big fire gems are delicate, y'know, they'll shatter at a careless blow—they dug under the broiling sun, day after day. A lot of these guys had less clothes than us now. A lot of 'em didn't eat as good, or as regular. Working their butts off. More accidents, more disease than here. There were fights, too, in plenty.

"But they lived for the future. Performed the most incredible feats of physical endurance for hope, all voluntary. They were obsessed. They were—well, you remind me a lot of them. They wouldn't quit for *nothing*. They turned a mountain into a chasm in a year, with hand trowels. It was nuts. I loved it.

"This place"—Suegar glanced around—"just makes me scared shitless." His right hand touched his rag rope bracelet. "It'll suck up your future, swallow you down—it's like death is just a formality, after that. Zombie town, suicide city. The day I stop trying, this place'll eat me."

"Mm," agreed Miles. They were nearing what Miles thought of as the farthest point of their circuit, across the camp from the women's group at whose now-permeable borders Miles and Suegar kept their sleeping mats.

A couple of men walking the perimeter from the opposite direction coalesced with another gray-pajama'd pair. As if casually and spontaneously, three more arose from their mats on Miles's right. He could not be sure without turning his head, but Miles thought he caught more peripheral motion closing in behind him.

The approaching four stopped a few meters in front of them. Miles and Suegar hesitated. Gray-clad men, all variously larger than Miles—who wasn't?—frowning, full of a fierce tension that arced to Miles and scree'd down his nerves. Miles recognized only one of them, an ex-surly brother he'd seen in Pitt's company. Miles didn't bother taking his eyes off Pitt's lieutenant to look around for Enforcers. For one thing, he was pretty sure one of the men in the company facing them *was* an Enforcer.

And the worst of it was, getting cornered—if you could call it that in here—was his own fault, for letting his movements fall into a predictable daily routine. A stupid, basic, beginner's mistake, that; inexcusable.

Pitt's lieutenant stepped forward, chewing on his lip, staring at Miles with hollowed eyes. *He's psyching himself up,* Miles realized. *If all he wanted was to beat me to a pulp, he could do it in his sleep.* The man slid a carefully braided rag rope through his fingers. A strangling cord... no, it wasn't going to be another beating. This time, it was going to be premeditated murder.

"You," said Pitt's lieutenant hoarsely. "I couldn't figure you out at first. You're not one of us. You could never have been one of us. Mutant... You gave me the clue yourself. Pitt wasn't a Cetagandan spy. *You* are!" And lunged forward.

Miles dodged, overwhelmed by onslaught and insight. Damn, he'd known there must be a good reason scragging Pitt that way had felt so much like a mistake despite its efficiency. The false accusation was two-edged, as dangerous to its wielder as its victim—Pitt's lieutenant might even believe *his* accusation true—Miles had started a witch-hunt. Poetic justice, that he be its first victim, but where would it end? No wonder their captors hadn't interfered lately. Their silent Cetagandan watchers must be falling off their station chairs laughing right now—mistake piled on mistake, culminating here by dying stupidly like vermin at the hands of vermin in this verminous hole...

Hands grabbed him; he contorted spasmodically, kicking out, but only half broke their hold. Beside him Suegar whirled, kicked, struck, shouted with demonic energy. He had reach, but lacked mass. Miles lacked both reach and mass. Still Suegar managed to break an assailant's hold on Miles for a moment.

Suegar's left arm, lashing out for a backhand blow, was caught and locked. Miles winced in sympathetic anticipation of the familiar muffled crack of breaking bones, but instead the man stripped off the rag rope bracelet from Suegar's wrist.

"Hey, Suegar!" the man taunted, dancing backward. "Look what I got!"

Suegar's head swiveled, his attention wrenched from his determined defense of Miles. The man peeled the wrinkled, tattered piece of paper from its cloth covering and waved it in the air. Suegar cried out in dismay and started to plunge toward him, but found himself blocked by two other bodies. The man tore the paper in half twice, then paused, as if momentarily puzzled how to dispose of it—then, with a sudden grin, stuffed the pieces in his mouth and started chewing. Suegar screamed.

"Dammit," cried Miles furiously, "it was me you wanted! You didn't have to do that—" He jammed his fist with all his strength into the smirking face of the nearest attacker, whose attention had been temporarily distracted by Suegar's show.

He could feel his bones shatter all the way back through his wrist. He was so damned *tired* of the bones, tired of being hurt again and again…

Suegar was screaming and sobbing and trying to gain on the paper chewer, who stood and chewed on through his grin. Suegar had lost all science in his attack, flailing like a windmill. Miles saw him go down, then had no attention left for anything but the anaconda coil of the strangling cord, settling over his own neck. He managed to get one hand between the cord and his throat, but it was the broken one. Cables of pain shuddered up his arm, seeming to burrow under his skin all the way to his shoulder. The pressure in his head mounted to bursting, closing down his vision. Dark purple and yellow moiré-patterned clouds boiled up in his eyes like thunderheads. A flashing brush of red hair sizzled past his tunneling vision…

He was on the ground then, with blood, wonderful blood, thudding back into his oxygen-starved brain. It hurt good, hot and pulsing. He lay for a moment not caring about anything else. It would be so good not to have to get up again…

The damned dome, cold and white and featureless, mocked his returning vision. Miles jerked onto his knees, staring around wildly. Beatrice, some Enforcers, and some of Oliver's commando buddies were chasing Miles's would-be assassins across the camp. Miles had probably only passed out for a few seconds. Suegar lay on the ground a couple of meters off.

Miles crawled over to Suegar. The thin man lay curled up around his stomach, his face pale green and clammy, involuntary shivers coursing through his body. Not good. Shocky. *Keep patient warm and administer synergine.* No synergine. Miles peeled clumsily out of his tunic and laid it over Suegar. "Suegar? You all right? Beatrice chased off the barbarians..."

Suegar looked up and smiled briefly, but the smile was reabsorbed almost immediately by distancing pain.

Beatrice came back eventually, mussed and breathing heavily. "You loonies," she greeted them dispassionately. "You don't need a bodyguard, you need a bloody keeper." She flopped onto her knees beside Miles to stare at Suegar. Her lips thinned to a pale slit. She glanced at Miles, her eyes darkening, the creases between her brows deepening.

I've changed my mind, Miles thought. *Don't start caring for me, Beatrice, don't start caring for anybody. You'll only get hurt. Over and over and over...*

"You better come back to my group," said Beatrice.

"I don't think Suegar can walk."

Beatrice rounded up some muscle, and the thin man was rolled onto a sleeping mat and carried, too much like Colonel Tremont's corpse for Miles's taste, back to their now-usual sleeping place.

"Find a doctor for him," Miles demanded.

Beatrice came back, strong-arming an angry, older woman.

"He's probably got a busted belly," snarled the doctor. "If I had a diagnostic viewer, I could tell you just what was busted. You got a diagnostic viewer? He needs synergine and plasma. You got any? I could cut him, and glue him back together, and speed his healing with electra-stim, if I had an operating theatre. Put him back on his feet in three days, no sweat. You got an operating theatre? I thought not.

"Stop looking at me like that. I used to think I was a healer. It took this place to teach me I was nothing but an interface between the technology and the patient. Now the technology is gone, and I'm just nothing."

"But what can we do?" asked Miles.

"Cover him up. In a few days he'll either get better or die, depending on what got busted. That's all." She paused, standing with folded arms and regarding Suegar with rancor, as if his injury was a personal affront. And so it was, for her: another load of grief and failure, grinding her hard-won healer's pride into the dirt. "I think he's going to die," she added.

"I think so, too," said Miles.

"Then what did you want me for?" She stomped off.

Later she came back with a sleeping mat and a couple of extra rags, and helped put them around and over Suegar for added insulation, then stomped off again.

Tris reported to Miles. "We got those guys who tried to kill you rounded up. What do you want done with 'em?"

"Let them go," said Miles wearily. "They're not the enemy."

"The hell they're not!"

"They're not my enemies, anyway. It was just a case of mistaken identity. I'm just a hapless traveler, passing through."

"Wake up, little man. I don't happen to share Oliver's belief in your 'miracle.' You're not passing through here. This is the last stop."

Miles sighed. "I'm beginning to think you're right." He glanced at Suegar, breathing shallowly and too fast, beside whom he crouched in watch. "You're almost certainly right, by this time. Nevertheless—let them go."

"Why?" she wailed, outraged.

"Because I said to. Because I asked you to. Would you have me beg for them?"

"Aargh! No. All right!" She wheeled away, running her hands through her clipped hair and muttering under her breath.

✦ ✦ ✦

A timeless time passed. Suegar lay on his side not speaking, though his eyes flicked open now and then to stare unseeing. Miles moistened his lips with water periodically. A chow call came and went without incident or Miles's participation; Beatrice passed by and dropped two rat bars beside them, stared at them with a carefully hardened gaze of general disapproval, and stalked off.

Miles cradled his injured hand and sat cross-legged, mentally reviewing the catalogue of errors that had brought him to this pass. He contemplated his seeming genius for getting his friends killed. He had a sick premonition that Suegar's death was going to be almost as bad as Sergeant Bothari's, six years ago, and he had known Suegar only weeks, not years. Repeated pain, as he had reason to know, made one more afraid of injury, not less, a growing, gut-wrenching dread. Not again, never again…

He lay back and stared at the dome, the white, unblinking eye of a dead god. And had more friends than he knew already been killed by this megalomanic escapade? It would be just like the Cetagandans, to leave him in here all unknowing, and let the growing doubt and fear gradually drive him crazy.

Swiftly drive him crazy—the god's eye blinked.

+ + +

Miles blinked in sympathetic nervous recoil, opened his eyes wide, stared at the dome as if his eyes could bore right through it. Had it blinked? Had the flicker been hallucinatory? Was he losing it?

It flickered again. Miles shot to his feet, inhaling, inhaling, inhaling.

The dome blinked out. For a brief instant, planetary night swept in, fog and drizzle and the kiss of a cold wet wind. This planet's unfiltered air smelled like rotten eggs. The unaccustomed dark was blinding.

"CHOW CALL!" Miles screamed at the top of his lungs.

Then limbo transmuted to chaos in the brilliant flash of a smart bomb going off beyond a cluster of buildings. Red light glared off the underside of an enormous billowing cloud of debris, blasting upward.

A racketing string of similar hits encircled the camp, peeled back the night, deafened the unprotected. Miles, still screaming, could not hear his own voice. A returning fire from the ground clawed the clouds with lines of colored light.

Tris, her eyes stunned, rocketed past him. Miles grabbed her by the arm with his good hand and dug in his heels to brake her, yanking her down so he could scream in her ear.

"This is it! Get the fourteen group leaders organized, make 'em get their first blocks of two hundred lined up and waiting all around the perimeter. Find Oliver, we've *got* to get the Enforcers moving to get the rest waiting their turn under control. If this goes exactly as we drilled it, we'll all get off." *I hope.* "But if they mob the shuttles like they used to mob the rat bar pile, none of us will. You copy?"

"I never believed—I didn't think—*shuttles*?"

"You don't have to think. We've drilled this fifty times. Just follow the chow drill. The *drill!*"

"You *sneaky* little sonofabitch!" The acknowledging wave of her arm, as she dashed off, was very like a salute.

A string of flares erupted in the sky above the camp, as if a white strobe of lightning went on and on, casting a ghastly illumination on the scene below. The camp seethed like a termite mound kicked over. Men and women were running every which way in shouting confusion. Not exactly the orderly vision Miles had had in mind— why, for example, had his people chosen a night drop and not a daytime one?—he would grill his staff later on that point, after he was done kissing their feet—

"Beatrice!" Miles waved her down. "Start passing the word! We're doing the chow call drill. But instead of a rat bar, each person gets a shuttle seat. Make 'em understand that—don't let anybody go haring off into the night or they'll miss their flight. Then come back here and stay by Suegar. I don't want him getting lost or trampled on. *Guard*, you copy?"

"I'm not a damn dog. What shuttles?"

The sound Miles's ears had been straining for penetrated the din at last, a high-pitched, multi-faceted whine that grew louder and louder. They loomed down out of the boiling scarlet-tinged clouds like monstrous beetles, carapaced and winged, feet extending even as they watched. Fully armored combat-drop shuttles, two, three, six… seven, eight… Miles's lips moved as he counted. Thirteen, fourteen, by God. They *had* managed to get #B-7 out of the shop in time.

Miles pointed. "*My* shuttles."

Beatrice stood with her mouth open, staring upward. "My God. They're beautiful." He could almost see her mind start to ratchet forward. "But they're not *ours*. Not Cetagandan either. Who the hell…?"

Miles bowed. "This is a paid political rescue."

"Mercenaries?"

"We're not something wriggling with too many legs that you found in your sleeping bag. The proper tone of voice is *Mercenaries!*—with a glad cry."

"But—but—but—"

"*Go*, dammit. Argue *later*."

She flung up her hands and ran.

Miles himself started tackling every person within reach, passing on the order of the day. He captured one of Oliver's tall commando buddies and demanded a boost on his shoulders. A quick look around showed fourteen coagulating knots of people in the mob scattered around the perimeter in nearly the right positions. The shuttles hovered, engines howling, then thumped to the ground one by one all around the camp.

"It'll have to do," Miles muttered to himself. He slapped the commando's shoulder. "Down."

He forced himself to walk to the nearest shuttle, a run on the shuttles being just the scenario he had poured out blood and bone and pride these last—three, four?—weeks to avoid.

A quartet of fully armed and half-armored troops were the first down the shuttle ramp, taking up guard positions. Good. They even had their weapons pointed in the right direction, toward the prisoners they were here to rescue. A larger patrol, fully armored, followed to gallop off double time, leapfrogging their own covering-fire range into the dark toward the Cetagandan installations surrounding the dome circle. Hard to judge which direction held the most danger—from the continuing fireworks, his fighter shuttles were providing plenty of external distraction for the Cetagandans.

At last came the man Miles most wanted to see, the shuttle's com officer.

"Lieutenant, uh"—he connected face and name—"Murka! Over here!"

Murka spotted him. He fumbled excitedly with his equipment and called into his audio pickup, "Commodore Tung! He's *here*, I *got* him!"

Miles peeled the com set ruthlessly from the lieutenant's head, who obligingly ducked down to permit the theft, and jammed it on his own head left-handed in time to hear Tung's voice reply tinnily, "Well, for God's sake don't lose him again, Murka. Sit on him if you have to."

"I want my staff," called Miles into the pickup. "Have you retrieved Elli and Elena yet? How much time have we got for this?"

"Yes, sir, no, and about two hours—if we're lucky," Tung's voice snapped back. "Good to have you back aboard, Admiral Naismith."

"You're telling me… Get Elena and Elli. Priority One."

"Working. Tung out."

Miles turned to find that the rat bar group leader in this section had actually succeeded in marshaling his first group of two hundred, and was engaged in making the second two hundred sit back down in a block to wait their turns. Excellent. The prisoners were being channeled up the ramp one at a time through a strange gauntlet. A mercenary slit the back of each gray tunic with a swift slice from a vibra-knife. A second mercenary slapped each prisoner across the back with a medical stunner. A third made a pass with a surgical hand-tractor, roughly ripping out the Cetagandan serial numbers encoded beneath the skin. He didn't bother to waste time on bandaging after. "Go to the front and sit five across, go to the front and sit five across, go to the front..." he chanted, droning in time to his hypnotically moving device.

Miles's sometime-adjutant Captain Thorne appeared, hurrying out of the glare and black shadows, flanked by one of the fleet's ship's surgeons and—praise be—a soldier carrying some of Miles's clothes, and boots. Miles dove for the boots, but was captured instead by the surgeon.

She ran a med stunner between his bare uneven shoulder blades, and zipped a hand-tractor across in its path.

"Ow!" Miles yelped. "Couldn't you wait one bleeding second for the stun to cut in?" The pain faded rapidly to numbness as Miles's left hand patted for the damage. "What's this all about?"

"Sorry, sir," said the surgeon insincerely. "Stop that, your fingers are dirty." She applied a plastic bandage. Rank hath its privileges. "Captain Bothari-Jesek and Commander Quinn learned something from their fellow Cetagandan prison monitors that we hadn't known before you went in. These encodes are permeated with drug beads, whose lipid membranes are kept aligned by a low-power magnetic field the Cetagandans were generating in the dome. An hour out of the dome, and the membranes start to break down, releasing a poison. About four hours later the subject dies—very unpleasantly. A little insurance against escapes, I guess."

Miles shuddered, and said faintly, "I see." He cleared his throat, and added more loudly, "Captain Thorne, mark a commendation—with *highest* honors—to Commander Elli Quinn and Captain Elena Bothari-Jesek. The, ah, our employer's intelligence service didn't even have that one. In fact, our employer's intelligence data lacked on a truly vast number of points. I shall have to speak to them—sharply—when I present the bill for this expanded operation. Before you put that away, doctor, numb my hand, please." Miles stuck out his right hand for the surgeon's inspection.

"Did it again, did you?" muttered the surgeon. "I'd think you'd learn..." A pass with the medical stunner, and Miles's swollen hand disappeared from his senses entirely, nothing left from the wrist down. Only his eyes assured him it was still attached to his arm.

"Yes, but will they pay for the expanded operation?" asked Captain Thorne anxiously. "This started out as a one-shot lightning strike to hook out one guy, just the sort of thing little outfits like us specialize in—now it's straining the whole Dendarii fleet. These damned prisoners outnumber *us* two to one. This wasn't in the original contract. What if our perennial mystery employer decides to stiff us?"

"They won't," said Miles. "My word. But—there's no doubt I'll have to deliver the bill in person."

"God help them, then," muttered the surgeon, and took herself off to continue pulling encodes from the waiting prisoners.

Commodore Ky Tung, a squat, middle-aged Eurasian in half-armor and a command channel headset, turned up at Miles's elbow as the first shuttles loaded with prisoners clapped their locks shut and screamed up into the black fog. They took off in first-come first-served positions, no waiting. Knowing Tung's passion for tight formations, Miles judged time must be their most dangerous limiting factor.

"What are we loading these guys onto, upstairs?" Miles asked Tung.

"We gutted a couple of used freighters. We can cram about five thousand in the holds of each. The ride out is going to be fast and nasty. They'll all have to lie down and breathe as little as possible."

"What are the Cetagandans scrambling to catch us?"

"Right now, barely more than some police shuttles. Most of their local space military contingent just happens to be on the other side of their sun just now, which is why we just happened to pick this moment to drop by… we had to wait for their practice maneuvers again, in case you were starting to wonder what was keeping us. In other words, the same scenario as our original plan to pull Colonel Tremont."

"Except expanded by a factor of ten thousand. And we've got to get in—what, four lifts? Instead of one," said Miles.

"Yeah, but get this." Tung grinned. "They sited these prison camps on this miserable outpost planet so's they wouldn't have to expend troops and equipment guarding them—counted on distance from Marilac, and the downgearing of the war there, to discourage rescue attempts. But in the period since you went in, half of their original guard complement has been pulled to other hot spots. Half!"

"They were relying on the dome." Miles eyed him. "And for the bad news?" he murmured.

Tung's smile soured. "This round, our total time window is only two hours."

"Ouch. Half their local space fleet is still too many. And they'll be back in two hours?"

"One hour, forty minutes, now." A sidewise flick of Tung's eyes betrayed the location of his ops clock, holovid-projected by his command headset into the air at a corner of his vision.

Miles did a calculation in his head, and lowered his voice. "Are we going to be able to lift the last load?"

"Depends on how fast we can lift the first three," said Tung. His ordinarily stoic face was more unreadable than ever, betraying neither hope nor fear.

Which depends in turn on how effectively I managed to drill them all... What was done was done; what was coming was not yet. Miles wrenched his attention to the immediate now.

"Have you found Elli and Elena yet?"

"I have three patrols out searching."

He hadn't found them yet. Miles's guts tightened. "I wouldn't have even attempted to expand this operation in midstream if I hadn't known they were monitoring me, and could translate all those oblique hints back into orders."

"Did they get 'em all right?" asked Tung. "We argued over some of their interpretations of your double-talk on the vids."

Miles glanced around. "They got 'em right... you got vids of all this?" A startled wave of Miles's hand took in the circle of the camp.

"Of you, anyway. Right off the Cetagandan monitors. They burst-transmitted them all daily. Very—er—entertaining, sir," Tung added blandly.

Some people would find entertainment in watching someone swallow slugs, Miles reflected. "Very dangerous... when was your last communication with them?"

"Yesterday." Tung's hand clamped on Miles's arm, restraining an involuntary leap. "You can't do better than my three patrols, sir, and I haven't any to spare to go looking for *you.*"

"Yah, yah." Miles slapped his right fist into his left palm in frustration before remembering that was a bad idea. His two coagents, his vital link between the dome and the Dendarii, missing. The Cetagandans shot spies with depressing consistency. After, usually, a series of interrogations that rendered death a welcome release... He tried to reassure himself with logic. If they'd blown their covers as Cetagandan monitor techs, and been interrogated, Tung would have run into a meat grinder here. He hadn't, ergo, they hadn't. Of course, they might have been killed by friendly fire, just now… Friends. He had too many friends to stay sane in this crazy business.

"You"—Miles retrieved his clothes from the still-waiting soldier—"go over there"—he pointed—"and find a red-haired lady named Beatrice and an injured man named Suegar. Bring them to me. Carry him carefully, he has internal injuries."

The soldier saluted and marched off. Ah, the pleasure again of being able to give a command without having to follow it up with a supporting theological argument. Miles sighed. Exhaustion waited to swallow him, lurking at the edge of his adrenaline-spurred bubble of hyperconsciousness. All the factors—shuttles, timing, the approaching enemy, distance to the getaway jump point, formed and reformed in all their possible permutations in his mind. Small variations in timing in particular multiplied into major troubles. But he'd known it would be like this back when he'd started. A miracle they'd got this far. No—he glanced at Tung, at Thorne— not a miracle, but the extraordinary initiative and devotion of his people. *Well done, oh, well done…*

Thorne helped him as he fumbled to dress himself one-handed. "Where the hell is my command headset?" Miles asked.

"We were told you were injured, sir, and in a state of exhaustion. You were scheduled for immediate evacuation."

"Damn presumptuous of somebody…" Miles bit back ire. No place in this schedule for running errands topside. Besides, if he had his headset, he'd be tempted to start giving orders, and he wasn't yet sufficiently briefed on the internal complexities of the operation from the Dendarii fleet's point of view. Miles swallowed his observer status without further comment. It did free him for rear guard.

Miles's batman reappeared, with Beatrice and four drafted prisoners, carrying Suegar on his mat to lay at Miles's feet.

"Get my surgeon," Miles said. His soldier obediently trotted off and found her. She knelt beside the semiconscious Suegar and pulled the encode from his back. A knot of tension unwound in Miles's neck at the reassuring hiss of a hypospray of synergine.

"How bad?" Miles demanded.

"Not good," the surgeon admitted, checking her diagnostic

viewer. "Burst spleen, oozing hemorrhage in the stomach—this one had better go direct to surgery on the command ship. Medtech—" she motioned to a Dendarii waiting with the guards for the return of the shuttle, and gave triage instructions. The medtech swathed Suegar in a thin foil heat wrap.

"I'll make sure he gets there," promised Miles. He shivered, envying the heat wrap a little as the drizzly acid fog beaded in his hair and coiled into his bones.

Tung's expression and attention were abruptly absorbed by a message from his com set. Miles, who had yielded Lieutenant Murka's headset back to him so that he might continue his duties, shifted from foot to foot in agony for news. *Elena, Elli, if I've killed you...*

Tung spoke into his pickup. "Good. Well done. Report to the A-Seven drop site." A jerk of his chin switched channels. "Sim, Nout, fall back with your patrols to your shuttle drop site perimeters. They've been found."

Miles found himself bent over with his hand supported on gelid knees, waiting for his head to clear, his heart lurching in huge slow gulps. "Elli and Elena? Are they all right?"

"They didn't call for a medtech... you sure you don't need one yourself? You're green."

"I'm all right." Miles's heart steadied, and he straightened up, to meet Beatrice's questing eyes. "Beatrice, would you please go get Tris and Oliver for me? I need to talk to them before the next shuttle relay goes up."

She shook her head helplessly and wheeled away. She did not salute. On the other hand, she didn't argue, either. Miles was insensibly cheered.

The booming racket around the dome circle had died down to the occasional whine of small-arms fire, human cry, or blurred amplified voice. Fires burned in the distance, red-orange glows in the muffling fog. Not a surgically clean operation... the Cetagandans were going to be extremely pissed when they'd counted their casualties, Miles judged. Time to be gone, and long gone. He tried to keep the poisoned encodes in mind, as anodyne to the vision of Cetagandan clerks and techs crushed in the rubble of their burning buildings, but the two nightmares seemed to amplify instead of cancelling each other out.

Here came Tris and Oliver, both looking a little wild-eyed. Beatrice took up station at Tris's right shoulder.

"Congratulations," Miles began, before they could speak. He had a lot of ground to cover and not much time left. "You have achieved an army." A wave of his arm swept the orderly array of prisoners—ex-prisoners—spread across the camp in their shuttle groups. They waited quietly, most seated on the ground. Or was it the Cetagandans who had ingrained such patience in them? Whatever.

"Temporarily," said Tris. "This is the lull, I believe. If things hot up, if you lose one or more shuttles, if somebody panics and it spreads—"

"You can tell anybody who's inclined to panic they can ride up with me if it'll make them feel better. Ah—better also mention that I'm going up in the *last* load," said Miles.

Tung, dividing his attention between this confab and his headset, grimaced in exasperation at this news.

"That'll settle 'em." Oliver grinned.

"Give them something to think about, anyway," conceded Tris.

"Now I'm going to give you something to think about. The new Marilac resistance. You're it," said Miles. "My employer originally engaged me to rescue Colonel Tremont, that he might raise a new army and carry on the fight. When I found him… as he was, dying, I had to decide whether to follow the letter of my contract, and deliver a catatonic or a corpse, or the spirit—and deliver an army. I chose this, and I chose you two. *You* must carry on Colonel Tremont's work."

"I was only a field lieutenant," began Tris in horror, in chorus with Oliver's, "I'm a grunt, not a staff officer. Colonel Tremont was a genius—"

"You are his heirs now. *I* say so. Look around you. Do I make mistakes in choosing my subordinates?"

After a moment's silence, Tris muttered, "Apparently not."

"Build yourselves a staff. Find your tactics geniuses, your technical wizards, and put 'em to work for you. But the drive, and the decisions, and the direction, must be yours, forged in this pit. It is you two who will remember this place, and so remember what it is you are doing, and why, always."

Oliver spoke quietly. "And when do we muster out of this army, Brother Miles? My time was up during the siege of Fallow Core. If I'd been anywhere else, I could have gone home."

"Until the Cetagandan army of occupation rolled down your street."

"Even then. The odds aren't good."

"The odds were worse for Barrayar, in its day, and they ran the Cetagandans right off. It took twenty years, and more blood than either of you have seen in your lives combined, but they did it," asserted Miles.

Oliver seemed more struck by this historical precedent than Tris, who said skeptically, "Barrayar had those crazy Vor warriors. Nuts who rushed into battle, who *liked* to die. Marilac just doesn't have that sort of cultural tradition. We're civilized—or we were, once..."

"Let me tell you about the Barrayaran Vor," cut in Miles. "The loonies who sought a glorious death in battle found it very early on. This rapidly cleared the chain of command of the accumulated fools. The survivors were those who learned to fight dirty, and live, and fight another day, and win, and win, and win, and for whom nothing, not comfort, or security, not family or friends or their immortal souls, was more important than winning. Dead men are losers by definition. Survival and victory. They weren't supermen, or immune to pain. They sweated in confusion and darkness. And with not one-half the physical resources Marilac possesses even now, they won. When you're Vor"—Miles ran down a little—"there is no mustering out."

After a silence Tris said, "Even a volunteer patriotic army must eat. And we won't beat the Cetagandans by firing spitballs at them."

"There will be financial and military aid forthcoming through a covert channel other than myself. If there is a Resistance command to deliver it to."

Tris measured Oliver by eye. The fire in her burned closer to the surface than Miles had ever seen it, coursing down those corded muscles. The whine of the first returning shuttles pierced the fog. She spoke quite softly. "And here I thought I was the atheist, Sergeant, and you were the believer. Are you coming with me—or mustering out?"

Oliver's shoulders bowed. With the weight of history, Miles realized, not defeat, for the heat in his eyes matched Tris's. "Coming," he grunted.

Miles caught Tung's eyes. "How we doing?"

Tung shook his head, held up fingers. "About six minutes slow, unloading upstairs."

"Right." Miles turned back to Tris and Oliver. "I want you both to go up on this wave, in separate shuttles, one to each troopship.

When you get there, start expediting the off-loading of your people. Lieutenant Murka will give you your shuttle assignment—" He motioned Murka over and packed them off.

Beatrice lingered. "I'm inclined to panic," she informed Miles in a distant tone. Her bare toe smudged whorls in the dampening dirt.

"I don't need a bodyguard anymore," Miles said. He grinned. "A keeper, maybe…"

A smile lighted her eyes that did not yet reach her mouth. *Later,* Miles promised himself. Later, he would make that mouth laugh.

The second wave of shuttles began to lift, even as the remnants of the returning first wave were still landing. Miles prayed everyone's sensors were operating properly, passing each other in this fog. Their timing could only get more ragged from now on. The fog itself was coagulating into a cold rain, silver needles pelting down.

The focus of the operation was narrowing rapidly now, more of machines and numbers and timing, less of loyalties and souls and fearsome obligations. An emotionally pathological mind, devoid of love and fear, might even call it fun, Miles thought. He began jotting scores left-handed in the dirt, numbers up, down, in transit, remaining, but the dirt was turning to gluey black mud and did not retain the impressions.

"Shit," Tung hissed suddenly through clenched teeth. The air before his face blurred in a flurry of vid-projected incoming information, his eyes flicking through it with practiced rapidity. His right hand bunched and twitched, as if tempted to wrench off his headset and stamp it into the mud in frustration and disgust. "That tears it. We just lost two shuttles out of the second wave."

Which two? Miles's mind screamed. *Oliver, Tris…* He forced his first question to be, "How?" *I swear, if they crashed into each other, I'm going to go find a wall and beat my head on it till I go numb…*

"Cetagandan fighter broke through our cordon. He was going for the troop freighters, but we nailed him in time. Almost in time."

"You got identifications on which two shuttles? And were they loaded or returning?"

Tung's lips moved in subvocalization. "A-Four, fully loaded. B-Seven, returning empty. Loss total, no survivors. Fighter Shuttle Five from the *Triumph* is disabled by enemy fire; pilot recovery now in progress."

He hadn't lost his commanders. His hand-picked and carefully nurtured successors to Colonel Tremont were safe. He opened his eyes, squeezed shut in pain, to find Beatrice, to whom the shuttle IDs meant nothing, waiting anxiously for interpretation.

"Two hundred dead?" she whispered.

"Two hundred six," Miles corrected. The faces, names, voices of the six familiar Dendarii fluttered through his memory. The two hundred ciphers must have had faces too. He blocked them out, as too crushing an overload.

"These things happen," Beatrice muttered numbly.

"You all right?"

"Of course I'm all right. These things happen. Inevitable. I am not a weepy wimp who folds under fire." She blinked rapidly, lifting her chin. "Give me… something to do. Anything."

Quickly, Miles added for her. *Right.* He pointed across the camp. "Go to Pel and Liant. Divide their remaining shuttle groups into blocks of thirty-three, and add them to each of the remaining third-wave shuttle groups. We'll have to send the third wave up overloaded. Then report back to me. Go quick, the rest will be back in minutes."

"Yessir." She saluted. For her sake, not his; for order, structure, rationality, a lifeline. He returned the salute gravely.

"They were already overloaded," objected Tung as soon as she was out of earshot. "They're going to fly like bricks with two-hundred-thirty-three squeezed on board. And they'll take longer to load on here and unload topside."

"Yes. God." Miles gave up scratching figures in the useless mud. "Run the numbers through the computer for me, Ky. I don't trust myself to add two and two just now. How far behind will we be by the time the main body of the Cetagandans comes in range? Come close as you can, no fudge factors, please."

Tung mumbled into his headset, reeled off numbers, margins, timing. Miles tracked every detail with predatory intensity. Tung concluded bluntly. "At the end of the last wave, five shuttles are still going to be waiting to unload when the Cetagandan fire fries us."

A thousand men and women.

"May I respectfully suggest, sir, that the time has come to start cutting our losses?" added Tung.

"You may, Commodore."

"Option One, maximally efficient; only drop seven shuttles in the last wave. Leave the last five shuttle loads of prisoners on the ground. They'll be retaken, but at least they'll be alive." Tung's voice grew persuasive on this last line.

"Only one problem, Ky. *I* don't want to stay here."

"You can still be on the last shuttle up, just like you said. By the way, sir, have I expressed myself yet, sir, on what a genuinely dumbshit piece of grandstanding that is?"

"Eloquently, with your eyebrows, a while ago. And while I'm inclined to agree with you, have you noticed yet how closely the remaining prisoners keep watching me? Have you ever watched a cat sneaking up on a horned hopper?"

Tung stirred uneasily, eyes taking in the phenomenon Miles described.

"I don't fancy gunning down the last thousand in order to get my shuttle into the air."

"Skewed as we are, they might not realize there were no more shuttles coming till after you were in the air."

"So we just leave them standing there, waiting for us?" *The sheep look up, but are not fed…*

"Right."

"You like that option, Ky?"

"Makes me want to puke, but—consider the nine thousand others. And the Dendarii fleet. The idea of dropping them all down the rat hole in a predoomed effort to pack up all these—miserable sinners of yours, makes me want to puke a lot more. Nine-tenths of a loaf is *much* better than none."

"Point taken. Let us go on to option two, please. The flight out of orbit is calculated on the speed of the slowest ship, which is…?"

"The freighters."

"And the *Triumph* remains the swiftest?"

"Betcher ass." Tung had captained the *Triumph* once.

"And the best armored."

"Yo. So?" Tung saw perfectly well where he was being driven. His obtuseness was but a form of oblique balking.

"So. The first seven shuttles up on the last wave lock onto the troop freighters and boost on schedule. We call back five of the *Triumph*'s fighter pilots and dump and destroy their craft. One's damaged already, right? The last five of these drop shuttles clamp to the *Triumph* in their place, protected from the now-arriving fire of the Cetagandan ships by the *Triumph*'s full shielding. Pack the prisoners into the *Triumph*'s corridors, lock shuttle hatches, boost like hell."

"The added mass of a thousand people—"

"Would be less than that of a couple of the drop shuttles. Dump and blow them too, if you have to, to fit the mass/acceleration window."

"—would overload life support—"

"The emergency oxygen will take us to the wormhole jump point. After jump the prisoners can be distributed among the other ships at our leisure."

Tung's voice grew anguished. "Those combat-drop shuttles are *brand new*. And my fighters—*five* of them—do you realize how hard it will be to recoup the funds to replace 'em? It comes to—"

"I asked you to calculate the time, Ky, not the price tag," said Miles through his teeth. He added more quietly, "I'll tack them on to our bill for services rendered."

"You ever hear the term *cost overrun*, boy? You will..." Tung switched his attention back to his headset, itself but an extension of the tactics room aboard the *Triumph*. Calculations were made, new orders entered and executed.

"It flies," sighed Tung. "Buys a damned expensive fifteen minutes. If nothing else goes wrong..." He trailed off in a frustrated mumble, as impatient as Miles himself with his inability to be three places at once.

"There comes my shuttle back," Tung noted aloud. He glanced at Miles, plainly unwilling to leave his admiral to his own devices, as plainly itching to be out of the acid rain and dark and mud and closer to the nerve center of operations.

"Get gone," said Miles. "You can't ride up with me anyway, it's against procedure."

"Procedure, hah," said Tung blackly.

With the lift-off of the third wave, there were barely two thousand prisoners left on the ground. Things were thinning out, winding down; the armored combat patrols were falling back now from their penetration of the surrounding Cetagandan installations, back toward their assigned shuttle landing sites. A dangerous turning of the tide, should some surviving Cetagandan officer recover enough organization to harry their retreat.

"See you aboard the *Triumph*," Tung emphasized. He paused to brace Lieutenant Murka, out of Miles's earshot. Miles grinned in sympathy for the overworked lieutenant, in no doubt about the orders Tung was now laying on him. If Murka didn't come back with Miles in tow, he'd probably be wisest not to come back at all.

+ + +

Nothing left now but a little last waiting. *Hurry up and wait.* Waiting, Miles realized, was very bad for him. It allowed his self-generated adrenaline to wear off, allowed him to feel how tired and hurt he really was. The illuminating flares were dying to a red glow.

There was really very little time between the fading of the labored thunder of the last third wave shuttle to depart, and the screaming whine of the first fourth wave shuttle plunging back. Alas that this had more to do with being skewed than being swift. The Marilacans still waited in their rat bar blocks, discipline still holding. Of course, nobody'd told them about the little problem in timing they faced. But the nervous Dendarii patrols, chivvying them up the ramps, kept things moving at a pace to Miles's taste. Rear guard was never a popular position to draw, even among the lunatic fringe who defaced their weapons with notches and giggled among themselves while speculating upon newer and more grotesque methods of blowing away their enemies.

Miles saw the semiconscious Suegar carried up the ramp first. Suegar would actually reach the *Triumph*'s sickbay faster in his company, Miles calculated, on this direct flight, than had he been sent on an earlier shuttle to one of the troop freighters and had to await a safe moment to transfer.

The arena they were leaving had grown silent and dark, sodden and sad, ghostly. *I will break the doors of hell, and bring up the dead...* there was something not quite right about the half-remembered quote. No matter.

This shuttle's armored patrol, the last, drew back out of the fog and darkness, electronically whistled in like a pack of sheepdogs by their master Murka, who stood at the foot of the ramp as liaison between the ground patrol and the shuttle pilot, who was expressing her anxiety to be gone with little whining revs on the engines.

Then from the darkness—plasma fire, sizzling through the rain-sodden, saturated air. Some Cetagandan hero—officer, troop, tech, who knew?—had crawled up out of the rubble and found a weapon—and an enemy to fire it at. Splintered afterimages, red and green, danced in Miles's eyes. A Dendarii patroller rolled out of the dark, a glowing line across the back of his armor smoking and sparking until quenched in the black mud. His armor legs seized up, and he lay wriggling like a frantic fish in an effort to peel out of it. A second plasma burst, ill-aimed, spent itself turning a few kilometers of fog and rain to superheated steam on a straight line to some unknown infinity.

Just what they needed, to be pinned down by sniper fire *now*… A pair of Dendarii rear guards started back into the fog. An excited prisoner—ye gods, it was Pitt's lieutenant again—grabbed up the armor-paralyzed soldier's weapon and made to join them.

"No! Come back later and fight on your own time, you jerk!" Miles sloshed toward Murka. "Fall back, load up, get in the air! Don't stop to fight! No time!"

Some of the last of the prisoners had fallen flat to the ground, burrowing like mudpuppies, a sound sensible reflex in any other context. Miles dashed among them, slapping rumps. "Get *aboard*, up the *ramp*, go, go, go!" Beatrice popped up out of the mud and mimicked him, shakily driving her fellows before her.

Miles skidded to a stop beside his fallen Dendarii and snapped the armor clamps open left-handed. The soldier kicked off his fatal carapace, rolled to his feet, and limped for the safety of the shuttle. Miles ran close behind him.

Murka and one patrolman waited at the foot of the ramp.

"Get ready to pull in the ramp and lift on my mark," Murka began to the shuttle pilot. "R—" His words were lost in an explosive pop as the plasma beam sliced across his neck. Miles could feel the searing heat from it pass centimeters above his head as he stood next to his lieutenant. Murka's body crumpled.

Miles dodged, paused to yank off Murka's com headset. The head came too. Miles had to brace it with his numb hand to pull the headset free. The weight of the head, its density and roundness, hammered into his senses. The precise memory of it would surely be with him until his dying day. He let it fall by Murka's body.

He staggered up the ramp, a last armored Dendarii pulling on his arm. He could feel the ramp sag peculiarly under their feet, glanced down to see a half-melted seam across it where the plasma arc that had killed Murka had passed on.

He fell through the hatchway, clutching the headset and yelling into it, "Lift, lift! Mark, now! Go!"

"Who is this?" came the shuttle pilot's voice back.

"Naismith."

"Yes, *sir*."

The shuttle heaved off the ground, engines roaring, even before the ramp had withdrawn. The ramp mechanism labored, metal and plastic complaining—then jammed on the twisted distortion of the melt.

"Get that hatch sealed back there!" the shuttle pilot's voice yowled over the headset.

"Ramp's jammed," Miles yowled back. "Jettison it!"

The ramp mechanism skreeled and shrieked, reversing itself. The ramp shuddered, jammed again. Hands reached out to thump on it urgently.

"You'll never get it that way!" Beatrice, across the hatch from Miles, yelled fiercely, and twisted around to kick at it with her bare feet. The wind of their flight screamed over the open hatchway, buffeting and vibrating the shuttle like a giant blowing across the top of a bottle.

To a chorus of shouting, thumping, and swearing, the shuttle lurched abruptly onto its side. Men, women, and loose equipment tangled across the tilting deck. Beatrice kicked bloodily at a final buggered bolt. The ramp tore loose at last. Beatrice, sliding, fell with it.

Miles dove at her, lunging across the hatchway. If he connected, he never knew, for his right hand was a senseless blob. He saw her face only as a white blur as she whipped away into the blackness.

It was like a silence, a great silence, in his head. Although the roar of wind and engines, screaming and swearing and yelling, went on as before, it was lost somewhere between his ears and his brain, and went unregistered. He saw only a white blur, smearing into the darkness, repeated again and again, replaying like a looping vid.

He found himself crouched on his hands and knees, the shuttle's acceleration sucking him to the deck. They'd got the hatch closed. The merely human babble within seemed muffled and thin, now that the roaring voices of the gods were silenced. He looked up into the pale face of Pitt's lieutenant, crouched beside him still clutching the unfired Dendarii weapon he'd grabbed up in that other lifetime.

"You'd better kill a whole lot of Cetagandans for Marilac, boy," Miles rasped to him at last. "You better be worth something to *somebody*, 'cause I've sure paid too much for you."

The Marilacan's face twitched uncertainly, too cowed even to try to look apologetic. Miles wondered what his own face must look like. From the reflection in that mirror, strange, very strange.

Miles began to crawl forward, looking for something, somebody... Formless flashes made yellow streaks in the corners of his vision. An armored Dendarii, her helmet off, pulled him to his feet.

"Sir? Hadn't you better come forward to the pilot's compartment, sir?"

"Yes, all right…"

She looped an arm around him, under his arm, so he didn't fall down again. They picked their way forward in the crowded shuttle, through Marilacans and Dendarii mixed. Faces were drawn to him, marked him fearfully, but none dared an expression of any kind. Miles's eye was caught by a silver cocoon, as they neared the forward end.

"Wait…"

He fell to his knees beside Suegar. *A hit of hope…* "Suegar. Hey, Suegar!"

Suegar opened his eyes to slits. No telling how much of this he was taking in, through the pain and the shock and the drugs.

"You're on your way now. We made it, made the timing. With all ease. With agility and speed. Up through the regions of the air, higher than the clouds. You had the scripture right, you did."

Suegar's lips moved. Miles bent his head closer.

"…wasn't really a scripture," Suegar whispered. "I knew it… you knew it… don't shit me…"

Miles paused, cold-stoned. Then he leaned forward again. "No, brother," he whispered. "For though we went in clothed, we have surely come out naked."

Suegar's lips puffed on a dry laugh.

Miles didn't weep until after they'd made the wormhole jump.

Elizabeth Moon's Vatta's War *debuted in 2003 with* Trading in Danger *and focuses on Kylara Vatta, a young member of the Vatta family, which runs the interstellar shipping corporation Vatta Enterprises. After forced resignation from the military academy, Ky captains an old trading ship for the corporation and finds her military training coming to good use. This action-packed story provides the bridge between the original five-book series and* Cold Welcome, *the first book of a brand-new series,* Vatta's Peace.

ALL IN A DAY'S WORK
ELIZABETH MOON

Ky Vatta, Grand Admiral of the fleet she had created, unpinned the decorations from her dress uniform and lifted the most recent—a broad purple-and-gold striped ribbon with an elaborate medal attached to it, courtesy of Moray System—over her head, wondering what she could possibly do with the rest of her life that would match what she'd already done.

She wasn't even thirty yet. She had accomplished miracles, people said, saved the lives of billions of people on uncounted planets, commanded the only combined space fleet in this corner of the galaxy. A fleet that was now recognized, supported by more and more of the systems that had told her the idea was impossible for anyone, let alone a young woman like her. But when she thought ahead—to the next round of official visits, the meetings with diplomats and politicians, the negotiations regarding contributions to the effort—the need for money and personnel and ships, the next award ceremony, the next budget cycle, and the next and the next and the next after that… she didn't want to think about it.

It wasn't that she wanted the war to come back. Most of her family had been wiped out, her childhood home obliterated, the Vatta headquarters destroyed. She had been injured, almost killed, more than once; that alternation of terror and rage and relief, over and over, had ruled her life for years until she finally defeated Turek's forces. Since then she'd seen the ruin, the cities left as piles of rubble, the land scorched and barren on the planets she had not been in time to save. And the bodies… no sane person could want war, just for the excitement of it. It had been the most intense years of her life, and during it—when she had a brief time to herself—she had yearned for peace.

So she could not be... what she felt like. She could not be... bored. It was ridiculous. Admirals did not get bored. Intelligent, capable adults did not get bored. There were things to do; there were always things to do, decisions to make, speeches to give, complaints and demands to hear.

And yet. She didn't want another war exactly, but she did want something interesting. Something even surprising. An idea bubbled up. A little harmless leisure.

"You know what I think we need?" she asked her flag captain, Pordre.

"What, Admiral?"

"I think we need a live-fire exercise on the way home. We need to go blow something up." He looked startled; she grinned at him. "I know the right place; only a slight detour."

✦ ✦ ✦

Vanguard II and the other three ships—*Eistfod*, *Quadlock*, and *Garnett*—emerged from jump a long light-gap from the former pirate base Ky had remembered. An empty system, no inhabited planets, no active human presence. Scan cleared; the techs, scan and comm, ran through the usual checks, putting the incoming data up for all to see and hear.

The signal was faint, but clearly a voice call. It sounded like gibberish to her, almost like the coded jargon the pirates had used years before. Her flag captain looked at her.

"Trap, Admiral?"

"Maybe. Let's find out." Ky felt a surge of energy; her earlier lethargy vanished. She'd wanted a surprise; the universe had provided one.

"Sir—it's a call for help." Selanyss, their new scan tech, said, wrist tentacles clamped on the back of his chair. He was a humod from Adelaide, one of those she'd rescued from Gretna early in the war.

"How do you know?" Ky asked.

"It's my native language, Mraldan. You know I'm from Polson, originally." He held up his hands, the wrist tentacles uncurling as he spoke.

"But you speak Trade," Pordre said. "I thought almost everyone did, at least as a second language."

"Not on Polson, sir. I learned it on Adelaide, after the admiral took us there." Selanyss's expression convinced Ky he wasn't telling her everything, but the message they'd received was more important.

"So… that was a call for help? From Polson? I thought it had been razed by Turek's troops."

"I don't think it was from Polson, Admiral, but somewhere closer. There's a ship track a couple of days old."

"Why don't people from Polson speak Trade?" Pordre asked. "It's the universal language—"

"We… didn't need to, sir."

Ky noticed that his tentacles had paled now, leaving a pattern of dark star-shaped spots. His face was paler, too. She had known he was more modded than most people when she hired him, but changing skin color and pattern surprised her. "What else was in the message?" she asked.

"They—a group of refugees from Polson—are being attacked."

"Well, that's what we're here for," Ky said briskly. "Rescue's our specialty. Let's track that down quickly. My guess is it's the old pirate base. Someone was left there, or moved in there after Turek's bunch left, and now someone else wants it. Com One, link me to the ship's ansible. Captain, prepare for combat conditions."

Her flagship, *Vanguard II*, had the most combat-experienced crew. *Eistfod*, the newest ship, just delivered by Moray on her visit there, had an all-Moray crew whose training she hadn't supervised. It matched *Vanguard* in size and had a newer suite of weapons control, but no experience. *Quadlock*, the smallest of the three warships, had a heavy weapons load and better resistance to damage. And lightly armed *Garnett*, their supply ship, would need to stay far back, out of any combat. Ky transmitted her orders to the others quickly, setting Garnett's captain free to find the best hiding spot she could.

"Scan's found only one ship track, so we should handle anything we find easily, but don't mix in. I'll call when we need you. Eistfod, go on and load your skimmers. We'll give them some exercise whether we actually need them or not. Hold your position on my starboard flank until we're closer. Quadlock, half on my port flank." The captains acknowledged.

Ky turned to Pordre. "Coordinates for microjump halfway to the old supply base—"

He recited them; Ky repeated them to the other captains. "Jump on my mark."

They emerged halfway to the base. *Eistfod* ended up ten kilometers ahead of mark, and before Ky could say anything, her captain apologized. "Recalibrating now, Admiral."

"Scan, where's that ship?"

"At a radiation source, Admiral. I think it's that base you talked about. It's not where it was…"

"It wouldn't be. It's a rock with buildings on it… it would be going somewhere. I remember a radiation source before, too. Probably a powerplant. Well, clearly that's where we should go. Any new transmissions?"

"Just a repeat of *Help, under attack,* Admiral. Should we reply?"

"No. Announcing ourselves this far out is too risky. We don't know what the attackers might do and we probably wouldn't like it. We need to be close enough to intervene. Nav, do you have any tighter coordinates?"

"Yes, Admiral; transmitting with margin of error."

"Next jump, two thirds of estimated distance, another pause for recalibration and assessment. Same formation. On my mark."

This time *Eistfod* emerged from jump exactly in position, as did the others. "Learning," Pordre commented.

"On mark," Navigation One said. "Margin of error 0.5 kilometers."

"Excellent," Ky said. "We want to come out of nowhere and scare the attackers—but be close enough to attack them, and far enough to have a decent delay before powered weapons can get to us."

Ky's group came out of the next microjump only about eighty kilometers from the base: weapons hot, and their automated challenge sending. NavOne scrambled to dump their residual velocity to match the base's.

The situation looked dire. A fat-bodied tradeship, smaller even than Quadlock, was firing at the former pirate base. Ky hadn't been this close to it in the war, the only time she'd been in that system before. Now she could see that the "base" must have started out as a deepspace automated mine, spreading out from its original control dome to form a complicated structure of pipes, drill stations, processing nodes, and warehouses for the final refined product, with several former docking points, only one of them still whole.

Selanyss stripped the beacon off the tradeship: *My Way,* out of Gretna.

"Any other ships in system?" Ky asked.

"No, Admiral. This is still the only one."

Gretna again. A society that engaged in human trafficking, as she'd found years before. That hated humods and considered them subhuman at best. Why had they come here? How had they known the Polsonites were here? Polson had been an all-humod world— was Gretna going after it just to kill humods?

Ky used the onboard ansible to contact her ships. "If any of the survivors are left, they'll be in those structures somewhere. The ship is Gretnan; we need to neutralize it without doing damage to the base, and we'll probably need to sending a boarding party to deal with any Gretnans—they're experienced in EVA."

Pordre spoke to Communications: "Match frequencies with any transmissions from the target, then enter our usual challenge hail." Ky listened to her recorded voice identifying her ships as Space Defense Force, demanding that the other ship cease fire and put its commanding officer on. The Gretnan ship answered with a badly aimed shot; the missile never came near them.

"Long range, underpowered," Pordre commented. "They should know better."

"You have no jurisdiction here," said a loud angry voice over the com. "This is our territory. Our colony."

"Identify yourself," Ky asked. The viewscreen remained blank. "We have received a distress call."

"I don't have to tell you anything. We filed claim on this entire system and you're trespassing."

"It was empty except for some squatters," another voice said. "Buncha them weirdos. Manufactured, claim to be human but they aren't."

"Shut *up*, Clive!" someone else said in the background.

"They're not human; they're like robots and they belong to their manufacturer."

"You are in territory patrolled by Space Defense Force; your beacon reports that your ship is out of Gretna. That's a long way from here; you need to identify yourself by name and provide evidence that you have a legal right here. In what court did you file your claim? Stand down your weapons, and prepare to be boarded. We will need to inspect and determine what's going on here."

"Oh, no you don't. You got no right to be here. Go away or we'll blow your ship to bits."

"You might want to look at your scan," Ky said. "You're outnumbered and outgunned."

Quadlock, on Ky's orders, had now maneuvered through a series of microjumps until it had a straight shot at the Gretnan ship without risking any of Ky's.

"You better not shoot at us! We got hostages!"

"I thought you said there were just robots here," Ky said. "Robots aren't hostages."

Selanyss gave her a startled look. "Admiral—"

She shook her head at him and went on. "I'm glad you finally noticed that you're in a hopeless position. Lock down your weapons, release your so-called hostages, and recall all your personnel to your ship. You will be required to allow a full inspection of your vessel..."

"No! You got no right. This is *our* ship, *our* base. It was abandoned and we've laid claim. These humods aren't real people and they're ours now. We got a right to do anything we want with them!"

"The dumber they are," Pordre said, "the easier the take-down."

"Not always," Ky said. "You weren't there when I met up with Gretnans before. They made holes in my ship. They're inbred for color, nasty, and short-sighted—no strategic sense—but they're not entirely stupid. They think they've got a way out."

A face showed up on the vid screen at last, the same near-albino coloring as those she'd seen on Gretna Station. The man sneered at her, a curl of lip that must be intended to show the crooked teeth. "You're that same cow shot up our station! I recognize you now! You come back and try that again and we'll blow you away."

Ky laughed, thumb over her mic. "They've probably never seen a cow."

"You're all nothing but perverts and godless cowards and trash!" That was a second face, similar in looks but the eyes had a hint of blue.

"And you're outnumbered and outgunned, so shut off all your weapons systems and prepare for inspection." Ky kept her voice level and firm.

On the auxiliary screen, the Gretnan ship emitted a plume of vapor.

"What are they doing?" Pordre asked.

"Breaking off from the base?" Nelson, sitting second scan didn't take his gaze off the screen.

"Maybe..."

"You like humods, you can have them! Dead!" The Gretnan ship's insystem drive came alive, and it powered away from the base. A long plume of vapor came out the docking arm: escaping air. "You won't get us!"

"They breached the airlock!" Pordre's tone expressed all the horror of any ship captain.

"Oh no you don't," Ky said, connecting to *Eistfod* and *Quadlock*. "Captains: pursue and destroy the Gretnan ship *My Way*; it has just breached the base, almost certainly costing lives. Don't let it reach jump radius." A small ship not near any large mass—it might jump in the next 35 seconds—and the debris from a hit might damage the base. "*Eistfod*, you have preferred angle."

"Engaging now," *Quadlock*'s captain said, an instant before *Eistfod*'s.

"Target acquired."

"Admiral—" That was Selanyss, now half-standing, gripping the back of his seat.

"Not now," Ky said. "Just a—" The screen flared, as *Eistfod*'s beam weapon steadied on the Gretnan ship; its shields flared, died, and the ship blew. "*Quadlock*: beam on high for debris cleanup."

"Beam on, wide sweep."

Ky turned back to the scan stations. "All right, Selanyss—what is it?"

"We have to go there, Admiral—"

"I will, but not until the debris field is clear."

"You don't understand—they may not be dead—the humods! We're—you know we're modded for different purposes. Some can live in hard vacuum for an hour, even. With very low atmospheric pressure, below what you could stand, for much longer. We need to get there fast."

Ky nodded. "All right, but we'll need to do it safely." Finally—a chance to do something useful herself. Better and better. She looked at Pordre. "Captain, you heard—we need to send a relief party to that base and save what lives we can. We have the pinnace and the shuttle: which?"

"Pinnace," he said at once. "Better shielding, smaller target. My exec can take it—"

"I'm going," Ky said.

"You can't—you're the admiral—"

"Of course I can; I'm not the captain," Ky said. "*You* have to stay with the ship; *I* don't."

He grimaced. "And if you get killed, you think it'll be fun for me to tell the others back on Greentoo?"

"No. But then I don't plan to be killed."

"No one ever does," Pordre said. "That's what worries me. I'll call down to the launch bay."

Ky looked at Selanyss. "Come on, Tech Selanyss; you're with me."

"Sir?" He looked confused.

"I don't speak their language; you do. I don't expect this will be easy, especially if some of the Gretnans are still on that thing. I need someone along who can communicate with them, convince them we aren't their enemies. Pordre, don't come in too close."

She was moving fast as she left the bridge, glad that she'd suited up as usual before coming out of jumpspace. "Selanyss, there'll be a suit for you in the launch bay; one of the other team members will get you fitted into it." She put on her helmet and locked it into the neck ring on the way to the launch bay; the pinnace pilot and boarding team were already aboard.

"Your weapons are racked inside, Admiral," said the launch chief.

"Thanks, Chief." Ky punched in at the lock, and entered the pinnace, Selanyss right behind her, then settled into the seat reserved for her. "Get Tech Selanyss suited and prepped," she said. "No weapons."

"Right away, sir." Kajan, head of the boarding team, took the suit from Selanyss, who still looked confused, popped the latches of the front opening, and said, "Right leg in here."

Ky looked around at the others, all familiar faces, and nodded to them. "Selanyss speaks the Polsons' language; he's our interpreter, so keep him alive. He says they can handle short periods of vacuum, and longer ones of low O2."

"They have mods for that?" Kajan stopped fastening and checking Selanyss's survival suit.

"Yes," Selanyss said. "Usually combined with the radiation-resistance and sensory suite. That's why some of them may be alive after a hull breach."

"Hold onto this," Kajan said to Selanyss. Then—"Wait—will your tentacle fit into the suit glove?"

"Not easily. I can't completely retract it." Selanyss looked at Ky. "Actually—my hand already has a glove on it. Over the others."

"The other what?"

"Um… this isn't the only tentacle."

"Well, how are we going to protect your hands?"

"They don't need it, really. Just let me get through the sleeve cuffs—"

Ky watched, fascinated, as Selanyss's hand seemed to ooze through the suit's cuff, followed by the wrist tentacle. He noticed her watching and shrugged. "It's really a thumb equivalent, just too big to fit into the thumb of a glove. Don't worry about it; the cuticle hardens in vacuum."

"Admiral, I'm getting a signal from the base." Ky yanked her attention away from Selanyss and her curiosity; her displays told her it was the pinnace pilot talking.

"Can you understand it?"

"Someone with minimal Trade is saying *Help, no kill* and then the same jabber we heard before."

"We need Selanyss," Ky said. "Kajan, get his helmet hooked up for multi-synch communications. Selanyss, the pilot's hearing someone alive on that base, who has very little Trade. Talk to him."

By the time the pinnace reached the docking tube, Ky knew there were almost a thousand Polson survivors in the old base, all transported to this base as slave labor for Turek's intended empire, and a small force of armed men from Gretna, left behind when their ship pulled away. Now that it had blown up, they were hunting the humods.

The damage to the docking arm was clear on the vid screen—the airlock had been wrenched askew, pulled partly away from the structure behind it.

"Getting in won't be the problem," Kajan said. "But if the humods don't have weapons, we're a small force to engage the remaining Gretnans."

"They will help us," Selanyss said.

"The best way they can help us is to stay out of the line of fire," Ky said. "And tell you what the layout is internally." Kajan nodded.

With the boarding party suited up, Kajan led the way into the open end of the docking tube. Selanyss stayed at the back of the group; he carried no weapon. Ky had pulled hers from the rack, but also stayed behind the leaders.

No Gretnans were in the open tube; the next airlock operated normally and though it took two cycles for them all to pass through, all made it safely, with no resistance from the Gretnans.

"The Gretnans are in the original drilling hub," Selanyss

reported. "They are looking for more weapons. Polsons don't think they've realized you're coming in."

"If we can take them from behind, all the better," Ky said. Another icon winked in her display. *Eistfod* had a boarding team ready to transfer, if she wanted it. "Come on. We're through one airlock, heading for the central area. No resistance yet."

The long docking arm finally went through another airlock and opened into a broader corridor where three of the humods greeted them with a torrent of Mraldan. Selanyss answered, then pulled on his own left hand—which Ky realized was actually a glove covering a writhing mass of tentacles, four about the same length and the wrist tentacle, stouter than the rest. A thumb indeed.

"They went down that corridor," Selanyss said, pointing. He spoke to the other humods in Mraldan and they answered. "Our people from Polson have moved into the next node, a warehouse."

"Tell them there's another boarding team coming in," Ky said. "From *Eistfod*. Do they have a good count on how many Gretnans are left? And if they're all in one group?"

"In one group, and about twenty. They're not sure, because three are being carried. They may have decompression injuries; they might even be dead."

Ky's display told her the *Eistfod* boarding party had entered the docking arm; she waited until they had cleared the airlock and were close enough to see. They saw nothing of the Gretnans, though they heard a rhythmic metallic clanging, until they entered the dome-shaped structure that housed the original automated mining station. A cluster of men in yellow gear were banging on a door with something metallic. Three were lying motionless on the floor.

"Drop your weapons!" Kajan yelled. Then, as the men swung around with their weapons ready, he said, "But they never do," and fired.

Ky grabbed Selanyss's arm and pulled him back flat against the corridor wall, while the second boarding team moved forward. "Just stay put," she said.

The firing stopped before she got into the chamber. The Gretnans had charged straight into the boarding parties and now lay in heaps on the floor.

"Sometimes you're lucky," Kajan said.

"Sometimes you're not!" One of the Gretnans rolled over, aiming at Kajan.

Ky fired before his finger touched the button. Kajan looked at her, eyes wide for a moment. "*He* certainly wasn't," Ky said. "Now let's meet our new allies and see what we can do about this mess."

The humods, via Selanyss, were glad to have the Gretnans dead and gone, but less happy with Ky's suggestion that they all move to Adelaide."

"Why not?" Ky asked, when Selanyss told her.

"We will be hunted. There is a… a genetically implanted code. We can be recognized."

"As humods? It's obvious you're humods, but they like humods on Adelaide."

"It's not the same. We're… registered. We have a trade mark… a patent… I don't know which you call it, but those who came to Polson were escapees. Were made, created as prototypes then bred for… for sale."

"But surely now—you'd been on Polson for a hundred years or more."

"The marker is genetic. Inherited. Can be read with the right reader. All it would take is someone from that corporation to be traveling through Adelaide and they would know."

"It could be gene-edited out, couldn't it?"

"How?"

"I don't know; I'm not a gene engineer but I know it's been done for some conditions. And anyway, you can't stay here. The base is ruined; you have no source of supply; you're vulnerable to anyone who comes along."

"Can you take us—them—then?"

"Not enough room in the warships, or even our supply ship." Ky grinned suddenly as she thought of it. "But I do have an idea." Stella would be furious, but she'd agree. She'd have to. "I can get you transportation, if you'll go. And Adelaide has very advanced medical technology."

While the humods discussed it, Ky made an ansible call back to Greentoo, and had her staff patch it to Cascadia and the Vatta Transport office.

+ + +

Eight hours later, back onboard *Vanguard II*, on the bridge as they headed out toward home, Ky rocked back on her heels and gave a long happy sigh. She glanced at her flag captain. He gave her a quizzical look. "You look happy, Admiral."

"I am. We got to rescue some good guys, blow up some bad guys, all while improving the navigation and combat efficiency of this unit, without a single casualty on our side. And I got to annoy my cousin Stella while actually doing Vatta Transport a good turn: a new and undoubtedly profitable route and a reputation as a company with a commitment to ethics and social welfare."

Pordre's eyebrows went up. "Annoying your cousin is part of a good day's work? I've met her."

Ky felt a twinge of guilt and pushed it away. "Annoying Stella is part of a game she and I have played on each other since childhood. She's older and taller and beautiful. I'm younger and shorter and an admiral." She shrugged. "It's a family thing."

"Routine, then," he said. "All in a day's work."

Dave Bara's Lightship Chronicles *is a newer space opera series—one with a classic feel but modern sensibilities and a growing fan base. His contribution for* Infinite Stars *takes place a few months before the events of* Impulse, *volume one of the Lightship Chronicles series, which also includes* Starbound *(volume two) and* Defiant *(volume three).*

LAST DAY OF TRAINING
DAVE BARA

It was hot in the cadet theater hall deep inside High Station Quantar, and we were all still sweating from our end of the day training shift. But we were almost there, almost done. Just one last day of training and we'd all officially be Lieutenants in the Unified Space Navy. Not Ensigns, not middies, not enlisted grunts. Graduates, even if the official ceremony wasn't for two more months. Lieutenant Peter Cochrane. I liked the sound of that.

There were twenty-two of us who had made it through the three-year set of classes to become junior officers, slated for our world's first faster than light ship in more than a century, H.M.S. *Starbound*. I was proud of that accomplishment, even more so as I hadn't enlisted or even thought about Navy service until the accident that had claimed my older brother Derrick's life almost three years ago. I was doing this for him, for his memory, as much as for myself.

Gunnery Sergeant Lukic was talking again, and I decided I had to at least tune into what he was saying out of courtesy.

"So, this final semester has been a bitch, eh, cadets?" he said. "Tomorrow will be your last day under my command, and I bet you're glad of that." There were grunts of acknowledgement all around the room. This final semester had been very physically taxing; EVAs, survival tests, lots of shuttle flying and plenty of just plain-assed hauling of materiel, in space and on the ground. The kind of stuff we'd never likely do on our permanent assignments, but that we had to be crossed-trained for anyway. Every one of us in this room was destined to be a Command Deck specialist, the best of the best, but that didn't mean it would always be easy.

My specialty was the longscope, the premier assignment that was up for grabs aboard *Starbound*, and since I was top of the class, that plum position would be mine. By chance and partly by design, my girlfriend for the last year, Natalie Decker, was getting the Astrogator's seat, and we'd be working closely together. A lot. And that was just fine with me.

Natalie was a dishwater blonde, very pretty with green eyes and a ready smile. She was also my first lover, and I hers. I felt that we were a particularly good match, but it was hard to think about the long-term future of our relationship when we were both still so young and not even full spacers yet. She held my hand now as she sat next to me, listening to Lukic speak.

"Your assignments for tomorrow will be ansible support. The Historian network is out on the rim, by High Station Candle, and that's quite a run from here, so it's going to be a long day. You'll be paired in twos for the maintenance work, one pilot and one EVA technician to do the actual repairs. Four ansible satellites each. You'll be heading out at 0700, so get your sleep," he said, glancing up at me and Natalie. "You had a good day today, now three hours of R&R and then hit your bunks. Understood, cadets?" Lukic finished, putting us in our place one last time.

"Understood, sir!" we all replied in unison, and with vigor.

"Good. Now get the hell out of here," he said, and that was that.

✦ ✦ ✦

We'd agreed to pose for pictures as a group on our last day, so we all gathered in our dress Quantar blues in front of the main atrium windows, with the spectacular view of our blue-green home world hanging above us. Duane Longer had volunteered to do the picture taking, as it was a hobby of his and he'd even put together a book for all of us to take with us of our favorite memories from the last three years together.

We were all there except for Natalie, and that had me concerned. I checked my watch and noted she was already ten minutes late. That wasn't like her. When I finally saw her walking up to the group my concerns were affirmed.

Her face was pale, as if she had just received some very bad news. I waited while she hugged many of the others. When she finally came to me I reached out and offered her my arms, and she hugged me gently before whispering in my ear.

"Is there someplace we can talk?" she said.

"After," I replied, then we shared a silent moment together, and

I could tell from the red in her eyes that she had been crying. A lot. She smiled wanly at me but then turned on her usual charm for the pictures. She looked very prim and proper in her dress blues and cap, hair cut to regulation hanging just above her shoulders. She held a black leather case tucked under one arm. I wondered if what was inside that case was at the core of her upset. She blinked back tears as she politely continued to converse, and then we all started posing for pictures.

I had the chance to watch her in several groups and I admired her poise under the circumstances. We had become close, perhaps closer than we should have allowed during our training, but being with her had been the best experience of my life, so far.

Duane Longer insisted that Natalie and I stand together for a picture, which was awkward. We both smiled as he took the shot three times. Finally, Natalie had enough.

"Thank you, Duane, no more please," she said testily. It was the first real crack of composure that I had seen from her.

"Aw c'mon, Nat! Just a few more!" Longer was nice enough, just not quick on the uptake.

"No, Duane. Really, no more." She waved a hand in front of the camera and started to walk away. He made the mistake of reaching out for her and catching her arm.

"C'mon, Nat! We're all heading over to the officer's lounge—"

"I said enough!" She swung her arm free and knocked his camera to the floor, where it bounced, then she stormed off in frustration.

"Hey! My camera! That cost me a week's cadet crowns!" he started after her. I had to step in with a firm hand to his chest.

"She said enough, Duane. I have to insist you give her some space," I said. He stiffened.

"Since when are you her watchdog?" I liked Duane, but I wasn't going to allow his overbearing good-naturedness to hurt Natalie. We were about the same height and he was two years older than me, but I had the better of him plenty of times in the gym.

"Since she asked you to let her go. Now please be smart and *let her go*." He hesitated as I pushed just a bit harder.

"What about my camera?"

"If it's broken I'll make sure it gets paid for. Good enough?" He eyed me hard, then turned back to his other friends.

"I guess so."

"Good." He leaned down to pick up the camera.

"You two sure got touchy enough," he said to my back as I strode away from him. A second later and I was out of hearing range and moving through the rapidly dissipating crowd. I knew where Natalie was headed, and I was going there as well.

+ + +

A quick lifter ride, and I was in the forward lounge in the dorm tower. It was a place we'd spent many quiet nights looking out on Quantar and dreaming of the stars. I came off the lifter and saw her in the front row of the small lounge, head bowed. The lounge had been a warm place for us as lovers, but now it seemed empty as space and nearly as cold.

I set the door code for privacy and then took off my cap and walked to the sofa, sitting down silently next to her. I knew her well enough to know that talking first wasn't the answer. She would let me know when she was ready. After a few moments she composed herself and turned to face me but didn't say anything.

"What's wrong?" I finally ventured. She handed me the leather case she'd been carrying without a word. I wasn't stupid. I knew what it was; assignment orders. I opened it. It indicated her new assignment request had been approved… to H.M.S. *Impulse*, the Carinthian Lightship that had been in service for six months.

"What's this?" I said. We were supposed to be together on *Starbound*, at least that was what I *thought* the plan was.

"I was approached by Captain Bergovic about a month ago," she said. Bergovic was the Headmaster of the Cadet Academy. "He asked me to consider an assignment aboard *Impulse*, as part of a Quantar technical team of twelve that would be assigned there. Something about mixing the Lightship crews to create more fraternity among the Navy. I told him I would consider it. Then this came last night."

"Can't you refuse?" I said. She took the case back from me.

"Did you read it, Peter? Those are my assignment *orders*. I leave in less than a week."

"I can get this undone," I said confidently. She frowned.

"Be realistic, Peter. You may be the Grand Admiral's son but you don't have that kind of power." I had no answer for that, so I stayed silent. She stood up quickly and started pacing.

"This is all your father's doing. And that goddamned Wesley," she said.

"You don't know that," I said, even though I knew she was probably right.

"I know enough, Peter. I know that we've been put as far away from each other as possible. I know that the daughters of military men aren't good enough for royal families, Union or not. And I know what ship the Feilberg family runs, and who the Astrogator is that will be swapped out with me to *Starbound*." That caught my attention. It was something that hadn't even occurred to me.

"You think my father and Admiral Wesley plan to put Karina Feilberg and me together?"

She sighed in frustration. "It's obvious, Peter. They want you to be in close quarters so that you'll be attracted to each other. She's an Astrogator, and you're a Longscope officer. Just like you and me. So the two of us had to be split up so that the two of *you* could be together. That's just the way things are." Now she was angry.

"Is that what you think?" I said. She turned and faced me.

"Yes, it's damned well what I think!" she said, almost yelling. "Are you really that naïve?"

"Natalie—"

"Answer my question. Do you really think hooking you up with a Carinthian princess isn't part of the overall agenda? You are the son of a royal, you know."

I took a deep breath and looked into her angry face, flushed red with emotion. "I suppose it could be," I admitted, looking away from her. Quantar's links to the old royal peerage system were weak, but I was still the only surviving son of the nominal Director, with my own titles and privileges bestowed on me by historical right.

"Uh-huh," she said, then walked off to stand alone at the view window. I waited only a moment, then followed her. I put my arms around her waist and spoke as softly and honestly as I could.

"Natalie, please. Let's not have this, not now. Besides, there was a chance we both wouldn't have made *Starbound*'s roster anyway." That wasn't really a lie, but I knew it was implausible. She turned back to me, face clear of tears even if her makeup was smudged beyond repair.

"How long do we have?" she asked. I looked at my watch.

"An hour of R&R left and eight more after that until we start our assignment," I said. She smiled bravely.

"Then let's not waste another moment fighting. Can you get George to vacate your dorm room?" she asked.

"I think so," I replied. She smiled again.

Now I smiled, then kissed her softly and took her by the hand to the lifter.

+ + +

I was able to get George Layton out of my bunk for the night, so I would owe him one. Natalie and I spent the night together making love, in the very real sense of the word. I finally fell asleep with her cradled in my arms, as much of her flesh pressed against mine as we both could manage. I wanted to remember her; her smell, touch, taste. It could be months before we saw each other again. Or years.

When I woke up she was already gone, back to her own room. There was a simple note stuck on my mirror:

> Peter,
> *Please forgive me for leaving this way. I think it's better for us both if we don't try to see each other again after today until we find a way to meet as friends, however long from now that might be. Take care, and be safe.*
>
> *I love you,*
> *Natalie*

And with that the first love affair of my life was over. I was taken aback by the finality of it. I had thought she would need me every moment until her departure time came. But I found myself admiring her strength to walk away of her own accord. Again I had underestimated her. I hung my head and sighed, then gave in and lay back down on my bed, pulling the sheets and covers back over my head, begging for my alarm not to go off.

+ + +

But go off it did, at precisely 0600. I showered quickly and made my way down to the Landing Deck. As I arrived, I gathered my EVA suit and helmet from the quartermaster and then was greeted by *Starbound*'s Earth Historian, Serosian, a tall dark-haired man who had served as my mentor during my time here at the Lightship Academy. He shook my hand as I came up.

"Good luck today, Peter. Almost done," he said with a smile. The Historians were known for their ruthless adherence to rules on sharing information with the developing star systems of the Union and rarely did I find them friendly or outgoing. Serosian was the uncommon exception to that rule.

"Almost done with training," I agreed. "But some other things have already ended," I said with a nod toward my repair pod. Natalie was already suited and inside our two-person maintenance craft, waiting for me. Serosian turned her way and then back to me with a look of sympathy on his face.

"Not all endings can be good endings, Peter," he said.

"This one is tougher than most," I replied. He smiled a bit.

"There will be other girls for a young man of your standing," he said. I thought about that. It didn't comfort me.

"I'm sure you're right. But for now there's only the one girl for me, and she's being sent away," I said.

Serosian shrugged. "I know this was Admiral Wesley's doing, but I hope in time you'll see it's for the best."

I just shook my head at that, then I raised my suit and helmet. "I've got to get in my gear," I said.

He nodded. "We'll talk again later. And be careful out there today, Peter. Don't let your emotions get in the way of doing your job."

"I'll try not to," I said, and with that he was gone and I got into my EVA suit.

Because I was doing the EVAs and Natalie was doing the piloting, we would be separated by an environmental barrier and we could only communicate by com. Natalie had a skin-tight survival suit, designed for non-EVA work inside a ship while mine was quite a bit bulkier and used for extended missions outside the ship. After passing flight check I got into my side of our repair pod and activated my com.

"Ready when you are, Nat," I said.

There was a pause, and then she said, "Can we keep it as professional as possible today, please?"

That pissed me off. "Of course, *Lieutenant*," I said sarcastically. "You've made your wishes clear in that regard, in more ways than one, and I will try and adhere to them."

"Good," she said, then fired up our pod and we queued up for liftoff. A few minutes later and we were well on our way out to the ansible ring near High Station Candle. The flight took us nearly three hours, which passed in silence. I even turned my com off and slept. Her job, after all, was flying the repair pod.

Mine didn't start until we had something to repair.

I was sound asleep when she used the priority override to wake me up. "We're here," she said loudly into my com. I looked up and checked my telemetry. We were four hundred meters from the first ansible on our list.

"You couldn't get us any closer than that?" I said, grumpy after being wakened from a sound sleep.

"It's within the guidelines," she snapped back.

"You know how crappy I am with free EVAs," I said back. It was true, free-floating EVAs, maneuvering with cone jets using small bursts of propellant, wasn't one of my specialties.

I ran the repair scan and everything came out nominal, so my only job was to swap out the data card and then recalibrate the longwave receptor nodes, but those were things that had to be done from the ansible itself. I collected the new data card and the key codes for the calibration, then started venting my cabin pressure. When the pressure hit zero I reached for the hatch release.

"Popping the hatch in 5… 4… 3…"

"No need to be so dramatic, Lieutenant," came Natalie's voice in my ear, so I shut up and just popped the thing before releasing my restraint straps.

"Anything we need at the grocery store, honey?" I said as I rose out of the pod. That got no response. She was really pissing me off now.

I aligned myself with the ansible and set my navigation mark.

"Don't blow your first burst, it's the most important," came her unwelcome advice in my ear. "And you know your propensity for getting too excited about things."

I tried to ignore that barb. "It will be easier to concentrate without you nagging in my ear," I said back, then hit the pre-calibrated jet burst. Within about a hundred meters it was clear I was off course.

"You need to correct," she said in my ear.

"I'm aware," I replied. "It wouldn't have been a problem if you could have got us closer." I re-ran my flight path and took the suit's recommended correction of a .45 second microburst from the right cone jet only. I loaded the correction and hit it. My course changed very subtly as I watched, a passenger on a very slow guided missile.

"Now you've over-corrected," came my ever-present critic's voice.

"I took the suit guide's recommended action," I snapped back.

"Yes, but you waited too long to execute. Next time don't hesitate. I'll feed the fix directly into your suit jet controls." She did, and now I was even more the passenger and my ego was bruised.

Once I was at the ansible, I started in on the recalibration work for the longwave receptor nodes. I entered in the key codes on the LED plasma panel and the system slowly chugged through its protocols, aligning itself with the other ansibles both up and down the line of communication. Then I started in on the data card. It was hard to get to and I struggled with my tools, trying to get the cover plate off, securing it to the ansible's hull, and then picking out the card that needed replacing. It took time, almost forty minutes, but I got it done.

"Coming home," I said, then reset my course back to the pod and headed back. Going home was easier than coming out, and I felt myself slowly getting the hang of it. Space-borne EVAs were never going to be my thing, but I at least owed it my full effort.

We proceeded from there to our second and then our third assignment, and each one went better than the previous one. Just one more to go, but we'd been out almost seven hours and we were both tired. Tired enough for the walls to come down, emotionally at least, if not the very solid physical barrier between our two compartments inside the pod.

"Just one more and you'll be rid of me," I said as we were about halfway to ansible number 4.

"Don't be stupid. I don't want to be rid of you," Natalie said.

"You could have fooled me."

She sighed. "I'm not blaming you for things, Peter. I just… I just want to protect myself. Emotionally."

"I understand that."

"There are other reasons. Things we need to discuss before I leave," she said in a much softer tone. That intrigued me.

"Do we have time to talk about them right now?" I asked.

She stayed silent for a moment, then, "Probably not. Fifteen minutes to the last ansible. We should stay focused on work. We'll talk on the trip home. We'll have plenty of time then."

"Okay," I said, but now my mind was spinning with thoughts of what other "things" we needed to discuss besides her assignment to a ship other than *Starbound*.

Presently we pulled up to the last ansible, but it looked like it was completely out of commission. It was still in place, but dark, and I got no readings on my scan of its systems.

"Well, shit, we're going to have to go in and lock on, I think. The power's out. We may need the pod's power to jump-start the ansible back up," I said.

"Got it," she replied, and then began the very delicate maneuver of piloting the repair pod to inside a meter of the ansible before locking onto the thing with the pod's clamps. "Locked down," she said after about ten minutes of difficult maneuvering. "Check your jet-fuel reserve before you go out."

"I've got enough, I think. Besides, we are locked on to the thing," I said.

"Always overconfident," she said, but I ignored her. I just wanted this mission to be over.

I emptied the environment from my side of the cabin and made my way out of the hatch again, using just a small burst of the jets to get clear. I managed to grab one of the EVA handles on the ansible pretty easily and then I made my way hand-over-hand to the control panel.

"I'm not an electrician, but this puppy looks dead to me," I said. I proceeded to activate my monitoring tool and scanned the whole unit. There was residual power in some of the components but the backup batteries were cold, indicating it had been offline for a while. The system was double-redundant though, like most space systems, meaning the ansible's failure wouldn't have been noticed by the overall system until we conducted our maintenance mission. I called up the repair procedure and it had me removing the power system panel and attempting a reboot. That took almost fifteen minutes and the reboot attempt was a no-go.

"You're going to have to extend me the power cord to re-fire this thing," I said.

"Acknowledged. Is there a matching plugin on the ansible?" I looked for a minute, and found it in a very inconvenient place.

"There is, but whoever designed this power panel never expected anyone to have to use it, based on its location. Complete crap design," I said. Natalie extended the power cord out and I had to go and retrieve it, no easy task, and I was using up more and more of my cone jet propellant sliding back and forth.

"You've only got twenty-two minutes of environment left in that suit," she said in my ear as I struggled to turn myself upside down and invert my position relative to the pod. "If you can't get the repair done in that time, you'll have to come back in and reload." That could take another thirty minutes, and I didn't want to waste that time.

"Understood. It should be doable," I said as I struggled with the cord, getting it wrapped around my arm and stuck under my shoulder before I finally got the thing in my left hand, stretching it out towards the ansible plugin. "Cripes, it's a dozen centimeters too short," I said.

"Are you sure? The repair kit says it should reach from this position."

"Well, since my arm is fully extended and the cord is taut, then yes, I'm pretty damn sure it's not long enough," I snapped.

"Maybe your arms are too short," she deadpanned.

"I think that's a conversation for another time," I said.

"Try again," she pushed me, without any further comments about my physical shortcomings. I stretched it again and felt it give a little, the connectors finally clicking together. As soon as I let go though, the connection broke.

"Shit. I'm going to have to hold this thing while you charge the line. It won't stay connected on its own," I said.

"Are you sure?"

"Yes, I'm sure!" I yelled. We were under pressure now, for time, environment, everything. "Sorry. Yes, I'm sure I'm going to have to hold it while you run power through the damn line."

"That's against the regs."

"Natalie…" I heard her sigh in my com.

"All right, but once the ansible is running you let go," she said.

"Agreed."

I waited as she ran through the power protocols, then extended my arm one more time until the connectors clicked.

"Ready here," I said.

"Okay. Power coming through the line in 3… 2… 1…"

I wasn't sure what happened next. There was a bright spark and I couldn't see for a few seconds. By the time I got my bearings all I could be sure of was that I wasn't attached to the ansible anymore. I looked out my visor and all I could see was that the ansible and pod were passing frequently in and out of my visor's line of sight, and growing more distant with each pass.

I was spinning away in free space.

I tried to determine the axis of my rotation, and as best I could I took a guess and fired a series of short bursts from my left cone jet. This had the desired effect of slowing down my spin rate but left me with essentially no propellant left in my suit. I eventually got my rotation stopped so that the ansible and pod were constantly in my line of sight.

I checked my com but it was dead, as were my environmental controls and all the suit's systems. Clearly I'd taken a jolt from the electrical system on board the ansible, possibly a spark from one of the internal components that stored energy. It wouldn't have taken much to create a feedback loop through the line that blew me off into space, but as I'd said, I was no electrician.

Then I looked up and I saw something else, something which disturbed me a lot. A blue-suited figure was floating free from the repair pod and coming right for me.

I watched as Natalie approached, maneuvering toward me much more skillfully than I could have done. Within a few minutes, she had me wrapped in her arms. I watched as she plugged in an auxiliary power line to my suit.

"Can you hear me?" she said into my now-functioning com.

"Yes," I said. "You can't stay out here in that skin suit. You won't last twenty minutes. It's not built for extended EVAs."

"I know that. And I used six minutes getting to you." She adjusted my arm panel, checking my vitals and environment. "Christ," she said. "You've got a leak somewhere." We both struggled to hold on to each other as we looked for the leak, and then found it readily enough. There was a burn hole on the outside of my left forearm. "That short knocked out everything in the pod, Peter. It's rebooting, but it will take twenty minutes to come back online."

"And you have less than fourteen minutes in that suit," I said. She turned my arm monitor panel to me so I could see it.

"At the rate you're losing air and heat, you've barely got six," she said.

"No chance of making it back to the pod?" She shook her head.

"I used almost all my propellant getting to you, and yours is nearly gone, too. We don't have enough to get back," she said.

"So we're going to die out here," I said. She said nothing to that, just looked at me through her visor.

"I managed to get off a distress call through my autonomous suit com, but without the longwave boost from the pod I doubt anyone heard it," she said. We stayed silent for a few moments, just holding each other.

"Maybe we should have that conversation we were going to have on the trip home now," I said. Maybe I just wanted to talk about something, anything, besides the fact that I was most probably going to die in my girlfriend's arms in a few minutes, and then she would die after me.

"Jesus, Peter," she said, looking away from me.

"Just tell me, Natalie." I could feel my mind beginning to fade, and I was starting to get very cold. I tried to focus on her face, but it was getting harder to see her. My visor was fogging up.

"There was another reason I wanted to switch assignments from *Starbound*," she said.

"Tell me."

There was a long pause, and I felt my life ebbing away. It was so damn cold...

"I'm pregnant, Peter. I'm going to have our baby. That trip we took to the Tasman Islands between semesters, I forgot to take my pregnancy repressors," she said.

I willed myself out of the fog, fighting hard for my life. To get back to her...

"I worried about that. I... I didn't take mine... either."

"Don't talk, just listen," I heard her say. "I didn't want to burden you, for you to feel obligated to stay with me. You had so much in front of you..." My eyes were closed now. All I could do was mumble some words, but I wanted to touch her, to hold her one last time, but we were separated by the damned suits, and the cold vacuum of space.

"I love you, Peter. I always will," I heard her say through tears and sobbing. And then everything was dark around me, I couldn't hear her voice anymore... and it was so cold...

+ + +

When I woke up for the third time, the doctors told me that I'd been in an induced coma for nine days and that I'd almost died. This time the information stuck. In some ways, I wished I had died. Serosian came to see me the second day, and I demanded to be let out of the hospital. It was him who had rescued both Natalie and me, in a small Downship used for diplomatic missions. Turned out he'd been tracking me, just in case. Something about me being "a valuable asset to the Union," or some such crap. Whatever. It didn't comfort me, at all.

Natalie, well, Natalie was gone off to Carinthia and her assignment on H.M.S. *Impulse*. She left me a small handwritten note stating that our child had been put in stasis pending adoption by a couple in New Auckland. I wouldn't be allowed to know their names, or anything more about them. I guessed it was the right choice, her choice, but it hurt me badly.

After a day out of the hospital Serosian came to see me again in my new stateroom on High Station, a serious upgrade over my Academy lodgings. The privileges of being a junior officer, I guessed.

"And how is our first Lightship Academy valedictorian?" he asked, sitting across from me.

I shrugged. "As well as can be expected, I suppose," I replied. "This has been quite an unpleasant ride for me. I missed all our Academy celebrations, the parties, seeing my friends, and I'm on forced leave for three more days before I can report to *Starbound*."

"And you've lost your girl."

I looked up at him. "Yes. That, and… other things."

Serosian leaned forward. "That's part of why I'm here, Peter. Natalie left me a note, too. A request, really. And I'm here to fulfill that request," he said.

"I don't know what you mean."

He stood up. "Get dressed, Lieutenant. I have something to show you," he said.

I did, and we went back down to the medical bay. Several medical technicians nodded to us as we passed, Serosian speaking softly to them. Eventually he led me into a darkened room where we both sat down and the thick soundproof door was quietly shut behind us. He leaned over to me and spoke in a whisper.

"Just listen," he said, and I did. As the room grew quieter I realized I could hear *something*, but not quite make out what it was. Then it dawned on me.

A heartbeat.

Slowly a light on the wall came up, and I could ever so faintly see a small object in extremely dim blue-green light floating in the dark. I stood up to get a better look. "Is this—" I whispered.

"This is your child, Peter. She's in stasis right now, growing very slowly, but eventually she'll be accelerated to full term and her adoptive parents will take her home."

"She?" I asked. Serosian nodded.

"You have a daughter," he said.

A tear came to my eye. "But only for a little while," I said. "Can I touch her?"

Serosian nodded. "That's what this chamber is for, to simulate the touch of a parent on a mother's womb. Go ahead," he said.

I went to the wall and touched the amniotic sack. It flexed and gave freely, so I put my arms around my daughter, for what I was sure would be the only time.

And I cried.

+ + +

Once more I stood in the observation lounge on High Station, staring out at the stars and wondering what might have been between Natalie and me. Serosian's parting words still hung in my memory.

"You still have *Starbound* to look forward to, Peter, and my guess is you'll have plenty of adventures ahead of you. This is just the beginning," he had said. I hoped that was true, because it felt like the end of something very big and very important in my life, and I hoped the next chapter would end with me being happier than I was now.

I thought of Natalie, and our love, one last time, and then I vowed to put it out of my mind and get myself ready for the job ahead.

I had a feeling that the Union Navy was going to need me to be prepared.

In 1995 Catherine Asaro's popular Skolian Empire series began in Primary Inversion *with a sort of intergalactic* Romeo and Juliet *story. Since then, many books and stories have followed. The author herself introduces this next chapter: "The choice made by the brothers in the 'Wages of Honor' plays a role in several of my books about the Ruby Dynasty. It features in* The Radiant Seas *after Soz becomes Imperator and must take the Radiance Fleet into the largest battles ever faced by the Skolian Imperialate. She has a decision to make, one that will affect the lives of millions, even billions of people. Sitting in the darkness of her quarters on the flagship of the fleet, she contacts her father during the last moments before all interstellar communications fail. She asks him who he thinks made the right decision in the War of the Clans, Eldrin or Althor. Her father tells her that he doesn't know, but that both of her brothers acted with honor. The decision Soz finally makes changes the course of an interstellar war. I've wanted to write this story for a long time, so when Bryan asked me if I would contribute a Skolian story to the anthology, I knew the time had come to put it into words."*

THE WAGES OF HONOR

CATHERINE ASARO

I. CHILD OF THE CATHEDRAL

Eldrin gripped the hilt of his great sword with both hands and swung the weapon in a wide arc. Light slanted through the Stained Glass Forest, dappling him with color while he practiced. Only two other sounds broke the drowsing silence of late afternoon, the chirp of prism-crickets and the rumble of a transport taking off from the tiny, distant starport. He circled his blade around and around, savoring the strain on his muscles. At sixteen years of age, he enjoyed the exertion; it created a hypnotic sense of motion that almost let him forget why he had come here. If only he could empty his mind and escape his thoughts. They threatened to spiral out of control, once again dropping him into the ice of his memories.

The ice of death.

No! He swung the sword faster, striving for an exhaustion that would blanket his mind. If only the serenity here could soothe him. The Stained Glass Forest reminded him of the library in his home, with its windows designed in mosaics of colored glass. He couldn't read the books, not even a few words, but he loved that room, the way sunlight pouring through the windows cast patterns of colored light across the floor. Here in the forest, the trees and their branches were poles of glasswood, each tree a single color: red, blue, green, or gold. Spheres of the same colors hung from the branches, some small enough to fit in the palm of his hand, others ten times that size. The two suns of the planet Lyshriol were setting behind the trees, the large amber sphere of Valdor partially eclipsed by Aldan's smaller gold orb. In their light, the forest glowed like a living cathedral of stained-glass windows.

Eldrin paused and poked his blade into a sphere above his head. It popped, showering him with glitter, the pollen that would someday grow more trees. He laughed, such a rare sound nowadays, and brushed the pollen off his loose shirt. He sang a few lines of an aria he had been composing, and the music soothed the ragged edges of his thoughts.

A voice rumbled behind him. "You fighting bubbles now?"

Eldrin looked around to see his brother Althor a few paces away, dressed in trousers and a dark shirt. He was holding his own great sword, the blade resting casually against his shoulder. Although only fourteen, two years younger than Eldrin, Althor already stood taller than him, taller indeed than any man in their village. His shoulders were broad, his muscles developed and large, and he was still growing. The light glinted on his curls, making him look even more like their mother, with the same metallic gold tinge to his skin and hair.

"Where did you come from?" Eldrin didn't want company; he had come out here to be alone.

Althor walked over to him. "I thought we were going to practice."

Damn, he had forgotten. He almost told Althor he didn't feel like it, but he didn't want to look weak to his "little" brother. So he said, "All right."

They faced each other, preparing, and began their practice. Eldrin swung at Althor with a fast cut, a move his other sparring partners almost never managed to counter. Althor easily parried and came at him from the other side, stopping his sword just short of Eldrin's hip. They swung again and again, and Althor countered him every time. Often he didn't even use two hands to hold the hilt, despite his weapon being a two-handed sword. Finally he did use both fists so he could swing with even more power. Their blades clanged and the strike sent Eldrin's sword flying out of his hand.

"Hah!" Althor grinned at him.

Eldrin nodded to his brother. "Well done." What else could he say? Often when Althor beat him, his anger surged, but today he just felt tired; not the fatigue of a good practice, but a deeper exhaustion that had nothing to do with his body. Althor wouldn't understand; he could practice all day, then go up to his bedroom and study quantum physics.

Althor was watching him. "Maybe we should practice later."

"All right." Eldrin retrieved his sword. Althor's intrusion had shattered his attempt to find peace, and he felt as if he would explode. He knew his brother hadn't meant to trespass; he only sought the closeness they had known in their youth. Althor had no idea of the ice within him, the frozen places where Eldrin died a little more each day.

✦ ✦ ✦

"Enough!" Eldrin swung his sword in a huge arc and slammed the blade into a console. The station shattered, spraying white shards of luminex up into the air. Designed from smart material that could alter its structure, the shards softened their jagged edges as they fell so they wouldn't tear apart whatever they hit—not even him, who deserved their excoriation.

"Eldrin, stop!" Tomas, his teacher, stared at him from the other side of the console. Bits of glowing debris swirled around him, a startling contrast to his dark hair and eyes. "This is a school. Your weapons have no place here."

"It's a lie!" Eldrin could no longer hold back his endlessly circling thoughts. When he had come in from practice, drenched with sweat, Tomas had simply offered him a book. And Eldrin had snapped.

Once, not so long ago, Eldrin had wanted to learn, yearned for knowledge so much that it burned within him even though he couldn't read even simple sentences. Last year, incredibly, for a few weeks, the written word had almost started to make sense, finally, after more than a decade of his struggling to learn. None of that mattered any more. It was too late. He didn't deserve the light of knowledge.

Today Tomas stood his ground, never flinching, but Eldrin knew him too well to deny the truth. His teacher, the mentor he had always admired, feared he was about to die. Eldrin recognized the dread in his eyes. He had known it himself last year when he fought at his father's side in the War of Clans. Three times in that war, Eldrin had killed another human being.

The memories crowded in on him, the chaos of battle, the pain, the *death*, until he thought he would crack under their onslaught. Desperate, he slashed at the air, but he misjudged the swing and his sword hit the wall, the blade vibrating as cracks splintered up to the ceiling.

"Don't!" The woman's shout came from behind him.

Eldrin spun around, raising his weapon. His mother, Roca Skolia, stood in the archway of the classroom, her windblown hair tousled across her shoulders, her blue leggings and tunic glowing in the sunlight slanting through the doorway. She was gold: her hair, her skin, even her eyelashes. She did truly resemble the goddess everyone in Dalvador believed her to be, impossibly beautiful, never aging, but Eldrin knew the truth. His mother was human, very human, and she could hurt just as deeply as anyone.

He lowered his sword. Behind him, Tomas exhaled.

"Saints almighty," his mother said. "What are you doing?"

Eldrin walked to her. She was a tall woman, but he looked down at her now, no longer the small child who had curled in the shelter of her arms. He had no answers. The days when she could fix his hurts had ended long ago. That child was lost, and a monster lived in his place, a frozen man who didn't deserve her love. He took a breath, wanting to speak, to reach out to her, but no words came. They were trapped within him. He knew only that he couldn't let her see him this way.

Eldrin walked out of the school.

✦ ✦ ✦

Roca stared at Tomas. "Are you all right?" She had to go after Eldrin, but first she had to make sure her son hadn't harmed his teacher.

Tomas came over to her. "I can't have him back in my school."

"Has he threatened you before?" She had known Tomas for years, since she and her husband had brought him here to teach their children—first Eldrin and then the others, ten in all now. She had never seen him look so pale.

"Not overtly." He hesitated. "Councilor, I don't want to overstep."

Roca spoke quietly. "I'm the Foreign Affairs Councilor only

when I go offworld to sit in the Imperialate Assembly. That is separate from my life here. You should feel free to talk to me about any of the children."

Tomas pushed his hand through his hair. "I kept hoping I could get through to him. He was making progress. He wants to learn, I'm sure of it, even if he says he doesn't care." His optimism faded. "But last year, after he came back from that war, everything had changed. He's closed to me."

Roca understood. She was losing Eldrin, and she didn't know how to reach him.

A voice rumbled. "Hoshma, what's wrong?"

She turned with a start to see Althor looming behind her.

"What's happened?" he asked.

Maybe he knew what had set off his brother. "Did you and Eldrin fight again?"

"No." Althor paused. "We did practice. It was fine, though. Why? Did he say something?"

"Not exactly. It's just—he's so angry."

"You're shaking." Althor watched her with concern. "Did he hurt you?"

"Well, no, of course not." What did you tell a boy when the older brother he had idolized was becoming someone none of them recognized?

Last year, when Eldrin had come home with his father from the War of the Clans, the people in Dalvador had greeted him as a shining hero. They knew nothing about the guilt Roca feared was destroying her oldest son.

✦ ✦ ✦

Althor stood at the window in his bedroom and watched the courtyard two stories below, an open area paved with blue flagstones. The sun shone in the clear air and on the blue turreted roofs of the village beyond the castle walls. Eldrin was in the courtyard playing jump-and-block with a youth from the village, a sturdy blacksmith who also trained in their father's army. Eldrin spent so much time outside that the sun had bleached his red hair with streaks of gold. The locks swung around his face as he dodged his opponent.

The smith did his best, but he didn't have the skill to beat Eldrin. No one did except Althor. Although Eldrin hid how he felt, Althor knew their practices upset him. Lately Althor bested him all the time, both at sports and weapons practice. Althor had begun to fear he would injure his sparring partners because he couldn't control his strength, which seemed to increase more every day. He had no wish to cause Eldrin pain, either physical or emotional. Maybe it was better if they quit practicing. Although Althor would miss spending time with his brother, he otherwise preferred the virtual war games he played on the interstellar meshes.

Several girls from the village were sitting on the wall of the courtyard, watching the game. They smiled or blushed whenever Eldrin glanced their way. They had started doing the same to Althor three years ago. People had told him he looked like a man even back then. The girls flirted. Althor hadn't cared, but it didn't matter. Eldrin would never forgive him for attracting the interest of a girl Eldrin had liked.

These days, Althor felt heavy all the time. He weighed too much for this planet. He had seen the images of his mother's father, a huge man over two meters tall. Someday Althor would be like him, or so everyone claimed. Althor had lived his entire life on Lyshriol, with its pretty landscapes and vicious wars, but he had to go soon. He wasn't like Eldrin, perfectly suited to this world. Althor wanted to pilot star fighters, not wield a sword.

Eldrin had everything a man needed to succeed here, the warrior who had become a hero. He liked this life, farming, living close to the land. He couldn't have cared less about the universe beyond Lyshriol. Eldrin even looked like a taller version of their sire, handsome in the way of the Lyshrioli people. Althor knew he could never live up to his older brother, the son their father wanted.

In the courtyard below, Eldrin rolled the smith over his hip, using an advanced throw. When the man hit the ground too hard and lay still, Eldrin froze, breathing heavily. Then he offered his hand. The smith took it, climbing to his feet, and bowed to Eldrin, acknowledging his win.

Althor knew why his brother had frozen for that instant. He feared he had injured the smith. Eldrin never wanted to cause pain. He liked to practice, loved it even, but he hated life-or-death battle. He empathized too strongly with the people he fought. Althor understood. They both shared that trait, inherited from their parents. They learned to block the moods of other people, but it was harder for Eldrin. He wouldn't even harm the gauzy shimmerflies that wandered into the house. He would never acknowledge that trait, not on a world where a man's worth was determined by his prowess in combat. What warrior preferred to sing rather than fight?

It didn't affect Althor the same way, for the battles he fought were all games played on the offworld meshes. His opponents were strewn across the stars, their interactions facilitated by a technology so advanced, his people had learned to surmount even the barriers of light speed. It gave him a layer of emotional protection that Eldrin would never know.

"You fight so hard, my brother," Althor said softly. "What demons are you trying to defeat?"

+ + +

"He's not fine!" Roca stared at her husband. "Damn it, Eldri, he almost ran Tomas through with that blasted sword you gave him."

Her husband, Eldrinson Valdoria, was standing in front of the window alcove of their bedroom, his body silhouetted against the tall glass panes. Beyond him, the view showed the plains of Dalvador rippling in the breeze. Supple reeds covered them like an ocean, each tipped by a bubble-pod. When the pods burst, they laid a sparkling sheen of pollen over the land, as if this were a place of fairytales instead of an atavistic land where warriors hacked each other to pieces with blades.

"He wouldn't hurt his teacher." Eldrinson was dressed simply today, like a farmer rather than a war leader, with a rough shirt and trousers. His wine-red locks brushed his ears, so much like their son's hair. "Tomas is like a member of the family."

"You didn't see what happened." Roca went over to him, standing at his height, meeting his gaze. "I should have refused to let Eldrin ride with you in the War of Clans."

"You did refuse." He spoke quietly. "You can't make us change what we are."

"He was too young."

"Eldrin is a man, Roca, not a child." He rubbed his neck as if the muscles ached. "I think, yes, it was hard for him. None of us wants to go to war. But he will be stronger for this."

"No. He won't." She didn't know how to make him see. "It's destroying him. It isn't just the war. It's everything, his confusion, his frustration that he can't learn what comes so easily to his siblings. If we don't find a way to help him, something inside him is going to break." She gave word to one of her greatest fears. "What if he loses control when he and Althor are fighting and one of them stabs the other? Those swords can be fatal."

"They would never do that!" He exhaled. "Yes, I know, they don't get along so well lately. But their bond as brothers is as strong as any I've ever seen. They will outgrow this rivalry."

"It isn't rivalry. It goes deeper." Somewhere distant, a man sang a haunting melody in a minor key. It had to be Eldrin; none of their other children had such a magnificent classical voice.

"They're so different," she said. "They don't understand each other."

"They'll work it out. They're good boys, Roca."

Her voice caught. "Yes. They are. But you don't see? Eldrin is dying inside."

"What help can you bring?" His face creased in lines that hadn't been there a few years ago. "Some offworld intruder who wants to mold him into a stranger? No. I won't do that to Eldrin. It goes against all that he knows here."

She forced out the words neither of them wanted to hear. "That's why he needs to leave. He has to get away from the contradictions of this life, to go someplace where they can help him learn to read, help him take pleasure in knowledge instead of endless frustration. And he needs someone who can help him heal; a psychiatrist. A doctor for the mind."

"No!" He stepped back from her. "You won't send him away."

Softly she said, "I don't want him to go, either. But we need to consider it."

"Will you send me away too?" After so many years, he no longer tried to hide his pain from her. "I will never learn to read either, Roca. I will never understand your physics, your histories, your mesh systems. Will you send me to specialists who dissect my mind and seek to change me into what I am not?"

"You are a miracle." She struggled to find the words for this dangerous ground they so rarely trod. "You and your people, you don't need the written word. Your minds are unique. You hold your knowledge, your histories, your identity in your phenomenal memories and your songs. I love you exactly the way you are." Roca willed him to understand. "But our son is half you and half me, and his two halves are breaking him apart. You feel joy in your life. Eldrin doesn't."

He lifted his hand, motioning as if to encompass all of Dalvador.

"The changes you have brought to my people, these things you call electricity, fiber optics, superconductors, the orbital defense system that guards our world, the medicine that heals my people—I have never understood them. Before your people rediscovered us, we had no memory of being a lost colony from an interstellar civilization. We're farmers, Roca. Not technocrats. We don't live this way because that is the only life we know. We do it because this is what we *are*." He shook his head. "We've been here so long, cut off from the rest of humanity, we've changed. Or I don't know, maybe the original settlers remade themselves using this thing you call genetic engineering. All I know is that we aren't like you. If you try to force us into that mold, it will destroy us."

Even now, did that fear haunt him? She had spent decades trying to show him otherwise, but nothing could erase their huge differences. Their son's refusal to take advanced technology into battle had been, for Roca, the breaking point. Neither Eldrin nor his father understood; they considered it a point of honor. A warrior engaged his enemy in a fair fight. For Eldrin to use the advances of his mother's people would be dishonorable, the height of cowardice. Roca didn't give a damn about that honor. She wanted her husband and children to live. Period.

And yet—when it came to the final moment, what could she have done? By the laws here, Eldrin was an adult at sixteen, able to make his own decisions. Imperialate law still considered him a child, but Eldrin would never have forgiven her if she denied him what he considered a man's path of honor. She couldn't stop him any more than she could someday stop Althor from going offworld to fight in an interstellar war with every advance their star-spanning culture could offer. Nor was it only Althor; their daughter Soz already showed signs of the military brilliance that would take her away from this pastoral land into the violence of an interstellar conflict unimaginable on this world. Was Eldrin's choice truly that different? In the end, she had watched him ride away to battle, a decision she had regretted ever since.

A tear gathered in her eye. "You know I have never forced my culture on yours."

His voice softened. "Yes. It is true. You have brought your ways gently. These changes, they never disrupt, they only enhance our lives. And I am grateful." He took a deep breath. "But how long before the workings of your universe break through that protection like huge cogs and grind up my culture in their relentless march of 'progress?'"

She rubbed the heel of her hand across her cheek, smearing away the tear. "Would you stop Eldrin from leaving even if it's better for him to go? If he stays here, we may lose him forever."

For a moment he didn't answer. Then he stepped forward and pulled her into his arms, laying his head against hers. "Ai, Rocalisa," he murmured. "I cannot bear to think of him going."

"Nor can I." She held him close, her voice barely audible. "But I think we must."

His breath stirred her hair. It was a long time before he whispered, "I know."

✦ ✦ ✦

Eldrin stood at the edge of the forest and gazed across the plains to the town of Dalvador. His family's home stood on the edge of the village. Crenellated walls surrounded the house, with turreted guard towers at each corner, all of it pale blue stone. It was a castle, really, though too small to amount to much. It provided a fortress that could protect people from the village during crises. Today the gates stood open, guarded by invisible security systems.

Round, white-washed houses clustered in the village, their roofs like upside-down tulips, either violet or blue. Eldrin had never heard of "flowers" before Tomas told him about roses and tiger lilies. When Eldrin asked his console for images, it showed him the astonishing diversity of life among the terraformed worlds of human-settled space. Flowers weren't as lovely, though, as the Dalvador Plains. Anyone walking through the shimmering reeds left a trail of tiny orbs and glittering pollen floating in their wake. A pretty effect, but also vital to the protection of Dalvador, which rose like an island in the ocean of reeds. Soldiers were hard-pressed to move in secrecy when the plains so easily betrayed their location.

Of course, the orbital positioning system could spy anywhere on the planet. Last year, his mother had found a way to let his father know that an army was gathering in secret, ready to restart the Clan Wars. She hadn't told him, only suggested a new route the scouts might ride during their patrols. That night, they had come upon the hidden army. Eldrin doubted his father realized what his mother had done, using the technology of her people to give him an edge that he never would have accepted, had he known. It conflicted Eldrin all the more because if she hadn't warned them, the battle could have ended in defeat instead of the victory they had won.

Although Eldrin couldn't read about life on other worlds, he listened voraciously when his console narrated his lessons in the privacy of his bedroom. Most animals fought and killed on instinct. Only humans developed codes of warfare. As Eldrin saw it, their ability to act with honor was what set humans apart from unthinking predators. To act without honor diminished their humanity. If he fought using advanced technology, it violated the codes of fair combat. And yet... without the warning his mother had given them, more people would have died. He couldn't reconcile the conflicted halves of his moral code. One of his worst arguments with Althor had been two years ago, a debate that culminated with his brother calling it "unmitigated idiocy" to hold "misplaced honor" above the advantage of technology. Eldrin didn't know which had angered him more, that Althor called him an idiot for the principles he valued or that his then twelve-year-old brother used the word "unmitigated," which Eldrin had never even heard before then, let alone understood.

Fine. He understood perfectly well now the unmitigated nature of his stupidity. He loved his brother, but he hated what Althor represented. Why the hell did he have to choose between honor and advantage? He had killed three people last year, two with his sword and one with his bare hands. He would live with that guilt for the rest of his life, knowing he had taken them from their families, their lives, their dreams. Were his mother's people better somehow, that with their star-spanning technology, they could kill millions instead of three? This was moral?

Eldrin closed his eyes. Breezes blew across his face, carrying the scent of the plains, yet even that sweetness couldn't soothe him. He had no sanctuary. Only the folk music of Dalvador helped. It offered simple melodies, the minor creations of a minor people on a minor world that had no real effect in the greater scheme of interstellar civilization. Limited it might be, but it gave him solace against the agony of his thoughts. Lifting his head, he took a deep breath.

And he sang.

+ + +

Althor straightened up, his back aching. His father's farm spread out across the plains, with Dalvador to the south and the Stained Glass Forest to the north. He enjoyed working here, unlike many of his other chores. He liked the physical labor. Today he harvested bubbles: small yellow ones with fruity pulp inside, pale and tart; long bubbles, crunchy, with flavor that burst on your tongue; translucent bubbles that spilled nectar when cut open. He didn't understand how people on other worlds ate. Their food had no constancy. Some of it was plant, some animal, some this, some that. How did they even know what to call food? He had to admit, though, that time he had eaten a prime rib steak, he hadn't minded. Not at all. Damn, that had tasted good.

Regardless, he wanted to be done with his work. He had a gaming session tonight with his JagWars team. His friends. He had far more of them on the interstellar mesh than here in the village. It gave him less privacy, though. Imperialate Space Command monitored the kids who played mesh games. Althor had realized it when military academies started sending him recruiting messages every time his team won a competition.

Music drifted over the plains. He paused, holding his scythe in one hand and a cluster of stalks in the other. All around him, people were stopping their work to listen, a woman in a pale tunic tilting her head to one side, a man with graying hair gazing toward the Stained Glass Forest, a child smiling as she stopped loading bubbles into her basket. The song floated on the air, incomparably beautiful. Althor closed his eyes, letting it wash over him. The melody spiraled in a baritone aria, then soared into a man's tenor range. A chill went through him. Yes, he knew that song. For all that he had never understood Eldrin, he stood in awe of his brother's voice.

Their friends knew only that they liked to hear Eldrin sing. He was the firstborn heir to the Bard, so it was fortunate he had a good voice. Althor saw what they didn't understand. The origins of the human settlement on Lyshriol had been lost after the fall of the Ruby Empire. By the time his mother's people regained star travel and found their ancient colonies, the settlement here had lost most of its technology. No one knew why the people on Lyshriol had neither written language nor the ability to learn one. However, the Memories, those women who studied their entire lives to preserve the knowledge of Dalvador, remembered their more recent history and culture with astonishing recall. They kept Dalvador in their minds—and the Bard sang their memories for his people.

Althor's family had been singers for as long as anyone remembered. Geneticists may have even engineered their ancestors for their incredible voices. Whatever the origins of that gift, Eldrin had inherited its full span. He had sung all his life, practicing without even thinking about it. His five-octave range outclassed even the most famous singers on the mesh. The only person Althor knew who sang better was their father. Neither he nor Eldrin seemed to comprehend their talent. They shrugged at the thought. The father was the Bard. Eldrin was his heir. Of course they could sing.

The people of Dalvador were fortunate Eldrin had been born first, because Althor knew he couldn't sing worth spit. He couldn't even figure out how you knew if you hit the right notes. At best, he croaked. Now he stood, awash in the glory of a voice that could have made Eldrin famous across a thousand worlds, and Althor felt small. He would never create anything as remotely spectacular—or as pure—as the music his father and brother took for granted, an ability to sing that for some inconceivable reason meant nothing to them, so much less than their ability to wield a sword.

Althor thought otherwise. Someday he would leave here to fight a war beyond anything either Eldrin or their father could imagine. What Althor excelled at—his ability to kill—had its true value in what it protected. He would fight because that was all he could do, unlike his father and brother, who had a greater calling.

He would fight so their voices could never be silenced.

II. CHILD OF THE SKY

The bow broke with a loud crack that vibrated in the air. Althor swore and dropped the pieces on the ground. He had rolled up his sleeves, and sunshine warmed his arms. The archery target stood at the other end of this clearing in the plains with several arrows stuck in its center, perfectly positioned. Too bad he couldn't shoot any more. He was done for the day. Again, damn it.

"Another one broke?" a man asked.

Althor turned to see his father watching him. "The glasswood is too brittle."

Eldrinson came over. "I had hoped this new bow would last longer."

"Apparently not." Althor scowled with his frustration. "What's the point of being this strong if either I hold back so much, I'm useless as an archer, or else I break my bows?" In the past two years, since Eldrin had gone offworld, Althor had kept growing, until he stood more than a head taller than his father. It wasn't just his height, either, but his musculature. Sometimes he felt as if he would sink into the ground with the weight of his body.

"I need a better bow," Althor said.

His father considered the broken pieces on the ground. "This is the best we've done. I don't think we can make it stronger."

Althor crossed his arms. "Yes. We can." He was working with an engineer at the starport to construct a bow from a composite material better suited to his needs than glasswood.

Eldrinson frowned. "Not a fair bow."

"You say as a man of honor, I must meet my opponent in fair combat." Althor lowered his arms. "How is it honor when I can't even use the same weapons?"

"You break the bows because of your strength." Eldrinson spoke as if this somehow answered the question. Althor supposed it did. His size and strength came from his offworld heritage.

"It still feels wrong," Althor said.

His father seemed more thoughtful than angry. He turned and walked toward the edges of the clearing. Beyond him, in the distance, Dalvador basked under the sun.

Eldrinson turned to him. "Ultimately the decision is yours. I won't deny you that choice."

Althor nodded. Beyond his father, he saw a trail of bubbles forming in the plains. Someone was running through the reeds; Soz it looked like. At twelve, she seemed less a child every day. She wore a blue dress like other girls in the village, but as she neared them, he saw the ripped sleeves and smudged hem. She had probably been planning military campaigns with her friends again and launching them against their confused brothers, who didn't know what to make of being attacked by girls. Althor suspected at least some of them liked it far more than they were willing to admit.

Althor smiled as she came up to them. "My greetings, commander."

Although Soz laughed, she shifted back and forth on her feet, too restless to stay still.

Eldrinson regarded her curiously. "What is it, Soshoni?"

"Mother says you need to come to the house." Soz glanced at Althor, then back at their father. "She said hurry."

"All right," Eldrinson said. "Tell her that I will be right there."

Soz nodded and took off running, leaving a floating river of pollen above the plains.

+ + +

"Come on." Soz tugged on Althor's arm. "We can hear them from the tower. They're in the room right next to it, that alcove that looks over the courtyard."

Althor pulled away his arm. "I'm not going to eavesdrop."

Soz glared at him. "Fine. Stay here." She headed up the spiral stairs of the tower, disappearing around its curve. Then she called, "It's only your life they're arguing about, after all."

"What?" Startled, Althor followed, ducking his head so it didn't hit the ceiling. "Why would they argue about me?" He rarely got into trouble, unlike Soz or their brother Del. He envied their willingness to push boundaries.

"Not you exactly," Soz said. They didn't have enough room to walk together, so she went first, maneuvering her way up the narrow tower much more easily than him. "But it affects you."

"What affects me?"

"Lord Avaril. Grandfather's cousin."

Althor froze. "What are you talking about?"

She turned to him, standing in the curve of the stairs. "Avaril has raised another army. They're coming through the mountains."

Althor stared at her. Lulled by more than two years of peace, he had assumed the failure of Avaril's last attack meant he was done. Of course it was a stupid assumption. This war had been going since their father's birth, when he became the Dalvador Bard instead of Avaril, and it would continue on through the generations until one clan decimated the other. And this time Althor was sixteen, a man in Dalvador, old enough to ride into battle.

"Come on." He motioned his sister up the stairs. "Climb faster."

✦ ✦ ✦

Eldrinson paced across the alcove, and Roca stood watching him. "What the hell did you expect me to do?" she said. "Pretend I didn't know they were coming?"

He came over to her. "You know how I feel about this."

She scowled. "I won't let your obsessed cousin attack our family again."

"You must leave it alone, Roca. This is my home, my people, and my world."

She didn't want this argument, not again. "Althor stays here."

Eldrinson just looked at her. He didn't even seem angry, only sad.

"Damn it," she said. "You can't take him with you."

THE WAGES OF HONOR

"It is his decision, not mine or yours."

"Like hell. By the laws of my people, he won't reach his full majority for another nine years."

Eldrinson banged his fist against his thigh. "We don't live with your people. We live with mine. He is an adult."

"He's still an Imperial citizen." Roca felt as if she were trying to climb an impossibly steep hill. "Legally he is a child. As his parent, I forbid him to go."

"You will tell him this yourself?"

She tried to project a certainty she didn't feel. "Yes."

"And then what? Will you also forbid his leaving home for this military school where he intends to apply next year? That won't work, either."

She hated knowing he was right. Yes, she could stop Althor now, even have soldiers from the battle cruiser in orbit come down and hold him in his room. To say he would never forgive her was the understatement of the century, even more so than with Eldrin, for Althor was a natural for the military, whereas Eldrin had never liked warfare. It would be hypocrisy to force Althor to stay here against his will and then let him go offworld to attend the Dieshan Military Academy.

"We can destroy Avaril's forces from orbit," Roca said. She would gladly blast his army into smoldering oblivion.

"This is my fight." Eldrinson took hold of her shoulders. "You say we have to follow the laws of your people. Well, your *own* laws don't allow you to interfere with my world." He lowered his arms. "You can't just go dropping bombs on my people when it suits your purposes."

"Colonel Majda agrees with me."

"Majda and her soldiers are up there to protect you. Not me."

"They protect my family."

He spoke coldly. "I can't stop your military from forcing Althor to stay here, nor can I stop you from having your orbital defense system obliterate my cousin's forces. But if you do this, Roca, don't come back to our home." His gaze never wavered. "I love you more than life, more than I ever believed a man could love a woman. But if you take away my self-determination, my pride, and my honor, I cannot live with you."

What could she say? She had spent decades fighting for her husband's right to be considered an equal among her people. The

Assembly had even tried to nullify the marriage when she first wed him, claiming an uneducated farmer on a backwater world had no business marrying an heir of their ancient royal line. She had stood up to them then and at every turn since. In return, Eldrinson accepted the changes she brought to his world, not only the technology but the differences in how she approached life. They had raised their children with her worldview as much as his, and because they worked together, the children thrived. The older ones constantly challenged them, but for all their youthful rebellions, they were miracles. Would she throw all that to the wind because she couldn't accept the results of the life she and Eldrinson had spent so many years building together? They had taught the children their principles of morality, and tomorrow Althor would act on those principles by riding with his father into war. She couldn't forbid him to go.

Roca didn't have to speak; she could tell Eldrinson knew her decision. Perhaps he saw the answer in her face or felt it in his ability to empathize with her. He pulled her close and they held each other, but she knew his grief as well as her own.

✦ ✦ ✦

The family gathered in the Hearth Room to listen to the broadcast. Althor knew it would play throughout settled space, sent by a technology that accessed a universe where the laws of relativistic physics didn't apply. It allowed them to enjoy a concert that took place light years away.

Del draped his lanky self across one of the armchairs in front of the fireplace, and Chaniece sat in the chair next to him. At fifteen, they were both a year younger than Althor, fraternal twins as different as fire and cool water.

Althor settled into the armchair next to Soz. She was sitting on one end of the sofa, taking apart a pulse revolver. She had filched it from the starport as if that were a perfectly normal act rather than a challenge to their parents. She was still simmering about the fight they had overheard today between their mother and father. Their words had left Althor with much to think about.

His brother Vyrl ambled into the room and sprawled on the other end of the sofa, exhausted from his daily work out, all long arms and legs at thirteen. Ten-year-old Denric sat in another armchair reading a holo-book, some adventure thing. Shannon was off somewhere, probably in the stables with the lyrine. Aniece was reading too, a book for seven-year-olds about fluffy animals. The toddler Kelric trundled around the room on pudgy legs, golden like their mother and large for his age.

"Opera," Del grumbled. "I hate it."

"That's because you yell instead of singing." Soz never looked up from her pulse revolver. "You sound awful."

"Oh, shut up," Del said.

"That's enough, you two." Roca walked into the room. "Del, you have such a beautiful voice. Why do you only sing those loud songs?"

Vyrl yawned and stretched his arms. "How long before this broadcast starts, anyway?" which fortunately covered Del's muttered *Fuck that* well enough that their mother didn't hear.

"Soz, for gods' sake, is that a gun?" their mother said. "Put it down."

Soz looked up at her. "It can't shoot. I took apart the ignition mechanism."

Their father came into the room. "My greetings, everyone," he said amiably. He took his seat in the armchair across from the fire, next to Althor, and stretched his booted feet out on the red-and-gold carpet. Roca was standing to one side, by the wall behind the circle of chairs. Althor suspected she was too nervous to sit. Kelric toddled over to her and she scooped him into her arms. He settled contentedly into her embrace.

"Soz, did you hear me?" their mother said. Almost simultaneously, their father said, "Denric, you need to put the book away. You too, Aniece."

Denric kept reading. "I'm almost finished."

"You don't have time to finish." Soz twisted the stock of the revolver. "The broadcast starts in less than two minutes."

"I told you both to put away your books." Eldrinson glanced at the sofa, then did a double take. "Soz, where the blazes did you get a gun? Give it to me."

"I'm hungry," Aniece said.

Denric turned off his novel. "Come on. Let's go to the kitchen."

"For flaming sake," their mother said. "Can't you all sit still for five minutes? Soz, I don't care what you took apart. Give it to your father. *Now.*"

"And no more solo visits to the port," Eldrinson told her, holding out his hand.

Soz glowered and didn't move, so Althor discreetly kicked her foot. If she didn't quit trying to provoke them, they wouldn't let her watch the broadcast. She turned her glare on him, but then she extended her arm across his torso, handing their father the dismantled gun. He took it with an odd look, as if he didn't know what to do with the offworld weapon.

Althor spoke quietly to him. "I can take it back to the port later."

Eldrinson nodded with a hint of relief in his gaze.

Before anyone could say anything else, a man's resonant voice filled the room. "Welcome to the Selei Opera Hall." His words came over the sound system their parents had set up for this gathering. With a hum, a translucent screen lowered in front of the hearth. A holographic image formed in the space before it showing them a great hall with a man standing on a circular stage. Even knowing the "hall" was a projection created for the sake of viewers, Althor found it impressive.

The man continued. "We are pleased to bring you tonight's performance via the top verification protocols in the Imperialate."

Vyrl opened his eyes and lifted his head. "The what?"

"Verification," Roca said.

Chaniece spoke in her melodic voice. "What would they need to verify?"

"That what we're going to hear is real," Soz said. "People can look up the protocols on the mesh if they don't believe it."

"Why the hell wouldn't it be real?" Del asked.

Roca scowled at him. "Watch your language, young man."

Del stiffened, but when Chaniece shook her head slightly at him, he let it go.

"You can do anything through the mesh," Althor said. "They want the audience to know they're hearing a genuine singer, not someone with an enhanced voice." He wished his mother didn't look so tired. It was killing him knowing how she worried about him and his father.

The view zoomed in on the stage as a second man walked out and joined the announcer. Gods above, it was Eldrin. He bore little resemblance to the youth who, two years ago, had bid his family goodbye at the port. Althor had never envied his brother as much as he did on that day when Eldrin left their world to see the stars. A stranger stood on the stage tonight, an elegant man in modern slacks and a white dress shirt. Although Eldrin still wore his hair longer than most Imperial men, he had trimmed it to his ears and brushed it back from his face. He was no longer a Dalvador farm boy. He had become an Imperialate prince.

"Holy shit," Soz said. She got away with it because Aniece said, "He looks so handsome," at the same time.

"Someone had better verify that's Eldrin," Vyrl said. "I don't believe it."

"Hoshpa!" Kelric waved his hands at the holo and laughed. "Two hoshpas!"

Their father smiled. "That isn't me, Kelli. It's your brother."

The announcer introduced him as Eldrin Valdoria, neglecting to mention the titles he had inherited from their mother or that he was heir to the Dalvador Bard, which no one would have understood anyway. He looked relaxed, but Althor recognized his brother's tells. Eldrin was scared. He had never sung in public before. He wouldn't tonight, either, not literally; he was on the sound stage of a holo studio. But his voice would go out to thousands, and depending on how many people downloaded the recording, millions might eventually hear him sing.

"He's been practicing," Roca said, more as if to reassure herself than the rest of them. "He'll be fine." She looked more nervous than Eldrin.

The announcer left the stage and Eldrin stood alone, against an ivory backdrop bordered by marble columns. Classical music curled through the air, and he began to sing.

Althor settled back in his chair, letting the music flow over him. Eldrin had chosen a Dalvador aria. His voice swelled as he crested the high notes, and then he slid into his lower register, where he rumbled. His tonality and vibrato sounded even better than his magnificent renditions of the song at home. He soared to the peak of the aria and held the highest note longer than Althor had thought a person could sing on one breath. Never taking a break, he swept down the scale in a wash of melodic sound.

The beauty of the music heightened Althor's conflicted thoughts. Like Eldrin before him, tomorrow he would ride into battle. Yes, he could fight. He was good at it. But to what purpose? So his father and Avaril could go at each other again and again, decade after decade? It would never stop. Althor couldn't imagine his younger siblings going into war. Del just wanted to sing his loud songs and sleep with girls. Chaniece loved their life on the farm. Vyrl was a dancer, another artist. None of his other siblings were cut out for combat except Soz, and she sure as hell wouldn't ride into combat on Lyshriol. More likely, she'd end up commanding the Imperialate military.

As much as Althor had argued with Eldrin in their youth, he understood the choices his brother and father had made three years ago. He also knew why Soz had brought the gun tonight. She wanted him to take it with him tomorrow.

Althor and the port engineer had finished his new bow today. It was a good weapon, made from a composite that bent with ease and never broke no matter how much strength he used. He could defeat many opponents with that bow. It was still a betrayal of the code of war, but less so than the gun. A compromise. Or he could do as Eldrin had done, forgoing any technological advantages. Althor knew he was a powerful fighter, that probably no one on Lyshriol could best him even if he couldn't use a bow.

What to choose? He didn't have an answer. He listened as Eldrin soared to his finale, his voice a testament to the beauty only humans created. Althor didn't know how to reconcile such heights of human achievement to the unparalleled ability of humanity to commit mayhem against itself.

✦ ✦ ✦

Dawn arrived, and the twin suns rose above the horizon, their gold light softening the world. Roca stood in the courtyard near the castle watching her husband and his men gather. The medic from the port arrived, bringing his supplies. Eldrinson had balked when she first asked him to take the doctor, but he finally gave in, she suspected because the art of healing was more universal than the esoteric physics that underlay modern military science.

Althor appeared around a corner of the house leading a black lyrine, a genetically engineered cross between a horse and a big-horned ram. It looked liked a stallion, with its speed and grace, but horns curved around its head. He brought the largest, most muscular animal in the stables, one of the few strong enough to carry his weight. They made an impressive pair, and people moved aside as he walked to his father.

What most drew Roca's attention was the bow Althor had strapped in a harness on his back. He covered it with a cloth as did all archers on Lyshriol. Pollen drifting in the air damaged the glasswood, trying to grow on it, so archers protected their bows until they went into battle. Roca doubted Althor's weapon needed that cover. He used it so no one would see that he carried a weapon designed from an offworld composite.

She closed her eyes and let out a breath, grateful for his decision. When she opened her eyes, Althor was talking to his father, the two of them half hidden among all the other soldiers and lyrine in the courtyard. Eldrinson glanced at the covered bow on Althor's back, but it didn't look as if he said anything about it. She suspected he was secretly grateful their son had found this compromise.

Roca made her way across the courtyard. The soldiers stepped aside for her and bowed from the waist, acknowledging their commander's queen. When she reached her husband and son, Eldrinson smiled at her. "You are a beautiful sight."

She tried to return his smile. "You two look impressive." They wore disk mail and leather armor over tunics and leggings, with knee boots protecting their legs.

Eldrinson pulled her to him. "Don't worry so." He kissed her, then drew back.

"Be careful, love." She looked up at Althor. "And you."

Her son spoke gently. "I'll protect him."

Eldrinson gave a snort. "Not so old yet that I can't defend myself, young man."

Althor smiled, but Roca couldn't read him. Sometimes she felt so attuned to her children, she knew their moods as if they were her own. Today Althor seemed shuttered. He had withdrawn, giving her a glimpse of the impassive starfighter pilot he would someday become—if he survived this war.

After the men mounted their lyrine, Roca retreated to the castle and went up the spiral stairs of a tower. She stood at the top, outside, and watched her husband's company ride out of the courtyard. More riders joined them, and the army flowed into the Dalvador Plains, stretching out in a long column, until their numbers swelled to nearly two hundred.

Roca tried not to think of the absurdity of an interstellar Assembly Councilor standing in a castle watching a sword-bearing army ride to battle. What stopped her from interfering weren't the laws that forbade her to violate the cultural sovereignty of her husband's people; it was her decades of respect for the man she loved, the father of her children, even if his choices broke her heart.

✦ ✦ ✦

The first time Althor had seen the Plains of Tyroll, in his childhood, he had loved that great expanse of wind-swept reeds. Located between a range of mountains and a solitary ridge that rose out of the plains like a giant wall, the serenity of Tyroll had spoken to him. Today, no hint of that peace remained. Two armies trampled the reeds, filling the land with the clang of swords and the shouts of warriors.

Althor rode through the chaos, his great sword gripped in one hand. He managed the blade with ease despite its weight. A warrior in the black-and-gold armor of Avaril's men came at him, raising a lighter sword. Althor deflected the blow and swung at his attacker. Their blades clanged, and Althor sent his opponent's weapon flying from his grip. He struck out again, but the man was already evading him, jerking his mount away. Althor's sword ripped across the lyrine's upper body, and the animal screamed, rearing on its hind legs. It threw its rider, and the man crashed to the ground. Althor didn't wait to see if he rose again; instead he turned and rode hard toward the tall ridge.

Avaril had brought three hundred and fifty men. They outnumbered Eldrinson's army by more than three to two. Althor had looked at the orbital images last night, after his father slept, and they hadn't shown this many fighters in the opposing army. Avaril must have hidden some of his men and brought them in this morning.

Someone shouted at Althor, something about his bow. Althor still hadn't removed the cover. He ignored the call and focused on the ridge, but he couldn't shut down his empathic response to the battle, the blood rage, fear, and violence. This was nothing like a virtual war; here you *felt* it all.

He kept going. Another of Avaril's men rode at him, bearing down with his blade. Althor parried the blow with so much force, his strike broke the other man's weapon in two. He felt as if he were moving in slow motion as he swung again. He thrust his blade into the man's chest, and blood spurted from the wound. The warrior stared at Althor with a stunned expression, as if he couldn't comprehend what had just happened. A massive shudder went through Althor. He had a sudden sense of *nothing* where a moment before he had felt a living man. Eldrin had once told him that during combat, a battle lust came over him, but Althor knew only the agony of the man's death and his own inescapable realization that he had just killed another human being.

He had reached the base of the tall ridge and the edge of the battle. He kept going, galloping around the wall of rock until it hid him from the conflict. No true warrior would ride *away* from combat. Althor shut the thought out of his mind. He had to stop thinking, or he would never finish what he had set out to do.

The noise of the fighting was muted on this side of the cliff. He scanned its base, looking—yes, there. A steep path climbed the ridge. He walked his mount to the base of the path, where rocks lay piled in clumps. The lyrine picked its way through the boulders and headed up the path. He guided the animal with care, letting it choose the best footing.

Coward. *A man without honor.*

Althor tried to empty his mind of the damning thoughts.

As he went higher, the sounds of battle grew more distant. The wind picked up, pulling at his clothes, keening over the ridge. He took off his helmet and left it on a crag that jutted out from the cliff face on his right. Jagged spires of rock rose on his left, so he rode along a chute of rock. Every now and then, between the spires, he glimpsed the plains to the south, away from the fighting in the west.

He continued to climb.

The path curved westward and he came out into open air, the top of the cliff level now with his shoulders. More rock formations blocked his view to the west, but it wouldn't be long before he rode above them as well. The wind ruffled his hair, blowing across the short curls. He continued upward, and the path opened out at the top of the ridge. He could see the Plains of Tyroll far below, the battle so distant, the armies looked like toy soldiers. He continued along the ridge. If anyone looked this way, they would see a large man on a lyrine silhouetted against the sky.

The path ended in an open space with boulders clumped on his right. He sat on his mount, looking out over the battle as it surged back and forth, hundreds of men fighting, on foot or mounted. Avaril's men were rolling war towers into place, tall scaffoldings of glasswood that resembled giant lyrine. Warriors climbed ladders up to platforms on the tower and shot arrows at the melee in the battlefield below. Eldrinson's men had too few defenses against the onslaught.

Althor felt as if he were moving in slow motion as he reached over his shoulder and dragged the protective cloth off his back. He let the cover go and the wind caught it, sending the cloth floating down the ridge. He reached back again—

And pulled the laser cannon out of its harness.

Althor had wrestled with his decision for hours last night. He had returned Soz's gun to the port and walked back out into the Lyshriol darkness, but he hadn't gone home. Instead, he boarded the military shuttle that sat on the tarmac. Its armaments included a laser carbine, more of a cannon than a gun. He knew how to disconnect it from the ship; he had used such a weapon a hundred times and more in the war games he played. He had never shot a cannon in real life, but he knew every nuance of that massive weapon. Only one aspect differed now from his virtual battles.

Death here was real.

The gun weighed far more than any broadsword, but he had no trouble holding its bulk. With a shove, he pushed the activator lever forward, and the cannon hummed. Lights flashed along its body, lines of red turning green as its systems activated. Althor pressed the controls in a pattern as familiar to him as speaking. He raised the weapon, tapping on its targeting systems, and aimed at the tallest of the two towers.

This endless war was crushing his people. So many had died and so many more would give their lives in the generations to come. Today he would lose any claim to honor, but he would be committing a far greater crime if he didn't protect the people and land he loved. His mother came from offworld. By law, she couldn't interfere. But he was a citizen of Lyshriol, born and raised here, a son of this land. They had sent him to fight a war, the weaponry on the transport was dedicated to protecting his mother's family, and his father had given him the choice to use or not use the technology of her people. He had meant only the enhanced bow, but Althor chose a different interpretation.

He fired the cannon.

The laser shot cut through the air like a lightning bolt. When it hit the war tower, the structure exploded and men fell from its cross-bars, screaming as they plunged to the ground. Multicolored flames erupted along the structure, incinerating the glasswood. Nausea surged in Althor, but he couldn't stop, not now, not until he ensured that the knowledge of this day became burned so deeply into the collective memory of his people that no one would ever again challenge his father to die.

Althor shoved the recharger forward and aimed at the tower on the other side of the field, moving with a surety born from years of practice. He fired again, the laser shot brilliant in the air, and destroyed the second tower. Men were shouting below, running, staring at the figure on the ridge who brought down lightning from the sky.

He toggled the magnifier, and the battlefield jumped into view, showing him which men wore the armor of Avaril's army. He narrowed the beam and cut a swath through the fighters, selectively picking off Avaril's warriors. This was no different from the combat simulations he had done—except that today, tears ran down his face. It felt as if he had been on this ridge for hours, an eternity, but the targeting display told him only seconds had passed. He kept firing, dying inside as he slaughtered his father's enemies.

When Avaril's few remaining men began to run from the field, Althor stopped and lowered the cannon. In the Plains of Tyroll, his father's men were standing utterly still or sitting on their mounts, staring at the ridge. The ashes and charred bodies of their enemies surrounded them. His father was walking toward the ridge, his face upturned. Althor couldn't see his expression, but he knew his shock. His second-born son had just pulverized every tradition of decency valued by their people.

Among the star-spanning military of the Imperialate, Althor knew he would be no more than one small cog in a massive, interstellar war machine that protected a thousand worlds and more, a trillion people living across the stars. He couldn't end that brutal, soul-parching conflict, but here on Lyshriol, he could preserve what he loved. He committed the ultimate sin for the greater good because no one on Lyshriol would ever dare go to war again, finally understanding the powers his mother's people could call down upon them.

And if his guilt destroyed him, only he would know.

✦ ✦ ✦

Roca stood at a window on the top level of the castle with Colonel Majda at her side. Dressed in the green uniform of an army officer in Imperial Space Command, Majda cut an imposing figure. Iron gray streaked the dark hair she wore pulled back from her aristocratic face. At their vantage point, they could see Eldrinson's army coming through the plains toward Dalvador. They had won the most dramatic battle in the known history of Lyshriol, yet they rode in subdued silence. Althor no longer covered the laser carbine strapped across his back. The weapon jutted up above his shoulder, its silver and black surfaces glinting in the sunlight.

"We knew as soon as he fired," Colonel Majda said. "It raised alarms in the orbital systems."

Roca felt too numb from shock to process it yet. Nor could she absorb that the golden child she carried as a baby had become this silent giant. "Will you arrest him?"

The colonel turned to her. "For what?"

"He killed over three hundred people." Roca heard the disbelief in her own voice.

"Your husband took him to fight." The colonel regarded her steadily. "So he fought."

Bitterness edged Roca's voice. "We give our children games of war, train them to kill, and then mourn when they do exactly what we taught them to do." Althor hadn't even stolen the carbine; as a member of the Ruby Dynasty, technically she owned the transport. She was a civilian, an elected member of a democratic Assembly, but she still carried the ancient title and was third in line for a red throne that no longer existed.

Majda spoke quietly. "I am sorry, Councilor. None of us wants our children killed or scarred by war. But even I've heard the news spreading among the people in Dalvador, and I can barely speak their language. The legend is already growing. Your husband will fight no more wars." She met Roca's gaze. "Yesterday, Althor made it possible for the people of Lyshriol to achieve a peace that may last for centuries, as long as your family and their descendants protect this world."

Roca turned to watch the army pouring from the plains into the village. She could see Althor better now, but his face remained unreadable. Softly, she said, "At what price?"

✦ ✦ ✦

By the time Roca came down to the Great Hall, using a discreet side entrance, Eldrinson was taking his seat on the dais. The anthropologists who chronicled life on Lyshriol loved to call him a king because his house resembled a castle and he had a big chair, but Roca knew the title baffled him. As the Bard, he did more than sing for his people, he also acted as a judge and commanded a relatively small army, but that hardly made him a "king." His chair wasn't a throne; it was simply where he sat when people came to him for rulings on their conflicts.

Today, all of that would change.

Eldrinson's warriors filed into the great hall. Althor appeared in the doorway. As he walked the length of the room, the soldiers all throughout the hall went down on one knee. They didn't rise until after he passed. Roca tried to feel his mood, but he had closed himself to all of them. He was terrifying, the huge warrior who commanded the lightning. But she knew the sixteen-year-old boy under that silent exterior; for all that Althor betrayed no emotion, inside he grieved.

Althor climbed the steps of the dais and went to stand next to his father, towering over the chair. Eldrinson glanced in Roca's direction. When he saw her and beckoned, she shook her head.

"You should go," Colonel Majda said.

Roca scowled at her. "I won't have these people thinking I am some fake goddess."

"They will think what they think. You should stand with your family. Let your husband's people know you support him." She put a hand on Roca's shoulder. "And Althor."

As much as Roca had no desire to feed the myths that had grown around her, she knew Majda was right. After what had happened, it could destabilize the stunned population of Dalvador if they thought the Bard's son and his wife were set against each other. She walked to the dais and went up the stairs. Standing on the other side of Eldrinson's chair from Althor, she looked out at the warriors in the hall. Three men entered at the far end, two Dalvador fighters with a third warrior between them, a youth in the gold-and-black armor of Lord Avaril's army. Roca thought he looked familiar, but she couldn't tell why from so far away.

The Dalvador men came forward, gripping the younger man's biceps, forcing him to walk with them. When they reached the dais, they shoved the youth. He stumbled and then stopped, looking up at Eldrinson. Taking a deep breath, he went up the dais steps. As he knelt to Eldrinson with his head bowed, Roca finally recognized him. Karl of Avaril—Lord Avaril's oldest son. The father must have died in the battle.

Althor spoke, and his deep voice rumbled. "Do you swear fealty to Dalvador?"

Karl looked up with a jerk, staring at Althor as if he had heard a war god instead of a youth his own age. "Yes." He looked at Eldrinson. "I swear my fealty."

"Do you swear," Althor said, "never to make war against Dalvador again, not against my family, not against the villages of the Plains, the Rillian Vales, the mountains of Ryder's Lost Memory, the Blue Dales, or any of the outlying provinces?"

"Yes." Karl's face paled. "I swear."

So it begins, Roca thought. Today they entered a new era, one born in great pain and yet offering an age of peace. No more of her children would ride into battle, not on Lyshriol. But as she watched Karl, she wondered if any of their children, here or among the stars, would ever heal from the violence their parents bequeathed to them.

+ + +

The holo-stage in the console room of the castle was discreet, set in a corner, small and unassuming, with a screen curving around one side. Althor waited on the stage. The holo of a man formed in front of him, the two of them facing each other as if they stood in the same room instead of light years apart. Eldrin seemed much the same now as during the concert, except his hair was tousled and his clothes less formal, a blue pullover and grey slacks.

He nodded to Althor. "My greetings."

"You look well." Althor thought of Eldrin's phenomenal performance, of how his brother's talent could lift the human spirit to such heights. "I liked your concert."

Eldrin spoke awkwardly. "Thanks."

Althor paused, uncertain how to talk to his brother. "So are you and Dehya staying in her home on the Orbiter?" He had yet to figure out how he felt about Eldrin's marriage.

"Always." Eldrin smiled. "You'd never know we were on a space habitat. The valley where we live is beautiful. The sky is bluer than on Lyshriol." He hesitated. "It's not a real sky. I mean, I could walk on it if I wanted to. But it looks real."

It had always struck Althor as odd, using so much of a habitat for a "sky," but he supposed it didn't matter. The Orbiter had plenty of room. "I've seen images. It's beautiful."

"Yes." Eldrin started to add more, then stopped. After a moment, he said, "I read about what happened."

Althor knew he meant the Plains of Tyroll. "How?"

"Dehya had a briefing report."

It suddenly hit Althor what his brother had said. "You read it? Yourself?"

"It took a while. But, yes. I'm learning." Eldrin's smile faded. "Are you all right?"

"I'm fine."

They stood in silence. When it became strained, Althor said, "Which of us do you think was right?" He regretted the question the moment he spoke. What could Eldrin say? Either he condemned himself or he condemned Althor.

"I don't know." Eldrin exhaled. "I truly don't, Althor. Maybe I never will."

"I'm sorry." Althor raked his hand through his curls. "I don't know why I bothered you."

Eldrin's voice gentled in a way Althor hadn't heard since they were too young to know what rivalry meant. "We chose different paths, you and I, but for each of us it was the right decision. You acted for what, ultimately, was the greater good."

Althor spoke in a flat voice. "It was an act of cowardice."

Eldrin shook his head. "You had the courage to do what you believed right. How many lives have you saved from future wars? We'll never know, Althor, because those people will never die. They will live. Because of you."

He heard the words, but they couldn't ease the darkness within him. "Perhaps."

"Give yourself time."

"You've changed." Althor smiled. "We've been here five minutes and haven't fought once."

Eldrin laughed, a resonant sound. "So we haven't."

They talked a while longer and then signed off. Afterward, Althor went to a balcony and gazed across the plains. His sister Aniece was running through the reeds, chasing bubbles. Farther on, Vyrl and his girlfriend Lily were spinning around. Soz and Chaniece ran circles around Del, daring him to catch them as he laughed. Kelric toddled along with Denric, who was holding his hand. Even Shannon had joined them today, running with his arms outstretched, stirring pollen into the air.

Althor doubted he would ever again share that freedom of spirit. He would help his father deal with the aftermath of the battle, and his mother would use her gifts of diplomacy to handle relations with the grieving Tyroll villages. Althor would go to the counselor his parents and Colonel Majda insisted he see, even if he couldn't talk about what had happened, not yet. Next year he would apply to the Dieshan Military Academy. Perhaps someday he could learn to deal with his inner darkness.

Watching his family helped. Lyshriol existed in an idyllic bubble protected from the greater battles that raged across the stars. For now, the people he loved were safe, and at least in that, he could find some small peace.

One of my favorite voices in science fiction today, Nnedi Okorafor writes from her Nigerian American heritage, telling stories from the point of view of African peoples and cultures that make her voice unique and compelling. Our next story won both the Hugo and the Nebula in 2016 as well as the British Fantasy Award for Best Novella. It is the first in an ongoing series of novellas (so far) of space opera about Africans in space. Awesome stuff. A sequel came out early in 2017, and here's hoping for lots more in this series.

BINTI

NNEDI OKORAFOR

I

I powered up the transporter and said a silent prayer. I had no idea what I was going to do if it didn't work. My transporter was cheap, so even a droplet of moisture, or more likely, a grain of sand, would cause it to short. It was faulty and most of the time I had to restart it over and over before it worked. *Please not now, please not now,* I thought.

The transporter shivered in the sand and I held my breath. Tiny, flat, and black as a prayer stone, it buzzed softly and then slowly rose from the sand. Finally, it produced the baggage-lifting force. I grinned. Now I could make it to the shuttle. I swiped *otjize* from my forehead with my index finger and knelt down. Then I touched the finger to the sand, grounding the sweet-smelling red clay into it. "Thank you," I whispered. It was a half-mile walk along the dark desert road. With the transporter working, I would make it there on time.

Straightening up, I paused and shut my eyes. Now the weight of my entire life was pressing on my shoulders. I was defying the most traditional part of myself for the first time in my entire life. I was leaving in the dead of night and they had no clue. My nine siblings, all older than me except for my younger sister and brother, would never see this coming. My parents would never imagine I'd do such a thing in a million years. By the time they all realized what I'd done and where I was going, I'd have left the planet. In my absence, my parents would growl to each other that I was to never set foot in their home again. My four aunties and two uncles who lived down the road would shout and gossip among themselves about how I'd scandalized our entire bloodline. I was going to be a pariah.

"Go," I softly whispered to the transporter, stamping my foot. The thin metal rings I wore around each ankle jingled noisily, but I stamped my foot again. Once on, the transporter worked best when I didn't touch it. "Go," I said again, sweat forming on my brow. When nothing moved, I chanced giving the two large suitcases sitting atop the force field a shove. They moved smoothly and I breathed another sigh of relief. At least some luck was on my side.

+ + +

Fifteen minutes later I purchased a ticket and boarded the shuttle. The sun was barely beginning to peak over the horizon. As I moved past seated passengers far too aware of the bushy ends of my plaited hair softly slapping people in the face, I cast my eyes to the floor. Our hair is thick and mine has always been *very* thick. My old auntie liked to call it "ododo" because it grew wild and dense like ododo grass. Just before leaving, I'd rolled my plaited hair with fresh sweet-smelling *otjize* I'd made specifically for this trip. Who knew what I looked like to these people who didn't know my people so well.

A woman leaned away from me as I passed, her face pinched as if she smelled something foul. "Sorry," I whispered, watching my feet and trying to ignore the stares of almost everyone in the shuttle. Still, I couldn't help glancing around. Two girls who might have been a few years older than me, covered their mouths with hands so pale that they looked untouched by the sun. Everyone looked as if the sun was his or her enemy. I was the only Himba on the shuttle. I quickly found and moved to a seat.

The shuttle was one of the new sleek models that looked like the bullets my teachers used to calculate ballistic coefficients during my A-levels when I was growing up. These ones glided fast over land using a combination of air current, magnetic fields, and exponential energy—an easy craft to build if you had the equipment and the time. It was also a nice vehicle for hot desert terrain where the roads leading out of town were terribly maintained. My people didn't like to leave the homeland. I sat in the back so I could look out the large window.

I could see the lights from my father's astrolabe shop and the sand storm analyzer my brother had built at the top of the Root—that's what we called my parents' big, big house. Six generations of my family had lived there. It was the oldest house in my village, maybe the oldest in the city. It was made of stone and concrete, cool in the night, hot in the day. And it was patched with solar planes and covered with bioluminescent plants that liked to stop glowing just before sunrise. My bedroom was at the top of the house. The shuttle began to move and I stared until I couldn't see it anymore. "What am I doing?" I whispered.

An hour and a half later, the shuttle arrived at the launch port. I was the last off, which was good because the sight of the launch port overwhelmed me so much that all I could do for several moments was stand there. I was wearing a long red skirt, one that was silky like water, a light orange wind-top that was stiff and durable, thin leather sandals, and my anklets. No one around me wore such an outfit. All I saw were light flowing garments and veils; not one woman's ankles were exposed, let alone jingling with steel anklets. I breathed through my mouth and felt my face grow hot.

"Stupid stupid stupid," I whispered. We Himba don't travel. We stay put. Our ancestral land is life; move away from it and you diminish. We even cover our bodies with it. *Otjize* is red land. Here in the launch port, most were Khoush and a few other non-Himba. Here, I was an outsider; I was outside. "What was I thinking?" I whispered.

I was sixteen years old and had never been beyond my city, let alone near a launch station. I was by myself and I had just left my family. My prospects of marriage had been 100 percent and now they would be zero. No man wanted a woman who'd run away. However, beyond my prospects of normal life being ruined, I had scored so high on the planetary exams in mathematics that the Oomza University had not only admitted me, but promised to pay for whatever I needed in order to attend. No matter what choice I made, I was never going to have a normal life, really.

I looked around and immediately knew what to do next. I walked to the help desk.

✦ ✦ ✦

The travel security officer scanned my astrolabe, a full *deep* scan. Dizzy with shock, I shut my eyes and breathed through my mouth to steady myself. Just to leave the planet, I had to give them access to my *entire* life—me, my family, and all forecasts of my future. I stood there, frozen, hearing my mother's voice in my head. "There is a reason why our people do not go to that university. Oomza Uni wants you for its own gain, Binti. You go to that school and you become its slave." I couldn't help but contemplate the possible truth in her words. I hadn't even gotten there yet and already I'd given them my life. I wanted to ask the officer if he did this for everyone, but I was afraid now that he'd done it. They could do anything to me, at this point. Best not to make trouble.

When the officer handed me my astrolabe, I resisted the urge to snatch it back. He was an old Khoush man, so old that he was privileged to wear the blackest turban and face veil. His shaky hands were so gnarled and arthritic that he nearly dropped my astrolabe. He was bent like a dying palm tree and when he'd said, "You have never traveled; I must do a full scan. Remain where you are," his voice was drier than the red desert outside my city. But he read my astrolabe as fast as my father, which both impressed and scared me. He'd coaxed it open by whispering a few choice equations and his suddenly steady hands worked the dials as if they were his own.

When he finished, he looked up at me with his light green piercing eyes that seemed to see deeper into me than his scan of my astrolabe. There were people behind me and I was aware of their whispers, soft laughter and a young child murmuring. It was cool in the terminal, but I felt the heat of social pressure. My temples ached and my feet tingled.

"Congratulations," he said to me in his parched voice, holding out my astrolabe.

I frowned at him, confused. "What for?"

"You are the pride of your people, child," he said, looking me in the eye. Then he smiled broadly and patted my shoulder. He'd just seen my entire life. He knew of my admission into Oomza Uni.

"Oh." My eyes pricked with tears. "Thank you, sir," I said, hoarsely, as I took my astrolabe.

I quickly made my way through the many people in the terminal, too aware of their closeness. I considered finding a lavatory and applying more *otjize* to my skin and tying my hair back, but instead I kept moving. Most of the people in the busy terminal wore the black and white garments of the Khoush people—the women draped in white with multicolored belts and veils and the men draped in black like powerful spirits. I had seen plenty of them on television and here and there in my city, but never had I been in a sea of Khoush. This was the rest of the world and I was finally in it.

As I stood in line for boarding security, I felt a tug at my hair. I turned around and met the eyes of a group of Khoush women. They were all staring at me; *everyone* behind me was staring at me.

The woman who'd tugged my plait was looking at her fingers and rubbing them together, frowning. Her fingertips were orange red with my *otjize*. She sniffed them. "It smells like jasmine flowers," she said to the woman on her left, surprised.

"Not shit?" one woman said. "I hear it smells like shit because it *is* shit."

"No, definitely jasmine flowers. It is thick like shit, though."

"Is her hair even real?" another woman asked the woman rubbing her fingers.

"I don't know."

"These 'dirt bathers' are a filthy people," the first woman muttered.

I just turned back around, my shoulders hunched. My mother had counseled me to be quiet around Khoush. My father told me that when he was around Khoush merchants when they came to our city to buy astrolabes, he tried to make himself as small as possible. "It is either that or I will start a war with them that I will finish," he said. My father didn't believe in war. He said war was evil, but if it came he would revel in it like sand in a storm. Then he'd say a little prayer to the Seven to keep war away and then another prayer to seal his words.

I pulled my plaits to my front and touched the *edan* in my pocket. I let my mind focus on it, its strange language, its strange metal, its strange feel. I'd found the *edan* eight years ago while exploring the sands of the hinter deserts one late afternoon. "*Edan*" was a general name for a device too old for anyone to know its functions, so old that they were now just art.

My *edan* was more interesting than any book, than any new astrolabe design I made in my father's shop that these women would probably kill each other to buy. And it was mine, in my pocket, and these nosy women behind me could never know. Those women talked about me, the men probably did too. But none of them knew what I had, where I was going, who I was. Let them gossip and judge. Thankfully, they knew not to touch my hair again. I don't like war either.

The security guard scowled when I stepped forward. Behind him I could see three entrances, the one in the middle led into the ship called *Third Fish*, the ship I was to take to Oomza Uni. Its open door was large and round leading into a long corridor illuminated by soft blue lights.

"Step forward," the guard said. He wore the uniform of all launch site lower-level personnel—a long white gown and gray gloves. I'd only seen this uniform in streaming stories and books and I wanted to giggle, despite myself. He looked ridiculous. I stepped forward and everything went red and warm.

When the body scan beeped its completion, the security guard reached right into my left pocket and brought out my *edan*. He held it to his face with a deep scowl.

I waited. What would he know?

He was inspecting its stellated cube shape, pressing its many points with his finger and eyeing the strange symbols on it that I had spent two years unsuccessfully trying to decode. He held it to his face to better see the intricate loops and swirls of blue and black and white, so much like the lace placed on the heads of young girls when they turn eleven and go through their eleventh-year rite.

"What is this made of?" the guard asked, holding it over a scanner. "It's not reading as any known metal."

I shrugged, too aware of the people behind me waiting in line and staring at me. To them, I was probably like one of the people who lived in caves deep in the hinter desert who were so blackened by the sun that they looked like walking shadows. I'm not proud to say that I have some Desert People blood in me from my father's side of the family, that's where my dark skin and extra-bushy hair come from.

"Your identity reads that you're a harmonizer, a masterful one who builds some of the finest astrolabes," he said. "But this object isn't an astrolabe. Did you build it? And how can you build something and not know what it's made of?"

"I didn't build it," I said.

"Who did?"

"It's… it's just an old, old thing," I said. "It has no math or current. It's just an inert computative apparatus that I carry for good luck." This was partially a lie. But even I didn't know exactly what it could and couldn't do.

The man looked as if he would ask more, but didn't. Inside, I smiled. Government security guards were only educated up to age ten, yet because of their jobs, they were used to ordering people around. And they especially looked down on people like me.

Apparently, they were the same everywhere, no matter the tribe. He had no idea what a "computative apparatus" was, but he didn't want to show that I, a poor Himba girl, was more educated than he. Not in front of all these people. So he quickly moved me along and, finally, there I stood at my ship's entrance.

I couldn't see the end of the corridor, so I stared at the entrance. The ship was a magnificent piece of living technology. *Third Fish* was a Miri 12, a type of ship closely related to a shrimp. Miri 12s were stable calm creatures with natural exoskeletons that could withstand the harshness of space. They were genetically enhanced to grow three breathing chambers within their bodies.

Scientists planted rapidly growing plants within these three enormous rooms that not only produced oxygen from the CO_2 directed in from other parts of the ship, but also absorbed benzene, formaldehyde, and trichloroethylene. This was some of the most amazing technology I'd ever read about. Once settled on the ship, I was determined to convince someone to let me see one of these amazing rooms. But at the moment, I wasn't thinking about the technology of the ship. I was on the threshold now, between home and my future.

I stepped into the blue corridor.

+ + +

So that is how it all began. I found my room. I found my group— twelve other new students, all human, all Khoush, between the ages of fifteen and eighteen. An hour later, my group and I located a ship technician to show us one of the breathing chambers. I wasn't the only new Oomza Uni student who desperately wanted to see the technology at work. The air in there smelled like the jungles and forests I'd only read about. The plants had tough leaves and they grew everywhere, from ceiling to walls to floor. They were wild with flowers, and I could have stood there breathing that soft, fragrant air for days.

We met our group leader hours later. He was a stern old Khoush man who looked the twelve of us over and paused at me and asked, "Why are you covered in red greasy clay and weighed down by all those steel anklets?" When I told him that I was Himba, he coolly said, "I know, but that doesn't answer my question." I explained to him the tradition of my people's skin care and how we wore the steel rings on our ankles to protect us from snakebites. He looked at me for a long time, the others in my group staring at me like I was a rare bizarre butterfly.

"Wear your *otjize*," he said. "But not so much that you stain up this ship. And if those anklets are to protect you from snakebites, you no longer need them."

I took my anklets off, except for two on each ankle. Enough to jingle with each step.

I was the only Himba on the ship, out of nearly five hundred passengers. My tribe is obsessed with innovation and technology, but it is small, private, and, as I said, we don't like to leave Earth. We prefer to explore the universe by traveling inward, as opposed to outward. No Himba has ever gone to Oomza Uni. So me being the only one on the ship was not that surprising. However, just because something isn't surprising doesn't mean it's easy to deal with.

The ship was packed with outward-looking people who loved mathematics, experimenting, learning, reading, inventing, studying, obsessing, revealing. The people on the ship weren't Himba, but I soon understood that they were still my people. I stood out as a Himba, but the commonalities shined brighter. I made friends quickly. And by the second week in space, they were *good* friends.

Olo, Remi, Kwuga, Nur, Anajama, Rhoden. Only Olo and Remi were in my group. Everyone else I met in the dining area or the learning room where various lectures were held by professors onboard the ship. They were all girls who grew up in sprawling houses, who'd never walked through the desert, who'd never stepped on a snake in the dry grass. They were girls who could not stand the rays of Earth's sun unless it was shining through a tinted window.

Yet they were girls who knew what I meant when I spoke of "treeing." We sat in my room (because, having so few travel items, mine was the emptiest) and challenged each other to look out at the stars and imagine the most complex equation and then split it in half and then in half again and again. When you do math fractals long enough, you kick yourself into treeing just enough to get lost in the shallows of the mathematical sea. None of us would have made it into the university if we couldn't tree, but it's not easy. We were the best and we pushed each other to get closer to "God."

Then there was Heru. I had never spoken to him, but we smiled across the table at each other during mealtimes. He was from one of those cities so far from mine that they seemed like a figment of my imagination, where there was snow and where men rode those enormous gray birds and the women could speak with those birds without moving their mouths.

Once Heru was standing behind me in the dinner line with one of his friends. I felt someone pick up one of my plaits and I whirled around, ready to be angry. I met his eyes and he'd quickly let go of my hair, smiled, and raised his hands up defensively. "I couldn't help it," he said, his fingertips reddish with my *otjize*.

"You can't control yourself?" I snapped.

"You have exactly twenty-one," he said. "And they're braided in tessellating triangles. Is it some sort of code?"

I wanted to tell him that there *was* a code, that the pattern spoke my family's bloodline, culture, and history. That my father had designed the code and my mother and aunties had shown me how to braid it into my hair. However, looking at Heru made my heart beat too fast and my words escaped me, so I merely shrugged and turned back around to pick up a bowl of soup. Heru was tall and had the whitest teeth I'd ever seen. And he was very good in mathematics; few would have noticed the code in my hair.

But I never got the chance to tell him that my hair was braided into the history of my people. Because what happened, happened. It occurred on the eighteenth day of the journey. The five days before we arrived on the planet Oomza Uni, the most powerful and innovative sprawling university in the Milky Way. I was the happiest I'd ever been in my life and I was farther from my beloved family than I'd ever been in my life.

I was at the table savoring a mouthful of a gelatinous milk-based dessert with slivers of coconut in it; I was gazing at Heru, who wasn't gazing at me. I'd put my fork down and had my *edan* in my hands. I fiddled with it as I watched Heru talk to the boy beside him. The delicious creamy dessert was melting coolly on my tongue. Beside me, Olo and Remi were singing a traditional song from their city because they missed home, a song that had to be sung with a wavery voice like a water spirit.

Then someone screamed and Heru's chest burst open, spattering me with his warm blood. There was a Meduse right behind him.

✦ ✦ ✦

In my culture, it is blasphemy to pray to inanimate objects, but I did anyway. I prayed to a metal even my father had been unable to identify. I held it to my chest, shut my eyes, and I prayed to it, *I am in your protection. Please protect me. I am in your protection. Please protect me.*

My body was shuddering so hard that I could imagine what it would be like to die from terror. I held my breath, the stench of *them* still in my nasal cavity and mouth. Heru's blood was on my face, wet and thick. I prayed to the mystery metal my *edan* was made of because that had to be the only thing keeping me alive at this moment.

Breathing hard from my mouth, I peeked from one eye. I shut it again. The Meduse were hovering less than a foot away. One had launched itself at me but then froze an inch from my flesh; it had reached a tentacle toward my *edan* and then suddenly collapsed, the tentacle turning ash gray as it quickly dried up like a dead leaf.

I could hear the others, their near substantial bodies softly rustling as their transparent domes filled with and released the gas they breathed back in. They were tall as grown men, their domes' flesh thin as fine silk, their long tentacles spilling down to the floor like a series of gigantic ghostly noodles. I grasped my *edan* closer to me. I am in your protection. Please protect me.

Everyone in the dining hall was dead. At least one hundred people. I had a feeling everyone on the ship was dead. The Meduse had burst into the hall and begun committing *moojh-ha ki-bira* before anyone knew what was happening. That's what the Khoush call it. We'd all been taught this Meduse form of killing in history class. The Khoush built the lessons into history, literature, and culture classes across several regions. Even my people were required to learn about it, despite the fact that it wasn't our fight. The Khoush expected everyone to remember their greatest enemy and injustice. They even worked Meduse anatomy and rudimentary technology into mathematics and science classes.

Moojh-ha ki-bira means the "great wave." The Meduse move like water when at war. There is no water on their planet, but they worship water as a god. Their ancestors came from water long ago. The Khoush were settled on the most water-soaked lands on Earth, a planet made mostly of water, and they saw the Meduse as inferior.

The trouble between the Meduse and the Khoush was an old fight and an older disagreement. Somehow, they had agreed to a treaty not to attack each other's ships. Yet here the Meduse were performing *moojh-ha ki-bira.*

I'd been talking to my friends.

My *friends.*

Olo, Remi, Kwuga, Nur, Anajama, Rhoden, and Dullaz. We had spent so many late nights laughing over our fears about how difficult and strange Oomza Uni would be. All of us had twisted ideas that were probably wrong... maybe partially right. We had so much in common. I wasn't thinking about home or how I'd *had* to leave it or the horrible messages my family had sent to my astrolabe hours after I'd left. I was looking ahead toward my future and I was laughing because it was so bright.

Then the Meduse came through the dining hall entrance. I was looking right at Heru when the red circle appeared in the upper left side of his shirt. The thing that tore through was like a sword, but thin as paper... and flexible and easily stained by blood. The tip wiggled and grasped like a finger. I saw it pinch and hook to the flesh near his collarbone.

Moojh-ha ki-bira.

I don't remember what I did or said. My eyes were open, taking it all in, but the rest of my brain was screaming. For no reason at all, I focused on the number five. Over and over, I thought, *5-5-5-5-5-5-5-5*, as Heru's eyes went from shocked to blank. His open mouth let out a gagging sound, then a spurt of thick red blood, then blood frothed with saliva as he began to fall forward. His head hit the table with a flat thud. His neck was turned and I could see that his eyes were open. His left hand flexed spasmodically, until it stopped. But his eyes were still open. He wasn't blinking.

Heru was dead. Olo, Remi, Kwuga, Nur, Anajama, Rhoden, and Dullaz were dead. Everyone was dead.

The dinner hall stank of blood.

✦ ✦ ✦

None of my family had wanted me to go to Oomza Uni. Even my best friend Dele hadn't wanted me to go. Still, not long after I received the news of my university acceptance and my whole family was saying no, Dele had joked that if I went, I at least wouldn't have to worry about the Meduse, because I would be the only Himba on the ship.

"So even if they kill everyone else, they won't even *see* you!" he'd said. Then he'd laughed and laughed, sure that I wasn't going anyway.

Now his words came back to me. Dele. I'd pushed thoughts of

him deep into my mind and read none of his messages. Ignoring the people I loved was the only way I could keep going. When I'd received the scholarship to study at Oomza Uni, I'd gone into the desert and cried for hours. With joy.

I'd wanted this since I knew what a university was. Oomza Uni was the top of the top, its population was only 5 percent human. Imagine what it meant to go there as one of that 5 percent; to be with others obsessed with knowledge, creation, and discovery. Then I went home and told my family and wept with shock.

"You can't go," my oldest sister said. "You're a master harmonizer. Who else is good enough to take over Father's shop?"

"Don't be selfish," my sister Suum spat. She was only a year older than me, but she still felt she could run my life. "Stop chasing fame and be rational. You can't just leave and fly across the *galaxy.*"

My brothers had all just laughed and dismissed the idea. My parents said nothing, not even congratulations. Their silence was answer enough. Even my best friend Dele. He congratulated and told me that I was smarter than everyone at Oomza Uni, but then he'd laughed, too. "You cannot go," he simply said. "We're Himba. God has already chosen our paths."

I was the first Himba in history to be bestowed with the honor of acceptance into Oomza Uni. The hate messages, threats to my life, laughter and ridicule that came from the Khoush in my city, made me want to hide more. But deep down inside me, I wanted… I *needed* it. I couldn't help but act on it. The urge was so strong that it was mathematical. When I'd sit in the desert, alone, listening to the wind, I would see and feel the numbers the way I did when I was deep in my work in my father's shop. And those numbers added up to the sum of my destiny.

So in secret, I filled out and uploaded the acceptance forms. The desert was the perfect place for privacy when they contacted my astrolabe for university interviews. When everything was set, I packed my things and got on that shuttle. I come from a family of *Bitolus*; my father is a master harmonizer and I was to be his successor. We *Bitolus* know true deep mathematics and we can control their current, we know systems. We are few and we are happy and uninterested in weapons and war, but we can protect ourselves. And as my father says, "God favors us."

I clutched my *edan* to my chest now as I opened my eyes. The Meduse in front of me was blue and translucent, except for one of its tentacles, which was tinted pink like the waters of the salty lake beside my village and curled up like the branch of a confined tree. I held up my *edan* and the Meduse jerked back, pluming out its gas and loudly inhaling. *Fear*, I thought. *That was fear.*

I stood up, realizing that my time of death was not here yet. I took a quick look around the giant hall. I could smell dinner over the stink of blood and Meduse gases. Roasted and marinated meats, brown long-grained rice, spicy red stews, flat breads, and that rich gelatinous dessert I loved so much. They were all still laid out on the grand table, the hot foods cooling as the bodies cooled and the dessert melting as the dead Meduse melted.

"Back!" I hissed, thrusting the *edan* at the Meduse. My garments rustled and my anklets jingled as I got up. I pressed my backside against the table. The Meduse were behind me and on my sides, but I focused on the one before me. "This will kill you!" I said as forcibly as I could. I cleared my throat and raised my voice. "You saw what it did to your brother."

I motioned to the shriveled dead one two feet away; its mushy flesh had dried and begun to turn brown and opaque. It had tried to take me and then something made it die. Bits of it had crumbled to dust as I spoke, the mere vibration of my voice enough to destabilize the remains. I grabbed my satchel as I slid away from the table and moved toward the grand table of food. My mind was moving fast now. I was seeing numbers and then blurs. Good. I was my father's daughter. He'd taught me in the tradition of my ancestors and I was the best in the family.

"I am Binti Ekeopara Zuzu Dambu Kaipka of Namib," I whispered. This is what my father always reminded me when he saw my face go blank and I started to tree. He would then loudly speak his lessons to me about astrolabes, including how they worked, the art of them, the true negotiation of them, the lineage. While I was in this state, my father passed me three hundred years of oral knowledge about circuits, wire, metals, oils, heat, electricity, math current, sand bar.

And so I had become a master harmonizer by the age of twelve. I could communicate with spirit flow and convince them to become one current. I was born with my mother's gift of mathematical sight. My mother only used it to protect the family, and now I was going to grow that skill at the best university in the galaxy... if I survived. "Binti Ekeopara Zuzu Dambu Kaipka of Namib, that is my name," I said again.

My mind cleared as the equations flew through it, opening it wider, growing progressively more complex and satisfying. $V—E + F = 2$, $a^2 + b^2 = c^2$, I thought. I knew what to do now. I moved to the table of food and grabbed a tray. I heaped chicken wings, a turkey leg, and three steaks of beef onto it. Then several rolls; bread would stay fresh longer. I dumped three oranges on my tray, because they carried juice and vitamin C. I grabbed two whole bladders of water and shoved them into my satchel as well. Then I slid a slice of white milky dessert on my tray. I did not know its name, but it was easily the most wonderful thing I'd ever tasted. Each bite would fuel my mental well-being. And if I were going to survive, I'd need that, especially.

I moved quickly, holding up the *edan*, my back straining with the weight of my loaded satchel as I held the large food-heavy tray with my left hand. The Meduse followed me, their tentacles caressing the floor as they floated. They had no eyes, but from what I knew of the Meduse, they had scent receptors on the tips of their tentacles. They saw me through smell.

The hallway leading to the rooms was wide and all the doors were plated with sheets of gold metal. My father would have spat at this wastefulness. Gold was an information conductor and its mathematical signals were stronger than anything. Yet here it was wasted on gaudy extravagance.

When I arrived at my room, the trance lifted from me without warning and I suddenly had no idea what to do next. I stopped treeing and the clarity of mind retreated like a loss of confidence. All I could think to do was let the door scan my eye. It opened, I slipped in and it shut behind me with a sucking sound, sealing the room, a mechanism probably triggered by the ship's emergency programming.

I managed to put the tray and satchel on my bed just before my legs gave. Then I sunk to the cool floor beside the black landing chair on the fair side of the room. My face was sweaty and I rested my cheek on the floor for a moment and sighed. Images of my friends Olo, Remi, Kwuga, Nur, Anajama, Rhoden crowded my mind. I thought I heard Heru's soft laughter above me... then the sound of his chest bursting open, then the heat of his blood on my face. I whimpered, biting my lip. "I'm here, I'm here, I'm here," I whispered. Because I was and there was no way out. I shut my eyes

tightly as the tears came. I curled my body and stayed like that for
several minutes.

I brought my astrolabe to my face. I'd made the casing with
golden sand bar that I'd molded, sculpted, and polished myself. It
was the size of a child's hand and far better than any astrolabe one
could buy from the finest seller. I'd taken care to fashion its weight
to suit my hands, the dials to respond to only my fingers, and its
currents were so true that they'd probably outlast my own future
children. I'd made this astrolabe two months ago specifically for my
journey, replacing the one my father had made for me when I was
three years old.

I started to speak my family name to my astrolabe, but then I
whispered, "No," and rested it on my belly. My family was planets
away by now; what more could they do than weep? I rubbed the on
button and spoke, "Emergency." The astrolabe warmed in my hands
and emitted the calming scent of roses as it vibrated. Then it went
cool. "Emergency," I said again. This time it didn't even warm up.

"Map," I said. I held my breath, waiting. I glanced at the door.
I'd read that Meduse could not move through walls, but even I knew
that just because information was in a book didn't make it true.
Especially when the information concerned the Meduse. My door
was secure, but I was Himba and I doubted the Khoush had given
me one of the rooms with full security locks. The Meduse would
come in when they wanted or when they were willing to risk death
to do away with me. I may not have been Khoush... but I was a
human on a Khoush ship.

My astrolabe suddenly warmed and vibrated. "Your location
is 121 hours from your destination of Oomza Uni," it said in its
whispery voice. So the Meduse felt it okay for me to know where
the ship was. The virtual constellation lit up my room with white,
light blue, red, yellow, and orange dots, slowly rotating globes from
the size of a large fly to the size of my fist. Suns, planets, bloom
territories all sectioned in the mathematical net that I'd always
found easy to read. The ship had long since left my solar system.
We'd slowed down right in the middle of what was known as "the
Jungle." The pilots of the ship should have been more vigilant. "And
maybe less arrogant," I said, feeling ill.

The ship was still heading for Oomza Uni, though, and that
was mildly encouraging. I shut my eyes and prayed to the Seven.
I wanted to ask, "Why did you let this happen?" but that was

blasphemy. You never ask why. It was not a question for you to ask.

"I'm going to die here."

✦ ✦ ✦

Seventy-two hours later, I was still alive. But I'd run out of food and had very little water left. Me and my thoughts in that small room, no escape outside. I had to stop crying; I couldn't afford to lose water. The toilet facilities were just outside my room so I'd been forced to use the case that carried my beaded jewelry collection. All I had was my jar of *otjize*, some of which I used to clean my body as much as possible. I paced, recited equations, and was sure that if I didn't die of thirst or starvation I'd die by fire from the currents I'd nervously created and discharged to keep myself busy.

I looked at the map yet again and saw what I knew I'd see; we were still heading to Oomza Uni. "But why?" I whispered. "Security will…"

I shut my eyes, trying to stop myself from completing the thought yet again. But I could never stop myself and this time was no different. In my mind's eye, I saw a bright yellow beam zip from Oomza Uni and the ship scattering in a radiating mass of silent light and flame. I got up and shuffled to the far side of my room and back as I talked. "But suicidal Meduse? It just doesn't make sense. Maybe they don't know how to…"

There was a slow knock at the door and I nearly jumped to the ceiling. Then I froze, listening with every part of my body. Other than the sound of my voice, I hadn't heard a thing from them since that first twenty-four hours. The knock came again. The last knock was hard, more like a kick, but not near the bottom of the door.

"L… leave me alone!" I screamed, grabbing my *edan*. My words were met with a hard bang at the door and an angry, harsh hiss. I screeched and moved as far from the door as my room would permit, nearly falling over my largest suitcase. *Think think think*. No weapons, except the *edan*… and I didn't know what made it a weapon.

Everyone was dead. I was still about forty-eight hours from safety or being blown up. They say that when faced with a fight you cannot win, you can never predict what you will do next. But I'd always known I'd fight until I was killed. It was an abomination to commit suicide or to give up your life. I was sure that I was ready. The Meduse were very intelligent; they'd find a way to kill me, despite my *edan*.

Nevertheless, I didn't pick up the nearest weapon. I didn't prepare for my last violent rabid stand. Instead, I looked my death square in the face and then… then I *surrendered* to it. I sat on my bed and waited for my death. Already, my body felt as if it were no longer mine; I'd let it go. And in that moment, deep in my submission, I laid my eyes on my *edan* and stared at its branching splitting dividing blue fractals.

And I saw it.

I *really* saw it.

And all I could do was smile and think, *How did I not know?*

+ + +

I sat in the landing chair beside my window, hand-rolling *otjize* into my plaits. I looked at my reddened hands, brought them to my nose and sniffed. Oily clay that sang of sweet flowers, desert wind, and soil. *Home*, I thought, tears stinging my eyes. I should not have left. I picked up the *edan*, looking for what I'd seen. I turned the *edan* over and over before my eyes. The blue object whose many points I'd rubbed, pressed, stared at, and pondered for so many years.

More thumping came from the door. "Leave me alone," I muttered weakly.

I smeared *otjize* onto the point of the *edan* with the spiral that always reminded me of a fingerprint. I rubbed it in a slow circular motion. My shoulders relaxed as I calmed. Then my starved and thirsty brain dropped into a mathematical trance like a stone dropped into deep water. And I felt the water envelop me as down down down I went.

My clouded mind cleared and everything went silent and motionless, my finger still polishing the *edan*. I smelled home, heard the desert wind blowing grains of sand over each other. My stomach fluttered as I dropped deeper in and my entire body felt sweet and pure and empty and light. The *edan* was heavy in my hands; so heavy that it would fall right through my flesh.

"Oh," I breathed, realizing that there was now a tiny button in the center of the spiral. This was what I'd seen. It had always been there, but now it was as if it were in focus. I pushed it with my index finger. It depressed with a soft "click" and then the stone felt like warm wax and my world wavered. There was another loud knock at the door. Then through the clearest silence I'd ever experienced, so clear that the slightest sound would tear its fabric, I heard a solid oily low voice say, "Girl."

I was catapulted out of my trance, my eyes wide, my mouth yawning in a silent scream.

"Girl," I heard again. I hadn't heard a human voice since the final screams of those killed by the Meduse, over seventy-two hours ago.

I looked around my room. I was alone. Slowly, I turned and looked out the window beside me. There was nothing out there for me but the blackness of space.

"Girl. You will die," the voice said slowly. "Soon." I heard more voices, but they were too low to understand. "Suffering is against the Way. Let us end you."

I jumped up and the rush of blood made me nearly collapse and crash to the floor. Instead I fell painfully to my knees, still clutching the *edan*. There was another knock at the door. "Open this door," the voice demanded.

My hands began to shake, but I didn't drop my *edan*. It was warm and a brilliant blue light was glowing from within it now. A current was running through it so steadily that it made the muscles of my hand constrict. I couldn't let go of it if I tried.

"I will not," I said, through clenched teeth. "Rather die in here, on *my* terms."

The knocking stopped. Then I heard several things at once. Scuffling at the door, not toward it, but *away*. Terrified moaning and wailing. More *voices*. Several of them.

"This is evil!"

"It carries shame," another voice said. This was the first voice I heard that sounded high-pitched, almost female. "The shame she carries allows her to mimic speech."

"No. It has to have sense for that," another voice said.

"Evil! Let me deactivate the door and kill it."

"Okwu, you will die if you…"

"I will kill it!" the one called Okwu growled. "Death will be my honor! We're too close now, we can't have…"

"Me!" I shouted suddenly. "O… Okwu!" Calling its name, addressing it so directly sounded strange on my lips. I pushed on. "Okwu, why don't you talk to me?"

I looked at my cramped hands. From within it, from my *edan*, possibly the strongest current I'd ever produced streamed in jagged connected bright blue branches. It slowly etched and lurched through the closed door, a line of connected bright blue treelike branches that shifted in shape but never broke their connection. The current was touching the Meduse. Connecting them to me. And though I'd created it, I couldn't control it now. I wanted to scream, revolted. But I had to save my life first. "I am speaking to you!" I said. "Me!"

Silence.

I slowly stood up, my heart pounding. I stumbled to the shut door on aching trembling legs. The door's organic steel was so thin, but one of the strongest substances on my planet. Where the current touched it, tiny green leaves unfurled. I touched them, focusing on the leaves and not the fact that the door was covered with a sheet of gold, a super communication conducter. Nor the fact of the Meduse just beyond my door.

I heard a rustle and I used all my strength not to scuttle back. I flared my nostrils as I grasped the *edan*. The weight of my hair on my shoulders was assuring, my hair was heavy with *otjize*, and this was good luck and the strength of my people, even if my people were far far away.

The loud bang of something hard and powerful hitting the door made me yelp. I stayed where I was. "Evil thing," I heard the one called Okwu say. Of all the voices, that one I could recognize. It was the angriest and scariest. The voice sounded spoken, not transmitted in my mind. I could hear the vibration of the "v" in "evil" and the hard breathy "th" in "thing." Did they have mouths?

"I'm not evil," I said.

I heard whispering and rustling behind the door. Then the more female voice said, "Open this door."

"No!"

They muttered among themselves. Minutes passed. I sunk to the floor, leaning against the door. The blue current sunk with me, streaming through the door at my shoulder; more green leaves bloomed there, some fell down my shoulder onto my lap. I leaned my head against the door and stared down at them. Green tiny leaves of green tiny life when I was so close to death. I giggled and my empty belly rumbled and my sore abdominal muscles ached.

Then, quietly, calmly, "You are understanding us?" this was the growling voice that had been calling me evil. Okwu.

"Yes," I said.

"Humans only understand violence."

I closed my eyes and felt my weak body relax. I sighed and said, "The only things I have killed are small animals for food, and only with swift grace and after prayer and thanking the beast for its sacrifice." I was exhausted.

"I do not believe you."

"Just as I do not believe you will not kill me if I open the door. All you do is kill." I opened my eyes. Energy that I didn't know I still had rippled through me and I was so angry that I couldn't catch my breath. "Like… like you… killed my friends!" I coughed and slumped down, weakly. "My friends," I whispered, tears welling in my eyes. "Oooh, my friends!"

"Humans must be killed before they kill us," the voice said.

"You're all stupid," I spat, wiping my tears as they kept coming. I sobbed hard and then took a deep breath, trying to pull it together. I exhaled loudly, snot flying from my nose. As I wiped my face with my arm, there were more whispers. Then the higher-pitched voice spoke.

"What is this blue ghost you have sent to help us communicate?"

"I don't know," I said, sniffing. I got up and walked to my bed. Moving away from the door instantly made me feel better. The blue current extended with me.

"Why do we understand you?" Okwu asked. I could still hear its voice perfectly from where I was.

"I… I don't know," I said, sitting on my bed and then lying back.

"No Meduse has ever spoken to a human… except long ago."

"I don't care," I grunted.

"Open the door. We won't harm you."

"No."

There was a long pause. So long that I must have fallen asleep. I was awakened by a sucking sound. At first I paid no mind to it, taking the moment to wipe off the caked snot on my face with my arm. The ship made all sorts of sounds, even before the Meduse attacked. It was a living thing and like any beast, its bowels gurgled and quaked every so often. Then I sat up straight as the sucking sound grew louder. The door trembled. It buckled a bit and then completely crumpled, the gold plating on the outside now visible. The stale air of my room whooshed out into the hallway and suddenly the air cooled and smelled fresher.

There stood the Meduse. I could not tell how many of them, for they were transparent and when they stood together, all I could see were a tangle of translucent tentacles and undulating domes. I clutched the *edan* to my chest as I pressed myself on the other side of the room, against the window.

It happened fast like the desert wolves who attack travelers at night back home. One of the Meduse shot toward me. I watched it come. I saw my parents, sisters, brothers, aunts, and uncles, all gathered at a remembrance for me—full of pain and loss. I saw my spirit break from my body and return to my planet, to the desert, where I would tell stories to the sand people.

Time must have slowed down because the Meduse was motionless, yet suddenly it was hovering over me, its tentacles hanging an inch from my head. I gasped, bracing myself for pain and then death. Its pink withered tentacle brushed my arm firmly enough to rub off some of the *otjize* there. *Soft*, I thought. *Smooth*.

There it was. So close now. White like the ice I'd only seen in pictures and entertainment streams, its stinger was longer than my leg. I stared at it, jutting from its bundle of tentacles. It crackled and dried, wisps of white mist wafting from it. Inches from my chest. Now it went from white to a dull light gray. I looked down at my cramped hands, the *edan* between them. The current flowing from it washed over the Meduse and extended beyond it. Then I looked up at the Meduse and grinned. "I hope it hurts," I whispered.

The Meduse's tentacles shuddered and it began to back away. I could see its pink deformed tentacle, part of it smeared red with my *otjize*.

"You are the foundation of evil," it said. It was the one called Okwu. I nearly laughed. Why did this one hate me so strongly?

"She still holds the shame," I heard one say from near the door.

Okwu began to recover as it moved away from me. Quickly, it left with the others.

✦ ✦ ✦

Ten hours passed.

I had no food left. No water. I packed and repacked my things. Keeping busy staved off the dehydration and hunger a bit, though my constant need to urinate kept reminding me of my predicament. And movement was tricky because the *edan*'s current still wouldn't release my hands' muscles, but I managed. I tried not to indulge in my fear of the Meduse finding a way to get the ship to stop producing and circulating air and maintaining its internal pressure, or just coming back and killing me.

When I wasn't packing and repacking, I was staring at my *edan*, studying it; the patterns on it now glowed with the current. I needed to know how it was allowing me to communicate. I tried different soft equations on it and received no response. After a while, when not even hard equations affected it, I lay back on my bed and let myself tree. This was my state of mind when the Meduse came in.

"What is that?"

I screamed. I'd been gazing out the window, so I heard the Meduse before I saw it.

"What?" I shrieked, breathless. "I… what is what?"

Okwu, the one who'd tried to kill me. Contrary to how it had looked when it left, it was very much alive, though I could not see its stinger.

"What is the substance on your skin?" it asked firmly. "None of the other humans have it."

"Of course they don't," I snapped. "It is *otjize*, only my people wear it and I am the only one of my people on the ship. I'm not Khoush."

"What is it?" it asked, remaining in the doorway.

"Why?"

It moved into my room and I held up the *edan* and quickly said, "Mostly… mostly clay and oil from my homeland. Our land is desert, but we live in the region where there is sacred red clay."

"Why do you spread it on your skins?"

"Because my people are sons and daughters of the soil," I said. "And… and it's beautiful."

It paused for a long moment and I just stared at it. Really looking at the thing. It moved as if it had a front and a back. And though it seemed to be fully transparent, I could not see its solid white stinger within the drapes of hanging tentacles. Whether it was thinking about what I'd said or considering how best to kill me, I didn't know. But moments later, it turned and left. And it was only after several minutes, when my heart rate slowed, that I realized something odd. Its withered tentacle didn't look as withered. Where it had been curled up tightly into itself, now it was merely bent.

✦ ✦ ✦

It came back fifteen minutes later. And immediately, I looked to make sure I'd seen what I knew I'd seen. And there it was, pink and not so curled up. That tentacle had been different when Okwu had accidently touched me and rubbed off my *otjize*.

"Give me some of it," it said, gliding into my room.

"I don't have any more!" I said, panicking. I only had one large jar of *otjize*, the most I'd ever made in one batch. It was enough to last me until I could find red clay on Oomza Uni and make more. And even then, I wasn't sure if I'd find the right kind of clay. It was another planet. Maybe it wouldn't have clay at all.

In all my preparation, the one thing I didn't take enough time to do was research the Oomza Uni planet itself, so focused I was on just *getting* there. All I knew was that though it was much smaller than earth, it had a similar atmosphere and I wouldn't have to wear a special suit or adaptive lungs or anything like that. But its surface could easily be made of something my skin couldn't tolerate. I couldn't give all my *otjize* to this Meduse; this was my *culture*.

"The chief knows of your people, you have much with you."

"If your chief knows my people, then he will have told you that taking it from me is like taking my soul," I said, my voice cracking. My jar was under my bed. I held up my *edan*.

But Okwu didn't leave or approach. Its curled pink tentacle twitched.

I decided to take a chance, "It helped you, didn't it? Your tentacle."

It blew out a great puff of its gas, sucked it in and left.

It returned five minutes later with five others.

"What is that object made of?" Okwu asked, the others standing silently behind it.

I was still on my bed and I pushed my legs under the covers. "I don't know. But a desert woman once said it was made from something called 'god stone.' My father said there is no such…"

"It is shame," it insisted.

None of them moved to enter my room. Three of them made loud puffing sounds as they let out the reeking gasses they inhaled in order to breathe.

"There is nothing shameful about an object that keeps me alive," I said.

"It poisons Meduse," one of the others said.

"Only if you get too close to me," I said, looking straight at it. "Only if you try and *kill* me."

Pause.

"How are you communicating with us?"

"I don't know, Okwu." I spoke its name as if I owned it.

"What are you called?"

I sat up straight, ignoring the fatigue trying to pull my bones to the bed. "I am Binti Ekeopara Zuzu Dambu Kaipka of Namib." I considered speaking its single name to reflect its cultural simplicity compared to mine, but my strength and bravado were already waning.

Okwu moved forward and I held up the *edan*. "Stay back! You know what it'll do!" I said. However, it did not try to attack me again, though it didn't start to shrivel up as it approached, either. It stopped feet away, beside the metal table jutting from the wall carrying my open suitcase and one of the containers of water.

"What do you need?" it flatly asked.

I stared, weighing my options. I didn't have any. "Water, food," I said.

Before I could say more, it left. I leaned against the window and tried not to look outside into the blackness. Feet away from me, the door was crushed to the side, the path of my fate was no longer mine. I lay back and fell into the deepest sleep I'd had since the ship left Earth.

+ + +

The faint smell of smoke woke me up. There was a plate on my bed, right before my nose. On it was a small slab of smoked fish. Beside it was a bowl of water.

I sat up, still tightly grasping the *edan*. I leaned forward, and sucked up as much water from the bowl as I could. Then, still holding the *edan*, I pressed my forearms together and worked the food onto them. I brought the fish up, bent forward and took a bite of it. Smoky salty goodness burst across my taste buds. The chefs on the ship fed these fish well and allowed them to grow strong and mate copiously. Then they lulled the fish into a sleep that the fish never woke from and slow-cooked their flesh long enough for flavor and short enough to maintain texture. I'd asked the chefs about their process as any good Himba would before eating it. The chefs were all Khoush, and Khoush did not normally perform what they called "superstitious ritual." But these chefs were Oomza Uni students and they said they did, even lulling the fish to sleep in a similar way. Again, I'd been assured that I was heading in the right direction.

The fish was delicious, but it was full of bones. And it was as I was using my tongue to work a long, flexible, but tough bone from my teeth that I looked up and noticed the Meduse hovering in the doorway. I didn't have to see the withered tentacle to know it was Okwu. Inhaling with surprise, I nearly choked on the bone. I dropped what was left, spat out the bone and opened my mouth to speak. Then I closed it.

I was still alive.

Okwu didn't move or speak, though the blue current still connected us. Moments passed, Okwu hovering and emitting the foul-smelling gas as it breathed and me sucking bits of fish from my mouth wondering if this was my last meal. After a while, I grasped the remaining hunk of fish with my forearms and continued eating.

"You know," I finally said, to fill the silence. "There are a people in my village who have lived for generations at the edge of the lake." I looked at the Meduse. Nothing. "They know all the fish in it," I continued. "There is a fish that grows plenty in that lake and they catch and smoke them like this. The only difference is that my people can prepare it in such a way where there are no bones. They remove them all." I pulled a bone from between my teeth. "They have studied this fish. They have worked it out mathematically. They know where every bone will be, no matter the age, size, sex of the fish. They go in and remove every bone without disturbing the body. It is delicious!" I put down the remaining bones. "This was delicious, too." I hesitated and then said, "Thank you."

Okwu didn't move, continuing to hover and puff out gas. I got up and walked to the counter where a tray had been set. I leaned down and sucked up the water from this bowl as well. Already, I felt much stronger and more alert. I jumped when it spoke.

"I wish I could just kill you."

I paused. "Like my mother always says, 'we all wish for many things,'" I said, touching a last bit of fish in my back tooth.

"You don't look like a human Oomza Uni student," it said. "Your color is darker and you…" It blasted out a large plume of gas and I fought not to wrinkle my nose. "You have *okuoko*."

I frowned at the unfamiliar word. "What is *okuoko*?"

And that's when it moved for the first time since I'd awakened. Its long tentacles jiggled playfully and a laugh escaped my mouth before I could stop it. It plumed out more gas in rapid succession and made a deep thrumming sound. This made me laugh even harder. "You mean my hair?" I asked shaking my thick plaits.

"*Okuoko*, yes," it said.

"*Okuoko*," I said. I had to admit, I liked the sound of it. "How come the word is different?"

"I don't know," it said. "I hear you in my language as well. When you said *okuoko* it is *okuoko*." It paused. "The Khoush are the color of the flesh of the fish you ate and they have no *okuoko*. You are red brown like the fish's outer skin and you have *okuoko* like Meduse, though small."

"There are different kinds of humans," I said. "My people don't normally leave my planet." Several Meduse came to the door and crowded in. Okwu moved closer, pluming out more gas and inhaling it. This time I did cough at the stench of it.

"Why have you?" it asked. "You are probably the most evil of your people."

I frowned at it. Realizing something. It spoke like one of my brothers, Bena. I was born only three years after him yet we'd never been very close. He was angry and always speaking out about the way my people were maltreated by the Khoush majority despite the fact that they needed us and our astrolabes to survive. He was always calling them evil, though he'd never traveled to a Khoush country or known a Khoush. His anger was rightful, but all that he said was from what he didn't truly know.

Even I could tell that Okwu was not an elder among these Meduse; it was too hotheaded and… there was something about it that reminded me of me. Maybe its curiosity; I think I'd have been one of the first to come see, if I were it, too. My father said that my curiosity was the last obstacle I had to overcome to be a true master harmonizer. If there was one thing my father and I disagreed on, it was that; I believed I could only be great if I were curious enough to seek greatness. Okwu was young, like me. And maybe that's why it was so eager to die and prove itself to the others and that's why the others were fine with it.

"You know nothing of me," I said. I felt myself grow hot. "This is not a military ship, this is a ship full of professors! Students! All dead!! You killed everyone!"

It seemed to chuckle. "Not your pilot. We did not sting that one."

And just like that, I understood. They would get through the university's security if the security people thought the ship was still full of living breathing unmurdered professors and students. Then the Meduse would be able to invade Oomza Uni.

"We don't need *you*. But that one is useful."

"That's why we are still on course," I said.

"No. We can fly this creature ship," it said. "But your pilot can speak to the people on Oomza Uni in the way they expect." It paused, then moved closer. "See? We never *needed* you."

I felt the force of its threat physically. The sharp tingle came in white bursts in my toes and traveled up my body to the top of my head. I opened my mouth, suddenly short of breath. *This* was what fearing death truly felt like, not my initial submission to it. I leaned away, holding up my *edan*. I was sitting on my bed, its red covers making me think of blood. There was nowhere to go.

"That shame is the only reason you are alive," it said.

"Your *okuoko* is better," I whispered, pointing at the tentacle. "Won't you spare me for curing that?" I could barely breathe. When it didn't respond, I asked, "Why? Or maybe there is no reason."

"You think we are like you humans?" it asked, angrily. "We don't kill for sport or even for gain. Only for purpose."

I frowned. They sounded like the same thing to me, gain and purpose.

"In your university, in one of its museums, placed on display like a piece of rare meat is the stinger of our chief," it said. I wrinkled my face, but said nothing. "Our chief is..." It paused. "We know of the attack and mutilation of our chief, but we do not know how it got there. We do not care. We will land on Oomza Uni and take it back. So you see? We have purpose."

It billowed out gas and left the room. I lay back in my bed, exhausted.

+ + +

But they brought me more food and water. Okwu brought it. And it sat with me while I ate and drank. More fish and some dried-up dates and a flask of water. This time, I barely tasted it as I ate.

"It's suicide," I said.

"What is... suicide?" it asked.

"What you are doing!" I said. "On Oomza Uni, there's a city where all the students and professors do is study, test, create *weapons*. Weapons for taking every form of life. Your own weapons were probably made there!"

"Our weapons are made within our bodies," it said.

"What of the current-killer you used against the Khoush in the Meduse–Khoush War?" I asked.

It said nothing.

"Suicide is death on purpose!"

"Meduse aren't afraid of death," it said. "And this would be honorable. We will show them never to dishonor Meduse again. Our people will remember our sacrifice and celebrate…"

"I… I have an idea!" I shouted. My voice cracked. I pushed forward. "Let me talk to your chief!" I shrieked. I don't know if it was the delicious fish I'd eaten, shock, hopelessness, or exhaustion. I stood up and stepped to it, my legs shaky and my eyes wild. "Let me… I'm a master harmonizer. That's why I'm going to Oomza Uni. I am the best of the best, Okwu. I can create harmony *anywhere*." I was so out of breath that I was wheezing. I inhaled deeply, seeing stars explode before my eyes. "Let me be… let me speak for the Meduse. The people in Oomza Uni are academics, so they'll understand honor and history and symbolism and matters of the body." I didn't know any of this for sure. These were only my dreams… and my experience of those on the ship.

"Now you speak of 'suicide' for the both of us," it said.

"Please," I said. "I can make your chief listen."

"Our chief hates humans," Okwu said. "Humans took his stinger. Do you know what…"

"I'll give you my jar of *otjize*," I blurted. "You can put it all over your… on every *okuoko*, your dome, who knows, it might make you glow like a star or give you super-powers or sting harder and faster or…"

"We don't like stinging."

"Please," I begged. "Imagine what you will be. Imagine if my plan works. You'll get the stinger back and none of you will have died. You'll be a hero." *And I get to live*, I thought.

"We don't care about being heroes." But its pink tentacle twitched when it said this.

✦ ✦ ✦

The Meduse ship was docked beside the *Third Fish*. I'd walked across the large chitinous corridor linking them, ignoring the fact that the chances of my returning were very low.

Their ship stank. I was sure of it, even if I couldn't smell it through my breather. Everything about the Meduse stank. I could barely concentrate on the spongy blue surface beneath my bare feet. Or the cool gasses Okwu promised would not harm my flesh even though I could not breathe it. Or the Meduse, some green, some blue, some pink, moving on every surface, floor, high ceiling, wall, or stopping and probably staring at me with whatever they stared with. Or the current-connected *edan* I still grasped in my hands. I was doing equations in my head. I needed everything I had to do what I was about to do.

The room was so enormous that it almost felt as if we were outside. Almost. I'm a child of the desert; nothing indoors can feel like the outdoors to me. But this room was huge. The chief was no bigger than the others, no more colorful. It had no more tentacles than the others. It was surrounded by other Meduse. It looked so much like those around it that Okwu had to stand beside it to let me know who it was.

The current from the *edan* was going crazy—branching out in every direction bringing me their words. I should have been terrified. Okwu had told me that requesting a meeting like this with the chief was risking not only my life, but Okwu's life as well. For the chief hated human beings and Okwu had just begged to bring one into their "great ship."

Spongy. As if it were full of the firm jelly beads in the milky pudding my mother liked to make. I could sense current all around me. These people had deep active technology built into the walls and many of them had it running within their very bodies. Some of them were walking astrolabes, it was part of their biology.

I adjusted my facemask. The air that it pumped in smelled like desert flowers. The makers of the mask had to have been Khoush women. They liked everything to smell like flowers, even their privates. But at the moment, I could have kissed those women, for as I gazed at the chief, the smell of flowers burst into my nose and mouth and suddenly I was imagining the chief hovering in the desert surrounded by the dry sweet-smelling flowers that only bloomed at night. I felt calm. I didn't feel at home, because in the part of the desert that I knew, only tiny scentless flowers grew. But I sensed Earth.

I slowly stopped treeing, my mind clean and clear, but much stupider. I needed to speak, not act. So I had no choice. I held my chin up and then did as Okwu instructed me. I sunk to the spongy floor. Then right there, within the ship that brought the death of my friends, the boy I was coming to love, my fellow Oomza Uni human citizens from Earth, before the one who had instructed its people to perform *moojh-ha ki-bira*, also called the "great wave" of death, on my people—still grasping the *edan*, I prostrated. I pressed my face to the floor. Then I waited.

"This is Binti Ekeopara Zuzu Dambu Kaipka of Namib, the one… the one who survives," Okwu said.

"You may just call me Binti," I whispered, keeping my head down. My first name was singular and two-syllabled like Okwu's name and I thought maybe it would please the chief.

"Tell the girl to sit up," the chief said. "If there is the slightest damage to the ship's flesh because of this one, I will have you executed first, Okwu. Then this creature."

"Binti," Okwu said, his voice was hard, flat. "Get up."

I shut my eyes. I could feel the *edan*'s current working through me, touching everything. Including the floor beneath me. And I could *hear* it. The floor. It was singing. But not words. Just humming. Happy and aloof. It wasn't paying attention. I pushed myself up, and leaned back on my knees. Then I looked at where my chest had been. Still a deep blue. I looked up at the chief.

"My people are the creators and builders of astrolabes," I said. "We use math to create the currents within them. The best of us have the gift to bring harmony so delicious that we can make atoms caress each other like lovers. That's what my sister said." I blinked as it came to me. "I think that's why this *edan* works for me! I found it. In the desert. A wild woman there once told me that it is a piece of old old technology; she called it a 'god stone.' I didn't believe her then, but I do now. I've had it for five years, but it only worked for *me* now." I pounded my chest. "For *me*! On that ship full of you after you'd all done… done that. Let me speak for you, let me speak to them. So no more have to die."

I lowered my head, pressing my *edan* to my belly. Just as Okwu told me. I could hear others behind me. They could have stung me a thousand times.

"You know what they have taken from me," the chief asked.

"Yes," I said, keeping my head down.

"My stinger is my people's power," it said. "They took it from us. That's an act of war."

"My way will get your stinger back," I quickly said. Then I braced myself for the rough stab in the back. I felt the sharpness press against the nape of my neck. I bit my lower lip to keep from screaming.

"Tell your plan," Okwu said.

I spoke fast. "The pilot gets us cleared to land, then I leave the ship with one of you to negotiate with Oomza Uni to get the stinger back… peacefully."

"That will take our element of surprise," the chief said. "You know nothing about strategy."

"If you attack, you will kill many, but then they will kill you. All of you," I said. "Ahh," I hissed as the stinger pointed at my neck was pressed harder against my flesh. "Please, I'm just…"

"Chief, Binti doesn't know how to speak," Okwu said. "Binti is uncivilized. Forgive it. It is young, a girl."

"How can we trust it?" the Meduse beside the chief asked Okwu.

"What would I do?" I asked, my face squeezed with pain. "Run?" I wiped tears from my face. I wiped and wiped, but they kept coming. The nightmare kept happening.

"You people are good at hiding," another Meduse sneered. "Especially the females like you." Several of the Meduse, including the chief, shook their tentacles and vibrated their domes in a clear display of laughter.

"Let Binti put down the *edan*," Okwu said.

I stared at Okwu, astonished. "What?"

"Put it *down*," it said. "You will be completely vulnerable. How can you be our ambassador, if you need that to stay safe from us?"

"It's what allows me to hear you!" I shrieked. And it was all I had.

The chief whipped up one of its tentacles and every single Meduse in that enormous room stopped moving. They stopped as if the very currents of time stopped. Everything stopped as it does when things get so cold that they become ice. I looked around and when none of them moved, slowly, carefully I dragged myself inches forward and turned to see the Meduse behind me. Its stinger was up, at the height of where my neck had been. I looked at Okwu, who said nothing. Then at the chief. I lowered my eyes. Then I ventured another look, keeping my head low.

"Choose," the chief said.

My shield. My translator. I tried to flex the muscles in my hands. I was greeted with sharp intense pain. It had been over three days. We were five hours from Oomza Uni. I tried again. I screamed. The *edan* pulsed a bright blue deep within its black and gray crevices, lighting up its loops and swirls. Like one of the bioluminescent snails that invaded the edges of my home's lake.

When my left index finger pulled away from the *edan*, I couldn't hold the tears back. The *edan*'s blue-white glow blurred before my eyes. My joints popped and the muscles spasmed. Then my middle finger and pinky pulled away. I bit my lip so hard that I tasted blood. I took several quick breaths and then flexed every single one of my fingers at the same time. All of my joints went *CRACK*! I heard a thousand wasps in my head. My body went numb. The *edan* fell from my hands. Right before my eyes, I saw it and I wanted to laugh. The blue current I'd conjured danced before me, the definition of harmony made from chaos.

There was a soft *pap* as the *edan* hit the floor, rolled twice, then stopped. I had just killed myself. My head grew heavy... and all went black.

✦ ✦ ✦

The Meduse were right. I could not have represented them if I was holding the *edan*. This was Oomza Uni. Someone there would know everything there was to know about the *edan* and thus its toxicity to the Meduse. No one at Oomza Uni would have really believed I was their ambassador unless I let go.

Death. When I left my home, I died. I had not prayed to the Seven before I left. I didn't think it was time. I had not gone on my pilgrimage like a proper woman. I was sure I'd return to my village as a full woman to do that. I had left my family. I thought I could return to them when I'd done what I needed to do.

Now I could never go back. The Meduse. The Meduse are not what we humans think. They are truth. They are clarity. They are decisive. There are sharp lines and edges. They understand honor and dishonor. I had to earn their honor and the only way to do that was by dying a second time.

I felt the stinger plunge into my spine just before I blacked out and just after I'd conjured up the wild line of current that I guided to the *edan*. It was a terrible pain. Then I left. I left them, I left that ship. I could hear the ship singing its half-word song and I knew it was singing to me. My last thought was to my family, and I hoped it reached them.

✦ ✦ ✦

Home. I smelled the earth at the border of the desert just before it rained, during Fertile Season. The place right behind the Root, where I dug up the clay I used for my *otjize* and chased the geckos

who were too fragile to survive a mile away in the desert. I opened
my eyes; I was on my bed in my room, naked except for my wrapped
skirt. The rest of my body was smooth with a thick layer of *otjize*. I
flared my nostrils and inhaled the smell of me. Home…

I sat up and something rolled off my chest. It landed in my
crotch and I grabbed it. The *edan*. It was cool in my hand and all
dull blue as it had been for years before. I reached behind and felt
my back. The spot where the stinger had stabbed me was sore and
I could feel something rough and scabby there. It too was covered
with *otjize*. My astrolabe sat on the curve of the window and I
checked my map and stared outside for a very long time. I grunted,
slowly standing up. My foot hit something on the floor. My jar. I put
the *edan* down and picked it up, grasping it with both hands. The
jar was more than half-empty. I laughed, dressed and stared out the
window again. We were landing on Oomza Uni in an hour and the
view was spectacular.

+ + +

They did not come. Not to tell me what to do or when to do it.
So I strapped myself in the black landing chair beside the window
and stared at the incredible sight expanding before my eyes. There
were two suns, one that was very small and one that was large but
comfortably far away. Hours of sunshine on all parts of the planet
were far more than hours of dark, but there were few deserts on
Oomza Uni.

I used my astrolabe in binocular vision to see things up close.
Oomza Uni, such a small planet compared to Earth. Only one third
water, its lands were every shade of the rainbow—some parts blue,
green, white, purple, red, white, black, orange. And some areas
were smooth, others jagged with peaks that touched the clouds.
And the area we were hurtling toward was orange, but interrupted
by patches of the dense green of large forests of trees, small lakes,
and the hard gray-blue forests of tall skyscrapers.

My ears popped as we entered the atmosphere. The sky started
to turn a light pinkish color, then red orange. I was looking out
from within a fireball. We were inside the air that was being ripped
apart as we entered the atmosphere. There wasn't much shaking
or vibrating, but I could see the heat generated by the ship. The
ship would shed its skin the day after we arrived as it readjusted
to gravity.

We descended from the sky and zoomed between monstrously beautiful structures that made the skyscrapers of Earth look miniscule. I laughed wildly as we descended lower and lower. Down down, we fell. No military ships came to shoot us out of the sky. We landed and, moments after smiling with excitement, I wondered if they would kill the pilot now that he was useless? I had not negotiated that with the Meduse. I ripped off my safety belt and jumped up and then fell to the floor. My legs felt like weights.

"What is…"

I heard a horrible noise, a low rumble that boiled to an angry-sounding growl. I looked around, sure there was a monster about to enter my room. But then I realized two things. Okwu was standing in my doorway and I understood what it was saying.

I did as it said and pushed myself into a sitting position, bringing my legs to my chest. I grasped the side of my bed and dragged myself up to sit on it.

"Take your time," Okwu said. "Your kind do not adjust quickly to *jadevia.*"

"You mean gravity?" I asked.

"Yes."

I slowly stood up. I took a step and looked at Okwu, then past it at the empty doorway. "Where are the others?"

"Waiting in the dining room."

"The pilot?" I asked

"In the dining room as well."

"Alive?"

"Yes."

I sighed, relieved, and then paused. The sound of its speech vibrating against my skin. This was its true voice. I could not only hear at its frequency, but I saw its tentacles quiver as it spoke. And I could understand it. Before, it had just looked like their tentacles were quivering for no reason.

"Was it the sting?" I asked.

"No," it said. "That is something else. You understand, because you truly are what you say you are—a harmonizer."

I didn't care to understand. Not at the moment.

"Your tentacle," I said. "Your *okuoko.*" It hung straight, still pink but now translucent like the others.

"The rest was used to help several of our sick," it said. "Your people will be remembered by my people."

The more it spoke, the less monstrous its voice sounded. I took another step.

"Are you ready?" Okwu asked.

I was. I left the *edan* behind with my other things.

+ + +

I was still weak from the landing, but this had to happen fast. I don't know how they broke the news of their presence to Oomza Uni authorities, but they must have. Otherwise, how would we be able to leave the ship during the brightest part of the day?

I understood the plan as soon as Okwu and the chief came to my room. I followed them down the hallway. We did not pass through the dining room where so many had been brutally killed, and I was glad. But as we passed the entrance, I saw all the Meduse in there. The bodies were all gone. The chairs and tables were all stacked on one side of the large room as if a windstorm had swept through it. Between the transparent folds and tentacles, I thought I glimpsed someone in the red flowing uniform of the pilot, but I wasn't sure.

"You know what you will say," the chief said. Not a question, but a statement. And within the statement, a threat.

I wore my best red shirt and wrapper, made from the threads of well-fed silkworms. I'd bought it for my first day of class at Oomza Uni, but this was a more important occasion. And I'd used fresh *otjize* on my skin and to thicken my plaited hair even more. As I'd palm rolled my plaits smooth like the bodies of snakes, I noticed that my hair had grown about an inch since I'd left home. This was odd. I looked at the thick wiry new growth, admiring its dark brown color before pressing the *otjize* onto it, making it red. There was a tingling sensation on my scalp as I worked the *otjize* in and my head ached. I was exhausted. I held my *otjize*-covered hands to my nose and inhaled the scent of home.

Years ago, I had snuck out to the lake one night with some other girls and we'd all washed and scrubbed off all our *otjize* using the lake's salty water. It took us half the night. Then we'd stared at each other horrified by what we'd done. If any man saw us, we'd be ruined for life. If our parents saw us, we'd all be beaten and that would only be a fraction of the punishment. Our families and people we knew would think us mentally unstable when they heard, and that too would ruin our chances of marriage.

But above all this, outside of the horror of what we'd done, we all felt an awesome glorious... shock. Our hair hung in thick clumps, black in the moonlight. Our skin glistened, dark brown. *Glistened*. And there had been a breeze that night and it felt amazing on our exposed skin. I thought of this as I applied the *otjize* to my new growth, covering up the dark brown color of my hair. What if I washed it all off now? I was the first of my people to come to Oomza Uni, would the people here even know the difference? But Okwu and the chief came minutes later and there was no time. Plus, really, this was Oomza Uni, someone would have researched and known of my people. And that person would know I was naked if I washed all my *otjize* off... and crazy.

I didn't want to do it anyway, I thought as I walked behind Okwu and the chief. There were soldiers waiting at the doorway; both were human and I wondered what point they were trying to make by doing that. Just like the photos in the books I read, they wore all-blue kaftans and no shoes.

"You first," the chief growled, moving behind me. I felt one of its tentacles, heavy and smooth, shove me softly in the back right where I'd been stung. The soreness there caused me to stand up taller. And then more softly in a voice that only tickled my ear with its strange vibration. "Look strong, girl."

Following the soldiers and followed by two Meduse, I stepped onto the surface of another planet for the first time in my life. My scalp was still tingling, and this added to the magical sensation of being so far from home. The first thing I noticed was the smell and weight of the air when I walked off the ship. It smelled jungly, green, heavy with leaves. The air was full of *water*. It was just like the air in the ship's plant-filled breathing chambers!

I parted my lips and inhaled it as I followed the soldiers down the open black walkway. Behind me, I heard the Meduse, pluming out and sucking in gas. Softly, though, unlike on the ship. We were walking toward a great building, the ship port.

"We will take you to the Oomza Uni Presidential Building," one of the soldiers said in to me in perfect Khoush. He looked up at the Meduse and I saw a crease of worry wrinkle his brow. "I don't know... their language. Can you..."

I nodded.

He looked about twenty-five and was dark-brown-skinned like me, but unlike the men of my people, his skin was naked, his hair shaven low, and he was quite short, standing a head shorter than me. "Do you mind swift transport?"

I turned and translated for Okwu and the chief.

"These people are primitive," the chief responded. But it and Okwu agreed to board the shuttle.

+ + +

The room's wall and floor were a light blue, the large open windows letting in sunshine and a warm breeze. There were ten professors, one from each of the ten university departments. They sat, stood, hovered, and crouched behind a long table of glass. Against every wall were soldiers wearing blue uniforms of cloth, color, and light. There were so many different types of people in the room that I found it hard to concentrate. But I had to or there would be more death.

The one who spoke for all the professors looked like one of the sand people's gods and I almost laughed. It was like a spider made of wind, gray and undulating, here and not quite there. When it spoke, it was in a whisper that I could clearly hear despite the fact that I was several feet away. And it spoke in the language of the Meduse.

It introduced itself as something that sounded like "Haras" and said, "Tell me what you need to tell me."

And then all attention was suddenly on me.

+ + +

"None of you have ever seen anyone like me," I said. "I come from a people who live near a small salty lake on the edge of a desert. On my people's land, fresh water, water humans can drink, is so little that we do not use it to bathe as so many others do. We wash with *otjize*, a mix of red clay from our land and oils from our local flowers."

Several of the human professors looked at each other and chuckled. One of the large insectile people clicked its mandibles. I frowned, flaring my nostrils. It was the first time I'd received treatment similar to the way my people were treated on Earth by the Khoush. In a way, this set me at ease. People were people, everywhere. These professors were just like anyone else.

"This was my first time leaving the home of my parents. I had never even left my own city, let alone my planet Earth. Days later, in the blackness of space, everyone on my ship but the pilot was killed, many right before my eyes, by a people at war with those who view my own people as near slaves." I waited for this to sink in, then continued. "You've never seen the Meduse, either. Only studied them... from afar. I know. I have read about them too." I stepped forward. "Or maybe some of you or your students have studied the stinger you have in the weapons museum up close."

I saw several of them look at each other. Some murmured to one another. Others, I did not know well enough to tell what they were doing. As I spoke, I fell into a rhythm, a meditative state very much like my math-induced ones. Except I was fully present, and before long tears were falling from my eyes. I told them in detail about watching Heru's chest burst open, desperately grabbing food, staying in that room waiting to die, the *edan* saving me and not knowing how or why or what.

I spoke of Okwu and how my *otjize* had really been what saved me. I spoke of the Meduse's cold exactness, focus, violence, sense of honor, and willingness to listen. I said things that I didn't know I'd thought about or comprehended. I found words I didn't even know I knew. And eventually, I told them how they could satisfy the Meduse and prevent a bloodbath in which everyone would lose.

I was sure they would agree. These professors were educated beyond anything I could imagine. Thoughtful. Insightful. United. Individual. The Meduse chief came forward and spoke its piece, as well. It was angry, but thorough, eloquent with a sterile logic. "If you do not give it to us willingly, we have the right to take back what was brutally stolen from us without provocation," the chief said.

After the chief spoke, the professors discussed among themselves for over an hour. They did not retreat to a separate room to do this. They did it right before the chief, Okwu, and me. They moved from the glass table and stood in a group.

Okwu, the chief, and I just stood there. Back in my home, the elders were always stoic and quiet and they always discussed everything in private. It must have been the same for the Meduse, because Okwu's tentacles shuddered and it said, "What kind of people are these?"

"Let them do the right thing," the chief said.

Feet away from us, beyond the glass table, these professors were shouting with anger, sometimes guffawing with glee, flicking antennae in each other's faces, making ear-popping clicks to get the attention of colleagues. One professor, about the size of my head, flew from one part of the group to the other, producing webs of gray light that slowly descended on the group. This chaotic method of madness would decide whether I would live or die.

I caught bits and pieces of the discussion about Meduse history and methods, the mechanics of the *Third Fish*, the scholars who'd brought the stinger. Okwu and the chief didn't seem to mind hovering there waiting. However, my legs soon grew tired and I sat down right there on the blue floor.

✦ ✦ ✦

Finally, the professors quieted and took their places at the glass table again. I stood up, my heart seeming to pound in my mouth, my palms sweaty. I glanced at the chief and felt even more nervous; its *okuoko* were vibrating and its blue color was deeper, almost glowing. When I looked at Okwu, where its *okuoko* hung, I caught a glimpse of the white of its stinger, ready to strike.

The spiderlike Haras raised two front legs and spoke in the language of the Meduse and said, "On behalf of all the people of Oomza Uni and on behalf of Oomza University, I apologize for the actions of a group of our own in taking the stinger from you, Chief Meduse. The scholars who did this will be found, expelled, and exiled. Museum specimen of such prestige are highly prized at our university, however such things must only be acquired with permission from the people to whom they belong. Oomza protocol is based on honor, respect, wisdom, and knowledge. We will return it to you immediately."

My legs grew weak and before I knew it, I was sitting back on the floor. My head felt heavy and tingly, my thoughts scattered. "I'm sorry," I said, in the language I'd spoken all my life. I felt something press my back, steadying me. Okwu.

"I am all right," I said, pushing my hands to the floor and standing back up. But Okwu kept a tentacle to my back.

The one named Haras continued. "Binti, you have made your people proud and I'd personally like to welcome you to Oomza Uni." It motioned one of its limbs toward the human woman beside it. She looked Khoush and wore tight-fitting green garments that clasped every part of her body, from neck to toe. "This is Okpala. She is in our mathematics department. When you are settled, aside from taking classes with her, you will study your *edan* with her. According to Okpala, what you did is impossible."

I opened my mouth to speak, but Okpala put up a hand and I shut my mouth.

"We have one request," Haras said. "We of Oomza Uni wish Okwu to stay behind as the first Meduse student to attend the university and as a showing of allegiance between Oomza Uni governments and the Meduse and a renewal of the pact between human and Meduse."

I heard Okwu rumble behind me, then the chief was speaking up. "For the first time in my own lifetime, I am learning something completely outside of core beliefs," the chief said. "Who'd have thought that a place harboring human beings could carry such honor and foresight." It paused and then said, "I will confer with my advisors before I make my decision."

The chief was pleased. I could hear it in its voice. I looked around me. No one from my tribe. At once, I felt both part of something historic and very alone. Would my family even comprehend it all when I explained it to them? Or would they just fixate on the fact that I'd almost died, was now too far to return home and had left them in order to make the "biggest mistake of my life"?

I swayed on my feet, a smile on my face.

"Binti," the one named Okpala said. "What will you do now?"

"What do you mean?" I asked. "I want to study mathematics and currents. Maybe create a new type of astrolabe. The *edan*, I want to study that and…"

"Yes," she said. "That is true, but what about your home? Will you ever return?"

"Of course," I said. "Eventually, I will visit and…"

"I have studied your people," she said. "They don't like outsiders."

"I'm not an outsider," I said, with a twinge of irritation. "I am…" And that's when it caught my eye. My hair was rested against my back, weighed down by the *otjize*, but as I'd gotten up, one lock had come to rest on my shoulder. I felt it rub against the front of my shoulder and I *saw* it now.

I frowned, not wanting to move. Before the realization hit me, I knew to drop into meditation, treeing out of desperation. I held myself in there for a moment, equations flying through my mind, like wind and sand. Around me, I heard movement and, still treeing, I saw that the soldiers were leaving the room. The professors were getting up, talking among themselves in their various ways. All except Okpala. She was looking right at me.

I slowly lifted up one of my locks and brought it forward I rubbed off the *otjize*. It glowed a strong deep blue like the sky back on earth on a clear day, like Okwu and so many of the other Meduse, like the uniforms of the Oomza Uni soldiers. And it was translucent. Soft, but tough. I touched the top of my head and pressed. They felt the same and… I felt my hand touching them. The tingling sensation was gone. My hair was no longer hair. There was a ringing in my ear as I began to breathe heavily, still in meditation. I wanted to tear off my clothes and inspect every part of my body. To see what else that sting had changed. It had not been a sting. A sting would have torn out my insides, as it did for Heru.

"Only those," Okwu said. "Nothing else."

"This is why I understand you?" I flatly asked. Talking while in meditation was like softly whispering from a hole deep in the ground. I was looking up from a cool dark place.

"Yes."

"Why?"

"Because you had to understand us and it was the only way," Okwu said.

"And you needed to prove to them that you were truly our ambassador, not prisoner," the chief said. It paused. "I will return to the ship; we will make our decision about Okwu." It turned to leave and then turned back. "Binti, you will forever hold the highest honor among the Meduse. My destiny is stronger for leading me to you." Then it left.

I stood there, in my strange body. If I hadn't been deep in meditation I would have screamed and screamed. I was so far from home.

✦ ✦ ✦

I'm told that news of what had happened spread across all Oomza Uni within minutes. It was said that a human tribal female from a distant blue planet saved the university from Meduse terrorists by sacrificing her blood and using her unique gift of mathematical harmony and ancestral magic. "Tribal": that's what they called humans from ethnic groups too remote and "uncivilized" to regularly send students to attend Oomza Uni.

Over the next two days, I learned that people viewed my reddened dark skin and strange hair with wonder. And when they saw me with Okwu, they grew tense and quiet, moving away. Where they saw me as a fascinating exotic human, they saw Okwu as a dangerous threat. Okwu was of a warlike people who, up until now, had only been viewed with fear among people from all over. Okwu enjoyed its infamy, whereas I just wanted to find a quiet desert to walk into so I could study in peace.

"All people fear decisive proud honor," Okwu proclaimed.

We were in one of the Weapons City libraries, staring at the empty chamber where the chief's stinger had been kept. A three-hour transport from Math City, Weapons City was packed with activity on every street and crowded with sprawling flat gray buildings made of stone. Beneath each of these structures were inverted buildings that extended at least a half-mile underground where only those students, researchers, and professors involved knew what was being invented, tested, or destroyed. After the meeting, this was where they'd taken me, the chief, and Okwu for the retrieval of the stinger.

We'd been escorted by a person who looked like a small green child with roots for a head, who I later learned was the head professor of Weapons City. He was the one who went into the five-by-five-foot case made of thick clear crystal and opened it. The stinger was placed atop a slab of crystal and looked like a sharp tusk of ice.

The chief slowly approached the case, extended an *okuoko*, and then let out a large bluish plume of gas the moment its *okuoko* touched the stinger. I'll never forget the way the chief's body went from blue to clear the moment the stinger became a part of it again. Only a blue line remained at the point of demarcation where it had reattached—a scar that would always remind it of what human beings of Oomza Uni had done to it for the sake of research and academics.

Afterward, just before the chief and the others boarded the *Third Fish* that would take them back to their own ship just outside the atmosphere, upon Okwu's request, I knelt before the chief and placed its stinger on my lap. It was heavy and it felt like a slab of solid water and the edge at its tip looked like it could slice into another universe. I smeared a dollop of my *otjize* on the blue scar where it had reattached. After a minute, I wiped some of it away. The blue scar was gone. Their chief was returned to its full royal translucence, they had the half jar of *otjize* Okwu had taken from me, which healed their flesh like magic, and they were leaving one of their own as the first Meduse to study at the great Oomza University. The Meduse left Oomza Uni happier and better off than when they'd arrived.

+ + +

My *otjize*. Yes, there is a story there. Weeks later, after I'd started classes and people had finally started to leave me be, opting to simply stare and gossip in silence instead, I ran out of *otjize*. For days, I'd known it would happen. I'd found a sweet-smelling oil of the same chemical makeup in the market. A black flower that grew in a series of nearby caverns produced the oil. But a similar clay was much harder to find. There was a forest not far from my dorm, across the busy streets, just beyond one of the classroom buildings. I'd never seen anyone go into it, but there was a path opening.

That evening, before dark, I walked in there. I walked fast, ignoring all the stares and grateful when the presence of people tapered off the closer I got to the path entrance. I carried my satchel with my astrolabe, a bag of nuts, my *edan* in my hands, cool and small. I squeezed my *edan* as I left the road and stepped onto the path. The forest seemed to swallow me within a few steps and I could no longer see the purpling sky. My skin felt near naked, the layer of *otjize* I wore was so thin.

I frowned, hesitating for a moment. We didn't have such places where I came from and the denseness of the trees, all the leaves, the small buzzing creatures, made me feel like the forest was choking me. But then I looked at the ground. I looked right there, at my sandaled feet and found precisely what I needed.

I made the *otjize* that night. I mixed it and then let it sit in the strong sunshine for the next day. I didn't go to class, nor did I eat that day. In the evening, I went to the dorm and showered and did that which my people rarely do: I washed with water. As I let the water run through my hair and down my face, I wept. This was all I had left of my homeland and it was being washed into the runnels that would feed the trees outside my dorm.

When I finished, I stood there, away from the running stream of water that flowed from the ceiling. Slowly, I reached up. I touched my "hair." The *okuoko* were soft but firm and slippery with wetness. They touched my back, soft and slick. I shook them, feeling them *otjize*-free for the first time.

I shut my eyes and prayed to the Seven; I hadn't done this since arriving on the planet. I prayed to my living parents and ancestors. I opened my eyes. It was time to call home. Soon.

I peeked out of the washing space. I shared the space with five other human students. One of them just happened to be leaving as

I peeked out. As soon as he was gone, I grabbed my wrapper and came out. I wrapped it around my waist and I looked at myself in the large mirror. I looked for a very very long time. Not at my dark brown skin, but where my hair had been. The *okuoko* were a soft transparent blue with darker blue dots at their tips. They grew out of my head as if they'd been doing that all my life, so natural looking that I couldn't say they were ugly. They were just a little longer than my hair had been, hanging just past my backside, and they were thick as sizable snakes.

There were ten of them and I could no longer braid them into my family's code pattern as I had done with my own hair. I pinched one and felt the pressure. Would they grow like hair? *Were* they hair? I could ask Okwu, but I wasn't ready to ask it anything. Not yet. I quickly ran to my room and sat in the sun and let them dry.

Ten hours later, when dark finally fell, it was time. I'd bought the container at the market; it was made from the shed exoskeleton of students who sold them for spending money. It was clear like one of Okwu's tentacles and dyed red. I'd packed it with the fresh *otjize*, which now looked thick and ready.

I pressed my right index and middle finger together and was about to dig out the first dollop when I hesitated, suddenly incredibly unsure. What if my fingers passed right through it like liquid soap? What if what I'd harvested from the forest wasn't clay at all? What if it was hard like stone?

I pulled my hand away and took a deep breath. If I couldn't make *otjize* here, then I'd have to… change. I touched one of my tentacle-like locks and felt a painful pressure in my chest as my mind tried to take me to a place I wasn't ready to go to. I plunged my two fingers into my new concoction… and scooped it up. I spread it on my flesh. Then I wept.

I went to see Okwu in its dorm. I was still unsure what to call those who lived in this large gas-filled spherical complex. When you entered, it was just one great space where plants grew on the walls and hung from the ceiling. There were no individual rooms, and people who looked like Okwu in some ways but different in others walked across the expansive floor, up the walls, on the ceiling. Somehow, when I came to the front entrance, Okwu would always come within the next few minutes. It would always emit a large plume of gas as it readjusted to the air outside.

"You look well," it said, as we walked down the walkway. We both loved the walkway because of the winds the warm clear seawater created as it rushed by below.

I smiled. "I *feel* well."

"When did you make it?"

"Over the last two suns," I said.

"I'm glad," it said. "You were beginning to fade."

It held up an *okuoko*. "I was working with a yellow current to use in one of my classmate's body tech," it said.

"Oh," I said, looking at its burned flesh.

We paused, looking down at the rushing waters. The relief I'd felt at the naturalness, the trueness of the *otjize* immediately started waning. *This* was the real test. I rubbed some *otjize* from my arm and them took Okwu's *okuoko* in my hand. I applied the *otjize* and then let the *okuoko* drop as I held my breath. We walked back to my dorm. My *otjize* from Earth had healed Okwu and then the chief. It would heal many others. The *otjize* created by my people, mixed with my homeland. This was the foundation of the Meduse's respect for me. Now all of it was gone. I was someone else. Not even fully Himba anymore. What would Okwu think of me now?

When we got to my dorm, we stopped.

"I know what you are thinking," Okwu said.

"I know you Meduse," I said. "You're people of honor, but you're firm and rigid. And traditional." I felt sorrow wash over and I sobbed, covering my face with my hand. Feeling my *otjize* smear beneath it. "But you've become my friend," I said. When I brought my hand away, my palm was red with *otjize*. "You are all I have here. I don't know how it happened, but you are..."

"You will call your family and have them," Okwu said.

I frowned and stepped away from Okwu. "So callous," I whispered.

"Binti," Okwu said. It plumed out gas, in what I knew was a laugh. "Whether you carry the substance that can heal and bring life back to my people or not, I am your friend. I am honored to know you." It shook its *okuoko*, making one of them vibrate. I yelped when I felt the vibration in one of mine.

"What is that?" I shouted, holding up my hands.

"It means we are family through battle," it said. "You are the first to join our family in this way in a long time. We do not like humans."

I smiled.

He held up an *okuoko*. "Show it to me tomorrow," I said, doubtfully.

"Tomorrow will be the same," it said.

When I rubbed off the *otjize* the burn was gone.

✦ ✦ ✦

I sat in the silence of my room looking at my *edan* as I sent out a signal to my family with my astrolabe. Outside was dark and I looked into the sky, at the stars, knowing the pink one was home. The first to answer was my mother.

CoDominium is a series of future history novels by Jerry Pournelle that began in 1973 with a A Spaceship For The King *and includes collaborations with Larry Niven. Both authors are famous for their space opera, and our next story, from 1982, is the prequel to the collaborative novel* The Mote In God's Eye, *which the two authors wrote together in 1974.*

REFLEX

LARRY NIVEN AND JERRY POURNELLE

"Throughout the past thousand years of history it has been traditional to regard the Alderson Drive as an unmixed blessing. Without the faster than light travel Alderson's discoveries made possible, humanity would have been trapped in the tiny prison of the Solar System when the Great Patriotic Wars destroyed the CoDominium on Earth. Instead, we had already settled more than two hundred worlds.

"A blessing, yes. We might now be extinct were it not for the Alderson Drive. But unmixed? Consider. The same tramline effect that colonized the stars, the same interstellar contacts that allowed the formation of the First Empire, allow interstellar war. The worlds wrecked in two hundred years of Secession Wars were both settled and destroyed by ships using the Alderson Drive.

"Because of the Alderson Drive we need never consider the space between the stars. Because we can shunt between stellar systems in zero time, our ships and ships' drives need cover only interplanetary distances. We say that the Second Empire of Man rules two hundred worlds and all the space between, over fifteen million cubic parsecs...

"Consider the true picture. Think of myriads of tiny bubbles, very sparsely scattered, rising through a vast black sea. We rule some of the bubbles. Of the waters we know nothing..."

—from a speech delivered by Dr. Anthony Horvath
at the Blaine Institute, AD 3029.

Any damn fool can die for his country.

—General George S. Patton.

3017 AD

The Union Republic War Cruiser *Defiant* lay nearly motionless in space a half billion kilometers from Beta Hortensi. She turned slowly about her long axis.

Stars flowed endlessly upward with the spin of the ship, as if *Defiant* were falling through the universe. Captain Herb Colvin saw them as a battle map, infinitely dangerous. *Defiant* hung above him in the viewport, its enormous mass ready to fall on him and crush him, but after years in space he hardly noticed.

Hastily constructed and thrown into space, armed as an interstellar cruiser but without the bulky Alderson Effect engines which could send her between the stars, *Defiant* had been assigned to guard the approaches to New Chicago from raids by the Empire. The Republic's main fleet was on the other side of Beta Hortensi, awaiting an attack they were sure would come from that quarter. The path *Defiant* guarded sprang from a red dwarf star four-tenths of a light year distant. The tramline had never been plotted. Few within New Chicago's government believed the Empire had the capability to find it, and fewer thought they would try.

Colvin strode across his cabin to the polished steel cupboard. A tall man, nearly two meters in height, he was thin and wiry, with an aristocratic nose that many Imperial lords would have envied. A shock of sandy hair never stayed combed, but he refused to cover it with a uniform cap unless he had to. A fringe of beard was beginning to take shape on his chin. Colvin had been clean-shaven when *Defiant* began its patrol twenty-four weeks ago. He had grown a beard, decided he didn't like it and shaved it off, then started another. Now he was glad he hadn't taken the annual depilation treatments. Growing a beard was one of the few amusements available to men on a long and dreary blockade.

He opened the cupboard, detached a glass and bottle from their clamps, and took them back to his desk. Colvin poured expertly despite the Coriolis effect that could send carelessly poured liquids sloshing to the carpets. He set the glass down and turned toward the viewport.

There was nothing to see out there, of course. Even the heart of it all, New Chicago—Union! In keeping with the patriotic spirit of the Committee of Public Safety, New Chicago was now called Union. Captain Herb Colvin had trouble remembering that, and

Political Officer Gerry took enormous pleasure in correcting him every damned time. Union was the point of it all, the boredom and the endless low-level fear; but Union was invisible from here. The sun blocked it even from telescopes. Even the red dwarf, so close that it had robbed Beta Hortensi of its cometary halo, showed only as a dim red spark. The first sign of attack would be on the bridge screens long before his eyes could find the black-on-black point that might be an Imperial warship.

For six months *Defiant* had waited, and the question had likewise sat waiting in the back of Colvin's head.

Was the Empire coming?

+ + +

The Secession War that ended the first Empire of Man had split into a thousand little wars, and those had died into battles. Throughout human space there were planets with no civilization, and many more with too little to support space travel.

Even Sparta had been hurt. She had lost her fleets, but the dying ships had defended the Capital; and when Sparta began to recover, she recovered fast.

Across human space men had discovered the secrets of interstellar travel. The technology of the Langston Field was stored away in a score of Imperial libraries; and this was important because the Field was discovered in the first place through a series of improbable accidents to men in widely separated specialties. It would not have been developed again.

With Langston Field and Alderson Drive, the Second Empire rose from the ashes of the First. Every man in the new government knew that weakness in the First Empire had led to war—and that war must not happen again. This time all humanity must be united. There must be no worlds outside the Imperium, and none within it to challenge the power of Emperor and Senate. Mankind would have peace if worlds must die to bring it about.

The oath was sworn, and when other worlds built merchantmen, Sparta rebuilt the Fleet and sent it to space. Under the fanatical young men and women humanity would be united by force. The Empire spread around Crucis and once again reached behind the Coal Sack, persuading, cajoling, conquering, and destroying where needed.

New Chicago had been one of the first worlds reunited with the Empire of Man. The revolt must have come as a stunning surprise. Now Captain Herb Colvin of the United Republic waited on blockade patrol for the Empire's retaliation. He knew it would come, and could only hope that *Defiant* would be ready.

He sat in the enormous leather chair behind his desk, swirling his drink and letting his gaze alternate between his wife's picture and the viewport. The chair was a memento from the liberation of the Governor General's palace on New Chicago. (On Union!) It was made of imported leathers, worth a fortune if he could find the right buyer. The Committee of Public Safety hadn't realized its value.

Colvin looked from Grace's picture to a pinkish star drifting upward past the viewport, and thought of the Empire's warships. Would they come through here, when they came? Surely they were coming.

In principal *Defiant* was a better ship than she'd been when she left New Chicago. The engineers had automated all the routine spacekeeping tasks, and no United Republic spacer needed to do a job that a robot could perform. Like all of New Chicago's ships, and like few of the Imperial Navy's, *Defiant* was as automated as a merchantman.

Colvin wondered. Merchantmen do not fight battles. A merchant captain need not worry about random holes punched through his hull. He can ignore the risk that any given piece of equipment will be smashed at any instant. He will never have only minutes to keep his ship fighting or see her destroyed in an instant of blinding heat.

No robot could cope with the complexity of decisions damage control could generate, and if there were such a robot it might easily be the first item destroyed in battle. Colvin had been a merchant captain and had seen no reason to object to the Republic's naval policies, but now that he had experience in warship command, he understood why the Imperials automated as little as possible and kept the crew in working routine tasks: washing down corridors and changing air filters, scrubbing pots and inspecting the hull. Imperial crews might grumble about the work, but they were never idle. After six months, *Defiant* was a better ship, but... she had lifted out from... Union with a crew of mission-oriented warriors. What were they now?

Colvin leaned back in his comfortable chair and looked around his cabin. It was too comfortable. Even the captain—especially the captain!—had little to do but putter with his personal surroundings, and Colvin had done all he could think of.

It was worse for the crew. They fought, distilled liquor in hidden places, gambled for stakes they couldn't afford, and were bored. It showed in their discipline. There wasn't any punishment duty either, nothing like cleaning heads or scrubbing pots, the duties an Imperial skipper might assign his crewmen. Aboard *Defiant* it would be make-work, and everyone would know it.

He was thinking about another drink when an alarm trilled.

"Captain here," Colvin said.

The face on the viewscreen was flushed. "A ship, sir," the Communications officer said. "Can't tell the size yet, but definitely a ship from the red star."

Colvin's tongue dried up in an instant. He'd been right all along, through all these months of waiting, and the flavor of being right was not pleasant. "Right. Sound battle stations. We'll intercept." He paused a moment as Lieutenant Susack motioned to other crew on the bridge. Alarms sounded through *Defiant*. "Make a signal to the fleet, Lieutenant."

"Aye aye, sir."

Horns were still blaring through the ship as Colvin left his cabin. Crewmen dove along the steel corridors, past grotesque shapes in combat armor. The ship was already losing her spin and orienting herself to give chase to the intruder. Gravity was peculiar and shifting. Colvin crawled along the handholds like a monkey.

The crew was waiting. "Captain's on the bridge," the duty NCO announced. Others helped him into armor and dogged down his helmet. He had only just strapped himself into his command seat when the ship's speakers sounded.

"ALL SECURE FOR ACCELERATION. STAND BY FOR ACCELERATION."

"Intercept," Colvin ordered. The computer recognized his voice and obeyed. The joltmeter swung hard over and acceleration crushed him to his chair. The joltmeter swung back to zero, leaving a steady three gravities.

The bridge was crowded. Colvin's comfortable acceleration couch dominated the spacious compartment. In front of him three helmsmen sat at inactive controls, ready to steer the ship if her main battle computer failed. They were flanked by two watch officers. Behind him were runners and talkers, ready to do the Captain's will when he had orders for them.

There was one other.

Beside him was a man who wasn't precisely under Colvin's command. *Defiant* belonged to Captain Colvin. So did the crew— but he shared that territory with Political Officer Gerry. The Political Officer's presence implied distrust in Colvin's loyalty to the Republic. Gerry had denied this, and so had the Committee of Public Safety; but they hadn't convinced Herb Colvin.

"Are we prepared to engage the enemy, Captain?" Gerry asked. His thin and usually smiling features were distorted by acceleration.

"Yes. We are doing so now," Colvin said. What the hell else could they be doing? But of course Gerry was speaking for the recorders.

"What is the enemy ship?"

"The hyperspace wake's just coming into detection range now, Mister Gerry." Colvin studied the screens. Instead of space with the enemy ship black and invisible against the stars, they showed a series of curves and figures, probability estimates, tables whose entries changed even as he watched. "I believe it's a cruiser, same class as ours," Colvin said.

"Even match?"

"Not exactly," Colvin said. "He'll be carrying interstellar engines. That'll take up room we use for hydrogen. He'll have more mass for his engines to move, and we'll have more fuel. He won't have a lot better armament than we do, either." He studied the probability curves and nodded. "Yeah, that looks about right. What they call a 'Planet Class' cruiser."

"How soon before we fight?" Gerry gasped. The acceleration made each word an effort.

"Few minutes to an hour. He's just getting under way after coming out of hyperdrive. Too damn bad he's so far away, we'd have him right if we were a little closer."

"Why weren't we?" Gerry demanded.

"Because the tramline hasn't been plotted," Colvin said. And I'm speaking for the record. Better get it right, and get the sarcasm out of my voice. "I requested survey equipment, but none was available. We were therefore required to plot the Alderson entry point using optics alone. I would be much surprised if anyone could have made a better estimate using our equipment."

"I see," Gerry said. With an effort he touched the switch that gave him a general intercom circuit. "Spacers of the Republic, your comrades salute you! Freedom!"

"Freedom!" came the response. Colvin didn't think more than

half the crew had spoken, but it was difficult to tell.

"You all know the importance of this battle," Gerry said. "We defend the back door of the Republic, and we are alone. Many believed we need not be here, that the Imperials would never find this path to our homes. That ship shows the wisdom of the government."

Had to get that in, didn't you? Colvin chuckled to himself. Gerry expected to run for office, if he lived through the coming battles.

"The Imperials will never make us slaves! Our cause is just, for we seek only the freedom to be left alone. The Empire will not permit this. They wish to rule the entire universe, forever. Spacers, we fight for liberty!"

Colvin looked across the bridge to the watch officer and lifted an eyebrow. He got a shrug for an answer. Herb nodded. It was hard to tell the effect of a speech. Gerry was said to be good at speaking. He'd talked his way into a junior membership on the Committee of Public Safety that governed the Republic.

A tiny buzz sounded in Colvin's ear. The Executive Officer's station was aft, in an auxiliary control room, where he could take over the ship if something happened to the main bridge.

By Republic orders Gerry was to hear everything said by and to the captain during combat, but Gerry didn't know much about ships. Commander Gregory Halleck, Colvin's exec, had modified the intercom system. Now his voice came through, the flat nasal twang of New Chicago's outback. "Skipper, why don't he shut up and let us fight?"

"Speech was recorded, Greg," Colvin said.

"Ah. He'll play it for the city workers," Halleck said. "Tell me, skipper, just what chance have we got?"

"In this battle? Pretty good."

"Yeah. Wish I was so sure about the war."

"Scared, Greg?"

"A little. How can we win?"

"We can't *beat* the Empire," Colvin said. "Not if they bring their whole fleet in here. But if we can win a couple of battles, the Empire'll have to pull back. They can't strip all their ships out of other areas. Too many enemies. Time's on our side, if we can buy some."

"Yeah. Way I see it, too. Guess it's worth it. Back to work."

It had to be worth it, Colvin thought. It just didn't make sense to put the whole human race under one government. Someday they'd get a really bad Emperor. Or three Emperors all claiming the throne at once. Better to put a stop to this now, rather than leave the problem to their grandchildren.

The phones buzzed again. "Better take a good look, skipper," Halleck said. "I think we got problems."

The screens flashed as new information flowed. Colvin touched other buttons in his chair arm. Lt. Susack's face swam onto one screen. "Make a signal to the fleet," Colvin said. "That thing's bigger than we thought. This could be one hell of a battle."

"Aye aye," Susack said. "But we can handle it."

"Sure," Colvin said. He stared at the updated information and frowned.

"What is out there, Captain?" Gerry asked. "Is there reason for concern?"

"There could be," Colvin said. "Mister Gerry, that is an Imperial battle cruiser. General class, I'd say." As he told the political officer, Colvin felt a cold pit in his guts.

"And what does that mean?"

"It's one of their best," Colvin said. "About as fast as we are. More armor, more weapons, more fuel. We've got a fight on our hands."

"Launch observation boats. Prepare to engage," Colvin ordered. Although he couldn't see it, the Imperial ship was probably doing the same thing. Observation boats didn't carry much for weapons, but their observations could be invaluable when the engagement began.

"You don't sound confident," Gerry said.

Colvin checked his intercom switches. No one could hear him but Gerry. "I'm not," he said. "Look, however you cut it, if there's an advantage that ship's got it. Their crew's had a chance to recover from their hyperspace trip, too." *If we'd had the right equipment—* No use thinking about that.

"What if it gets past us?"

"Enough ships might knock it out, especially if we can damage it, but there's no single ship in our fleet that can fight that thing one-on-one and expect to win."

He paused to let that sink in.

"Including us."

"Including us. I didn't know there was a battle cruiser anywhere in the trans-Coalsack region."

"Interesting implications," Gerry said.

"Yeah. They've brought one of their best ships. Not only that, they took the trouble to find a back way. Two new Alderson tramlines. From the red dwarf to us, and a way into the red dwarf."

"Seems they're determined." Gerry paused a moment. "The Committee was constructing planetary defenses when we lifted out."

"They may need them. Excuse me…" Colvin cut the circuit and concentrated on his battle screens.

The master computer flashed a series of maneuver strategies, each with the odds for success if adopted. The probabilities were only a computer's judgment, however. Over there in the Imperial ship was an experienced human captain who'd do his best to thwart those odds while Colvin did the same. Game theory and computers rarely consider all the possibilities a human brain can conceive.

The computer recommended full retreat and sacrifice of the observation boats—and at that gave only an even chance for *Defiant*. Colvin studied the board. "ENGAGE CLOSELY," he said.

The computer wiped the other alternatives and flashed a series of new choices. Colvin chose. Again and again this happened until the ship's brain knew exactly what her human master wanted, but long before the dialogue was completed the ship accelerated to action, spewing torpedoes from her ports to send H-bombs on random evasion courses toward the enemy. Tiny lasers reached out toward enemy torpedoes, filling space with softly glowing threads of bright color.

Defiant leaped toward her enemy, her photon cannons pouring out energy to wash over the Imperial ship. "Keep it up, keep it up," Colvin chanted to himself. If the enemy could be blinded, her antennas destroyed so that her crew couldn't see out through her Langston Field to locate *Defiant*, the battle would be over.

Halleck's outback twang came through the earphones. "Looking good, boss."

"Yeah." The very savagery of unexpected attack by a smaller vessel had taken the enemy by surprise. Just maybe—

A blaze of white struck *Defiant* to send her screens up into the orange, tottering toward yellow for an instant. In that second *Defiant* was as blind as the enemy, every sensor outside the Field vaporized. Her boats were still there, though, still sending data on the enemy's position, still guiding torpedoes.

"Bridge, this is damage control."

"Yeah, Greg."

"Hulled in main memory bank area. I'm getting replacement elements in, but you better go to secondary computer for a while."

"Already done."

"Good. Got a couple other problems, but I can handle them."

"Have at it." Screens were coming back online. More sensor clusters were being poked through the Langston Field on stalks. Colvin touched buttons in his chair arm. "Communications. Get number three boat in closer."

"Acknowledged."

The Imperial ship took evasive action. She would cut acceleration for a moment, turn slightly, then accelerate again, with constantly changing drive power. Colvin shook his head. "He's got an iron crew," he muttered to Halleck. "They must be getting the guts shook out of them."

Another blast rocked *Defiant*. A torpedo had penetrated her defensive fire to explode somewhere near the hull. The Langston Field, opaque to radiant energy, was able to absorb and redistribute the energy evenly throughout the Field; but at cost. There had been an overload at the place nearest the bomb: energy flaring inward. The Langston Field was a spaceship's true hull. Its skin was only metal, designed only to hold pressure. Breach it and—

"Hulled again aft of number two torpedo room," Halleck reported. "Spare parts, and the messroom brain. We'll eat basic protocarb for a while."

"If we eat at all." Why the hell weren't they getting more hits on the enemy? He could see the Imperial ship on his screens, in the view from number two boat. Her field glowed orange, wavering to yellow, and there were two deep purple spots, probably burnthroughs. No way to tell what lay under those areas. Colvin hoped it was something vital.

His own Field was yellow tinged with green. Pastel lines jumped between the two ships. After this was over, there would be time to remember just how *pretty* a space battle was. The screens flared, and his odds for success dropped again, but he couldn't trust the computer anyway. He'd lost number three boat, and number one had ceased reporting.

The enemy ship flared again as *Defiant* scored a hit, then another. The Imperial's screens turned yellow, then green; as they cooled back toward red another hit sent them through green to blue.

"Torps!" Colvin shouted, but the master computer had already done it. A stream of tiny shapes flashed toward the blinded enemy. "Pour it on!" Colvin screamed. "Everything we've got!" If they could keep the enemy blind, keep him from finding *Defiant* while they poured energy into his Field, they could keep his screens hot enough until torpedoes could get through. Enough torpedoes would finish the job. "Pour it on!"

The Imperial ship was almost beyond the blue, creeping toward the violet. "By God we may have him!" Colvin shouted.

The enemy maneuvered again, but the bright rays of *Defiant*'s lasers followed, pinning the glowing ship against the star background. Then the screens went blank.

Colvin frantically pounded buttons. Nothing happened. *Defiant* was blind. "Eyes! How'd he hit us?" he demanded.

"Don't know." Susack's voice was edged with fear. "Skipper, we've got problems with the detectors. I sent a party out but they haven't reported—"

Halleck came on. "Imperial boat got close and hit us with torps."

Blind. Colvin watched his screen color indicators. Bright orange and yellow, with a green tint already visible. Acceleration warnings hooted through the ship as Colvin ordered random evasive action. The enemy would be blind too. Now it was a question of who could see first. "Get me some eyes." he said. He was surprised at how calm his voice was.

"Working on it," Halleck said. "I've got minimal sight back here. Maybe I can locate him."

"Take over gun direction," Colvin said. "What's with the computer?"

"I'm not getting damage reports from that area," Halleck said. "I have men out trying to restore internal communications, and another party's putting out antennas—only nobody really wants to go out to the hull edge and work, you know."

"Wants!" Colvin controlled blind rage. Who cared what the crew wanted? His ship was in danger!

Acceleration and jolt warnings sounded continuously as *Defiant* continued evasive maneuvers. Jolt, acceleration, stop, turn, jolt—

"He's hitting us again." Susack sounded scared.

"Greg?" Colvin demanded.

"I'm losing him. Take over, skipper."

Defiant writhed like a beetle on a pin as the deadly fire followed her through maneuvers. The damage reports came as a deadly litany. "Partial collapse, after auxiliary engine room destroyed. Hulled in three places in number five tankage area, hydrogen leaking to space. Hulled in the after recreation room."

The screens were electric blue when the computer cut the drives. *Defiant* was dead in space. She was moving at more than a hundred kilometers per second, but she couldn't accelerate.

"See anything yet?" Colvin asked.

"In a second," Halleck replied. "There. Wups. Antenna didn't last half a second. He's yellow. Out there on our port quarter and pouring it on. Want me to swing the main drive in that direction? We might hit him with that."

Colvin examined his screens. "No. We can't spare the power." He watched a moment more, then swept his hand across a line of buttons.

All through *Defiant* nonessential systems died. It took power to maintain the Langston Field, and the more energy the Field had to contain the more internal power was needed to keep the Field from radiating inward. Local overloads produced burnthroughs, partial collapses sending bursts of energetic photons to punch holes through the hull. The Field moved toward full collapse, and when that happened, the energies it contained would vaporize *Defiant*. Total defeat in space is a clean death.

The screens were indigo and *Defiant* couldn't spare power to fire her guns or use her engines. Every erg was needed simply to survive.

"We'll have to surrender," Colvin said. "Get the message out."

"I forbid it!"

For a moment Colvin had forgotten the Political Officer.

"I forbid it!" Gerry shouted again. "Captain, you are relieved from command. Commander Halleck, engage the enemy! We cannot allow him to penetrate to our homeland!"

"Can't do that, sir," Halleck said carefully. The recorded conversation made the executive officer a traitor, as Colvin was the instant he'd given the surrender order.

"Engage the enemy, Captain." Gerry spoke quietly. "Look at me, Colvin."

Herb Colvin turned to see a pistol in Gerry's hands. It wasn't a sonic gun, not even a chemical dart weapon as used by prison guards. Combat armor would stop those. This was a slugthrower—no. A small rocket launcher, but it looked like a slugthrower. Just the weapon to take to space.

"Surrender the ship," Colvin repeated. He motioned with one hand. Gerry looked around, too late, as the quartermaster pinned his arms to his sides. A captain's bridge runner launched himself across the cabin to seize the pistol.

"I'll have you shot for this!" Gerry shouted. "You've betrayed everything. Our homes, our families—"

"I'd as soon be shot as surrender," Colvin said. "Besides, the Imperials will probably do for both of us. Treason, you know. Still, I've a right to save the crew."

Gerry said nothing.

"We're dead, Mister. The only reason they haven't finished us off is we're so bloody helpless the Imperial commander's held off firing the last wave of torpedoes to give us a chance to quit. He can finish us off any time."

"You might damage him. Take him with us, or make it easier for the fleet to deal with him—"

"If I could, I'd do that. I already launched all our torpedoes. They either got through or they didn't. Either way, they didn't kill him, since he's still pouring it on us. He has all the time in the world— look, damn it! We can't shoot at him, we don't have power for the engines, and look at the screens! Violet! Don't you understand, you blithering fool, there's no further place for it to go! A little more, a miscalculation by the Imperial, some little failure here, and that field collapses."

Gerry stared in rage. "Maybe you're right."

"I know I'm right. Any progress, Susack?"

"Message went out," the communications officer said. "And they haven't finished us."

"Right." There was nothing else to say.

A ship in *Defiant*'s situation, her screens overloaded, bombarded by torpedoes and fired on by an enemy she cannot locate, is utterly helpless; but she has been damaged hardly at all. Given time she can radiate the screen energies to space. She can erect antennas to find her enemy. When the screens cool, she can move and she can shoot. Even when she has been damaged by partial collapses, her enemy cannot know that.

Thus, surrender is difficult and requires a precise ritual. Like all of mankind's surrender signals it is artificial, for man has no surrender reflex, no unambiguous species-wide signal to save him from death after defeat is inevitable. Of the higher animals, man is alone in this.

Stags do not fight to the death. When one is beaten, he submits, and the other allows him to leave the field. The three-spine stickleback, a fish of the carp family, fights for its mates but recognizes the surrender of its enemies. Siamese fighting fish will not pursue an enemy after he ceases to spread his gills.

But man has evolved as a weapon-using animal. Unlike other animals, man's evolution is intimately bound with weapons and tools; and weapons can kill farther than man can reach. Weapons in the hand of a defeated enemy are still dangerous. Indeed, the Scottish *skean dhu* is said to be carried in the stocking so that it may be reached as its owner kneels in supplication…

Defiant erected a simple antenna suitable only for radio signals. Any other form of sensor would have been a hostile act and would earn instant destruction. The Imperial captain observed and sent instructions.

Meanwhile, torpedoes were being maneuvered alongside *Defiant*. Colvin couldn't see them. He knew they must be in place when the next signal came through. The Imperial ship was sending an officer to take command.

Colvin felt some of the tension go out of him. If no one had volunteered for the job, *Defiant* would have been destroyed.

Something massive thumped against the hull. A port had already been opened for the Imperial. He entered carrying a bulky object: a bomb.

"Midshipman Horst Staley, Imperial Battlecruiser *MacArthur*," the officer announced as he was conducted to the bridge. Colvin could see blue eyes and blonde hair, a young face frozen into a mask of calm because its owner did not trust himself to show any expression at all. "I am to take command of this ship, sir."

Captain Colvin nodded. "I give her to you. You'll want this," he added, handing the boy the microphone. "Thank you for coming."

"Yes, sir." Staley gulped noticeably, then stood at attention as if his captain could see him. "Midshipman Staley reporting, sir. I am on the bridge and the enemy has surrendered." He listened for a few seconds, then turned to Colvin. "I am to ask you to leave me alone on the bridge except for yourself, sir. And to tell you that if anyone else comes on the bridge before our Marines have secured this ship, I will detonate the bomb I carry. Will you comply?"

Colvin nodded again. "Take Mr. Gerry out, quartermaster. You others can go, too. Clear the bridge."

The quartermaster led Gerry toward the door. Suddenly the political officer broke free and sprang at Staley. He wrapped the midshipman's arms against his body and shouted, "Quick, grab the bomb! Move! Captain, fight for your ship, I've got him!"

Staley struggled with the political officer. His hand groped for the trigger, but he couldn't reach it. The mike had also been ripped from his hands. He shouted at the dead microphone.

Colvin gently took the bomb from Horst's imprisoned hands. "You won't need this, son," he said. "Quartermaster, you can take your prisoner off this bridge." His smile was fixed, frozen in place, in sharp contrast to the midshipman's shocked rage and Gerry's look of triumph.

The spacers reached out and Horst Staley tried to escape, but there was no place to go as he floated in free space. Suddenly he realized that the spacers had seized his attacker, and Gerry was screaming.

"We've surrendered, Mister Staley," Colvin said carefully. "Now we'll leave you in command here. You can have your bomb, but you won't be needing it."

Jean Johnson's "Theirs Not To Reason Why" stories span novels and short fiction for more than a decade now, and have prompted compliments from the likes of Gail Carriger, among others. This next story is the latest entry. Technically as much military sci-fi as space opera, the series crosses both, but what's interesting here is how much the feel of the classic "sword and planet" subgenre is reflected.

✦ ✦ ✦

Author's Acknowledgment: This story is dedicated to Gary Larson, creator of The Far Side, *and thus is the inadvertent, unwitting, and utterly unassociated inspiration for the main character of this story. Alas, poor Gary; you know not what you begat. (Thank you!)*

   Mitch's adventures are canonical to what my fans have decided to call the "Ia-verse," aka my main science fiction universe. The actual infiltration and battle scenes take place on September 17, 2498 Terran Standard, while the writing portion takes place a few hours past midnight Terran Standard (the equivalent of Greenwich Mean Time) on September 18, 2498.

   For those who are curious or are just trying to keep track, that places this story solidly during the events of "Theirs Not to Reason Why", early on in the timeline for Damnation, *the fifth and final book of that series. Also, please note that all views being expressed on who or what qualifies as a barbarian are Mitch's and not mine. Mitch makes no apologies if someone else thinks he got it wrong; barbarians don't apologize for the opinions of civilized people on how barbarians "should" exist or behave.*

—Jean

HOW TO BE A BARBARIAN IN THE LATE 25TH CENTURY
JEAN JOHNSON

PROLOGUE

Barbarian – / ˌbärˈberēən /
1. In ancient times, a member of a community or tribe not belonging to one of the great civilizations: Greek, Roman, Chinese, Indian, Egyptian, et cetera, though the Greeks

considered the Egyptians barbarians at times, too.

2. Of or relating to ancient barbarians; a person perceived to be uncivilized or primitive compared to current or local standards.

3. PFC Mitch "the Turk" Turman, TUPSF-SF 9th Cordon, 1st Division, 1st Battalion, 1st Brigade, "Ia's Damned" A Company, 2nd Platoon, E Squadron Beta.

+ + +

SEPTEMBER 18, 2498
SIC TRANSIT, TUPSF DAMNATION

Glaring at the form waiting for him on his workstation screen, Mitch Turman contemplated mutiny for the one thousandth or so time. The damned cursor blinked at him in silent accusation, demanding the most repugnant of efforts. But when he lifted his hand to give the appropriate crude gesture of defiance—based on the two-fingered salute of the ancient barbaric Britons versus their more civilized French counterparts during the Hundred Years' War, mocking the defeated archers who had lost those fingers—his ribs twinged with more than enough pain to make him grunt.

That caught the attention of the wench tidying their quarters. "I hear grunting."

"Barbarians are supposed to grunt, woman!" Mitch retorted. "And I am in pain. I have every reason to grunt."

"Yes, but I don't hear any typing." She shut a cabinet with the double-click that said the safety latches had taken hold, and came over to him while he grumbled wordlessly under his breath. Leaning carefully over the back of his chair, she kissed his head. "You know the rule, first the After Action Report, *then* the 'real' account of what happened."

"It's a stupid rule," he muttered. "Why did I make it up?"

"Aw, is my barbarian pouting?" she sympathized, caressing his light-brown arm with her pale-cream hand. She would have caressed his head, but though his braids had cushioned most of the blow and modern medicine had done much to ease the pain, he still had bruises and cuts from combat at the back of his scalp.

His muscles tightened under her touch, showing off the well-defined biceps he knew she loved. Especially when she traced over the curves and indents he made. "Barbarians do not *pout*, wench. We *brood*."

"Yes, I know, dear. Put all that mighty brooding power to good use and kill the After Action Report with ruthless efficiency, then you can have fun," Lilith told him.

"I can't have fun," he muttered. "Mishka said no lovemaking until my ribs are healed."

"She said don't move around a lot," his wife reminded him. "Which includes more than just lovemaking."

Mitch perked up at that. "So I can put off writing my—"

Lilith pointed at the workstation console. "No! Write! Your Warlady has commanded it must be done before you retire for the night."

Sighing roughly—his Warlady was his Warlady, whom he had sworn to follow into and out of battle—Mitch put his callused fingers on the keys, and started typing. Under SOLDIERS PRESENT, he typed in all ten names from the 2nd Platoon, E Squadron. Corporal Jin Bottomley, Private First Class, Kzin Kozak of E Squad Alpha, then himself and Lilith for E Squad Beta. Gamma was PFC Leonne Prudhomme and PSC Merry Rudolph. It was only September, but Merry had already gone around to the crew on her monthly chore, threatening them with various inventive forms of bodily harm if they even just *thought* about humming Christmas tunes in her direction before December 1st. Not that she'd know, since she wasn't a telepath like him, but Mitch admired the creativity of her threats.

Delta Team on E Squad, 2nd Platoon, consisted of PFC Franklin Jacoe and Private Second Grade Willow Thompson, stolen from the TUPSF-Navy to serve on General Ia's crew back when it first formed. Epsilon had PFG Derek Schwadel, and the "new guy", PSG Maximus Nesbit, who had replaced Finnimore Hollick when Finn died a heroic death a few years back, rescuing civilians on Mars from a breached transport tunnel during the war. Maximus had an awesome name, and a great sense of humor, but if he had been born into a barbarian tribe, he'd have been a skald or a bard at most, and not a stalwart warrior. Famed for his storytelling abilities, but only modestly for his fighting abilities.

No one else's name was needed, so he tabbed through some of the drop-down menus, and got down to the first entry box for what happened. Calling up the recordings from his headset camera, he matched the date—yesterday, the 17th—and the time—**13:35** Terran Standard—to the action.

✦ ✦ ✦

13:25 TS, The operation began with our planetary insertion on the Solarican colonyworld of Au'Aurrran. Touchdown of our transport took place at a landing port, Kokitllum, a settlement in the northern hemisphere. The shuttle was piloted by Chief Yeoman Maeve O'Keefe, 2nd A Alpha. Upon disembarkation, 2nd E Squad was met by an escort of Solarican forces of the local 115th Wing, who subsequently led E Squad into the subterranean passages of the region.

✦ ✦ ✦

Boring boring boring boring boring… "Lilith?"

"Yes, love?" his wife asked.

"I require that brown foreigner drink you know how to make."

"Caf' or cocoa?" she asked.

"Cocoa. And put the corpse of a mallow plant in the boiling brew."

"One big one, or several little ones?" she asked. Seeing him perk up, his beautiful, clever, sable-haired wife grinned at him. When she did that, and what she said next, melted his heart yet again toward her despite the way she insisted he fill out the deadly dull report; while she was no muscle-thewed warrioress, Lilith Turman *was* a crafty sneak with a heart of precious gold. "I stole a bag of mini marshmallows from the aft galley."

"Strew the battlefield with the corpses of our miniscule enemies!" he decided. She laughed and headed for the mini-galley in their quarters, which mostly contained a small fridge, a sink, and the drinks dispenser. The cocoa came from packets, the same as the hybrid Terran/V'Dan coffee did, but he just liked the way it tasted when she pushed the buttons.

"…I'm not hearing any typing!" she called over her shoulder.

"Slave driver," he muttered, but returned his fingers to the keyboard, ignoring the twinge in his ribs. Whatever modern medical miracle drug had been injected into the sites of each break would repair them swiftly under the bandaging holding them in the proper shape, and would have it repaired within two full days at most, but it still hurt in the meantime.

✦ ✦ ✦

We traveled by hexawalker and by foot for over two hours. During that time, we saw predominantly Solarican soldiers and various colonial militia members of the different races. They guarded our passage, as per General Ia's precognitively pre-arranged orders. Attached is a log of the spatial coordinates and a compressed vidfile of this timeframe, but otherwise nothing of note or interest happened.

+ + +

Sneaking a glance over his shoulder, he checked to make sure Lilith was still busy waiting for the machine to do its business, and opened his private writing file. Slapping a quick working title onto the first line, *Mitch the Mighty Turk versus the Kraken Warriors of the Catmen Catacombs*, he started writing.

+ + +

Upon command of our Great Warlady, whose name resounds like a red hawk's cry and whose dark Shamanic visions had bespoke of foul danger amongst our distant allies, I journeyed with my stalwart companions to the cavernous realms of the Au'Aurrran kingdom at the far-flung reaches of the land. There, the Feline Ones greeted us with ceremonial chest thumpings and the displaying of mighty claws and teeth. I flexed my thews and exchanged tales of prowess as we moved, but while they are an admirably fierce yet hospitable race, we did not linger to rest, let alone feast upon the tasty flesh of the local beasts, for we had far to go.

As we hiked, the Catmen passed some of us rations of jerked meat from some sort of dragonish beast, long and lizard-like with an unholy preference for the near-boiling waters of the subterranean caverns that grace their otherwise glacially plagued home. The others did not care for the strong gamey flavor, but I found it stimulating, and soon amassed a decent ration for fueling myself later in our quest. My companions, foolish, did not even request in exchange for it any of the blander fare which we had been given to put in our packs before departing for this land.

The natives had illuminated most of our way via the magical lights crafted by their sorcerers, but there came a point where the supplied illumination ended, and we were forced to spend our own magics—

+ + +

"That is *not* the After Action Report."

Rolling his eyes, Mitch sighed and eyed the cup of cocoa. "Fine. I'll write more of the Report."

Lilith held his cup aloft, high enough that when he tried to reach for it, he grunted in pain. She spoke mercilessly. "You have to write four more time-stamped entries before I will let you have a sip."

"Wife!" Mitch complained, scowling.

"Husband!" she shot back. She lowered the cup so that he could see the marshmallows bobbing in the top. Using a food-safe pen, she had inked little scowling or terrified faces on each of the marshmallows, which explained what had taken her so long. "Write fast, or they'll all perish before you'll have a chance to enjoy their misfortune."

"*Augh!* Fine!" Shifting to the form, Mitch wrote fast and terse entries. His wife indulged him in his barbarian imagination, and he loved her for it, but dammit, mini marshmallows melted fast!

+ + +

15:44 TS, E Squad arrived at the coordinates for the insertion point for Operation Generator Shutdown 151-679, insertion point located at 49°16'16.48" N 122°45'46.75" W. at a depth from the surface of 147.65m. The access tunnel through the bedrock had suffered multiple collapses from earthquakes in the two centuries since the First Salik War, and we knew in advance we could only take light armor, so we had left our mechsuits back on board the TUSPF *Damnation* as per General Ia's precognitive orders.

16:03 TS, E Squad located and entered the passageway leading to the backdoor access of the First Salik War Insurgency Camp Gwosh-Plik 3-32.

16:09 TS, E Squad encountered the first obstacle to our ingress, a section of fallen but stable rock reducing the aperture of the passageway to roughly 1.0m. All Squad members were able to transit the opening in adequate time.

16:13 TS, E Squad encountered the second obstacle to our ingress, an aperture of 0.79m with a twist. All Squad members were able to transit the opening in adequate time.

16:26 TS, E Squad encountered a divergence of three possible paths. E Squadron followed the directives of General Ia, taking the least likely-looking passage, aperture 0.67m at an elevation of 3.73m above passage floor on a rock fall slope. All Squad members were able to transit the opening in adequate time.

+ + +

"There! *Five* entries," he told her.

She handed over the mug, and kissed the braids covering his scalp. The front, not the back where he had hit his head a few hours before. Then frowned and rubbed her fingers over the nubbly, wiry locks near his brow. "We'll need to redo your braiding, soon. It's growing out again."

"It'll have to wait until my ribs heal," he reminded her. "You know how much I love it when you play with my unbound hair. I don't want to have to restrain myself."

"Mmm, yes. Because I get tumbled into the bedfurs most vigorously when I play with your hair." She kissed his head again, and returned to her own workstation seat. "You can have five minutes to write in your novel, and then it's back to the Report."

"Slave driver," he muttered again, but smiled when he saw what she'd drawn on the treats in his cocoa. "Awww, that one has a little Senatorial laurel wreath on its head. I love the look of horror on its little face."

"I put it in first, to represent the moral decay caused by soft, decadent, 'civilized' life," Lilith said, smiling. "That's why it's melting faster than the rest."

"You really do get me, woman," Mitch muttered, sipping at the hot, sweet liquid. Clipping the mug into its holder, he quickly started typing, not wanting to waste his five minutes.

✦ ✦ ✦

With the magical crystals given to us by our sorcerers, we crept along the tunnels leading to the stronghold where the Kraken Warriors had set up their foul war camp. The way was close and difficult. The very earth had been shaken by the Gods during the last great battle, crushing passages and crumbling safe routes. The Catmen could go no further, for by escorting us even this far, they had left some of their villages under-defended. We saluted them vigorously and parted company. Two turnings later, we came to a narrow defile in the underground labyrinth of this remote land.

Fallen rocks seemingly barred our way, but the fierce warrioress Merry—she of the swift blade and who earned the nickname Thumb-Breaker in battle against me when I improperly teased her about the winestain birthmark coloring her nose—discovered an opening which we could crawl through. Ever fearless, she took the lead, and proved the passage went through. Her shieldsister Leonne the Lioness followed, and our warband leader, Jin the Monk, ordered me to go through, as the largest of the warband.

It was an easy fit, even in my leather armor, decorated in the sigils of protection and blessed by blacksmiths with plates of that new, shiny metal, iron.

✦ ✦ ✦

"Your five minutes are up. More After Action, less Barbarian Action."

"You are *only* this forward and sassy because you know I cannot fling you over my shoulder and spank your rump, until after my ribs are healed," Mitch pointed out, dragging his attention reluctantly back to the dull, boring form on the left side of his screen.

"I know. And I also know you would be *bored* with a mate who doesn't stand up to you," she told him, her tone smug. A peek showed her naturally rosy lips were curved in an equally smug smile. "Barbarians don't like shy maidens who faint at the slightest raised voice."

"Of course not. We respect strength. Strong barbarian women beget strong, healthy barbarian children." Even if they couldn't *have* any children while they served in the war. *One day*, he thought to himself. *One day, we will have a lot of strong, healthy children.* Then checked to make sure his psychic shields were in place. He knew the thought of being restricted from starting a family depressed her, but they both agreed the war was too important to win to bow out just yet.

Of course, Mitch wasn't a strong telepath; he wasn't weak enough that he needed to touch people, but he did need them to be within a few meters of him. That telepathy came with a touch of xenopathy. That, in turn, allowed him to sense alien minds before alien warriors could ambush him... but again, only if they were close.

His greatest strength as a psi lay in another ability, pyrokinesis. Specifically, micropyrokinesis. He was an expert at spot-welding circuitry, which as far as the Terran United Planets Space Force was concerned made him an outstanding maintenance engineer, enough to pay him high bonuses for signing up and serving, though the military structure was not all that compatible with his personal lifestyle preferences. But as far as his Commanding Officer was concerned, even being a barbarian at heart made him a vital part of her crew.

✦ ✦ ✦

16:28 TS, E Squad encountered the smallest transitable aperture of 0.63m in a gypsum macrocrystal cavern, created by the collapse of bedrock around multiple gypsum shafts. We followed the precognitive instructions provided to us by General Ia to determine exactly which aperture was large enough for us to use. The gridwork of crystalline shafts had grown in an average diameter 1.3m and average lengths in excess of 6m, and the estimated tonnage of the shafts would have exceeded full mechsuit lifting capacities several times over.

16:30 TS, After group consultation, the Squadron determined to send the smallest and largest members through the aperture. The reasoning was that if the largest member got stuck, the remainder of the Squad could pull on that soldier's legs while the smallest member in the vanguard position could shove on the stuck soldier's head and shoulders to attempt to force them back through, and with only one soldier in the vanguard position, only two soldiers would be put at risk if any Salik forces registered our presence in the vicinity of their stronghold.

16:31 TS, Squad Leader Corporal Jin Bottomley, A Alpha, was determined to be the most slender member of the Squadron; our Corporal entered the aperture in vanguard position without hesitation after removing her armaments and equipment harness to ensure she fit. Immediately after she made the transit, her teammate PFC Kzin Kozak passed her harness and armaments to her so she could secure the next segment of our ingress. Corporal Bottomley as usual remained alert and attuned to her surroundings throughout her transit.

16:32 TS, As the largest member of E Squadron, 2nd Platoon, A Company, I passed my armaments through to Corporal Bottomley through the aperture, and attempted to climb through the opening. It was a tight fit, and I had to retreat and regroup. Manual assistance was needed from the rearguard to extract me. However, after removing my light armor and upper uniform, I was able to clear the aperture within 18 seconds.

✦ ✦ ✦

"There. Four entries. I demand more dying senatorial sloths of the corrupt civilization type as sacrifices to appease my distaste for this... boring business. Please," he added as soon as he finished crosschecking the vidstreams to make sure he had all the numbers correct. Barbarians could be polite, when the target of their request was deemed worthy.

Lilith rose from her workstation to his right, and paused to kiss him on that side of his head. As she did so, she tickled just under his chin where his beard always started to grow in fastest, making him smile at the affectionate touch. He returned his attention to his personal document while she crossed behind him to fetch and decorate more miniature marshmallows.

✦ ✦ ✦

The pathway emerged onto a sight most wondrous: great crystalline shafts large enough to have formed the pillars of some grand and glorious temple crisscrossed the vast cavern. We walked with wonder, leaping from shaft to perilous shaft, climbing up angled slopes and affixing ropes to assist each other. Our Warlady had communed with the spirit of her Patron God, Chronos the Temporal, and had plotted a path for us to a hidden crevice halfway up one awe-inspiring wall. If we had not had the touch of the Gods blessing our quest, we should never have found the opening.

Not even the greatest and mightiest of ogres could have moved those three shafts even so much as a thumb-width farther apart. Such mischief was our plight, for the opening looked too small to transit. Had they been grown at the hands of faeries? Mischievous sprites of nature, the kind who would take an unholy delight in crafting crystals of gargantuan stature in such a seemingly obstructive position?

Jin, our warband leader, decreed that she, as the smallest if most cunning of our warriors, should go through the opening first, to scout the far side. Should it prove the right one—the error would have been ours if it were not, for our Warlady is rarely ever wrong—then the largest of us would go through next. As I was the only true barbarian born and raised amongst my boon companions, though I had since adopted the others into learning proper barbarian ways, I knew that I would be the one to test the opening's girth against my resilence and determination. Tall as a tree in height, broad as a mountain in muscles, if I could make it through, the rest of our warband could survive.

I strove with stoic expression to ignore the suggestions made by Maximus—he of a formerly civilized land, and thus uncouth in his jests—that Jin could always stomp on my head and shoulders to dislodge me like a wine cork, should I become lodged in place. My mate, clever and wise, pointed out that he was a reed in shape, and fuzzy-faced enough to serve as a pipe cleaner. If I was the cork for this bottle mouth, she reasoned, then he could be inserted and rubbed back and forth through the opening in the hopes of his facial bristles scouring it wider.

In the span of their jests, Warleader Jin the Monk had stripped her armor and handed most of her precious weapons to her shieldbrother, Kzin. She took with her a simple crossbow for a weapon and wriggled through—

Lilith dropped three toga-drawn marshmallows into his cocoa, kissed him, and continued drawing more at her desk. Mitch smiled, sipped, and continued.

—wriggled through the opening. Her efforts were ungraceful at best, but none of us would dare voice a jest at her expense. She had long earned our respect with her leadership, standing tall, if thin. As I peered through the opening in the crystalline lattice, she crawled farther up the passage, stood up—I could see her from calf to hip through the mix of gypsum and rock—then turned back and beckoned to me to join her.

Stripping my armor, and all my weapons but for a knife in my teeth, I attempted to enter the opening. Even my tunic proved problematic, however. Removing it, I angled my shoulders a little more, and with a great shove of my feet and a heave of my arms, I made it through, though the rock stole a sacrifice of red life's blood from my chest and shoulder. Still, there was leverage when I reached with my arms, and the geomancer's vice did not hold me more than a few moments at best.

Flush with triumph, I turned around and reached through the opening for my things. Lilith, clever wench, passed through my trusty labrys first, knowing I would rather be bereft of all coverings than be left bereft of any armaments. A barbarian without the means to fight is truly naked, even if he wears a dozen layers of clothes. She is, however, my mate, and insisted I re-don my armor once it, too, was passed through.

I indulged her because we have not yet completed the trials demanded of us by our people, to prove ourselves beyond all doubt in battle before we can have the right to raise the next generation. We must be able to teach them how to survive and thrive in the face of all adversaries, all foes, whether they be of weather, warriorship, or witchcraft. Once these damned Kraken Warriors are defeated, my wench and I will fill the world with our well-earned progeny, and true strength and honor shall rule! Until then, we make do. I helped her dress, and made certain her weapons, like mine, were well-maintained and intact, unharmed by our long journey, while we waited for the rest to come through.

Though they were not as broad-shouldered as me, most of the others in our warband elected to remove their armor and pass it through, too. Franklin, broad-shouldered to a degree, almost needed to remove his shirt as well. I suspect he refused because he knew that after the display of my great muscles and intimidating battle scars, his physique would seem puny by comparison when exposed to the glow of our witch-lights.

Perhaps it was partially out of want to ensure they remembered my thews that I placed my tunic upon the opening we had used, but I knew that on this side of the rock wall, there were several openings that seemed almost of a similar size, but which would be too tight to traverse if we were forced to retreat by the cruel cunning of the Kraken Empire. Picking the wrong opening could leave us vulnerable to being trapped in a slaughter. I could afford the loss of my warband tunic; our Warlady is generous with our pay, so long as we are diligent in not wasting our resources needlessly…

✦ ✦ ✦

Lilith cleared her throat, displayed the carefully decorated cylindrical "captives" in her hand, hovered them without releasing any over his cocoa cup… and then gave the workstation screen a pointed look. Rolling his eyes, Mitch went back to writing in the official dry, dull, boring Report form. He input a few more entries, ending with:

16:45 TS, E Squad encountered the "back door" emergency hatch into the Salik Base. Mission specialist PFC Leonne Prudhomme deployed and applied a pair of SASU-17 to the control panel. As per General Ia's precognition probability of 72%, the first code which the General gave us functioned adequately, neutralizing surveillance and alarm systems; her coding took only 18 seconds from application of the SASUs to the final command input. The outer airlock-style door unlocked and opened, but only partway due to structural compression from earthquake damage. This left an aperture of 0.17m, insufficient ingress for our squadron.

+ + +

A glance at Lilith showed her busy on her own report. Sneaking his cursor over to his document, Mitch continued the tale. The real one, not the boring military-ese version.

+ + +

Just a short journey through the crystalline catacombs allowed us to reach the postern gate of the Kraken Fortress. Built in the ancient style of yesteryear, it stood there, still formidable in its cladding of iron and stone, stalwart despite the passing of time. Dust coated its crevices, and no signs of sentries graced its wall. Why should it? To the Kraken mind, no one of anything but the puniest of strength and weakest of skills could have navigated the earthquake-wrought passage to this point. Their hubris would be their undoing, in expecting soft, civilized soldiers to have been picked for a true warrior's task.

The Lioness, cunning and wise in the ways of witchery, pulled forth the necromantic creations of artifice and artwork. Shaped like a dead Kraken's tendrils, each talisman bore strange magics that would allow her to cast spells upon the runic magics sealing the portal shut. Our Dark Lady, Warlady and Shaman, had given us scrolls to consult. Should the signs and portends be favorable, by following the first of the spells scribed therein, the portal should open without sign nor sound, our entry guaranteed.

Such work requires craft and cunning, a keen mind and a close attention to detail. Our Warlady, disciple of Chronos, had given us instructions for contingency upon contingency... yet when the door of the postern gate unsealed its eldrich wardings and creaked open on the first spell's try, we could not rejoice. What the God of Time could predict in part, the God of Earthquakes could still counter. The great metal gate lodged less than a hand-span wide, too narrow a gap for even the most slender of our warband.

Silence was our ally. Noise, our foe. To use explosive magics would have announced our presence, and a hundred vicious Kraken soldiers would have descended upon us like carrion beetles, each one determined to bite off chunks of our flesh and chew whilst we screamed. As the others sank into a fierce, if hissed debate, I perceived the door to be only a hand-span thick, and the dip in the ceiling causing the door to move no farther only occurred at one spot.

I had brought my battleaxe, not a mace or a sledgehammer; merely bashing my foes into a pulp would not have delivered a swift enough end to the cunning, treacherous Krakens. Breaking the stone was neither possible, nor quiet enough. But doors, I realized, had hinges… and these hinges were metal. Stretching out my will, I summoned up the power that burned within, the blessing of Ogun, Orisha of Fire, God of Warriors and Crafters, and my personal patron from my Yoruban roots.

Such a gift of fire as I have been granted is not the big flash of an explosion. It is not large, and it is not showy. It is more akin to the slow creep of lava seeping with deadly heat down a mountainside, powerful yet subtle. The pungent scent of burning dust reached my nostrils, pleasing me despite the way it assaulted my senses. Soon, the death of neglect found itself swept aside by the more pleasing scent of the forge, of heated metal waiting for the striking of the hammer. But not to forge a sword into a plowshare like the civilized folks do. No, this was forging a set of door hinges into a way to pry open the door.

My mate scented the smoke, saw my outstretched arm, and exhorted the others to grab the door. With the effort of four, and the protection of their stout gloves, they managed to pull the panel away from its molten metal shackles. Glowing gold dripped onto the floor in its wake, but they shifted the door away from its obstruction and set it aside. Ogun, my patron, granted me the power to extract the heat of holy fire, and within seconds, the edge was safe to touch. But no free passage awaited us. This was a sally port, a barbican with two gates to block the way.

Again, the Lioness progressed, and applied her talisman of Kraken-shaped enchanted hands… and again, the door opened, but only opened partially when by its artifice, she applied the spells to pacify the eldritch powers set to watch in an eternal vigil over this neglected, forgotten entrance. The damage of Tullgrrah, Catman God of Quakes upon the entryway made it necessary to unleash my fury at the delay upon the metal hinges and frame so that the new portal, too, could be forced to give way.

+ + +

"That doesn't look like a dry, boring account," Lilith said… and ate one of his mini marshmallow men.

"That prisoner was mine to destroy!" Mitch protested.

She continued munching unrepentantly, typing into her report. "I drew it, and… I am *done* with my report."

"Good, you can finish mine," he grunted.

"Absolutely not," she countered, unmoved.

"I am injured, woman!"

"You can still write."

"Ruthless wench!"

"Absolutely." Her fingers touched another of the little caricatures, lifting it to her lips. Placed on the console on the far side from her husband, they were not going to be close enough for him to snatch at the rest, and she clearly knew it. "Better hurry, I only drew ten… whoops, sorry, only eight are left."

Munch.

Glaring at her, Mitch brooded a few moments in mutiny, then sighed roughly and resumed writing his damned report. He typed in the dry, boring, factual details on how they disabled the surveillance system via a control console inside near the back entrance, looping the vids so that the broadcasts showed nothing but empty, dusty, unused back corridors. Dutifully logged the timestamp for the moment when they heard movement as they progressed through those corridors—17:01 Terran Standard—and how they reached the cavern holding the geothermally powered generators for the whole base at 17:07 TS.

He described how he and a handful of the others silently took up guard positions around the machinery, while Prudhomme, Schwadel, and Nesbit applied their suction-hand devices to the consoles to input General Ia's codes on how to shut down the generators and lock out the Salik forces from remote reactivation.

+ + +

17:12 TS, PSG Willow Thompson, E Delta, hearing movement and what sounded like Sallhash being spoken in the distance, alerted the rest of us on our HUD headsets to make no noise while we stood guard. I continued to peruse the large body of water located behind the main grouping of geothermal ductwork. Sensing that danger was nearby, though I could not xenopathically discern the exact direction, I elected to hold ready my Non-Standard Melee Weapon, specifically my NSMW 506-78, instead of my standard-issue HK-74 laser rifle, under the precognition-authorized assertion of my CO to "…just be yourself while you're down there, Mitch."

+ + +

"Hmm… that'll do." Four miniature marshmallow prisoners plopped into Mitch's cocoa cup. Four more awaited release. Lilith gave him a pointed look. "Quoting the CO on that particular point almost sounds exciting. Are you sure you want to include it?"

"That is exactly what she told me to do, and I *succeeded*. If I'd been using my laser rifle, I could've shot up some of the equipment and set off an alarm," he retorted. Deliberately, he shifted his cursor over to his writing. "I wrote several entries in the report, I get to reward myself with the story."

"Yes, love. For a few minutes," Lilith replied serenely. And patted one of the remaining four marshmallows with a gentle little *squish squish* of its cylindrical head. Silently warning him to earn his treat.

By Conan, she's so... so... Magnificently annoying! Amused, Mitch quickly wrote out what happened next in the story, eager to get to the exciting part.

+ + +

...Dread crept through my veins, a prickling of warning, of cold, malicious, rapacious thoughts dragging along my shamanic senses like a wet river weed leaving muddy slime in its wake. Just before they struck, I sensed their intentions and hissed a warning: Through cunning and guile, three Kraken Warrior-Smiths had lurked in the waters, hiding upon hearing our initial approach.

Just as the Lioness and her two companions neutralized the first of the eldritch spell-wardings holding off the hordes of the Catmen Empire, they launched themselves with their mighty, fearsome, monstrously powerful legs out of the water, clearing the pipes drawing earth-energies up out of the bedrock. Ready with my labrys, I lashed out and cleaved through the first and nearest of the descending monsters' limbs. Gore splattered and blood flowed profusely, but mine was not the only debilitating blow.

My mate, swift in reflex and sure of aim, flung her dagger straight into the skull of a descending Kraken, impaling its wits even as she rolled out of its way. Sure in my faith that she could and would kill her foe, I finished my swing with a spin, slamming the bit of my battleaxe into the brains of my enemy—only to be grappled by the slimy squid-like tentacles of the third Kraken warrior. With a heaving grasp, he crushed my ribs, attempting to paralyze me so he could bite off a chunk of my flesh, in the foul manner of his kind.

Grimacing in pain, I cracked my head back against his mouth, breaking his teeth at the expense of stars exploding across my vision. Releasing one hand from my labrys, I reached up and back, grasped the eyestalk of the beast-man, and proved my strength was more than equal to his by crushing one eye, rendering him blind. With a mouthful of my hair, the beast could not roar loudly; with a stab of her other knife, my mate slaughtered the Kraken, robbing his life before he could devour mine.

He slumped against me, paining me from the pressure on my broken ribs. Some of the suckers ripped free, leaving welts that perhaps shall scar, testament to my surviving the attack of the cannibal Kraken. With aid from my companions, I peeled off the rest, and expressed my rage by decapitating all three—a task well-suited to the swinging of a labrys, and never to be underestimated in the hands of one as well-trained as I in the art of the battleaxe.

Coated in the gore of my enemies, their blood splashed across my body and drenching the floor, I stood guard while Willow, the Tree-Witch, applied her medical magics to my frame and wrapped my ribs with bandaging to ensure the broken ends would not shift should battle occur again. The sounds of our combat had not been loud enough to draw the rest of the stronghold's warriors, so when the last of the eldritch counterspelling had been chanted and drawn upon the mystical artifacts, I was able to move with the rest of the warband out of the cavern and back to our base camp beyond the doors I had melted free of the earth's grip...

+ + +

"More Action Report, dear," his mate reminded him.

He reached for his cup, sipped, and made a face. "My cocoa is getting cold."

"Write faster. I'll even make you a fresh one if you finish the report in the next ten minutes," she added. "And I'll throw in some Kraken marshmallows, this time."

The irony of "eating" Salik-decorated marshmallows, when that race literally wanted to eat humans alive, appealed to him. Focusing through the dull ache of his ribs and the faint throbbing of his head, he finished the report, ending with the last few timestamped moments worth mentioning, and gave the shortest answers possible in the analysis fields.

+ + +

19:44 TS, The 3rd Platoon of "Clan Calygos," the TUPSF-SF 19th Cord. 6th Div. 4th Batt. 1st Brig. 2nd Leg., B Company, reached our position. Corporal Bottomley exchanged the pre-designated sign-and-countersign confirming our respective identities.

19:49 TS, 3rd Platoon of Clan Calygos Company extracted E Squad, 2nd Platoon of Ia's Damned out through the front door. I expressed my relief and gratitude at not having to contort my broken ribs through any small apertures. We then headed out under vehicular escort to our extraction point. There were no further incidents to report during our entire retreat.

23:31 TS, E Squadron, 2nd Platoon, A Company reunited with our shuttlecraft and returned to the TUPSF *Damnation*.

23:57 TS, Commander Mishka reported that my ribs were broken, not just cracked, and applied bone-setting compounds along with biokinetic healing, then put me on medical leave for the next five days while my ribs heal. My skull was pronounced "not cracked" and I was given antibiotics to counter any potential xenobiotic infection or sepsis from the cuts made by the Salik technician's teeth.

What went wrong: Nothing, really. All obstacles were successfully overcome in the course of our mission.

What could have been done better: I need to be faster with my battleaxe next time. I should've been able to cut off those tentacles before they grappled me.

Any condemnations of your comrades: Absolutely none; everyone did an excellent job, as usual.

Any additionally commendations of your comrades: Commendations were noted in the timesheet where appropriate.

+ + +

"Done... and sent! Now, my beloved, bring me the effigies you have made of my enemies, so that I may drown them in the boiling brown lava that is the Drink of the Gods!" he commanded.

"Yes, my love," Lilith agreed, and kissed the non-injured top of his head one more time before moving to dispense another mug of hot cocoa for her barbarian mate. "You have definitely earned it."

He really was quite lucky, Mitch acknowledged, watching her out of the corner of his eye since turning that way fully hurt his ribs too much. Whether of the 5th century variety or of the 25th, not every barbarian had such a willful, wonderful, helpful mate.

As mentioned in Robert Silverberg's introduction, writers Edmond Hamilton and Leigh Brackett separately are key influences on space opera. In this case, Hamilton joins his wife for her final Eric John Stark story, their only formal collaboration, in the sword-and-planet story tradition, a related subgenre that went on to influence space opera, but flowed out of fantasy. Rousing adventure stories set on other planets, and usually featuring Earthmen as protagonists, the term "sword and planet" derives from the stories' heroes typically engaging their adversaries in hand-to-hand combat, primarily with simple melée weapons such as swords, even in a setting that often boasts advanced technology. Buried for years, "Stark and the Star Kings" first appeared in 2010 in a Brackett Stark collection, and has only been reprinted a couple of times. It follows dozens of others about the beloved character who here confronts a peril of unending doom.

STARK AND THE STAR KINGS

LEIGH BRACKETT AND EDMOND HAMILTON

The great Rift Valley runs southeast just below the equator, a stupendous gash across the dry brown belly of Mars. Two and a half thousand miles it runs in length, and as much as twenty thousand feet in depth, and all that enormous emptiness is packed and brimming over with the myths and superstitions of more thousands of years than even the Martians can count.

Along the nighted floor of the valley, Eric John Stark went alone.

The summons had been for him alone. It had reached him unexpectedly in the gritty chill of a Dryland camp. A voice of power had spoken in his mind. A quiet voice, as compelling as death.

"Oh, N'Chaka," the voice had said. "Man-Without-a-Tribe. The Lord of the Third Bend bids you come."

All Mars knew that the one who called himself Lord of the Third Bend had laired for many lifetimes in the hidden depths of the Great Rift Valley. Human? No one could say. Even the Ramas, those nearly immortal Martians with whom Stark had once done battle in the dead city of Sinharat, had known nothing about him. But they feared his strength.

Stark had thought about it for perhaps an hour, watching red dust blow across a time-eaten land made weird and unfamiliar by the strangely diminished sunlight.

It was odd that the summons should come now. It was odd that the Lord of the Third Bend should know enough about him to call him by that name that few men knew and fewer still ever used; not his true patronymic but his first-name, given him by the sub-human tribe that had reared him. It was odd, in fact, that the Lord of the Third Bend should call him by any name, at any time, as though he might have need of him.

Perhaps he did.

And in any case, it was not often that one was invited into the presence of Legend.

So Stark was riding his scaly beast through the perpetual night of the valley, toward the Third Bend. Although that voice of power had not spoken again in his mind, he had known exactly how to reach his destination.

He was approaching it now.

Far ahead, to the right, a little light showed. The rays were as feeble as though strangled at birth, but the light was there. It grew slowly brighter, shifting in his view as the beast changed direction. They were rounding the Third Bend.

The ruddy glow of light strengthened, contracting from a vague glow into a discrete point.

The beast shied suddenly. It turned its ungainly head and hissed, staring through the darkness to the left.

"And now what?" Stark asked it, his hand going to the weapon at his belt.

He could see nothing. But it seemed to him that he heard a faint sound as of laughter, and not in a human voice.

He took his hand away from his weapon. Stark did not doubt that the Lord of the Third Bend had servants, and there was no reason that the servants need be human.

Stark cuffed his mount and rode on, looking neither to right nor left. He had been invited here, and he was damned if he would show fear.

The beast padded on reluctantly, and the far-off witch-laughter drifted through the darkness, now louder and again soft and far away. The point of ruddy light ahead expanded and became an upright rectangle, partly veiled by mists that seemed to curl through it from beyond.

The glowing rectangle was a great open door, with a light beyond it. The door was in the side of a building whose shape and dimensions were unguessable in the shrouding darkness. Stark got the impression of a huge somber citadel going up into the perpetual night of the abyss and showing only this one opening.

He rode up to the portal and dismounted, and went through into the curling mists beyond. He could see nothing of whatever hall or cavern he had entered, but there was a feeling of space, of largeness.

He stopped and waited.

For a time there was no sound at all. Then, from somewhere in the mist, whispered the sweet and evil laughter that was not quite human.

Stark said to it, "Tell your master that N'Chaka awaits his pleasure."

There were hidden titterings and scurryings that seemed to circle upon themselves, and then that quiet compelling voice he remembered spoke to him. He was not sure for a moment whether he heard it with his ears or with his mind. Perhaps both. It said,

"I am here, N'Chaka."

"Then show yourself," said Stark. "I bargain with no one whose face I cannot see."

No one appeared, and the voice said with infinite softness, "Bargain? Was there mention of bargaining? Does the knife in one's hand bargain with its owner?"

"This knife does," said Stark. "You must have need of me or you would not have brought me here. If you have need of me, you will not destroy out of mere annoyance. Therefore show yourself, and let us talk."

"Here in my remoteness," said the voice, "the winds have told me much of the Earthman with two names who is not of Earth. It appears that what I heard was true."

There came a sound of sandals upon the stone. The mists rolled back. The Lord of the Third Bend stood before Stark.

He was a young man, dressed in the very old High Martian costume of a toga-like garment whose ends brushed the floor. His smooth face was incredibly handsome.

"You may call me Aarl," he said. "It was my man-name once, long ago."

Stark felt the hairs lift on the back of his neck. The eyes in that young face were as black as space, as old, and as deep. They were eyes of knowledge and strength beyond anything human, eyes to steal a man's soul and drown it. They frightened him. He felt that if he looked full into them he would be shattered like flawed glass. Yet he was too proud to glance away. He said,

"Am I to understand that you have existed in this shape for all these ages?"

"I have had many shapes," said Aarl. "The outward semblance is only illusion."

"Perhaps for you," said Stark. "Mine is somewhat more integral. Well. I have come far and I am tired, hungry, and thirsty. Are wizards above the laws of hospitality?"

"Not this one," said Aarl. "Come with me."

They began walking through what Stark took, from the echoes, to be a high-roofed hall of some length. There was no more sound from the unseen servitors.

The mists drew farther back. Now Stark could see walls of dark stone that went up to a great height. Upon them were designs of fire, shining arabesques that constantly moved and changed shape. Something about them bothered Stark. After a moment he realized that the fiery designs were corroded, tarnished, like the sunlight of upper Mars.

"So," he said. "The darkness is here, too."

"It is," said Aarl. He glanced sideling at Stark as they walked. "How do the wise men of science explain this darkness to the people of the nine worlds?"

"You already know that, of course."

"Yes. Nevertheless, tell me."

"They say that the whole solar system has moved into a cosmic dust cloud that is dimming the sun."

"Do they believe that, these wise men with all their instruments?"

"I don't know. That is what they must say, of course, to forestall panic."

"Do you believe it?"

"No."

"Why not?"

"I have been among the tents of the Dryland nomads. Their wise men say differently. They say it is not an inert thing but an active force."

"They are wise indeed. It is not a dust cloud. It is more than that, very much more than that."

Aarl stopped walking and spoke with feverish intensity.

"Can you conceive of a vampire something that drinks energy, that steals it from across a great void... a greater void than you imagine? A thing that will, if it is not stopped, devour not only the light of the sun but even the force of gravity that holds this family of worlds together? That will literally destroy the solar system?"

Stark stared at him appalled, not wanting to believe yet knowing somehow that it was so.

The Lord of the Third Bend reached out and grasped Stark's wrist with an icy hand.

"I'm afraid, Stark. My powers are great, but against this they're useless without help. That is why I need you. Yes. *Need* you. Come, and I'll show you why."

✦ ✦ ✦

They sat in a mist-bordered chamber high in the citadel. And Stark was remembering the words of an ancient bardic chant.

Fear the Lord of the Third Bend. Fear him, for he is the master of time.

"The great void of which I spoke," said Aarl, "is not only a dimension of space. Look."

Stark looked at the curtain of mist. And was caught by the incredible scene that formed within it.

A panorama of stars, the great glooms of the void a background for a wilderness of flaring suns. He felt himself drawn into that immensity, to rush through it at incredible speed. Chains of stars rose up before him, mountain ranges of high-piled, shining nebulae loomed on either hand. He swept past them in all their glory and left them far behind.

The view shifted, changed perspective. And Stark beheld ships ahead of him, gleaming starships that raced through the celestial jungle.

He saw them brilliant and small as toys. With a vertiginous wrench he returned to the reality of his own body and the coldness of the stone he sat upon.

"You are adept," he said, "at putting all this into my mind. Which is what you're doing."

"True," said Aarl. "But it is not mere imagining. You see what I have seen across two hundred thousand years of time. You see the future."

Stark believed it. The Lord of the Third Bend had not acquired his stature in the minds of generations of men by means of fraud. The sort of shabby trickery known to any village thaumaturgist would not have stood the test. Aarl wielded the lost knowledge of forgotten Mars, a science that differed greatly from the science of Earth but was none the less a science.

He looked at the vision on the screen of mist. Two hundred thousand years.

"Those ships," said Aarl, "those very powerful ships that travel with such speed, are the ships of the Star Kings."

That name, heard for the first time, rang in Stark's mind like the strident call of a bugle.

"The Star Kings?"

"The men who rule that future umiverse, each in his own kingdom, principality, or barony."

"Ah," said Stark, and looked again. "That is right and fitting. The starlands are too bright for grubby clerks, and bureaucrats in rumpled suits each trying to be more common than the next. Yes. Let there be Star Kings."

"You must go there, Stark. Into the future."

A small pulse began to beat beneath the angle of Stark's jaw. "Into the future. Bodily? Your knowledge can send me bodily across two hundred thousand years?"

"Two years or two million. It is all the same."

"Can you bring me back? Bodily."

"If you survive."

"Hm," said Stark, and looked again at the vision. "How would I go? I mean, in what capacity?"

"As an envoy, a messenger. Someone must go and meet these Star Kings face to face." Aarl's voice was angry. "I have ascertained that this menace to our solar system exists in their time. I have attempted to contact them by mental arts, without success. They simply did not hear. That is why I sent for you, Stark."

"You sent for N'Chaka," Stark said, and smiled. N'Chaka, the Man-without-a-tribe who could not remember his real parents, naked fosterling of the beast-folk of wild sun-shattered Mercury; N'Chaka, who wore his acquired humanity like an uncomfortable garment and who still tended to use his teeth when angered. "Why N'Chaka as an ambassador to the courts of the Star Kings?"

"Because N'Chaka is an animal at heart, though he has a man's brain. Animals do not lie, they do not turn traitor because of greed for money or power, or because of that worse tempter, philosophical doubt." Aarl studied him with those space-deep eyes. "In other words, I can trust you."

"You think that if someone offered me a throne at Algol or Betelgeuse, I wouldn't take it?" Stark laughed. "The Lord of the Abyss overestimates the purity of the beast."

"I think not."

"And anyway, why a bastard Earthman? Why not a Martian?"

"We're too concerned with our past, too deeply rooted in our own sacred soil. You have no roots. You do have a devouring curiosity, and a rare capacity for survival. Otherwise you would not be here." He held up his hand to forestall comment. "Look."

The scene on the mist-curtain changed abruptly. Now a madman's dream of space appeared, a tangled nightmare of crowding suns, dead stars, filamentary nebulae. Stark seemed to be racing at blinding speed through this cosmic jungle.

"The region at the western limb of the galaxy," said Aarl. "It is called, in that future time, The Marches of Outer Space. It holds a number of the smaller star-kingdoms. It also holds this."

Two old red suns like ruby brooches pinned a ragged veil of darkness across the starfield. Stark plunged into the gloom of the dark nebula, past dim drowned stars dragging their nighted planets. The coiling dust seemed to tear like smoke with the wind of his passing. Out on the other side there was light again, but it was strangely bent, distorted around an area of blankness, of nothingness quite different from the dusty darkness of the nebula. He could not see into it. The vision seemed to recoil, as though struck back by a blow.

"Not even my arts can penetrate that blind area," said Aarl. "But it is from there that the force comes, leaping back through time, draining the energy from our solar system."

"And my task, if I go, will be a simple one," Stark said. "Find out what that force is, who is responsible for it, and put an end to it." He shook his head. "Your faith in my abilities is touching, but do you know what I think, Aarl? I think you've lived in this dark hole far too long. I think your senses have left you."

He stood up, turning his back to the screen of mist.

"The task is impossible, and you know it."

"Yet it must be done."

"If it's a natural phenomenon, some freak warping of the continuum…"

"Then of course we are helpless. But I don't think it is." Aarl rose. He seemed to have grown taller and his eyes were hypnotic in their intensity. "You have no love for Earth because of what Earthmen did to your foster-tribe, yet I think you would not truly wish all those millions dead and the planet with them, long before its time. And what of Mars, which has been something of a home to you? She too has a while to go before the night overtakes her."

The pulse hammered more strongly under Stark's jaw. "I wouldn't even know where to start. It could take a lifetime."

"We do not have a lifetime," said Aarl, "nor even half of one. The energy-drain is accelerating rapidly. And I can tell you where to begin. With a man named Shorr Kan, King of Aldeshar in the Marches. The most powerful of the petty kings, and wily enough for two. You will find him sympathetic."

"How so?"

"Because this strange force is causing *him* immediate trouble. You must find a way to enlist his help."

"You speak as though I've already made my decision."

"You have."

Stark turned and looked at the mist-curtain again. It was blank now, only mist and nothing more. Yet he could still see the ships of the Star Kings and the untamed jungle of the Marches. The future, undiscovered, unexplored. Could he have the chance to see it, and refuse?

He said, "I suppose you're right."

Aarl nodded. "You had no choice, really. I was sure of that before I summoned you."

Stark shrugged. Suppose he tried and failed; it was better than sitting helplessly. And he could make his own decision about coming back.

He followed Aarl out of the chamber.

They came at length into a long hall crowded with objects. Stark recognized several instruments of modern Earth science; there was a fine seismograph, spectroscopic equipment, an array of electronic items, the latest in lasers. There were other things that seemed to have survived out of ancient Mars, arrangements of crystalline shapes that had no meaning whatever for Stark. There were yet other objects that he surmised had been constructed by the Lord of the Third Bend himself.

One of these was a sort of helical cage of crystal ribbons whose upper part spiraled away toward the high-vaulted roof. It appeared to vanish up there. Stark attempted to follow its progressively blurring outlines and was forced to stop, overcome with vertigo.

Aarl took his place within the lower part of the cage. "This helix amplifies my mental powers and enables me to manipulate the time-dimension. Stand anywhere. I shall be able to retain contact with your mind, since we are now attuned to communication, but I shall not waste precious energy on conversation. When you are ready to come back, tell me."

He did something with his hands. The crystal ribbons began to run with subtle fires.

"When you awaken you will be in the future, and I shall have given you such knowledge of it as I possess."

Before the darkness took him, Stark felt an incongruous pang of hunger. Aarl's promised hospitality had not been forthcoming.

✦ ✦ ✦

He had a strange dream. He was infinite. He was transparent. The spaces between his atoms were large enough to let whole constellations through. He moved, but his motion was neither forward nor backward; it was a sly sneaky sidelong slither through… what?

In his dream the motion made him very sick. He felt like vomiting, but there was nothing inside him and so he could only retch.

Perhaps that was why Aarl had not bothered to feed him.

Retching, he awoke.

And saw that he had stopped moving. There was solid ground beneath his feet. His stomach received this information gratefully.

The light was peculiar. It was greenish. He looked up and saw a green sun blazing in a blue-green sky flecked with minty clouds.

He recognized the sun. It was Aldeshar, in the Marches of Outer Space.

The planet whose solidity was so welcome to him must be Altoh, the throne-world.

He had appeared, materialized, reassembled… whatever it was he had done… on a low ridge above an alien city. It was a pleasant city, low-roofed and rambling, with here and there a tall fluted tower for variety. The people had done without the ugly cubism of functional building. A network of canals glittered in the sunlight. There was a profusion of trees and flowering shrubs. The wandering streets were thronged with people and the canals were busy with boats. There seemed to be no motorized traffic on the surface, so the air was blessedly clean.

All the movement in the streets seemed to be converging toward a point in the southwestern sector of the city, where he could see a clump of more imposing buildings, with taller towers and an enormous square. The city was Donalyr, the capital, and the buildings would be Shorr Kan's palace and the administrative center of the star-kingdom.

A vast deep-bass humming sound suddenly filled the heavens, drawing Stark's attention away from the city. Down across the sky, ablaze with light and roaring with the thunder of God, a colossal ship slanted into its landing pattern. Stark's gaze followed it down, to a starport far out beyond the northern boundaries of Donalyr. The ground trembled beneath him, and was still.

Stark went down to the city. In the time it took him to reach the outskirts, three more ships had landed.

He let himself be carried along with the flow of people toward the palace square. He found that Aarl had supplied him with a working knowledge of the language; he could understand the chatter around him. The folk of Altoh were tall and strong, with ruddy tan skins and sharp eyes and faces. They wore loose brightly colored garments suitable to the mild climate. But there were many foreigners, in this place where the starships came and went, men and women and a sprinkling of non-humans, in all shapes and sizes and colors, wearing every sort of dress. Donalyr, apparently, was quite used to strangers.

Even so, the people he passed turned their heads to look at Stark. Perhaps it was his height and the way he moved, or perhaps it was something arresting about the harsh planes of his face and the peculiar lightness of his eyes, accentuated by a skin-color that spoke of long exposure to a savage sun. They sensed some difference in him. Stark ignored them, secure in the knowledge that they could not possibly guess the degree of his differentness.

Ships continued to drop in rolling thunder out of the sky. He had counted nine by the time he reached the edge of the great square. He looked upward to watch number ten come in, and he felt the tiniest movement close to him in the crowd, the lightest of touches as though a falling leaf had brushed him. He whipped his right hand round behind him, snapped it shut on something bony, and turned to see what he had caught.

A little old man stared up at him with the bright, unrepentant face of a squirrel caught stealing nuts from someone else's hoard.

"You're too fast," he said. "Even so, you'd never have had me if your clothing wasn't so unfamiliar. I thought I knew where every pocket and purse in the Marches is situated. You must come from way back in."

"Far enough," said Stark. The old man wore a baggy tunic of no particular color, neither light nor dark, brilliant nor dull. If you didn't look hard at him you wouldn't see him in the throng. Beneath the hem he showed knobby knees and pipestem shanks. "Well," said Stark, "and what shall we do with you, Grandfather?"

"I took nothing," said the old man. "And it's my word against yours… you can't prove that I even tried."

"Hm," said Stark. "How good is your word?"

"What a question to ask!" said the old man, drawing himself up.

"I'm asking it."

The old man shot off on another tack. "You're a stranger here. You'll need a guide. I know every stone of this city. I can show you all of its delights. I can keep you out of the hands of…"

"…of thieves and pickpockets. Yes." Stark pulled his captive around to a more comfortable position. "What's your name?"

"Song Durr."

"All right, Song Durr. There's no hurry, we can always decide later what to do." He kept a strong hold on the thin wrist. "Tell me what's going on here."

"The Lords of the Marches are gathering for a conference with Shorr Kan." He laughed. "Conference, my eye. What's your name, by the way?" Stark told him. "That's an odd one. I don't seem to place the world of origin."

"I am also called N'Chaka."

"Ah. From Strior, perhaps? Or Naroten?" He looked keenly at Stark. "Well, no matter." His voice dropped. "Perhaps that is your Brotherhood name?"

A brotherhood of thieves, of course. Stark shrugged and let the old man interpret the gesture as he would. "Why did you say, 'Conference, my eye'?"

"Some starships have been lost. The rulers of a dozen or so little kingdoms are hopping mad about it. They suspect that Shorr Kan is responsible." Song Durr cackled admiringly. "And I wouldn't be surprised if he were. He's the hell and all of a king. Give him a little more time and he'll rule all the Marches. Him, that didn't have a pan to cook in when he first came here." He added, "My hand will be quite ruined, Brother N'Chaka."

"Not just yet. How were these ships lost?"

"They simply disappeared. Somewhere out beyond Dendrid's Veil."

"Dendrid's Veil. That would be a dark nebula? Yes. And who is Dendrid?"

"The Goddess of Death."

It seemed a fitting name. "And why do they blame Shorr Kan?"

Song Durr stared at him. "You *must* be from way back in. That's no-man's-land out there, and there's been a lot of pawing and picking at it... quarrels over boundaries, annexations, all that. A lot of it is still unexplored. Shorr Kan has been the most daring and ambitious in his activities, or the most unscrupulous, whichever way you want to put it, though they'd all do the same themselves if they had the courage. Also, *we* haven't lost any ships." He rubbed his skinny nose and grinned. "I'd like to be a fly on the wall when they have that conference."

Stark said, "Brother Song Durr, let us be two flies."

The old man's eyes popped. "You mean, get right inside the palace?" He pulled sharply against Stark's grip. "Oh, no."

"You mistake me," Stark said. "I don't mean to break in like thieves. I mean to walk in, like kings."

Or like ambassadors. Envoys, from another time and place. Stark wondered if Aarl were listening, in his misty Martian citadel two hundred thousand years ago.

Song Durr stood, rigid in all his stringy sinews, while Stark told him what he was going to have to do if he wanted to keep his freedom.

In the end, Song Durr began to smile.

"I think I would like that," he said. "Yes, I think that would be better than another stay in the convict pens. I don't know why... if it were anyone but you, Brother N'Chaka, I'd take the pens, but somehow you make me believe that we can get away with it." He shook his head. "You do have large ideas, for a country boy."

Cackling, he led the way toward the surrounding streets.

"We'll have to hurry, Brother. The Star Kings will be arriving soon, and we mustn't be late to the party!"

+ + +

The procession of the Star Kings glittered its way from the landing place at the far end of the palace square, where the hover-cars came down, along the central space held open by rows of tough-looking guardsmen in white uniforms, toward the palace itself. There were jewels enough and royal costumes of divers sorts, and faces of many colors, four of them definitely non-human; a brilliant pageant, Stark thought, and suitable to the place, with the magnificent towers looming above in the fierce green glare of the sun, the vast crowd, the humming silence, the intricately carved and fluted portico where Shorr Kan, Sovereign Lord of Aldeshar, sat upon a seat of polished stone… a tiny figure at this distance, but somehow radiating power even so, a signal brightness among grouped and shining courtiers.

The brazen voice of a chamberlain echoed across the square, reproduced from clusters of speakers.

"Burrul Opis, King of the worlds of Maktoo, Lord Paramount of the Nebula Zorind. Kan Martann, King of the Twin Suns of Keldar. Flane Fell, King of Tranett and Baron of Leth…"

One by one the Star Kings approached the seat of Shorr Kan and were greeted, and passed on into the palace with their retinues.

"Now," said Stark, and pushed Song Durr forward. From between two of the guardsmen the old man cried out,

"Wait! Wait, there! One other is here to confer with our sovereign lord! Eric John Stark, Ambassador Ex…"

His voice squeaked off as the guardsmen grabbed him. The chamberlain who was turning away from the last departing hover-car, looked with surprised annoyance at the commotion.

Stark stepped forward, thrusting the guardsmen apart. "Eric John Stark, Ambassador Extraordinary from the worlds of Sol."

He had shed his travel-stained garments, still patched with the red dust of Mars. He was clad all in black now, a rich tunic heavy with embroidery over soft trousers and fine boots. Song Durr had stolen them from one of the best shops catering to off-worlders. He had wanted to steal some jewels as well, but Stark had settled for a gold chain. For a moment everything went into a tableau as the chamberlain stared at Stark and the guardsmen hesitated over whether or not they should kill him where he stood.

Stark said to the chamberlain, "Tell your master that my mission is urgent, and deals with the subject of the conference."

"But you were not on the list. Your credentials…"

"I have travelled a very long way," said Stark, "to speak with your king. What I have to say concerns the death of suns. Are you a man of such courage that you dare turn me away?"

"I am not a brave man at all," said the chamberlain. "Hold them." The guardsmen held. The chamberlain sent an attendant scurrying toward the palace. Shorr Kan had paused in his rising, his attention drawn to the interruption. There was some hurried talk, and Stark saw Shorr Kan make a decisive gesture. The attendant came scurrying back.

"The Ambassador from Sol may approach, with an escort."

The chamberlain looked relieved. He nodded to the guardsmen, who stepped out of line, weapons at the ready, and positioned themselves behind Stark and Song Durr, who was now gloriously robed in crimson. The little man was breathing hard, holding himself nervously erect.

They strode through a rising babble as the crowd pushed and craned to see this new curiosity. They mounted the palace steps. And Stark stood before Shorr Kan, King of Aldeshar in the Marches of Outer Space.

King he might be, but he had not grown fat on it, nor un-watchful. He was still the hunting tiger, the cool-eyed predator with prey under his paw and his whiskers a-twitch with eagerness to get more. He looked at Stark with a kind of deadly good humor, baring strong white teeth in a strong hard face.

"Ambassador Extraordinary from the worlds of Sol. Tell me, Ambassador… where is Sol?"

That was a good question, and one Stark did not attempt to answer. "Very far away," he said, "but even so, of interest to Your Majesty."

"How so?"

"The problem facing you here in the Marches also affects us. When I heard of the conference, I didn't wait to present my credentials in the normal manner. It's vital that I attend." Was Shorr Kan ignorant of Sol because of its distance and unimportance, or because it no longer existed? In which case… Stark forced the thought resolutely away. If he let his mind become involved with time paradoxes he would never get anywhere.

"Vital," Shorr Kan was asking, "to whom?"

"This power beyond Dendrid's Veil, whatever it may be, is killing our sun, our solar system. Yours may be next. I would say it's vital to all of us to find out what that power is."

Deep in the tiger eyes Stark saw the stirring of a small shadow and recognized it for what it was. Fear.

Shorr Kan nodded his dark head once. "The Ambassador from Sol may enter."

The guardsmen stepped back. Stark and Song Durr followed the king and his courtiers through the great portal.

"I almost believed you myself," Song Durr whispered. His step was light now, his face crinkled in a greedy smile. "For a country boy, you do well."

Stark wondered how he would feel about that later on.

The conference was a stormy one, held in a huge high-vaulted hall that made kings and courtiers seem like dressed-up children huddled in the midst of its ringing emptiness. Some predecessor of Shorr Kan's had designed it most carefully. The dwindling effect of the architecture was deliberate. The throne-chair was massive, set so high that everyone must look up and become aware, not only of the throne and its occupant, but of the enormous winged deities that presided on either side of the dais. They had identical faces, very fierce and jut-nosed and ugly. Eyes made of precious stones glared down at the lesser kings. Stark surmised that the original of those unpleasant faces had been the builder's own.

Shorr Kan sat there now, and listened to his enemies.

Flane Fell, King of Tranett, seemed to be spokesman for the group, and the foremost in angry accusation. His skin was the color of old port, his features vulturine. He wore gray, with a diamond sunburst on his breast, and his bald skull, narrow as a bird's, was surmounted by a kind of golden tower. After a great deal of bickering and shouting he cried out,

"If you are not responsible for the loss of our ships, then who is? What is? Tell us, Shorr Kan!"

Shorr Kan smiled. He was younger than Stark had expected, but then youth was nothing against a conqueror.

"You believe that I am developing some great secret weapon out there beyond Dendrid's Veil. Why?"

"Your ambitions are well known. You'll rule the Marches alone, if you can."

"Of course," said Shorr Kan. "Isn't that true of every one of us? It's not my ambitions you fear, it's my ability. And I'd remind you that I've not needed any secret weapons so far." All their silken plumage rustled with indignation, and he laughed. "You have formed an alliance against me, I'm told."

"Yes."

"How do you propose to use it?"

"Force," said Flane Fell, and the others shouted agreement. "Overwhelming force, if you drive us to it. Your navy is powerful, but against our combined fleets Aldeshar couldn't stand for a week."

"True," said Shorr Kan, "but consider. What if I do in fact possess a secret weapon? What would happen then to your lovely fleets? I doubt if you'll take that chance."

"Don't be too sure, upstart," said Kan Martann furiously. "We've all lost ships, all but you, Shorr Kan. If you have no weapon, and you're truly ignorant of the force beyond Dendrid's Veil, why are you preserved from misfortune?"

"Because I'm smarter than you are. After the first ship disappeared, I kept mine out of there." He made a sweeping gesture, bringing Stark into the group. "I present to you Eric John Stark, Ambassador Extraordinary from the worlds of Sol. Perhaps we ought to hear what he has to say. It seems to have some bearing on our quarrel."

Stark knew from the beginning that he was talking against the barrier of completely closed minds. Still, he told them the meticulous truth, leaving out only the mention of time and characterizing Aarl simply as a scientist. They barely let him finish.

"What did you hope to gain by this?" asked Flane Fell, addressing the throne. "The fellow is an obvious imposter, intended to convince us that because some mythical system on the other side of the galaxy is being attacked by this menace, you could have nothing to do with it. Did you think we'd believe it?"

"I think you're a parcel of fools," said Shorr Kan, when the clamor had subsided. "Suppose he's telling the truth. If this thing can kill one sun, it can kill another... Aldeshar, Tranett, Maktoo, the Twins of Keldar."

"We're not that easily deceived!"

"Which simply means that you're frightened out of your royal wits. You want to believe in a weapon controlled by me because you feel you can do something about that. But suppose it's a weapon *not* controlled by me? Suppose it's some wild freak of nature not controlled, or controllable, by anyone? Wouldn't you be wiser to find out?"

"We've tried," said Flane Fell grimly. "We lost ships and gained no knowledge. Now it's up to you. This is our ultimatum, Shorr Kan. Dismantle your weapon, or give us proof that the thing is not of your making. In one month's time an unmanned vessel will be sent beyond the Veil. If it vanishes, and your proofs have not been forthcoming, it means war."

They lifted their clenched fists all together and shouted, "War!"

"I hear you, brother kings. Now go."

The group departed with a clatter of jewelled heels on the echoing floor.

"You, too," said Shorr Kan, and dismissed his courtiers. "Stay," he said to Stark. "And you, little thief…"

"Majesty," said Song Durr, "I am chamberlain to the Ambassador…"

"Don't lie to me," said Shorr Kan. "I was one of the Brotherhood myself, before I became a king. You have my permission to steal, if you can do it without being caught, as much as will not bulge that borrowed finery. In one hour I shall send men to hunt for you, but they will not look beyond the palace doors."

"Majesty," said Song Durr, "I embrace your knees. And yours, country boy. We were well met indeed. Good luck to you." He scampered away, thin shanks twinkling beneath his robe.

"His worries are small," said Shorr Kan, and smiled.

"But you don't envy him."

"If I did, I would be in his place." Shorr Kan came down from the throne and stood before Stark. "You're a strange man, Ambassador. You make me uneasy, and you bring disturbing news. Perhaps I ought to have you killed at once. That is what my brother kings would do. But I'm not a born king, you see, I'm an upstart, and so I keep my eyes and ears and especially my mind wide open. Also, I have another advantage over my colleagues. I know I'm telling the truth when I say that I have no secret weapon, and I do not know what force this is that eats up ships and stars. Do you believe me, Ambassador?"

"Yes."

"Why?"

"If you controlled the force, you'd use it."

Shorr Kan laughed. "You see that, do you? Of course you do.

That pack..." He jerked his chin contemptuously at the doorway. "Their spite blinds them. Their chief hope is to be rid of me, no matter what else befalls them."

"You must admit they've mousetrapped you rather neatly."

"They think they have. But they are only petty kings, Ambassador, and there is nothing more petty than a petty king."

He looked up and around the great hall. "Hideous, isn't it? And those two fellows there beside the throne, with their ugly great faces. I've thought of putting hats on them, but they look silly enough already. Aldeshar was always a petty kingdom, always will be. But first steps must be small, Ambassador. There are larger thrones ahead."

Ambition, intelligence, energy, ruthlessness, shone in him like a brilliant light. They made him beautiful, with the beauty of things which are perfect in their design and flawless in their functioning.

"Now there is a problem to be solved, eh?" The tiger eyes came back to Stark, fixed on him. "Why did you come to me, Ambassador? All this long, long way from Sol."

"It seemed that we might help each other."

"You need help from me," said Shorr Kan. "Do I need help from you?"

"How can I answer that until we know what threatens us?"

Shorr Kan nodded. "I have a feeling about you, Ambassador Stark. We shall be great friends, or great enemies, and if it's the latter, I'll not hesitate to kill you."

"I know that."

"Good, we understand each other. Now, there is much to do. My scientific advisors will want to hear your story. Then..."

"Your Majesty," said Stark, "of your mercy... it's been a long time since I tasted food."

A scant two hundred thousand years.

+ + +

Two old red suns like ruby brooches pinned a ragged curtain of darkness across the starfield. Dendrid's Veil, looking exactly as Stark had seen it in the mist of Aarl's citadel chamber. The view was still a projection, this time on the simulator screen of a Phantom scout, the fastest ship in Shorr Kan's fleet, loaded with special gear.

Stark and Shorr Kan stood together studying the simulator. Beneath Stark and around him, tormenting the whole of the ship's fabric and his own flesh, was the throb and hum of the FTL drive, a subliminal sense of wrenching displacement coupled with a suffocating feeling of being trapped inside a shell of unimaginable power like an unhatched chick in an egg. The image on the screen was an electronic trick no more genuine than Aarl's, except that the actual nebula was ahead.

The flight was no spur-of-the-moment thing. There had been endless hasslings with counsellors; scientific advisors, military and civilian advisors, all of whom pulled furiously in totally different directions. In the end, Shorr Kan had had his way.

"A king is made for ruling. When he ceases to have the courage and the vision necessary to perform that function, he had damn well better abdicate. My kingdom is threatened with destruction by two things, war and the unknown. Unless the unknown is made known, war is inevitable. Therefore it is my duty to find out what lies beyond Dendrid's Veil."

"But not in person," said his counsellors. "The risk is too great."

"The risk is too great to send anyone but myself," said Shorr Kan. Nobility radiated from him, illumined the throne and the ugly genies. It was easy to see how he drew his followers to him. "What is a king, if he does not think first of the safety of his people? Prepare a ship."

After all the orders were given and the counsellors sent off to deal with them, Shorr Kan grinned at Stark. They were alone then in the great hall.

"Nobility is all very well, but one must be practical too. Do you see my point, Ambassador?"

Stark's patience had worn somewhat with the wrangling and delay. He had been conscious of an increasing urgency, as though Aarl were putting a silent message into his mind: "*Hurry!*"

He said rather curtly, "At best you'll bait your brother kings to follow you because they'll be afraid to let you go alone. You may find a way to destroy them, or use them as allies, whichever seems advisable at the time. At worst, with a fast ship under you, you may hope to have a line of escape open if things go too far wrong. How can you be sure they won't simply blow you out of space, thus negating both possibilities?"

"They'll want me to lead them to the weapon. I think they'll wait." Shorr Kan put his hand confidently on Stark's shoulder. "And since you'll be with me, you had better hope that I'm right. I've made some enquiries about you, Ambassador."

"Oh?"

"I thought perhaps you might be a spy for my brother kings, or even an assassin. You do have the look of one, you know. But my agents could find no trace of you, and you don't seem to have sprung from any of our local planets. So I must believe you're what you say you are. There's only one small problem…" He smiled at Stark. "We still haven't been able to locate Sol. So I'm keeping you by me, Ambassador, close by, as an unknown quantity."

An unknown quantity, Stark thought, to be used or discarded. Yet he could not help liking Shorr Kan.

And now he stood in the bridge of the scout and wondered whether Shorr Kan had read his brother kings aright. Because the ships of the Kings of the Marches had followed them, were following, at a discreet distance but hanging stubbornly in their wake.

"We'll make planetfall in the nebula," said Shorr Kan. "Ceidri, the farthest inhabited world we know and the closest to the edge of this unknown power. They're strange folk, the Ceidrins, but the Marches are full of strange folk, the beginnings of new evolutions and the rags and bobtails of old ones driven out here by successive waves of interstellar conquest. Perhaps they can tell us something."

"They're scientists?"

"In their own peculiar way."

The chief of the scientists who had accompanied the battery of instruments mounted aboard made a derisive sound.

"Sorcerors. And not even human."

"And what have you been able to tell us?" Shorr Kan demanded. "That there is an area of tremendous force beyond the Veil, force sufficient to warp space around it, destroying everything that comes near it? We knew that. Can you tell us how to approach this force, how to learn its source without being destroyed ourselves?"

"Not yet."

"When you know, tell me. Until then, I'll take whatever knowledge I can get regardless of the source."

Time passed, time that was running out for all of them, here and now and for the nine little worlds of Sol two hundred thousand years in the past. The ship plunged into the dark nebula as into a cloud of smoke, and it was as Stark had seen it on Aarl's misty curtain, the coiling wraiths seeming to shred away with the speed of the ship's passing. An illusion, and then the ship dropped out of FTL into normal space. Here at the edge of the nebula the veil was thin and a half-drowned star burned with a lurid light, hugging one small planet close to it for warmth.

Through the torn openings of Dendrid's Veil, Stark could see what lay beyond, the area of blankness, secret and strange.

It seemed to have grown since last he saw it.

They landed on the planet, a curious shadowed world beneath its shrouded sun, a hothouse of pale vegetation. There was a town, with narrow lanes straggling off among the trees and houses that were themselves like clumps of vegetation, woven of living vines that bloomed heavily with dark flowers.

The people of Ceidri were dark too, and small, deep-eyed and shambling, with clever hands and coats of rich glossy fur that shed the rain. They received their visitors out of doors, where there was room for them to stand erect. Night came on and the sky glowed with twisting dragon-shapes of dull fire where the parent star lit drifts of dust.

Talk was through an interpreter, but Stark was aware of more than the spoken words. There were powerful undercurrents of both fear and excitement.

"It is growing," said the chief, "it reaches, grasps, sucks. It is a strong child. It has begun to think."

There came a silence over the clearing. A shower of rain fell lightly and passed on.

"You are saying," said Shorr Kan in a strangely flat voice, "that that thing out there is alive? Interpreter, make certain of the meaning!"

"It lives," said the chief. His eyes glowed in his small snubby face. "We feel it." And he added, "It will kill us soon."

"Then it is evil?"

"Not evil. No." His narrow shoulders lifted. "It lives."

Shorr Kan turned to his scientists. "Can this be possible? Can a force… a… nothing be alive?"

"It has been postulated that the final evolution might be a creature of pure energy, alive in the sense that it would feed on energy, as all life-forms do in one form or another, and be sentient… to what degree we can only guess, anything from amoeboid to God-like."

The chief of the scientists stared at the heavens, and then at the small brown creatures who watched with their strange eyes. "We cannot accept it. Not on this evidence. Such a momentous occurrence…"

"…ought to have been discovered by the proper authorities," said Shorr Kan, and added a short word. "It may be so, it may not be so, but let us keep an open mind." To the headman of the Ceidrins he said urgently, "Can you speak to the thing? Communicate?"

"It does not hear us. Do you hear the cry of the organisms in the air you breathe or the water you drink?"

"But you can hear… it?"

"Oh, yes, we hear. It grows swiftly. Soon we shall hear nothing else."

"Can you make us able to hear?"

"You are men, and men tend to be deafened by their own noises. But there is one here…" His glossy head turned. His eyes met Stark's. "One here is not like the rest, he is not quite deaf. Perhaps we can help him to hear."

"Very well, Ambassador," said Shorr Kan, "you came to learn what it is that eats your sun. Here is your chance."

They told him what to do. He knelt upon the ground and they formed a ring of small dark shapes around him, with the dark flowers shedding a heavy scent, and the dragon sky above. He looked into the glowing eyes of the chief, and felt his mind becoming malleable, being drawn out, a web of sensitive threads, stretching, linking with the circled minds.

Gradually, he began to hear.

He heard imperfectly with his limited human brain, and he was glad instinctively that this was so. He could not have supported the full blaze of that consciousness. Even the echo of it stunned him.

Stunned him with joy.

The joy of being alive, of being sentient and aware, of being young, thrusting, vibrant, strong. The joy of *being*.

There was no evil in that joy, no cruelty in the strength that pulsed and grew, sucking life from the cradling universe as simply and naturally as a blade of grass sucks nourishment from the soil. Energy was its food and it ate and was not conscious of life destroyed. That conception was impossible to it. In its view nothing could be destroyed, only changed from one form to another. It saw all of creation as one vast source of fuel for its eternal fires, and that creation now included all of time as well as space. The tremendous force gathering at the heart of the thing had begun to twist the fabric of the continuum itself, deforming it so fantastically that the Sol of two hundred thousand years ago was as accessible as the drowned sun of Ceidri.

It was very young. It was without sin. Its mental potential spanned parsecs. Already it had intimations of its own greatness. It would *think*, and grow, while the myriad wheeling galaxies swarmed like bees in the sheer beauty of their being, and in due course it would create. God knew what it would create, but all its impulses shone and were pure.

It was innocent. And it was a killer.

Yet Stark yearned to be a part of that divine strength and joyousness. He desired to be lost forever within it, relieved of self and all the petty agonies that went with human living. He felt that he had almost achieved this goal when the contract was broken and he found himself still kneeling with the Ceidrins round him and a soft rain falling. The rain had wet his cheeks, and he was desolate.

Shorr Kan spoke to him, and he answered.

"It is alive. A new species. And it means the end of ours, if we don't kill it. If it can be killed."

He stood up, and he saw their faces staring at him, the King of Aldeshar and his scientists and his experts in war and weaponry, doubtful and afraid. Afraid to believe, afraid not to believe.

And Stark added, "If it should be killed."

The voices began then, clamoring all at once, until they were silenced by a new sound.

Down across the dragon sky, the ships of the Star Kings came to land.

Shorr Kan said, "We'll wait for them here." He looked at Stark. "While your mind was straining at its tether to be gone, I had a report from my ship. The power cells are being drained. Only an infinitesimal loss so far, but definite. I wonder what my brother kings will make of it all."

His brother kings were jubilant. They had left their heavy cruisers standing off Ceidri, an overwhelming force against Shorr Kan's scout. They were delighted to have caught their fox so easily.

"If you have a weapon, you can't use it against us now without using it against yourself," Flane Fell told him. He had laid aside his silks and jewels, and his golden crown. Like the others, he was dressed for war.

"If I had a weapon," said Shorr Kan tranquilly, "that thought would have occurred to me. I imagine you're having the planet searched for hidden installations, possible control centers, and the like?"

"We are."

"And do you still suppose that any human agency could possibly create or control the force that lies out there?"

"All the evidence will be fairly evaluated, Shorr Kan."

"That gives me great comfort. In the meantime, have your technicians monitor the power cells of your ships with great care. Have them monitor mine as well. And don't be too long about your decision."

"Why?" demanded Flane Fell.

Shorr Kan beckoned to Stark. "Tell them."

Stark told them.

The Kings of the Marches, the human kings, looked at the Ceidrins and Flane Fell said, "What are these that we should believe them? Little lost brute-things on a lost planet. And as for this so-called ambassador..."

He did not finish. One of the non-human kings had stepped forward to confront him. This fellow's dawn-ancestor had bequeathed to him a splendid rangy build, a proud head with an aristocratic snout and only a suggestion of fangs, and a suit of fine white fur banded handsomely with gray. His smile was fearsome.

"As a brute-thing myself," he said, "I speak for my fellow kings of the minority, and I say that the hairless son of an ape is no less a brute-thing than we, and no more competent to judge truthfulness in any form. We ourselves will speak with the Ceidrins."

They went to do so. Shorr Kan smiled. "The King of Tranett has already given me allies. I'm grateful."

Stark had gone apart. He looked at the sky and remembered.

The morning came dark with drifting rain. When the clouds broke it seemed to Stark that the shrouded sun was dimmer than he remembered, but that of course was imagination. The four non-human kings rejoined the group. Their faces were solemn, and the chief of the Ceidrins was with them.

"The man Stark spoke truly," said the gray-barred king. "The thing has already begun to draw the life from this sun. The Ceidrins know they're doomed, and so shall we be in our turn if this thing is not destroyed."

Reports came in from the ships, those that had landed and those still free in space awaiting orders. All had unexplained losses of energy from the power cells.

"Well, brother kings," said Shorr Kan, "what is your decision?"

The four non-humans ranged themselves with the King of Aldeshar. "Our fleets are at your disposal, and the best of our scientific minds." The gray-barred king looked at Flane Fell with blazing golden eyes. "Leave your little spites behind, apeling, or all our kind, all things that breathe and move, are foredone."

Shorr Kan said, "You can always kill me later on, if we live."

Flane Fell made an angry gesture. "Very well. Let all our efforts be combined, to the end that this thing shall die."

✦ ✦ ✦

"Let all our efforts be combined..."

Messages were flashed to the scientific centers of the far-flung star-worlds. Messages all asking the same question.

How can this thing be killed, before it kills us?

The ships had left Ceidri and returned to the hither side of the nebula, where they hung like a shoal of fingerlings against the Veil, catching palely the light of distant suns. They waited for answers. Answers began to come.

"Energy!" said Shorr Kan, and cursed. "The thing *is* energy. It devours energy. It lives on suns. How can it be destroyed with energy?"

Narin Har, chief of the joint scientific missions now aboard Flane Fell's flagship, that being the largest and possessed of the most sophisticated communications center, answered Shorr Kan.

"We have results from the three great computers at Vega, Rigel, and Fomalhaut. They all agree that we must use energy against energy, in the form of our most potent missiles."

Shorr Kan said, "Anti-matter?"

"Yes."

"But won't that simply feed its strength?"

"They're working on the equations now. But judging from the relatively slow rate at which it is presently absorbing energy from the stars it has attacked, we ought to be able to introduce the violent energy of anti-matter missiles into it in such quantities that it will be unable to assimilate rapidly enough. The result is expected to be total annihilation."

"How many missiles?"

"That is the information we're waiting for now."

It came.

Narin Har read the figures to the Kings of the Marches,

assembled in the flagship. These figures meant little to Stark, who was present, but he could see by the faces of the kings that the impact of them was staggering.

"We must ask for every ship available from every ruler in the galaxy," said Shorr Kan. "Every available anti-matter missile, which may not be enough since the supply is limited, and a full complement of conventional atomics. We must beg for them, and with all speed."

The scout ship, sent back through the Veil, had brought word that the thing was growing now with frightening rapidity.

The message was sent, backed by all the scientific evidence they could muster.

Again they waited.

Beyond the Veil the thing fed contentedly and dreamed its cosmic dreams. And grew.

"If the Empire sends its ships," said Shorr Kan, "the rest will follow." He pounded his fist on the table. "How long does it take the fools to deliberate? If they insist on waggling their tongues forever..." He stood up. "I'll speak with Jhal Arn myself."

"Jhal Arn?" asked Stark.

"You are a country boy, Ambassador. Jhal Arn is ruler of the Mid-Galactic Empire, the most potent force in the galaxy."

"You sound as though you don't love him."

"Nor the Empire. That is beside the point now. Come along, if you like."

In the communications room, Stark watched the screen of the sub-space telecom spring to life.

"The Hall of Suns," said Shorr Kan, "at Throon, royal planet of Canopus and center of the Empire. Ah, yes. The Imperial Council is in session."

The hall was vast, splendid with the banners and insignia of a thousand star-kingdoms, Stark caught only a fleeting glimpse of that magnificence, and of the many alien personages... ambassadors, he thought, representing their governments at this extraordinary session, princes and nobles from worlds he did not know. The view narrowed in upon the throne chair, where a tall man sat looking into the apparatus before him so that he seemed to be staring straight at Shorr Kan. Which he was, across half a galaxy.

Shorr Kan wasted no time on regal courtesies.

"Jhal Arn," he said, "you have no cause to love me, nor I you, and you have no cause to trust me, either. Still, we are both citizens of this galaxy, and here we both must live or die, and all our people with us. We of the Marches are committed, but we have not the strength to fight this thing alone. If you do not lead the way for the Star Kings, if you do not send the ships we need, then you will have condemned your own Empire to destruction."

Jhal Arn had a fine strong face, worn with the strain of governing. There was wisdom in his eyes. He inclined his head slightly.

"Your feelings, and mine, are of equal unimportance, Shorr Kan. The lords of the Council have now understood that. We have conferred with all our scientists and advisors. The decision has been taken. You shall have the ships."

The screen went dark.

And they waited, watching the blank heavens where the far suns burned, while the great blazing wheel of the galaxy turned on its hub of stars, one infinitesimal fraction of a revolution so long that only a computer could comprehend it.

At last the ships came.

Stark watched them on the screens as they came, dropping out of the void. Shorr Kan told him what they were. The squadrons of Fomalhaut Kingdom, with the blazon of the white sun on their bows. The ships of Rigel and Deneb, Algol and Altair, Antares and Vega. The fleets of wide-flung Kingdoms of Lyra and Cygnus and Cassiopeia, of Lepus and Corvus and Orion. The ships of the Barons of Hercules, ensigned with the golden cluster. And on and on until Stark's head was ringing with star names and giddy with the sheer numbers of that mustering.

Last of all, huge sombre shadows of interstellar war, came the great battle-cruisers of the Empire.

The ships of the Star Kings, in massed rendezvous off Dendrid's Veil. The heavens were aglitter with them.

There was much coming and going of star-captains, discussions of strategy, endless pawings-over of data and clackings of on-board computers. The vast armada hung in the starshine, and Stark remembered the battle plans he had made in his own life, in a former time; the plotted charges of the men of Kesh and Shun in the Martian Drylands, the deadly tribal prowlings in the swamps and seas of Venus. Exercises for prattling babes. Here, on the screen, was magnificence beyond belief.

And on the other side of the Veil was an adversary beyond his former imagining.

He wondered if Aarl still waited and listened. He wondered if the worlds of Sol still lived.

At length Shorr Kan told him, "We are ready. The combined fleets will move in exactly six units, Galactic Arbitrary Time."

+ + +

The fleets of the Star Kings moved. Rank on shining rank, they plunged into the gloom of the nebula, crashed headlong through the coiling clouds of dust to burst into open space beyond where the twisted enigma waited, sprawled carelessly across space and time.

Stark stood with Shorr Kan by the screens of the small scout, attached now to Shorr Kan's navy, three heavy cruisers and a swarm of lighter craft, everything that could carry a missile.

Aldeshar's fleet was in the first attack wave, with the other fleets of the Marches. The scout leaped away from the nebula, fired its conventional atomics into the looming blankness of the thing ahead, then spiraled upward and away, skirting the edges of destruction. It took up station where it could see, and if necessary, run. Shorr Kan was again being practical.

The first wave struck like a thunderbolt, loosing the full batteries of their missiles and swerving away a complicated three-dimensional dance of death, carefully plotted to avoid being swallowed by the enemy and to leave the way clear for the following wave.

And they came, the silver fleets with their proud insignia of suns and clusters and constellations; the might of the Star Kings against the raw power of creation.

They poured their salvos of unthinkable energy into the child of energy, lighting smothered flares across the parsecs, pounding at the fabric of the universe with which the creature was entwined until space itself was shaken and the scout ship lurched in the backlash as though upon a heavy sea.

The creature, roused, struck back.

Bolts of naked force shot from its blind face, spearing ships, wiping the heavens clean. Yet more ships came on, more missiles sped to seed the thing with deadly anti-matter. More dark lightnings flashed. But the thing still lived, and fought, and killed.

"It's defending itself," Stark said. "Not only itself, but its whole species, just as we are."

He could sense the bewilderment it felt, the fear, the outraged anger. Probably his previous contact through the Ceidrins had given him that ability, and he was sorry it had, dim though the echo was. The creature was still, he thought, unaware of living beings as such. It only knew that this sudden bursting of strange energy within it was dangerous. It had located the source of that energy and was trying to destroy it.

It appeared to have succeeded.

The fleets drew off. There was a cessation of all action. The lightnings ceased. The thing lay apparently untouched, undiminished.

Stark said, "Have we lost?" He was soaked with sweat and shaking as though he had himself been fighting.

Shorr Kan only said, "Wait."

The ships of the Barons of Hercules detached themselves from the massed ranks of the fleet. They sped away as though in flight.

"Are they running?" asked Stark.

Again Shorr Kan said, "Wait."

Presently Stark understood. Far away, greatly daring along the uncharted flank of this creature, the fleet of the Cluster struck. Annihilating lightnings danced and flared, and the creature struck out at those ships, forgetting the massed fleets that had now moved into a pattern of semi-englobement. It was after all a child, and ignorant of even simple strategies.

The fleets charged, loosing a combined shellfire of raving energies at a single area of the creature's being.

This time the fires they lit did not go out.

They spread. They burned and brightened. Great gouts of energy burst nova-like from out of that twisted blankness, catching ships, destroying them, but without aim or purpose. The savage bolts were random now, blind emissions of a dying force.

The fleets regrouped, pouring in all they had left to them of death.

And Stark heard... felt, with the atoms of his flesh... the last unbelieving cry of despair, the anguish of loss as strength and joy faded and the wheeling galaxies in all their beauty went from sight, a flight of brilliant butterflies swept away on a cruel wind.

It died.

The fleets of the Star Kings fled from the violence of that dying, while space rocked around them and stars were shattered, while the insane fury of total destruction blazed and roiled and fountained across the parsecs and the stuff of the universe trembled.

The ships took refuge beyond Dendrid's Veil. They waited, afraid that the chain-reaction they had set in motion might yet engulf them. But gradually the turbulence quietened, and when their instruments registered only normal radiation, the scout ship and a few others ventured to return.

The shape of the nebula was altered. Ceidri and its dim sun had vanished. Out beyond, there was a new kind of blankness, the empty blankness of death.

Even Flane Fell was awed by the enormity of what they had done. "It is a heavy thing to be God."

"Perhaps a heavier one to be man," said Shorr Kan. "God, as I recall, never doubted He was right."

They turned back then, and the fleets of the Star Kings, such as had survived that killing, dispersed, each one homing on its separate star.

Shorr Kan returned to Aldeshar.

In the hall of the ugly genie he spoke to Stark. "Well, Ambassador? Your little sun is safe now, if salvation didn't come too late. Will you return there, or will you stay with me? I could make your fortune."

Stark shook his head. "I like you, King of Aldeshar. But I'm no good running mate, and sooner or later we'd come to that enmity you spoke of. Besides, you're born for trouble, and I prefer to make my own."

Shorr Kan laughed. "You're probably right, Ambassador. Though I'm sorry. Let us part friends."

They shook hands. Stark left the palace and walked through the streets of Donalyr toward the hills, and through all the voices and the sounds around him he could still hear that last despairing cry.

He went up on the ridge above the city. And Aarl brought him home.

+ + +

They sat in the mist-bordered chamber high in the ancient citadel.

"We ought not to have killed it," Stark said. "You never touched its consciousness. I did. It was… God-like."

"No," said Aarl. "Man is God-like, which is to say creator, destroyer, savior, kind father and petty tyrant, ruthless, bloodthirsty, bigoted, merciful, loving, murderous, and noble. This creature was far beyond mere godliness, and so perhaps more worthy than we to survive… *but it did not survive*. And that is the higher law."

Aarl fixed him with those space-black eyes.

"No life exists but at the expense of other life. We kill the grain to make our bread, and the grain in time kills the soil it grows in. Do not reproach yourself for that. In due course another such super-being may be born which will survive in spite of us, and then it will be our turn to go. Meanwhile, *we* survive, and that is our proof of right. There is no other."

He led Stark down the long and winding ways to the portal, where his saddled beast was waiting. Stark mounted and rode away, turning his back forever on the Third Bend.

And so he had seen the future, and touched beauty, and the thing was done, for better or worse. Beauty had died beyond Dendrid's Veil, and high above, where the walls of the Great Rift Valley towered against the sky, the sun was shining on the old proud face of Mars. Some good, some evil, and perhaps in the days to come Aarl's words would soothe his conscience.

And conscience or not, he would never forget the splendor of the ships of the Star Kings massed for battle.

A series of novels about a cocky, rich hero, Lord Thomas Kinago, Jody Lynn Nye's Imperium series is laced with humor. Her brand-new story for Infinite Stars *fits into the timeline in between two novels that are still forthcoming— not yet contracted, even! They are* Scenes from the Imperium *and* Race for the Imperium, *in which Kinago becomes enthusiastic about one hobby after another, spends the first novel becoming involved in a theater company, and the intrigue going on both in front of and behind the curtains.*

IMPERIUM IMPOSTOR

JODY LYNN NYE

I was in a spot, both literally and figuratively. As a covert operative in the service of the Imperium Secret Service, my erstwhile task was to provide a figurehead, a delicious and irresistible tidbit for a pack of potentially perilous personnel. Somehow, in a manner that still escaped me, I had just failed to be kidnapped.

"Lord Thomas," asked Ensign Nesbitt, my sole companion at the moment, "what just happened?"

"That," I said, staring at the blue-enameled airlock that had just sealed shut in our faces, "is a very good question. The only fact that I can reliably ascertain is that the Bluts have taken Commander Parsons prisoner instead of me."

"They're going to be sorry," Nesbitt said, with sincere feeling writ upon his large and florid face.

"I have no doubt as to that," I replied, feeling more at sea than I had at the age of fifteen whilst marooned alone in the middle of my home planet Keinolt's largest ocean when my watercraft's ion engines had unexpectedly ceased to function. My aide-de-camp was a formidable opponent, possessed of every useful skill and the keen intelligence to make use of them. I flicked an imaginary mote of dust from the breast of my immaculate, bespoke white dress tunic with salmon flashings at wrist and shoulder, baffled as to how they could have mistaken a man clad entirely in black from my sartorial splendor. "Almost as sorry as I am."

"We gotta get him back, my lord! We have to tell the captain they took him!"

I glanced over my shoulder at the corridor. At the far end of the ship lay a meeting with a covert operative that Parsons was supposed to have attended once the alarm was raised regarding my abduction, providing useful cover so the agent's presence would not be noted. My understanding was that the information carried by the operative was vital to Imperium security which must be imparted without delay. Parsons's absence would not raise quite the same hue and cry as mine. After all, he was a senior officer in the Imperium Navy as well as a highly placed agent and my mentor, but I was a member of the Imperium family, cousin to the Emperor himself, and not at all least, son of the First Space Lord. I made the only decision I could.

"No, my friend," I said. "Go and inform Captain Ranulf that it was I who was abducted, as we planned. I must make that meeting before Parsons's agent leaves this ship."

Nesbitt stared at me, his mouth agape. "*You're* gonna pretend to be *Commander Parsons*?"

"No," I said, straightening my shoulders, as if feeling the ponderous weight that had unexpectedly descended upon them. "But I must be the contact that the agent expects to find."

✦ ✦ ✦

I departed the airlock bay through the engineering access hatch before the inevitable arrival of the security officers. The security chief herself knew of our mission, so the automated cameras which were even now recording my movements would not report to the Officer of the Day and thence to the captain, who had more than enough to worry about. Having studied the plans of the Imperium Destroyer *Enceladus* in excruciating detail before we shipped out on her, I reached my cabin in no time. A hidden eye identified me even as I dropped from a ceiling hatch and opened the door. With a glance to either side of the corridor to make certain I was not observed, I dashed inside.

"Double-secure, code Zeta 922 licorice-allsorts dolphin rupture Melvin oyster," I said, also displaying upon my viewpad the image of a panda cub wearing a hat. The door closed behind me, and all manner of security programming took effect. Electrified mesh descended into the ductwork. Even the mirror above my bathroom sink became obscured.

"Lt. Lord Thomas," CF-202m, my assigned LAI valetbot, came bustling up to me. Coffee stood as tall as I did, but was composed mainly of narrow metal struts on a wheeled assembly that allowed it to glide nearly as smoothly as Parsons. Its upper extremities terminated in nimble, glovelike hands, only with three thumbs instead of one. "How may I serve, sir?"

Without waiting, I threw open the doors to my wardrobe, and began to peruse it for the appropriate outfit for my meeting. My plan ought to succeed. Parsons was a trifle taller than my lofty height and of a similar slim build. If the contact did not know him personally, the superficial resemblance which I planned to significantly enhance might fool it. Instead of the high-fashion garments, the choice of which I prided myself, I reached for the simplest and least-adorned of all my tunics and plain trousers. I need not worry about insignia; Parsons never wore any. If I hadn't known him since I was small, I wouldn't know his rank or distinguished history. I donned these self-effacing items.

Enceladus, properly speaking, was a warship, pride of His Highness the Emperor Shojan XII, ruler of the vast extent of space in which *Enceladus* flew and my cousin. *Enceladus* had been chosen as a meeting point for periodic renegotiation of trading terms among the many neighbors that bordered the Imperium. It had been readily agreed by the Uctu Autocracy owing, I add with all due modesty, to my recent efforts as envoy to Her Serenity the Autocrat Visoltia. Her representative here, Lord Steusan, minister of agriculture, knew me well. I needed to avoid being recognized by him as well as the crew. Fortunately, the Uctu were easily confused when it came to telling human beings apart.

I sat down before the mirror. By Imperium law, I was not permitted to make physical changes to the natural lineaments of my face or body. No member of the noble house was. The reason was lost in antiquity to all but a few, a number to which I was proud and humbled to be a member: the noble class had been genetically modified, millennia ago, to be completely bilaterally symmetrical and of surpassing beauty. The rest of the citizens of the Imperium, but particularly humans, had been modified at the same time to respond to our extremes of symmetry and handsomeness with an overwhelming willingness to obey the rule of law. They loved us because they had been born to do so. That visual-neural link helped to keep the Imperium, spread across thousands of stars, from fragmenting into chaos over the intervening years, even when no more than a three-dimensional image of the Emperor or

Empress was present. As a result, the nobility was forbidden from intermarrying with common folk, or from altering themselves genetically, so as not to dilute the necessary gene pool for producing future leaders. The very cohesion of the Imperium depended upon those strictures.

However, in matters of temporary cosmetics and pigmentation, the law was vague. I intended to wrap myself in that obscurity, for the best cause in the world.

"Coffee, listen carefully," I addressed the valetbot's reflection, "I need you to do something rather unusual..."

+ + +

Reflected in the glossy golden wall of the reception corridor, the tall, slender figure sauntered with expressionless mien toward the concealed doorway that lay hidden around the next turn. Black clothes, which matched the wearer's black hair and dark eyes, gave him the appearance of a shadow as he passed virtually unnoticed through the crowd of diplomats gathered at the entrance to the small amphitheater that served as the meeting hall. I watched my own reflection in the shining wall opposite the doorway, and felt deeply impressed at how well my valetbot had made me up to look like my aide-de-camp. I was much better looking, of course. CF-202m had used sophisticated layering of cosmetic surface filler to change the lines of my face as well as to tint it to match Parsons's complexion. Some subtle artistic rendering had thrown off the perfect symmetry that was a mark of my familial descent. Every time I saw that irregularity, it shocked me. But the subterfuge worked. No one addressed me by my name.

In fact, no one addressed me at all. They were all engaged in groups of two or three, or in one case, six, speaking in low tones. I had to strain to eavesdrop. I slowed down beside the largest group, representatives of the Trade Union, the Imperium's largest neighbor, all blondes with broad faces and rather flat noses. The only reason I could distinguish the ambassador was that the other five deferred to her. I dared not pass too closely to the gecko-like Uctu trio lest Lord Steusan detect any traits that would allow him to identify me.

The subject under discussion by most of the attendees was not matters of trade, but my abduction. The murmurs confirmed that all of the ship's systems were on high alert, turning the attention outward, in search of the vessel on which "I" was not a prisoner.

The landing bay had become the busiest site on the ship, as small-range fighters zipped in and out, dropping off a tired pilot in exchange for a fresh one. Most of them speculated on the reason for my capture, wondering what the ramifications would be for kidnapping the son of a high-ranking government official. I did my best to avoid reacting. It was rather like attending my own funeral, without the distinct inconvenience of actually being dead. I heard a few words of praise and admiration that I took to my heart, as well as expressions of deep concern for my well-being.

"No, ma'am," Lt. Philomena Anstruther said in a low voice as I edged by her. The slender, dark-haired human female was a member of my personal crew—or rather, that assigned to my ship, the *Rodrigo*, a small scout vessel that was at this moment patrolling around the *Enceladus* under the steady hands of Oskelev, my Wichu pilot. Her pale face was chalky with concern. "No word yet on Lord Thomas. I hope he's all right."

"Confound him," Captain Ranulf said. She was a sturdily built human with small features set in a large, pugnacious ochre face and very short dark-blonde hair. "The First Space Lord is going to tear my arms off if I don't come home with him! Why didn't he just muster out when he graduated like the rest of his class?"

Anstruther glanced away. Her large eyes lit upon me, now ten meters farther down the hall. I saw recognition dawn, but she covered it in a nanosecond. Inwardly, I cheered. I knew I could count upon her not to reveal my disguise. As the information specialist of my small crew, she had a skyrocketing intelligence coupled with a banker's grasp of secrecy. She turned her gaze back to Ranulf.

"The visitors from the Autocracy like him, Captain," she said. Her voice was slightly shaken, like a good cocktail, but Ranulf didn't notice. "He amuses them."

I felt like strutting with pride, but did my best to proceed with a Parsons-like glide, drawing no more attention from the assemblage than a breath of wind. I had to admit it was more difficult than I thought. My natural inclination is to dress and walk in order to draw all possible eyes, and optical receptors needed to be suppressed lest the rumor of my disappearance be disproved. I had to channel my recent enthusiasm of theater to absorb the personality of he whom I pretended to be.

"Sir!" exclaimed an officer in formal dress, bursting forth from an office at the end of the corridor. To my dismay, his eyes were fixed on *me*. Quelling the butterflies that had begun a lively cotillion in my midsection, I assumed a cool expression and returned his nod. "Commander!"

I relaxed. He had taken my appearance at face value.

"Lieutenant Commander Schiele," I said, keeping all inflection from my tone, as would my friend and associate. Schiele offered me a glance that was both admiring and fearful. I imagine my own address to Parsons bore some of the same characteristics.

"I want you to know, Commander, that we are doing everything we can to retrieve Lord Thomas! Please reassure Admiral Kinago Loche that we will retrieve her son safely."

"I know that you will do your best," I said, careful not to allow myself to sound as though I believed it in the least. Schiele quivered and rushed on, catching up with a pair of security officers who stood at the edge of the diplomatic crowd.

I congratulated myself with another inward cheer. I had fooled one pair of eyes at least. Now, to carry on with the mission at hand.

Our presence and subterfuge on board the *Enceladus* was to enable Parsons to meet with another operative of the Imperium Covert Services Operations, a Croctoid whose code name was Dolly. I had been present for part of the briefings, which had been delivered by my mother and another senior official, but had paid less than rapt attention, since my role was solely camouflage. The Bluts, who were, not to put too fine a point on it, not part of the Covert Services operation, had been provoked into making the attack on the *Enceladus* by having their ambassador's invitation accidentally but very publicly rescinded across the Infogrid, the main means of communication, record-keeping and socializing throughout the Imperium and beyond. By law, all persons over the age of literacy were required to maintain an up-to-date and accurate file on the Infogrid, so the Bluts' humiliation was widespread. In addition, it was bruited about that it was *my* doing that caused the withdrawal of the invitation. It had been carefully noted, though not in my personal file, that I would be on the *Enceladus*, in that vulnerable and easily exploited location, at a certain time. If one wanted to educate me on the niceties of Blut diplomacy, that would be the opportune moment. I still had a knockout spray in my sleeve that I would have deployed to prevent physical damage, should that diplomacy extend to physical interaction. In any case, the moment the kidnapping had occurred, a secondary message had gone out saying that there had been a grave misunderstanding, and the Blut representative was not only welcome but vital to the conference.

The Croctoid's scout ship, disguised as an Imperium fighter, will have hung off the *Enceladus*, lying low without any lights or unnecessary emissions before flying into the landing bay under cover of the hue and cry out for me. As he or she would be wearing Imperium fighter uniform, no notice would be taken of him as he entered.

The agent was risking his life to meet with Parsons. He carried evidence of something that was of grave importance to the summit conference. I wished that I had listened more intently to that part of the mission. I taunted my memory centers with scorn, demanding that they remember everything. I had less than ten meters before my portrayal must be perfect.

I ambled with purpose toward my rendezvous, hoping that the agent's first words would spur mnemonic recall in me.

I turned the corner, waited until a yet another blond man in Trade Union beige with the air of a harried assistant passed me, then slipped through the door. To my surprise, the chamber was not an office or a meeting room, but a janitor's closet, cluttered with trash receptacles, buckets, bottles and jars of high-smelling fluids, and various small cleanerbots, currently disabled. Fortunately, the Croctoid had already arrived.

I admired his adherence to subterfuge: he was dressed in the pale-gray costume of a maintenance worker, down to the pail of some noxious-smelling organic compound he was pouring down the drain in the corner. Croctoids, with their scaly, greenish skin, long, toothy jaws, knobby heads, clawed hands and feet, and thick, heavy tails, were rather unlovely to the human eye, though attractive to one another, I had no doubt.

The Croctoid looked up at my approach.

"What do you want… sir?"

Excellent! That was exactly what the briefing had said was the first of the coded exchange.

"I was just passing through," I said blithely. "Lovely day if it doesn't rain."

"Raining on a starship?" the Croctoid replied, narrowing one beady eye at me.

I halted. Perhaps I was recalling the lines incorrectly. He was supposed to respond with "I have no time for umbrellas."

"How do you feel about weather protection?" I prompted him.

The Croctoid looked alarmed. "Is something going wrong with the hydroponics section, sir?"

"No!" I said. "At least, I do not believe it is malfunctioning." We had diverted from one set of coded phrases to another which I had never heard. I smiled at him, doing my best to be charming. It did not work. My natural advantage was lost because of the seeming asymmetry of my features. I needed to fall back upon authority. I fixed him with a stern, Parsons-like gaze. "Perhaps an umbrella would be a useful device."

The Croctoid, instead of picking up on my cue, started to edge toward the door.

"I'll just go look in the gardens, sir," he said, his scaly brow twitching nervously. "I'd better go…"

"But what about my umbrella?" I asked, as he retreated down the corridor.

A heavy hand fell upon my shoulder. I jumped.

"I have no time for umbrellas," a throaty voice said from behind me. I glanced back in alarm. Another Croctoid stood, or rather leaned there, a much larger specimen than the janitor, his lower half contained within one of the round trash barrels. He stared down his long snout at me with small black eyes like dull onyx. "Well?"

I realized that I had made a mistake in identity. I hastened to recover myself.

"There was a lovely crop of rutabagas this year," I said.

The Croctoid in the trash barrel nodded curtly.

"Greens are good for gout," he said. "Who *writes* these absurd exchanges, anyhow?"

"I don't know," I replied, relieved. I held out a hand to assist him in removing himself from the receptacle. "My understanding is that their author is lost to the mists of antiquity."

He showed his impressive rows of jagged, yellowed teeth. "That would make a better countersign. I'm Dolly. You're Mask?"

"That's right." Thank goodness he knew my code name. I was certain I'd never heard it.

"I can't believe you mistook a sanitation worker for me!"

I shrugged, channeling Parsons's magnificent indifference to cover my chagrin.

"It amused me. I had to test you. I wondered if your handler might have sent a decoy."

"No time for that," Dolly hissed. Croctoids had very short tempers. "Come with me."

He departed the room at a rapid pace. I have a long stride, but even I had to hurry to keep up with Dolly. He pushed through the busy crowd near the entrance to the landing bay. Before we went through the airlock, he grabbed a spare breather helmet off the racks near the door and tossed it to me.

"Where are we going?" I asked. "I thought we were going to confer back there."

He gave me a pitying look and his tail lashed, slapping me in the leg.

"Can't talk here!" He donned his own helmet. Assuming my own, I followed him through into the chill air. He wove among the personnel on duty with the air that he belonged there. I didn't usually think about the professions of Covert informers when they were not delivering reports. "Dolly" was clearly used to command, perfectly at ease in this milieu. My guess was that he was an officer in the Imperium navy, who had risen through the ranks by virtue of competence and loyalty. How long that had taken him, I did not know. I was not good at guessing a Croctoid's age. It would have been against protocol to try and trace him later on via the Infogrid, but I admit to an aching curiosity as to his quotidian identity.

Ninety percent of the time, the bay of a destroyer was quiet and echoingly empty except for LAI and AI bots maintaining the small fighters and support vehicles. During that remaining ten percent, orderly chaos reigned. Banks of lights flashed out coded messages and warnings to pilots and ground crew. Small, triangular fighter craft flew in and out of the bay, piercing the vacuum barrier that kept atmosphere circulating at the inner end. When they landed, bots checked the fuel rods and structural integrity, emptied and filled tanks, and made way for the next pilot or pilots to jump in and continue the battle or patrol or what mission was the rule of the day. In this case, it was the ongoing search for me.

Dolly led me behind a repair gurney to a two-seat fighter that looked like all the others, and bundled me into the rear seat. The life-support system automatically sealed around my long frame and fitted itself to the valves in the helmet. The communications system ran through its sound check, beeping a series of tones in my ears, and raised the heads-up scope to my eye level. Before I could give the traditional thumbs up, Dolly blasted the fighter out of the landing bay, past the sequencing red-and-green lights, and into the black breadth of space. The g-force thrust my body back into the crash padding. I gasped for breath until the pressure equalized. It was not a pleasant sensation. The wearer of the helmet before me must have had a dry throat. The padding bore an eye-watering odor of menthol and eucalyptus.

I had never been allowed to operate one of these fighters on my own, despite being the winner of multiple prestigious space races and atmosphere flitter rallies, because these were short-range vessels, essentially a bubble of air fitted with an engine and guns, and no real safeguards beyond rudimentary shielding. Sometimes it was a trial having my life safeguarded so closely. Under Dolly's expert management, the fighter swooped and turned on a wingtip, following nearly invisible ion traces on the navigational scope projected before my eyes. I was enchanted.

"May I fly her?" I asked, as we rose over the bulk of the *Enceladus*'s knobbly engine cluster in pursuit of a minuscule ion trail. The blackness of space swallowed up most of the destroyer's massive form except where lights indicated service access and entryway hatches. In my peripheral vision, I spotted tiny, moving flecks of light that were other fighters searching for "my" abductors.

"No! Do you even know how to fly a search pattern?"

I scanned the controls. "I assume that the navigational computer does most of the work."

"No, it doesn't! This isn't *fun*, Mr. Mask. Don't waste my time."

On the scope, I could see why the *Enceladus*'s contingent was having trouble seeing where the Blut's ship had gone. Thanks to the arrival of all the diplomatic vessels, some of which orbited the warship's hulk, what would normally have been empty space was full of traces and microscopic particles, hiding the ion trail which would otherwise have been as visible as a neon tri-tennis ball in the snow. Other black shapes, the craft belonging to the ambassadorial visitors and their attendant protective ships and fighters, intermittently blotted out distant stars as they traversed from one to another and, not incidentally, creating still more ion trails. Still, we joined the chase, following traces until they petered out or we determined that they belonged to an identified craft in the landing bay or a visitor's vessel. Comparing the traces took time, which meant we had a window in which to talk.

"No, you are correct," I said, re-establishing my assumed

character, while my inner child beat its fists and feet on the floor in frustration. "Pray impart your information. Why was it necessary to make contact now, in the midst of this very sensitive conference?"

"That's exactly why it was necessary," Dolly snapped. "There's an impostor among the diplomats. Word came through covert channels that there's a plot to disrupt the conference."

"How cunning. In what way?"

"Blowing it up. All the attendees and the ship, too. Maybe take out all the visitors' vessels as well."

Even my inner child looked up at that statement. Imperium safety, indeed!

"They can't do that!" I declared. "How would they manage to smuggle enough explosives on board to cause such a catastrophic explosion?"

"Figure it out, Mr. Mask," Dolly said dryly. "Diplomatic ships. People come and go from them all the time. No one searches the vessels or the personnel, out of mutual courtesy. A stupid custom, just begging to be corrupted. All those beings, dozens of representatives from every major power in this part of the galaxy, all wiped out in one blast. The blame would fall on the Imperium."

My inner child lowered its tiny brow in a frown.

"What do you need me to do?"

"Find it and neutralize it," Dolly said, steering beneath a faint trail that showed in blue on the navigation scope.

"Who is the spy?"

"A human. This is what I got from a contact who knows a contact who knows someone undercover." A file popped up on the scope, replacing the forward view. I peered at it. It was a short digitavid of a human with hair the color of my cousin Erita's—in other words, a dirty blonde, but apart from a faint impression of complexion— medium light—I could gain no insight into its identity, not height nor body mass nor gender. Luckily, I did not have to tease out such fine details to pick out the would-be assassin. I compared the image with the complement of diplomats and crew. From the crowd of visitors whom I had met or seen on board, this almost certainly had to be a member of the Trade Union delegation.

The image had been enhanced many times until it became a series of minute colored blocks, shifting as the person in it shifted, but the real identifier was a snatch of voice, a low alto or high tenor, with the thick accent typical of the TU central systems. I played the brief excerpt over and over, trying to hear what the operative was saying.

"...Device... undetec—... no... failure..."

"Is this all you have?" I asked in frustration.

"I suppose you want a whole Infogrid file with vacation pictures?" I could hear the sneer in Dolly's voice. "This is it. We haven't been able to re-establish the chain back to the original source to get more information. We've got to assume that that person's been *neutralized*."

The final word chilled me by its depersonalized character.

"But what is the substance of their complaint? Few would go to the trouble of violently disrupting a meeting if they did not have a serious grievance against our government."

"Is this a test? Because I'm not putting up with it!" Dolly growled.

I put on my very best Parsons hauteur.

"Good Croctoid, there are many problems which come to the attention of the Covert Services. Do I need to run through a list of the serious matters that erupt and disturb the serenity of our realm so you can tell me if I am 'hot' or 'cold'?"

"Good point," Dolly said, with grudging admiration. "It's Maxwellington-5, otherwise known as Drixol. Manufacturing and mining. Plenty of good jobs, or up until the last year or two. The protesters are angry with the government for letting corporations run the place just on the edge of the law. They're running sweatshops, where they haven't pushed out human workers entirely, cheating suppliers, replacing good materials with cheap stuff, fixing prices. A bunch of bad apples."

"Why isn't the government of Drixol stepping forward to uphold the law?"

"*I* don't know." Dolly put the fighter into a hard turn and hared off to follow another faint trail. The cold of space began to permeate the pilot's compartment, but the real chill lay in my belly. "But it's getting bad. Drixol has been gathering supporters in a private file on the Infogrid to secede from the Imperium. They're up to over a hundred thousand."

I rocked back in my seat, shocked to the core. I knew the governor. Like many of the highest officials, she was a member of the noble family. "Lady Margaretha Kinago Tan Dunwoody Olathe is my third cousin. She's terribly responsible. She would never let corporations act in such a clear violation of ethics. I cannot believe such a tale!"

Dolly snorted. "Your cousin? You have ties to the Imperium family?"

I pressed my face into a thin smile. "All humans are somewhat related."

"Well, you all look alike to me," Dolly said, turning the fighter to return to the landing bay of the *Enceladus*. "You've got the data. The mission is up to you now. I must return to my ship and join the cohort retrieving your other agent."

"He will be all right," I said, wondering if by now Parsons had managed to lock up all the Bluts and was at this moment steering their ship back toward our location. "Thank you for your service, Dolly."

"That is not the correct countersign," Dolly admonished me.

I nodded. "Oh, look! A panda wearing a hat!"

"You never know who is shopping in these places," Dolly said. "Bah! Whoever created these exchanges should pay more attention to context."

"I imagine that the very incongruousness of the phrases makes them useful," I said.

Dolly snorted. As soon as we landed, he ordered me out of the cockpit without any further pleasantries, not only typical Croctoid behavior, but appropriate as an operative moving in deep cover. The backwash of air as he departed made me stagger. I removed my helmet, wiping the eucalyptus fug from my eyes.

"Hey!" shouted a flight deck manager, running toward me. "Who was that? Something's wrong with his fighter's transponder!"

"I know," I said, with a cool Parsonian gaze that brought him to a halt. "He will return for repairs as soon as the crisis has ended."

Insurgency! My mind had been racing ever since Dolly had told me about the suspected explosive device. The very thought made the *Hesperiidae* resume dancing in my stomach. The Imperium had been calm for so many centuries, it was easy to take peace for granted. With my family as figureheads, citizens had been inclined to cooperate and band together. I knew that the bonding was a matter of genetic manipulation with my family at its core. To see the Emperor's face was to instantly wish to please him. The rest of us possessed that charisma to an extent, the reason that our family was constrained not to mate or even to interact with the general population more than was strictly necessary. All other Imperium citizens were the product of a different kind of genetic manipulation that made them obedient to us. I wondered what had gone wrong for Margaretha that her people were able to rebel against her. In the meantime, I had to identify the perpetrator. A lesser being would be daunted by plunging back into an environment that might be on the edge of exploding, but I was a noble of the Imperium house. It was my duty to help protect and further the Emperor's cause.

I would inform the captain as to the potential calamity, but was there anything that I could do to shorten the process of finding the impostor and gleaning the location of the bomb? I did not fear death, but the very thought of searching kilometers of ship for anything that seemed out of place bored me beyond words, even assuming we had the time to find it. I wished I had Parsons there beside me. He would be able to take command of this situation and weed out the bomber and get to the bottom of the situation in short order.

But, he was still on the Blut ship, somewhere in the darkness. I could not rely upon his common sense and shockingly keen intelligence to unwrap this riddle. The chill in my belly annoyed the butterflies. The best being for the job was far away, out of reach.

No, I realized. I had someone better—someone who could compel the truth from any Imperium-born soul. I had *me*.

Running for the inner airlock, I clicked into my private channel via the viewpad on my hip.

"Coffee, meet me in the landing bay lavatory. Bring cold cream."

✦ ✦ ✦

"Lord Thomas!" Captain Ranulf was the first to spot me as I sauntered down the corridor from the washroom with my valet trundling along at my heels. "You're safe!"

Anstruther detached herself from her conversation and ran toward me, beaming. Even at the distance, anyone could see that her pupils spread wide. I recognized that involuntary response as a sign that my natural appearance had been restored, although serving members of the military were treated with a system that suppressed the obedience impulse. It prevented me or my relatives staging a shipbound mutiny, which on the whole was a good thing, considering our somewhat frivolous natures. Other human beings, whether or not their genealogy had been subjected to alteration, exhibited a similar pleasure-response. She clasped my hand, a number of unspoken questions in her eyes.

"All shall be revealed," I promised her.

Then, I was surrounded by well-wishers who wanted to slap me on the shoulder or shake my hand. Lord Steusan came forward to exchange happy expressions with me. The Wichu representative lifted me off my feet in a massive hug. Even the petite Donre ambassador left off haranguing his interpreter to kick me in the shins, a sign of cordial approbation among his people. Several of the Trade Union representatives milled about, offering pleasantries.

"Very happy to see you safe," Ambassador Cheutlie said, beaming. I assumed she was the ambassador. The chorus line of nearly identical aides smiled. I kept my expression bland, trying to match the tone of Dolly's recording with his voice. Similar, albeit not identical.

"Where did they take you?" Ranulf demanded.

"Oh, out there." I gestured with a vague hand. "I had some stern things shouted at me, I must admit."

"Well, you're back," the captain said, looking infinitely relieved and not a little impatient. "I don't know what I would have said to your mo—I mean, to Commander Parsons." She looked around. "Where is he, by the way?"

"Detained," I said, leading her aside and dropping my voice. "I have information, er, obtained by Commander Parsons that there is a credible threat to this ship."

Her eyes went wide.

"What threat?" she asked, lowering her own tone. "My security chief has not informed me of any potential attacks."

I reduced my volume still further, in case any of the visitors, who had now resumed their private conversations, had eavesdropping technology. I explained the data that Dolly had given me.

"A bomb?" she squeaked. It would have taken a monolith not to let out an ejaculation of concern, but it was without a doubt a squeak. She shot a wary glance toward the party at my back. "And one of the... those... are responsible? How are we going to figure out which one is the spy without causing an interstellar incident?"

I smiled, although I admit the expression might have been a trifle insufferable.

"By asking them," I said. I turned to Cheutlie and the entire Trade Union contingent. They regarded me with pleasant, blank countenances.

I had not really taken in on my first brief introduction to them that they were rather a handsome group, for commoners. Their shades of hair varied from deep amber to lightest honey gold, and their wide-set eyes from dark green to pale blue. The skin tones, however, came close to being identical, the pale-brown shade of ground mustard seeds. None of them could have been distinguished from the general gene pool from which they had sprung. The traitor among them had clearly been chosen for his or her resemblance to the ambassador's preference. Anything that did not fit the mold could have been altered. But at base, the mole from the Imperium would still bear the genetic hallmark of his or her birth. I fixed them with a flirtatious expression, doing my best to appear as adorable and approachable as I could.

"Kiss me," I said. I admired the set of their squarish jaws, and lips with a pointed cupid's bow that parted faintly at my request. I would have been happy for any one of them to kiss me. But it was the young man on the end, with amber hair and green eyes, who stepped forward and placed a shy peck on my right cheek. He withdrew, blinking, as if shocked at his own action. His fellows stared at him in open astonishment. I turned back to the captain. "Ask him."

The captain was baffled, as I knew she would be.

"Ask him what?"

"Where he planted the bomb," I said.

"What?" the ambassador demanded. "You accuse sabotage from one of my people?"

"He's not one of yours," I said. "His DNA on my cheek will prove it."

Alas, but my words broke the spell. The young man realized that he had betrayed himself, though not how. He bounded forward and shoved me backward. I fell over Coffee, bowling over the security personnel in my wake. The spy leaped over me and fled around the corner.

"Stop him!" I shouted.

The captain spoke into her viewpad.

"Security! Seal the doors on level 22 between the conference center and the landing bay!"

I sprang to my feet and set off in pursuit.

The heavy metal doors should have been slamming closed all along the high, square corridor. Ahead of me, I could see a bright-blue light in the spy's hand, no doubt a device to prevent the portals from obeying. I had to catch him.

A brief glance over my shoulder told me that two security personnel had joined the chase, weapons drawn. They wouldn't be fast enough. I opened out my stride.

I am swift on my feet, but the impostor must have been genetically crossed with an eland. The airlock doors stood ajar, wreathed in red as alarms blared shrill warnings. The spy passed through them, and the blue light in his hand blinked. The glass portals began to slide shut. I measured the narrowing gap with my eye. I had to make it through. With every ounce of strength I had, I dove in between the panels.

I landed on the cold metal floor beside a couple of pilots on break, with coffee cups in one hand and their helmets in the other. They scrambled to help me to my feet.

Ahead of me, the spy bounded toward a small craft where a pilot was just mounting the boarding ladder. With a leap far from one of which an ordinary human was capable, he shoved her off the platform and jumped in. The canopy dropped, and the small craft shot off into the darkness.

"Excuse me," I said. I plucked the helmet out of the arms of one of the pilots and dashed toward another craft preparing to launch. I jumped into the second seat behind the white-furred aeronaut and popped on my protective headgear. "Follow that fighter!"

"Aye, sir," the Wichu pilot said.

We rocketed off the bay floor. Rings of light danced around the exit to the flight deck. I assumed that the spy's device had prevented his ship from being remotely disabled.

Thanks to my excursion with Dolly, I knew the geography of *Enceladus* and the general area around her. Emerging into darkness, the heads-up scope showed me a hot new ion trail that led up and over the hulking body toward the tail. If memory served, that was the direction of the last jump point through which *Enceladus* had emerged. If the spy succeeded in passing through it, we would lose him.

Over the intership communications link, I could hear the captain giving orders.

"...Find that fighter and bring it back here! I repeat, tail number EHX-80. We need the pilot unharmed and conscious, if at all possible. Give all aid and assistance to Lieutenant Kinago in EHX-67. He is in pursuit. I expect a running report. Captain out!"

We attained a point of vantage as we crested the bulk of the ship. I spotted a couple of small craft who had been engaged in either perimeter patrols or seeking out the Blut ship. Out on the far edge of the scope was a receding dot that had to be the spy's craft. He had not disabled the telemetry, so the code numbers scrolled up underneath the computerized image. I pointed.

"There it is! Top speed!"

"I got him, sir." The small craft veered sharply away from the *Enceladus* and shot toward the small dot. I had struck lucky. Wichu were natural space pilots. They never suffered disorientation or motion sickness, and their nimble hands were surprisingly fast on the controls.

"Good soul!" I said absently, chafing in frustration as the bright dot receded ahead of us. She was being too direct in her approach. We were going to lose him! "I… I didn't get your name."

"Lieutenant Wagelev," she replied. "We'll get him."

The spy wove a skilled dance among the crowd of ships floating in space in between us and the jump point. Without needing the computer to plot it, I saw a series of angles that would bring me out in front of him.

"Let me have the controls," I pleaded.

"Are you rated for a combat fighter?" she countered.

"No, but I have a great deal of experience in small craft… Are you a fan of flitter racing?"

"Who isn't?" the Wichu pilot responded avidly.

"I am Lord Thomas Kinago," I said. "The last race I won was the Gogatar Rally."

"Controls over to you, my lord!" she said. "An image for my Infogrid file when we land?"

I smiled. "Of course."

The navigational controls of a standard fighter were made as intuitive in function as possible, aided by AI as required. I leaned into them, compelling every erg that the engines could produce. I veered slight left then slight right, feeling for her responsiveness. She handled much like the steering of a racing flyer. I knew where I was, then. I could concentrate on catching up with the fugitive.

"On your left!" I shouted into the audio pickup as I flipped the fuselage ninety degrees and slid in between a supply ship and the Donre cruiser. Two tiny war craft, a helmeted pilot in each, fell in behind me, peppering me with low-level energy bolts. I bent my flyer down in a right-angled spiral and dove under the Donre ship, hoping that they would leave me alone. "Confound it, I'm trying to help keep your ambassador alive!"

"Shields holding," Wagelev informed me. "What's their problem?"

"Terminal contrariness," I said, my eyes fixed on the scope. The ion trail we were following took a sharp loop upward and to the right. It led straight into an explosion of ion particles. The spy was cleverer than I had given him credit for. He had flown straight toward a group of small ships, causing them to scatter outward, burying his trail.

I nodded to myself. It didn't matter. I knew where he must go.

I angled up and through the cloud. Ion trails etched in pale gray on the blackness led outward from it in all directions, but only one continued on in the direction of the jump point. I poured on all the speed of which the fighter was capable, but it didn't respond with the leap I hoped for.

"Divert power from shields and weapons," I instructed Wagelev.

"Sir, we'll be defenseless if someone fires on us!"

"Nothing else matters if we can't catch him, Lieutenant," I said. I felt the small ship surge under my fingertips as the rest of the available energy transferred to navigation and helm.

The jump point lay on the heliopause of the nearest star, a red giant in its final stages before collapsing into a brown dwarf. We were several thousand kilometers away from the anomaly, so I still had a chance to get ahead of him and block his access.

Ahead and below my eyeline, the tiny bright dot and its attendant statistics reappeared on my scope. As if he had sensed me, he began weaving in an irregular corkscrew pattern, seeking to throw me off as to which angle he planned to approach the wormhole. I assessed the motions with an experienced eye. Seeing him as a racing competitor, I should be able to intuit what he was going to do next. He would have to try to elude me and get into a chicane, in this case the jump point, before I could. But what more? I had no tractor beams in this fighter. If I shot him down, I could not learn the location of the bomb, possibly before it was too late.

"Is there any way to speak to him?" I asked. The tiny dot in space grew almost imperceptibly larger. We were gaining on him. "Can you open communication frequencies that he might hear?"

"Sure. We only use three. The others are locked out."

"Open them all." I waited until the graphic appeared in the bottom corner of the screen. I toggled the controls so that it would broadcast my face to the fleeing fighter's scope. "This is Lord Thomas Kinago. Please stop your current trajectory and return to the *Enceladus*. You need to tell me where you have hidden the explosive device."

"Where he hid what?" Wagelev demanded, her voice on a rising note.

"Sh!" I hissed. "I know you can hear me, my friend. Turn back now, and we will work together to allay your concerns."

"No one listens to us!" came the wail from the speakers.

"I'm listening," I said, in a soothing tone. My craft closed in steadily on the mark on my screen. Soon, I could actually see the tiny vessel in the distance. "I'm rather good at listening. Or so my cousins tell me. Did you know that the Emperor is one of my cousins? Quite a handsome fellow, really. I'm green with envy at how well he photographs. Would you like to see a tri-dee of him? I have his entire speech from the feast to celebrate Workers' Day."

Undoubtedly, my babbling puzzled the fighters I could see coming up behind us, like the peloton in a cycle race. They would all be too late to make a difference, unless I could force the spy back again.

The fleeing craft seemed to hesitate as my image and the sound of my voice impinged upon the pilot's consciousness. I continued to chatter, knowing how it distracted my cousins when we played games that required concentration. His serpentine flight wavered, then became a straight line. We were less than a thousand kilometers away from the jump point.

Aha! I took the opportunity to underfly him and come up between him and the nebulous corona that indicated the entry to the tame wormhole. Now I was racing ahead, a hundred kilometers ahead, trying to keep him in my wake. I flipped the craft around end over end, so I flew backward, facing him.

"Hah! You're a way better pilot than he is, my lord!" Wagelev crowed.

"No!"

Red bolts lanced from the fighter's weapons. I realized all too late that the circuits from both seats were open to the communication channel. I had to veer off and reverse my nose once again to dodge the deadly blasts. As I did, he shot past us toward the void.

"Oops, sorry," the Wichu said, as the momentum threw us

both sideways against our seats' crash padding. "Switching to full shields."

"No!" I cried. "I need the maneuverability!"

"But he'll kill us," Wagelev said.

"No," I said, doggedly holding onto the controls with both hands. "No, he won't."

With all the skill of which I was capable, I thrust the fighter forward, causing it to describe a corkscrew path around the spy. At one point, one of our fins nearly scraped the canopy over his head. He blasted energy bolts in every direction, hoping to hit us. The telemetry indicated that he had clipped the port thruster, knocking part of the housing off into space.

We were nearing the perilous beauty of the jump point. If I let myself get drawn into its maelstrom, I could be swept anywhere from millions of kilometers to light years away from my present position. The small fighter might or might not be strong enough to withstand its gravitational force. The same went for the spy. We had to get him back safely, but I had no means of grappling him back.

Perhaps no means but charm. I opened up all frequencies to him again, and ripped the helmet off my head. The air was thin but just breathable.

"What's your name, my friend?" I asked, focusing on the scope as if addressing him directly. I spoke gently, omitting any hint of threat or authority from my tone. "I want to know about you. We hardly had time to connect, back in the ship."

"M... Malcolm..."

I smiled the meltingly wistful smile that hardly ever worked on my maternal unit when I sought to escape punishment for something I had done.

"I am Thomas. I hear you come from Drixol. Is that so?"

"...Yes."

"Lady Margaretha is my cousin. Why do you want to harm others to get her attention?"

Malcolm became agitated, shifting back and forth in his crash couch.

"Our cause is just!"

"But destroying countless innocent lives won't aid your cause," I said. "Tell me what you want. Then I might be able to discuss it with her."

"...Could you?"

"I certainly could," I said. He wavered.

"We're getting too close, my lord," Wagelev said, on a rising note of concern, if not panic. "We're gonna go through in a second!"

I gestured outside of the range of the tri-dee pickup for her to stay silent.

"Come back with me. Tell me where the device is, and we'll meet with Margaretha about your concerns."

"There are too many!" the spy said.

In the scope behind us, I could see more craft coming up behind me, flanked by two larger craft, an Imperium corvette and the Blut ship. *Parsons!* I thought in delight.

"You may write your manifesto in prison!" Captain Ranulf's voice interrupted. "Stop now, and we won't blow you into atoms!"

"Captain, really," Parsons's dry voice interjected, a mild rebuke compared with what I wanted to say. I dearly wished that I could reach through the spaceways and stifle the captain into silence.

Distracted from my voice, the spy stopped flying evasive patterns and made straight for the wavering light, a candle in the darkness. I hurtled after him, knowing that I could not pull him back. He would reach the jump point, and all lives aboard *Enceladus* would be lost.

In desperation, I played my last card.

"If you pass through that portal, you will never see me again, Malcom," I said plaintively. "Never again to behold my countenance, nor that of my majestic cousin, Emperor Shojan. How sad that would be."

The craft arrowed toward the pinpoint wormhole, with half the contingent of the *Enceladus* and the Blut ship behind it. Then, it veered away.

"May I have a tri-dee of you to keep?" Malcolm asked, in a voice nearly as wistful as mine.

"I will even personalize it," I said firmly.

The small craft went limp in space. The Blut ship beat the rest of the peloton to the floating fighter and fixed it with a tractor beam.

+ + +

The DNA sample from my cheek was sufficient to confirm Malcolm as a denizen of the Imperium, not a citizen of the Trade Union. I was able to deliver the promised tri-dee before he was bundled firmly in the direction of the brig.

I returned to my cabin, where I found Parsons already in situ. He stood to one side out of harm's way as I gladly shed the dull black carapace of my disguise and sought through my wardrobe for suitable party clothes.

"I knew you would be able to restore yourself to our bosom," I said. "I think I did as well at my end in performing efficiently extemporaneous action, don't you think? I communicated successfully incognito with your contact, revealed the spy and convinced him to give himself up, as well as providing proof to the authorities. The ship is saved!"

A tiny motion of the area above his left eyebrow was a noncommittal reaction, not approving or disapproving as far as I can tell.

"My lord, you could have found a less ostentatious and less hazardous way of obtaining the DNA," he said. "And also of compelling the spy to surrender. You could have communicated with him via tri-dee broadcast, and never exposed yourself to the hazards of space in a craft as unprotected as a fighter."

"I could," I said, shrugging into a coat that had been sewn for me with illuminated threads woven into the complicated sapphire-blue damask. Coffee swooped in to do up the complicated silk frogs down the front. With a critical eye, I turned back and forth in front of the mirror. I did look absolutely splendid. I beamed up at Parsons, satisfied on all fronts. "But where would have been the fun in that?"

Hawaiian author Linda Nagata's military scifi series *The Red*, set on near-future Earth, has wracked up accolade after accolade. Her trilogy started out self-published and then got picked up by a major publisher after the reviews and critical praise, and she continues the saga here with a brand-new short story that parallels the main action in *The Red* trilogy. It takes place in a different theater of operations, but shares the idea of the augmented infantry soldiers who make up a Linked Combat Squad.

REGION FIVE

LINDA NAGATA

I was a soldier not a human fly, but Trident swore the battle AI could make it work. My helmet's audio quieted the sounds of shouts and screams and gunfire from the streets below, and the rumble of helicopters above the city, so that it was easy for me to hear Trident as he spoke over a private channel from his post at the Guidance office in Charleston: "You've got to trust me, Josh. We've got a viable route for you. But it's only going to work if you move out when I call it. No hesitation."

I wondered when we'd gotten to a first-name basis. Trident was the lieutenant's remote handler, but the lieutenant was dead in a checkpoint blast that had been just one in a simultaneous wave of attacks that brought our peacekeeping efforts to an abrupt end.

It had been "Sergeant Miller" when Trident first opened a persistent link with my helmet's audio, informing me of what I already knew: that I was now in command of my Linked Combat Squad. *We'll work together*, he'd told me. *I'll help you get out of there.* That was thirty minutes ago, as a guerilla army of RPs poured up out of the subway tunnels, and barricades were going up in the streets. Time enough for our relationship to get tight—but I didn't like what he was asking me to do next.

Asshole, I thought, but I focused a little too hard on the sentiment. My wired skullcap picked up the cerebral pattern, my tactical AI interpreted it, and a synthesized voice spoke the thought for me in a flat artificial tone that went out over the persistent channel linking me to Trident. "Asshole," it said.

"Oops," I added out loud.

Trident took it well. "You just need to get the squad to the roof, Josh."

"I understand the goal." I just didn't like the route.

I was crouched on the edge of an abyss, behind a concrete pillar that had once framed the now-blown-out glass wall of an office suite on the thirty-eighth floor of an eighty-eight story skyscraper designated as building 21-North. The suite was a temporary refuge for my LCS—my Linked Combat Squad. Fifteen soldiers, twelve of us still alive. We'd set up booby traps to be triggered by the battle AI when the door was inevitably breached. Of course we planned to be gone by then.

I looked past glittering fragments of shattered glass at a forest of high-rise buildings, a hundred or more: the once-affluent city center of Region Five. Scattered fires billowed and blazed in offices that had been hit by rocket fire, and black smoke from burning cars wended up from the street, poisoning the air between the buildings.

Beyond the towers, just visible through the smoke, were the mixed districts. Green marked the gated neighborhoods with their large parks and luxury homes; gray was the color of the ugly, low-rise concrete block apartments that served as middle-class housing; and sealing the spaces between them—like multicolored mold—were the slums. A vast, interconnected maze of tumble-down homes that sprawled all the way to the glittering airport, ten miles out.

The airport was our goal, our destination. Home base. Safety in a region gone mad, and it was my task to get my LCS there before the RPs got to us. But car bombs and barricades had closed the roads out of the city center, and snipers held posts in most of the buildings, waiting to pick off any foreign soldier unwise enough to set foot in the streets. So Command had decided that our only way out was up.

I felt pressure on my shoulder. Turned to see Kat's hand, inside an armored glove. Leaning down, she asked off-com: "How long we gonna be here, Sergeant?" Her voice crisp, calm, reflecting the focused state of her baseline mood.

"Not long. We'll be going as soon as the route is clear."

We'd decimated the crew of RPs that had followed us up the stairwell, but there would be more. We didn't call them "Replacement Parts" for nothing. RPs were shock troops drawn from the slums, the expendable weapons of a warlord who crapped in gold-plated toilets while he claimed to be fighting for the poor. RP training was minimal, but they came in such numbers and jacked up so high on designer drugs it hardly mattered. We'd probably killed thirty or more, just getting into 21-North. I hoped their signing bonus was worth it.

Kat dropped into a crouch beside me. "Busy out there," she observed, still off-com so the rest of the squad wouldn't hear her.

"Robot war," I agreed, answering the same way as we watched a pair of cheap kamikazes dart past in the gulf below us. They were small UAVs—four-foot wingspans, electric engines, propeller driven—fast and agile. They peeled off, heading in opposite directions down an adjacent avenue.

Trident had sworn that we'd won the initial air war. Enemy UAVs had been eliminated while we climbed the tower, and anything still in flight belonged to us. Maybe it was true.

I flinched as another kamikaze dropped out of the sky. It shot past us in a dive so steep I thought it was aimed at a target in the street. But fifteen or twenty floors below our position, it shifted its trajectory, pulling up, and then accelerating through a shattered window in the building across the street. Red flames ballooned at the point of impact.

"You know why this city is code-named Region Five?" Kat asked.

"Not sure I want to know." Kat's theories were rarely comforting.

She told me anyway. "It's because this fucked-up city is the fifth circle of Hell. The fifth circle is ruled by anger—and as you know, everyone in Region Five is mad as hell."

Sad truth.

Trident interrupted our little exercise in philosophy. "This is it, Josh. You are clear to move out."

"Roger that."

Trident wanted me to trust him. I'd told him the relationship was moving a little fast, but hell, it's not like I had a choice. He had access to up-to-the-second intelligence summaries prepared by Command's analytical AIs, and to angel-sight from surveillance drones, and to every camera and mic in our squad. All of that gave him a better grasp of the battlefield's dynamics than I could hope to have, despite him being thousands of miles away. I needed his guidance, his input, his oversight. I had to trust him.

I stood, rising easily to my feet despite the weight of my pack, buoyed up by the powerful joints of my exoskeleton. Kat stood too, and together we turned to the squad. *Gen-com*, I thought.

My skullcap picked up the request and shifted my audio channel. "Heads up," I said, speaking softly, trusting the com system to boost my voice.

Ten anonymous black visors turned in my direction.

We looked like invaders from space.

The uniform was ordinary gray-brown urban camo, but we were bulked up by body armor, backpacks, and by the arm and leg struts of our exoskeletons, looking like gray external bones. Each of us carried a Harkin Integrated Tactical Rifle—a HITR, naturally—double-triggered to fire both 7.62-millimeter rounds and programmable grenades from the underslung launcher. Wired skullcaps were the external component of our brain–computer interface. Over the skullcap, we wore a helmet with a full-face opaque black visor. The local kids had loved the look of our rigs. To them, we'd been alien heroes, come to Region Five to restore order.

Kids could still dream.

I spoke quickly, quietly. "We're moving out. I'm on point. Follow in your designated order, keep your interval, stick to your projected route, and do not look down." This last was advice to myself. "*Hoo-yah*," I added.

A soft round of responses came back to me over gen-com. "*Hoo-yah.*"

The dead stood on the periphery of the living: the lieutenant and two privates, held up by their rigs but slumped—burned and bloodied—heads bowed, faces mercifully hidden behind black visors spider-webbed by impacts. They would move out with us, their exoskeletons operated by the battle AI, judiciously mimicking the pattern of movement it observed in the rest of the squad.

The dead were never left behind. Not the bodies or the gear. It was a matter of honor, sure, but we were also fighting a propaganda war and Command would pancake this building before they allowed the bodies of our brothers and sisters to be mutilated or left to hang in the streets.

I turned back to the abyss, insulated from a direct assault of grief by the constant manipulations of my skullcap. Its activity triggered cascades of neurochemicals intended to keep me focused and alert, in a baseline state of wary intensity. It didn't automatically eliminate fear though, because fear could be a useful emotion in my profession.

I drew a deep breath, all too aware of my racing heart and the tremor in my hands. I reminded myself that if I fucked up, a Kevlar rope would limit my fall. Kat was the anchor, backed up by Porter and Chan. "Don't drop me," I muttered to them.

"Don't get shot," Kat told me.

"And move fast," Trident added. "We took out the last known sniper, but there are always going to be ten more Replacement Parts for every one that falls."

My team, always positive.

I leaned out into the void.

We'd left the stairwell because, two floors up, surveillance showed close to seven hundred civilians waiting to get past an RP checkpoint. They were being identified, searched, and robbed of any useful valuables, before being allowed to cross a sky bridge that led to the relative safety of 21-South. The RPs on that level were vigilant. They had guards set up in the stairwells, and while we could fight our way through, a renewed battle would certainly panic the civilians and lead to unacceptable casualties.

So Command had decided stealth was our best option. We would avoid a fight by climbing unseen up the outside of the tower, until we were past the civilian-occupied floors. Our route was out of sight of the sky bridge, on the opposite side of the building, nestled in an angle of 21-North's postmodern exterior where two semicircular walls intersected.

A rush of a warm wind growled past the rim of my helmet. I refused to look down. Instead, I twisted around, looking up at the side of the building, and as I did, my route appeared as an overlay of reality projected on my visor. I saw two handholds, indicated by right and left hand prints inside of bright-green circles. Clutching the window frame, I grabbed the first hold—a narrow lip of concrete. I set my arm hook over it, and held on with my fingers too, as backup. Then I let go of the window frame and reached for the second handhold. I did not look down.

I did not *want* to look down.

But I could feel, in the base of my brain, in the back of my neck, just how far I'd fall if the rope broke, if I let go. My hands were shaking. I swear every hair on my body was standing on end as I used my exoskeleton's powered arm struts to haul myself up.

That's when I realized I *had* to look down.

"*Shit*," I whispered off-com. I lowered my gaze, looking for another green circle, knowing it would be there, and it was. This one had a barefoot graphic—and far, far below it was the street. How long would it take me to fall that far? What would I be thinking on the way down?

Then I saw someone run the experiment. A man, dressed in business casuals, took flight from a floor that I guessed to be at least fifteen stories below me. I heard his high-pitched scream. Another man followed after him. I saw it happen this time. I saw the arms that shoved him out a shattered window.

I wrenched my gaze away before they hit. I focused on the projected footprint, jamming the climbing hook of my rig against another lip of concrete, praying it would hold my weight. I boosted myself higher. Found the next foothold. Released an arm hook and used that to secure the next handhold.

The hook slipped. It scraped across concrete, sending dried pigeon dung peppering across my visor. I think I stopped breathing. I know my legs were trembling. Not from strain. Physically, the climb was easy because my exoskeleton was doing most of the work. But goddamn, we were thirty-eight stories up, I'd just seen two men plummet to the street, and my skin was puckering. I'd never trained to do this. None of us had. And I hated being this scared. I prayed I'd get shot before I fell.

"Try it again, Josh," Trident said in a voice so calm it irritated the fuck out of me.

I looked again at the next handhold. It had shifted toward center. I set the hook against it. Got my fingers set. Past gritted teeth, I told Trident, "I'm feeling a little tense." In truth, I was hoping I wouldn't puke. "Maybe you could fix that for me."

I hated having to ask, but what the fuck. Guidance was supposed to take care of my headspace. My skullcap was there to monitor brain activity and to influence it at need. It seemed to me a good time for some artificial rebalancing of my mood chemistry.

Trident spoke slowly, choosing his words. "I don't have a... uh, a *precedent* that will allow me to address this situation on my own, but I submitted a request for a prescription."

I didn't ask how long a response would take. It didn't matter, because with or without a fix, I had four floors to climb. So I made myself do it:

Haul up.

Move my right foot.

My left hand.

Left foot.

Right hand.

The rope trailing behind me while I schooled myself to think of nothing but the climb. I moved as fast as I dared, knowing I was an easy target for any sniper who'd evaded the kamikazes, but also concerned for my squad. They were due to follow me, and the sooner the better. If the RPs found them, the door of that office suite would not hold up against a rocket-propelled grenade.

But as much as I wanted to climb that wall with the speed of a circus act, fear made me slow and clumsy. My hands trembled, my armored gloves were wet with sweat, the tiny fans running inside my helmet were not enough to cool the flush that heated my face, and every time I slipped it got worse.

I kept on that way for one and a half floors, and then Trident came to my rescue. "Got your prescription approved," he said.

"Hit me."

He sent the fix to my skullcap, triggering a neurochemical response—and confidence blossomed in my brain. The transition was so extreme I wondered if it was a mistake, an overdose, because Guidance had never let me feel anything that good before. It was a heroic mindset, high, energized, but not manic. No. The opposite: a machinelike focus, and the certainty that I *could* do this without making a mistake.

I sucked in a sharp breath. "I think that's going to work," I told Trident. I looked up, set my grip. Looked down, placed my foot. Repeated that sequence, climbing steadily now. Resisting a subsurface temptation to reflect on what I was doing, or what was being done to me.

Deep down, I knew my prescription confidence wasn't going to last long. There is a limit to how long brain cells can be artificially stimulated before they become exhausted and cease to react. But I let the concern go unexamined, and climbed.

Four floors up, Command had put a rocket through the glass wall of another office suite. The blast had opened the door to the hall, allowing Guidance to send in a palm-sized seeker to scout the floor.

"You got an update for me, Trident?" I asked as I got close.

"The entire floor reads empty, and quiet."

That's what I liked to hear.

I reached the suite and crawled in, onto carpet strewn with

broken glass. A glance around showed charred desks and smoldering chairs and artwork and fine ceramics and children's drawings tossed haphazardly against blackened walls. My high drained away, and in just a couple of seconds I returned to real life—that familiar baseline state in which I was wary, alert, and intensely focused on my surroundings. I didn't mind. It's an outlook that's kept me alive through multiple combat missions. Heroic confidence doesn't do that. Soldiers convinced of their invulnerability tend not to last.

I looked toward the door of the suite. It was hanging open on broken hinges. The sight left me feeling exposed. I paused to listen, but the only sounds I heard came from the battle outside. Trident was right. It was quiet up here. There was no hint of the civilian chaos I knew to be unfolding two floors below.

"Okay, Kat," I said. "I'm going to pull up the rope."

"Roger that. We are ready."

I used the single rope to pull up four more, securing them to anchor points already mapped for me in the room. "Okay, let's move."

My soldiers started to climb, four at a time. I lay flat on the glass-strewn floor, looking down, watching their progress. Their gray adaptive camo did a good job of blending with the gray concrete. I listened to their whispers over gen-com as they began the ascent. *Holy fuck*, and *Sweet Jesus*. They sounded impressed, but not scared, because Josh made sure they were high.

Still, "Focus," I reminded them over gen-com. "Move one limb at a time."

The replies came in quiet confidence:

"No worries, Sergeant."

"I'm good."

"I got this."

On-demand confidence. As soon as the first cohort joined me, the second started up. No one hesitated like I had. No one freaked out. They made the ascent quickly, moving from hold to hold as if they'd done this trick a hundred times because belief made it easy, and Guidance was making damn sure they believed.

On the third wave, we hauled up the dead. And then Kat, Lopez, and Fields made the climb.

"Confirm all present," I told Trident.

"Confirmed."

I switched to gen-com. "Next phase commences now."

+ + +

There were two stairwells inside 21-North's concrete core. The doors to both were closed. That meant I could not send the seeker ahead to investigate. We had to go ourselves.

The closest stairwell was just a few steps away down the darkened hall. The seeker waited for us by the door, hovering at head height, a soft hum emanating from its rotors. I moved up, taking a position to one side of the door, my HITR ready. Raymond took the opposite side. Boldin and Young stacked behind us.

"Ready," I said, and reached out, nudging the door open a crack. Through the gap there came a slice of light and the jumbled voices of a crowd—not close—but not so far away either. The tone was angry, fearful. I couldn't understand the language, but I recognized a shouted threat, a desperate wail. "That's got to be from the checkpoint," Young whispered. A spillover of noise from civilians desperate to cross the sky bridge.

"Agreed." I nudged the door wider and shoved the muzzle of my HITR through the gap, panning it, so the battle AI could use the feed from the muzzle cams to evaluate what was on the other side. As I did, I watched the feed on my visor's display. It showed an empty stairwell lit by emergency LEDs. No debris, no bodies, no booby traps or IEDs in sight.

"Clear to advance," Trident said.

I opened the door wider. The seeker moved first, darting past the door and then zipping down the stairwell—but it descended only a single flight before wheeling around and returning. "Clear below," Trident said. He sent the seeker upstairs next, to reconnoiter hazards above us.

"Young, Raymond." I gestured at them to move toward the lower stairs. "Guard the downstairs approach. Fall in when the squad is past."

I pulled a button camera from my vest pocket, peeled off the backing, and stuck it against the wall, placing it as high as I could reach. Trident would monitor the feed. We'd know if any hostiles passed this point.

"All right," I said, speaking softly over gen-com. "This is it. We should be past the worst of it. All we need to do now is reach the roof. We've got helicopters ready to come in and pick us up. So let's move fast, but keep it quiet. Do not alert the enemy that we are here, and we'll get to enjoy hot showers and home cinema tonight."

I knew the skullcap was working again when I felt another sudden shift in my mood. This time my ready state ramped up, leaving me primed and eager to tackle the last half of our climb. The taut posture of my soldiers reflected a similar mood shift.

"Move out," I said, taking the lead as we set off up the stairs.

This was not the way I'd expected to spend the day.

✦ ✦ ✦

Fifteen million people. That was the estimated population of the urban maze we called Region Five. For three years, the city's good citizens had worked hard to whittle that number down by killing each other in a brutal civil war. On one side was a dictator who'd accumulated vast wealth and an army of ruthless enforcers. On the other was a revolutionary warlord who'd risen to power on a cult of personality while accumulating a fortune of his own. Reviled by both sides was the tiny educated class—the engineers, administrators, lawyers, skilled contractors and technicians, and the business people, who, together, possessed the thin skin of knowledge every urban complex needs to function. Most had fled during the worst of the hostilities, and what was left of Region Five's infrastructure quickly fell apart.

The threat of mass starvation had proven sufficient to get a peace treaty signed. A few hundred of the essential expats agreed to return, and a coalition of 7,000 peacekeeping troops was promised as "a show of international support." That's how Captain Tardiff had put it, though he'd looked like he had a bad taste in his mouth. "We won't be here long," he'd promised us.

I don't know. We'd been seven weeks in-country. It felt like a long time—but it wasn't time enough for the Coalition to get their act together. We were still operating with half the promised troop numbers. Three thousand soldiers, assigned to occupy a city of fifteen million. The math just wasn't going to work. So we limited our operation to the city center, where people seemed happy to have us around.

But that morning, out on patrol, we all knew something was up. I'd felt the battle AI's anxiety bleeding through my skullcap. We all did.

And then at ten hundred local time, the hammer came down.

In that moment, when I understood we were about to be overrun, I'd felt shock, fear, horror—until a switch in my brain toggled, and I was in battle mode. Maybe it was the skullcap. Maybe it was me. My training. My experience. I'd like to think so, but I don't know.

It didn't really matter. We just had to get the fuck out.

It was a bloody street fight to 21-North. I can see it all in my mind, hear the screams, the gunfire, smell the burn of smoke in the back of my throat, and remember the rage and the grief I'd felt over our dead—but looking back, it feels emotionally distant, as if the memory belongs to someone else.

We wear the skullcaps to ensure it will feel that way. The skullcaps are an interface to keep us focused and on topic, and to distance us from the worst of what we've seen and done.

It's hard sometimes to know what's real.

✦ ✦ ✦

We moved fast, assured by the seeker that the stairwell above us was clear. Boot plates thumping in soft percussive rhythm, faint hiss of exoskeleton joints, creak of backpacks, low whirr of fans, and the white-noise of breath drawn under duress. My helmet audio should have screened out those noises, but I wanted to hear them. I wanted to focus on them instead of on the distant boom of slamming doors, the screamed threats and the wailing, the occasional crack of gunfire. The tactical AI picked up on that, and allowed it.

We'd climbed only five flights when I felt a tremor in the concrete. It startled me badly. I ducked down against the wall just as the roar of an explosion reached us. My ears popped, and I winced against the pressure in my skull. Lopez was right behind me. He was crouched on the stairs too, with Chan behind him, huddled in a corner of the landing.

Trident spoke over gen-com. "We had four RPs investigating the suite you evacuated. The battle AI triggered the explosives."

Trident had probably watched it happen. That was part of his job: sitting in an air-conditioned office, facing a bank of screens, overseeing the last moments of people he'd helped to target for death. I hoped Command had him wired up too.

"Roger that," I said.

Recovering my composure, I told Lopez, "You still got a button camera, right? Stick it to the wall. I want to leave more eyes behind us."

We renewed our climb, deploying cameras every few floors.

Our seeker had scouted the stairwell above us, and confirmed it to be clear, but we had no data on who occupied the floors we were passing. That left me feeling like I was in some stupid video game. Every few seconds, I would stride up another flight, turn the corner, see the fire door ahead, the number of the floor painted on it in cool blue. I trained my HITR on each door that I passed, imagining it slamming open to admit a shattering of gunfire from an endless spawn of suicidal characters encroaching from the other side.

Trident interrupted this fantasy with a reality update: "Pursuit is on the way. Enemy seeker has just passed the first wall cam."

I was moving too fast to check my squad map, but I knew Kat would have taken her usual place at the end of our column. I snatched words from between panting breaths. "Kat, that one's yours. Take it out."

"You got it, Sergeant."

"Trident. RPs?"

"Not in sight yet, and I can't hear anything coming."

"Other stairwell, you think?"

"Could be."

We didn't have any devices in place to monitor that route.

I flinched at the harsh report of a three-round burst.

"Seeker down," Kat reported.

"Haul ass," I told her.

The enemy knew now where we were—but the elevators weren't running. They'd have to come up the stairs after us, and I wasn't going to give them a chance to catch up. "Close up any gap in the line," I ordered. "This is a sprint."

Of course it was possible the RPs had personnel already in place above us, positioned out of sight on one of the floors, waiting to launch an ambush.

"Here they come," Trident said. "Enemy now passing the first wall camera. We've got nine... no, eleven RPs on your trail. Armed with automatic rifles, a couple of grenade launchers. Manual grenades."

We were way ahead of them.

✦ ✦ ✦

How long does it take to climb forty stories? We were advancing two or three stairs at a time, each stride powered by our exoskeletons. We still had to work for it, but if no one got in our way, it was only going to take a few minutes to reach the top. "You got our ride incoming?" I asked Trident.

Silence on his side, extending several seconds, long enough to make me worry about a communications issue. I reached the next landing.

"Stairwell's blocked ahead," Trident said. "At least a hundred people—"

"*What?*" I pulled up so abruptly Lopez had to dodge to keep from crashing into me.

"I think they're mostly civilians—"

"What do you mean, you *think*?"

"They knocked down the seeker before I could do a full assessment. I can confirm noncombatants, though. Children. Unarmed women and men. Approach cautiously. Don't shoot unless the AI marks a target."

My LCS was gathering on the stairs below me. On the landing, the fire door told me we were on the seventy-fifth floor. "Why don't I hear them, Trident?" I whispered. "That many civilians, just a few floors up, I should hear voices. Are they alive?"

"*Yes*. Yes, they're alive. They're quiet. They're hushing each other."

That told me they were afraid. They didn't want to be found—but we were going to run right into them, and the RPs would follow.

Trident said, "Intelligence is analyzing the video we were able to get. Using facial recognition to identify them."

Resentment stirred inside me, though at what, I wasn't sure. Maybe at Trident's feigned ignorance as he pretended there was some question about who was hiding on the stairs above. I put an end to that. "They're the expats," I said, starting to climb again. "The technicians, the bureaucrats, the ones who came back to help rebuild this city. The ones the RPs have been throwing out the windows."

The expats had abandoned their country, fled the fighting, only to return in the company of foreign troops. That made them an enemy of the people they'd left behind, right?

"Confirming your guess," Trident said. "But there could be RPs with them."

I snorted. *That* wasn't likely. I reached the seventy-seventh floor. "They're here because they were promised protection, Trident." I knew now why I felt bitter. "Looks like that job falls to us."

So much for an easy run to the roof. I already had three dead soldiers walking behind me up the stairs. How many more of us would become casualties as we waited for a hundred civilians to be evacuated ahead of us?

Trident's voice was soft, apologetic, as he said exactly the opposite of what I expected to hear: "Negative, Josh. Command says you will continue up the stairs to the roof, where you will be evacuated."

"You mean ahead of the civilians?"

To my shock, Captain Tardiff broke in. "The civilians are the responsibility of the Coalition leadership and will be evacuated by them. *My* responsibility is to you and the rest of my people. My orders are to get all of you out safely, with no additional casualties. So you will proceed past the civilians—"

"But Captain Tardiff, sir, the enemy is just a few minutes behind us."

I shouldn't have interrupted him, but his orders weren't making sense to me. That fed my resentment, helped it grow into anger— though I still wasn't sure who or what I should be angry with. The civilians, for getting in my way? The Coalition, for this FUBAR'd operation? The captain, for ordering me to walk away and do nothing to prevent a slaughter? Or myself, because I'd been wishing for an excuse to do exactly that.

The captain sorted it all out nicely: "It's not a matter for debate, Miller. You *will* take your LCS directly to the roof and stand ready to evacuate. Is that understood?"

Yeah, I'm slow, but I do catch on. We'd been brought to Region Five to support the peace process. No one had asked us if we wanted to come. But the expats had volunteered. Now the whole affair was revealed as an empty gesture, a stunt, a performance put on so that afterwards the politicians could shrug and say, *Hey, we tried!*

Sure, the expats had hoped for more—but they should have known better.

+ + +

Trident monitored the progress of the RPs through the wall cameras we'd left behind. The civilians monitored us through their cell phones.

We saw the first phone tucked into a corner of the stairwell on the eighty-first floor. I knew the local cell system was down, but with peer-to-peer capabilities, the phones could be useful within the building. So I cradled my weapon, and as I passed the phone, I held up a gloved hand and flashed an OK, making sure the American flag on my uniform was visible. I didn't want any resistance when we caught up with them.

Another phone, two floors up, passively observing.

The third phone spoke as I reached it. A woman's voice. I slowed to listen: "We are no threat," she said in crisp English. "Please, there are children with us—"

Some part of my mind wanted to sympathize with her, but what was the point? I couldn't help her. So I cut her off with gruff instructions. "Ma'am, I want to see everyone's hands when I turn the corner. You communicate that to your people. Cooperate, and no one needs to get hurt."

They weren't fools. They did as they were told. I saw them as I approached the eighty-seventh floor. They were packed onto the flight above, mostly men in pale button-down shirts and conservative slacks, watching me between the rails, their hands held shoulder high, palms out. The battle AI assessed the visual feeds received through my helmet cams. It highlighted no weapons.

I noted that they'd left no room to get past them.

Two women, apparently serving as their advance team, waited for me on the landing. One was slim and young, dressed in a dark business suit too hot for this climate, the other middle-aged, a round figure in a flowing brown and beige gown. Both stood with hands up. I guessed the rest of the women and the children were above, on the next flight of stairs which should be the last flight, just below the door to the roof.

The older woman spoke to me in a low, cautious voice. "You are Americans, part of the coalition that invited us here. Will you help us?"

"We're trying to get to the roof, ma'am."

"As are we. We cannot go down. If the revolutionaries find us, they will kill us. We tried to call for help, but the cell system is down. So we resolved to go to the roof, where the Coalition could find us, help us—but the door at the top of the stairs is locked. We can't get through."

I knew I should feel sympathetic. Who wouldn't? We owed these people… didn't we? Still, I had my orders. I kept my voice carefully neutral when I assured her, "My people will get the door open, ma'am. But you need to stand aside. Let us pass."

The young woman clutched at her companion's arm, her dark eyes fearful. "You will help us, then? You'll let the Coalition know we are here?"

"They already know you're here, ma'am."

A door slammed somewhere below. I didn't want to question Trident aloud in front of the civilians, so I asked silently, *Trident, how far?* Letting my skullcap pick up the thought and translate it into words that he could hear.

"A few minutes," he assured me. "It's a hard climb and they're getting tired. You've got time to get your LCS to the roof." But then his tone shifted. He didn't sound quite as confident when he said, "They're smashing cameras as they come. I can't be sure of their numbers."

Lopez had moved up beside me. He asked the women, "How many of you are there?"

I raised my hand to cut him off, even as the older woman answered: "One hundred twenty-eight. Thirty-two children."

"Geez, Sergeant. What are we going to do?"

"We're going to get the fucking door open," I snapped, feeling my poisonous resentment on the rise again. From behind my anonymous black visor, I addressed the frightened expats. "This is what I need you to do. I want everyone to move down at least two flights. Keep close to the wall while you do it. Leave the railing clear, so we can get past. We're going to blow the door."

That gave them hope, so they cooperated, opening a lane alongside the railing. I started up, at the same time whispering instructions over gen-com. "Let's move. Quickly. Forget the interval. Stay close. Look for weapons as we go, and push back against any resistance."

Kat protested. "RPs' gonna be here soon, Sergeant. You want me to set up a rear guard, buy some time?"

"Negative." I reached the next flight. The women and children were there. They were moving down while I strode up. They stayed quiet, not wanting to alert any roving RPs, but they watched me, frightened eyes wanting to harbor hope, but unsure if it was a good bet. A little boy reached out, his tiny fingers brushing my exoskeleton's thigh strut as I passed. "We stay together," I told Kat. I knew that once we blew the door, the RPs would come fast and the civilians would panic. "I'm not going to risk a rear guard getting trapped on the wrong side of this mob."

"Yes, Sergeant." She sounded reluctant. She sounded like my conscience.

All of the civilians were behind me when I looked up the last, empty flight of stairs. Another closed steel fire door was at the top.

Mounted above the door was an illuminated green sign. I couldn't read it, but the battle AI tagged it with a translation. *Exit*. Yeah? Only if you have the key.

I sent Lopez and Chan ahead to rig the door. Then I eyed my squad map, assuring myself that everyone, even Kat, was obeying orders and coming up behind me. We gathered on the landing, or on the stairs just below. Kat was one level down, last in line. "Civilian coming up fast," she warned.

I heard the quick footsteps, the panting breath. I told Lopez, "Once you get the door open, get outside and take down the antennas. Make it safe for the helicopters."

"Yes, Sergeant."

I leaped down a full flight of stairs to the lower landing, letting the shocks on my rig absorb the impact. My sudden appearance startled the young woman in the business suit who we'd talked to before. The expats crowded behind her, looking frightened, like they wanted to try for the roof again. What would we have to do to hold them back, when panic hit?

The woman's gaze fixed on me, as if she could see my eyes past my visor. She said very softly, "The killers are coming, sir. They're close. A phone picked up their voices."

Over gen-com, Lopez announced, "Fire in the hole."

"Hold up," I told him.

Once the explosives were triggered, the RPs would come after us, berserker style, because that's how they fought—and they'd cut right through the civilians.

I'd known that before, but I had my orders.

"Sergeant?" Lopez asked over gen-com, sounding puzzled.

"These people," I whispered to Trident. "We can't just leave them here."

The woman in the suit looked at me, wide eyed, her worst suspicions confirmed, while Kat backed me up. "It's true, Sergeant. We have a duty."

But Captain Tardiff was speaking again too. "Sergeant Miller, I don't like this anymore than you do, but we are under orders to evacuate. We did what we could, but the mission is over."

My heart was beating fast, my anxiety rising, my conscience white hot. "Captain, it's only ten miles to the airport. That's nothing. You can take the civilians out first. Thirty at a time. Drop them off, turn the helicopter around. We can hold the roof—"

"*Negative.* There are over seven hundred coalition soldiers to be airlifted out. If you're not on the roof to meet your flight, your LCS goes to the back of the line—and God knows if we'll even have a functional ship by then."

I couldn't believe what I was hearing. "Captain Tardiff, I understand the urgency—"

"Do you? Do you understand what will happen to you if any of you are captured? Do you understand the propaganda cost to future operations? Get your people to the roof *now*, Miller." His tone changed. He wasn't talking to me anymore when he said, "Make it happen, Trident."

Fear. That's what they hit me with. Raw fear from out of nowhere, triggered by some formula that Trident sent to my skullcap. I teetered on the edge of a panic attack. Cold sweat, racing heart, shallow breathing, and a spine-deep desire to get out, to get away. I'd never felt an artificial load like that before. A skullcap is supposed to moderate fear, maintain an alert state, cocoon traumatic memories. It was not supposed to take away my good judgment. It was not supposed to make me too afraid to do what was right.

It was abusive to mess with my head like that—and it was *illegal.* I was a US Army soldier and I had rights. I clung to that thought. "Do not *fuck* with my head," I whispered. "Or I am going to take the goddamn skullcap off."

It was a move that would end my career, no question, but in that moment I did not care. I wanted my head clear. The fear eating at me was real, but I knew it wasn't mine and I wasn't going to let it control me. What belonged to me was my resolve that I was not going to let Trident, or the Captain, or the US Army rewrite the core formula of who I was. And that resolve was enough to let me stand firm against Trident's artificial panic.

At the same time, I recognized the truth—I should have seen it before—but Trident must have been in and out of my head ever since we'd discovered the civilians. I felt shame remembering how, just a minute ago, I'd been thinking of them as just an obstacle to be gotten around, not as people with hopes and dreams and core truths of their own.

Kat had known something was wrong with me.

"Get out of my head, Trident," I warned. "Get out *now*."

"*Shit,*" Trident whispered. It was the first time I'd heard him swear. But he switched off the artificial fear and brought me back to baseline. He said, "I think you're going to get me fired, Josh."

"You and me, both."

But I was starting to feel like myself again—what I thought of as me—although nothing about our situation was changed. We were in trouble, with an attack by the RPs imminent. "Lopez!" I barked.

"Sergeant?"

"I'm taking Kat. We're going back down. We're going to set up a rear guard. On my word, you blow the door. Make the roof safe, enforce order, and get the civilians out. See that they're evacuated first. I don't care what kind of flack you get. Understood?"

"Roger that, Sergeant."

"Captain Tardiff, you still there?"

"You're going to find yourself up on charges, Miller," he answered. "Assuming you survive."

Was I more determined, because they'd tried to make me panic? It didn't matter. "Command can spin this, Captain. You know they can. Commandeer a helicopter for this building. Prioritize the civilians. You know that's going to make for positive propaganda anyway."

"Goddamn it," he said softly.

I turned to Kat, and off-com I asked her, "You with me?"

"Yeah, Sergeant. Let's do this right."

More of my squad spoke up, volunteering for the rear guard. I took only Young and Porter, assigning the rest to help Lopez, or to assist with crowd control.

The civilians squeezed out of the way as we headed down again. They asked no questions. Once we were past them, I whispered to Lopez, "Trigger it."

My helmet blunted the sharp crack of the explosives, but not the fearful cries of the civilians or the chorus of angry shouts and scattered gunfire from below.

Kat leaned over the railing, aiming her HITR straight down. "Movement," she reported.

"Hit 'em," I said. "Grenade."

Alastair Reynolds' award-winning space opera is of a more contemporary bent than some, featuring more realistic science and definite modern sensibilities. Part of the British New Space Opera movement that also includes Peter F. Hamilton, Iain Banks, Neal Asher, and others, his offering for us in a new story in his Revelation Space saga, set 200 years before the events of the titular novel and deals with the discovery of the first "Shroud," a giant alien artifact which plays a role in some of the other books and stories. This story, however, has all new characters.

NIGHT PASSAGE
ALASTAIR REYNOLDS

If you were really born on Fand then you will know the old saying we had on that world.

Shame is a mask that becomes the face.

The implication being that if you wear the mask long enough, it grafts itself to your skin, becomes an indelible part of you—even a kind of comfort.

Shall I tell you what I was doing before you called? Standing at my window, looking out across Chasm City as it slid into dusk. My reflection loomed against the distant buildings beyond my own, my face chiselled out of cruel highlights and pitiless, light-sucking shadows. When my father held me under the night sky above Burnheim Bay, pointing out the named colonies, the worlds and systems bound by ships, he told me that I was a very beautiful girl, and that he could see a million stars reflected in the dark pools of my eyes. I told him that I didn't care about any of that, but that I did want to be a starship captain.

Father laughed. He held me tighter. I do not know if he believed me or not, but I think it scared him, that I might mean exactly what I said.

+ + +

And now you come.

You recognise me, as he would not have done, but only because you knew me as an adult. You and I never spoke, and our sole meeting consisted of a single smile, a single friendly glance as I welcomed the passengers onto my ship, all nineteen thousand of them streaming through the embarkation lock—twenty if you include the Conjoiners.

Try as I might, I can't picture you.

But you say you were one of them, and for a moment at least I'm inclined to give you the time of day. You say that you were one of the few thousand who came back on the ship, and that's possible—I could check your name against the *Equinoctial*'s passenger manifest, eventually—and that you were one of the still fewer who did not suffer irreversible damage due to the prolonged nature of our crossing. But you say that even then it was difficult. When they brought you out of reefersleep, you barely had a personality, let alone a functioning set of memories.

How did I do so well, when the others did not? Luck was part of it. But when it was decreed that I should survive, every measure was taken to protect me against the side-effects of such a long exposure to sleep. The servitors intervened many times, to correct malfunctions and give me the best chance of coming through. More than once I was warmed to partial life, then submitted to the auto-surgeon, just to correct incipient frost damage. I remember none of that, but obviously it succeeded. That effort could never have been spread across the entire manifest, though. The rest of you had to take your chances—in more ways than one.

Come with me to the window for a moment. I like this time of day. This is my home now, Chasm City. I'll never see Fand again, and it's rare for me to leave these rooms. But it's not such a bad place, Yellowstone, once you get used to the poison skies, the starless nights.

Do you see the lights coming on? A million windows, a million other lives. The lights remain, most of the time, but still they remind me of the glints against the Shroud, the way they sparked, one after the other. I remember standing there with Magadis and Doctor Grellet, finally understanding what it was they were showing me— and what it meant. Beautiful little synaptic flashes, like thoughts sparking across the galactic darkness of the mind.

But you saw none of that.

+ + +

Let me tell you how it started. You'll hear other accounts, other theories, but this is how it was for me.

To begin with no one needed to tell me that something was wrong. All the indications were there as soon as I opened my eyes, groping my way to alertness. Red walls, red lights, a soft pulsing alarm tone, the air too cold for comfort. The *Equinoctial* was supposed to warm itself prior to the mass revival sequence, when we reached Yellowstone. It would only be this chilly if I had been brought out of hibernation at emergency speed.

"Rauma," a voice said. "Captain Bernsdottir. Can you understand me?"

It was my second-in-command, leaning in over my half-open reefersleep casket. He was blurred out, looming swollen and pale.

"Struma." My mouth was dry, my tongue and lips uncooperative. "What's happened? Where are we?"

"Mid-crossing, and in a bad way."

"Give me the worst."

"We've stopped. Engines damaged, no control. We've got a slow drift, a few kilometres per second against the local rest frame."

"No," I said flatly, as if I was having to explain something to a child. "That doesn't happen. Ships don't just stop."

"They do if it's deliberate action." Struma bent down and helped me struggle out of the casket, every articulation of bone and muscle sending a fresh spike of pain to my brain. Reefersleep revival was never pleasant, but rapid revival came with its own litany of discomforts. "It's sabotage, Captain."

"What?"

"The Spiders..." He corrected himself. "The Conjoiners woke up mid-flight and took control of the ship. Broke out of their area, commandeered the controls. Flipped us around, slowed us down to just a crawl."

He helped me hobble to a chair and a table. He had prepared a bowl of pink gelatinous pap, designed to restore my metabolic balance.

"How..." I had too many questions and they were tripping over themselves trying to get out of my head. But a good captain jumped to the immediate priorities, then backtracked. "Status of the ship. Tell me."

"Damaged. No main drive or thruster authority. Comms lost." He swallowed, like he had more to say.

I spooned the bad-tasting pink pap into myself. "Tell me we can repair this damage, and get going again."

"It can all be fixed—given time. We're looking at the repair schedules now."

"We?"

"Six of your executive officers, including me. The ship brought us out first. That's standard procedure: only wake the captain under dire circumstances. There are six more passengers coming out of freeze, under the same emergency protocol."

Struma was slowly swimming into focus. My second-in-command had been with me on two crossings, but he still looked far too young and eager to my eyes. Strong, boyish features, an easy smile, arched eyebrows, short, dark curls neatly combed even in a crisis.

"And the..." I frowned, trying to wish away the unwelcome news he had already told me. "The Conjoiners. What about them. If you're speaking to me, the takeover can't have been successful."

"No, it wasn't. They knew the ship pretty well, but not all of the security procedures. We woke up in time to contain and isolate the takeover." He set his jaw. "It was brutal, though. They're fast and sly, and of course they outnumbered us a hundred to one. But we had weapons, and most of the security systems were dumb enough to keep on our side, not theirs."

"Where are they now?"

"Contained, what's left of them. Maybe eight hundred still frozen. Two hundred or so in the breakout party—we don't have exact numbers. But we ate into them. By my estimate there can't be more than about sixty still warm, and we've got them isolated behind heavy bulkheads and electrostatic shields."

"How did the ship get so torn up?"

"It was desperate. They were prepared to go down fighting. That's when most of the damage was done. Normal pacification measures were never going to hold them. We had to break out the heavy excimers, and they'll put a hole right through the hull, out to space and anything that gets in the way—including drive and navigation systems."

"We were carrying excimers?"

"Standard procedure, Captain. We've just never needed them before."

"I can't believe this. A century of peaceful cooperation. Mutual advancement through shared science and technology. Why would they throw it all away now, and on my watch?"

"I'll show you why," Struma said.

Supporting my unsteady frame, he walked me to an observation port and opened the radiation shutters. Then he turned off the red emergency lighting so that my eyes had a better chance of adjusting to the outside view.

I saw stars. They were moving slowly from left to right, not because the ship was moving as a whole but because we were now on centrifugal gravity and our part of the *Equinoctial* was rotating. The stars were scattered into loose associations and constellations, some of them changed almost beyond recognition, but others—made up of more distant stars—not too different than those I remembered from my childhood.

"They're just stars," I told Struma, unsurprised by the view. "I don't…"

"Wait."

A black wall slid into view. Its boundary was a definite edge, beyond which there were no stars at all. The more we rotated, the more blackness came into our line of sight. It wasn't just an absence of nearby stars. The Milky Way, that hobbled spine of galactic light, made up of tens of millions of stars, many thousands of light years away, came arcing across the normal part of the sky then reached an abrupt termination, just as if I were looking out at the horizon above a sunless black sea.

For a few seconds all I could do was stare, unable to process what I was seeing, or what it meant. My training had prepared me for many operational contingencies—almost everything that could ever go wrong on an interstellar crossing. But not this.

Half the sky was gone.

"What the hell is it?"

Struma looked at me. There was a long silence. "Good question."

✦ ✦ ✦

You were not one of the six passenger-delegates. That would be too neat, too unlikely, given the odds. And I would have remembered your face as soon as you came to my door.

I met them in one of the mass revival areas. It was similar to the crew facilities, but much larger and more luxurious in its furnishings. Here, at the end of our voyage, passengers would have been thawed out in groups of a few hundred at a time, expecting to find themselves in a new solar system, at the start of a new phase in their lives.

The six were going through the same process of adjustment I had experienced only a few hours earlier. Discomfort, confusion—and a generous helping of resentment, that the crossing had not gone as smoothly as the brochures had promised.

"Here's what I know," I said, addressing the gathering as they sat around a hexagonal table, eating and drinking restoratives. "At some point after we left Fand there was an attempted takeover by the Conjoiners. From what we can gather one or two hundred of them broke out of reefersleep while the rest of us were frozen. They commandeered the drive systems and brought the ship to a standstill. We're near an object or phenomenon of unknown origin. It's a black sphere about the same size as a star, and we're only fifty thousand kilometres from its surface." I raised a hand before the obvious questions started raining in. "It's not a black hole. A black hole this large would be of galactic mass, and there's no way we'd have missed something like that in our immediate neighbourhood. Besides, it's not pulling at us. It's just sitting there, with no gravitational attraction that our instruments can register. Right up to its edge we can see that the stars aren't suffering any aberration or redshift... Yes?"

One of the passengers had also raised a hand. The gesture was so polite, so civil, that it stopped me in my tracks.

"This can't have been an accident, can it?"

"Might I know your name, sir?"

He was a small man, mostly bald, with a high voice and perceptive, piercing eyes.

"Grellet. Doctor Grellet. I'm a physician."

"That's lucky," I said. "We might well end up needing a doctor."

"Luck's got nothing to do with it, Captain Bernsdottir. The protocol always ensures that there's a physician among the emergency revival cohort."

I had no doubt that he was right, but it was a minor point of procedure and I felt I could be forgiven for forgetting it.

"I'll still be glad of your expertise, if we have difficulties."

He looked back at me, something in his mild, undemonstrative manner beginning to grate on me. "Are we expecting difficulties?"

"That'll depend. But to go back to your question, it doesn't seem likely that the Conjoiners just stumbled on this object, artefact, whatever we want to call it. They must have known of its location, then put a plan in place to gain control of the ship."

"To what end?" Doctor Grellet asked.

I decided truthfulness was the best policy. "I don't know. Some form of intelligence gathering, I suppose. Maybe a unilateral first contact attempt, against the terms of the Europa Accords. Whatever the plan was, it's been thwarted. But that's not been without a cost. The ship is damaged. The *Equinoctial*'s own repair systems will put things right, but they'll need time for that."

"Then we sit and wait," said another passenger, a woman this time. "That's all we have to do, isn't it? Then we can be on our way again."

"There's a bit more to it than that," I answered, looking at them all in turn. "We have a residual drift toward the object. Ordinarily it wouldn't be a problem—we'd just use the main engines or steering thrusters to neutralise the motion. But we have no means of controlling the engines, and we won't get it until the repair schedule is well advanced."

"How long?" Doctor Grellet asked.

"To regain the use of the engines? My executive officers say four weeks at the bare minimum. Even if we shaved a week off that, though, it wouldn't help us. At our present rate of drift we'll reach the surface of the object in twelve days."

There was a silence. It echoed my own, when Struma had first informed me of our predicament.

"What will happen?" another passenger asked.

"We don't know. We don't even know what that surface is made of, whether it's a solid wall or some kind of screen or discontinuity. All we do know is that it blocks all radiation at an immeasurably high efficiency, and that its temperature is exactly the same as the cosmic microwave background. If it's a Dyson sphere... or something similar... we'd expect to see it pumping out in the infrared. But it doesn't. It just sits there being almost invisible. If you wanted to hide something, to conceal yourself in interstellar space... impossibly hard to detect, until you're almost on top of it... this would be the thing. It's like camouflage, a cloak, or—"

"A shroud," Doctor Grellet said.

"Someone else will get the pleasure of naming it," I said. "Our concern is what it will do. I've ordered the launch of a small instrument package, aimed straight at the object. It's nothing too scientific—we're not equipped for that. Just a redundant spacesuit with some sensors. But it will give us an idea what to expect."

"When will it arrive?"

"In a little under twenty-six hours."

"You should have consulted with the revival party before taking this action, Captain," Doctor Grellet said.

"Why?"

"You've fired a missile at an object of unknown origin. You know it isn't a missile, and so do we. But the object?"

"We don't know that it has a mind," I responded.

"Yet," Doctor Grellet said.

✦ ✦ ✦

I spent the next six hours with Struma, reviewing the condition of the ship at first hand. We travelled up and down the length of the hull, inside and out, cataloguing the damage and making sure there were no additional surprises. Inside was bearable. But while we were outside, travelling in single-person inspection pods, I had that black wall at my back the whole time.

"Are you sure there weren't easier ways of containing them, other than peppering the ship with blast holes?"

"Have you had a lot of experience with Conjoiner uprisings, Captain?"

"Not especially."

"I studied the tactics they used on Mars, back at the start of the last century. They're ruthless, unafraid of death, and totally uninterested in surrender."

"Mars was ancient history, Struma."

"Lessons can still be drawn. You can't treat them as a rational adversary, willing to accept a negotiated settlement. They're more like a nerve gas, trying to reach you by any means. Our objective was to push them back into an area of the ship that we could seal and vent if needed. We succeeded—but at a cost to the ship." From the other inspection pod, cruising parallel to mine, his face regarded me with a stern and stoic resolve. "It had to be done. I didn't like any part of it. But I also knew the ship was fully capable of repairing itself."

"It's a good job we have all the time in the world," I said, cocking my own head at the black surface. At our present rate of drift, it was three kilometres nearer for every minute that passed.

"What would you have had me do?" Struma asked. "Allow them to complete their takeover, and butcher the rest of us?"

"You don't know that that was their intention."

"I do," Struma said. "Because Magadis told me."

I let him enjoy his moment before replying.

"Who is Magadis?"

"The one we captured. I wouldn't call her a leader. They don't have leaders, as such. But they do have command echelons, figures trusted with a higher level of intelligence processing and decision-making. She's one of them."

"You didn't mention this until now?"

"You asked for priorities, Captain. I gave you priorities. Anyway, Magadis got knocked around when she was captured. She's been in and out of consciousness ever since, not always lucid. She has no value as a hostage, so her ultimate usefulness to us isn't clear. Perhaps we should just kill her now and be done with it."

"I want to see her."

"I thought you might," Struma said.

Our pods steered for the open aperture of a docking bay.

✦ ✦ ✦

By the time I got to Magadis she was awake and responsive. Struma and the other officers had secured her in a room at the far end of the ship from the other Conjoiners, and then arranged an improvised cage of electrostatic baffles around the room's walls, to screen out any possible neural traffic between Magadis and the other Conjoiners.

They had her strapped into a couch, taking no chances with that. She was shackled at the waist, the upper torso, the wrists, ankles, and neck. Stepping into that room, I still felt unnerved by her close proximity. I had never distrusted Conjoiners before, but Struma's mention of Mars had unlocked a head's worth of rumour and memory. Bad things had been done to them, but they had not been shy in returning the favour. They were human, too, but only at the extreme edge of the definition. Human physiology, but boosted for a high tolerance of adverse environments. Human brain structure, but infiltrated with a cobweb of neural enhancements, far beyond anything carried by Demarchists. Their minds were cross-linked, their sense of identity blurred across the glassy boundaries of skulls and bodies.

That was why Magadis was useless as a hostage. Only part of her was present to begin with, and that part—the body, the portion of her mind within it—would be deemed expendable. Some other part of Magadis was still back with the other Conjoiners.

I approached her. She was thin, all angles and edges. Her limbs, what I could see of them beyond the shackles, were like folded blades, ready to flick out and wound. Her head was hairless, with a distinct cranial ridge. She was bruised and cut, one eye so badly swollen and slitted that I could not tell if it had been gouged out or still remained.

But the other eye fixed me well enough.

"Captain." She formed the word carefully, but there was blood on her lips and when she opened them I saw she had lost several teeth and her tongue was badly swollen.

"Magadis. I'm told that's your name. My officers tell me you attempted to take over my ship. Is that true?"

My question seemed to amuse and disappoint her in equal measure.

"Why ask?"

"I'd like to know before we all die."

Behind me, one of the officers had an excimer rifle pointed straight at Magadis's head.

"We distrusted your ability to conduct an efficient examination of the artefact," she said.

"Then you knew of it in advance."

"Of course." She nodded demurely, despite the shackle around her throat. "But only the barest details. A stellar-size object, clearly artificial, clearly of alien origin. It demanded our interest. But the present arrangements limited our ability to conduct intelligence gathering under our preferred terms."

"We have an arrangement. Had, I should say. More than a century of peaceful cooperation. Why have you endangered everything?"

"Because this changes everything."

"You don't even know what it is."

"We have gathered and transmitted information back to our mother nests. They will analyse the findings accordingly, when the signals reach them. But let us not delude ourselves, Captain. This is an alien technology—a demonstration of physics beyond either of our present conceptual horizons. Whichever human faction understands even a fraction of this new science will leave the others in the dust of history. Our alliance with the Demarchists has served us well, as it has been of benefit to you. But all things must end."

"You'd risk war, just for a strategic advantage?"

She squinted from her one good eye, looking puzzled. "What other sort of advantage is there?"

"I could—should—kill you now, Magadis. And the rest of your Conjoiners. You've done enough to give me the right."

She lifted her head. "Then do so."

"No. Not until I'm certain you've exhausted your usefulness to me. In five and half days we hit the object. If you want my clemency, start thinking of ways we might stop that happening."

"I've considered the situation," Magadis said. "There are no grounds for hope, Captain. You may as well execute me. But save a shot for yourself, won't you? You may come to appreciate it."

+ + +

We spent the remainder of that first day confirming what we already knew. The ship was crippled, committed to its slow but deadly drift in the direction of the object.

Being a passenger-carrying vessel, supposed to fly between two settled, civilised solar systems, the *Equinoctial* carried no shuttles or large extravehicular craft. There were no lifeboats or tugs, nothing that could nudge us onto a different course or reverse our drift. Even our freight inventory was low for this crossing. I know, because I studied the cargo manifest, looking for some magic solution to our problem: a crate full of rocket motors, or something similar.

But the momentum of a million-tonne starship, even drifting at a mere fifty metres a second, is still immense. It would take more than a spare limpet motor or steering jet to make a difference to our fate.

Exactly what our fate was, of course, remained something of an open question.

Soon we would know.

+ + +

An hour before the suit's arrival at the surface I gathered Struma, Doctor Grellet, the other officers and passenger delegates in the bridge. Our improvised probe had continued transmitting information back to us for the entire duration of its day-long crossing. Throughout that time there had been little significant variation in the parameters, and no hint of a response from the object.

It remained black, cold, and resolutely starless. Even as it fell within the last ten thousand kilometres, the suit was detecting no trace radiation beyond that faint microwave sizzle. It was pinging sensor pulses into the surface and picking up no hint of echo or backscatter. The gravitational field remained as flat as any other part of interstellar space, with no suggestion that the black sphere exerted any pull on its surroundings. It had to be made of something, but even if there had been only a moon's mass distributed throughout that volume, let alone a planet or a star, the suit would have picked up the gradient.

So it was a non-physical surface—an energy barrier or discontinuity. But even an energy field ought to have produced a measurable curvature, a measurable alteration in the suit's motion.

Something else, then. Something—as Magadis had implied—that lay entirely outside the framework of our physics. A kink or fracture in spacetime, artfully engineered. There might be little point in attempting to build a conceptual bridge between what we knew and what the object represented. Little point for baseline humans, at least. But I thought of what a loom of cross-linked, genius-level intelligences might make of it. The Conjoiners had already developed weapons and drive systems that were beyond our narrow models, even as they occasionally drip-fed us hints and glimpses of their "adjunct physics," as if to reassure their allies that they were only a step or two behind.

The suit was within eight thousand kilometres of the surface when its readings began to turn odd. It was small things to start with, almost possible to put down to individual sensor malfunctions. But as the readings turned stranger, and more numerous, the unlikelihood of these breakdowns happening all at once became too great to dismiss.

Dry-mouthed, I stared at the numbers and graphs.

"What?" asked Chajari, one of the female passengers.

"We'll need to look at these readings in more detail…" Struma began.

"No," I said, cutting him off. "What they're telling us is clear enough as it is. The suit's accelerometers are going haywire. It feels as if it's being pulled in a hundred directions at once. Pulled and pushed, like a piece of putty being squashed and stretched in someone's hand. And it's getting worse…"

I had been blunt, but there was no sense in sugaring things for the sake of the passengers. They had been woken to share in our decision-making processes, and for that reason alone they needed to know exactly how bad our predicament was.

The suit was still transmitting information when it hit the seven-thousand-kilometre mark, as near as we could judge. It only lasted a few minutes after that, though. The accelerational stresses built and built, until whole blocks of sensors began to black out. Soon after that the suit reported a major loss of its own integrity, as if its extremities had been ripped or crushed by the rising forces. By then it was tumbling, sending back only intermittent chirps of scrambled data.

Then it was gone.

I allowed myself a moment of calm before proceeding.

"Even when the suit was still sending to us," I said, "it was being buffeted by forces far beyond the structural limits of the ship. We'd have broken up not long after the eight-thousand mark—and it would have been unpleasant quite a bit sooner than that." I paused and swallowed. "It's not a black hole. We know that. But there's something very odd about the spacetime near the surface. And if we drift too close we'll be shredded, just as the suit was."

It reached us then. The ship groaned, and we all felt a stomach-heaving twist pass through our bodies. The emergency tone sounded, and the red warning lights began to flash.

Had we been a ship at sea, it was as if we had been afloat on calm waters, until a single great wave rolled under us, followed by a series of diminishing after-ripples.

The disturbance, whatever it had been, gradually abated.

Doctor Grellet was the first to speak. "We still don't know if the thing has a mind or not," he said, in the high, piping voice that I was starting to hate. "But I think we can be reasonably sure of one thing, Captain Bernsdottir."

"Which would be?" I asked.

"You've discovered how to provoke it."

✦ ✦ ✦

Just when I needed some good news, Struma brought it to me.

"It's marginal," he said, apologising before he had even started. "But given our present circumstances…"

"Go on."

He showed me a flowchart of various repair schedules, a complex knotted thing like a many-armed octopus, and next to it a graph of our location, compared to the sphere.

"Here's our present position, thirty-five thousand kilometres from the surface."

"The surface may not even be our worst problem now," I pointed out.

"Then we'll assume we only have twenty-five thousand kilometres before things get difficult—a bit less than six days. But it may be enough. I've been running through the priority assignments in the repair schedule, and I think we can squeeze a solution out of this."

I tried not to cling to false hope. "You can?"

"As I said, it's marginal, but…"

"Spare me the qualifications, Struma. Just tell me what we have or haven't got."

"Normally the ship prioritises primary drive repairs over anything else. It makes sense. If you're trying to slow down from lightspeed, and something goes wrong with the main engines at a high level of time-compression… well, you want that fixed above all else, unless you plan on over-shooting your target system by several light years, or worse." He drew a significant pause. "But we're not in that situation. We need auxiliary control now, enough to correct the drift. If it takes a year or ten to regain relativistic capability, we'll still be alive. We can wait it out in reefersleep."

"Good…" I allowed.

"If we override all default schedules, and force the repair processes to ignore the main engines—and anything we don't need to stay alive for the next six days—then the simulations say we may have a chance of recovering auxiliary steering and attitude control before we hit the ten-thousand-kilometre mark. Neutralise the drift, and reverse it enough to get away from this monster. Then worry about getting back home. And even if we can't get the main engines running again, we can eventually transmit a request for assistance, then just sit here."

"They'd have to answer us," I said.

"Of course."

"Have you… initiated this change in the schedule?"

He nodded earnestly. "Yes. Given how slim the margins are, I felt it best to make the change immediately."

"It was the right thing to do, Struma. You've given us a chance. We'll take it to the passenger-representatives. Maybe they'll forgive me for what happened with the suit."

"You couldn't have guessed, Captain. But this lifeline… it's just a chance, that's all. The repair schedules are estimates, not hard guarantees."

"I know," I said, patting him on the shoulder. "And I'll take them for what they are."

✦ ✦ ✦

I went to interview Magadis again, deciding for the moment to withhold the news Struma had given me. The Conjoiner woman was still under armed guard, still bound to the chair. I took my seat in the electrostatic cage, facing her.

"We're going to die," I said.

"This is not news," Magadis answered.

"I mean, not in the way we expected. A clean collision with the surface—fast and painless. I'm not happy about that, but I'll gladly take it over the alternative."

"Which is?"

"Slow torture. I fired an instrument probe at the object—a suit stuffed full of sensors."

"Was that wise?"

"Perhaps not. But it's told me what we can expect. Spacetime around the sphere is... curdled, fractal, I don't know what. Restructured. Responsive. It didn't like the suit. Pulled it apart like a rag doll. It'll do the same to the ship, and us inside it. Only we're made of skin and bone, not hardware. It'll be worse for us, and slower, because the suit was travelling quickly when it hit the altered spacetime. We'll take our time, and it'll build and build over hours."

"I could teach you a few things about pain management," Magadis said. "You might find them useful."

I slapped her across the face, drawing blood from her already swollen lip.

"You were prepared to meet this object. You knew of its prior existence. That means you must have had a strategy, a plan."

"I did, until our plan met your resistance." She made a mangled smile, a wicked, teasing gleam in her one good eye. I made to slap her again, but some cooler part of me stilled my hand, knowing how pointless it was to inflict pain on a Conjoiner. Or to imagine that the prospect of pain, even drawn out over hours, would have any impact on her thinking.

"Give me something, Magadis. You're smart, even disconnected from the others. You tried to commandeer the ship. Your people designed and manufactured some of its key systems. You must be able to suggest something that can help our chances."

"We have gathered our intelligence," she told me. "Nothing else matters now. I was always going to die. The means don't concern me."

I nodded at that, letting her believe it was no more or less than I had expected.

But I had more to say.

"You put us here, Magadis—you and your people. Maybe the others will see things the same way you do—ready and willing to accept death. Do you think they will change their view if I start killing them now?"

I waited for her answer, but Magadis just looked at me, nothing in her expression changing.

Someone spoke my title and name. I turned from the prisoner to find Struma, waiting beyond the electrostatic cage.

"I was in the middle of something."

"Before it failed, the suit picked up an echo. We've only just teased it out of the garbage it was sending back in the last few moments."

"An echo of what?" I asked.

Struma drew breath. He started to answer, then looked at Magadis and changed his mind.

+ + +

It was another ship. Shaped like our own—a tapering, conic hull, a sharp end and a blunter end, two engines on outriggers jutting from the widest point—but smaller, sleeker, darker. We could see that it was damaged to some degree, but it occurred to me that it could still be of use to us.

The ship floated eight thousand kilometres from the surface of the object. Not orbiting, since there was nothing to hold it on a circular course, but just stopped, becalmed.

Struma and I exchanged thoughts as we waited for the others to reconvene.

"That's a Conjoiner drive layout," he said, sketching a finger across one of the blurred enhancements. "It means they made it, they sent it here—all without anyone's knowledge, in flagrant violation of the Europe Accords. And it's no coincidence that we just found it. The object's the size of a star, and we're only able to scan a tiny area of it from our present position. Unless there are floating wrecks dotted all around this thing, we must have been brought close to it deliberately."

"It explains how they knew of the object," I mused. "An earlier expedition. Obviously it failed, but they must have managed to transmit some data back to one of their nests—enough to make them determined to get a closer look. I suppose the idea was to rendezvous and recover any survivors, or additional knowledge captured by that wreck." My fingers tensed, ready to form a fist. "I should ask Magadis."

"I'd give up, if I were you. She's not going to give us anything useful."

"That's because she's resigned to death. I didn't tell her about the revised repair schedule."

"That's still our best hope of survival."

"Perhaps. But I'd be remiss if I didn't explore all other possibilities, just in case the repair schedule doesn't work. That ship's too useful a prize for me to ignore. It's an exploratory craft, obviously. Unlike us, it may have a shuttle, something we can use as a tug. Or we can use the ship itself to nudge the *Equinoctial*."

Struma scratched at his chin. "Nice in theory, but it's floating well inside the point where the suit started picking up strange readings. And even if we considered it wise to go there, we don't have a shuttle of our own to make the crossing."

"It's not wise," I admitted. "Not even sane. But we have the inspection pods, and one of them ought to be able to make the crossing. I'm ready to try, Struma. It's better than sitting here thinking of ways to hurt Magadis, just to take my mind off the worse pain ahead for the rest of us."

He considered this, then gave a grave, dutiful nod. "Under the circumstances, I think you're right. But I wouldn't allow you to go out there on your own."

"A Captain's prerogative…" I started.

"Is to accept the assistance of her second-in-command."

✦ ✦ ✦

Although I was set on my plan, I still had to present it to the other officers and passenger-representatives. They sat and listened without question, as I explained the discovery of the other ship and my intention of scavenging it for our own ends.

"You already know that we may be able to reverse the drift. I'm still optimistic about that, but at the same time I was always told to have a back-up plan. Even if that other ship doesn't have anything aboard it that we can use, they may have gathered some data or analysis that can be of benefit to us."

Doctor Grellet let out a dry, hopeless laugh. "Whatever it was, it was certainly of benefit to them."

"A slender hope's better than none at all," I said, biting back on my irritation. "Besides, it won't make your chances any worse. Even if Struma and I don't make it back from the Conjoiner ship, my other officers are fully capable of navigating the ship, once we regain auxiliary control."

"The suit drew a response from the object," Grellet said. "How can you know what will happen if you approach it in the pods?"

"I can't," I said. "But we'll stop before we get as deep as the suit did. It's the best we can do, Doctor." I turned my face to the other passenger-representatives, seeking their tacit approval. "Nothing's without risk. You accepted risk when you consigned yourselves into the care of your reefersleep caskets. As it stands, we have a reasonable chance of repairing the ship before we get too close to the object. That's not good enough for me. I swore an oath of duty when I took on this role. You are all precious to me. But also I have twenty thousand other passengers to consider."

"You mean nineteen thousand," corrected Chajari diplomatically. "The Conjoiners don't count any more—sleeping or otherwise."

"They're still my passengers," I told her.

+ + +

No plan was ever as simple as it seemed in the first light of conception. The inspection pods had the range and fuel to reach the drifter, but under normal operation it would take much too long to get there. If there were something useful on the Conjoiner wreck I wanted time to examine it, time to bring it back, time to make use of it. I also did not want to have to depend on some hypothetical shuttle or tractor to get us back. That meant retaining some reserve fuel in the pods for a return trip to the *Equinoctial*. Privately, if my ship was going down then I wanted to be aboard when it happened.

There was a solution, but it was hardly a comfortable one.

Running the length of the *Equinoctial* was a magnetic freight launcher, designed for ship-to-ship cargo transfer. We had rarely used it on previous voyages and since we were travelling with only a low cargo manifest I had nearly forgotten it was there at all. Fortunately, the inspection pods were easily small enough to be attached to the launcher. By being boosted out of the ship on magnetic power, they could complete the crossing in a shorter time and save some fuel for the round-trip.

There were two downsides. The first was that it would take time to prepare the pods for an extended mission. The second was that the launcher demanded a punishing initial acceleration. That was fine for bulk cargo, less good for people. Eventually we agreed on a risky compromise: fifty gees, sustained for four seconds, would give us a final boost of zero point two kilometres per second. Hardly any speed at all, but it was all we could safely endure if we were going to be any use at the other end of the crossing. We would be unconscious during the launch phase and much of the subsequent crossing, both to conserve resources and spare us the discomfort of the boost.

Slowly the *Equinoctial* was rotated and stabilised, aiming itself like a gun at the Conjoiner wreck. Lacking engine power, we did this with gyroscopes and controlled pressure venting. Even this took a day. Thankfully the aim didn't need to be perfect, since we could correct for any small errors during the crossing itself.

Six days had now passed since my revival, halving our distance to the surface. It would take another three days to reach the Conjoiner ship, by which time we would have rather less than three days to make any use of its contents. Everything was now coming down to critical margins of hours, rather than days.

I went to see Magadis before preparing myself for the departure.

"I'm telling you my plans just in case you have something useful to contribute. We've found the drifter you were obviously so keen on locating. You've been going behind our backs all this time, despite all the assurances, all the wise platitudes. I hope you've learned a thing or two from the object, because you're going to need all the help you can find."

"War was only ever a question of time, Captain Bernsdottir."

"You think you'll win?"

"I think we'll prevail. But the outcome won't be my concern."

"This is your last chance to make a difference. I'd take you with me if I thought I could trust you, if I thought you wouldn't turn the systems of that wreck against me just for the spite. But if there's something you can tell me, something that will help all our chances…"

"Yes," she answered, drawing in me a little glimmer of hope, instantly crushed. "There's something. Kill yourselves now, while you have the means to do it painlessly. You'll thank me for it later."

I stepped out of the cage, realising that Doctor Grellet had been observing this brief exchange from a safe distance, his hands folded before him, his expression one of lingering disapproval.

"It was fruitless, I suppose?"

"Were you expecting something more?"

"I am not the moral compass of this ship, Captain Bernsdottir. If you think hurting this prisoner will serve your ends, that is your decision."

"I didn't do that to her. She was bruised and bloodied when she got here."

He studied me carefully. "Then you never laid a hand on her, not even once?"

I made to answer, intending to deny his accusation, then stopped before I disgraced myself with an obvious lie. Instead I met his eyes, demanding understanding rather than forgiveness. "It was a violent, organised insurrection, Doctor. They were trying to kill us all. They'd have succeeded, as well, if my officers and I hadn't used extreme measures."

"In which case it was a good job you were equipped with the tools needed to suppress that insurrection."

"I don't understand."

He nodded at the officer still aiming the excimer rifle at Magadis. It was a heavy, dual-gripped laser weapon—more suited to field combat than shipboard pacification. "I am not much of a historian, Captain. But I took the time to study a little of what happened on Mars. Nevil Clavain, Sandra Voi, Galiana, the Great Wall and the orbital blockade of the first nest…"

I cut him off. "Is this relevant, Doctor Grellet?"

"That would depend. My recollection from those history lessons is that the Coalition for Neural Purity discovered that it was very difficult to take Conjoiners prisoner. They could turn almost any weapon against its user. Keeping them alive long enough to be interrogated was even harder. They could kill themselves quite easily. And the one thing you learned never to do was point a sophisticated weapon at a Conjoiner prisoner."

✦ ✦ ✦

For the second time in nine days I surfaced to brutal, bruising consciousness through layers of confusion and discomfort. It was not the emergence from reefersleep this time, but a much shallower state of sedation. I was alone, pressed into acceleration padding, a harness webbed across my chest. I moved aching arms and released the catch. The cushioning against my spine eased. I was weightless, but still barely able to move. The inspection pod was only just large enough for a suited human form.

I was alive, and that was something. It meant that I had survived the boost from the *Equinoctial*. I eyed the chronometer, confirming that I had been asleep for sixty-six hours, and then I checked the short-range tracker, gratified to find that Struma's pod was flying close to mine. Although we had been launched in separate boosts, there had been time for the pods to zero-in on each other without eating into our fuel budgets too badly.

"Struma?" I asked across the link.

"I'm here, Captain. How do you feel?"

"About as bad as you, I'm guessing. But we're intact, and right now I'll take all the good news I can get. I'm a realist, Struma: I don't expect much to come of this. But I couldn't sit back and do nothing, just hoping for the best."

"I understood the risks," he replied. "And I agree with you. We had to take this chance."

Our pods had maintained a signals lock with the *Equinoctial*. They were pleased to hear from us. We spent a few minutes transmitting back and forth, confirming that we were healthy and that our pods had a homing fix on the drifter. The Conjoiner ship was extremely dark, extremely well-camouflaged, but it stood no chance of hiding itself against the perfect blackness of the surface.

I hardly dared ask how the repair schedule had been progressing. But the news was favourable. Struma's plan to divert the resources had worked well, and all indications were that the ship would regain some control within thirteen hours. That was cutting it exceedingly fine: *Equinoctial* was now only three days' drift from the surface, and only a day from the point where the suit's readings had begun to deviate from normal spacetime. We had done what we could, though—given ourselves a couple of slim hopes where previously there had been none.

Struma and I reviewed our pod systems one more time, then

began to burn fuel, slowing down for our rendezvous with the drifter. We could see each other by then, spaced by a couple of kilometres but still easily distinguished from the background stars, pushing glowing tails of plasma thrust ahead of us.

We passed the ten-thousand-kilometre mark without incident. I felt sore, groggy and dry-mouthed, but that was to be expected after the acceleration boost and the forced sleep of the cruise phase. In all other respects I felt normal, save for the perfectly sensible apprehension anyone would have felt in our position. The pod's instruments were working properly, the sensors and readouts making sense.

At nine thousand kilometres I started feeling the change.

To begin with it was small things. I had to squint to make sense of the displays, as if I was seeing them underwater. I put it down to fatigue, initially. Then the comms link with the *Equinoctial* began to turn thready, broken up with static and drop-outs.

"Struma…" I asked. "Are you getting this?"

When his answer came back, he sounded as if he was just as far away as the ship. Yet I could see his pod with my own eyes, twinkling to port.

"Whatever the suit picked up, it's starting sooner."

"The surface hasn't changed diameter."

"No, but whatever it's doing to the space around it may have stepped up a notch." There was no recrimination in his statement, but I understood the implicit connection. The suit had provoked a definite change, that ripple that passed through the *Equinoctial*. Perhaps it had signified a permanent alteration to the environment around the surface, like a fortification strengthening its defences after the first strike.

"We go on, Struma. We knew things might get sticky—it's just a bit earlier than we were counting on."

"I agree," he answered, his voice coming through as if thinned-out and Doppler-stretched, as if we were signalling each other from halfway across the universe.

At least the pods kept operating. We passed the eight-thousand-five-hundred mark, still slowing, still homing in on the Conjoiner ship. Although it was only a quarter of the size of the *Equinoctial*, it was also the only physical object between us and the surface, and our exhaust light washed over it enough to make it shimmer into visibility, a little flake of starship suspended over a sea of black.

There would be war, I thought, when the news of this treachery reached our governments. Our peace with the Conjoiners had never been less than tense, but such infringements that had happened to date had been minor diplomatic scuffles compared to this. Not just the construction and operation of a secret expedition, in violation of the terms of mutual cooperation, but the subsequent treachery of Magadis's attempted takeover, with such a cold disregard for the lives of the other nineteen thousand passengers. They had always thought themselves better than the rest of us, Conjoiners, and by certain measures they were probably correct in that assessment. Cleverer, faster, and certainly more willing to be ruthless. We had gained from our partnership, and perhaps they had found some narrow benefits in their association with us. But I saw now that it had never been more than a front, a cynical expediency. Behind our backs they had been plotting, trying to leverage an advantage from first contact with this alien presence.

But the first war had pushed them nearly to extinction, I thought. And in the century since they had shared many of their technologies with us—allowing for a risky normalisation in our capabilities. Given that the partnership had worked for so long, why would they risk everything now, for such uncertain stakes?

My thoughts flashed back to Doctor Grellet's parting words about our prisoner. My knowledge of history was nowhere near as comprehensive as his own, but I had no reason to doubt his recollection of those events. It was surely true, what he said about Conjoiner prisoners. So why had Magadis tolerated that weapon being pointed at her, when she could have reached into its systems and made it blow her head off?

Unless she wanted to stay alive?

"Struma..." I began to say.

But whatever words I had meant to say died unvoiced. I felt wrong. I had experienced weightlessness and gee-loads, but this was something completely new to me. Invisible claws were reaching through my skin, tugging at my insides—but in all directions.

"It's starting," I said, tightening my harness again, for all the good it would do.

The pod felt the alteration as well. The readouts began to indicate anomalous stresses, outside the framework of the pod's extremely limited grasp of normal conditions. I could still see the Conjoiner ship, and beyond the surface's black horizon the stars remained at a fixed orientation. But the pod thought it was starting to tumble.

Thrusters began to pop, and that only made things worse.

"Go to manual," Struma said, his voice garbled one instant, inside my skull the next. "We're close enough now."

Two hundred kilometres to the ship, then one hundred and fifty, then one hundred, slowing to only a couple of hundred metres per second now. The pod was still functioning, still maintaining life-support, but I'd had to disengage all of its high-level navigation and steering systems, trusting to my own ragged instincts. The signal lock from the *Equinoctial* was completely gone, and when I twisted round to peer through the rear dome, the stars seemed to swim behind thick, mottled glass. My guts churned, my bones ached as if they had been shot through with a million tiny fractures. A slow growing pressure sat behind my eyes. The only thing that kept me pushing on was knowing that the rest of the ship would be enduring worse than this, if we did not reverse the drift.

Finally the Conjoiner ship seemed to float out of some distorting medium, becoming clearer, its lines sharper. Fifty kilometres, then ten. Our pods slowed to a crawl for the final approach.

And we saw what we had not seen before.

Distance, the altered space, and the limitations of our own sensors and eyes had played a terrible trick on us. The state of decay was far worse than we had thought from those long-range scans. The ship was a frail wreck, only its bare outline surviving. The hull, engines, connecting spars were present… but they had turned fibrous, gutted open, ripped or peeled apart in some places, reduced to lacy insubstantiality in others. The ship looked ready to break apart, ready to become dust, like some fragile fossil removed from its preserving matrix.

For long minutes Struma and I could only stare, our pods hovering a few hundred metres beyond the carcass. All the earlier discomforts were still present, including the nausea. My thoughts were turning sluggish, like a hardening tar. But as I stared at the Conjoiner wreck, nothing of that mattered.

"It's been here too long," I said.

"We don't know."

"Decades… longer, even. Look at it, Struma. That's an old, old ship. Maybe it's even older than the Europa Accords."

"Meaning what, Captain?"

"If it was sent here before the agreement, no treaty violation ever happened."

"But Magadis…"

"We don't know what orders Magadis was obeying. If any." I swallowed hard, forcing myself to state the bleak and obvious truth. "It's useless to us, anyway. Too far gone for there to be anything we could use, even if I trusted myself to go inside. We've come all this way for nothing."

"There could still be technical data inside that ship. Readings, measurements of the object. We have to see."

"No," I said. "Nothing would have survived. You can see that, can't you? It's a husk. Even Magadis wouldn't be able to get anything out of that now." My heart was starting to race. Besides the nausea, and the discomfort, there was now a quiet, rising terror. I knew I was in a place where simple, thinking organisms such as myself did not belong. "We failed, Struma. It was the right thing to attempt, but there's no sense deluding ourselves. Now we have to pray that the ship can slow itself down without any outside help."

"Let's not give up without taking a closer look, Captain. You said it yourself—we've come this far."

Without waiting for my assent he powered his pod for the wreck. The Conjoiner ship was much smaller than the *Equinoctial*, but still his pod diminished to a tiny bright point against its size. I cursed, knowing that he was right, and applied manual thrust control to steer after him. He was heading for a wide void in the side of the hull, the skin peeled back around it like a flower's petals. He slowed with a pulse of thrust, then drifted inside.

I made one last attempt to get a signal lock from the main ship, then followed Struma.

Maybe he was right, I thought—thinking as hard and furiously as I could, so as to squeeze the fear out of my head. There might still be something inside, however unlikely it looked. A shuttle, protected from the worst of the damage. A spare engine, with its control interface miraculously intact.

Once I was inside, though, I knew that such hopes were forlorn. The interior decay was just as bad, if not worse. The ship had rotted from within, held together by only the flimsiest traces of connective tissue. With my pod's worklights beaming out at full power, I drifted through a dark, enchanted forest made of broken and buckled struts, severed floors and walls, shattered and mangled machinery.

I was just starting to accept the absolute futility of our expedition when something else occurred to me. There was no sign of Struma's pod. He had only been a few hundred metres ahead of me when he passed out of sight, and if nothing else I should have picked up the reflections from his worklights and thrusters, even if I had no direct view of his pod.

But when I dimmed my own lights, and eased off on the thruster pod, I fell into total darkness.

"Struma," I said. "I've lost you. Please respond."

Silence.

"Struma. This is Rauma. Where are you? Flash your lights or thrusters if you can read me."

Silence and darkness.

I stopped my drift. I must have been halfway into the innards of the Conjoiner ship, and that was far enough. I turned around, rationalising his silence. He must have gone all the way through, come out the other side, and the physical remains of the ship must be blocking our communications.

I fired a thruster pulse, heading out the way I had come in. The ruined forms threw back milky light. Ahead was a flower-shaped patch of stars, swelling larger. Not home, not sanctuary, but still something to aim for, something better than remaining inside the wreck.

I saw him coming just before he hit. He must have used a thruster pulse, just enough to move out of whatever concealment he had found. When he rammed my pod the closing speed could not have been more than five or six metres per second, but it was still enough to jolt the breath from me and send my own pod tumbling. I gasped for air, fighting against the thickening heaviness of my thoughts to retain some clarity of mind. I crashed into something, collision alarms sounding. A pod was sturdy enough to survive the launch boost, but it was not built to withstand an intentional, sustained attack.

I jabbed at the thruster controls, loosened myself. Struma's pod was coming back around, lit in the strobe-flashes of our thrusters. Each flash lit up a static tableau, pods frozen in mid-space, but from one flash to the next our positions shifted.

I wondered if there was any point reasoning with him.

"Struma. You don't have to do this. Whatever you think you're going to achieve..." But then a vast and calm understanding settled over me. It was almost a blessing, to see things so clearly. "This was staged, somehow. This whole takeover attempt. Magadis... the others... it wasn't them breaking the terms of the Accord, was it?"

His voice took on a pleading, reasoning tone.

"We needed this intelligence, Rauma. More than we needed them, and certainly more than we needed peace."

Our pods clanged together. We had no weapons beyond mass and speed, no defences beyond thin armour and glass.

"Who, Struma? Who do you speak for?"

"Those who have our better interests in mind, Rauma. That's all you need to know. All you *will* know, shortly. I'm sorry you've got to die. Sorry about the others, too. It wasn't meant to be this bad."

"No government would consent to this, Struma. You've been misled. Lied to."

He came in again, harder than before, keeping thruster control going until the moment of impact. I blacked out for a second or ten, then came around as I drifted to a halt against a thicket of internal spars. Brittle as glass, they snapped into drifting, tumbling whiskers, making a dull music as they clanged and tinkled against my hull.

A fissure showed in my forward dome, pushing out little micro-fractures.

"They'd have found out about the wreck sooner or later, Rauma—just as we did. And they'd have found a way to get here, no matter the costs."

"No," I said. "They wouldn't. Maybe once they'd have been that ruthless—as would we. But we've learned to work together, learned to build a better world."

"Console yourself. When I make my report, I'll ensure you get all the credit for the discovery. They'll name the object after you. Bernsdottir's Object. Bernsdottir's Shroud. Which would you prefer?"

"I'd prefer to be alive." I had to raise my voice over the damage alarm. "By the way, how do you expect to make a report, if we never get home?"

"It's been taken care of," Struma said. "They'll accept my version of events, when I return to the *Equinoctial*. I'll say you were trapped in here, and I couldn't help you. I'll make it sound suitably heroic."

"Don't go to any trouble on my account."

"Oh, I wouldn't. But the more they focus on you, the less they'll focus on me."

He rammed me one more time, and I was about to try and dive around him when I let my hands drift from the thruster controls. My pod sailed on, careening into deepening thickets of ruined ship. I bounced against something solid, then tumbled on.

"You'd better hope that they manage to stop the drift."

"Perhaps they will, perhaps they won't. I don't need the ship, though. There's a plan—a contingency—if all else were to fail. I abandon the ship. Catapult myself out of harm's way in a reefersleep casket. I'll put a long-range homing trace on it. Out between the stars, the casket will have no trouble keeping me cold. Eventually they'll send another ship to find me."

More thruster flashes, but not from me. For an instant the sharp, jagged architecture of this place was laid stark. Perhaps I saw a body somewhere in that chaos, stirred from rest by our rude intrusion, tumbling like a doll, a fleshless, sharp-crested skull turning its blank eyes to mine.

"I'm glad you trust your masters that well."

"Oh, I do."

"Who are they, Struma? A faction within the Demarchists? One of the non-aligned powers?"

"Just people, Rauma. Just good, wise people with our long-term interests in mind."

Struma came in again, lining up for a final ram. He must have heard that damage alarm, I thought, and took my helpless tumble as evidence that I had suffered some final loss of thruster control.

I let him fall closer. He picked up speed, his face seeming to swell until it filled his dome. His expression was one of stony resolve, filled more with regret than anger. Our eyes must have met in those last strobe-lit instants, and perhaps he saw something in my own face, some betrayal of my intentions.

By then, though, it would have been much too late.

I jammed my hands back onto the controls, thrusting sideways, giving him no time to change his course. His pod slid into the space where mine had been only an instant earlier, and then onward, onto the impaling spike of a severed spar. It drove through armour, into Struma's chest, and in the flicker of my own thrusters I watched his body undergo a single violent convulsion, even as the air and life raced from his lungs.

Under better circumstances, I would have found a way to remove his body from that wreck. Whatever he had done, whatever his sins, no one deserved to be left in that place.

But these were not better circumstances, and I left him there.

+ + +

Of the rest, there isn't much more I need to tell you. Few things in life are entirely black and white, and so it was with the repair schedule. It completed on time, and *Equinoctial* regained control. I was on my way back, using what remained of my fuel, when they began to test the auxiliary engines. Since they were shining in my direction, I had no difficulty making out the brightening star that was my ship. Not much was being asked of it, I told myself. Surely now it would be possible to undo the drift, even reverse it, and begin putting some comfortable distance between the *Equinoctial* and the object.

As my pod cleared the immediate influence of the surface, I regained a stable signal and ranging fix on the main ship. Hardly daring to breathe, I watched as her drift was reduced by a factor of five. At ten metres per second a human could have outpaced her. It was nearly enough—tantalising close to zero.

Then something went wrong. I watched the motors flicker and fade. I waited for them to restart, but the moment never came. Through the link I learned that some fragile power coupling had overloaded, strained beyond its limits. Like everything else, it could be repaired—but only given time that we did not have. The *Equinoctial*'s rate of drift had been reduced, but not neutralised. Our pods had detected changes at nine thousand kilometres from the surface. At its present speed, the ship would pass that point in four days.

We did not have time.

I had burned almost all my fuel on the way back from the wreck, leaving only the barest margin to rendezvous with the ship. Unfortunately that margin proved insufficient. My course was off, and by the time I corrected it, I did not have quite enough fuel to complete my rendezvous. I was due to sail past the ship, carrying on into interstellar space. The pod's resources would keep me alive for a few more days, but not enough for anyone to come to my rescue, and eventually I would freeze or suffocate, depending on which got me first. Neither option struck me as very appealing. But at least I would be spared the rending forces of the surface.

That was not how it happened, of course.

My remaining crew, and the passenger-representatives, had decreed that I should return to the ship. And so the *Equinoctial*'s alignment was trimmed very carefully, using such steering control as the ship now retained, and I slid back into the maw of the cargo launcher. It was a bumpy procedure, reversing the process that had boosted me out of the ship in the first place, and I suffered concussion as the pod was recaptured by the launch cradle and brought to a punishing halt.

But I was alive.

Doctor Grellet's was the first face I saw when I returned to awareness, lying on a revival couch, sore around the temples, but fully cognizant of what had happened.

My first question was a natural one.

"Where are we?"

"Two days from the point where your pods began to pick up the altered spacetime." He spoke softly, in the best bedside manner. "Our instruments haven't picked up anything odd just yet, but I'm sure that will change as we near the boundary."

I absorbed his news, oddly resentful that I had not been allowed to die. But I forced a captain-like composure upon myself. "It took until now to revive me?"

"There were complications. We had to put you into the auto-surgeon, to remove a bleed on the brain. There were difficulties getting the surgeon to function properly. I had to perform a manual override of some of its tasks."

No one else was in the room with me. I wondered where the rest of my executive staff were. Perhaps they were busy preparing the ship for its last few days, closing logs and committing messages and farewells to the void, for all the hope they had of reaching anyone.

"It's going to be bad, Doctor Grellet. Struma and I got a taste of it, and we were still a long way from the surface. If there's nothing we can do, then no one need be conscious for it."

"They won't be," Doctor Grellet said. "Only a few of us are awake now. The rest have gone back into reefersleep. They understand that it's a death sentence, but at least it's painless, and some sedatives can ease the transition into sleep."

"You should join them."

"I shall. But I wanted to tell you about Magadis first. I think you will find it interesting."

When I was ready to move Doctor Grellet and I made our way to the interrogation cell. Magadis was sitting in her chair, still bound. Her head swivelled to track me as I entered the electrostatic cage. In the time since I had last seen her, the swelling around her bad eye had begun to reduce, and she could look at me with both eyes.

"I told the guard to stand down," Doctor Grellet said. "He was achieving nothing anyway."

"You told me about the prisoners on Mars."

He gave a thin smile. "I'm glad some of that sunk in. I didn't really know what to make of it at the time. Why hadn't Magadis turned that weapon on herself, or simply reached inside her own skull to commit suicide? It ought to have been well within her means."

"Why didn't you?" I asked her.

Magadis levelled her gaze at Doctor Grellet. Although she was still my prisoner, her poise was one of serene control and dominance. "Tell her what you found, Doctor."

"It was the auto-surgeon," Grellet said. "I mentioned that there were problems getting it to work properly. No one had expected that it would need to be used again, I think, and so they had taken no great pains to clear its executive memory of the earlier workflow."

"I don't understand," I said.

"The auto-surgeon had been programmed to perform an unusual surgical task, something far outside its normal repertoire. Magadis was brought out of reefersleep, but held beneath consciousness. She was put into the auto-surgeon. A coercive device was installed inside her."

"It was a military device," Magadis said, as detached as if she were recounting something that had happened to someone else entirely, long ago and far away. "An illegal relic of the first war. A Tharsis Lash, they called it. Designed to override our voluntary functions, and permit us to be interrogated and serve as counter-propaganda mouthpieces. While the device was installed in me, I had no volition. I could only do and say what was required of me."

"By Struma," I said, deciding that was the only answer that made any sense.

"He was obliged to act alone," Magadis answered, still with that same icy calm. "It was made to look like an attempted takeover of your ship, but no such thing was ever attempted. But we had to die, all of us. No knowledge of the object could be allowed to reach our mother nests."

"I removed the coercive device," Doctor Grellet said. "Of course, there was resistance from your loyal officers. But they were made to understand what had happened. Struma must have woken up first, then completed the work on Magadis. Struma then laid the evidence for an attempted takeover of the ship. More Conjoiners were brought out of reefersleep, and either killed on the spot or implanted with cruder versions of the coercive devices, so that they were seen to put up a convincing fight. The other officers were revived, and perceived that the ship was under imminent threat. In the heat of the emergency they had no reason to doubt Struma."

"Nor did I," I whispered.

"It was vital that the Conjoiners be eliminated. Their cooperation was required for the existence and operation of this ship, but they could not be party to the discovery and exploration of the object."

"What about the rest of us?" I asked. "We were all part of it. We'd have spoken, when we got back home."

"You would have accepted Struma's account of the Conjoiner takeover, as you very nearly did. As I did. But it was a mistake to put her under armed guard, and another mistake to allow me a close look at that auto-surgeon. I suppose we can't blame Struma for a few slips. He had enough to be concentrating on."

"You were worried about war," Magadis said evenly. "Now it may still happen. But the terms of provocation will be different. A faction inside one of your own planetary governments engineered this takeover bid." She held her silence for a few moments. "But I do not want war. Do you believe in clemency, Rauma Bernsdottir?"

"I hope so."

"Good." And Magadis stood from her chair, her bindings falling away where they had clearly never been properly fastened. She took a step nearer to me, and in a single whiplash motion brought her arm up to my chin. Her hand closed around my jaw. She held me with a vicelike force, squeezing so hard that I felt my bones would shatter. "I believe in clemency as well. But it takes two to make it work. You struck me, when you thought I was your prisoner."

I stumbled back, crashing against the useless grid of the electrostatic cage. "I'm sorry."

"Are you, Captain?"

"Yes." It was hard to speak, hard to think, with the pain she was inflicting. "I'm sorry. I shouldn't have hit you."

"In your defence," Magadis said, "you only did it the once. And although I was under the control of the device, I saw something in your eyes. Doubt. Shame." She relinquished her hold on me. I drew quick breaths, fully aware of how easily she could still break me. "I'm minded to think you regretted your impulse."

"I did."

"Good. Because someone has to live, and it may as well be you."

I reached up and nursed the skin around my jaw. "No. We're finished—all of us. All that's left is reefersleep. We'll die, but at least we'll be under when it happens."

"The ship can be saved," Magadis answered. "And a small number of its passengers. This will happen. Now that knowledge of the object has been gathered, it must reach civilisation. You will be the vector of that knowledge."

"The ship can't be saved. There just isn't time."

Magadis turned to Doctor Grellet. "Perhaps we should show her, Doctor. Then she would understand."

+ + +

They took me to one of the forward viewports. Since the ship was still aimed at the object all that was presently visible was a wall of darkness, stretching to the limit of vision in all directions. I stared into that nothingness, wondering if I might catch a glimpse of the Conjoiner wreck, now that we were so much closer. They had asked me very little of what happened to Struma, as if my safe return was answer enough.

Then something flashed. It was a brief, bright scintillation, there and gone almost before it had time to register on my retinas. Wondering if it might have been a trick of the imagination, I stayed at the port until I saw another of the flashes. A little later came a third. They were not happening in the same spot, but clustered near enough to each other not to be accidental.

"You saved us," Doctor Grellet said, speaking quietly, as if he might break some sacred spell. "Or at least, showed us the way. When you and Struma used the cargo launcher to accelerate your pods, there was an effect on the rest of the ship. A tiny but measurable recoil, reducing some of her speed."

"It's no help to us," I said, taking a certain bleak pleasure in pointing out the error in his thinking. "If we had a full cargo manifest, tens of thousands of tonnes, then maybe we could shoot enough of it ahead of the ship to reverse the drift. But we haven't. We're barely carrying any cargo at all."

Another flash twinkled against the surface.

"It's not cargo," Magadis said.

I suppose I understood even then. Some part of me, at least. But not the part that was willing to face the truth.

"What, then?"

"Caskets," Doctor Grellet said. "Reefersleep caskets. Each about as large and heavy as your inspection pod, each still containing a sleeping passenger."

"No." My answer was one of flat denial, even as I knew there was no reason for either of them to lie.

"There are uncertainties," Magadis said. "The launcher is under strain, and its efficiency may not remain optimal. But it seems likely that the ship can be saved with the loss of only half the passenger manifest." Some distant, alien sympathy glimmered in her eyes. "I understand that this is difficult for you, Rauma. But there is no other way to save the ship. Some must die, so that some must live. And you in particular must be one of the living."

The flashes continued. Now that I was attuned to their rhythm, I picked up an almost subliminal nudge in the fabric of the ship, happening at about the same frequency as the impacts. Each nudge was the cargo launcher firing another casket away, the ship's motion reducing by a tiny value. It produced a negligibly small effect. But put several thousand negligibly small things together and they can add up to something useful.

"I won't sanction this," I said. "Not for the sake of the ship. Not murder, not suicide, not self-sacrifice. Nothing's worth this."

"Everything is worth it," Magadis said. "Firstly, knowledge of the artefact—the object—must reach civilisation, and it must then be disseminated. It cannot remain the secretive preserve of one faction or arm of government. It must be universal knowledge. Perhaps there are more of these objects. If there are, they must be mapped and investigated, their natures probed. Secondly, you must speak of peace. If this ship were lost, if no trace of it were ever to return home, there would always be speculation. You must guard against that."

"But you..."

She carried on speaking. "They would accept your testimony more readily than mine. But do not think this is suicide, for any of us. It has been agreed, Rauma—by a quorum of the living, both baseline and Conjoiner. A larger subset of the sleeping passengers was brought to the edge of consciousness, so that they could be polled, their opinions weighed. I will not say that the verdict was unanimous... but it carried, and with a healthy majority. We each take our chances. The automated systems of the ship will continue ejecting caskets until the drift has been safely reversed, with a comfortable margin of error. Perhaps it will take ten thousand sleepers, or fifteen thousand. Until that point has been reached, the selection is entirely random. We return to reefersleep knowing only that we have a better than zero chance of surviving."

"It's enough," Doctor Grellet said. "As Magadis says, better that one of us survives than none of us."

"It would have suited Struma if you butchered us all," Magadis said. "But you didn't. And even when there was a hope that the repairs could be completed, you risked your life to investigate the wreck. The crew and passengers evaluated this action. They found it meritorious."

"Struma just wanted a good way to kill me."

"The decision was yours, not Struma's. And our decision is final." Magadis's tone was stern, but not without some bleak edge of compassion. "Doctor Grellet and I will return to reefersleep now. Our staying awake was only ever temporary, and we must also submit our lives to chance."

"No," I said again. "Stay with me. Not everyone has to die—you said it yourselves."

"We accepted our fate," Doctor Grellet said. "Now, Captain Bernsdottir, you must accept yours."

✦ ✦ ✦

And I did.

I believed that we had a better than even chance. I thought that if one of us survived, thousands more would also make it back. And that among those sleepers, once they were woken, would be witnesses willing to corroborate my version of events.

I was wrong.

The ship did repair itself, and I did make it back to Yellowstone. As I have mentioned, great pains were taken to protect me from the long exposure to reefersleep. When they brought me back to life, my complications were minimal. I remembered almost all of it from the first day.

But the others—the few thousand who were spared—they were not so fortunate. One by one they were brought out of hibernation, and one by one they were found to have suffered various deficits of memory and personality. The most lucid among them, those who had come through with the least damage, could not verify my account with the reliability demanded by public opinion. Some recalled being raised to minimal consciousness, polled as to the decision to sacrifice some of the passengers—a majority, as it turned out—but their recollections were vague and sometimes contradictory. Under other circumstances such things would have been put down to revival amnesia, and there would have been no blemish on my name. But this was different. How could I have survived, out of all of them?

You think I didn't argue my case? I tried. For years, I recounted exactly what had happened, sparing nothing. I turned to the ship's own records, defending their veracity. It was difficult, for Struma's family back on Fand. Word reached them eventually. I wept for what they had to bear, with the knowledge of his betrayal. The irony is that they never doubted my account, even as it burned them.

But that saying we had on Fand—the one I spoke of earlier. *Shame is a mask that becomes the face.* I mentioned its corollary, too—of how that mask can become so well-adapted to its wearer that it no longer feels ill-fitting or alien. Becomes, in fact, something to hide behind—a shield and a comfort.

I have come to be very comfortable with my shame.

True, it chafed against me, in the early days. I resisted it, resented the new and contorting shape it forced upon my life. But with time the mask became something I could endure. By turns I became less and less aware of its presence, and then one day I stopped noticing it was there at all. Either it had changed, or I had. Or perhaps we had both moved towards some odd accommodation, each accepting the other.

Whatever the case, to discard it now would feel like ripping away my own living flesh.

I know this surprises you—shocks you, even. That even with your clarity of mind, even with your clear recollection of being polled, even with your watertight corroboration, I would not jump at the chance for forgiveness. But you misjudge me if you think otherwise.

Look out at the city now.

Tower after tower, like the dust columns of stellar nurseries, receding into the haze of night, twinkling with a billion lights, a billion implicated lives.

The truth is, they don't deserve it. They put this on me. I spoke truthfully all those years ago, and my words steered us from the brink of a second war with the Conjoiners. A few who mattered—

those who had influence—they took my words at face value. But many more did not. I ask you this now: why should I offer them the solace of seeing me vindicated?

They can sleep with their guilt when I'm dead.

I hear your disbelief. Understand it, even. You've gone to this trouble, come to me with this generous, selfless intention—hoping to ease these final years with some shift in the public view of me. It's a kindness, and I thank you for it.

But there's another saying we used to have on Fand. You'll know it well, I think.

A late gift is worse than no gift at all.

Would you mind leaving me now?

Poul Anderson began his career in the Golden Age of science fiction, with famed editor John W. Campbell publishing his first story in 1947. His Time Patrol series of space operas are among the most famous contributions to our genre. "Duel on Syrtis" appeared in March 1951 in Planet Stories *and tells the tale of Riordan, a wealthy human who has hunted game on all the planets in the solar system, from Mercury to Pluto. He has come to Mars to bag the Martian owlie, a sentient being who is protected from hunters. However, the law is no more an obstacle to Riordan than the hostile environment through which he must move.*

DUEL ON SYRTIS
POUL ANDERSON

Bold and ruthless, he was famed throughout the System as a big-game hunter. From the firedrakes of Mercury to the ice-crawlers of Pluto, he'd slain them all. But his trophy-room lacked one item; and now Riordan swore he'd bag the forbidden game that roamed the red deserts… a Martian!

✦ ✦ ✦

The night whispered the message. Over the many miles of loneliness it was borne, carried on the wind, rustled by the half-sentient lichens and the dwarfed trees, murmured from one to another of the little creatures that huddled under crags, in caves, by shadowy dunes. In no words, but in a dim pulsing of dread which echoed through Kreega's brain, the warning ran—

They are hunting again.

Kreega shuddered in a sudden blast of wind. The night was enormous around him, above him, from the iron bitterness of the hills to the wheeling, glittering constellations light-years over his head. He reached out with his trembling perceptions, tuning himself to the brush and the wind and the small burrowing things underfoot, letting the night speak to him.

Alone, alone. There was not another Martian for a hundred miles of emptiness. There were only the tiny animals and the shivering brush and the thin, sad blowing of the wind.

The voiceless scream of dying traveled through the brush,

from plant to plant, echoed by the fear-pulses of the animals and the ringingly reflecting cliffs. They were curling, shriveling and blackening as the rocket poured the glowing death down on them, and the withering veins and nerves cried to the stars.

Kreega huddled against a tall gaunt crag. His eyes were like yellow moons in the darkness, cold with terror and hate and a slowly gathering resolution. Grimly, he estimated that the death was being sprayed in a circle some ten miles across. And he was trapped in it, and soon the hunter would come after him.

He looked up to the indifferent glitter of stars, and a shudder went along his body. Then he sat down and began to think.

+ + +

It had started a few days before, in the private office of the trader Wisby.

"I came to Mars," said Riordan, "to get me an owlie."

Wisby had learned the value of a poker face. He peered across the rim of his glass at the other man, estimating him.

Even in God-forsaken holes like Port Armstrong one had heard of Riordan. Heir to a million-dollar shipping firm which he himself had pyramided into a System-wide monster, he was equally well known as a big-game hunter. From the firedrakes of Mercury to the ice-crawlers of Pluto, he'd bagged them all. Except, of course, a Martian. That particular game was forbidden now.

He sprawled in his chair, big and strong and ruthless, still a young man. He dwarfed the unkempt room with his size and the hard-held dynamo strength in him, and his cold green gaze dominated the trader.

"It's illegal, you know," said Wisby. "It's a twenty-year sentence if you're caught at it."

"Bah! The Martian Commissioner is at Ares, halfway round the planet. If we go at it right, who's ever to know?" Riordan gulped at his drink. "I'm well aware that in another year or so they'll have tightened up enough to make it impossible. This is the last chance for any man to get an owlie. That's why I'm here."

Wisby hesitated, looking out the window. Port Armstrong was no more than a dusty huddle of domes, interconnected by tunnels, in a red waste of sand stretching to the near horizon. An Earthman in airsuit and transparent helmet was walking down the street and a couple of Martians were lounging against a wall. Otherwise nothing—a silent, deadly monotony brooding under the shrunken sun. Life on Mars was not especially pleasant for a human.

"You're not falling into this owlie-loving that's corrupted all Earth?" demanded Riordan contemptuously.

"Oh, no," said Wisby. "I keep them in their place around my post. But times are changing. It can't be helped."

"There was a time when they were slaves," said Riordan. "Now those old women on Earth want to give 'em the vote." He snorted.

"Well, times are changing," repeated Wisby mildly. "When the first humans landed on Mars a hundred years ago, Earth had just gone through the Hemispheric Wars. The worst wars man had ever known. They damned near wrecked the old ideas of liberty and equality. People were suspicious and tough—they'd had to be, to survive. They weren't able to—to empathize with the Martians, or whatever you call it. Not able to think of them as anything but intelligent animals. And Martians made such useful slaves—they need so little food or heat or oxygen, they can even live fifteen minutes or so without breathing at all. And the wild Martians made fine sport—intelligent game, that could get away as often as not, or even manage to kill the hunter."

"I know," said Riordan. "That's why I want to hunt one. It's no fun if the game doesn't have a chance."

"It's different now," went on Wisby. "Earth has been at peace for a long time. The liberals have gotten the upper hand. Naturally, one of their first reforms was to end Martian slavery."

Riordan swore. The forced repatriation of Martians working on his spaceships had cost him plenty. "I haven't time for your philosophizing," he said. "If you can arrange for me to get a Martian, I'll make it worth your while."

"How much worth it?" asked Wisby.

+ + +

They haggled for a while before settling on a figure. Riordan had brought guns and a small rocketboat, but Wisby would have to supply radioactive material, a "hawk," and a rockhound. Then he had to be paid for the risk of legal action, though that was small. The final price came high.

"Now, where do I get my Martian?" inquired Riordan. He gestured at the two in the street. "Catch one of them and release him in the desert?"

It was Wisby's turn to be contemptuous. "One of them? Hah! Town loungers! A city dweller from Earth would give you a better fight."

The Martians didn't look impressive. They stood only some four feet high on skinny, claw-footed legs, and the arms, ending in bony four-fingered hands, were stringy. The chests were broad and deep, but the waists were ridiculously narrow. They were viviparous, warm-blooded, and suckled their young, but gray feathers covered their hides. The round, hook-beaked heads, with huge amber eyes and tufted feather ears, showed the origin of the name "owlie." They wore only pouched belts and carried sheath knives; even the liberals of Earth weren't ready to allow the natives modern tools and weapons. There were too many old grudges.

"The Martians always were good fighters," said Riordan. "They wiped out quite a few Earth settlements in the old days."

"The wild ones," agreed Wisby. "But not these. They're just stupid laborers, as dependent on our civilization as we are. You want a real old-timer, and I know where one's to be found."

He spread a map on the desk. "See, here in the Hraefnian Hills, about a hundred miles from here. These Martians live a long time, maybe two centuries, and this fellow Kreega has been around since the first Earthmen came. He led a lot of Martian raids in the early days, but since the general amnesty and peace he's lived all alone up there, in one of the old ruined towers. A real old-time warrior who hates Earthmen's guts. He comes here once in a while with furs and minerals to trade, so I know a little about him." Wisby's eyes gleamed savagely. "You'll be doing us all a favor by shooting the arrogant bastard. He struts around here as if the place belonged to him. And he'll give you a run for your money."

Riordan's massive dark head nodded in satisfaction.

+ + +

The man had a bird and a rockhound. That was bad. Without them, Kreega could lose himself in the labyrinth of caves and canyons and scrubby thickets—but the hound could follow his scent and the bird could spot him from above.

To make matters worse, the man had landed near Kreega's tower. The weapons were all there—now he was cut off, unarmed and alone save for what feeble help the desert life could give. Unless he could double back to the place somehow—but meanwhile he had to survive.

He sat in a cave, looking down past a tortured wilderness of sand and bush and wind-carved rock, miles in the thin clear air to the glitter of metal where the rocket lay. The man was a tiny speck in the huge barren landscape, a lonely insect crawling under the deep-blue sky.

Even by day, the stars glistened in the tenuous atmosphere. Weak pallid sunlight spilled over rocks tawny and ocherous and rust-red, over the low dusty thorn-bushes and the gnarled little trees and the sand that blew faintly between them. Equatorial Mars!

Lonely or not, the man had a gun that could spang death clear to the horizon, and he had his beasts, and there would be a radio in the rocketboat for calling his fellows. And the glowing death ringed them in, a charmed circle which Kreega could not cross without bringing a worse death on himself than the rifle would give—

Or was there a worse death than that—to be shot by a monster and have his stuffed hide carried back as a trophy for fools to gape at? The old iron pride of his race rose in Kreega, hard and bitter and unrelenting. He didn't ask much of life these days—solitude in his tower to think the long thoughts of a Martian and create the small exquisite artworks which he loved; the company of his kind at the Gathering Season, grave ancient ceremony and acrid merriment and the chance to beget and rear sons; an occasional trip to the Earthling settling for the metal goods and the wine which were the only valuable things they had brought to Mars; a vague dream of raising his folk to a place where they could stand as equals before all the universe. No more. And now they would take even this from him!

He rasped a curse on the human and resumed his patient work, chipping a spearhead for what puny help it could give him. The brush rustled dryly in alarm, tiny hidden animals squeaked their terror, the desert shouted to him of the monster that strode toward his cave. But he didn't have to flee right away.

✦ ✦ ✦

Riordan sprayed the heavy-metal isotope in a ten-mile circle around the old tower. He did that by night, just in case patrol craft might be snooping around. But once he had landed, he was safe—he could always claim to be peacefully exploring, hunting leapers or some such thing.

The radioactive had a half-life of about four days, which meant that it would be unsafe to approach for some three weeks—two at the minimum. That was time enough, when the Martian was boxed in so small an area.

There was no danger that he would try to cross it. The owlies had learned what radioactivity meant, back when they fought the humans. And their vision, extending well into the ultra-violet, made it directly visible to them through its fluorescence—to say nothing of the wholly unhuman extra senses they had. No, Kreega would try to hide, and perhaps to fight, and eventually he'd be cornered.

Still, there was no use taking chances. Riordan set a timer on the boat's radio. If he didn't come back within two weeks to turn it off, it would emit a signal which Wisby would hear, and he'd be rescued.

He checked his other equipment. He had an airsuit designed for Martian conditions, with a small pump operated by a power-beam from the boat to compress the atmosphere sufficiently for him to breathe it. The same unit recovered enough water from his breath so that the weight of supplies for several days was, in Martian gravity, not too great for him to bear. He had a .45 rifle built to shoot in Martian air, that was heavy enough for his purposes. And, of course, compass and binoculars and sleeping bag. Pretty light equipment, but he preferred a minimum anyway.

For ultimate emergencies there was the little tank of suspensine. By turning a valve, he could release it into his air system. The gas didn't exactly induce suspended animation, but it paralyzed efferent nerves and slowed the overall metabolism to a point where a man could live for weeks on one lungful of air. It was useful in surgery, and had saved the life of more than one interplanetary explorer whose oxygen system went awry. But Riordan didn't expect to have to use it. He certainly hoped he wouldn't. It would be tedious to lie fully conscious for days waiting for the automatic signal to call Wisby.

He stepped out of the boat and locked it. No danger that the owlie would break in if he should double back; it would take tordenite to crack that hull.

He whistled to his animals. They were native beasts, long ago domesticated by the Martians and later by man. The rockhound was like a gaunt wolf, but huge-breasted and feathered, a tracker as good as any Terrestrial bloodhound. The "hawk" had less resemblance to its counterpart of Earth: it was a bird of prey, but in the tenuous atmosphere it needed a six-foot wingspread to lift its small body.

Riordan was pleased with their training.

The hound bayed, a low quavering note which would have been muffled almost to inaudibility by the thin air and the man's plastic helmet had the suit not included microphones and amplifiers. It circled, sniffing, while the hawk rose into the alien sky.

Riordan did not look closely at the tower. It was a crumbling stump atop a rusty hill, unhuman and grotesque. Once, perhaps ten thousand years ago, the Martians had had a civilization of sorts, cities and agriculture and a neolithic technology. But according to their own traditions they had achieved a union or symbiosis with the wildlife of the planet and had abandoned such mechanical aids as unnecessary.

Riordan snorted.

The hound bayed again. The noise seemed to hang eerily in the still, cold air; to shiver from cliff and crag and die reluctantly under the enormous silence. But it was a bugle call, a haughty challenge to a world grown old—stand aside, make way, here comes the conqueror!

The animal suddenly loped forward. He had a scent. Riordan swung into a long, easy low-gravity stride. His eyes gleamed like green ice. The hunt was begun!

✦ ✦ ✦

Breath sobbed in Kreega's lungs, hard and quick and raw. His legs felt weak and heavy, and the thudding of his heart seemed to shake his whole body.

Still he ran, while the frightful clamor rose behind him and the padding of feet grew ever nearer. Leaping, twisting, bounding from crag to crag, sliding down shaly ravines and slipping through clumps of trees, Kreega fled.

The hound was behind him and the hawk soaring overhead. In a day and a night they had driven him to this, running like a crazed leaper with death baying at his heels—he had not imagined a human could move so fast or with such endurance.

The desert fought for him; the plants with their queer blind life that no Earthling would ever understand were on his side. Their thorny branches twisted away as he darted through and then came back to rake the flanks of the hound, slow him—but they could not stop his brutal rush. He ripped past their strengthless clutching fingers and yammered on the trail of the Martian.

The human was toiling a good mile behind, but showed no sign of tiring. Still Kreega ran. He had to reach the cliff edge before the hunter saw him through his rifle sights—had to, had to, and the hound was snarling a yard behind now.

Up the long slope he went. The hawk fluttered, striking at him, seeking to lay beak and talons in his head. He batted at the creature with his spear and dodged around a tree. The tree snaked out a branch from which the hound rebounded, yelling till the rocks rang.

The Martian burst onto the edge of the cliff. It fell sheer to the canyon floor, five hundred feet of iron-streaked rock tumbling into windy depths. Beyond, the lowering sun glared in his eyes. He paused only an instant, etched black against the sky, a perfect shot if the human should come into view, and then he sprang over the edge.

He had hoped the rockhound would go shooting past, but the animal braked itself barely in time. Kreega went down the cliff face, clawing into every tiny crevice, shuddering as the age-worn rock crumbled under his fingers. The hawk swept close, hacking at him and screaming for its master. He couldn't fight it, not with every finger and toe needed to hang against shattering death, but—

He slid along the face of the precipice into a gray-green clump of vines, and his nerves thrilled forth the appeal of the ancient symbiosis. The hawk swooped again and he lay unmoving, rigid as if dead, until it cried in shrill triumph and settled on his shoulder to pluck out his eyes.

Then the vines stirred. They weren't strong, but their thorns sank into the flesh and it couldn't pull loose. Kreega toiled on down into the canyon while the vines pulled the hawk apart.

Riordan loomed hugely against the darkening sky. He fired, once, twice, the bullets humming wickedly close, but as shadows swept up from the depths the Martian was covered.

The man turned up his speech amplifier and his voice rolled and boomed monstrously through the gathering night, thunder such as dry Mars had not heard for millennia: "Score one for you! But it isn't enough! I'll find you!"

The sun slipped below the horizon and night came down like a falling curtain. Through the darkness Kreega heard the man laughing. The old rocks trembled with his laughter.

+ + +

Riordan was tired with the long chase and the niggling insufficiency of his oxygen supply. He wanted a smoke and hot food, and neither was to be had. Oh, well, he'd appreciate the luxuries of life all the more when he got home—with the Martian's skin.

He grinned as he made camp. The little fellow was a worthwhile quarry, that was for damn sure. He'd held out for two days now, in a little ten-mile circle of ground, and he'd even killed the hawk. But Riordan was close enough to him now so that the hound could follow his spoor, for Mars had no watercourses to break a trail. So it didn't matter.

He lay watching the splendid night of stars. It would get cold before long, unmercifully cold, but his sleeping bag was a good-enough insulator to keep him warm with the help of solar energy stored during the day by its Gergen cells. Mars was dark at night, its moons of little help—Phobos a hurtling speck, Deimos merely a bright star. Dark and cold and empty. The rockhound had burrowed into the loose sand nearby, but it would raise the alarm if the Martian should come sneaking near the camp. Not that that was likely—he'd have to find shelter somewhere too, if he didn't want to freeze.

The bushes and the trees and the little furtive animals whispered a word he could not hear, chattered and gossiped on the wind about the Martian who kept himself warm with work. But he didn't understand that language which was no language.

Drowsily, Riordan thought of past hunts. The big game of Earth, lion and tiger and elephant and buffalo and sheep on the high sun-blazing peaks of the Rockies. Rainforests of Venus and the coughing roar of a many-legged swamp monster crashing through the trees to the place where he stood waiting. Primitive throb of drums in a hot wet night, chant of beaters dancing around a fire—scramble along the hell-plains of Mercury with a swollen sun licking against his puny insulating suit—the grandeur and desolation of Neptune's liquid-gas swamps and the huge blind thing that screamed and blundered after him—

But this was the loneliest and strangest and perhaps most dangerous hunt of all, and on that account the best. He had no malice toward the Martian; he respected the little being's courage as he respected the bravery of the other animals he had fought. Whatever trophy he brought home from this chase would be well earned.

The fact that his success would have to be treated discreetly didn't matter. He hunted less for the glory of it—though he had to admit he didn't mind the publicity—than for love. His ancestors had fought under one name or another—Viking, Crusader, mercenary, rebel, patriot, whatever was fashionable at the moment. Struggle was in his blood, and in these degenerate days there was little to struggle against save what he hunted.

Well—tomorrow—he drifted off to sleep.

✦ ✦ ✦

He woke in the short gray dawn, made a quick breakfast, and whistled his hound to heel. His nostrils dilated with excitement, a high keen drunkenness that sang wonderfully within him. Today—maybe today!

They had to take a roundabout way down into the canyon and the hound cast about for an hour before he picked up the scent. Then the deep-voiced cry rose again and they were off—more slowly now, for it was a cruel stony trail.

The sun climbed high as they worked along the ancient river-bed. Its pale chill light washed needle-sharp crags and fantastically painted cliffs, shale and sand and the wreck of geological ages. The low harsh brush crunched under the man's feet, writhing and crackling its impotent protest. Otherwise it was still, a deep and taut and somehow waiting stillness.

The hound shattered the quiet with an eager yelp and plunged forward. Hot scent! Riordan dashed after him, trampling through dense bush, panting and swearing and grinning with excitement.

Suddenly the brush opened underfoot. With a howl of dismay, the hound slid down the sloping wall of the pit it had covered. Riordan flung himself forward with tigerish swiftness, flat down on his belly with one hand barely catching the animal's tail. The shock almost pulled him into the hole too. He wrapped one arm around a bush that clawed at his helmet and pulled the hound back.

Shaking, he peered into the trap. It had been well made—about twenty feet deep, with walls as straight and narrow as the sand would allow, and skillfully covered with brush. Planted in the bottom were three wicked-looking flint spears. Had he been a shade less quick in his reactions, he would have lost the hound and perhaps himself.

He skinned his teeth in a wolf-grin and looked around. The owlie must have worked all night on it. Then he couldn't be far away—and he'd be very tired—

As if to answer his thoughts, a boulder crashed down from the nearer cliff wall. It was a monster, but a falling object on Mars has less than half the acceleration it does on Earth. Riordan scrambled aside as it boomed onto the place where he had been lying.

"Come on!" he yelled, and plunged toward the cliff.

For an instant a gray form loomed over the edge, hurled a spear at him. Riordan snapped a shot at it, and it vanished. The spear glanced off the tough fabric of his suit and he scrambled up a narrow ledge to the top of the precipice.

The Martian was nowhere in sight, but a faint red trail led into the rugged hill country. *Winged him, by God!* The hound was slower in negotiating the shale-covered trail; his own feet were bleeding when he came up. Riordan cursed him and they set out again.

They followed the trail for a mile or two and then it ended. Riordan looked around the wilderness of trees and needles which blocked view in any direction. Obviously the owlie had backtracked and climbed up one of those rocks, from which he could take a flying leap to some other point. But which one?

Sweat which he couldn't wipe off ran down the man's face and body. He itched intolerably, and his lungs were raw from gasping at his dole of air. But still he laughed in gusty delight. What a chase! What a chase!

✦ ✦ ✦

Kreega lay in the shadow of a tall rock and shuddered with weariness. Beyond the shade, the sunlight danced in what to him was a blinding, intolerable dazzle, hot and cruel and life-hungry, hard and bright as the metal of the conquerors.

It had been a mistake to spend priceless hours when he might have been resting working on that trap. It hadn't worked, and he might have known that it wouldn't. And now he was hungry, and thirst was like a wild beast in his mouth and throat, and still they followed him.

They weren't far behind now. All this day they had been dogging him; he had never been more than half an hour ahead. No rest, no rest, a devil's hunt through a tormented wilderness of stone and sand, and now he could only wait for the battle with an iron burden of exhaustion laid on him.

The wound in his side burned. It wasn't deep, but it had cost him blood and pain and the few minutes of catnapping he might have snatched.

For a moment, the warrior Kreega was gone and a lonely, frightened infant sobbed in the desert silence. *Why can't they let me alone?*

A low, dusty-green bush rustled. A sandrunner piped in one of the ravines. They were getting close.

Wearily, Kreega scrambled up on top of the rock and crouched low. He had backtracked to it; they should by rights go past him toward his tower.

He could see it from here, a low yellow ruin worn by the winds of millennia. There had only been time to dart in, snatch a bow and a few arrows and an axe. Pitiful weapons—the arrows could not penetrate the Earthman's suit when there was only a Martian's thin grasp to draw the bow, and even with a steel head the axe was a small and feeble thing. But it was all he had, he and his few little allies of a desert which fought only to keep its solitude.

Repatriated slaves had told him of the Earthlings' power. Their roaring machines filled the silence of their own deserts, gouged the quiet face of their own moon, shook the planets with a senseless fury of meaningless energy. They were the conquerors, and it never occurred to them that an ancient peace and stillness could be worth preserving.

Well—he fitted an arrow to the string and crouched in the silent, flimmering sunlight, waiting.

The hound came first, yelping and howling. Kreega drew the bow as far as he could. But the human had to come near first—

There he came, running and bounding over the rocks, rifle in hand and restless eyes shining with taut green light, closing in for the death.

Kreega swung softly around. The beast was beyond the rock now, the Earthman almost below it.

The bow twanged. With a savage thrill, Kreega saw the arrow go through the hound, saw the creature leap in the air and then roll over and over, howling and biting at the thing in its breast.

Like a gray thunderbolt, the Martian launched himself off the rock, down at the human. If his axe could shatter that helmet—

He struck the man and they went down together. Wildly, the Martian hewed. The axe glanced off the plastic—he hadn't had room for a swing. Riordan roared and lashed out with a fist. Retching, Kreega rolled backward.

Riordan snapped a shot at him. Kreega turned and fled. The

man got to one knee, sighting carefully on the gray form that streaked up the nearest slope.

A little sandsnake darted up the man's leg and wrapped about his wrist. Its small strength was just enough to pull the gun aside. The bullet screamed past Kreega's ear as he vanished into a cleft.

He felt the thin death-agony of the snake as the man pulled it loose and crushed it underfoot. Somewhat later, he heard a dull boom echoing between the hills. The man had gotten explosives from his boat and blown up the tower.

He had lost axe and bow. Now he was utterly weaponless, without even a place to retire for a last stand. And the hunter would not give up. Even without his animals, he would follow, more slowly but as relentlessly as before.

Kreega collapsed on a shelf of rock. Dry sobbing racked his thin body, and the sunset wind cried with him.

Presently he looked up, across a red and yellow immensity to the low sun. Long shadows were creeping over the land, peace and stillness for a brief moment before the iron cold of night closed down. Somewhere the soft trill of a sandrunner echoed between low wind-worn cliffs, and the brush began to speak, whispering back and forth in its ancient wordless tongue.

The desert, the planet and its wind and sand under the high cold stars, the clean open land of silence and loneliness and a destiny which was not man's, spoke to him. The enormous oneness of life on Mars, drawn together against the cruel environment, stirred in his blood. As the sun went down and the stars blossomed forth in awesome frosty glory, Kreega began to think again.

He did not hate his persecutor, but the grimness of Mars was in him. He fought the war of all which was old and primitive and lost in its own dreams against the alien and the desecrator. It was as ancient and pitiless as life, that war, and each battle won or lost meant something even if no one ever heard of it.

You do not fight alone, whispered the desert. *You fight for all Mars, and we are with you.*

Something moved in the darkness, a tiny warm form running across his hand, a little feathered mouse-like thing that burrowed under the sand and lived its small fugitive life and was glad in its own way of living. But it was a part of a world, and Mars has no pity in its voice.

Still, a tenderness was within Kreega's heart, and he whispered gently in the language that was not a language, *You will do this for us? You will do it, little brother?*

+ + +

Riordan was too tired to sleep well. He had lain awake for a long time, thinking, and that is not good for a man alone in the Martian hills.

So now the rockhound was dead too. It didn't matter, the owlie wouldn't escape. But somehow the incident brought home to him the immensity and the age and the loneliness of the desert.

It whispered to him. The brush rustled and something wailed in darkness and the wind blew with a wild mournful sound over faintly starlit cliffs, and it was as if they all somehow had a voice, as if the whole world muttered and threatened him in the night. Dimly, he wondered if man would ever subdue Mars, if the human race had not finally run across something bigger than itself.

But that was nonsense. Mars was old and worn-out and barren, dreaming itself into slow death. The tramp of human feet, shouts of men and roar of sky-storming rockets, were waking it, but to a new destiny, to man's. When Ares lifted its hard spires above the hills of Syrtis, where then were the ancient gods of Mars?

It was cold, and the cold deepened as the night wore on. The stars were fire and ice, glittering diamonds in the deep crystal dark. Now and then he could hear a faint snapping borne through the earth as rock or tree split open. The wind laid itself to rest, sound froze to death, there was only the hard clear starlight falling through space to shatter on the ground.

Once something stirred. He woke from a restless sleep and saw a small thing skittering toward him. He groped for the rifle beside his sleeping bag, then laughed harshly. It was only a sandmouse. But it proved that the Martian had no chance of sneaking up on him while he rested.

He didn't laugh again. The sound had echoed too hollowly in his helmet.

With the clear bitter dawn he was up. He wanted to get the hunt over with. He was dirty and unshaven inside the unit, sick of iron rations pushed through the airlock, stiff and sore with exertion. Lacking the hound, which he'd had to shoot, tracking would be slow, but he didn't want to go back to Port Armstrong for another. No, hell take that Martian, he'd have the devil's skin soon!

Breakfast and a little moving made him feel better. He looked with a practiced eye for the Martian's trail. There was sand and brush over everything, even the rocks had a thin coating of their own erosion. The owlie couldn't cover his tracks perfectly—if he tried, it would slow him too much. Riordan fell into a steady jog.

Noon found him on higher ground, rough hills with gaunt needles of rock reaching yards into the sky. He kept going, confident of his own ability to wear down the quarry. He'd run deer to earth back home, day after day until the animal's heart broke and it waited quivering for him to come.

The trail looked clear and fresh now. He tensed with the knowledge that the Martian couldn't be far away.

Too clear! Could this be bait for another trap? He hefted the rifle and proceeded more warily. But no, there wouldn't have been time—

He mounted a high ridge and looked over the grim, fantastic landscape. Near the horizon he saw a blackened strip, the border of his radioactive barrier. The Martian couldn't go further, and if he doubled back Riordan would have an excellent chance of spotting him.

He turned up his speaker and let his voice roar into the stillness: "Come out, owlie! I'm going to get you, you might as well come out now and be done with it!"

The echoes took it up, flying back and forth between the naked crags, trembling and shivering under the brassy arch of sky. *Come out, come out, come out—*

The Martian seemed to appear from thin air, a gray ghost rising out of the jumbled stones and standing poised not twenty feet away. For an instant, the shock of it was too much; Riordan gaped in disbelief.

Kreega waited, quivering ever so faintly as if he were a mirage.

Then the man shouted and lifted his rifle. Still the Martian stood there as if carved in gray stone, and with a shock of disappointment Riordan thought that he had, after all, decided to give himself to an inevitable death.

Well, it had been a good hunt. "So long," whispered Riordan, and squeezed the trigger.

Since the sandmouse had crawled into the barrel, the gun exploded.

✦ ✦ ✦

Riordan heard the roar and saw the barrel peel open like a rotten banana. He wasn't hurt, but as he staggered back from the shock Kreega lunged at him.

The Martian was four feet tall, and skinny and weaponless, but he hit the Earthling like a small tornado. His legs wrapped around the man's waist and his hands got to work on the airhose.

Riordan went down under the impact. He snarled, tigerishly, and fastened his hands on the Martian's narrow throat. Kreega snapped futilely at him with his beak. They rolled over in a cloud of dust.

The brush began to chatter excitedly.

Riordan tried to break Kreega's neck—the Martian twisted away, bored in again.

With a shock of horror, the man heard the hiss of escaping air as Kreega's beak and fingers finally worried the airhose loose. An automatic valve clamped shut, but there was no connection with the pump now—

Riordan cursed, and got his hands about the Martian's throat again. Then he simply lay there, squeezing, and not all Kreega's writhing and twistings could break that grip.

Riordan smiled sleepily and held his hands in place. After five minutes or so Kreega was still. Riordan kept right on throttling him for another five minutes, just to make sure. Then he let go and fumbled at his back, trying to reach the pump.

The air in his suit was hot and foul. He couldn't quite reach around to connect the hose to the pump—

Poor design, he thought vaguely. *But then, these airsuits weren't meant for battle armor.*

He looked at the slight, silent form of the Martian. A faint breeze ruffled the gray feathers. What a fighter the little guy had been! He'd be the pride of the trophy room, back on Earth.

Let's see now— He unrolled his sleeping bag and spread it carefully out. He'd never make it to the rocket with what air he had, so it was necessary to let the suspensine into his suit. But he'd have to get inside the bag, lest the nights freeze his blood solid.

He crawled in, fastening the flaps carefully, and opened the valve on the suspensine tank. Lucky he had it—but then, a good hunter thinks of everything. He'd get awfully bored, lying here till Wisby caught the signal in ten days or so and came to find him, but he'd last. It would be an experience to remember. In this dry air, the Martian's skin would keep perfectly well.

He felt the paralysis creep up on him, the waning of heartbeat and lung action. His senses and mind were still alive, and he grew aware that complete relaxation has its unpleasant aspects. Oh, well— he'd won. He'd killed the wiliest game with his own hands.

Presently Kreega sat up. He felt himself gingerly. There seemed to be a rib broken—well, that could be fixed. He was still alive. He'd been choked for a good ten minutes, but a Martian can last fifteen without air.

He opened the sleeping bag and got Riordan's keys. Then he limped slowly back to the rocket. A day or two of experimentation taught him how to fly it. He'd go to his kinsmen near Syrtis. Now that they had an Earthly machine, and Earthly weapons to copy—

But there was other business first. He didn't hate Riordan, but Mars is a hard world. He went back and dragged the Earthling into a cave and hid him beyond all possibility of human search parties finding him.

For a while he looked into the man's eyes. Horror stared dumbly back at him. He spoke slowly, in halting English: "For those you killed, and for being a stranger on a world that does not want you, and against the day when Mars is free, I leave you."

Before departing, he got several oxygen tanks from the boat and hooked them into the man's air supply. That was quite a bit of air for one in suspended animation. Enough to keep him alive for a thousand years.

A.C. Crispin's StarBridge saga for young adult readers is a series of novels and stories that was ahead of its time. From progressive roles for women to its views of crosscultural interaction with alien species, sexuality, and more, StarBridge has been cited as an influence by many writers who followed, Seanan McGuire among them. This next story was part novel excerpt, part new material written for me by Crispin as a standalone for my 2013 anthology Raygun Chronicles: Space Opera For A New Age. *It turned out to be the last words Crispin ever wrote as she died of cancer before the book was released. To me, it remains one of my favorite first contact stories, and an example of a brilliant, ahead of its time space opera series by a leading space opera author who wrote everything from originals to Star Trek and Star Wars novels and more, and who was taken from us too soon.*

TWILIGHT WORLD

A.C. CRISPIN

Mahree Burroughs crouched on the ill-fitting seat designed for non-human crew members, her eyes never leaving the chrono that was counting down how long she had to live.

Despite her studies, she couldn't yet read the Simiu written language fluently, but numbers were easy. The chrono was silent as the numbers counted down the alien time-units. Mahree did a rough computation in her head and realized that they had just a little under a Terran day to live. About twenty-three hours until the three inhabitants of the little courier ship they'd dubbed *Rosinante* used up the last of the oxygen in the ship's air supply. Less than a day's worth of breathable air. She fought back panic, twisting her long, dark braid in her hands until it hurt, then forcing herself to breathe slowly through her nose, then out through her mouth.

Breathing was such a simple, basic act, she thought. People hardly ever even thought about it. *Until the air runs out.* Then the need for air, just simple air, overwhelmed everything. In a day, the two humans and one Simiu aboard *Rosinante* would be dead. Mahree Burroughs, her Simiu friend Dhurrrkk', and Rob Gable, the ship's physician from the trading vessel *Désirée*… all of them, dead. Unless, of course the alarm they'd rigged on the ship's sensors sounded, alerting them that they'd found a world with a breathable oxygen atmosphere.

Some rescue mission, Mahree thought bitterly. *Here we are, trying to bring about a peaceful solution between our peoples, only to die out here when our air runs out.*

Sixteen-year-old Mahree and her young Simiu friend, Dhurrrkk', out of all the human crew of the trading ship *Désirée* and the Simiu world of Hurrreeah, were the only two of their respective species who had learned to actually speak each other's language. The trading ship crew and the authorities of Hurrreeah had relied on computer translations to communicate—translations that had led to a tragic misunderstanding between the two peoples. Now the two species stood poised on the brink of violence, possibly outright war.

Mahree and Dhurrrkk' had decided that they couldn't let that happen. Dhurrrkk' had confided in Mahree that there was an interstellar organization of all the Known Worlds that might be able to help. The headquarters of the Cooperative League of Systems was located on a giant space station near the bright star Mizar. Dhurrrkk' was a pilot. Together, they'd stolen this ship, and set off for Shassiszss. Only one thing had gone wrong with their escape. Rob Gable had come upon them just as they were about to leave, and Mahree had to bring him along—at gunpoint.

Yeah, not only do I get myself and Dhurrrkk' killed on this escapade, she thought, *I've condemned Rob to die, too.*

The alien numbers continued to count down, measuring out the Simiu equivalent of seconds, minutes, and hours.

Mahree tried not to think about what it would be like at the end. Gasping for oxygen, lungs straining, eyes bulging, their faces suffusing with blood as their O2-starved tissues died. Would it hurt before they passed out? Would they feel as though they were strangling, or being choked? Or would the three of them just quietly pass out? Who would go first?

Death by asphyxiation didn't sound very appealing. *And all we were trying to do was help... who could have anticipated that human effluvia and exhalations would kill the oxygen-producing plants in the hydroponics lab?*

At first, everything had gone well. Once Mahree and Dhurrrkk' had explained their mission, Rob had thrown himself into the rescue effort, and the two humans had spent days growing accustomed to eating Simiu food, living under the slightly heavier Simiu gravity, sleeping on Simiu bedding, and, most challenging of all, utilizing Simiu plumbing. But then, about ten days out from Hurrreeah, Dhurrrkk' had come to them, visibly upset. His usually bright violet eyes were dimmed, his forehead crest of fur drooped, and his mane was ragged, as if he'd been clawing at it with his long, tough nails. "There is trouble, my friends," he said, in his harshly accented English. "An emergency in the hydroponics lab. Come see for yourselves."

Rob and Mahree had scrambled up from the Simiu sleeping pads, and followed their four-footed friend into the bowels of the little courier ship. One glance at the plants in the hydroponics lab had shown them sickly, drooping vegetation, obviously dying. Nearly all of the species were affected. "I have checked everything repeatedly," Dhurrrkk' told them, sitting back on his haunches rather like a Terran baboon. "Nothing has changed in the ship's environment except for your presence. The plant life is dying because it has been exposed to human exhalations and effluvia. At this rate we will not have sufficient oxygen in our air to reach Shassiszss."

The three of them had stared at each other in shock. At first, Mahree had thought it must be some kind of nightmare, but the danger was real, and there seemed to be no solution.

The chrono continued its inexorable countdown.

"Mahree," came a human voice from behind her. Mahree started, then turned to see Rob Gable, short and dark-haired, his good-looking features lined with concern. "Are you still staring at that thing? Come and get some sleep. You'll use less air that way, and staring at that chrono would drive anyone round the bend."

"I don't want to waste my last day sleeping," she protested.

"I can't think of a better strategy," he pointed out. "Maybe you'll have good dreams."

"I doubt it. Last time I slept I had nightmares."

"Well, give it a try. It really will help to conserve our remaining air."

She frowned, but let herself be persuaded. She *was* tired... her eyes were heavy and sore. Following Rob into the cabin they'd converted for human use, she lay down beside him, taking some comfort in his nearness. Her heavy eyes gradually closed and her breathing became regular...

+ + +

Dhurrrkk' wailed, clutching his chest as it heaved, seeking air—but there was none. Mahree's face was contorted and purple as she, too, shrilled a high, keening scream. Both of them tumbled to the deck, thrashing convulsively, their mouths opening and closing, emitting that never-ending shrieking wail—

Rob jerked awake, carrying that last hideous dream-image before his eyes so vividly that it took him a moment to realize that it was, indeed, only a nightmare. And still the wailing shrilled that insistent, nerve-wracking shriek of—*of Dhurrrkk's alarm!*

Rob sat up, eyes wide. "Whatthe*hell*?"

Mahree was staring at him, eyes wide with incredulous hope.

Minutes later, the alarm silenced, the three travelers stared dubiously at the data on the screens. Mahree was able to translate the information for Rob, whose frown deepened as she continued. "That rinky-dink little thing?" he exclaimed, eyeing the red dwarf occupying the middle of *Rosinante's* main viewscreen. "Good grief, it's only 170,000 kilometers in diameter—barely bigger than Jupiter!"

"It's the only system we've found," Mahree reminded him, "so be nice."

Dhurrrkk' nodded. "It is indeed very small," he admitted.

Mahree translated from the screen data. "It's got two planets— one a frozen hunk not even big enough to be spherical, the other about six-tenths the size of Earth. That's the one with the atmosphere. It orbits the star at a distance of about four million kilometers, and it's tidally locked, so it always keeps the same face toward its sun. Its year is a whopping four and a half days."

"But there are definite readings of oxygen in its atmosphere," Dhurrrkk' pointed out. "Not as high oxygen content as we could have wished, perhaps, but at this point, we have no alternative. We will need to find and harvest whatever plants are emitting that oxygen."

Mahree nodded. "Let's set her down, then go find us some air."

+ + +

Mahree stood in the control room hatch, wearing her spacesuit, her helmet tucked under her arm. She listened intently as Rob and Dhurrrkk' completed the atmospheric analysis of the chill little worldlet where *Rosinante* now rested.

"That's all very well and good," she broke in, interrupting their jargon-laden exchange impatiently after a few minutes, "but what's the bottom line? Can we *breathe* out there?"

Rob scowled at his link, considering. "Doubtful," he concluded. "At least, not for more than a minute or so. Nothing in the air can *hurt* us to breathe it, but the overall oxy level is like being on top of a high mountain, Earthside. The slightest exertion, and we'd pass out in short order."

"Could we breathe it while we're resting? Sit down and take off our helmets to conserve our breathing packs?"

"*You* might—and I stress *might*—be able to, for a short time, because you were raised on Jolie, which has a lower oxygen content than Earth or Hurrreeah, but I wouldn't risk either Dhurrrkk' or me trying it."

Mahree bit her lip. "What about the plants?" she said.

Rob shook his head, obviously bewildered. "I just don't know," he said. "It's an extremely peculiar situation out there. Certain locations have significantly higher concentrations of O2 than others—but there's no consistent correlation between those oxy concentrations and the patches we identified as vegetation during our low-level sweep. Sometimes they coincide, sometimes they don't. We're not too far from one of the higher concentrations of oxygen, so we'll just have to take a look."

"How can there be higher concentrations of oxygen? Doesn't the gas dissipate into the atmosphere?"

"Sure—some. But this place has fixed tides, hardly any weather. The temperature is a constant four degrees, just above freezing, and that doesn't vary, because there's no night. So there's no wind to move the atmosphere around. And oxygen is a comparatively heavy gas, so that when it's emitted under these circumstances, it tends to stay in one place, at least for a while." He glanced at his watch. "We'd better get going. Air's awasting."

Within minutes, the three explorers were ready. The doctor carried a sensing device to help them locate and analyze the local vegetation in their search for the oxygen concentrations.

"The gravity is low," he warned Mahree as Dhurrrkk' began cycling the air out of the airlock into storage, where it could be reused. "About half a gee. Be careful."

"Does Dhurrrkk' know that?" she asked. The two humans could talk to each other, but there had been no time to adjust their suit radios to the Simiu wavelength. They could communicate sketchily by touching helmets and shouting, but that form of conversation had obvious limits.

"Yeah, he knows."

The outer doors split apart, then opened wide. Mahree stepped cautiously down the ramp, watching her footing, because the ramp was steep, and her feet had an alarming tendency to slip in the low gravity—gravity which felt doubly light, because she'd spent days now living at one and a half gee.

Finally she was standing safely on solid ground, free to look around. Mahree caught her breath with excitement, thrilled despite their desperate situation to actually be standing on an alien world. *I'm the first human to ever tread here,* she realized. *One giant step, and all that stuff.*

Slowly, searching for any patches of the vegetation that had so puzzled Rob, she rotated 360 degrees, staring avidly.

It was a bleak vista that met her eyes—cold, yet washed everywhere with a hellish scarlet illumination from the red dwarf overhead. The ground beneath her feet was hard, black-brown rock, with a thin, damp layer of dark grayish-brown soil overlaying it. A dank red mist lay close along the ground, pooling deeper in any depressions. Mahree could see for a long way in most directions, because the ground, though rock-strewn and broken, was relatively flat.

She lifted her face to the sun, and her faceplate's polarizing ability automatically cut in—but the protection was hardly necessary. The light level was dim, about that of a cloudy twilight. *Dhurrrkk"'s going to be nearly blind,* she realized, and said as much to Rob.

"We'll have to keep him right with us," he agreed. "Will you *look* at that sun!"

"I'm looking," she said, awed. "It doesn't look small from here, does it?"

Overhead, the unnamed red dwarf dominated the cloudless sky, appearing five times the diameter of Sol or Jolie's sun. As it flamed dully in the deep purply red sky, it appeared almost close enough to touch; Mahree and Rob could clearly make out solar prominences lashing outward from its disk.

"It probably flares every so often," Mahree said, remembering one of Professor Morrissey's astronomy lectures. "Let's hope it doesn't decide to belch out a heavy concentration of X-rays while we're here."

"Let's hope it doesn't," Rob agreed fervently.

After a minute, Dhurrrkk' touched her arm, and Mahree came out of her reverie with a start. "We'd better go," she said. "We can't waste air just standing here gawking."

The three set off across the rocky ground, Rob in the lead, Dhurrrkk' and Mahree close behind him. Once the girl caught the toe of her boot on one of the multitudes of small, jagged outcrops and stumbled badly, but her fall was slow enough that she was able to catch herself on her hands.

"*Easy*," Rob said, pulling her up one-handed in the light gravity. "One of these volcanic ridges could rip your suit. You okay?"

"Fine," she said, trying not to gasp with reaction to her near disaster. "You'd think walking in gravity this low would be easy, but it's not; the ground's so broken."

The explorers halted when they reached the little lake they'd charted during the flyby. Crimson mist obscured its surface, reflecting the light of the red sun.

"How deep is that water? Any vegetation down there?" Mahree asked Rob, stepping cautiously onto the dark rocks of the "shore."

He examined his scanning device. "Not very deep. About two meters in the middle. And yes, there's plant life down there."

"Is it giving off oxygen?"

"Yes, but we can't use these plants, because the Simiu hydroponics lab, unlike *Désirée*'s, is set up for land-based vegetation. The tanks are way too shallow. Not to mention that I can't envision any way of hauling enough of this water aboard to support a significant amount of plant life. Even at one-half gee, water's *heavy*."

They walked on, frequently having to detour around patches of the mist that were thick enough to obscure their footing, and skirting an occasional head-high upthrust of the black rock.

Finally, they reached the closest large patch of vegetation. The alien plants filled an entire shallow "basin" in the rocky surface, and were clumped together so closely they resembled thick moss. Each plant stood only a few centimeters above the soil that nourished its roots. The moss-plants were a dull, dark green in color, with tiny, fleshy-thick "leaves."

His boots hidden by a knee-high patch of mist, Rob bent over to carefully scan the plants. After a moment, he shook his head. "No O2?" Mahree asked numbly.

"Some, but not enough. These plants photosynthesize, but… he trailed off, then burst out, "they *can't* be the source of those higher O2 levels I was reading!"

"How many of these moss-plants would we need to keep us going?"

"Half an acre of them," Rob said disgustedly. "Forget it."

Dhurrrkk' tugged on Mahree's arm, and she leaned over to touch helmets. After conveying the bad news, she straightened. "Okay, where's that higher O2 concentration you mentioned, Rob?"

He consulted the instrument and pointed. "Thataway."

"Let's get going."

They trudged toward the area he had indicated. Mahree checked the homing grid displayed just above eye level in her helmet, and discovered that they were now well over a straight-line kilometer away from *Rosinante*. The strangely close horizon made estimating distances by eye difficult. She cast a swift, nervous glance at the gauge showing the status of her breathing pack. *Just about two hours left. The walking's so difficult that I'm using more air than I realized.*

The thought made her want to stride faster, but she forced herself to move deliberately, fighting off the sensation of a cold hand slowly tightening around her throat. *Fear uses up oxygen*, she told herself sternly. *Calm down.*

A few minutes later, as though he had read her thoughts, Rob said, "How's your air holding out?"

"One hundred and sixteen minutes," she said. "How about yours?"

"One hundred and eight," he said. "As we predicted, I'm burning my O2 supply faster than you are."

"That means that Dhurrrkk' has a little more than ninety minutes left," Mahree calculated, her mouth going dry. "The Simiu breathing packs hold less than ours do, and Simiu lungs require more oxygen than human lungs. And we can't share our air with him, because our packs won't fit his suit couplings!"

"I know," Rob agreed bleakly. "Nearly half his air's gone. Maybe we ought to tell him to go back to the ship and wait for us there, while we continue searching."

Mahree shook her head. "Dhurrrkk' won't do it. We'd just be wasting time and air trying to convince him. He'd regard leaving us out here as being cowardly and dishonorable. I know that without even asking."

"Well, then, we'll just have to allow enough air for all of us to make it back to *Rosinante*."

She licked her lips, trying unsuccessfully to moisten them. "What for, Rob?" Resisting the urge to slam her gloved hand against the nearest rock in frustration, she managed to keep her voice calm. "What's the point of that? We'd just be postponing the inevitable for a few hours. I'd rather spend our last minutes out here *trying*, than lying around the ship watching those final seconds tick by. I don't think I have enough courage to face that. Do you?"

Rob did not reply.

A few minutes later he abruptly halted, announcing, "Right in front of us are the O2 coordinates I pinpointed earlier."

Both of them hurried forward, then Mahree let out a low cry of disappointment. There was nothing to see.

Nothing.

Nothing but the bare, upthrust ridges of blackish rock, small, tumbled boulders, pebbles that lay nearly buried in a comparatively deep layer of the soil, and a growth of the fleshy-leaved moss-plants. The ubiquitous mist drifted as their feet displaced it, eddying away from them, then settled again.

Rob's voice filled her helmet, harsh with dismay. "But... but these are the right coordinates; I *swear* I didn't make a mistake! This is crazy! These are the same plants as before, but there aren't nearly enough of them to cause the O2 concentration I measured just a couple of hours ago!"

"Is the oxygen level any higher, here?"

He consulted the instrument again. "The overall oxygen level is a little higher, but it's dropped considerably from what I saw earlier. I just don't understand it!"

Mahree felt sick with defeat. She bent over, staring intently at the ground. "These plants look funny," she observed, after a moment. "They're shinier than the ones we saw earlier, though they appear to be the same species."

"You're right," he said. "That's odd."

She walked slowly around, peering down at all the plants in the area. "They're all the same," she reported. "Could there be some kind of natural process going on that causes the change from dull to shiny, producing oxygen as it does so?"

Rob shook his head dubiously. "Maybe. That makes as much sense as anything on this crazy planet. But I don't see any agent that could be the cause of such a change. No other vegetation, nothing. It's also possible that these plants represent a different variety of the basic species. You know, like long- and short-stemmed roses—one type is naturally shiny, and the other is naturally dull."

"I've never seen a rose, except on a holo-vid," Mahree reminded him. *And it looks like I'm never going to see one now.* Resolutely, she squelched that train of thought. "Look, Rob, we have to discover one of those patches that's still emitting O2 so we can find out where the oxygen readings are coming from. I think we should search this entire area. Maybe your coordinates were just a little off?"

"Not a chance," he replied grimly. "I checked those readings four times, and then Dhurrrkk' verified them after me. But we might as well do as you suggest—there's nothing else we can do, except keep trying."

Mahree leaned over to touch her helmet to Dhurrrkk's, and explained what had happened. The Simiu nodded silently.

"I'll go first from now on. You watch the scanner, Rob," she said, beckoning them to follow her. Trying to choose the clearest path, she increased her pace until she was traveling at the fastest walk possible, given the broken ground.

The three explorers began circling around the area Rob's coordinates had indicated, searching for any sign of the mysterious higher-oxygen pockets. Dhurrrkk' gamely followed the two humans' lead, but Mahree knew that her Simiu friend was nearly blind in the dim light, and thus would be of little help.

Ninety minutes of air left, she noted, reading from her gauge, and had to clench her jaw against panic.

They kept going as the minutes slipped by, Mahree in the forefront, picking the smoothest path possible, Rob behind her, scarcely taking his eyes off his sensing device, and Dhurrrkk' bringing up the rear.

Eighty-two minutes.

Grimly, Mahree fought the urge to glance constantly at her air gauge; avoiding obstacles on the rocky ground required all her concentration. But every so often, she just *had* to look up.

Seventy-one minutes.

Rob's breathing sounded harsh in her ears. Mahree thought of what it would be like to have to helplessly listen to that sound falter and cease, and fought the desire to ask him how much air he had left. *You're better off not knowing*, she thought. *Keep your mind on your job.*

Fifty-four minutes.

Now there was no question of trying to head back for *Rosinante* and the few hours of air remaining aboard the ship. *Rob's taken me at my word*, she realized, grimly. *We're going to keep going until we drop in our tracks.*

She swallowed as she realized that Dhurrrkk' had little more than a half hour of air remaining. *Exactly how many minutes?* she wondered, mentally comparing the ratio, but losing track of the numbers in her growing panic. She tried to fight the fear, but it was like a live creature writhing inside her, gnawing at her mind, until she wanted to shriek and run away.

Calm, calm. You have to stay calm! Dhurrrkk's life may depend on you not losing your head! Breathe slowly... slowly. In... out... in... out... Gradually, her fear ebbed; she was able to control her breathing.

Seconds later, Mahree turned a corner around a low outcrop of rock, then halted so abruptly that Rob bumped into her. "Look! What are those things?"

"Damned if I know," he said, staring.

The ground before them was covered with the moss-plants, but lying among them, obscuring them in patches, were five large, thick, phosphorescent shapes. They shone white-violet in the red dimness and were roughly rectangular.

Each faintly glowing growth was a meter or so long by three-quarters of a meter wide. They were entirely featureless. The moment she saw them, Mahree found herself irresistibly reminded of a fuzzy white baby blanket her brother Steven had dragged around with him until it fell apart—these things were exactly the same size and shape, and even their edges were ragged, just like Steven's security blanket.

She turned eagerly to regard Rob as he scanned the patch. "Have we found the O2 emitters?" she asked.

He shook his head, and even in the vacuum suit she could see his shoulders sag. "Negative," he said, in a voice that betrayed the fact that he'd experienced a flash of hope, too. "The oxy level's a little higher here, true enough, just like in the shiny-leaved place, but these things aren't emitting anything. I scan no photosynthesizing capability at all—which fits. Look at their color."

Mahree walked out into the midst of the moss-plants, wisps of red mist swirling around her boots. Feeling a strange reluctance to get too near any of them, she placed her boots with exaggerated care. "Are they plants?"

"No. More like fungi." Rob checked his readings again. "Actually, they share some kinship with lichens, too. They must derive nourishment from the moss-plants as they decay."

Mahree glanced at her air gauge and squared her shoulders. *Forty-nine minutes.* "We'd better keep going," she said.

Rob raised his hand to halt her. "Wait. I want Dhurrrkk' to stay here. This place is easily recognizable, and I've got its coordinates. You and I can circle around and wind up back here in fifteen or twenty minutes. Tell him to lie down and conserve his air. That'll increase his time by five minutes or so. Otherwise, he doesn't have a prayer."

"He'll never agree, Rob!"

"Try, dammit!" he insisted. "Tell him that if he insists on accompanying us until he drops, we'll just end up using the last of our air carrying him."

"That's a good point," she admitted. Kneeling beside the Simiu, Mahree touched her helmet to his, repeating Rob's plea.

The Simiu looked uncertain. Then, slowly, he nodded and deliberately lay down in the midst of the plants, also being careful not to touch any of the phosphorescent growths.

Surprised, because she hadn't expected him to give in so easily, Mahree peered down into Dhurrrkk's helmet, trying to make out his features in the dim light. *He looks kind of funny,* she thought, worried. *Abstracted. Glassy-eyed. Could the Simiu equivalent of hypoxia be hitting him already? Or is he praying or something like that?*

Once more, she touched helmets. "Dhurrrkk', are you okay?"

"I feel fine, FriendMahree," the alien said remotely, as though he was listening to her with only part of his mind. "I promise that I will wait for you here."

✦ ✦ ✦

As he followed Mahree away from the recumbent Simiu, Robert Gable couldn't resist a last glance back at the alien. *He's got about twenty-five minutes to live,* he thought, *give or take five minutes. And I've got twenty-eight minutes and forty seconds.*

"How you fixed for air?" he asked Mahree.

"Forty-five minutes and thirty seconds. You?"

"I'm okay," he replied. "Thirty-nine minutes, here."

Her voice was puzzled and suspicious in his radio. "But before, you were *eight* minutes less than me," she said. "You *gained* a couple of minutes?"

"It takes a lot more effort to lead out here than to follow," he said, using his most reasonable tone. "You're burning O2 much faster now that you're going first."

She started to say something else, but Rob snapped, "Watch out! You nearly snagged your leg on that rock!"

"I did not!" She increased her pace a bit, and Rob struggled to match it without stumbling. "I hope Dhurrrkk' is okay," she muttered. "He looked sort of odd."

"If there's something wrong with him, there's not a damned thing either of us can do about it," Rob pointed out. "The only chance any of us has, now, is for us to locate the source of the oxygen emissions—pronto."

"And if we do?"

"Then you can take off your helmet, lie down, and wait there, while I use the last air in both our breathing packs to carry Dhurrrkk' back to the ship. Then he can take off and pilot *Rosinante* closer to the oxygen emissions source, and I'll come back and get you—then we'll both collect the plants."

"Why do I have to be the one that stays, while you go rescue Dhurrrkk'? Why not the other way around?" Mahree demanded irritably.

"Because you need less O2 to breathe, and I'm stronger than you are," Rob replied calmly, forcing himself not to glance at his air gauge. "Dhurrrkk's no lightweight, even at a half gee."

"Oh. But how will you come back to get me if you use up the last of our breathing packs carrying Dhurrrkk' back to the ship?"

"I've got a two-hour supply of pure oxygen in the oxy pack in my medical kit. I can use it to recharge two breathing packs. Pure oxygen will last us longer than standard airmix. That'll give us each slightly more than an hour's worth of air."

"Oh," Mahree said again. After a moment, she asked hesitantly, "Rob… do you really think that plan will work?"

"No," the doctor said tightly. "I don't think it has a snowball's chance in hell of really working. But if you can think of anything better, I'm all ears."

Mahree had no response. Rob was relieved, because his powers of invention were drying up. He glanced at his air gauge. *Twenty-one minutes.*

Knowing full well that he would use up his air faster than Mahree, the doctor had decided before they left *Rosinante* that their only hope might lie in keeping her going as long as possible. So he had surreptitiously disabled the emergency broadcast unit in his suit. Otherwise, as his breathing pack ran out, she would have been warned as to his status. *Worrying about me running out of air would only make her use her own supply faster*, he thought, repressing a twinge of guilt. *But if by some miracle we both survive this, she's going to be pissed.*

Struggling to keep up the swift pace Mahree set, while checking the sensing device he carried, Rob had little time to note his surroundings. He knew from the location grid in his helmet that Mahree was leading them in a wide circle, gradually taking them back to the spot where Dhurrrkk' waited.

A flat, computer-generated voice suddenly spoke inside the doctor's helmet. "Automatic reminder to the occupant of this suit. You have fifteen minutes of air remaining. Fifteen minutes of air."

Fifteen minutes to live. I feel like Dorothy when the witch turns over that big hourglass. Fifteen minutes...

Rob found himself remembering how he'd arrived at this moment. Memories of his parents, his sisters, of medical school, and the Lotis Plague flicked through his mind like flat, grainy images from one of his antique black-and-white films. He grinned wryly as he followed Mahree, careful to keep glancing at his sensing device every few seconds. *So it's true, what they say—your life does flash before your eyes...*

"Automatic reminder to the occupant of this suit. You have ten minutes of air remaining. Ten minutes of air. You are advised to change breathing packs within the next five minutes."

Rob listened to Mahree's breathing over the radio, remembering the first day they'd met, the nearly instantaneous rapport between them; only she, of all the people aboard *Désirée*, had matched his own eagerness for making the First Contact—not because doing so would make them famous or rich, but because she, too, had an abiding belief that contact with extraterrestrial beings would be a good thing for the human race.

And then his own belief had wavered and nearly toppled... along with Raoul's and the rest of the human crew—and, to hear Dhurrrkk' tell it, the Simiu had lost faith, too. Only Mahree and Dhurrrkk' had managed to retain their belief in each other's continuing goodwill. Was that because they were so young that they hadn't had as much opportunity to have their hopes and ideals trampled?

"Rob, how much air do you have left?"

The doctor sneaked a glance at his readout. *Seven minutes.*

"Seventeen minutes," he lied glibly. *There's nothing she can do about it*, he rationalized, repressing a stab of guilt for lying to her, *and worrying will just make her use air even faster. Our only chance is for Mahree to stay on her feet and locate those oxygen concentrations.* "How about you?" he asked.

"Twenty-seven minutes," she replied. "How far are we from Dhurrrkk'? He must be almost out of air by now."

"We're close," Rob said, checking the location grid. "Here, you carry this." *So I won't drop it or damage it when I fall.*

She took the instrument without question, and they pressed on. Rob watched her stride forward, forcing herself onward, though he knew she must be at least as tired as he was. *Not one complaint*, he thought. *Not even the suggestion of a whimper. I wonder if she'd concede that this counts as courage...*

The doctor experienced a sudden rush of affection for Mahree; they'd grown to know each other so well during this strange odyssey. Comrades, friends... in some ways, Rob mused, Mahree had become one of the closest friends he'd ever had. *Too bad I won't get to see her all grown up; she'd have been something, I'd bet.*

"Automatic reminder to the occupant of this suit. You have five minutes of air remaining. Five minutes of air. If breathing pack is not replaced within four minutes, hypoxia will commence."

Oh, shut up, he thought irritably. *There's not a goddamned thing I can do about it.* Acting on a sudden impulse, he twisted his head around and deliberately tongued the two manual controls that would shut off his suit readouts. The air gauge and location grid went dark. *There, that's better.*

Rob found himself thinking back over his relationships with women. He'd had liaisons with several while he'd been in school (and was proud that, after the affairs had ended, he'd remained friends with all of them)—but he'd never been *in love*.

If there's anything I regret, Rob thought, pushing himself after Mahree with dogged persistence, and realizing with a sinking feeling that he was beginning to gasp a little, and not from exertion, *it's that I never felt that way about...*

"There he is!" Mahree cried, as they caught sight of the moss-plant hollow and the phosphorescent growths. Dhurrrkk' lay sprawled among them, hands clutching his helmet.

"Is he breathing?" Rob asked, coming to a halt on the edge of the hollow. His voice sounded strange in his own ears, tinny and far away. *But I'm not far away; I'm right here*, he thought fuzzily. He tried to move forward, staggered a little, then recovered by bracing himself on a low outcrop of rock. He let himself slide down until he was sitting atop it. All his limbs felt pleasantly heavy, and his mind was beginning to float.

Like drifting off to sleep after a few beers, he realized detachedly. Somewhere a portion of his brain was shrieking "apoxia!" but the word meant nothing. His head nodded, and his eyelids began to close.

"He's still alive!" Mahree's voice reached him, and Rob had to think hard to remember whom she was talking about. "But he's barely breathing!"

He forced his eyes open, saw Mahree crouched on the ground beside Dhurrrkk'. *I should get up*, he thought. *Go help...*

But his body would not obey him. Black spots danced before his eyes, and he closed them again because they were making him so terribly dizzy.

"*Rob!*" screamed a voice over his radio. The doctor opened his eyes again as he felt himself being shaken violently. He saw Mahree bent over him, her own eyes wide and terrified behind the faceplate of her helmet.

"Rob, how much air do you have left? Don't lie to me this time, goddammit!"

He tried to tell her that he had turned off his readouts, that it was okay, it didn't hurt, but his tongue moved sluggishly, and no sound emerged. All the black spots coalesced suddenly into an all-encompassing darkness that swooped toward him like a live creature, enfolding him past all struggle.

With a sigh, Rob gave in and let it carry him away.

✦ ✦ ✦

"Oh, God!" Mahree sobbed, catching her companion as he tumbled over bonelessly. "God, help me! Somebody please, please help me, someone—anyone!"

How much air does he have left?

She lowered Rob onto the moss-plants, beside Dhurrrkk', then turned him half over so she could read his breathing pack's outside gauge, located on his right hip.

The first thing she saw was the flash of the red "Low Oxygen Level—Condition Critical" reading on the indicator as it pulsed steadily in the dimness, then before her eyes it changed.

ZERO O2, it read, in double-size letters. HYPOXIA IMMINENT—CHANGE PACK IMMEDIATELY.

Reflexively, then, Mahree looked up at her own display. *Eighteen minutes.*

Eighteen long minutes…

I cannot sit here for eighteen minutes and watch them die, Mahree realized, feeling a calm that went beyond despair. *No way.*

Moving as quickly and surely as if she'd rehearsed the procedure hundreds of times, she detached Rob's used breathing pack in a matter of moments, and just as quickly replaced it with her own. *I'm sorry, Rob*, she thought, hearing the sounds of his gasping breaths ease as his oxygen-starved lungs took in the new air. *This is a rotten thing to do to you, love, but I just don't have the courage to let you go first. If we're both lucky, you won't even wake up.*

Then she sat back between the two prone figures, and, picking up Rob's gloved hand, held it in her lap between her own two. *I've got maybe ninety seconds' worth of air left in my suit*, she thought, still calm. *How should I spend them?*

Her early religious training argued that she ought to pray, but the only prayer Mahree could remember at the moment was the one with the line about, "If I should die before I wake."

Talk about stating the obvious, she thought, with grim amusement. *No, I guess praying is out.*

As she sat there, waiting, Mahree found that she was fighting a growing urge to take off her helmet.

It's the hypoxia, she thought dazedly. *It must be. The first thing to go is judgment.*

A conviction that, if she would just remove her helmet, everything would be all right filled her mind. Mahree glanced around, seeing the phosphorescent growths gleaming weirdly in the sanguine light. *What's happening to me? My mind feels as though it's not mine anymore!* By now she was panting, suffocating, her lungs laboring as they strained frantically to gasp in the last vestiges of oxygen her suit air contained.

Darkness crouched on the edges of her vision, an expanding, hungry darkness without end. But the darkness would go away if she would just get rid of her helmet.

Mahree blinked, dazed, and realized that, without being aware of her actions, she'd released the fastenings of her helmet, and now had both hands on its sides, preparatory to twisting it, then lifting it free of her shoulders. The urge to remove it was a driving imperative within her now, a command that she had no strength left to fight.

What am I doing? she wondered frantically as she twisted, breaking the helmet's seal. She was in agony now, her lungs stabbing fire as they rebelled against the surfeit of carbon dioxide. *Oxygen!* something deep within her mind was insisting. *There will be oxygen! Take the helmet off!*

With a final, lung-tearing gasp, Mahree tore her helmet free, dropping it onto the moss-plants beside her. Cold, moist atmosphere smote her sweaty face like a blow. As blackness flowed across her vision, she inhaled deeply...

Slowly, the blackness began to recede.

Moments later, Mahree realized that she was crouched on hands and knees between Rob and Dhurrrkk', her head hanging down, and that she was *breathing.*

Oxygen! she thought, hardly able to believe this wasn't some dying hallucination. *Something here is emitting oxygen!*

A strong sense of affirmation filled her, affirmation mixed with concern. Mahree hastily groped for the fastenings of Dhurrrkk's helmet. Her gloved fingers couldn't grasp the alien shapes, and, with a sob of impatience, she unsealed her gloves, ripping them off. She fumbled again at the Simiu's helmet, and found, to her astonishment, that the seals had already been released. But the helmet was stuck; she had to use all her strength and leverage to twist it free. Finally it gave.

Seconds later, she had rolled the Simiu onto his back. She could not tell whether he was breathing, or whether his heart was still beating.

"Dhurrrkk'!" she yelled, then slapped his face.

When he did not respond, Mahree hastily scuttled around him until she was kneeling facing his feet, then she grasped his chin and pulled the alien's head toward her, tilting it back. His jaw opened, and she peered into his mouth to check the location of his tongue. It was hard to tell in the dimness, but she *thought* she now had a clear airway.

Cupping both hands hard around his muzzle to seal his mouth shut, Mahree inhaled a deep breath of the blessedly oxygenated air, then she bent, placed her own mouth tightly over his nostrils, and blew as hard as she could.

First she gave him four quick, hard breaths to deliver an initial jolt of oxygen; then she tried to settle into a regular rhythm. Mahree *thought* she felt the sense of resistance that meant she'd achieved a proper airway and seal, but she couldn't be sure.

Darkness gathered again at the fringes of her vision as she continued to suck in air, then blow it hard into the unmoving alien's nostrils.

Come on, Dhurrrkk', she thought, *I'll pass out if I keep this up much longer, so come on!*

As Mahree dizzily raised her head for the next gulp of air, she started and barely prevented herself from recoiling violently. A hand-span away from Dhurrrkk's head lay a spectrally glowing, faintly pulsing mass.

My God, it's the baby blanket! It moved!

She missed half a beat, then resolutely inhaled again and blew. Her dizziness returned, but as she snatched a quick gasp for her own lungs, it abated. *That fungus has to be what's giving off the oxygen,* she thought, with sudden certainty. *And right now it's giving off extra oxygen, as if it knows how much I really need it! But that would mean that it's—*

Beneath her fingers, Dhurrrkk"s muzzle twitched. *Right! That's it!* she cheered him on, drawing in another lungful of oxygen-rich air. She blew again, and this time when she turned toward the blanket to gulp air, she unmistakably felt a faint tickle of warm exhalation against her cheek.

Another breath. This time she *saw* his exhaled breath steam in the cold, damp air. Another breath… and yet another…

Dhurrrkk' abruptly gasped, twitched, then gasped again. *He's breathing!*

Mahree hovered, ready to resume the artificial respiration if necessary, but the Simiu no longer needed her help. Soon Dhurrrkk's violet eyes opened and focused on her.

"Do not try to move, FriendDhurrrkk'. You passed out, but now that we have air, you will be fine," Mahree managed to say, though her abused throat rebelled more than usual at the Simiu syllables. "Just lie still, please. I must check on Rob."

She turned around to regard the doctor, then glanced at the breathing pack's external gauge. *Fourteen minutes.* She shook her head and looked again. *Fourteen minutes? I don't believe it! All that, and it's only been four minutes?*

Hastily, she pulled off his helmet, then disconnected the airflow from the breathing pack to conserve the remainder. Rob did not stir. Mahree pulled up an eyelid, then touched her fingers to the pulse in his throat. *He's okay… just out cold.*

She smiled as an idea occurred to her, then, after making sure Dhurrrkk' wasn't watching, she bent over and kissed her unconscious companion lingeringly on the mouth. "Call it my fee for saving your ass, you oh-so-noble bastard," she muttered, remembering how he'd lied to her about how much air he had left.

Then, grasping his limp form beneath the arms, she dragged him over the moss-plants until he, too, was lying with his face close to the phosphorescent growth. "Here, Blanket," she gasped, "you can give *him* some oxygen, too. Please."

Then she sat down, gazing wonderingly at the fungus-creature. Their savior.

When Rob scanned them earlier, they weren't emitting any oxygen. But when we were in danger of dying, they—or this one at least—started to emit it. And, just when I was getting ready to pass out, the creature moved closer, and gave off additional oxygen. That has to mean that—

Mahree wiped cold sweat off her forehead, then licked her lips nervously. *That's impossible! This is a fungus, one of the simplest forms of life around! Don't be crazy, Mahree!*

She bent over, peering closely at the faintly shining growth. It was completely featureless, except for millions of short, threadlike cilia on its top-side. She lay down on her side amid the moss-plants, then squinted up at the fungus's underside. *It moved; it must have. How the hell can it move?*

The blanket's bottom side was covered with tiny appendages nearly the length of her little finger. They moved constantly, rippling over the moss-plants like minuscule tentacles. "So *that's* how you get around," Mahree muttered.

Scrambling back up to hands and knees, she cautiously inched closer to the phosphorescent creature, until her nose was only a hand-span away. "Hi, Blanket," she said, feeling ridiculous—*I'm talking to a fungus? I must have cleared my jets!*—"My name is Mahree Burroughs. I really appreciate your helping us out, just now. We desperately needed that oxygen. I hope you folks don't suddenly stop emitting it." She shook her head. "I don't know why I'm talking. You don't have ears, so you can't possibly hear or understand me, can you?"

Slowly, the edge of the phosphorescent growth lifted clear of the moss-plants, extending itself toward her face.

Mahree couldn't help it—she let out a startled yelp and jerked back. Her heart slammed in her chest. Biting her lip savagely, she steadied her breathing, forcing herself to inhale and exhale lightly and evenly. There wasn't sufficient oxygen in the hollow to sustain her if she hyperventilated.

Maybe it was just exhibiting some kind of involuntary reflex in response to movement? she thought, watching the baby blanket settle back down onto the moss-plants.

Slowly, she leaned forward again. "If you can understand me, Blanket, *don't* move. Stay still, okay?"

Mahree moved so close that her nose nearly brushed the blanket's side, but the phosphorescence did not stir.

"Ohhh-kay," she muttered. "If you can understand me, Blanket, please move *now.*"

The edge of the creature rippled, then rose until it was a full hand-span above the moss-plants.

"Holy shit," Mahree gulped. "I was right. You're *sentient.*"

Again the sense of affirmation filled her mind.

"And telepathic, right? You can make what you're thinking and feeling go from your 'mind'—or whatever equivalent you've got—into mine?"

Affirmation.

A human groan interrupted her "conversation." Mahree turned to see that Dhurrrkk' was sitting up, holding Rob's hands, and that the doctor was stirring. "Excuse me a moment, please, Blanket," she said. "I must check on my friend. I will return."

Affirmation.

Mahree hastily crawled over to put a hand on Dhurrrkk''s shoulder. "FriendDhurrrkk'," she said. "How do you feel?"

The Simiu put a hand on his forehead. "There is pain here," he said. "But otherwise I am fine."

"Just promise me you'll take it easy for a while. You were pretty far gone."

"I promise, FriendMahree." The Simiu's violet eyes were full of emotion. Slowly, minus his customary ease and grace, he reached over to grasp her hand. "You gave me your own breath, so that I could live," he said, switching to her own language. "I will be forever grateful, my friend. We are honor-bound, you and I. For as long as

I may live, your honor and your life will be as important to me as my own."

"Dhurrrkk'..." Mahree tried to think of something to say, but words failed her. Instead, she gripped his six-fingered hand hard, nodding.

He motioned to Rob. "Honored HealerGable is awakening." Mahree hastily turned around, to find the doctor lying there with his eyes open. "Hi," she said softly, bending over him. "How are you feeling?"

"I'm breathing," he whispered, his eyes filled with profound bewilderment. "Why am I still alive?"

"Because we've found the source of the oxygen emissions, Rob," she told him. "And a lot more besides."

"Huh? You located one of the O2 sources?"

"Yes," she said, seeing that he was still weak and disoriented. The rest of her news could wait.

He put out a hand. "Are you sure you're really here?" he mumbled uncertainly. "I'm not hallucinating?"

For an answer, Mahree took his gloved hand, unsealed it, pulled off the covering, then grasped his bare fingers tightly. "I'm really here," she said. "Feel."

"Feels good," he mumbled, smiling. "Squeeze tight." After a moment, he shakily sat up, then looked at the Simiu. "Honored Dhurrrkk', I'm glad to see that you're all right."

The alien made the formal greeting gesture of his people. "Honored HealerGable," he said in English, with a twinkle, "I'm pleased to observe the same about you."

The doctor shook his head, confusion filling his eyes. "But I don't understand how we got here—wherever we are. I was out of air. I must've passed out." He glanced down at his side.

"*Waitaminit!* This says I've got twelve minutes left on this pack." He looked back up, glaring at Mahree. "You switched breathing packs, didn't you? Gave me the last of your air?"

"It was the least I could do, after you lied to me," she said acerbically. "One dirty trick deserves another." She returned his glare with interest. "And if you dare to tell me that it was for my own good, you're going to find yourself stretched out on these damned moss-plants again."

"I knew you'd be pissed," he mumbled, obviously deeply touched by his discovery of the switched breathing pack. "But I didn't figure

I'd live to hear about it. Forgive me?"

Rob sounded so uncharacteristically meek that Mahree had to laugh. "Let's call it even."

The doctor glanced around him, and his eyes widened as he recognized their location. "Hey, this is the same place as we left Dhurrrkk'." He scratched his head. "Now, let me get this straight. We came back here to get Dhurrrkk', only this time there was oxygen in this hollow? But how?"

"Thank *them*," Mahree said, pointing to the blanket-creatures. "They're the things that have been emitting the O2."

"*Them?* The fungi?" He blinked. "That's impossible. Crazy. They can't even photosynthesize."

"You *ain't seen* crazy, yet. Brace yourself, Rob. They're *sentient*. We've just made a First Contact."

He stared at her in silence, no expression on his face. "Sentient," he repeated, finally.

"They *are*," Mahree insisted. "They knew we needed oxygen, so they convinced me to take off my helmet, so I could breathe. And when I'd taken it off, this one"—she pointed to the closest blanket-creature—"crawled over just so it could give me extra O2 when I was giving Dhurrrkk' artificial respiration."

He hesitated. "Uhhhhh... that's hard to believe," he said, finally, using a carefully neutral tone. "Are you *sure*?"

"Honored Mahree is correct," Dhurrrkk' interjected, in English. "Before I lost my awareness of my surroundings, I was conscious of something contacting my mind, something that touched and questioned with intelligent purpose. It instructed me to take off my helmet, but I was unable to comply."

"That's because it was stuck," she told him.

Rob stared at both of them. Then he looked down at the blanket. "You're telling me this *thing* is sentient," he said, in a this-can't-be-happening-to-me tone of voice. "*This* thing"—he pointed—"this phosphorescent patch of fungus?"

"It's not a *thing*, it's a *person*, Rob. Mind your manners," Mahree admonished. "Watch, I'll prove it."

Turning back to "her" blanket, Mahree ran through the same demonstration that she had earlier. Finally, she said to the being, "This is my friend, Robert Gable—Rob, as he's called. This is what he looks like." She glanced at the doctor's face. "And this is my friend Honored Dhurrrkk'." She looked at the Simiu. "Now, if you don't mind, Blanket, I'd like you to move over and stop in front of Rob, so he'll know for sure that you can understand me."

With surprising speed, the alien creature crawled unhesitatingly over to Rob, stopped, then raised one edge into the air and waved at him.

The doctor paled as he stared at the being, eyes wide, then suddenly he bent forward until his forehead rested on the moss-plants before him.

"Good grief, Rob," Mahree exclaimed, "you don't have to *pray* to it! Just say 'hello'!"

He drew several long breaths. "I'm not praying, you idiot," he said crossly in a muffled voice. "If I hadn't gotten my head down, I would've fainted. Give me a break, sweetheart. It's been a long, hard day."

After a minute Rob sat back up, his color much improved. "I'll be damned," he whispered softly, eyeing the fungus-being. He cleared his throat. "How do you do, uh, Blanket? It's a real pleasure."

Mahree concentrated, and received a clear sense of inquiry. "It's telepathic—or something—" she said. "Right now, it wants to know about us. How we got here."

"It is asking me the same thing," Dhurrrkk' said.

Trying to be as clear and simple as she could, Mahree thought slowly, deliberately, of how they had come to this world, aboard *Rosinante*, and why. She tried to make her images of the ship as vivid as possible, knowing instinctively that the creature before her could have no concept of technology or artificial constructions.

Finally, she turned to Dhurrrkk'. "Did you tell it?"

"Yes," he said. "As clearly as I could. Communication with the being is growing easier for me, the more I do it."

Mahree felt a prickle of envy. "It's still pretty hard for me," she admitted.

Rob was watching them. "I can feel it now, too," he said. "A sense of inquiry, and curiosity, right?" When they nodded, he continued, "But it's sure nothing like what Great-Aunt Louise used to do. She spoke in words, except they were silent."

"Maybe Blanket can learn words, eventually," Mahree said. "At first it just communicated faint impressions. Now they're getting stronger."

"It would like to help us," Dhurrrkk' announced suddenly.

"It already *has* helped us," Rob said. "Though I have to admit that it might have been kinder if it hadn't interfered when we passed out. Spending the rest of my life here in this hollow, while we slowly die of thirst, isn't a very appealing prospect."

Dhurrrkk' said, "It is giving me images, now. It thinks it knows a way."

Mahree felt an absurd sense of abandonment as she realized that "her" blanket was now communicating most effectively with the Simiu. *Don't be stupid*, she thought sternly. *It obviously has discovered that a Simiu brain is easier for it to reach.*

She and Rob waited as the Simiu sat there, an abstracted expression on his face. Finally, he raised his violet eyes to theirs. "I have learned something about these beings. Each of these creatures is very, very old, and each is intelligent. Normally, they are not interested in much outside of pursuing their own obscure musings, mental games, and philosophical reflections. However, the one that Mahree calls 'Blanket' is different. For one thing, it is younger—perhaps only a million or so of my years old."

Mahree and Rob gasped sharply. "A *million* years old?" she repeated, and the Simiu nodded soberly.

"Blanket is far more interested in external stimuli and events than its companions. It is intrigued by the notion of our ship, and traveling through space. It likes us. It does not want us to perish, and it is willing to help us safely reach our destination. If we would like it to, Blanket has volunteered to join us aboard *Rosinante*, and provide us with oxygen. In return, we must promise to bring it back here, when it asks to be returned to its own world."

"Can it give off that much oxygen?" Rob said skeptically, after he'd spent a moment assimilating the Simiu's words. "Doesn't it need its oxygen for itself?"

"No, the blankets themselves require very little oxygen. It is a by-product they produce during digestion. It has no part in their breathing process."

They fart oxygen? Mahree thought, wildly, and giggled shrilly before she could stop herself. Rob reached over to put a steadying hand on her shoulder.

"We will need to provide Blanket with native rock and moss-plants, sufficient to allow it ample nourishment for the duration of our journey," Dhurrrkk' concluded.

"Well, if it tells us how much it needs, we'll be happy to do that," Rob said. "But there's just one thing. How the hell do we get out of this hollow, and back to *Rosinante*?"

"Blanket has asked its companions to assist, and they have agreed. They think their companion foolish for wishing to depart this world in order to aid us," the Simiu paused, then continued, as he evidently received additional information, "but none of them wish to see us perish. As long as they can remain here, the others are willing to help us reach the ship."

"How do they propose to help us?"

"You will see. Please remain still. They mean no harm." Rob started as two more of the creatures stirred, then began moving across the moss-plants toward them.

Mahree's "Blanket" began crawling back toward her. She felt a moment of pleased satisfaction that it had evidently elected to return to her instead of staying with Dhurrrkk', then the creature moved past her, out of her line of sight unless she turned her head. *What is it going to do?*

Mahree swallowed hard as she both heard and felt something brush against the material of her vacuum suit, then the front collar of the suit was pressed against her throat as something heavy begin pulling itself up her back. She clenched her fists, squeezing her eyes shut, as Blanket slowly inched its way up. *It's saving your life*, she thought, repeatedly. *That's not a fungus crawling up your body, it's a person. A good, kind person. It's saving your life...*

Finally, the creature lay over her shoulders and down her back like a phosphorescent cape. At the extreme edge of her peripheral vision, she caught movement, then two glowing narrow "fingers" appeared as Blanket extruded two corners across her cheeks.

Mahree shivered, forcing herself to sit quietly. She closed her eyes as she felt the cold, admittedly damp substance of the alien being creep across her skin, until both pseudopods met, linking together across her upper lip.

She opened her eyes to find Rob staring down at the phosphorescent mass moving toward him. The doctor was chalky pale and runnels of sweat coursed down his face. He was trembling violently.

"Rob!" she said sharply. "*Rob!*"

Slowly, he looked up.

"Don't pull a Simon Viorst on us, Rob! They're helping us; just keep telling yourself that."

The doctor took several deep breaths, then finally nodded. A touch of color reappeared in his lips. "Okay. Don't worry about me, honey. I'm okay now."

He sat still as the phosphorescent mass crept slowly up his back. "I just wish," he said, and the control he was exerting over himself was palpable, "that I hadn't watched that nineties version of *The Puppet Masters* so *many* times. Remind me to show it to you if we ever get home."

Mahree drew a deep breath of relief, then picked up her helmet and gloves. "Everybody ready?" she said, standing. She discovered that, even with her head above the level of the hollow, she was breathing easily—the O2 level was no thinner than what she'd experienced camping in the mountains on Jolie.

"Ready," Dhurrrkk' said, handing Rob his helmet to carry. His blanket-creature was draped over his neck and back like a second, glowing mane.

"Ready," Rob said. "Let's rock."

"Rock?" echoed Dhurrrkk', as the three blanket-caped explorers picked their way out of the moss-plant hollow. "We must gather a number of rocks, true, along with harvesting plants, but don't you believe, FriendRob, that we would be better served to do that closer to our ship? Rocks are heavy to carry."

"Uh… yeah," Rob said, giving Mahree a wink, and speaking with some difficulty because of the pseudopods linked across his upper lip, "you're right, FriendDhurrrkk'. Rocks *are* heavy."

Bennett R. Coles' Astral Saga is a newer space opera/military science fiction novel series by an up-and-coming author of growing significance. This short story is based midway between Ghosts of War *and* March of War, *books two and three of the Virtues of War trilogy. It provides just a glimpse into the life of one of the trilogy's main characters during those chaotic times.*

TWENTY EXCELLENT REASONS
BENNETT R. COLES

The lieutenants were stressing again. It seemed to be what they did best. Sublieutenant Jack Mallory didn't care if they stressed on their off-time, but the quiet spectacle of hissed whispers and dagger glares was affecting all ranks. The ship's bridge was crowded, and Jack kept tucked against a console to avoid getting shouldered out of the way.

He tried to distract himself by gazing up at the vision of outside space projected on the inner sphere of the bridge. Stars gleamed in the blackness across three quarters of the sphere, but low and forward the brown and green crescent of the planet Thor floated amidst a swarm of tactical symbols representing ships in orbit. The nearby star, Asgard, was a dazzling, orange orb a few degrees to the left. Jack let his gaze sweep across the starscape and spotted the single, brighter point of light that was Asgard's companion star, Vanaheim. They and their planets made up the youngest human colony, Valhalla, which was widely considered to be a backwater in this ongoing rebellion. But Jack had been here long enough to know the rebels were still dangerous, fighting a guerilla campaign that was wearing the Astral Force down.

Maybe, he conceded, the lieutenants had reason to be stressed.

All he ever had to worry about was his Hawk. But even that suddenly wasn't the same anymore. The Astral Force, in its wisdom, had decided that every Hawk pilot would now be augmented by a tactical crewmember. He turned again to glance at his new assistant.

Master Rating Daisy Singh stood beside him, watching the briefing preparations with a clear discomfort. Almost his height but looking very slight under her regulation coveralls, long black hair tied in a braid, she didn't look old enough to have already been promoted twice, which spoke either to her incredible abilities or to the fact that too many people were dying in this war.

She caught his gaze.

"Is the bridge always like this?"

"Just when we're at war."

She stared at him for a moment, then scoffed.

"Glad I'm not in charge," she said.

"Welcome to my world," he added. "Have you ever flown in a Hawk before?"

"I did the training course on the simulator," she said, dark cheeks flushing. "Before that I was a sensors tech."

Jack kept his face neutral, even as his heart sank. Not only did he have to change his ingrained patterns in the cockpit, he had a newbie riding shotgun.

"Well, you'll have to tell me what you can do. I'm used to doing it all myself."

"Yes, sir."

Jack was tempted to keep talking, to learn more about this poor kid being thrown in as his backseat. But Lieutenant Dawson tapped him sharply on the shoulder.

"Jack, we're starting the mission brief—get in your damn spot."

Jack followed his boss toward the open area of the bridge in front of the raised command chairs. The lieutenants were gathered literally at the feet of *Frankfurt*'s commanding officer, Commander Rossato. She, at least, didn't look quite as grim as her officers.

The briefing started. Jack hoisted in the specific updates on rebel positions, but the presentation didn't contain any surprises for him. There was a group of hostages being held in a rebel hideout on Thor.

It was an increasingly common tactic for the rebels. Jack felt an unusual emotion well within him: anger. He knew only too well what it meant to be a hostage, knew what it meant to be beaten nearly to death and displayed as a spectacle for all the worlds to see. He caught his fingers brushing over the reconstructed bones in his cheek and pulled his hand down. The doctors had done their job well, and no one need ever know what had happened. But he knew.

He felt a new determination to get this mission done.

Both of *Frankfurt*'s Hawks were going to be used for the extraction, each carrying four armed crewmembers to deal with resistance and to load the hostages. Astral Special Forces had a pair of operatives already in position to neutralize the rebels on site.

It wasn't at all the sort of mission the Hawk had originally been designed for, but war was the great driver of innovation. Jack himself had already done more orbital insertions in his single year in the cockpit than most pilots did in their entire careers. Lieutenant Dawson, though, looked quite pale.

The briefing concluded with words from the captain.

"This is a quick mission," Commander Rossato said quietly but firmly. "Get down, get the hostages, get back up to the ship. There are no other Astral assets in the area so we'll be providing you cover fire. And we will hold our position in low orbit"—she glared down at her bridge officers—"until you return. That means *Frankfurt* will take a pounding, so don't dawdle on the ground."

✦ ✦ ✦

The fires of atmo entry had faded and Jack manhandled his controls against the wall of tortured air through which his Hawk plunged. Switching to terrestrial reckoning he noted his altitude at ten kilometers, dropping fast, and speed slowing to hypersonic. His controls rattled against the air rushing over the Hawk's flight surfaces. He calmed himself with a slow breath and reacquainted himself with the feel of atmo flight.

"It's gonna be bumpy the whole way," he said to Singh, seated over his left shoulder at her tactical console. "It's not like space flight."

"Roger," she said, the tension clear in her voice.

Up ahead, Jack saw the flashes of *Frankfurt*'s orbital bombardment batteries pounding known rebel anti-aircraft positions. Like a precise, focused meteor shower, dazzling orbs struck down from orbit. Jack was still too high to see the results of the impacts, but there was no doubt the rebels knew he was coming. Dawson's Hawk was in the lead. They were dropping fast and maintaining speed, attempting to get under the rebel defence network before it got organized.

The Hawks leveled out at one kilometer, the landscape flashing by in a brownish blur splashed with green. Jack felt comfortable with the controls and knew he had a few moments to look ahead. It was always risky taking his hands off the stick and throttle to manipulate his sensors, but then he remembered Singh behind him.

"Project battlespace," he ordered.

It took a few moments, but then his canopy was lit up with

tactical symbols of rebel positions and units that were being tracked by *Frankfurt* in orbit. Jack scanned the augmented view of the landscape.

An alarm sounded in Jack's headset, indicating hostile weapons tracking. He jinked right then left, ignoring the g-forces that wrenched him. He saw Dawson's Hawk break left and launch countermeasures. Jack dropped to five hundred meters before settling out on course. The alarm faded from his ears as hostile tracking was lost.

The hostage location was fast approaching. Dawson's Hawk was still ahead to port, nearly a thousand meters higher. It was starting to drift backward as Dawson reduced speed for landing. Jack scanned his own approach vector and the area to the south of the target position. At this altitude, he wanted a bit more space between Hawks.

He hauled his stick to the right, then reversed his turn and brought the Hawk around in a wide arc, bleeding off speed while never settling onto a new course. If there were hidden rebel guns down there, they'd have a hell of a time getting a lock.

He finally steadied up, due south of the landing site—a small farm surrounded by open fields. The final ridge flashed by beneath him and he visually surveyed the farm, watching as Dawson landed in the closest field to the cluster of buildings. Seconds later, he fired thrusters and burned off the last of his speed into a pair of scorched trenches in the Thorian ground. The Hawk thumped down.

"Open the rear hatch!" he ordered.

There was a familiar hiss as the aft ramp decoupled from its locks and dropped to the ground. Jack felt a breeze of warm air wash through the cabin, tinged with the strange, oily quality unique to Thor's atmosphere. Through the canopy he saw armed crewmen emerge from Dawson's Hawk, advancing cautiously forward toward the enemy farm. From around the bulk of his own Hawk he saw four crewmen shuffling forward, rifles up.

There was one dead body within easy reach of his Hawk, a rebel with a slit throat. Closer to the farm were the splattered remains of at least three other fighters who had clearly been hit with Astral exploding rounds.

"*Axe flight*," came a new, deep voice in his headset, "*this is Astral Special Forces. We see you outside and we are exiting the farmhouse with hostages, over.*"

Jack heard Dawson acknowledge, then saw the main farmhouse

door open. A large figure emerged, his muscular bulk clear beneath some sort of pressure suit, hands raised cautiously as he walked forward. His face was hidden beneath a form-fitting helmet, and his head moved in a slow, careful scan of the two Hawks. Behind him, a gaggle of civilians began to emerge, many limping heavily and at least two being carried.

Jack had to fight to stay in his seat. Torturing hostages was still in fashion with the rebels, it seemed. And what was his own crew doing, standing there watching?

"Axe flight," he barked over the mission circuit, "get over there with stretchers and help those hostages!"

Stretchers were collected from within the two Hawks and hurried over to where the wounded were gathering outside. The large, unarmed man was clearly in charge and within moments the hostages were being loaded up and carried back toward the Hawks. Jack watched as another Special Forces operative emerged from the building, hefting an assault rifle. The two operatives waited until all the hostages were in motion before each headed for a different Hawk. The larger of the two, still apparently unarmed, escorted the evacuees into Jack's Hawk.

Jack turned in his seat, looking past Singh toward the main cabin. The first of the crew and hostages were ascending the rear ramp, but Jack watched for the operative. His bulk quickly came into view and he slipped with surprising grace through the crowded cabin. His pressure suit was black, with no obvious external life support, no control systems and no markings. He loomed over Singh and stared down at Jack.

"Good to see you again, Mr. Mallory."

Jack saw the surprised look on Singh's face which no doubt mirrored his own expression. Then he looked more closely at the operative and realized that they had met before, on a Research ship in orbit around Earth just hours before the opening battle of the war.

"Sergeant Chang." He wondered if some sort of witty remark was expected in moments like this. Something world-weary and withering? His imagination failed him. "Ready to lift off?"

Chang paused before answering, staring absently into space. Then he nodded as he took the seat next to Singh, over Jack's right shoulder.

"Yes, sir—both Hawks are loaded. Heavy casualties amongst the hostages."

"Closing rear hatch," Singh said, reaching for her controls.

Jack turned forward in his seat and saw Axe-One already lifting into the air.

"All personnel buckle in," he announced as he eased open his own throttle. "We're airborne."

With a full load of passengers, the Hawk was noticeably sluggish as Jack gained altitude, but he tucked under Dawson's wing and continued accelerating. He heard Dawson report, and *Frankfurt's* response that rebel forces were closing the area in force. Up ahead, orbital bombardment pounded down on scattered positions.

"*Axe-Two, this is One,*" he heard Dawson call, "*prepare for hard ascent.*"

Anti-air fire was already lighting up the sky ahead of them. Multiple tracking alarms sounded in his headset. They needed to get out of here, and fast. Flak and tracers exploded past them.

"*Axe-One on ascent!*"

The other Hawk nosed upward into a vertical climb, engines firing on full burn as countermeasures launched. Jack pulled back on his own stick and pushed open the throttle.

"Fire counter—"

His words were cut off by a bang against the hull. The Hawk shuddered and lurched to starboard. Another bang knocked him in his seat. He fought the stick as his own craft started to roll. The horizon came into view at the edge of his vision, swinging wildly. A series of thuds wrenched his stick and alarms lit up across his flight surfaces panel. His view suddenly filled with the mottled brown of the surface as the Hawk began to dive.

His flight surfaces were shredded, turning his Hawk into an unguided bomb strapped to a pair of rockets. He throttled back and switched to thruster control. Ill-equipped to fighting air resistance, the thrusters strained to push him out of his dive. Leveling out at under a kilometer, Jack blinked the sweat from his eyes and took stock of the tactical symbols still projected on the canopy before him.

There were too many hostiles—way too many. Looking up, he saw the blue symbol for *Frankfurt* in orbit, but no sign of Lieutenant Dawson.

"Location Axe-One," he snapped to Singh.

"Zero-four-five, fifty kilometers," she replied.

"Altitude?"

She didn't respond immediately. He repeated the question.

"No reading," she finally said.

He didn't have time for this newbie's confusion. Hauling on his stick he turned the Hawk toward the northeast to get a visual. His sightline was cluttered with enemy symbols scattered across the landscape.

"Clear tactical!"

The sea of symbols vanished.

And amidst all the anti-aircraft fire, Jack spotted a single, black trail of smoke tracing down.

"Axe-One this is Two," he said, "confirm status, over."

There was no response, except new targeting alarms.

"Singh, you fire countermeasures whenever those bastards get a lock on us!"

"Yes, sir," she replied.

He repeated his hail to Dawson. He hailed *Frankfurt*.

"Forest this is Axe-Two, confirm Axe-One status?"

"*This is Forest. Lost tracking on Axe-One,*" came *Frankfurt's* reply. "*Assess she's down.*"

"Sir," rumbled Chang in his ear, "there are survivors at the Axe-One crash site."

Jack had no idea how the operative knew that, but he didn't question it.

"Forest this is Axe-Two. Roger, I'm closing to recover survivors."

"*This is Forest. Assess rebel forces closing Axe-One's position in brigade strength, leading elements ETA ten mikes.*"

Ten minutes until Axe-One was overrun by rebels. Ten minutes until the survivors of the crash were prisoners once again. Visions of horror flashed through Jack's mind of his own captivity. He scanned his instruments. Fuel was draining fast, either through the constant thruster use or something more ominous. If he didn't break for orbit soon he might never make it at all. But there were survivors on the ground, and he knew what fate awaited them if they were captured. In ten minutes.

He pushed his throttle forward.

"This is Axe-Two, roger. Expediting recovery."

There was a long pause from orbit before, finally: "*Roger.*"

"Display tactical," he said to Singh.

The growing swarm of enemy contacts filled his vision again. There were dozens of them, but with sudden clarity he realized that not all were a threat.

"Give me weapons ranges of the nearest hostiles," he ordered quietly.

Shaded hemispheres appeared over the three rebel positions within range. The Hawk was headed through all of them.

"Stand by with countermeasures."

"Standing by," she said.

Jack pushed the stick forward, plunging toward the surface. Leveling out at an altitude far below what any spacefaring craft was ever designed to maintain, he weaved between outcrops. Rebel trackers followed him, but couldn't lock on.

Over one more ridge and Jack spotted the dissipating smoke of Axe-One's final dive. The Hawk was mostly intact, but a trail of debris was scattered across the rocky ground. Normally he'd conduct a flyover to assess safety before landing, but with only eight minutes left he flew straight in, thrusters screaming as he killed his speed and thumped down next to his broken wingman.

"Get that ramp down and load survivors," he shouted, unstrapping and climbing out of his own seat. To Singh he said, "Check for any critical failures in propulsion systems."

Pushing past the stunned crewmembers in the main cabin, he grabbed an engineering satchel and ran down the ramp. He coughed as the hot, oily air filled his lungs, shielding his eyes from the brilliant orange light of Asgard low in the sky. He saw a woman emerge from the Axe-One wreckage, her uniform revealing her as one of *Frankfurt*'s crew. Bright, terrified eyes stared at him through a dust-caked face.

"How many survivors?" he demanded.

"Eight," she croaked.

Crew from Axe-Two were running up with stretchers. As more survivors pulled themselves clear of the wreckage, Jack did a quick calculation. His Hawk was already weighed down with sixteen souls, and it was rated for no more than twenty. He had no problem exceeding official ratings for his bird, but between them the two Hawks had thirty-two people—there was no way he could carry a payload sixty percent in excess of tolerance into orbit.

He grabbed the nearest crewmember with a stretcher, but shouted loud enough for all to hear above the wind.

"Survivors only—we don't have the power to get the deceased to orbit."

The frantic activity around him paused, and Jack knew that in that moment he'd just earned the hatred of some of the crew. But no one argued.

He scrabbled over loose rocks to inspect his Hawk visually. As expected the stubby wings were mangled, but he was getting out on brute engine power. The nose was scraped but intact. The port side, however, was riddled with dents and holes.

And from one of them, he saw, dripped a dark liquid. The Hawk was losing fuel. Ripping open the satchel he grabbed a sealant can. He pressed it to the leak and watched the thick, grey putty ooze across the tortured metal. He had no idea how much was enough, but in seconds the dripping had ceased.

A scrape of rock alerted him to Singh's approach. Her dark skin shone with perspiration and her features were locked down in a mask of shock.

"Engineering report," she gasped. "Starboard main engine is good but port engine is showing alerts in some relays. It's reporting eighty percent efficiency but I don't know what's wrong and whether it will get worse."

Jack nodded, rising to his feet and running his hand along the warm surface of the hull. He didn't see any more punctures amidst the scarring, but there was no telling what the impacts might have done to internal systems.

"Thrusters?" he asked quietly.

"Operational."

He reached the stern of the Hawk, watched as the last survivors from Axe-One were carried aboard. The second Special Forces operative darted up the ramp, too fast for Jack to get a look at the face, but a light build and graceful movements suggested Chang's partner was a woman. Chang himself stepped into view down the ramp.

"We're loaded, sir. Twenty-four souls including you two."

Jack ascended into the Hawk's dark interior, stepping carefully over the wounded on the deck and the other crewmembers crouched over them. Other crew strapped themselves into the seats lining either side of the cabin. Most wore expressions of shock, but more than one glare followed him as he weaved his way forward.

"Close the ramp," he ordered Singh as he sat down and surveyed his control.

Even before he heard the aft hatch seal he nudged the throttles forward. The Hawk's engines increased in pitch, but the craft didn't move. Jack increased power and fired his thrusters. Through the rattling he felt the Hawk lift off the ground, but not by much, and not for long.

He pulled back and let the Hawk settle down again. On the tactical projection ahead he could see the first red symbols of rebel ground forces coming over the nearest rise. He had less than four minutes before his position was overrun. The ship was too heavy, and one engine was already weakening.

He glanced over his left shoulder at Singh, then over his right at Chang. The only one way the Hawk was getting airborne was if it lost some passengers. Hating himself anew, Jack climbed out of his seat and faced Chang.

The operative stared back at him, face as hard as granite. Beyond him, the cabin was crowded with frightened crewmembers and hostages. Everyone had noticed that the pilot was out of his seat when he should be flying them to safety, and soon all eyes were on him.

"Sergeant Chang," Jack whispered. "We're too heavy. I need to lose a couple of passengers."

Chang's eyes flickered back toward the cabin. After a moment he nodded. "I'll assess the two most badly injured and get them unloaded."

Jack felt his jaw drop, and for a moment he struggled to even understand the cold calculation in Chang's simple statement. The operative was moving to rise, but Jack pressed a hand against the huge man's shoulder. "No, Sergeant. I need you and your partner to get off the Hawk."

Real emotion flashed over Chang's features for the first time. A tiny part of Jack was terrified at what an operative might do if threatened, and he suddenly wished there was a lieutenant here to start barking orders. But Lieutenant Dawson was dead, and any other help was high in orbit.

"Sergeant Chang," Jack forced from his lips, "I am the commander of this mission and I'm ordering you and your partner to disembark."

Chang stared at him in silence, but something in his eyes indicated that he was engaged in far more than just listening to Jack.

"I'm sure you have an alternate escape route," Jack persisted. "None of my people do. And there is no fucking way I'm leaving any of them to the mercy of the rebels."

Chang rose to his feet, towering over Jack in the tiny space. Jack took a half step back into his own chair, trying to match stares with the operative and wondering if, after surviving his own time as a hostage and countless combat missions, he was going to die at the hands of Astral Special Forces.

"Good luck, sir," is all Chang said, before ordering Singh to open the rear ramp.

Amidst cries of alarm the ramp hissed open once again, but before anyone could protest Chang and his partner descended to the dusty ground outside.

Jack avoided the stares of the assembled passengers, glancing at Singh. She looked up at him in horror.

"Shut the ramp," he said, "and stand by countermeasures."

Strapping in again, he fired his thrusters at maximum and slammed the throttle forward. Amidst a swirling cloud of dust, the Hawk lifted into the air. It was sluggish, but slowly responded to his commands. He turned east and started to climb. He caught one last glimpse of Axe-One, and a pair of dark-suited figures moving amongst the wreckage.

Weighted down, the Hawk could never attempt a vertical climb into orbit. Jack kept the throttle at full and steered east, hoping the momentum he'd gained simply from Thor's rotation would help propel him upward. Scanning the tactical situation, he saw *Frankfurt* overhead and a sea of rebel forces swarming the landscape before him. Staying low to avoid anti-air fire was no longer an option. Heavy jinking was impossible with the Hawk so fat. If he wanted to reach orbit, all Jack could do was continue his straight, gentle climb through the hostile sky. He could feel the rebel guns lining him up in their sites right now.

Frankfurt was still dropping orbital bombardment, a steady stream of meteors striking down all across the landscape. With nothing else to do for a moment, Jack watched the bombardment pattern, noting how the strikes were alternating to his port and starboard. But those rebel batteries weren't the threat—it was the guns directly in front of him that had a clear shot.

"Highlight the rebel batteries dead ahead," he ordered Singh.

Moments later, a cone of enemy symbols stretching out in front of the Hawk shone more brightly.

"Forest, this is Axe-Two," he signaled. "Bound for orbit but heavy and no maneuvering ability. Request bombardment support against highlighted hostiles."

There was no change in the bombardment pattern.

"*This is Forest, negative. Highlighted are inside your danger zone for friendly fire.*"

His own ship wasn't going to protect him for fear of hitting him?

"This is Axe-Two. I cannot maneuver and I'm a sitting duck. Take highlighted hostiles. Concentrate fire on those closest to my position."

Jack watched as the bombardment paused. The Hawk continued to climb. He heard the tracking alarm in his ear and felt the thump of countermeasures firing. Then a new rain of fire dropped out of the sky directly ahead of him. He kept his eyes down on his controls as bombardment strikes blazed past him. The firing frequency increased, and even from his altitude Jack saw a long line of black smoke carpeting the surface. The bombardment probably wasn't hitting anything with accuracy, but Jack didn't care. If the rebels were too busy keeping their heads down, they weren't paying attention to him. And as he gained speed he only needed a few seconds to get past any single gun.

The sky was darkening as he climbed, the curved surface of Thor becoming clearer. He was out of range of the surface guns and *Frankfurt*'s blue symbol was beckoning ahead. There was still enough atmo to keep the ride bumpy, but the Hawk's thrusters were back in their element. He got the nose up more and did his best at a full climb.

A flashing red light caught his eye. He scanned his console and swore.

"What is it, sir?" Singh asked.

Obviously he'd sworn louder than intended.

"Low fuel," he said. "And we're not out of the gravity well yet."

She didn't respond, but he heard her tapping quickly at her console. No doubt she was using the computer to figure out what Jack's pilot experience had already discovered: they didn't have the fuel to reach *Frankfurt*'s position.

"Forest, this is Axe-Two," he signaled. "Fuel emergency. Request you close my position at best speed."

The acknowledgement came back immediately and Jack saw the vector on *Frankfurt*'s symbol alter dramatically as the destroyer changed course. Within moments the ship was moving toward him, but the vector still pointed high above. Jack checked his altitude. Not high enough. *Frankfurt* was a vessel designed purely for vacuum, and his Hawk was still fighting through the soup of atmo. He needed to get higher.

The engines were already on full burn, or at least as full as the limping port engine could manage. Checking his external mountings, Jack ejected his pair of self-defence missiles and the countermeasures pod. There was nothing to fight up here, and the loss of their deadweight gave him a few more seconds of thrust.

Jack scanned his console again, searching for anything else he could drop. There was nothing more externally mounted—the only thing left to dump was fuel, and he needed every last drop of that to propel him upward.

Up ahead, he could actually see the bright outline of *Frankfurt* through the blue symbol on his projection. Ordering Singh to remove the tactical display, he visually assessed the destroyer's movement, wondering why she was so visible. Terran warships were colored a dark charcoal specifically so that they were not easy to see in space. Why was she shining?

Because, Jack suddenly realized, she was pushing through the upper reaches of atmo, and super-heated gases were creating a bow wave. The damn destroyer was coming to him.

And if Commander Rossato was willing to risk everything, so was he. Jack knew he had one last way to push his Hawk upward. Pointing his thrusters directly aft, he fired them all. His fuel readings began to plummet, but he watched as his rate of climb crept higher.

"Forest, this is Axe-Two, firing all thrusters as boosters." He paused, not sure what the correct military lingo was for his next request. "Request you... catch me."

Frankfurt's fiery form was looming large overhead, closing from his starboard side. Jack kept his course steady and felt the fuel burn through his engines and thrusters. The Hawk climbed. And climbed.

Silence fell in the cockpit. The pressure against his seat faded to nothing. The tanks were empty, and the engines ceased. He could see *Frankfurt* bearing down on him, shuddering within an envelope of fire as she edged lower. He'd built up a lot of speed in his climb, but she was madly decelerating from a stable orbit.

"Sir," Singh whispered in the still cockpit. "What's going on?"

Jack could feel the effects of zero-g in his body. The controls were useless in his hands. His eyes remained on the approaching mass of *Frankfurt*. The fires were fading as she slowed, but the big ship was growing in his vision at an alarming rate.

"All personnel," he said calmly over the internal speaker, "brace for impact."

The Hawk's nose was beginning to dip. In another few moments it would top out in its ballistic arc and start its long descent back to Thor. *Frankfurt* loomed closer, filling half the sky with her dark bulk. Thrusters fired and she swung to expose her port-side hangar door.

Jack felt a sharp tug of gravity, gasping as he felt the Hawk begin to fall. But training kicked in and he scanned his instruments— altitude was steady. And the sense of falling was sideways, not down. *Frankfurt's* arrestor beams had grabbed his craft and were even now pulling him into the airlock. Mechanical clamps then reached out and secured themselves to the Hawk. He watched as the brilliant surface of Thor disappeared behind the dark floor of the airlock, felt as the Hawk thumped down onto the hard surface. The last of the planetary glow vanished as the airlock outer door closed.

✦ ✦ ✦

A hot shower always helped, but even scrubbed clean and wearing fresh coveralls Jack felt terrible. Lieutenant Dawson was dead. His body and those of the other victims had been left behind on the surface. Left behind by Jack. Safely in deep space and relaxing after the mission, everyone in *Frankfurt* seemed thrilled at his "success" but all he could picture in his mind were the dead bodies left behind.

But there was one bright memory from the mission. It took a bit of asking around, but Jack eventually found Master Rating Daisy Singh in the gym.

He heard her before he saw her, the steady thump of gloves against a heavy bag punctuated by the odd smack of a roundhouse kick. She was stripped down to shorts and a muscle shirt, skin shining with sweat as she pummeled the bag with furious blows. Jack couldn't help but be impressed. She'd appeared tiny and slight under her coveralls, but now he saw that her bird-like frame was taut with muscle.

She noticed him. With one last cross-hook combination she stepped back from the bag, breathing heavily as she stared at him.

"Sorry to interrupt," he said, walking up to her.

"It's okay, sir," she gasped.

"You did really good today."

"Thanks," she said automatically. Her expression didn't reveal gratitude, though. Her face was tight, eyes puffy. This close to her Jack realized that there were tears mixed in with the sweat on her cheeks.

They stared at each other for a long moment, the silence punctuated only by heavy breathing which she was already bringing under control.

Jack figured now was the time for him as the officer to say something inspirational; to reassure his crewmember that all was well in the worlds. But it wasn't, and he couldn't insult her with some patronizing speech.

"That mission went to shit," he said finally. "But we made it back and I couldn't have done it without you."

She nodded, blinking away fresh tears. One of her gloves rose slightly, as if she was going to punch the bag again, but she held back.

"So most missions aren't like that?"

He considered. The silence stretched again.

"How could you leave those people behind?" She blurted out. "I know we were heavy, but…"

"No buts—that's it. We could never have lifted off if we'd tried to evacuate the bodies, and now we'd all be dead or captured."

And there was no way, Jack thought, pushing down his own memories yet again, that he was being a prisoner again.

Was that it? Was he so afraid of his own fate that he was willing to sacrifice anyone? He didn't actually know if Chang and his partner had an alternate escape route.

"I'm just glad you're in charge," Singh said. "I wouldn't want that on my conscience."

Thanks. Jack suddenly had to blink away his own tears.

"Well, I'm sure Fleet will send us a new lieutenant soon enough," he said. "And then they can be in charge and I'll just go back to flying."

She was about to speak, but her gaze suddenly shifted to the gym's entrance behind him. She nodded for him to look.

Turning, Jack instinctively straightened to attention. Commander Rossato was walking toward him.

"Good evening, Mr. Mallory."

"Good evening, ma'am." He gestured to Singh. "Do you know my Hawk's new operator? Master Rating Singh did an excellent job today."

"Yes, you both did." She looked at them with a quiet understanding. "It was a tough mission, but a lot of good came from it."

Jack glanced at Singh. She was stone-faced but the moisture in her eyes revealed the emotions just below the surface. He turned his gaze back to Rossato. "I didn't think destroyers were atmo-capable, ma'am."

"They're not," Rossato said, a strange smile playing at her lips. "I didn't think Hawks were strike fighters, but you sure flew yours like one. I got inspired."

Once upon a time he would have loved a compliment like that. Now it just made him feel tired.

Rossato was no fool.

"Some days are worse than others, Jack." She nodded to Singh. "Daisy. But you did an amazing thing today. I'm not telling you to be proud of it, or inspired by it, or any of that BS. But you saved twenty lives today, and that's twenty excellent reasons to cut yourself some slack."

"Yes, ma'am."

"Congratulations, Lieutenant Mallory."

He looked up, surprised she'd make a mistake like that. "Ma'am, it's sublieutenant."

"I said *lieutenant*." She reached into her pocket and pulled out a pair of epaulettes, each with two silver bars. "And so does the admiral."

Having a lone commander swap out the subbie rank on his coveralls in the middle of the ship's gym wasn't exactly how Jack had pictured his first promotion. Nor had he ever thought he'd feel quite this miserable having the additional bar plunked on his shoulder.

She shook his hand and turned to go, calling over her shoulder. "Command brief is in one hour—as the flight department head you'll be expected to attend."

Jack's heart sank. There was no cavalry coming. No one was going to step into Dawson's shoes and take responsibility. It was all on him.

"I got your back, sir."

He turned. Singh extended one of her gloves toward him, knuckles out. Her expression had cleared and he saw in it something he hadn't seen since they met: hope.

He fist-bumped her glove. Then figured he'd better get some kind of flight department report put together for the evening brief.

"See you around, Singh."

1969's "The Ship Who Sang" is the first story in what became the Brainship series, written by Anne McCaffrey—creator of the Dragonriders of Pern— and others. The protagonist is a brainship, a ship which literally can sing. In 1994, McCaffrey called the resulting novel—for which this story served as the first chapter—the book of which she was most proud, and the story itself her favorite personal work. A very famous space opera, and a true classic.

THE SHIP WHO SANG
ANNE MCCAFFREY

She was born a thing and as such would be condemned if she failed the encephalograph test required of all newborn babies. There was always the possibility that though the limbs were twisted, the mind was not, that though the ears would only hear dimly, the eyes see vaguely, the mind behind them was receptive and alert.

The electro-encephalogram was entirely favorable, unexpectedly so, and the news was brought to the waiting grieving parents. There was the final harsh decision, to give their child euthanasia or permit it to become an encapsulated "brain," a guiding mechanism in any one of a number of curious professions. As such, their offspring would suffer no pain, live a comfortable existence in a metal shell for several centuries, performing unusual service to Central Worlds.

She lived and was given a name, Helva. For her first three vegetable months she waved her crabbed claws, kicked weakly with her clubbed feet and enjoyed the usual routine of the infant. She was not alone, for there were three other children in the big city's special nursery. Soon they all were removed to the Central Laboratory School, where their delicate transformation began.

One of the babies died in the initial transferal, but of Helva's "class," seventeen thrived in the metal shells. Instead of kicking feet, Helva's neural responses started her wheels; instead of grabbing with hands, she manipulated mechanical extensions. As she matured, more and more neural synapses would be adjusted to operate other mechanisms that went into the maintenance and running of a space ship. For Helva was destined to be the "brain" half of a scout ship, partnered with a man or woman, whichever she chose, as the mobile half. She would be among the elite of her kind. Her initial intelligence tests registered above normal and her adaptation index was unusually high. As long as her development within her shell lived up to expectations, and there were no side-effects from the pituitary thinking, Helva would live a rewarding, rich, and unusual life, a far cry from what she would have faced as an ordinary, "normal" being.

However, no diagram of her brain patterns, no early I.Q. tests recorded certain essential facts about Helva that Central must eventually learn. They would have to bide their official time and see, trusting that the massive doses of shell-psychology would suffice her, too, as the necessary bulwark against her unusual confinement and the pressures of her profession. A ship run by a human brain could not run rogue or insane with the power and resources Central had to build into their scout ships. Brain ships were, of course, long past the experimental stages. Most babies survived the perfected techniques of pituitary manipulation that kept their bodies small, eliminating the necessity of transfers from smaller to larger shells. And very, very few were lost when the final connection was made to the panels of ship or industrial combine. Shell-people resembled mature dwarfs in size whatever their natal deformities were, but the well-oriented brain would not have changed places with the most perfect body in the Universe.

So, for happy years, Helva scooted around in her shell with her classmates, playing such games as Stall, Power-Seek, studying her lessons in trajectory, propulsion techniques, computation, logistics, mental hygiene, basic alien psychology, philology, space history, law, traffic codes. All the et ceteras that eventually became compounded into a reasoning, logical, informed citizen. Not so obvious to her, but one of more importance to her teachers, Helva ingested the precepts of her conditioning as easily as she absorbed her nutrient fluid. She would one day be grateful to the patient drone of the subconscious-level instruction.

Helva's civilization was not without busy, do-good associations, exploring possible inhumanities to terrestrial as well as extraterrestrial citizens. One such group, Society for the Preservation of the Rights of Intelligent Minorities, got all incensed over shelled "children" when Helva was just turning fourteen. When they were forced to, Central Worlds shrugged its shoulders, arranged a tour of the Laboratory Schools and set the tour off to a big start by showing the members case histories complete with photographs. Very few committees ever looked past the first few photos. Most of the original objections about "shells" were overridden by the relief that these hideous (to them) bodies were mercifully concealed.

Helva's class was doing fine arts, a selective subject in her crowded program. She had advanced one of her microscopic tools which she would later use for minute repairs to various parts of her control panel. Her subject was large, a copy of the Last Supper, and her canvas small, the head of a tiny screw. She had tuned her sight to the proper degree. As she worked she absentmindedly crooned, producing a curious sound. Shell-people used their own vocal chords and diaphragms, but sound issued through microphones rather than mouths. Helva's hum, then, had a curious vibrancy, a warm, dulcet quality even in its aimless chromatic wanderings.

"Why, what a lovely voice you have," said one of the female visitors.

Helva "looked" up and caught a fascinating panorama of regular, dirty craters on a flaky pink surface. Her hum became a gurgle of surprise. She instinctively regulated her "sight" until the skin lost its cratered look and the pores assumed normal proportions.

"Yes, we have quite a few years of voice training, madam," remarked Helva calmly. "Vocal peculiarities often become excessively irritating during prolonged intrastellar distances and must be eliminated. I enjoyed my lessons."

Although this was the first time that Helva had seen unshelled people, she took this experience calmly. Any other reaction would have been reported instantly.

"I meant that you have a nice singing voice... dear," the lady said.

"Thank you. Would you like to see my work?" Helva asked, politely. She instinctively sheered away from personal discussions, but she filed the comment away for further meditation.

"Work?" asked the lady.

"I am currently reproducing the Last Supper on the head of a screw."

"Oh, I say," the lady twittered.

Helva turned her vision back to magnification and surveyed her copy critically.

"Of course, some of my color values do not match the old Master's and the perspective is faulty, but I believe it to be a fair copy."

The lady's eyes, unmagnified, bugged out.

"Oh, I forget," and Helva's voice was really contrite. If she could have blushed, she would have. "You people don't have adjustable vision."

The monitor of this discourse grinned with pride and amusement as Helva's tone indicated pity for the unfortunate.

"Here, this will help," said Helva, substituting a magnifying device in one extension and holding it over the picture.

In a kind of shock, the ladies and gentlemen of the committee bent to observe the incredibly copied and brilliantly executed Last Supper on the head of a screw.

"Well," remarked one gentleman who had been forced to accompany his wife, "the good Lord can eat where angels fear to tread."

"Are you referring, sir," asked Helva politely, "to the Dark Age discussions of the number of angels who could stand on the head of a pin?"

"I had that in mind."

"If you substitute 'atom' for 'angel,' the problem is not insoluble, given the metallic content of the pin in question."

"Which you are programmed to compute."

"Of course."

"Did they remember to program a sense of humor, as well, young lady?"

"We are directed to develop a sense of proportion, sir, which contributes the same effect."

The good man chortled appreciatively and decided the trip was worth his time.

If the investigation committee spent months digesting the thoughtful food served them at the Laboratory School, they left Helva with a morsel as well.

"Singing" as applicable to herself required research. She had, of course, been exposed to and enjoyed a music appreciation course that had included the better known classical works such as "Tristan and Isolde," "Candide," "Oklahoma," and "Le Nozze di Figaro," along with the atomic age singers, Birget Nilsson, Bob Dylan, and Geraldine Todd, as well as the curious rhythmic progression of the Venusians, Capellan visual chromatics, the sonic concert of the Altairians and Reticulan croons. But "singing" for any shell-person posed considerable technical difficulties. Shell-people were schooled to examine every aspect of a problem or situation before making a prognosis. Balanced properly between optimism and practicality, the nondefeatist attitude of the shell-people led them to extricate themselves, their ships, and personnel from bizarre situations. Therefore, to Helva, the problem that she couldn't open her mouth to sing, among other restrictions, did not bother her. She would work out a method, bypassing her limitations, whereby she could sing.

She approached the problem by investigating the methods of sound reproduction through the centuries, human and instrumental. Her own sound production equipment was essentially more instrumental than vocal. Breath control and the proper enunciation of vowel sounds within the oral cavity appeared to require the most development and practice. Shell-people did not, strictly speaking, breathe. For their purposes, oxygen and other gases were not drawn from the surrounding atmosphere through the medium of lungs but sustained artificially by solution in the shells. After experimentation, Helva discovered that she could manipulate her diaphragmic unit to sustain tone. By relaxing the throat muscles and expanding the oral cavity well into the frontal sinuses, she could direct the vowel sounds into the felicitous position for proper reproduction through her throat microphone. She compared the results with tape recordings of modern singers and was not unpleased, although her own tapes had a peculiar quality about them, not at all unharmonious, merely unique. Acquiring a repertoire from the Laboratory library was no problem to one trained to perfect recall. She found herself able to sing any role and any song which struck her fancy. It would not have occurred to her that it was curious for a female to sing bass, baritone, tenor, mezzo, soprano, and coloratura as she pleased. It was, to Helva, only a matter of the correct reproduction and diaphragmic control required by the music attempted.

If the authorities remarked on her curious avocation, they did so among themselves. Shell-people were encouraged to develop a hobby so long as they maintained proficiency in their technical work.

On the anniversary of her sixteenth year, Helva was unconditionally graduated and installed in her ship, the XH-834. Her permanent titanium shell was recessed behind an even more indestructible barrier in the central shaft of the scout ship. The neural, audio, visual, and sensory connections were made and sealed. Her extendibles were diverted, connected or augmented and the final, delicate-beyond-description brain taps were completed while

Helva remained anesthetically unaware of the proceedings. When she woke, she was the ship. Her brain and intelligence controlled every function from navigation to loading as a scout ship of her class needed. She could take care of herself, and her ambulatory half, in any situation already recorded in the annals of Central Worlds and any situation its most fertile minds could imagine.

Her first actual flight, for she and her kind had made mock flights on dummy panels since she was eight, showed her to be a complete master of the techniques of her profession. She was ready for her great adventures and the arrival of her mobile partner.

There were nine qualified scouts sitting around collecting base pay the day Helva reported for active duty. There were several missions that demanded instant attention, but Helva had been of interest to several department heads in Central for some time and each bureau chief was determined to have her assigned to his section. No one had remembered to introduce Helva to the prospective partners. The ship always chose its own partner. Had there been another brain ship at the base at the moment, Helva would have been guided to make the first move. As it was, while Central wrangled among itself, Robert Tanner sneaked out of the pilots' barracks, out to the field and over to Helva's slim metal hull.

"Hello, anyone at home?" Tanner said.

"Of course," replied Helva, activating her outside scanners. "Are you my partner?" she asked hopefully, as she recognized the Scout Service uniform.

"All you have to do is ask," he retorted in a wistful tone.

"No one has come. I thought perhaps there were no partners available and I've had no directives from Central."

Even to herself Helva sounded a little self-pitying, but the truth was she was lonely, sitting on the darkened field. She had always had the company of other shells and, more recently, technicians by the score. The sudden solitude had lost its momentary charm and become oppressive.

"No directives from Central is scarcely a cause for regret, but there happen to be eight other guys biting their fingernails to the quick just waiting for an invitation to board you, you beautiful thing."

Tanner was inside the central cabin as he said this, running appreciative fingers over her panel, the scout's gravity-chair, poking his head into the cabins, the galley, the head, the pressured-storage compartments.

"Now, if you want to goose Central and do us a favor all in one, call up the barracks and let's have a ship-warming partner-picking party. Hmmmm?"

Helva chuckled to herself. He was so completely different from the occasional visitors or the various Laboratory technicians she had encountered. He was so gay, so assured, and she was delighted by his suggestion of a partner-picking party. Certainly it was not against anything in her understanding of regulations.

"Cencom, this is XH-834. Connect me with Pilot Barracks."

"Visual?"

"Please."

A picture of lounging men in various attitudes of boredom came on her screen.

"This is XH-834. Would the unassigned scouts do me the favor of coming aboard?"

Eight figures galvanized into action, grabbing pieces of wearing apparel, disengaging tape mechanisms, disentangling themselves from bedsheets and towels.

Helva dissolved the connection while Tanner chuckled gleefully and settled down to await their arrival. Helva was engulfed in an unshell-like flurry of anticipation. No actress on her opening night could have been more apprehensive, fearful or breathless. Unlike the actress, she could throw no hysterics, china objets d'art or grease-paint to relive her tension. She could, of course, check her stores for edibles and drinks, which she did, serving Tanner from the virgin selection of commissary.

Scouts were colloquially known as "brawns" as opposed to the ship "brains." They had to pass as rigorous a training program as the brains and only the top one percent of each contributory world's highest scholars were admitted to Central Worlds Scout Training Program. Consequently the eight young men who came pounding up the gantry into Helva's hospitable lock were unusually fine-looking, intelligent, well coordinated and adjusted young men, looking forward to a slightly drunken evening, Helva permitting, and all quite willing to do each other dirt to get possession of her.

Such a human invasion left Helva mentally breathless, a luxury she thoroughly enjoyed for the brief time she felt she should permit it.

She sorted out the young men. Tanner's opportunism amused but did not specifically attract her; the blond Nordsen seemed too simple; dark-haired Alatpay had a kind of obstinacy with which she felt no compassion; Mir-Ahnin's bitterness hinted an inner darkness she did not wish to lighten, although he made the biggest outward play for her attention. Hers was a curious courtship, this would be only the first of several marriages for her, for brawns retired after 75 years of service, or earlier if they were unlucky. Brains, their bodies safe from any deterioration, were indestructible. In theory, once a shell-person had paid off the massive debt of early care, surgical adaptation and maintenance charges, he or she was free to seek employment elsewhere. In practice, shell-people remained in the service until they chose to self-destruct or died in the line of duty. Helva had actually spoken to one shell-person 322 years old. She had been so awed by the contact she hadn't presumed to ask the personal questions she had wanted to.

Her choice of a brawn did not stand out from the others until Tanner started to sing a scout ditty, recounting the misadventures of the bold, dense, painfully inept Billy Brawn. An attempt at harmony resulted in cacophony and Tanner wagged his arms wildly for silence.

"What we need is a roaring good tenor. Jennan, besides palming aces, what do you sing?"

"Sharp," Jennan replied with easy good humor.

"If a tenor is absolutely necessary, I'll attempt it," Helva volunteered.

"My good woman," Tanner protested.

"Sound your 'A'," laughed Jennan.

Into the stunned silence that followed the rich, clear, high "A," Jennan remarked quietly, "Such an A, Caruso would have given the rest of his notes to sing."

It did not take them long to discover her full range.

"All Tanner asked for was one roaring good lead tenor," Jennan said jokingly, "and our sweet mistress supplied us an entire repertory company. The boy who gets this ship will go far, far, far."

"To the Horsehead Nebula?" asked Nordsen, quoting an old Central saw.

"To the Horsehead Nebula and back, we shall make beautiful music," said Helva, chuckling.

"Together," Jennan said. "Only you'd better make the music and, with my voice, I'd better listen."

"I rather imagined it would be I who listened," suggested Helva.

Jennan executed a stately bow with an intricate flourish of his crush-brimmed hat. He directed his bow toward the central control pillar where Helva was. Her own personal preference crystallized at that precise moment and for that particular reason, Jennan, alone of the men, had addressed his remarks directly at her physical presence, regardless of the fact that he knew she could pick up his image wherever he was in the ship and regardless of the fact that her body was behind massive metal walls. Throughout their partnership, Jennan never failed to turn his head in her direction no matter where he was in relation to her. In response to this personalization, Helva at that moment and from then on always spoke to Jennan through her central mike, even though that was not always the most efficient method.

Helva didn't know that she fell in love with Jennan that evening. As she had never been exposed to love or affection, only the drier cousins, respect and admiration, she could scarcely have recognized her reaction to the warmth of his personality and thoughtfulness. As a shell-person, she considered herself remote from emotions largely connected with physical desires.

"Well, Helva, it's been swell meeting you," said Tanner suddenly as she and Jennan were arguing about the baroque quality of "Come All Ye Sons of Art." "See you in space some time, you lucky dog, Jennan. Thanks for the party, Helva."

"You don't have to go so soon?" asked Helva realizing belatedly that she and Jennan had been excluding the others from this discussion.

"Best man won," Tanner said, wryly. "Guess I'd better go get a tape on love ditties. Might need 'em for the next ship, if there're any more at home like you."

Helva and Jennan watched them leave, both a little confused.

"Perhaps Tanner's jumping to conclusions?" Jennan asked.

Helva regarded him as he slouched against the console, facing her shell directly. His arms were crossed on his chest and the glass he held had been empty for some time. He was handsome, they all were; but his watchful eyes were unwary, his mouth assumed a smile easily, his voice (to which Helva was particularly drawn) was resonant, deep, and without unpleasant overtones or accent.

"Sleep on it, at any rate, Helva. Call me in the morning if it's your opt."

She called him at breakfast, after she had checked her choice through Central. Jennan moved his things aboard, received their joint commission, had his personality and experience file locked into her reviewer, gave her the coordinates of their first mission. The XH835 officially became the JH-834.

Their first mission was a dull but necessary priority (Medical got Helva), rushing a vaccine to a distant system plagued with a virulent spore disease. They had only to get to Spica as fast as possible.

After the initial, thrilling forward surge at her maximum speed, Helva realized her muscles were to be given less of a workout than her brawn on this tedious mission. But they did have plenty of time for exploring each other's personalities. Jennan, of course, knew what Helva was capable of as a ship and partner, just as she knew what she could expect from him. But these were only facts and Helva looked forward eagerly to learning that human side of her partner which could not be reduced to a series of symbols. Nor could the give and take of two personalities be learned from a book. It had to be experienced.

"My father was a scout, too, or is that programmed?" began Jennan their third day out.

"Naturally."

"Unfair, you know. You've got all my family history and I don't know one blamed thing about yours."

"I've never known either," Helva said. "Until I read yours, it hadn't occurred to me I must have one, too, someplace in Central's files."

Jennan snorted. "Shell psychology!"

Helva laughed. "Yes, and I'm even programmed against curiosity about it. You'd better be, too."

Jennan ordered a drink, slouched into the gravity couch opposite her, put his feet on the bumpers, turning himself idly from side to side on the gimbals.

"Helva, a made-up name..."

"With a Scandinavian sound."

"You aren't blonde," Jennan said positively.

"Well, then, there're dark Swedes."

"And blonde Turks and this one's harem is limited to one."

"Your woman in purdah, yes, but you can comb the pleasure houses," Helva found herself aghast at the edge to her carefully trained voice.

"You know," Jennan interrupted her, deep in some thought of his own, "my father gave me the impression he was a lot more

married to his ship, the *Silvia*, than to my mother. I know I used
to think *Silvia* was my grandmother. She was a low number so she
must have been… a great-great-grandmother at least. I used to talk
to her for hours."

"Her registry?" asked Helva, unwittingly jealous of everyone
and anyone who had shared his hours.

"422. I think she's TS now. I ran into Tom Burgess once."

Jennan's father had died of a planetary disease, the vaccine for
which his ship had used up in curing the local citizens.

"Tom said she'd got mighty tough and salty. You lose your sweetness and I'll come back and haunt you, girl," Jennan threatened.

Helva laughed. He startled her by stamping up to the column
panel, touching it with light, tender fingers.

"I wonder what you look like," he said softly, wistfully.

Helva had been briefed about this natural curiosity of scouts.
She didn't know anything about herself and neither of them ever
would or could.

"Pick any form, shape, and shade and I'll be yours obliging," she
countered, as training suggested.

"Iron Maiden, I fancy blondes with long tresses," and Jennan
pantomimed Lady Godiva-like tresses. "Since you're immolated in
titanium, I'll call you Brunehilde, my dear," and he made his bow.

With a chortle, Helva launched into the appropriate aria just as
Spica made contact.

"What'n' Hell's that yelling about? Who are you? And unless
you're Central Worlds Medical go away. We've got a plague. No
visiting privileges."

"My ship is singing, we're the JH-834 of Worlds and we've got
your vaccine. What are our landing coordinates?"

"Your ship is singing?"

"The greatest S.A.T.B. in organized space. Any request?"

The JH-834 delivered the vaccine but no more arias and received
immediate orders to proceed to Leviticus IV. By the time they got
there, Jennan found a reputation awaiting him and was forced to
defend the 834's virgin honor.

"I'll stop singing," murmured Helva contritely as she ordered
up poultices for his third black eye in a week.

"You will not," Jennan said through gritted teeth. "If I have to
black eyes from here to the Horsehead to keep the snicker out of the
title, we'll be the ship who sings."

After the "ship who sings" tangled with a minor but vicious narcotic ring in the Lesser Magellanics, the title became definitely respectful. Central was aware of each episode and punched out a "special interest" key on JH-834's file. A first-rate team was shaking down well.

Jennan and Helva considered themselves a first-rate team, too, after their tidy arrest.

"Of all the vices in the universe, I hate drug addiction," Jennan remarked as they headed back to Central Base. "People can go to hell quick enough without that kind of help."

"Is that why you volunteered for Scout Service? To redirect traffic?"

"I'll bet my official answer's on your review."

"In far too flowery wording. 'Carrying on the traditions of my family, which has been proud of four generations in Service,' if I may quote your words."

Jennan groaned. "I was very young when I wrote that. I certainly hadn't been through Final Training. And once I was in Final Training, my pride wouldn't let me fail...

"As I mentioned, I used to visit Dad on board the *Silvia* and I've a very good idea she might have had her eye on me as a replacement for my father because I had had massive doses of scout-oriented propaganda. It took. From the time I was seven, I was going to be a scout or else." He shrugged as if deprecating a youthful determination that had taken a great deal of mature application to bring to fruition.

"Ah, so? Scout Sahir Silan on the JS-44 penetrating into the Horsehead Nebulae?"

Jennan chose to ignore her sarcasm.

"With you, I may even get that far. But even with Silvia's nudging, I never day-dreamed myself that kind of glory in my wildest flights of fancy. I'll leave the whoppers to your agile brain henceforth. I have in mind smaller contributions to space history."

"So modest?"

"No. Practical. We also serve, et cetera." He placed a dramatic hand on his heart.

"Glory hound?" scoffed Helva.

"Look who's talking, my Nebula-bound friend. At least I'm not greedy. There'll only be one hero like my dad at Parsaea, but I would like to be remembered for some kudo. Everyone does. Why else do or die?"

"Your father died on his way back from Parsaea, if I may point out a few cogent facts. So he could never have known he was a hero for damming the flood with his ship. Which kept Parsaean colony from being abandoned. Which gave them a chance to discover the antiparalytic qualities of Parsaea. Which he never knew."

"I know," said Jennan softly.

Helva was immediately sorry for the tone of her rebuttal. She knew very well how deep Jennan's attachment to his father had been. On his review a note was made that he had rationalized his father's loss with the unexpected and welcome outcome at the Affair at Parsaea.

"Facts are not human, Helva. My father was and so am I. And basically, so are you. Check over your dial, 834. Amid all the wires attached to you is a heart, an underdeveloped human heart. Obviously!"

"I apologize, Jennan," she said.

Jennan hesitated a moment, threw out his hands in acceptance and then tapped her shell affectionately.

"If they ever take us off the milkruns, we'll make a stab at the Nebula, huh?"

As so frequently happened in the Scout Service, within the next hour they had orders to change course, not to the Nebula, but to a recently colonized system with two habitable planets, one tropical, one glacial. The sun, named Ravel, had become unstable; the spectrum was that of a rapidly expanding shell, with absorption lines rapidly displacing toward violet. The augmented heat of the primary had already forced evacuation of the nearer world, Daphis. The pattern of spectral emissions gave indication that the sun would sear Chloe as well. All ships in the immediate spatial vicinity were to report to Disaster Headquarters on Chloe to effect removal of the remaining colonists.

The JH-834 obediently presented itself and was sent to outlying areas on Chloe to pick up scattered settlers who did not appear to appreciate the urgency of the situation. Chloe, indeed, was enjoying the first temperatures above freezing since it had been flung out of its parent. Since many of the colonists were religious fanatics who had settled on rigorous Chloe to fit themselves for a life of pious reflection, Chloe's abrupt thaw was attributed to sources other than a rampaging sun.

Jennan had to spend so much time countering specious

arguments that he and Helva were behind schedule on their way to the fourth and last settlement.

Helva jumped over the high range of jagged peaks that surrounded and sheltered the valley from the former raging snows as well as the present heat. The violent sun with its flaring corona was just beginning to brighten the deep valley as Helva dropped down to a landing.

"They'd better grab their toothbrushes and hop aboard," Helva said. "HO says speed it up."

"All women," remarked Jenna in surprise as he walked down to meet them. "Unless the men on Chloe wear furred skirts."

"Charm 'em but pare the routine to the bare essentials. And turn on your two-way private."

Jennan advanced smiling, but his explanation of his mission was met with absolute incredulity and considerable doubt as to his authenticity. He groaned inwardly as the matriarch paraphrased previous explanations of the warming sun.

"Revered mother, there's been an overload on that prayer circuit and the sun is blowing itself up in one obliging burst. I'm here to take you to the spaceport at Rosary—"

"That Sodom?" The worthy woman glowered and shuddered disdainfully at his suggestion. "We thank you for your warning but we have no wish to leave our cloister for the rude world. We must go about our morning meditation which has been interrupted—"

"It'll be permanently interrupted when that sun starts broiling you. You must come now," Jennan said firmly.

"Madame," said Helva, realizing that perhaps a female voice might carry more weight in this instance than Jannan's very masculine charm.

"Who spoke?" cried the nun, startled by the bodiless voice.

"I, Helva, the ship. Under my protection you and your sisters-in-faith may enter safely and be unprofaned by association with a male. I will guard you and take you safely to a place prepared for you."

The matriarch peered cautiously into the ship's open port.

"Since only Central Worlds is permitted the use of such ships, I acknowledge that you are not trifling with us, young man. However, we are in no danger here."

"The temperature at Rosary is now 99°," said Helva. "As soon as the sun's rays penetrate directly into this valley, it will also be 99°, and it is due to climb to approximately 180° today. I notice your buildings are made of wood with moss chinking. Dry moss. It should fire around noontime."

The sunlight was beginning to slant into the valley through the peaks and the fierce rays warmed the restless group behind the matriarch. Several opened the throats of their furry parkas.

"Jennan," said Helva privately to him, "our time is very short."

"I can't leave them, Helva. Some of the girls are barely out of their teens."

"Pretty, too. No wonder the matriarch doesn't want to get in."

"Helva."

"It will be the Lord's will," said the matriarch stoutly and turned her back squarely on rescue.

"To burn to death?" shouted Jennan as she threaded her way through her murmuring disciples.

"They want to be martyrs? Their opt, Jennan," said Helva dispassionately. "We must leave and that is no longer a matter of option."

"How can I leave, Helva?"

"Parsaea?" Helva asked tauntingly as he stepped forward to grab one of the women. "You can't drag them all aboard and we don't have time to fight it out. Get on board, Jennan, or I'll have you on report."

"They'll die," muttered Jennan dejectedly as he reluctantly turned to climb on board.

"You can risk only so much," Helva said sympathetically. "As it is we'll have just enough time to make a rendezvous. Lab reports a critical speedup in spectral evolution."

Jennan was already in the airlock when one of the younger women, screaming, rushed to squeeze in the closing port. Her action set off the others. They stampeded through the narrow opening. Even crammed back to breast, there was not enough room inside for all the women. Jennan brought out spacesuits to the three who would have to remain with him in the airlock. He wasted valuable time explaining to the matriarch that she must put on the suit because the airlock had no independent oxygen or cooling units.

"We'll be caught," said Helva in a grim tone to Jennan on their private connection. "We've lost eighteen minutes in this last-minute rush. I am now overloaded for maximum speed and I must attain maximum speed to outrun the heat wave."

"Can you lift? We're suited."

"Lift? Yes," she said, doing so. "Run? I stagger."

Jennan, bracing himself and the women, could feel her sluggishness as she blasted upward. Heartlessly, Helva applied thrust as long as she could, despite the fact that the gravitational force mashed her cabin passengers brutally and crushed two fatally. It was a question of saving as many as possible. The only one for whom she had any concern was Jennan and she was in desperate terror about his safety. Airless and uncooled, protected by only one layer of metal, not three, the airlock was not going to be safe for the four trapped there, despite the spacesuits. These were only the standard models, not built to withstand the excessive heat to which the ship would be subjected.

Helva ran as fast as she could but the incredible wave of heat from the exploding sun caught them halfway to cold safety.

She paid no heed to the cries, moans, pleas, and prayers in her cabin. She listened only to Jennan's tortured breathing, the missing throb in his suit's purifying system and the sucking of the overloaded cooling unit. Helpless, she heard the hysterical screams of his three companions as they writhed in the awful heat. Vainly, Jennan tried to calm them, tried to explain they would soon be safe and cool if they could be still and endure the heat. Undisciplined by their terror and torment, they tried to strike out at him despite the close quarters. One flailing arm became entangled in the leads to his power pack and the damage was quickly done. A connection, weakened by heat and the dead weight of the arm, broke.

For all the power at her disposal, Helva was helpless. She watched as Jennan fought for his breath, as he turned his head beseechingly toward her, and died.

Only the iron conditioning of her training prevented Helva from swinging around and plunging back into the cleansing heart of the exploding sun. Numbly she made rendezvous with the refugee convoy. She obediently transferred her burned, heat-prostrated passengers to the assigned transport.

"I will retain the body of my scout and proceed to the nearest base for burial," she informed Central dully.

"You will be provided escort," was the reply.

"I have no need of escort."

"Escort is provided, XH-834," she was told curtly. The shock of hearing Jennan's initial severed from her call number cut off her half-formed protest. Stunned, she waited by the transport until her screens showed the arrival of two other slim brain ships. The cortege proceeded homeward at unfunereal speeds.

"834? The ship who sings?"

"I have no more songs."

"Your scout was Jennan."

"I do not wish to communicate."

"I'm 422."

"Silvia?"

"Silvia died a long time ago. I'm 422. Currently MS," the ship rejoined curtly. "AH-640 is our other friend, but Henry's not listening in. Just as well, he wouldn't understand it if you wanted to turn rogue. But, I'd stop him if he tried to deter you."

"Rogue?" The term snapped Helva out of her apathy.

"Sure. You're young, You've got power for years. Skip. Others have done it. 732 went rogue twenty years ago after she lost her scout on a mission to that white dwarf. Hasn't been seen since."

"I never heard about rogues."

"As it's exactly the thing we're conditioned against, you sure wouldn't hear about it in school, my dear," 422 said.

"Break conditioning?" cried Helva, anguished, thinking longing-ly of the white, white furious hot heart of the sun she had just left.

"For you I don't think it would be hard at the moment," 422 said quietly, her voice devoid of her earlier cynicism. "The stars are out there, winking."

"Alone?" cried Helva from her heart.

"Alone!" 422 confirmed bleakly.

Alone with all of space and time. Even the Horsehead Nebula would not be far enough away to daunt her. Alone with a hundred years to live with her memories and nothing... nothing more.

"Was Parsaea worth it?" she asked 422 softly.

"Parsaea?" 422 repeated, surprised. "With his father? Yes. We were there, at Parsaea when we were needed. Just as you... and his son... were at Chloe. When you were needed. The crime is not knowing where need is and not being there."

"But I need him. Who will supply my need?" said Helva bitterly.

"834," said 422 after a day's silent speeding, "Central wishes your report. A replacement awaits your opt at Regulus Base. Change course accordingly."

"A replacement?" That was certainly not what she needed... a reminder inadequately filling the void Jennan left. Why, her hull was barely cool of Chloe's heat. Atavistically, Helva wanted time to mourn Jennan.

"Oh, none of them are impossible if you're a good ship," 422 remarked philosophically. "And it is just what you need. The sooner the better."

"You told them I wouldn't go rogue, didn't you?" Helva said.

"The moment passed you even as it passed me after Parsaea, and before that, after Glen Arthur, and Betelgeuse."

"We're conditioned to go on, aren't we? We can't go rogue. You were testing."

"Had to, Orders. Not even Psych knows why a rogue occurs. Central's very worried, and so, daughter, are your sister ships. I asked to be your escort. I… didn't want to lose you both."

In her emotional nadir, Helva could feel a flood of gratitude for Silvia's rough sympathy.

"We've all known this grief, Helva. It's no consolation, but if we couldn't feel with our scouts, we'd only be machines wired for sound."

Helva looked at Jennan's still form stretched before her in its shroud and heard the echo of his rich voice in the quiet cabin.

"Silvia! I couldn't help him," she cried from her soul.

"Yes, dear, I know," 422 murmured gently and then was quiet.

The three ships sped on, wordless, to the great Central Worlds base at Regulus. Helva broke silence to acknowledge landing instructions and the officially tendered regrets.

The three ships set down simultaneously at the wooded edge where Regulus' gigantic blue trees stood sentinel over the sleeping dead in the small Service cemetery. The entire Base complement approached with measured step and formed an aisle from Helva to the burial ground. The honor detail, out of step, walked slowly into her cabin. Reverently they placed the body of her dead love on the wheeled bier, covered it honorably with the deep blue, star-splashed flag of the Service. She watched as it was driven slowly down the living aisle which closed in behind the bier in last escort.

Then, as the simple words of interment were spoken, as the atmosphere planes dipped in tribute over the open grave, Helva found voice for her lonely farewell.

Softly, barely audible at first, the strains of the ancient song and requiem swelled to the final poignant measure until black space itself echoed back the sound of the ship who sang.

Charles Gannon's Terran Republic series has grown rapidly to have a major fanbase. His story here, "A Taste of Ashes," is part of the main story arc of the series, but is primarily focused on the character of Trevor Corcoran, Caine's ostensibly-soon-to-be brother-in-law and fellow cast-away and prisoner of war during the opening acts of the second book in the series, Trial By Fire. *When Trevor's path parts from Caine's to lead an assault team into occupied Indonesia and coordinate the final attack upon the combined enemy forces, he suffers even more than Caine in the course of events, so this is Trevor's story through to the end of* Trial By Fire.

A TASTE OF ASHES
CHARLES E. GANNON

"For I have eaten ashes like bread, and
mingled my drink with weeping."
Psalms, 102.9

NOVEMBER 14, 2119
OUTBOUND FROM BARNEY DEUCY, BARNARD'S STAR

The cell door opened without warning; an Arat Kur guard scuttled hesitantly into the strangely spacious chamber in which Trevor Corcoran had been imprisoned. Despite the exosapient's smoothly articulated armor, it still looked like a cross between a horseshoe crab and a mammalian cockroach. Muffled by the hardsuit, the Arat Kur's pensive chittering was audible before the translator in its multi-purpose backset began converting it to English. "You will please refrain from any unpermitted movements. To do otherwise would necessitate the use of lethal force." The Arat Kur started back for the cell door. "Please follow me."

Corcoran resisted the urge to shake his head. Even though the Arat Kur looked like hell, they were unfailingly polite. Even when they were about to destroy you. Which they had just done to thousands of Trevor's fellow servicepersons at Barnard's Star. He imagined the Arat Kur crews clicking and buzzing apologies every time they fired another X-ray laser, railgun, or missile at the human ships that had rushed to protect the Pearl: the biggest human naval base beyond Earth's own. Although the Pearl was located well beneath the surface and soupy-white atmosphere of Barnard's Star II C (which everyone called Barney Deucy), the defense of the base had been futile, albeit spirited.

The Arat Kur swayed slightly, but rapidly, from side to side: a sign of anxiety. "You must comply, Captain Corcoran. Please follow me."

Trevor nodded before he could remind himself that only a few of the exosapients had any familiarity with human gestures or body language. "I will comply." He walked forward at a measured pace, partially because he was not too eager to obey any instructions from his jailers, partially because the Arat Kur always seemed a little skittish when interacting with humans—skittish enough that any overly rapid motions might alarm them into using the lethal force his captor had mentioned at the outset. So, better safe than sorry.

The Arat Kur led the human out of the cell, keeping a respectable distance between them.

Some conquerors, thought Trevor.

✦ ✦ ✦

They didn't travel very far and never passed through any security checkpoint indicating their exit from what Corcoran had come to think of as the brig. However, after a dozen meters, the rather narrow passageway began intersecting with others that were several times as wide and half as high: designed for the subterranean Arat Kur, who were agoraphobic and preferred their ceilings close overhead. Which suggested that this entire section of the rotational habitat was specially constructed for taller species such as their Hkh'Rkh allies, or humans. So the reason they hadn't passed any security stations was because the Arat Kur, in keeping with their mannerly nature and passive xenophobia, had created this space to accommodate *all* their interactions with aliens. Including incarceration.

Somewhere in the course of their short walk through the gently sloped corridors, several almost noiseless quadrotor drones had drifted in behind Trevor, not coming closer than two meters—but that was close enough for him to make out the muzzle of some kind of underslung weapon. Nonetheless, when Trevor began increasing his pace, the guard did also, apparently with the intent of maintaining at least three meters between them. Having no neck and an inflexible body, the Arat Kur had a sizable rear blind-spot: it was logical they didn't like having anyone except for trusted friends too close behind them.

Without any explanatory preamble, Trevor's guard/guide angled toward a round hatchway that slid open at his approach. Trevor followed, ducking to get under the thin coaming of the portal.

Three Arat Kur were waiting within, sitting in what Corcoran had come to think of as their belly loungers. A single human was sitting before them in one of two conventional chairs, his arms crossed. He glanced sideways, smiled. "Welcome to the party, Trevor."

"Nice to be included," Corcoran responded with a smile of his own. "How long have you been here, Caine?"

The recently mustered-out Caine Riordan—a commander who was really just a civilian specialist dragooned into service—thought a minute. "About five minutes, I'd say."

Corcoran settled into the chair next to his friend. "Anything exciting to report?"

"Nope."

"No wild dancing or racy stories?"

"Trevor, given that I'm hoping to marry your sister when we get home, I have sworn off all debauchery." Which was particularly ironic coming from Riordan: he may not have been a Boy Scout as a kid, but he was certainly making up for it as an adult.

"Y'know," Trevor drawled, leaning back, "I'm not sure I believe your squeaky clean act, anyhow..."

The centrally seated Arat Kur raised his front claws, clacking them for attention. "I presume your inappropriate banter is a form of levity. I am aware that among your species, close associates often use situationally incongruous jocularity as a form of greeting, particularly if the situation is uncertain or perilous. I trust you have now dispelled any anxiety arising from your current circumstances. We have matters that require discussion."

Although Trevor only had scant contact with the Arat Kur during the two days that he'd been their prisoner, he'd nonetheless discovered that they were as devoid of clownery as they were overlavish with courtesy. It wasn't that the Arat Kur were humorless (not all of them, at least) but they always seemed to be so very— well, earnest. Trevor sighed. "I suppose that since you have now questioned us separately, you're going to put us together and see if any new information comes to light by playing us off against each other? Amateurish: rarely produces results."

The Arat Kur was either annoyed or puzzled: his mandibles clattered. "You misperceive. We have completed our interviews of you. This time, our purpose is different. And you will find that I am a very different interlocutor. We surmise that your initial unwillingness to cooperate more readily may have been motivated by a perception that your ranks, and thus opinions, were not fully appreciated by us. We correct that now. I am Urzueth Ragh, Personal Expediter for First Delegate Hu'urs Khraam. I am empowered to speak for him and make binding agreements in his stead."

Riordan shook his head. "Where's Darzhee Kut, the Arat Kur whom we rescued?"

Urzueth Ragh trilled faintly before his translator kicked in. "Speaker-to-Nestless Darzhee Kut is occupied with other tasks."

"Probably being debriefed about his time with us," muttered Trevor.

"That is correct," Urzueth Ragh confirmed guilelessly. "Furthermore, it is deemed unwise to include him in these discussions. It is only reasonable that your time together while stranded on the damaged spacecraft, and your cooperative efforts to contact rescuers, might compromise his objectivity."

"So you don't trust him."

"On the contrary, I trust Darzhee Kut implicitly. He is my friend and rock-sibling, whom I have known since we were tutored on Homerock. Were our roles reversed—had I been the one with whom you worked to effect a rescue—he would be speaking to you now, not I."

Riordan glanced at Trevor, shrugged. "Not so different from our own protocols."

Trevor hitched a shoulder in reply. "Yep."

Urzueth Ragh's mandibles twitched. "It gratifies me that you understand why Darzhee Kut may not be part of our exchanges. It is likely that you will see him, though, before we arrive at your homeworld."

Trevor leaned forward sharply, kept his elbows on his knees. "So when does the invasion start, Expediter Ragh?"

The Arat Kur, even the armored guard, flinched back: the guard drones whined closer. When it was clear that Trevor's sudden motion did not presage an attack, Urzueth returned to his forward-canted recumbency. "We shall spend nearly two weeks refueling and preaccelerating to effect out-shift. It is difficult to say when we shall arrive at Earth itself, but shortly thereafter, I suspect. No more than five days, at the most." Urzueth sounded slightly annoyed, probably at having quailed before an unarmed human that was already in the cross-hairs of his security forces.

Riordan had folded his arms. "So if you are not hoping to extract more totally useless information from us, why are we here?"

"So that we may formally request one of you to carry our surrender terms to your World Confederation."

Trevor shrank back. "No way."

Riordan leaned forward. "Why us?"

"Is it not obvious? You are both accustomed to working as interspecies liaisons. You were both members of your species' delegation to the Convocation of the Accord."

"Which the Arat Kur Wholenest intentionally undermined," Corcoran added sharply.

Urzueth's flexible mandibles frisked outward. "The matter of your intrusion upon our territory at 70 Ophiuchi—"

"You mean our *unwitting* intrusion—"

Riordan held up a hand. "Expediter, you no doubt understand our reluctance to cooperate with your people. You attacked without provocation or declaration of war, even though we are still a protected species. Under the rules of the Accord, we are therefore excluded from its political processes, to say nothing of attack from two of its four member-states."

Urzueth Ragh's mandibles wilted, curled under themselves. "I agree that the circumstances are singularly awkward. But we feel that the possibility of peace, and our intents, will be better understood if they are conveyed by humans."

Trevor glanced at Riordan, who was nodding slowly. Corcoran knew what that nodding meant: Caine's gesture of careful listening and receptivity was also buying him time to think. "Please expand upon that, Expediter."

Urzueth relaxed into his belly-lounger. "You have both seen how swiftly and completely our fleet defeated the very best ships of your most advanced nations and blocs. You have also seen that we are not cruel or inhospitable to prisoners, that we do not seek punitive concessions from your species, and that, in general, we are not eager to wage war."

"Strange that you'd start one then," Trevor muttered.

Urzueth faltered. Caine frowned at Corcoran, who detected the faintest hint of a smile under the superficially disapproving facial expression. *Okay: so you want me to keep Urzueth rattled. So I'll keep playing the bad cop to your good cop. Lead on, Riordan.*

Who held up an apparently restraining hand toward his friend while speaking to the Arat Kur. "It is, as you said, an awkward situation."

"Most assuredly," Urzueth replied, a nervous chittering rising up in counterpoint to the voice emerging from the translator. "I appreciate that you would normally be unwilling to help us. I am making this request in the hope that you will see the circumstances as I do: that this is the only way to help your own people."

Trevor didn't need to act angry: he already was. "Help them how? By convincing them they should just surrender and welcome their new Arat Kur overlords?"

Urzueth made what sounded like dysfunctionally repetitive clacking noises—the Arat Kur equivalent of a startled stutter?—before the translator began to emit a response. "We have no desire to be Earth's overlords. We merely wish for you to withdraw from 70 Ophiuchi and adjust your political structures to conform with the encyclopedic self-reference you presented in your bid for Accord Membership."

"Oh, is that all?"

Riordan "interceded" once again. "Expediter Ragh, no polity on Earth has the power, or the moral cowardice, to enact arbitrary changes dictated by a would-be conqueror. Furthermore, the Custodians would not approve of our doing so, any more than they will approve of your flagrant violation of the Accords by invading us. However, I understand the humanitarian intent behind your hope that we will bear the terms for an armistice to the powers-that-be on Earth."

"Mr. Riordan, I am afraid you are mistaken. I repeat: we request that you impart our terms of *surrender*, not armistice."

"With respect, Expediter, I am not mistaken. I am simply unwilling to carry terms of surrender to my homeworld. I am, however, willing to carry conditions whereby an armistice may be established so that the proper authorities may enter into negotiations. If, that is, you can prove that it is in the interests of Earth to enter into such an armistice."

Urzueth Ragh stopped in mid claw-wave. "Mister Riordan, I am not sure I heard you correctly."

"I assure you that you did. I remain unconvinced that an armistice, let alone surrender, are in the interests of my species and my homeworld."

Trevor overcame his own surprise enough to nod vigorously even while he thought: *Damn, I hope you know what you're doing, Caine. They just kicked our ass at Barnard's Star and are probably less than a month away from putting Earth itself in the bag.*

Urzueth's mandibles clicked asynchronously once again. "But… but you have just witnessed the destruction of your fleet. With the exception of a few lighter hulls that escaped outsystem, and one shift-carrier that was completing preacceleration for out-shift when we arrived, all your ships were destroyed. They inflicted few losses upon our formation. How then can you remain unconvinced that it is not in the best interests of Earth to seek an armistice, at least?"

"Because I have not seen conclusive evidence that your victory was won by superior technology. You forget, Expediter: Mr. Corcoran and I were trapped in an auxiliary command module, adrift, for the great majority of the engagement. We had no opportunity to witness *how* you won the battle. We only know that you did indeed prevail. For all we know, you may have retained saboteurs to ensure the outcome you are now claiming to be the proof of your technological superiority."

"We had no contact with Earth until you came to the Convocation, less than five weeks ago."

Riordan smiled. "Considering how much advance knowledge you had of Earth, I cannot help but consider that assertion ingenuous, Expediter." And he sat calmly, still smiling.

Urzueth spent several moments either considering, or being stunned by, Riordan's counter-assertion. "So I surmise that you require some form of proof, of evidence?"

"We do, if you wish us to carry your official terms for an armistice to our authorities. Neither Captain Corcoran nor I are eager for history to remember us as playing a role in facilitating Earth's possible capitulation. But if doing so saves lives, then we would take up that mantle of responsibility"—Caine glanced at Trevor, who nodded—"but only if we are convinced that our defeat is, in fact, inevitable."

"Very well. And what evidence do you require to be certain?"

Riordan shrugged. "The records of the recent combat. Sensor and visual recordings."

Urzueth's mandibles drooped. "I am not sure I am familiar with the recordings of which you speak."

Riordan sighed. "Expediter, we will not cooperate if you

start becoming coy. No military rises to your—or our—level of sophistication without ensuring that there are multiple sensor streams generated and recorded during every encounter. Planners use them to determine points of failure and success in tactics and equipment, to enable forensic analysis of adversaries' technology and doctrine, and to corroborate or disprove the reports of combatants. And it is imperative that we screen them within the next five minutes. Otherwise we cannot be certain that we are screening unedited images and sensor results. In which case you would have to find someone else to carry your words to our leaders."

Urzueth's rear legs moved fretfully. "That would be most inconvenient. There are few survivors. And none with your rank or experience as interspeciate liaisons." He swayed up out of his belly-couch. "Very well, but we shall attend you as you screen our recordings. And there are some—not many, but some—which we will not share. They are highly classified, even among our own people."

"I expected as much. We do not require comprehensive data: merely enough to prove that your fleet prevailed because of technological superiority and any other factors which you would bring to bear during an invasion of our homeworld."

Urzueth may have been in communication with his superiors, or they may have been listening in or watching all along. Either way, he bobbed curtly and announced, "Permission has been granted." Polyps just beyond his mandibles licked out, apparently manipulating a set of controls mounted on the sides of his mouth. A concentric pattern of small spheres emerged from the ceiling and the floor. In the space between, an array of holographic images appeared. "You may choose what you will. My assistants"—he dipped toward the two Arat Kur flanking him—"shall control the imaging."

"Control—or modify?" Trevor asked.

Urzueth's translator imparted the impatience of his reply. "You are welcome to attempt to manipulate the controls yourself, Mr. Corcoran, but I think you will find them somewhat challenging. Neither your mouth nor your extremities have the shape or flexibility of our own."

The lights dimmed slightly and Trevor settled back, careful not to look at Riordan. Damn it if Caine hadn't gotten the two of them a peek at the enemy's play book. Of course, the enemy knew that and probably didn't care because they had swept the field today. But if Earth ever got the chance to strike back…

Ten minutes later, Trevor was already struggling to keep alive the thought, let alone the hope, of a successful human counterattack. The footage and integrated sensor results depicted the same basic outcomes again and again and again: a human craft ripped asunder by an unseen beam, or torn apart by a missile impact, secondaries erupting and further ravaging the hull as magazines and fuel tanks exploded. In some cases, on the larger ships with fusion plants, a blue-white sphere bloomed out of the afterdecks, annihilating everything and often blanking the screen: engine containment had been lost. In most cases, the interval between first damage and final destruction was under half a minute: not enough time for any surviving crew to get into lifeboats or pods. So Urzueth Ragh probably wasn't exaggerating when he asserted that Trevor and Riordan were the two most senior humans left.

Riordan never looked away from the scenes. Rather, he called for them one after another, with increasing speed as the minutes wore on. Trevor had already committed key items of technical intelligence to memory: the superior speed and endurance of the Arat Kur drones, their higher efficiency MAP thrusters, and the curious absence of nuke-pumped X-ray laser missiles from their armamentarium. But Caine seemed to be looking for something else.

Urzueth evidently noticed the defense-analyst's same fixation upon the images. "Are you seeking something in particular, Mr. Riordan?"

"In fact, I am." Riordan leaned back with a frown. "But you do not seem to be willing to show it."

"If you make a request with which I may comply, I will be happy to do so."

"I've been watching our ships being destroyed. That is somewhat informative, but not as conclusive as watching your ships mount their attacks."

Urzueth paused, possibly conferring with his superiors, before replying: "How would that be conclusive?"

"Because if saboteurs had access to our ships, then the destruction I'm watching may not be the result of the weapons your craft carry. It could be the result of charges secreted aboard our hulls. In particular, the rapid destruction of so many of our larger craft—many by catastrophic fusion containment failure—is particularly hard to understand. How is that being accomplished?"

"X-ray laser."

"I have not seen any such weapons discharging."

"That is because our technology is different from yours."

"Evidently. And that is the technology I must explain to my superiors, if they are to believe our fight is futile."

"Very well." Urzueth gestured to one of his assistants.

The image abruptly changed from the jagged, blackened ribs of a gutted Russlavic destroyer to a smoothly attenuated delta: an Arat Kur shift-cruiser, viewed from off its starboard beam. The image—evidently relayed from another of the Arat Kurs' ubiquitous microsensors—moved forward along the ship's gray flank until it reached the bow. For a moment, Trevor suspected that their captors had pulled up the wrong sequence. This ship's prow had a hole akin to one where a spinal railgun's muzzle emerged, not the dome-like cap that typically concealed a laser's redirectional mirrors. But the raised rim around the weapon aperture glowed slightly at the same moment that the sensor results—streaming on the left side of the screen—jumped wildly. Warning guidons from the Arat Kur microsensor indicated thermal spikes at both the cruiser's nose and the shallow hillock at her stern.

Riordan nodded slightly. "This will help us make your case," he murmured in Urzueth's direction.

"Indeed? Why so?"

"Because this shows how you won your decisive victory against us. And how you would do it again."

Urzueth's mandibles clicked once. "I comprehend. Our spinal mounted X-ray lasers: you do not have their equivalent."

"We do not. Our nuke-pumped X-ray laser missiles are much less effective."

A similar scene depicted another shift-cruiser firing its X-ray laser: again, the watching microsensor painted thermal indicators at the ship's prow and the stern. "These weapons allow you to strike with much greater power from much greater distance. Clearly, this was the decisive factor in the engagement."

Urzueth seemed reluctant to agree. "That is an overly hasty conclusion, Mr. Riordan. Our advantages were many. In every comparable class or type of ship, ours had superior acceleration and endurance. Also, the enhanced autonomy of our drones allows them to operate more effectively and at greater remove from our control sloops, affording us a much greater direct response envelope."

Riordan nodded agreeably. "Yes, this is consistent with what

I saw. But these latter advantages can only be conceived in broad terms. Your spinal-mounted X-ray laser"—he pointed at the third, analogous scene now unfolding within the holo-round—"provides immediate, visual evidence of your superiority. I suspect it could prove the decisive element in convincing Earth's leaders that capitulation is their only reasonable option."

"Would it be helpful to see more?"

Unless Trevor was much mistaken, the corner of Riordan's mouth twitched—the way it often did when he was laboring to suppress a smile. "The more evidence, the better, Expediter."

+ + +

Instead of being shown back to their separate cells, Trevor and Caine were deposited in what was essentially a suite, but outfitted in a style that recalled a budget hotel trying to appear opulent. Before Urzueth could leave, Corcoran turned a slow circle, hands raised in a gesture that took in the entirety of the *nouveau gauche* furnishings. "Is this a prison cell?"

"No, Mr. Corcoran. Insofar as you have agreed to be our liaisons to the governments of Earth when we arrive there, these are ambassadorial quarters, suitable for your species. We hope they are to your liking."

Trevor struggled to find an adequate answer: it was a whole lot better than the cell he'd been in, but was so oddly laid out and appointed that he couldn't come up with an honest statement which might not also offend his and Caine's captor-hosts. They'd evidently put in a great deal of greatly flawed effort into making these quarters comfortable for them, but still—"We appreciate your consideration," he stammered at Urzueth's withdrawing carapace.

When the hatchway had contracted and sealed behind the exosapient and his entourage, Corcoran turned to Riordan, who was trying to get comfortable on a couch that looked like it had been rescued from a clearance sale of off-beat office furniture. "So, you found the destruction of our fleet riveting viewing?"

"I did," Caine said brightly. As he did, he shook his head from side to side. Twice.

"No?" Hmm, so you found what you were looking for in that final footage. But no way to talk about what it was, or what it means, here in our opulent and presumably bugged quarters. Trevor sat in a chair that appeared completely correct for human use but was an

ergonomic nightmare. "Guess there's nothing to do except for wait for dinner, then?"

"Which will probably be every bit as wonderful as the furniture and amenities," Riordan opined with an irony so bright that it was unlikely to be detected by the Arat Kur.

His prediction—including that of a gustatorily disastrous dinner—proved to be prophetic.

✦ ✦ ✦

NOVEMBER 17–29, 2119
BEYOND THE HELIOPAUSE, BARNARD'S STAR

Trevor and Caine discovered a means for confidential communications after the third day in their new but consistently irksome quarters. Although the Arat Kur did not keep them under constant surveillance—as their towering and ferocious Hkh'Rkh allies repeatedly urged—the humans were also rarely alone. The Arat Kur proved to be naturally congenial critters, and so did not presume that the humans wished to keep their own company most of the time. This meant there were always one or more distressingly attentive, yet politely distant, Arat Kur underfoot.

Trevor remembered the one time he had felt a similar sensation: during a family vacation in France when very young, his father had taken them to a private dinner at a 17th-century palace. The four of them—Dad, Mom, Elena, and himself—were the only guests in that immense, high-ceilinged dining room. Also, apparently in keeping with the period decor, there were no less than eight servers of different station and function arrayed around the periphery of the room like so many wax figures. Then there were the various chefs who emerged from the kitchen, the *sommelier*, and some guy who was less than the owner but more than the *maitre d'hotel*. All for four people. Trevor couldn't remember what his family talked about, or what they ate, or even the name of the damned palace: all he could remember was thinking, *Why are all these waiters here? Are they all even waiters? And what exactly do they do—other than, well, wait? And for what?*

Being a guest of the Arat Kur was a little like that, Trevor discovered. And so, while he and Caine were neither separated nor intruded upon, they also lacked the privacy for secure communications. It took a day or two to figure out a solution, which ironically presented itself through a strongly shared human and Arat Kur trait: attention to hygiene. Specifically, toilet hygiene.

Evidently, the Arat Kur were extremely fastidious about anything having to do with the excretion of wastes and had attitudes similar to humans about expecting privacy while doing so. Although the Arat Kur seemed only indifferently prepared to provide for human eating and sleeping requirements, they had obviously made a considerable study of human excretory habits. Caine and Trevor were somewhat dumbfounded to discover they had been furnished with a very reasonable approximation of a human toilet and an equally reasonable equivalent of toilet paper. The accompanying sink was large enough to bathe a toddler in and the amount of soap provided could have lasted them for many years.

After two days, however, it became evident that the Arat Kur were mildly distressed by the humans' toilet etiquette, but were too polite to say why—or perhaps the translation device wasn't furnished with the right terms (which was pretty understandable). Trevor found the whole situation mildly amusing; Caine, on the other hand, considered it a phenomenon of intense interest and started a fairly hilarious (unintentionally so, but still hilarious) set of experiments to discover what, specifically, about the human toilet habits so distressed the Arat Kur. Everything became a variable to be tested—often with rather ridiculous results. But ultimately, he hit upon the factor that changed the Arat Kur's reactions: the duration between flushing and exiting the bathroom. The longer the interval, the more—well, relieved—the Arat Kur appeared to be.

Caine urged Trevor to extend his time in the fresher as well, and they both began testing other changes in their routine: more or less washing; more or less soap used; more or less grooming. A clear trend emerged: the more fastitidious the humans were in their post-excretory habits, the more relaxed the Arat Kur became. What was for a human a thorough handwashing was, for an Arat Kur, the equivalent of a quick spit on each palm and a vigrous rub on either pant leg. Their captor-hosts seemed to approve of no less than five minutes of detailed scrubbing, nail-checking, and repeated hot-water rinsings. Which—because of their warders immediately changed attitudes as soon as they emerged from the other side of the apartment's closed bathroom door—all but proved that the Arat Kur had taken the fairly obvious precaution of putting visual (and probably audio) bugs in the privy. But still, it provided Trevor and Caine with an idea…

By day four, the two of them began to express the need to use the single toilet facility in quick sequence, occasionally overlapping, the second entering while the first was still washing his hands. And there, with the tap running and soap foaming and toilet flushing, they found short intervals of time in which they could hold an unmonitorable whispered conversation: maybe a dozen words worth. They tested their presumption of privacy by feigning a joint decision to commit suicide that night at dinner—and discovered no enhanced security precautions. If anything, the only reaction of their captors was a faintly greater measure of approval and appreciation for the humans' increased attention to hygiene.

Trevor and Caine maintained the new routine, but did not immediately exchange further information, reasoning that if there wasn't even the faintest hint that these intervals were being used to facilitate secret communications, even the most suspicious Arat Kur would eventually come to accept this as a normative behavior. And that seemed to be, in fact, what occurred.

They waited until a full week after Urzueth Ragh had displayed the wholesale destruction of the Commonwealth and Russlavic fleets at Barnard's Star before they started their brief exchanges. Ultimately, it took five days of intermittently overlapping visits to the restroom to compile even a brief conversation.

It was Trevor who started it, noisily working up enough lather to wash a small dog. "So I'm guessing that up until the footage of their shift-cruisers wiping out our ships, I saw pretty much what you did. Every analogous system on their hulls is both smaller and more powerful than the ones on ours."

Riordan nodded. "Yeah. But the X-ray laser was the game-changer, no matter what Urzueth said."

It was five hours later before Trevor got the opportunity to express his doubt. "Urzueth was trying to mislead us. No way that was an X-ray laser. Can't be. Damn ship would have vaporized itself."

"Yes, if it was nuke-pumped. But this one wasn't."

"Then how do they get all those X-rays at that energy level?"

"They're using their drive."

"You mean, antimatter? Still won't selectively give you—"

"No: it's not tapping an antimatter reaction. Not directly. They're powering it with their shift-generator, their analog of the Wasserman drive."

"Wait: are you saying that they're using a baby borderline black hole as a… a capacitor?"

Riordan answered the next day. "Not merely a capacitor: you can't store X-rays, and you can't generate them selectively."

"Then how—?"

"They've found a way to keep the drive's incipient event horizon stable for more than a microsecond. That gives them both the power levels and the X-rays."

"Well, X-rays and pretty much everything else that would be spat out by a field-effect constantly trying to become a cosmic catastrophe."

"Yeah—unless they've found a way to bleed off the X-rays selectively, directionally."

Trevor was able to follow up on Riordan's startling hypothesis a few hours later. "If they can do that, they've got a much better grasp of high-energy physics than we do."

"They'd have to in order to maintain an IEH for even a few seconds. And judging from the thermal spike back near their engine decks every time they fired that X-ray laser, that's exactly what they're doing: juicing their field effect generator."

Trevor frowned, then smiled. "That must be awfully expensive. In terms of antimatter, that is."

Riordan's only response was an answering smile as they finished washing for dinner.

✦ ✦ ✦

DECEMBER 2, 2119
INBOUND TO EARTH, THE SOLAR SYSTEM

Several days later, their part of the Arat Kur fleet shifted into Earth's backyard, somewhat above the ecliptic and off the shoulder of Jupiter. Dazhee Kut, who had managed to visit them briefly the day before, sent a message as they arrived, explaining that he hoped to speak with them soon again and to put their mission in context. However, for reasons they never learned, that second confab never materialized. Trevor and Caine shared the same suspicion regarding what had prevented him: Darzhee Kut might have appeared a tad too sympatico with his human co-survivors for his superiors' comfort.

So it was Urzueth Ragh who arrived to explain where they

were, that the human home fleet had now been defeated also, and that, very soon now, one of them would be sent home. The other would remain as a more permanent diplomatic liaison, at least until the current difficulties had passed. This was deemed essential since Trevor and Caine's fellow humans had still not acceded to the invaders' surrender demands; consequently, further unpleasantness was sure to follow.

"Just how much more unpleasant do you expect things to get?" Trevor asked in a tone of voice that made the Arat Kur administrator flinch slightly and his security staff inch closer.

"It is difficult to tell," Urzueth admitted. "The remaining ships of your home defense fleet appear to be regrouping for another pass at us. There are signs that Earth itself is preparing for resistance. It will be quite futile, I'm afraid. The outcome is not in question, once we hold the high ground."

Trevor felt sweat break out at various parts of his body. "You mean you'd actually use an asteroid to—?"

Urzueth Ragh started; his mandibles clacked in alarm. "Mr. Corcoran! We would never countenance such a barbarous act. It is not our intent to exterminate, or even conquer, your species: simply to compel you to agree to constraints that will ensure our own safety."

Riordan's smile was mirthless, his eyes narrow. "I wonder if that fine moral posture, of eschewing genocide, is just a bit easier to maintain since you fear the possibility of retaliation by the Custodians. Unfortunately, you *are* already in the process of perpetrating the worst violation of the Accords: attacking another species' homeworld."

Trevor glared at the Arat Kur. "Yeah, but since they're already here, maybe they figure they might as well swing for the fences: if you're going to break the law, you might as well go all the way. After all, someone tried to play 'drop the rock' on us about 35 years ago. Maybe that was you—and maybe this is just your up-close-and-personal return to make sure the job gets done this time."

Urzueth made a noise that sounded like choked wheezing. "Gentlemen! The Wholenest does not annihilate entire species, let alone biospheres. If you seek further reassurance, I will endeavor to provide it. Or, if it is your intent to insult us with such questions, you have succeeded."

Trevor was too mannerly to spit, but thought about it. "You're *insulted*? That's pretty funny, actually—given your treachery since Convocation."

Urzueth's mandibles froze, his wheezing diminished. He was either paralyzed by rage or shame. Trevor didn't know enough Arat Kur body language to tell, and frankly, didn't care.

"However," Riordan followed, "we are somewhat reassured at your response, Urzueth."

"And why do *you* believe my response is genuine, Mr. Riordan?"

"Because—well, you're not a very good actor."

Urzueth's respiration did not just grow more regular; it stopped. "Is that an insult or levity?"

"Well," Riordan confessed, "probably a bit of both."

Urzueth resumed breathing, and shut off his translator as he clacked and chittered at his escort. "Very well," he continued, "I presume that we may now continue our conversation in a productive fashion."

Yeah, don't bet on it. But Trevor remained silent and folded his arms.

Caine nodded slowly, carefully. "You mentioned that you intend to send one of us planetside and keep the other with your fleet."

"That is correct."

"And you are giving us the choice of who shall fulfill which role?"

"That, too, is correct. Although there was considerable resistance to that suggestion."

I'll bet, Trevor thought.

"And who was kind enough to propose that?" Riordan asked.

"Speaker-To-Nestless Kut was the first to suggest that you should be allowed to choose your respective roles. He was also the most dogged advocate when that proposition ran into strong opposition."

"Opposition from whom?"

"The Hkh'Rkh. They do not believe you should have any choice in this matter. Or any other."

Riordan smiled. "I suspect some of them wanted us to be left back at Barney Deucy. Without our space suits."

Urzueth made a buzzing sound deep in his thorax: even to human ears, it sounded uneasy, awkward. "Some of them expressed... similar sentiments."

" 'Some?' " Trevor glanced at Caine. "Sounds like a majority to me."

Urzueth started forward. "It would not have mattered even if they had been unanimous in their insistence. We conferred diplomatic status upon you. We will not fail to honor the implicit protections and commitments."

Damn, sometimes the Arat Kur spoke English as if they'd swallowed a dictionary and had to vomit up the bigger words. But Urzueth was earnest in his assertion. Just as he had been about rejecting any Arat Kur intention of destroying Earth in toto, Trevor had to admit. "Well, then—thank you for taking our side in that argument."

"You need not thank me. I did not do it for you. I did it because it was the right thing to do. The Arat Kur are beings of law, Mr. Corcoran—despite what you may think, given our recent actions."

"Thank you, just the same," added Riordan. "Now, if we are to take proper advantage of the right to select our upcoming roles, I must ask that you also provide us with complete privacy."

"I shall vacate your apartment at once." The Arat Kur turned to go.

"I'm sorry, Administrator Urzueth, but I do not simply mean that we wish to be alone. I must insist that we are allowed to discuss the matter in an environment where we may be certain that there is no possibility of surveillance."

Urzueth had rotated back toward the humans. For a moment, Trevor feared the exosapient might try to deny that they'd been monitored as closely as circumstances allowed during their entire time aboard the ship. But instead, he sagged slightly on his legs: the Arat Kur equivalent of a shrug and sigh. "And how may we assure you of that?"

Riordan smiled. "It is very kind of you to ask…"

✦ ✦ ✦

"Seriously?" Trevor muttered between chattering teeth.

"If you had a better idea, you were free to suggest it at any time," Riordan replied, wrapping his arms tightly about himself.

The cavernous interior of the recently emptied liquid hydrogen fuel tank creaked and groaned as the warmer air forced unusually rapid thermal equalization. Riordan and Corcoran had, as requested, watched the Arat Kur pump the fuel over into an adjoining tank. They entered and were sealed in as soon as the temperature rose to a bearable level, wearing as many layers as they could fit under the space suits in which they had been rescued. Even so, they were still shivering. Trevor rubbed his sides briskly. "Okay, so what's our best play?"

"The most important thing is that they take you straight to D.C. and you get a meeting with the POTUS so that—"

"Hey, hold on: I'm not the one going home. You—"

"It has to be you, Trevor. You've got the credentials, the experience, and the leverage to bring Richard Downing in line if he starts trying to control too much of the information flow himself."

"Me? Control my Uncle Richard, and through him, intelligence operatives all over the world? Are you nuts?"

"Probably, but that's a discussion for another time. The plain facts are that you're the war-hero son of the late Admiral Nolan Corcoran, that you've been a known quantity to D.C. insiders ever since you graduated from Annapolis, and that Richard owes you for all the cloak-and-dagger crap he pulled after your father died."

"Don't remind me—of any of it."

"Sorry, but I have to. Besides, you have another duty to perform."

"What's that?"

"To see your mother. You haven't been home since your father died."

Trevor didn't know whether to thank Caine for his compassion or punch him in the face. He dodged, instead: "Elena's there by now."

"I don't have time to put this delicately, but you know that's not the same. Elena was closer to your dad, and you to your mother."

"Don't try to play family counselor, Riordan."

"Not my intention. But you need to be home to help patch the hole your father left. He wasn't—couldn't be—there for your mom, or for you, not after returning from deflecting the Doomsday Rock and learning that we had interstellar neighbors who were trying to bash us back to the Bronze Age. And later? Well, shit: famous fathers and the sons who don't want to follow in their footsteps. It's hardly a unique family scenario."

Well, that was true. You couldn't swing a cat in the halls of the Academy and not hit a half-dozen midshipmen who didn't have a similar story. "Okay. You've said your piece and made good points. Here's my reply: there's not a chance in hell I'm going to leave you here. And it's not about saving you. *That's* what I'm doing for my family."

"What do you mean?"

"I mean you've got some personal business with Elena that needs settling, and quick. Six months ago, you reappeared after thirteen years of cold sleep—thirteen years while she grappled with the hinky reports that you'd died on Luna. So I'm not about to leave you behind in an enemy invasion fleet. I'm not going to make my sister a widow before she's married, and my nephew fatherless before he's met his father." Trevor watched Caine's expression closely, looking for any hint that he was less than completely moved by these appeals: if he was, he had no business being in the Corcoran family. Hell, you really didn't know about people until they were teetering on the horns of a dilemma like this one. Rather than detecting any vacillation, Trevor was gratified to see grim resolve firm Riordan's jaw, instead.

But that resolve took a direction Trevor hadn't intended. Caine frowned. "It's possible that staying with the invaders means I might be killed," he admitted, "but it's a slim possibility. At most. On the other hand, we can be quite sure of what those invaders will do if their collaborators on Earth discover and reveal that you are still on the active duty roster in the US military databanks. The Hkh'Rkh will rightly claim that you didn't disclose your active rank and your status as a combatant when you accepted your diplomatic status. They'll have you executed in a heartbeat, and the Arat Kur will not be able to intervene."

"You're military, now, too," Trevor rebutted in a tense whisper.

"Yeah, I was military—for a whopping total of twenty-nine days. All of it spent—from induction to retirement into the Reserves—on the Pearl. And what do you bet that paperwork never left Admiral Perduro's office, but was vaporized during the attack? If so, you and Downing are the only two humans who even know I've worn the blue. Meaning that I'm safe, that I've never been in the military as far as the invaders, or their turncoat pals in our megacorporations, know."

Trevor said, "Yeah, but"—and stopped because he couldn't find a sufficient objection.

"Besides," Caine continued, "there's a practical side to this as well. You're the one who has almost twenty years of military experience. The intel analysts are going to be able to get details from you regarding enemy ship architecture and other strategically and tactically relevant observations that I just didn't see, because I don't know what I was looking at."

"Bullshit. You're a defense analyst and writer. You see plenty. Like the Arat Kur's shipboard X-ray laser, and that they only mount it in their shift cruisers."

"Okay, so I catch some esoteric details. But most of the details the tech intel people are looking for are buried in the nitty-gritty stuff that veterans become familiar with by seeing it—or turning it over in their hands—time after time. Like you've done. For almost two decades." Riordan shook his head. "I've got too much book-learning and not enough experience.

"Now flip it around: no matter how this invasion shakes out, it's more likely we're going to need a diplomat next to the invaders than a warrior. Not that I'm a diplomat, really—"

Trevor shrugged. "You're a better diplomat than most of the real diplomats I've seen." And then Trevor knew, in that moment of casual agreement, he'd definitively lost the debate.

So did Riordan: his smile was slow, and a bit sad. "When you see Elena, tell her... tell her I've been thinking about her."

"Tell her yourself," Trevor countered. "You'll be together soon enough."

And then he looked away because he knew he was lying.

✦ ✦ ✦

DECEMBER 7, 2119
WASHINGTON D.C., EARTH

Trevor, waiting at the very end of the Metro platform, stepped forward as the train emerged from the tube with a faltering hum, and watched the dull, reflective gleam of the passing windows as it slowed and sank back down onto its primary track-wheels. As the last car drew abreast of him, he saw that it was almost entirely empty. His strategic waiting spot had paid the dividend he had hoped for: solitude.

He strolled alongside the now creeping car, slipped through the doors as soon as they parted, moved to the last seat and sank into it gratefully. It was both a relief and a little disorienting not to be the center of attention, not to have a dozen pairs of eyeballs—including those of the POTUS, the Joint Chiefs, Director of the CIA, Secretary of State—all boring into him, hanging on every word he uttered. And knowing that each one of those words was being recorded, sent out to the leaders of all five blocs, and examined from every angle.

Instead of resting after the two-day, closeted debrief, his first stop had been his father's office—or now, Uncle Richard's. One of the first to go up after the D.C. construction height codes had been revised in 2062, the building had beautiful views of the National Mall from its position directly south of the Washington Monument. A view Trevor had never seen until today.

Because Nolan Corcoran hadn't been like other kids' fathers. He never made it to school plays or games, was rarely in the same time-zone when parent-teacher meetings occurred. Hell: he'd rarely set foot in his own office. He'd always been on the road, always wheeling and dealing to achieve god knew what.

Until Riordan had confirmed First Contact just over a year ago and it turned out that Nolan Corcoran—and his shadowy umbrella intelligence cooperative known as IRIS—had been preparing for that fateful day ever since his team had found evidence of exosapient tampering during their intercept of the Earth-bound Doomsday Rock in 2083. As if an omen of things to come, the mission had kept him from being present for Trevor's birth and had saddled him with secrets which would dog Nolan to his untimely death half a year ago—possibly at the hands of an assassin.

The train pulled into L'Enfant Plaza: the platform was less crowded than usual. And, whether by chance or some subtle hint of body language, none of the dozen people who boarded the last car approached any of the seats near Trevor.

His collarcom—a burner furnished by the CIA—toned. *Damn it.* Trevor rose and exited just before the doors closed. The platform was now nearly empty: the influx of late afternoon commuters was light, probably because so many businesses and government offices had closed down in anticipation of whatever the Arat Kur might elect to do when the deadline for a response to their armistice proposal ran out. This year, instead of scanning the skies for Santa, kids—and their parents—were trying to pick out the slow, dim specks that marked the closest enemy ships as they moved along their orbital tracks.

Trevor tapped the collarcom after the seventh page: the first step confirming it was a legitimate contact. "Verify ID."

"Downing. Winter thorn. Two. Delta-Foxtrot."

Trevor waited for the collarcom to process the vocal biometrics and the digitized retinal scan which was required even to accept a voice-only call. The com clicked rapidly as it checked the data against a secure file in his belt-carried palmtop, then opened the channel. "How can I help you, sir?" Trevor wondered if he'd ever feel comfortable calling him "Uncle Richard" again.

Richard Downing's BBC-reader accent was stronger than usual: he tended to play it up when he was trying to sound avuncular. "I'm sorry you're still angry, Trevor."

"Yeah, well, I don't like being manipulated."

"See here, lad: this is wartime. I had to have you drop by today, had to pass along the mission—"

"Cut the crap. You weren't just 'passing along a mission' to me. You were twisting emotional thumbscrews to get me willingly on board for the shittiest op I've ever been handed."

"Trevor, if there was anyone else who could—"

"Just stop it; stop it now. In the future, if you're going to order me to prepare a surgical strike against the same people—well, *beings*— that allowed me to return to Earth on a diplomatic parole, don't give me the duty and country bullshit. Just give me the order—and don't bring Dad, or what he'd want, into it. Now: why are you calling?"

Downing sighed. "I need to get some additional guidance from you regarding the Arat Kur."

"Richard, just I spent two long days getting debriefed by all the experts. Then you had me in your own office for another hour. I assure you: I haven't held anything back."

"No, not intentionally, of course. But I'm not looking for specifics so much as impressions, suspicions: the kind of insights that wouldn't have been solicited during your official debriefing or which you didn't touch on when you joined us at my office."

Where "us" had included Major Opal Patrone, who was still not giving him the time of day, largely because she was still technically Caine's dedicated bodyguard, even though he remained a captive of the Arat Kur. Or at least that's what Trevor chose to believe. "So why didn't you ask me this when I was there?"

"Because you might reveal something that the others in my office were not cleared to hear."

"Well, then why the hell do you think it's a good idea to ask me over a comm line, encrypted or not?"

"Because, my boy, your burner collarcom has at least fifteen secure minutes before it can be hacked. Assuming anyone is even scanning for you: fewer than four hundred people know you were returned to us with the terms of the armistice. Besides, anyone who is trying to find a crack in our intel wall today is not wasting their time on random monitoring, which is the only way they'll find this link. Unless, that is, you keep asking me more questions and delay the process. Now: are you in a place where you can be overheard?"

"Do you really think I'm that stupid, Uncle Richard? It's been about a minute since I flashed my ID and walked out on the maintenance walkway in the eastbound tube. So let's make this quick: I don't want to be here when the next train comes rushing past within half a meter of my nose." And that was when Trevor realized he'd slipped and called him Uncle Richard. *Well, old habits die hard.*

"Right then: straight to it. I want your cultural take on the Arat Kur."

Trevor frowned. "Cultural? That's not exactly my speciality."

"I don't mean their preferences in art and music, lad. I mean how they approach war as a species. Not their technology and strategy: I'm after their mindset. You've been a professional warfighter for almost two decades. What sort of warfighters are they?"

Trevor discovered he was shaking his head even though Richard couldn't see the motion: he stopped it abruptly. "They're not really warfighters at all. The Arat Kur seem to find everything about war not just horrible, but distasteful—almost embarassing. As if they're ashamed to be caught up in an activity that is so barbarous. Or primitive."

Downing was silent a moment before replying. "That could prove very useful, Trevor. Tell me: do you have any hypothesis—no matter how subjective—as to the origins of that reaction?"

Trevor kept from shrugging. "Before we were rescued, Darzhee Kut told us that the Arat Kur have not had a major physical dispute, let alone a war or even a battle, in living memory. And some of them seem to live a *long* time. So part of their aversion arises because they never become accustomed to physical violence, either indivdiually or as a day-to-day social possibility. They find it so repulsive that they rejected a Hkh'Rkh offer to school them in all the dirty tricks that a war-fighting species is accustomed to: feints, misinformation, deception."

"Hmm. Were they any more attentive to the lessons they might have learned from our media about *our* conduct of war?"

"I don't think so. From what I could tell—which wasn't much— the Hkh'Rkh conducted exhaustive analyses of whatever signals they've picked up from us over the past century or so. But not the Arat Kur. They avoid thinking about violence the same way you and I would avoid jumping into a sewer if we could at all help it—even if there was something really important down in the muck."

"Yes—but we'd still do it if we had to."

"Yeah, but only to a point. And not with any natural eagerness. We'd never acquire an 'aptitude' for it: we'd tolerate it for just as long as we needed to and then, up out of that sewer. Although I think the Arat Kur may have an additional reservation."

"And what might that be?"

"I think that whatever dirty tricks they have up their sleeves"— Trevor's subconscious concocted the impossible image of an Arat Kur wearing a dress shirt—"they're not willing to reciprocate, to share them with the Hkh'Rkh."

"Because they're not sure how durable their current alliance is?"

"That's my suspicion. The two species couldn't be more dissimilar. And I got the impression that if the Arat Kur feel the Hkh'Rkh to be base, the Hkh'Rkh consider the Arat Kur to be cowards and more akin to prey animals."

Trevor could imagine Downing nodding as he murmured his reply. "Natural, given their evolutionary differences. And the Arat Kur are prudent to fear an end to the alliance. If the Hkh'Rkh remain stuck at their current shift-range, they may start eyeing the worlds of the neighbors they can *already* reach: the Arat Kur. So it makes sense that the Arat Kur refrain from sharing their own doctrinal secrets and advantages with them, but instead, keep the Hkh'Rkh at arm's length. That could be very useful for us. Very useful indeed. Thank you, Trev. You've certainly done all that could be expected of you. And more."

"And still not enough to avoid being sent to their Indonesian beachhead as a glorified hit man."

"Trevor, lad, I'm sorry, but as I explained, you're the only one the Arat Kur are likely to trust long enough to—"

"Yeah. I heard the speech. I don't need to hear it again."

He broke the link without saying goodbye: the next train was just pulling in.

✦ ✦ ✦

FEBRUARY 3, 2120
SPECIAL OPERATIONS COMPOUND "SPOOKY HOLLOW,"
PERTH, EARTH

The knock on the trailer door was unexpected and unwelcome. Trevor considered replying with the most satisfying response: "Fuck off." However, during the last two weeks of post-Jarkarta debriefings, he had been in daily contact with, and therefore might still be visited by, plenty of top brass. Wouldn't do to suggest an admiral or general should perform a biologically impossible act—no matter how much some of them might deserve being forced to try. So he settled on a compromise: "Have a good reason."

"Trevor," said a muffled voice beyond the door, "it's Ri—your Uncle Richard."

"Not a good reason," Trevor replied, taking a swig from the long neck of the bottle of Canadian rye.

"Trevor, don't do this. Don't make me pull rank."

"Oh, well then, I'm sorry, sir," he drawled loudly. "Please do come in."

Downing pushed open the door, paused on the threshold— probably because he hadn't been expecting to find the trailer unlit and all the blinds shut tight. Not that they could keep out pencil-thin bands of the punishing midday sun that should have, by all rights, beaten Perth back down into the barren near-equatorial ground from which it had arisen.

Downing, a black cutout framed by the blinding daylight, murmured. "Sorry, but I can't see a thing."

"Close the door. You'll see better in a moment. Whether you come in or not." Downing closed the door behind him. *Ah, worse luck.* "How may I be of assistance, sir?"

Downing found his way to a chair. He squinted at Trevor. "Trev, are you drunk?"

"No, sir. Sober and ready for duty."

"I wonder if a blood-alcohol test would agree with you."

"I am confident it would, sir. I take one sip every quarter hour. No more. And no less."

"Yes," Downing affirmed as he stared at the four empties lined up on the coffee table like a firing squad, "I can see that."

"Excellent. Your eyes are adjusting. To what do I owe the honor of the visit, sir?"

"I wanted to see how you're doing, lad."

"Never better, sir. Thanks for inquiring." Trevor picked up the rye again.

"I thought you took one sip every fifteen minutes."

"When I'm off-duty, yes, sir. When I'm on the clock or have official visitors, I step up the pace. Helps ward off the boredom, you see."

"Well, I'm sorry I'm boring you."

"No apology needed, sir. I've been bored quite a lot, of late. I was bored by the weeks of fighting through the Javanese jungle. Terribly bored being caught between non-stop waves of friendly and enemy fire and missile bombardment during the liberation of Jakarta. Almost took a snooze when the already-surrendered threat forces turned and shot both Caine and Elena in the back. Yawned when the Custodians arrived and slapped them into medical cryocells in the hope of being able to operate on them eventually. And could hardly bear the dullness of watching Major Opal Patrone bleed out and die. To say nothing of several of my oldest, sweatiest friends in the Teams. To whom I dedicate this drink. Hooyah." And he swigged from the bottle—longer than he usually did.

Downing was silent for a long time. "Trevor, I know you've had a beastly run of luck—"

"Luck, sir? I don't believe in luck. I believe in facts and orders. You ordered me here. You ordered all of us here. And fact: here we all died. Or damn near."

"See here, Trevor: I had no control over—"

"Yes, sir. I see, sir: you had no control. Although you're the director of the most highly classified intel group in existence, you had no control. Very understandable. Hands tied from higher up, no doubt." Trevor considered taking another swig; decided against it.

Downing rose. "I'm sorry to have disturbed you. Now that you were finally out of debrief, and the dust is settling a bit, I figured I might stop by to see if—" He stopped, waited, restarted. "Captain, you might be interested in knowing that the intelligence you brought back from Barnard's Star, both technical and cultural, proved to be decisive in ensuring the defeat of the Arat Kur fleet. You should also be aware that I will be leaving soon. For the Arat Kur homeworld. We have the means to carry the fight back to them, possibly force them to capitulate."

Trevor searched inside, tried to find a part of him that was concerned that his Uncle Richard might be going into harm's way, and at a great remove from any possibility of relief or help. Nope: nothing. "Godspeed, sir."

"Yes. Quite. Before I depart, I must also relay your next assignment."

Ah, now we come to it. "Of course, sir. I am eager to be out of barracks, sir."

"Then you'll like this assignment: it will take you very far away from your barracks. You will join a flotilla we're dispatching to chase down the most distant Arat Kur unit of which we're aware. You will provide our flotilla's CO with tactical and cultural insight on the enemy and guide the pursuit until combat is joined."

Trevor sat up: strange duty for a ground-pounder such as himself. But hell; it was a change of pace. And this time, it wouldn't involve watching his friends or family getting shot into bloody, flying pieces: that would be a bonus, for sure. "That's an unusual mission, sir."

"Not really. Although the Arat Kur had some superficial contact with civilians during both the occupation and liberation of Indonesia, not many of them, or our experts, really got to know anything about them. You have, and familiarity with their mindset and behavior could be crucial to the success of the flotilla's mission."

"How soon do I leave, sir?"

"It will be several weeks, yet. The counterattack fleet, the one I'm shipping out with, has first priority for preparation and logistical support. Your group will go next."

"So I'm headed back to Barnard's Star?"

"And beyond to Ross 154, which is where you'll rendezvous with the flotilla. The intelligence we've gleaned from captured Arat Kur hulls indicates that the force they left in Barnard's Star itself will have fled back across their border by now."

"So the flotilla is heading further down the line, then?"

"Yes. The same intelligence tells us that they sent a small detachment to commandeer the chokepoint at Ross 154 and then pushed onward to drop off Hkh'Rkh commerce raiders in Epsilon Indi. You'll follow them along that presumed path, locate them, engage them, compel surrender if you can."

"And if we cannot?"

"Then you destroy them."

"Sir, with all due respect: destroy them *how*? The Arat Kur were still vastly superior to us, ship to ship, during the battle for Earth. If the Custodians hadn't helped us by disabling their C4I systems with a virus, you and I would be in a prison camp—or a mass grave—now."

"You will not need superior firepower to complete your mission: just an adequate understanding of why the Arat Kur were more willing to kill themselves than surrender at the end of the invasion."

"Yes; that was odd. They never struck me as the courageous type."

"Oh, they're quite courageous, Captain. But not in the way we usually think of the word."

Trevor found that his resentment and desire for isolation were being nudged aside by growing curiosity. "I presume, sir, that an understanding of why the Arat Kur chose suicide instead of surrender is what you expect me to bring to the mission?"

"Yes. I shall arrange for one of our experts to explain what we know and what we suspect about that."

"If it's not too much trouble, I'd appreciate it if *you* might explain it to me. Sir."

Downing hesitated, then sat again. "I shall endeavor to do so, Captain."

+ + +

MAY 6, 2120
TRANSITING THE HELIOPAUSE, ROSS 154

"Captain Corcoran, are you sure you wouldn't be more comfortable in your acceleration couch?"

Trevor shook his head, didn't bother to look at the ensign who'd been assigned as his (thoroughly pointless) adjutant shortly after he'd boarded UCS *Valiant* a week ago. Instead, Corcoran kept staring at the stars on the main screen and enduring the constant two-gee acceleration.

In fact, that downward pressure felt good, was something to resist, something that unobtrusively reminded him that he was still alive, even as he devoted his full attention to the immobile starfield. In particular, he kept his eyes on the one irregular, and more luminous, speck that stood out from the smaller pinpricks of light: the Arat Kur shift-carrier which they'd been chasing for the past one hundred hours.

Valiant had found her prey just three days after Corcoran arrived on board. Detecting a slightly more coherent particle trail that grew in density as they pushed deeper into Ross 154's outer system, *Valiant*'s Aussie skipper, Steve Cameron, gambled that the fragmentary data from the system's remaining microsensors was accurate: that the enemy ship had not stopped to pick up any rearguard elements. Instead, she had headed straight toward a refueling site.

But since Ross 154's port facilities had been the first targets of the attackers four months ago, taking on a load of deuterium now meant a long layover at a gas giant. Refueling at the inner system's large gas giants was both more time consuming and more hazardous, due to their extremely high gravity and radiation levels. So after picking up Trevor from the temporary space station that had been deployed in place of the pre-war highport that was now a debris cloud, Captain Cameron had laid in a course for the small gas giant in the fourth orbit.

As anticipated and hoped, they detected signs that the Arat Kur shift-carrier was there, hanging in the lee of the innermost of the six moons swinging around the blue-white sphere that was Ross 154 Four. Careful observation—largely by passive microsensors that had been lying dormant nearby—revealed thermal trails skimming along the outermost edges of the planet's predominantly hydrogen atmosphere: tankers trailing drogue scoops to collect the fuel their parent ship would need for preacceleration and a shift to safety.

Captain Steve Cameron was both competent and direct: he'd wanted to rail-launch the drone resources of his flotilla—*Valiant* and three destroyers—into an interception net which, remaining inert as they coasted closer, would almost be upon the enemy before they were aware of his more distant ships. However, Corcoran—who, despite equal rank, was holding special orders which made his the final word on when and how to engage—urged that *Valiant* and her escorts crowd gees immediately and startle the Arat Kur, forcing them to break off fueling and spend energy less efficiently by fleeing at their best speed. Which they would have to do, lest the humans' smaller, swifter ships catch them. Cameron had been unconvinced that it was the best course of action, but relented when Trevor told him that, this way, there was an excellent chance that they'd be able to complete their mission without firing a shot.

So the crew of *Valiant* was now in the fourth day of a chase that was roundly held to be more boring than drills. At least during drills, circumstances changed and there were unexpected situations requiring active response. In contrast, this pursuit was only exciting to the number-crunchers in Logistics, who were constantly sending estimates of how long the flotilla could maintain a two-gee pursuit, how much fuel their ships would have left when and if they made intercept, how much hydrogen the enemy hull might have taken on, and if *Valiant* could, in fact, catch her in time. The odds looked promising: the flotilla was slowly but steadily gaining on the Arat Kur shift-carrier.

An hour ago, when *Valiant* finally neared the extreme edge of their own weapons envelope, Trevor had carried out the first of his orders from Joint Command: that the Arat Kur be sent a message, through one of their own translators, to stand down, deccelerate, and surrender. There had been no reply, and the deadline for a response was rapidly nearing.

Trevor heard his adjutant step back just as the helmsman—it was always the helmsman—started yet another round of contagious yawning. Within three minutes, every crewperson on the bridge would succumb to the same, weary reflex, suppressing it as much as possible. Cameron did not approve of yawning and did what he could to keep the crew on their toes. But make-work was only a temporary solution to the monotonous reality of a chase in space: so very different from what movies and recruiting flats promised.

Corcoran smiled at the stillness of the stars in the main viewer. If you hadn't spent years in the Force, you could never completely understand how full of shit the space-navy action shows were. There, ships were perpetually flashing past each other (each near-miss would have been a navigation offense warranting a court martial), making dramatic whooshing sounds (not possible in the vacuum of space), firing bright-colored beams (you only saw a beam in vacuum if you were looking straight at its source, which meant you were dead before the image reached your brain), or launching missiles at perilously close enemies (if you decided to wait for visual contact before launching your missiles, you'd never get to do so).

No, thought Trevor as he folded his hands behind his back and let his eyes wander out into the motionless stars, this was the reality you saw standing the eyeball watch on a genuine, working navy ship. Minute after minute, hour after hour, of the same uneventful view.

Dramatic shifts of perspective were rare. Usually, they occurred only when, in order to deccelerate, you tumbled the ship (which, incongruously, films often depicted as taking place in ultra-slow motion). The other possible cause for a 180-degree attitude change, and much more infrequent, were emergency maneuvers—which you did *not* want to experience. Ever.

Emergency maneuvers meant that something was wrong: a navigational error, unexpected debris, a thruster failure, a possibly hostile contact. The great irony of naval service, reflected Trevor as even Cameron succumbed to a slight squirm as he sat the conn, was that most servicepersons had enlisted for the "excitement" of wearing the blue, and kept hoping for excitement as they endured one uneventful patrol tour after another. But once they found themselves in a real shooting war, they rapidly came to have a deep and abiding appreciation for every passing day of the same unremarkable routine. Because when something went noticeably, dramatically wrong in space, it usually went very wrong indeed. Particularly during wartime.

But *Valiant*'s war had been uneventful. Originally part of the reserves posted to Delta Pavonis, she was one of the few ships which had been left behind when the Relief Fleet had come out of hiding and dealt the Arat Kur invasion a mortal blow at Earth. Only after the great bulk of the enemy fleet had been destroyed or chased back through Barnard's Star had *Valiant* been tasked to track down this final straggler.

The portside lift toned, opened, and revealed a tall young woman wearing civvies and an eyepatch. She waited for Cameron's acknowledgement, and, at his nod, stepped on to the bridge as if she was making a stage entrance, her gait suggesting she had spent a lot of time moving *en pointe*.

Trevor glanced at Cameron. "Who is she?"

"Reporter. IINS."

"Okay. But why is she on the bridge? And why now?"

"Because in ten minutes, if the Arat Kur have not responded, we will be moving to battle stations."

"So?"

"Ms. Thiri Za has been given clearance to witness the resolution of this engagement."

"And who gave her that clearance?"

"Joint Command."

Trevor looked back toward the stars. "So now our engagements are being recorded for the tabloids."

"On the contrary," Thiri objected, a bit too brightly. "I'm here to record events for posterity. This is the last major engagement of the war that will take place in our territory. It's a historical moment: the last of the invaders are being repelled."

I'm glad you're so sure of that. "Forgive me if I don't roll out the red carpet for you, Ms. Thiri, but I've had some bad experiences with embedded journalists."

"You mean we get in the way?"

"I mean that you get dead."

"I'm sure you also believe that we put your forces at increased risk. But I suppose I can understand that, since so many of us probably look just like the enemies you're used to fighting." She leaned her face aggressively towards his, winked with her one eye.

Trevor turned back toward her, and glanced at the eyepatch again. "Just because I've fought against enhanced insurgents doesn't make me cybigot, ma'am."

"No? Then why did you order the removal of—how did your intellience officers put it?—my 'hackable cybernetic enhancements' for the duration of my assignment?"

"I didn't order it. And I'm not your enemy, Ms. Thiri."

"Really? So what makes you so much more 'understanding' than everyone else on board this ship?"

"Because I've spent time in your part of the world."

"And what part is that?"

"The part where there's never enough food, never enough clean water, never enough electricity, never enough bandwidth." He glanced at her tailored clothes, manicured nails, finely coiffed hair. "And here you are, far away from all that. You did what you had to. To get out."

She seemed marginally mollified. "And yet you at least *approved* the removal of my eye, didn't you?"

Trevor shrugged. "Of course I did. That's a universal shipboard security protocol. Has been since the EMPidemic of 2081." A grotesque misnomer, but it had stuck, even though eighty percent of the problems had been caused by hacking rather than electromagnetic pulses. "Unfortunately, the most detailed security check into your background still won't show us a sleeper virus hidden in your implants."

"Yeah, I heard that all the time when I was first looking for work in the Pures."

Souders, the communication officer, frowned uncertainly. "The Pures?"

Thiri smirked at her. "Don't get out of your ivory tower much, do you, sib?"

Trevor interceded sharply. "It's short for Purelands, Lieutenant Souders. Those parts of the globe where performance-enhancing implants and modifications are outlawed."

"Yeah, and where they're not needed so much," Thiri added with an impatient glare. "You Pures have genetic screening and optimization: hardly any worries about disease, defects, neonatal impacts on IQ. And if you're not the sharpest knife in the drawer, so what? In the Developed World, there's always plenty of money and resources and computing power to get ahead.

"But where I grew up, we didn't have any of that. Still don't. So it's like the captain says: you grab any advantage you can. I did well in school, had a knack for getting into places, to talk with people, see things—sometimes things I shouldn't. So I got an ocular implant. Still working off the debt, too."

Cameron's timely interruption prevented what might have extended into an uncomfortable silence. He gestured toward the mission clock. "If the Arat Kur plan on replying, they're really taking it down to the wire. Do you think they know how hopeless their situation is?"

As if I care. But Trevor stayed professional. "I doubt it. They couldn't have received an actual report of their fleet's defeat at Earth; they were already on their way to Epsilon Indi to drop off the Hkh'Rkh commerce raiders. And because that was their whole load, this ship has none of its own defensive craft in her cradles." He folded his arms. "They can't fight; they can only run."

Thiri crossed her arms. "So if they've been out of contact with the rest of the Arat Kur forces, how do they even know they're in trouble? Because when they shifted back here, none of their ships were on station anymore?"

Trevor shrugged. "That and a null signal."

Thiri frowned. "A null signal?"

Souders explained. "It's the commo equivalent of a dead-man switch. If any component of an invasion force is not heard from by a specific time, the other elements will presume it's been lost or compromised. In this case, if the fleet which invaded our home system went silent, the other Arat Kur units were to assume that their entire campaign was a bust and to retreat immediately."

Cameron nodded briskly. "Unfortunately for this lot, 'immediately' wasn't soon enough. Gunnery, has our railgun been reconfigured for drone launch?"

"Yes, sir. And the drones have been rigged for high-gee acceleration."

As Cameron gave the order for the drone launches to begin, Thiri leaned closer. "I thought drones were already built to withstand high gees."

Cameron nodded. "Most of them can pull ten gees or more using their on-board engines. But the railgun will boost them a lot more during their flight up the spinal tube."

"How much more?"

"We've recently declassified the weapon specs on the *Gettysburg* class cruiser, the last of which was laid down six years ago. Her spinal tube puts fifteen gees of acceleration behind drones and other deployables. This cruiser, a *Heroic* class, exceeds that rating."

"And you're not going to tell me by how much, are you?" When Cameron didn't respond, she turned toward Corcoran.

Trevor shrugged. "Sorry. None of us are allowed to tell you, ma'am."

"Just call me Za."

Trevor detected the faint change in Thiri Za's tone and posture; it was subtly more casual. And perhaps, behind that, an additional hint of receptivity to less strictly professional interactions. At another time, Corcoran might have acted on it, or at least been flattered, but now, he couldn't care less. Actually, it was a faint annoyance, a reminder that the mere memory of Opal Patrone was vastly superior to any present realities. And would continue to be so, as far as he could tell. Trevor did not reply to Thiri Za.

With all *Valiant*'s sensor drones now heading toward the enemy shift-carrier, Cameron ordered the weaponized varieties and larger missiles into the launch tube. He glanced at the mission clock above the central view screen. "The deadline has come and gone, Captain Corcoran. But I believe your OpOrd gives you discretion to extend the time in which the Arat Kur may respond."

Trevor Corcoran shook his head sharply. "If they were going to communicate with us, they'd have done so long ago. They're just hoping we'll sit on our hands until they reach their shift-point."

Cameron studied the navplot. "Judging from their course, they're making for the optimal coordinates to 70 Ophiuchi. Unless they're trying to trick us, that is."

Corcoran shook his head again. "They don't need to trick us. It's 9.32 light years to 70 Ophiuchi. They can make that hop. We can't. And once they get there, we'll never catch them."

Cameron nodded. "They'll go to the companion system, 70 Ophiuchi B, which is uninhabited. Probably spend a week to ten days refueling and creating antimatter, and then preaccelerate for their next shift. Of course, it will take us that long just to preaccelerate and out-shift from here. And by the time we could get one hop closer to 70 Ophiuchi following the shorter links we have to use, the Arat Kur would have shifted twice again and reached their own systems."

Thiri looked from one captain to the other. "So we catch them here or not at all."

Trevor nodded.

Souders was staring at the data readouts. "Could still be a while before we actually catch her, though. She's making better speed than she should for her class. About 10 percent over observed maximum. Could she be equipped with auxiliary thrust modules?"

Cameron shrugged, glanced toward Sensor Ops, "Anything unusual about her thrust characteristics?"

"No, sir: energy and thermal signatures are consistent with her class."

Cameron nodded, ignored Thiri when she stepped closer to the conn. "But they could still get away and—"

Trevor interrupted. "The Arat Kur ship is moving faster than usual because she's light. That's one of the reasons we were sure that she has no ships from her own integral defense squadron in her cradles."

Thiri frowned, as if that answer was somehow disappointing. "But when we get closer, the shift-carrier could still attack us with its own spinal weapon, right?"

Trevor shrugged. "It could, but it won't. The shift-carrier can't accelerate and attack at the same time."

"Because of the energy it requires to power its main weapon?"

"No, because of her architecture, which puts the business end of that weapon at her bow. So, since we're stern-chasing her, she would have to tumble to fire her spinal weapon. And when she tumbles, her engines are pointed the wrong way: against the direction she wants to accelerate. So every second she's aligned to shoot at us, she's not continuing to accelerate to her shift point. Which means we gain just that much more on her."

"She could have other offensive options." Thiri sounded more stubborn than self-assured.

"Not unless she has some missiles left. And I doubt she does. She'd have launched by now, to keep us at bay while she crowds gees. No, she's running for shift. That's really the only option she has left, although it's pretty hopeless."

"Why?"

"Because given the boost from our railgun, our combat drones will catch up with her long before she makes it. And once our remote platforms start forcing her to take evasive action to avoid their long-range attacks and feints, she won't be able to hold her course. Our flotilla will get into effective range within a few hours."

Thiri stared at the schematic of the stern-heavy Arat Kur ship, displayed on the screen directly above the navplot. "Even so, how are we going to catch them? Their engines are huge."

Cameron leaned forward. "Ms. Thiri Za, those big engine decks mostly house inertial fusion drives. They're incredibly fuel-efficient and have extraordinary endurance: perfect for building preacceleration velocity over weeks or months. But fusion engines don't make you a jackrabbit. That's what MAP drives are for."

"You mean, our thrusters?"

"I mean MAP. There are a lot of different types of thrusters. On warships, MAP—Magnetically-Accelerated Plasmoid—drives are the gold standard. They give us decent periods of two and even three gees of acceleration. On this ship, they are our primary thrust agencies. On the Arat Kur ship"—Cameron pointed at the main screen—"they are secondary to its main purpose: to preaccelerate for days or weeks at a time, preparatory to achieving shift. That hull has just enough MAP thrusters to maneuver or to get out of trouble until help arrives—which it won't, here. Bottom line: if we push our MAPs to flank speed, we can close the gap and engage before we run out of fuel."

Thiri nodded. "So we're a well-armed sprinter overtaking a marathon runner."

"An *unarmed* marathon runner," Souders amended. "Strange

that she doesn't even have any defense drones."

Trevor shrugged. "My guess is that the naval reserves at Epsilon Indi made her expend whatever deployables she had left. And if she was being pursued during her withdrawal, then she wouldn't have had enough time to scoop up any drones that survived the engagement."

Cameron answered with a nod of his own. "Which means she probably remote-scuttled them."

Trevor nodded slowly. "That would be the Arat Kur SOP. They tried mass suicide after they lost the battle around Earth, in an attempt to deny us access to their space technology. Logically, this ship would have been given the same directives."

Cameron leaned to take a closer look at the holoplot. "Which I suspect they're regretting about now. The first of the recon drones should be drawing abreast of them within fifteen minutes."

Thiri sounded both anxious and eager. "And how close are *we* going to get, Captain?"

It was Corcoran who answered. "As close as we have to."

Cameron smiled. "Careful, now, Captain. You'll make my crew believe you have a death wish."

Trevor saw Thiri flinch—but out of discomfort, not fear. Cameron noticed, looked away to study the readouts—a bit too intently. He was clearly aware that he had said something inappropriate but had no idea what.

Of course, not having been on Earth in at least a year, Cameron had no way to know what Thiri obviously did: that over the course of the war, Trevor had lost almost everything he loved, often in well-publicized events. His father and the first woman he'd loved in years had been killed. His sister was in an alien intensive-care cryocell, in such critical condition that human medicine was incapable of saving her. Her long-lost love—and Trevor's friend—Caine was in pretty much the same straits.

Souders' brow had furrowed slightly during the awkward silence. She tried to restart the conversation. "Well, no matter the range, it should be a relatively short engagement."

Trevor shook his head. "Unless I'm much mistaken, it's going to be even shorter than you think."

"What do you mean?"

Trevor just kept watching the screen. The lopsided, glimmering speck winked and pulsed as if distressed.

The sensor operator explained the changes. "Target is maneuvering to get outside the pattern of the approaching drone envelope."

Cameron nodded. "Remote ops, move the drones to match her course. Keep the target in the center of their expanding cone."

"Compensating for target's movement, sir. She's piling on the thrust."

Cameron nodded approvingly. "That's more fuel she won't have later on. Time until our drone lasers reach effective range?"

"Twelve minutes, sir."

"And to contact, for impact-weapons?"

"Thirty-four minutes, sir."

The enemy shift-cruiser changed her heading again. With little difficulty, the widening cone of drones kept their formattion centered on the enemy's trajectory, bracketing her.

Cameron glanced at Trevor. "Captain, we're about to commence the part of the mission where authority must transfer to the conn."

Trevor nodded. "Soon, now."

Cameron waited, sighed. "In anticipation of that transfer, I propose to sound general quarters."

Trevor nodded. "By all means."

Cameron nodded to Souders, who sent the announcement echoing through the ship in between the peals of the klaxon.

The bridge crew perked up noticeably; the long dull hours of pursuit were coming to their inevitable denouement. Comchatter surged as stations conducted readiness checks, both of personnel and systems. Cameron nodded as the reports trickled in, informing the bridge that *Valiant* was indeed ready for battle. Thiri had moved forward a step. Her eyes were wide, her lips parted slightly. Trevor had seen that response before: the "reporter rush," he had mentally nicknamed it. The journalists who found their way into the field were rarely indifferent to the action: although they might decry it in their articles, they were frequently drawn to it like addicts to a drug of choice.

"Ten minutes to range, sir," the sensor officer announced.

Trevor stepped over to Souders at the Comms station. "Are the Arat Kur jamming our signals, Lieutenant?"

"No, sir. They've never even tried."

"Then please open a channel."

Cameron leaned forward. "Captain Corcoran, I think it's time to start using our *weapons* to communicate our intentions."

Trevor turned to him, smiled. "Sometimes, Captain, words are weapons. The deadliest of all. Lieutenant Souders?"

"Direct link established. Channel open, but they're still not talking. I'm just getting a carrier wave."

That will do. He nodded and Souders leaned back to give him room. "This is Captain Trevor Corcoran, mission commander aboard the UCS *Valiant*. As you are no doubt aware, the deadline to signal your willingness to surrender has now passed. You will also observe that our drones will soon surround you and that you cannot outmaneuver or outpace them.

"We know your ship to be without practicable defenses, and we will overtake you before you achieve your preacceleration velocity or the shift-point to 70 Ophiuchi. Any attempt to use your spinal weapon will simply shorten what remains of the pursuit. Lastly, our intelligence on your operations in this system and Epsilon Indi, along with recently captured technical data on your class of ship, indicate that you do not have enough antimatter reserves to effect out-shift prior to attaining your nominal preacceleration velocity.

"I am therefore contacting you—as a diplomatic courtesy—to convey our intents. Having captured many of your ships during and after the Battle of Earth, we are confident in our ability to cripple, rather than destroy, your hull. To this effect, the drones that shall soon be surrounding you will systematically degrade your point-defense lasers, and eventually, your thrusters and inertial fusion drives. We will, however, decline to bring our own ships into proximity with yours, since you might still be willing and able to scuttle your vessel to destroy any that come alongside. Rather, we will conduct boarding operations via small craft.

"If you wish to reconsider your refusal to surrender, this is your last opportunity to return our signals. Corcoran out."

The line was silent. And stayed so for twenty tense seconds.

Cameron leaned back. "A good, and humane, effort, Captain, but apparently they're not paying any attention to it. We should—"

Trevor raised his chin slightly. "Give them another minute."

Thiri looked at him, one eyebrow raised. "What do you expect them to—?"

"That," Trevor interrupted, pointing at the suddenly brighter main screen.

The glinting speck that was the Arat Kur shift carrier had

abruptly blossomed into a blue-white sphere. Just before it became uncomfortably actinic, like the flame of an arc welder, the screen's automatic filters cut in; the entire starfield faded.

"What was that? What happened?" Thiri almost shouted.

Cameron shook his head at the scrolling data. "They engaged their shift-drive."

"They're gone?" She was stunned.

"In a manner of speaking," Cameron responded. "They destroyed themselves. If the rest mass energy of a ship has not been elevated sufficiently by preacceleration, the shift-drive doesn't create an incipient event horizon: it just becomes a huge antimatter bomb. Which we just saw detonate."

"They destroyed themselves, just like they did at Earth," Thiri murmured, and then looked at Trevor. "And you knew it; you knew they would."

Trevor shrugged. "'Knew?' No. Strongly suspected? Yes."

Souders smiled. "So, yes, sir: a very short battle after all."

He smiled back at her. "I think we've expended enough weapons—and spent enough lives—fighting the Arat Kur."

Thiri seemed to be getting more annoyed by the moment. "But you might have been able to capture their ship, might have won another victory against—"

"Ms. Thiri, you were at Earth, too, so you know the bottom line of this engagement: there was no way the Arat Kur were going to surrender themselves or their ship. They are creatures of law, of duty, and have the courage of their convictions. If we had spent another few days hammering away at their ship's defenses and then trying to cripple her drives, it would have made no difference: in the end, they would still have destroyed themselves. And if we'd disabled their drive, they could still have scuttled themselves simply by forcing their antimatter containment fields to glitch. The explosion wouldn't have been as big, but the result would have been the same: total annihilation."

"So that's it?" she almost shouted. "I came out here—travelled for months, with my cybereye in a lockbox back on Earth—to see a split-second flash and drift through our enemy's ashes?"

Instead of her bright, angry eyes and flushed cheeks, Trevor saw the face of each dead teammate he had left behind in Jakarta. And his father's face, and his sister's, and Caine's, and Opal's. But then, he was always seeing Opal's face.

He spoke to Thiri as he continued to see the ghost-faces around him. "You came out here to report on war, Ms. Thiri. And you'll be able to make an accurate report. Because what you just witnessed is the nature of war. No drama or triumph. Just sharp, painful flashes and then, a taste of ashes." He walked past her and into the lift.

And in his wake, he felt the shades of those whom he had loved hovering close behind him.

As if they would follow him for the rest of his days.

Two supernovae, a black hole, and a neutron—significant celestial bodies—are at the center of our next story, by a science fiction star himself, Grand Master Robert Silverberg, who wrote the introduction to this volume. Silverberg began writing science fiction before the genre's Golden Age and sold his first tales as a teen, so adventure pulp is at the root of his fandom and inspiration. Our next tale, a stand-alone space opera, was written in 1987 for an anthology titled The Universe, *and is a terrific "first contact" story, too.*

THE IRON STAR

ROBERT SILVERBERG

The alien ship came drifting up from behind the far side of the neutron star just as I was going on watch. It looked a little like a miniature neutron star itself: a perfect sphere, metallic, dark. But neutron stars don't have six perky little out-thrust legs and the alien craft did.

While I paused in front of the screen the alien floated diagonally upward, cutting a swathe of darkness across the brilliantly starry sky like a fast-moving black hole. It even occulted the real black hole that lay thirty light-minutes away.

I stared at the strange vessel, fascinated and annoyed, wishing I had never seen it, wishing it would softly and suddenly vanish away. This mission was sufficiently complicated already. We hadn't needed an alien ship to appear on the scene. For five days now we had circled the neutron star in seesaw orbit with the aliens, a hundred eighty degrees apart. They hadn't said anything to us and we didn't know how to say anything to them. I didn't feel good about that. I like things direct, succinct, known.

Lina Sorabji, busy enhancing sonar transparencies over at our improvised archaeology station, looked up from her work and caught me scowling. Lina is a slender, dark woman from Madras whose ancestors were priests and scholars when mine were hunting bison on the Great Plains. She said, "You shouldn't let it get to you like that, Tom."

"You know what it feels like, every time I see it cross the screen? It's like having a little speck wandering around on the visual field of your eye. Irritating, frustrating, maddening—and absolutely impossible to get rid of."

"You want to get rid of it?"

I shrugged. "Isn't this job tough enough? Attempting to scoop a sample from the core of a neutron star? Do we really have to have an alien spaceship looking over our shoulders while we work?"

"Maybe it's not a spaceship at all," Lina said cheerily. "Maybe it's just some kind of giant spacebug."

I suppose she was trying to amuse me. I wasn't amused. This was going to win me a place in the history of space exploration, sure: Chief Executive Officer of the first expedition from Earth ever to encounter intelligent extraterrestrial life. Terrific. But that wasn't what IBM/Toshiba had hired me to do. And I'm more interested in completing assignments than in making history. You don't get paid for making history.

Basically the aliens were a distraction from our real work, just as last month's discovery of a dead civilization on a nearby solar system had been, the one whose photographs Lina Sorabji now was studying. This was supposed to be a business venture involving the experimental use of new technology, not an archaeological mission or an exercise in interspecies diplomacy. And I knew that there was a ship from the Exxon/Hyundai combine loose somewhere in hyperspace right now working on the same task we'd been sent out to handle. If they brought it off first, IBM/Toshiba would suffer a very severe loss of face, which is considered very bad on the corporate level. What's bad for IBM/Toshiba would be exceedingly bad for me. For all of us.

I glowered at the screen. Then the orbit of the *Ben-wah Maru* carried us down and away and the alien disappeared from my line of sight. But not for long, I knew.

As I keyed up the log reports from my sleep period I said to Lina, "You have anything new today?" She had spent the past three weeks analysing the dead-world data. You never know what the parent companies will see as potentially profitable.

"I'm down to hundred-meter penetration now. There's a system of broad tunnels wormholing the entire planet. Some kind of pneumatic transportation network, is my guess. Here, have a look."

A holoprint sprang into vivid life in the air between us. It was a sonar scan that we had taken from ten thousand kilometers out, reaching a short distance below the surface of the dead world. I saw odd-angled tunnels lined with gleaming luminescent tiles that still pulsed with dazzling colors, centuries after the cataclysm that had destroyed all life there. Amazing decorative patterns of bright lines were plainly visible along the tunnel walls, lines that swirled and overlapped and entwined and beckoned my eye into some adjoining dimension.

Trains of sleek snub-nosed vehicles were scattered like caterpillars everywhere in the tunnels. In them and around them lay skeletons, thousands of them, millions, a whole continent full of commuters slaughtered as they waited at the station for the morning express. Lina touched the fine scan and gave me a close look: biped creatures, broad skulls tapering sharply at the sides, long apelike arms, seven-fingered hands with what seemed like an opposable thumb at each end, pelvises enlarged into peculiar bony crests jutting far out from their hips. It wasn't the first time a hyperspace exploring vessel had come across relics of extinct extraterrestrial races, even a fossil or two. But these weren't fossils. These beings had died only a few hundred years ago. And they had all died at the same time.

I shook my head somberly. "Those are some tunnels. They might have been able to convert them into pretty fair radiation shelters, is my guess. If only they'd had a little warning of what was coming."

"They never knew what hit them."

"No," I said. "They never knew a thing. A supernova brewing right next door and they must not have been able to tell what was getting ready to happen."

Lina called up another print, and another, then another. During our brief fly-by last month our sensors had captured an amazing panoramic view of this magnificent lost civilization: wide streets, spacious parks, splendid public buildings, imposing private houses, the works. Bizarre architecture, all unlikely angles and jutting crests like its creators, but unquestionably grand, noble, impressive. There had been keen intelligence at work here, and high artistry. Everything was intact and in a remarkable state of preservation, if you make allowances for the natural inroads that time and weather and I suppose the occasional earthquake will bring over three or four hundred years. Obviously this had been a wealthy, powerful society, stable and confident.

And between one instant and the next it had all been stopped dead in its tracks, wiped out, extinguished, annihilated. Perhaps they had had a fraction of a second to realize that the end of the world had come, but no more than that. I saw what surely were family groups huddling together, skeletons clumped in threes or fours or fives. I saw what I took to be couples with their seven-fingered hands still clasped in a final exchange of love. I saw some kneeling in a weird elbows-down position that might have been one of—who can say? Prayer? Despair? Acceptance?

A sun had exploded and this great world had died. I shuddered, not for the first time, thinking of it.

It hadn't even been their own sun. What had blown up was this one, forty light-years away from them, the one that was now the neutron star about which we orbited and which once had been a main-sequence sun maybe three or four times as big as Earth's. Or else it had been the other one in this binary system, thirty light-minutes from the first, the blazing young giant companion star of which nothing remained except the black hole nearby. At the moment we had no way of knowing which of these two stars had gone supernova first. Whichever one it was, though, had sent a furious burst of radiation heading outward, a lethal flux of cosmic rays capable of destroying most or perhaps all life-forms within a sphere a hundred light-years in diameter.

The planet of the underground tunnels and the noble temples had simply been in the way. One of these two suns had come to the moment when all the fuel in its core had been consumed: hydrogen had been fused into helium, helium into carbon, carbon into neon, oxygen, sulphur, silicon, until at last a core of pure iron lay at its heart. There is no atomic nucleus more strongly bound than iron. The star had reached the point where its release of energy through fusion had to cease; and with the end of energy production the star no longer could withstand the gravitational pressure of its own vast mass. In a moment, in the twinkling of an eye, the core underwent a catastrophic collapse. Its matter was compressed—beyond the point of equilibrium. And rebounded. And sent forth an intense shock wave that went rushing through the star's outer layers at a speed of 15,000 kilometers a second.

Which ripped the fabric of the star apart, generating an explosion releasing more energy than a billion suns.

The shock wave would have continued outward and outward across space, carrying debris from the exploded star with it, and interstellar gas that the debris had swept up. A fierce sleet of radiation would have been riding on that wave, too: cosmic rays, X-rays, radio waves, gamma rays, everything, all up and down the spectrum. If the sun that had gone supernova had had planets close by, they would have been vaporized immediately. Outlying worlds of that system might merely have been fried.

The people of the world of the tunnels, forty light-years distant, must have known nothing of the great explosion for a full generation after it had happened. But, all that while, the light of that shattered star was traveling toward them at a speed of 300,000 kilometers per second, and one night its frightful baleful unexpected glare must have burst suddenly into their sky in the most terrifying way. And almost in that same moment—for the deadly cosmic rays thrown off by the explosion move nearly at the speed of light—the killing blast of hard radiation would have arrived. And so these people and all else that lived on their world perished in terror and light.

All this took place a thousand light-years from Earth: that surging burst of radiation will need another six centuries to complete its journey toward our home world. At that distance, the cosmic rays will do us little or no harm. But for a time that long-dead star will shine in our skies so brilliantly that it will be visible by day, and by night it will cast deep shadows, longer than those of the Moon.

That's still in Earth's future. Here the fatal supernova, and the second one that must have happened not long afterwards, were some four hundred years in the past. What we had here now was a neutron star left over from one cataclysm and a black hole left over from the other. Plus the pathetic remains of a great civilization on a scorched planet orbiting a neighboring star. And now a ship from some alien culture. A busy corner of the galaxy, this one. A busy time for the crew of the IBM/Toshiba hyperspace ship *Ben-wah Maru*.

+ + +

I was still going over the reports that had piled up at my station during my sleep period—mass-and-output readings on the neutron star, progress bulletins on the setup procedures for the neutronium scoop, and other routine stuff of that nature—when the communicator cone in front of me started to glow. I flipped it on. Cal Bjornsen, our communications guru, was calling from Brain Central downstairs.

Bjornsen is mostly black African with some Viking genes salted in. The whole left side of his face is cyborg, the result of some extreme bit of teenage carelessness. The story is that he was gravity-vaulting and lost polarity at sixty meters. The mix of ebony skin, blue eyes, blond hair, and sculpted titanium is an odd one, but I've seen a lot of faces less friendly than Cal's. He's a good man with anything electronic.

He said, "I think they're finally trying to send us messages, Tom."

I sat up fast. "What's that?"

"We've been pulling in signals of some sort for the past ninety minutes that didn't look random, but we weren't sure about it. A dozen or so different frequencies all up and down the line, mostly in the radio band, but we're also getting what seem to be infra-red pulses, and something flashing in the ultraviolet range. A kind of scattershot noise effect, only it isn't noise."

"Are you sure of that?"

"The computer's still chewing on it," Bjornsen said. The fingers of his right hand glided nervously up and down his smooth metal cheek. "But we can see already that there are clumps of repetitive patterns."

"Coming from them? How do you know?"

"We didn't, at first. But the transmissions conked out when we lost line-of-sight with them, and started up again when they came back into view."

"I'll be right down," I said.

Bjornsen is normally a calm man, but he was running in frantic circles when I reached Brain Central three or four minutes later. There was stuff dancing on all the walls: sine waves, mainly, but plenty of other patterns jumping around on the monitors. He had already pulled in specialists from practically every department—the whole astronomy staff, two of the math guys, a couple from the external maintenance team, and somebody from engines. I felt preempted. Who was CEO on this ship, anyway? They were all babbling at once. "Fourier series," someone said, and someone yelled back, "Dirichlet factor," and someone else said, "Gibbs phenomenon!" I heard Angie Seraphin insisting vehemently, "—continuous except possibly for a finite number of finite discontinuities in the interval—pi to pi—"

"Hold it," I said. "What's going on?"

More babble, more gibberish. I got them quiet again and repeated my question, aiming it this time at Bjornsen.

"We have the analysis now," he said.

"So?"

"You understand that it's only guesswork, but Brain Central gives a good guess. The way it looks, they seem to want us to broadcast a carrier wave they can tune in on, and just talk to them while they lock in with some sort of word-to-word translating device of theirs."

"That's what Brain Central thinks they're saying?"

"It's the most plausible semantic content of the patterns they're transmitting," Bjornsen answered.

I felt a chill. The aliens had word-to-word translating devices? That was a lot more than we could claim. Brain Central is one very smart computer, and if it thought that it had correctly deciphered the message coming in, then in all likelihood it had. An astonishing accomplishment, taking a bunch of ones and zeros put together by an alien mind and culling some sense out of them.

But even Brain Central wasn't capable of word-to-word translation out of some unknown language. Nothing in our technology is. The alien message had been *designed* to be easy: put together, most likely, in a careful high-redundancy manner, the computer equivalent of picture-writing. Any race able to undertake interstellar travel ought to have a computer powerful enough to sweat the essential meaning out of a message like that, and we did. We couldn't go farther than that though. Let the entropy of that message—that is, the unexpectedness of it, the unpredictability of its semantic content—rise just a little beyond the picture-writing level, and Brain Central would be lost. A computer that knows French should be able to puzzle out Spanish, and maybe even Greek. But Chinese? A tough proposition. And an *alien* language? Languages may start out logical, but they don't stay that way. And when its underlying grammatical assumptions were put together in the first place by beings with nervous systems that were wired up in ways entirely different from our own, well, the notion of instantaneous decoding becomes hopeless.

Yet our computer said that their computer could do word-to-word. That was scary.

On the other hand, if we couldn't talk to them, we wouldn't begin to find out what they were doing here and what threat, if any, they might pose to us. By revealing our language to them we might be handing them some sort of advantage, but I couldn't be sure of that, and it seemed to me we had to take the risk.

It struck me as a good idea to get some backing for that decision, though. After a dozen years as CEO aboard various corporate ships I knew the protocols. You did what you thought was right, but you didn't go all the way out on the limb by yourself if you could help it.

"Request a call for a meeting of the corporate staff," I told Bjornsen.

It wasn't so much a scientific matter now as a political one. The scientists would probably be gung-ho to go blasting straight ahead with making contact. But I wanted to hear what the Toshiba people would say, and the IBM people, and the military people. So we got everyone together and I laid the situation out and asked for a Consensus Process. And let them go at it, hammer and tongs.

Instant polarization. The Toshiba people were scared silly of the aliens. We must be cautious, Nakamura said. Caution, yes, said her cohort Nagy-Szabo. There may be danger to Earth. We have no knowledge of the aims and motivations of these beings. Avoid all contact with them, Nagy-Szabo said. Nakamura went even further. We should withdraw from the area immediately, she said, and return to Earth for additional instructions. That drew hot opposition from Jorgensen and Kalliotis, the IBM people. We had work to do here, they said. We should do it. They grudgingly conceded the need to be wary, but strongly urged continuation of the mission and advocated a circumspect opening of contact with the other ship. I think they were already starting to think about alien marketing demographics. Maybe I do them an injustice. Maybe.

The military people were about evenly divided between the two factions. A couple of them, the hair-splitting career-minded ones, wanted to play it absolutely safe and clear out of here fast, and the others, the up-and-away hero types, spoke out in favor of forging ahead with contact and to hell with the risks.

I could see there wasn't going to be any consensus. It was going to come down to me to decide.

By nature I am cautious. I might have voted with Nakamura in favor of immediate withdrawal; however, that would have made my ancient cold-eyed Sioux forebears howl. Yet in the end what swayed me was an argument that came from Bryce-Williamson, one of the fiercest of the military sorts. He said that we didn't dare turn tail and run for home without making contact, because the aliens would take that either as a hostile act or a stupid one, and either way they might just slap some kind of tracer on us that ultimately would enable them to discover the location of our home world. True caution, he said, required us to try to find out what these people were all about before we made any move to leave the scene. We couldn't just run and we couldn't simply ignore them.

I sat quietly for a long time, weighing everything.

"Well?" Bjornsen asked. "What do you want to do, Tom?"

"Send them a broadcast," I said. "Give them greetings in the name of Earth and all its peoples. Extend to them the benevolent warm wishes of the board of directors of IBM/Toshiba. And then we'll wait and see."

✦ ✦ ✦

We waited. But for a long while we didn't see.

Two days, and then some. We went round and round the neutron star, and they went round and round the neutron star, and no further communication came from them. We beamed them all sorts of messages at all sorts of frequencies along the spectrum, both in the radio band and via infra-red and ultraviolet as well, so that they'd have plenty of material to work with. Perhaps their translator gadget wasn't all that good, I told myself hopefully. Perhaps it was stripping its gears trying to fathom the pleasant little packets of semantic data that we had sent them.

On the third day of silence I began feeling restless. There was no way we could begin the work we had been sent here to do, not with aliens watching. The Toshiba people—the Ultra Cautious faction— got more and more nervous. Even the IBM representatives began to act a little twitchy. I started to question the wisdom of having overruled the advocates of a no-contact policy. Although the parent companies hadn't seriously expected us to run into aliens, they had covered that eventuality in our instructions, and we were under orders to do minimum tipping of our hands if we found ourselves observed by strangers. But it was too late to call back our messages and I was still eager to find out what would happen next. So we watched and waited, and then we waited and watched. Round and round the neutron star.

We had been parked in orbit for ten days now around the neutron star, an orbit calculated to bring us no closer to its surface than 9,000 kilometers at the closest skim. That was close enough for us to carry out our work, but not so close that we would be subjected to troublesome and dangerous tidal effects.

The neutron star had been formed in the supernova explosion that had destroyed the smaller of the two suns in what had once been a binary star system here. At the moment of the cataclysmic collapse of the stellar sphere, all its matter had come rushing inward with such force that electrons and protons were driven into each other to become a soup of pure neutrons. Which then were squeezed so tightly that they were forced virtually into contact with one another, creating a smooth globe of the strange stuff that we call neutronium, a billion billion times denser than steel and a hundred billion billion times more incompressible.

That tiny ball of neutronium glowing dimly in our screens was the neutron star. It was just eighteen kilometers in diameter but its mass was greater than that of Earth's sun. That gave it a gravitational field a quarter of a billion billion times as strong as that of the surface of Earth. If we could somehow set foot on it, we wouldn't just be squashed flat, we'd be instantly reduced to fine powder by the colossal tidal effects—the difference in gravitational pull between the soles of our feet and the tops of our heads, stretching us towards and away from the neutron star's center with a kick of eighteen billion kilograms.

A ghostly halo of electromagnetic energy surrounded the neutron star: X-rays, radio waves, gammas, and an oily, crackling flicker of violet light. The neutron star was rotating on its axis some 550 times a second, and powerful jets of electrons were spouting from its magnetic poles at each sweep, sending forth a beacon-like pulsar broadcast of the familiar type that we have been able to detect since the middle of the twentieth century.

Behind that zone of fiercely outflung radiation lay the neutron star's atmosphere: an envelope of gaseous iron a few centimeters thick. Below that, our scan had told us, was a two-kilometers-thick crust of normal matter, heavy elements only, ranging from molybdenum on up to transuranics with atomic numbers as high as 140. And within that was the neutronium zone, the stripped nuclei of iron packed unimaginably close together, an ocean of strangeness nine kilometers deep. What lay at the heart of *that*, we could only guess.

We had come here to plunge a probe into the neutronium zone and carry off a spoonful of star-stuff that weighed 100 billion tons per cubic centimeter.

No sort of conventional landing on the neutron star was possible or even conceivable. Not only was the gravitational pull beyond our comprehension—anything that was capable of withstanding the tidal effects would still have to cope with an escape velocity requirement of 200,000 kilometers per second when it tried to take off, two thirds the speed of light—but the neutron star's surface temperature was something like 3.5 million degrees. The surface temperature of our own sun is six thousand degrees and we don't try to make landings there. Even at this distance, our heat and radiation shields were straining to the limits to keep us from being cooked. We didn't intend to go any closer.

What IBM/Toshiba wanted us to do was to put a miniature hyperspace ship into orbit around the neutron star: an astonishing little vessel no bigger than your clenched fist, powered by a fantastically scaled-down version of the drive that had carried us through the space-time manifold across a span of a thousand light-years in a dozen weeks. The little ship was a slave-drone; we would operate it from the *Ben-wah Maru*. Or, rather, Brain Central would. In a maneuver that had taken fifty computer-years to program, we would send the miniature into hyperspace and bring it out again *right inside the neutron star*. And keep it there a billionth of a second, long enough for it to gulp the spoonful of neutronium we had been sent here to collect. Then we'd head for home, with the miniature ship following us along the same hyperpath.

We'd head for home, that is, unless the slave-drone's brief intrusion into the neutron star released disruptive forces that splattered us all over this end of the galaxy. IBM/Toshiba didn't really think that was going to happen. In theory a neutron star is one of the most stable things there is in the universe, and the math didn't indicate that taking a nip from its interior would cause real problems. This neighborhood had already had its full quota of giant explosions, anyway.

Still, the possibility existed. Especially since there was a black hole just thirty light-minutes away, a souvenir of the second and much larger supernova bang that had happened here in the recent past. Having a black hole nearby is a little like playing with an extra wild card whose existence isn't made known to the players until some randomly chosen moment midway through the game. If we destabilized the neutron star in some way not anticipated by the scientists back on Earth, we might just find ourselves going for a visit to the event horizon instead of getting to go home. Or we might not. There was only one way of finding out.

I didn't know, by the way, what use the parent companies planned to make of the neutronium we had been hired to bring them. I hoped it was a good one.

But obviously we weren't going to tackle any of this while there was an alien ship in the vicinity. So all we could do was wait. And see. Right now we were doing a lot of waiting, and no seeing at all.

✦ ✦ ✦

Two days later Cal Bjornsen said, "We're getting a message back from them now. Audio only. In English."

We had wanted that, we had even hoped for that. And yet it shook me to learn that it was happening.

"Let's hear it," I said.

"The relay's coming over ship channel seven."

I tuned in. What I heard was an obviously synthetic voice, no undertones or overtones, not much inflection. They were trying to mimic the speech rhythms of what we had sent them, and I suppose they were actually doing a fair job of it, but the result was still unmistakably mechanical-sounding. Of course there might be nothing on board that ship but a computer, I thought, or maybe robots. I wish now that they had been robots.

It had the absolute and utter familiarity of a recurring dream. In stiff, halting, but weirdly comprehensible English came the first greetings of an alien race to the people of the planet of Earth. "This who speak be First of Nine Sparg," the voice said. Nine Sparg, we soon realized from context, was the name of their planet. First might have been the speaker's name, or his—hers, its?—title; that was unclear, and stayed that way. In an awkward pidgin-English that we nevertheless had little trouble understanding, First expressed gratitude for our transmission and asked us to send more words. To send a dictionary, in fact: now that they had the algorithm for our speech they needed more content to jam in behind it, so that we could go on to exchange more complex statements than Hello and How are you.

Bjornsen queried me on the override. "We've got an English program that we could start feeding them," he said. "Thirty thousand words: that should give them plenty. You want me to put it on for them?"

"Not so fast," I said. "We need to edit it first."

"For what?"

"Anything that might help them find the location of Earth. That's in our orders, under Eventuality of Contact with Extraterrestrials. Remember, I have Nakamura and Nagy-Szabo breathing down my neck, telling me that there's a ship full of boogiemen out there and we mustn't have anything to do with them. I don't believe that myself. But right now we don't know how friendly these Spargs are and we aren't supposed to bring strangers home with us."

"But how could a dictionary entry—"

"Suppose the sun—*our* sun—is defined as a yellow G2 type star," I said. "That gives them a pretty good beginning. Or something about the constellations as seen from Earth. I don't know, Cal. I just want to make sure we don't accidentally hand these beings a road-map to our home planet before we find out what sort of critters they are."

Three of us spent half a day screening the dictionary, and we put Brain Central to work on it too. In the end we pulled seven words—you'd laugh if you knew which they were, but we wanted to be careful—and sent the rest across to the Spargs. They were silent for nine or ten hours. When they came back on the air their command of English was immensely more fluent. Frighteningly more fluent. Yesterday First had sounded like a tourist using a Fifty Handy Phrases program. A day later, First's command of English was as good as that of an intelligent Japanese who has been living in the United States for ten or fifteen years.

It was a tense, wary conversation. Or so it seemed to me, the way it began to seem that First was male and that his way of speaking was brusque and bluntly probing. I may have been wrong on every count.

First wanted to know who we were and why we were here. Jumping right in, getting down to the heart of the matter. I felt a little like a butterfly collector who has wandered onto the grounds of a fusion plant and is being interrogated by a security guard. But I kept my tone and phrasing as neutral as I could, and told him that our planet was called Earth and that we had come on a mission of exploration and investigation.

So had they, he told me. Where is Earth?

Pretty straightforward of him, I thought. I answered that I lacked at this point a means of explaining galactic positions to him in terms that he would understand. I did volunteer the information that Earth was not anywhere close at hand.

He was willing to drop that line of inquiry for the time being. He shifted to the other obvious one:

What were we investigating?

Certain properties of collapsed stars, I said, after a bit of hesitation.

And which properties were those?

I told him that we didn't have enough vocabulary in common for me to try to explain that either.

The Nine Sparg captain seemed to accept that evasion too. And provided me with a pause that indicated that it was my turn. Fair enough.

When I asked him what *he* was doing here, he replied without any apparent trace of evasiveness that he had come on a mission of historical inquiry. I pressed for details. It has to do with the ancestry of our race, he said. We used to live in this part of the galaxy, before the great explosion. No hesitation at all about telling me that. It struck me that First was being less reticent about dealing with my queries than I was with his; but of course I had no way of judging whether I was hearing the truth from him.

"I'd like to know more," I said, as much as a test as anything else. "How long ago did your people flee this great explosion? And how far from here is your present home world?"

A long silence: several minutes. I wondered uncomfortably if I had overplayed my hand. If they were as edgy about our finding their home world as I was about their finding ours, I had to be careful not to push them into an overreaction. They might just think that the safest thing to do would be to blow us out of the sky as soon as they had learned all they could from us.

But when First spoke again it was only to say, "Are you willing to establish contact in the visual band?"

"Is such a thing possible?"

"We think so," he said.

I thought about it. Would letting them see what we looked like give them any sort of clue to the location of Earth? Perhaps, but it seemed far-fetched. Maybe they'd be able to guess that we were carbon-based oxygen-breathers, but the risk of allowing them to know that seemed relatively small. And in any case we'd find out what *they* looked like. An even trade, right?

I had my doubts that their video transmission system could be made compatible with our receiving equipment. But I gave First the go-ahead and turned the microphone over to the communications staff. Who struggled with the problem for a day and a half. Sending the signal back and forth was no big deal, but breaking it down into information that would paint a picture on a cathode-ray tube was a different matter. The communications people at both ends talked and talked and talked, while I fretted about how much technical information about us we were revealing to the Spargs. The tinkering went on and on and nothing appeared on screen except occasional strings of horizontal lines. We sent them more data about how our television system worked. They made further adjustments in their transmission devices. This time we got spots instead of lines. We sent even more data. Were they leading us on? And were we telling them too much? I came finally to the position that trying to make the video link work had been a bad idea, and started to tell Communications that. But then the haze of drifting spots on my screen abruptly cleared and I found myself looking into the face of an alien being.

An alien face, yes. Extremely alien. Suddenly this whole interchange was kicked up to a new level of reality.

A hairless wedge-shaped head, flat and broad on top, tapering to a sharp point below. Corrugated skin that looked as thick as heavy rubber. Two chilly eyes in the center of that wide forehead and two more at its extreme edges. Three mouths, vertical slits, side by side: one for speaking and the other two, maybe for separate intake of fluids and solids. The whole business supported by three long columnar necks as thick as a man's wrist, separated by open spaces two or three centimeters wide. What was below the neck we never got to see. But the head alone was plenty.

They probably thought we were just as strange.

With video established, First and I picked up our conversation right where we had broken it off the day before. Once more he was not in the least shy about telling me things.

He had been able to calculate in our units of time the date of the great explosion that had driven his people far from home world: it had taken place 387 years ago. He didn't use the word "supernova," because it hadn't been included in the 30,000-word vocabulary we had sent them, but that was obviously what he meant by "the great explosion." The 387-year figure squared pretty well with our own calculations, which were based on an analysis of the surface temperature and rate of rotation of the neutron star.

The Nine Sparg people had had plenty of warning that their sun was behaving oddly—the first signs of instability had become apparent more than a century before the blow-up—and they had devoted all their energy for several generations to the job of packing up and clearing out. It had taken many years, it seemed, for them to accomplish their migration to the distant new world they had chosen for their new home. Did that mean, I asked myself, that their method of interstellar travel was much slower than ours, and that they had needed decades or even a century to cover fifty or a hundred light-years? Earth had less to worry about, then. Even if they wanted to make trouble for us, they wouldn't be able easily to reach us, a thousand light-years from here. Or was First saying that their new world was really distant—all the way across the galaxy, perhaps, seventy or eighty thousand light-years away, or even in some other galaxy altogether? If that was the case, we were up against truly superior beings. But there was no easy way for me to question him about such things without telling him things about our own hyperdrive and our distance from this system that I didn't care to have him know.

After a long and evidently difficult period of settling in on the new world, First went on, the Nine Sparg folk finally were well enough established to launch an inquiry into the condition of their former home planet. Thus his mission to the supernova site.

"But we are in great mystery," First admitted, and it seemed to me that a note of sadness and bewilderment had crept into his mechanical-sounding voice. "We have come to what certainly is the right location. Yet nothing seems to be correct here. We find only this little iron star. And of our former planet there is no trace."

I stared at that peculiar and unfathomable four-eyed face, that three-columned neck, those tight vertical mouths, and to my surprise something close to compassion awoke in me. I had been dealing with this creature as though he were a potential enemy capable of leading armadas of war to my world and conquering it. But in fact he might be merely a scholarly explorer who was making a nostalgic pilgrimage, and running into problems with it. I decided to relax my guard just a little.

"Have you considered," I said, "that you might not be in the right location after all?"

"What do you mean?"

"As we were completing our journey toward what you call the

iron star," I said, "we discovered a planet forty light-years from here that beyond much doubt had had a great civilization, and which evidently was close enough to the exploding star system here to have been devastated by it. We have pictures of it that we could show you. Perhaps *that* was your home world."

Even as I was saying it the idea started to seem foolish to me. The skeletons we had photographed on the dead world had had broad tapering heads that might perhaps have been similar to those of First, but they hadn't shown any evidence of this unique triple-neck arrangement. Besides, First had said that his people had had several generations to prepare for evacuation. Would they have left so many millions of their people behind to die? It looked obvious from the way those skeletons were scattered around that the inhabitants of that planet hadn't had the slightest clue that doom was due to overtake them that day. And finally, I realized that First had plainly said that it was his own world's sun that had exploded, not some neighboring star. The supernova had happened here. The dead world's sun was still intact.

"Can you show me your pictures?" he said.

It seemed pointless. But I felt odd about retracting my offer. And in the new rapport that had sprung up between us I could see no harm in it.

I told Lina Sorabji to feed her sonar transparencies into the relay pickup. It was easy enough for Cal Bjornsen to shunt them into our video transmission to the alien ship.

The Nine Sparg captain withheld his comment until we had shown him the batch.

Then he said, "Oh, that was not our world. That was the world of the Garvalekkinon people."

"The Garvalekkinon?"

"We knew them. A neighboring race, not related to us. Sometimes, on rare occasions, we traded with them. Yes, they must all have died when the star exploded. It is too bad."

"They look as though they had no warning," I said. "Look: can you see them there, waiting in the train stations?"

The triple mouths fluttered in what might have been the Nine Sparg equivalent of a nod.

"I suppose they did not know the explosion was coming."

"You suppose? You mean you didn't tell them?"

All four eyes blinked at once. Expression of puzzlement.

"Tell them? Why should we have told them? We were busy with our preparations. We had no time for them. Of course the radiation would have been harmful to them, but why was that our concern? They were not related to us. They were nothing to us."

I had trouble believing I had heard him correctly. A neighboring people. Occasional trading partners. Your sun is about to blow up, and it's reasonable to assume that nearby solar systems will be affected. You have fifty or a hundred years of advance notice yourselves, and you can't even take the trouble to let these other people know what's going to happen?

I said, "You felt no need at all to warn them? That isn't easy for me to understand."

Again the four-eyed shrug.

"I have explained it to you already," said First. "They were not of our kind. They were nothing to us."

✦ ✦ ✦

I excused myself on some flimsy excuse and broke contact. And sat and thought a long long while. Listening to the words of the Nine Sparg captain echoing in my mind. And thinking of the millions of skeletons scattered like straws in the tunnels of that dead world that the supernova had baked. A whole people left to die because it was inconvenient to take five minutes to send them a message. Or perhaps because it simply never had occurred to anybody to bother.

The families, huddling together. The children reaching out. The husbands and wives with hands interlocked.

A world of busy, happy, intelligent, people. Boulevards and temples. Parks and gardens. Paintings, sculpture, poetry, music. History, philosophy, science. And a sudden star in the sky, and everything gone in a moment.

Why should we have told them? They were nothing to us.

I knew something of the history of my own people. We had experienced casual extermination too. But at least when the white settlers had done it to us it was because they had wanted our land.

For the first time I understood the meaning of alien.

I turned on the external screen and stared out at the unfamiliar sky of this place. The neutron star was barely visible, a dull red dot, far down in the lower left quadrant; and the black hole was high.

Once they had both been stars. What havoc must have attended their destruction! It must have been the Sparg sun that blew first, the one that had become the neutron star. And then, fifty or a hundred years later, perhaps, the other, larger star had gone the same route. Another titanic supernova, a great flare of killing light. But of course everything for hundreds of light-years around had perished already in the first blast.

The second sun had been too big to leave a neutron star behind. So great was its mass that the process of collapse had continued on beyond the neutron-star stage, matter crushing in upon itself until it broke through the normal barriers of space and took on a bizarre and almost unthinkable form, creating an object of infinitely small volume that was nevertheless of infinite density: a black hole, a pocket of incomprehensibility where once a star had been.

I stared now at the black hole before me.

I couldn't see it, of course. So powerful was the surface gravity of that grotesque thing that nothing could escape from it, not even electromagnetic radiation, not the merest particle of light. The ultimate in invisibility cloaked that infinitely deep hole in space.

But though the black hole itself was invisible, the effects that its presence caused were not. That terrible gravitational pull would rip apart and swallow any solid object that came too close; and so the hole was surrounded by a bright ring of dust and gas several hundred kilometers across. These shimmering particles constantly tumbled toward that insatiable mouth, colliding as they spiraled in, releasing flaring fountains of radiation, red-shifted into the visual spectrum by the enormous gravity: the bright green of helium, the majestic purple of hydrogen, the crimson of oxygen. That outpouring of energy was the death-cry of doomed matter. That rainbow whirlpool of blazing light was the beacon marking the maw of the black hole.

I found it oddly comforting to stare at that thing. To contemplate that zone of eternal quietude from which there was no escape. Pondering so inexorable and unanswerable an infinity was more soothing than thinking of a world of busy people destroyed by the indifference of their neighbors. Black holes offer no choices, no complexities, no shades of disagreement. They are absolute.

Why should we have told them? They were nothing to us.

After a time I restored contact with the Nine Sparg ship. First came to the screen at once, ready to continue our conversation.

"There is no question that our world once was located here," he said at once. "We have checked and rechecked the coordinates. But the changes have been extraordinary."

"Have they?"

"Once there were two stars here, our own and the brilliant blue one that was nearby. Our history is very specific on that point: a brilliant blue star that lit the entire sky. Now we have only the iron star. Apparently it has taken the place of our sun. But where has the blue one gone? Could the explosion have destroyed it too?"

I frowned. Did they really not know? Could a race be capable of attaining an interstellar spacedrive and an interspecies translating device, and nevertheless not have arrived at any understanding of the neutron star/black hole cosmogony?

Why not? They were aliens. They had come by all their understanding of the universe via a route different from ours. They might well have overlooked this feature or that of the universe about them.

"The blue star—" I began.

But First spoke right over me, saying, "It is a mystery that we must devote all our energies to solving, or our mission will be fruitless. But let us talk of other things. You have said little of your own mission. And of your home world. I am filled with great curiosity, Captain, about those subjects."

I'm sure you are, I thought.

"We have only begun our return to space travel," said First. "Thus far we have encountered no other intelligent races. And so we regard this meeting as fortunate. It is our wish to initiate contact with you. Quite likely some aspects of your technology would be valuable to us. And there will be much that you wish to purchase from us. Therefore we would be glad to establish trade relations with you."

As you did with the Garvalekkinon people, I said to myself.

I said, "We can speak of that tomorrow, Captain. I grow tired now. But before we break contact for the day, allow me to offer you the beginning of a solution to the mystery of the disappearance of the blue sun."

The four eyes widened. The slitted mouths parted in what seemed surely to be excitement.

"Can you do that?"

I took a deep breath.

"We have some preliminary knowledge. Do you see the place

opposite the iron star, where energies boil and circle in the sky? As we entered this system, we found certain evidence there that may explain the fate of your former blue sun. You would do well to center your investigations on that spot."

"We are most grateful," said First.

"And now, Captain, I must bid you good night. Until tomorrow, Captain."

"Until tomorrow," said the alien.

+ + +

I was awakened in the middle of my sleep period by Lina Sorabji and Bryce-Williamson, both of them looking flushed and sweaty. I sat up, blinking and shaking my head.

"It's the alien ship," Bryce-Williamson blurted. "It's approaching the black hole."

"Is it, now?"

"Dangerously close," said Lina. "What do they think they're doing? Don't they know?"

"I don't think so," I said. "I suggested that they go exploring there. Evidently they don't regard it as a bad idea."

"You sent them there?" she said incredulously.

With a shrug I said, "I told them that if they went over there they might find the answer to the question of where one of their missing suns went. I guess they've decided to see if I was right."

"We have to warn them," said Bryce-Williamson. "Before it's too late. Especially if we're responsible for sending them there. They'll be furious with us once they realize that we failed to warn them of the danger."

"By the time they realize it," I replied calmly, "it *will* be too late. And then their fury won't matter, will it? They won't be able to tell us how annoyed they are with us. Or to report to their home world, for that matter, that they had an encounter with intelligent aliens who might be worth exploiting."

He gave me an odd look. The truth was starting to sink in.

I turned on the external screens and punched up a close look at the black hole region. Yes, there was the alien ship, the little metallic sphere, the six odd outthrust legs. It was in the zone of criticality now. It seemed hardly to be moving at all. And it was growing dimmer and dimmer as it slowed. The gravitational field had it, and it was being drawn in. Blacking out, becoming motionless. Soon it would have gone beyond the point where outside observers could perceive it. Already it was beyond the point of turning back.

I heard Lina sobbing behind me. Bryce-Williamson was muttering to himself: praying, perhaps.

I said, "Who can say what they would have done to us—in their casual, indifferent way—once they came to Earth? We know now that Spargs worry only about Spargs. Anybody else is just so much furniture." I shook my head. "To hell with them. They're gone, and in a universe this big we'll probably never come across any of them again, or they us. Which is just fine. We'll be a lot better off having nothing at all to do with them."

"But to die that way—" Lina murmured. "To sail blindly into a black hole—"

"It is a great tragedy," said Bryce-Williamson.

"A tragedy for them," I said. "For us, a reprieve, I think. And tomorrow we can get moving on the neutronium-scoop project." I tuned up the screen to the next level. The boiling cloud of matter around the mouth of the black hole blazed fiercely. But of the alien ship there was nothing to be seen.

Yes, a great tragedy, I thought. The valiant exploratory mission that had sought the remains of the Nine Sparg home world has been lost with all hands. No hope of rescue. A pity that they hadn't known how unpleasant black holes can be.

But why should we have told them? They were nothing to us.

David Drake's RCN series (also known as the "Lt. Leary" series) consists of stand-alone novels and short stories centering around Daniel Leary, an officer in the Republic of Cinnabar Navy (RCN) and Adele Mundy, a librarian and spy. Drake describes it as an "SF version of the Aubrey/Maturin series" by Patrick O'Brian. More character driven than his Hammer's Slammers, the plots of the RCN stories tend to be based on historical incidents. In his brand new story for us, which takes place before the first novel in the series, a fresh out of the academy Leary, his friend Pennyroyal, and a few fellow cadets invite trouble when they sneak off ship for a night of fun...

CADET CRUISE

DAVID DRAKE

Pennyroyal knew that Cadet Leary was supposed to have remained aboard the *Swiftsure* until 1700 hours with the rest of the Starboard Watch. That said, she'd gotten to know Daniel Leary pretty well during their three years at the Academy. When she couldn't locate him in their accommodation block or the cable tier where he was supposed to be on duty until 1630, she suspected that Leary had managed to slip ashore with the Port Watch.

It was more out of whim than from any real expectation of finding the other cadet that Pennyroyal went out on the hull through a forward airlock. The Dorsal A antenna was raised while the *Swiftsure* was docked in Broceliande Harbor. Daniel was sliding down a forestay, his rigging gauntlets sparking against the steel wire. A bosun's mate named Janofsky was following him down.

"You're supposed to be inspecting cable, Leary," Pennyroyal called, amazed and a little exasperated at what her friend got up to. "If an officer catches you fooling around in the sunshine, you'll lose your liberty. At *least* your liberty."

Daniel Leary wasn't any more interested in astrogation theory than Pennyroyal herself was, but he had an obvious gift for astrogation. He could be a valuable officer of the Republic of Cinnabar Navy—if he weren't booted out of the Academy before he graduated. Leary treated discipline the way he did religion: it was all very well for others, if they really wanted to go in for it.

"Pardon, ma'am, but that's just what we're doing," said Janofsky, touching his cap. "I directed Cadet Leary to inspect the standing rigging of Dorsal A under my supervision."

In theory the cadets were classed as landsmen: they were junior to able spacers, let alone to a warrant officer like Janofsky. In practice, outside of actual training many of the *Swiftsure's* cadre treated cadets like the officers they would become when they graduated.

Now with the Republic of Cinnabar and the Alliance of Free Stars in an all-out war, spacers were valuable commodities. It was necessary to provide cadets with practical experience before they were commissioned, but a training ship's complement tended to be made up of personnel who for one reason or another could be spared from front-line combat vessels.

Some of the *Swiftsure's* cadre had persistent coughs, stiff limbs, or were simply old: Janofsky probably wouldn't see seventy again. Others drank or drugged or were a little funny in the head.

But no few were ring-tailed bastards who were doubly hard on cadets. Cadets had the chance of bright futures, which none of those in a training ship's cadre could imagine would dawn for them.

"Ah," said Pennyroyal. She didn't believe the story, but it couldn't be disproved if Janofsky was willing to swear to it. Captain Landrieu herself couldn't punish Cadet Leary, and a veteran spacer like Janofsky knew that he was effectively beyond discipline. Old though he was, the bosun's mate carried out his duties—both working ship and training—with a skill that set him above most of the cadre.

"Come to that, Penny," Leary said, "you knocked off early yourself, not so?"

"I was on galley duty," Pennyroyal said. "With three quarters of the crew ashore, there was bugger all to do by mid shift. Cookie excused me and the other cadets. I wanted to find you."

Janofsky had gone below, leaving the two of them alone on the ship's spine. Though the *Swiftsure* was nearly sixty years old, she was still a battleship. She loomed over not only the rest of the harbor traffic but the buildings of Broceliande, none of which were over six stories high.

Foret was subject to the Cinnabar Empire—a Friend of Cinnabar if you wanted to be mealy-mouthed. It was a pleasant enough planet but of no real importance in galactic politics, making it a natural port call for an RCN training vessel. Part of what an RCN officer needed to know was how to behave on worlds which had their own cultures. Foret provided that, and the trouble you could get into on Broceliande stopped short of being eaten by the locals. There were ports where that wasn't true.

"I didn't mean to seem mysterious, Penny," Daniel said after glancing around. "Janofsky was doing a favor for me and I didn't want to embarrass him in front of a stranger. Which you pretty much are to him."

"And you're not?" said Pennyroyal. The sun, setting beyond the harbor mouth, stained pink the white-washed facades of buildings. The landscape beyond the city was heavily wooded. The ordinarily dark-green native foliage had a purplish cast in slanting light.

"I met Janofsky when I was six, in my Uncle Stacey's shipyard," Daniel said. "I didn't remember that—remember Janofsky, I mean. There must've been hundreds of spacers dropping by to give their regards to their old captain. Janofsky had been a young rigger on the *Granite*, the dedicated exploration vessel that Uncle Stacey made his Long Voyage in."

"When they discovered twenty-seven worlds that'd been lost to civilization for two thousand years?" Pennyroyal said. She had known that Daniel's "Uncle Stacey" had been in the RCN, but until now she hadn't connected the name with Commander Stacey Bergen, the most famous explorer in Cinnabar history. "No wonder you're such an astrogator!"

"I had a leg up," Daniel agreed with a slight smile. "Uncle Stacey never got rich, but the spacers who served under him say he was the greatest man who ever lived. The greatest captain, anyway. Janofsky asked about Uncle Stacey when I came aboard the *Swiftsure*, and I asked him to make some contacts for me in the shore establishment here when he went on liberty yesterday."

"Well, as a matter of fact," Pennyroyal said, "it was about liberty that I wanted to talk to you. You remember that story Vondrian and Ames told, about going on liberty on Broceliande with a ship's corporal?"

"Yes, I certainly do," Daniel said, his expression suddenly guarded. The corporals were the assistants to the master-at-arms, the ship's policemen. "They went to a gambling house that was raided by the police. One of the guards started shooting. If Vondrian hadn't been able to bribe the police to release him and the other cadets, they'd have been jailed for conspiracy to murder."

"Well, I always suspected that was a set-up," Pennyroyal said. "Today I heard that one of the ship's corporals, Platt, had offered to guide a group of cadets to a place at a distance from the harbor where the drinks were higher class. I remembered Vondrian's story and thought we ought to warn the others."

Pennyroyal could have done that herself, but she knew that if the story came from Leary it would be believed. If *she* told people what she'd heard during a night of drinking with two friends from an earlier class at the Academy, she'd be mocked as faint-hearted. An RCN officer with a reputation for cowardice wouldn't stay an RCN officer long.

There were plenty of people, instructors as well as cadets, who thought Daniel Leary was bumptious, a fool, and even certifiably mad. The rumor about him pleasuring the Commandant's daughter in the Academy chapel justified any of those descriptions—and Pennyroyal, who had been on watch in the choir loft, knew the story was true.

Nobody thought Leary was a coward.

"Well, as it chances..." Daniel said carefully. "I *had* heard about the expedition and thought I'd join it. I'm not fancy about what I drink, but Platt says the women are higher class too. They *do* interest me."

"Are you joking?" said Pennyroyal, but he clearly wasn't. There had to be something behind Leary's bland smile, though.

Another thought struck her. "Say!" she said. "Is your man Hogg going along? I don't doubt he's a real bruiser even if he does look like a hayseed with maybe two brain cells to rub together, but you can't muscle your way through a dozen cops!"

"Umm, Steward's Mate Hogg has business of his own to attend to tonight, he told me," Daniel said. "He's not really my man, you know. He insisted on following me from the Bantry estate when I broke with my father and entered the Academy, but I can't afford to keep him. He's living on his pay and whatever he might add to that by playing cards."

Hogg's winnings were greater than his RCN pay, from what Pennyroyal had seen in the galley; but however the former Leary tenant made his living, he continued to refer to Daniel as "the young master." Still, Hogg doubtless had a life beyond service to Cadet Leary.

Pennyroyal stared at her friend. "What are you planning, Leary?" she said. "You've got *something* on."

Daniel shrugged. "I plan to go to a high-class entertainment establishment…" he said. "And have a good time. That's all."

"If you're going, then I'm going along," Pennyroyal said. "That's flat. Understood?"

This time Daniel grinned. "You know I'm always glad to have you beside me, Penny," he said. "But don't act surprised at anything you may hear, all right?"

"All right," said Pennyroyal, grinning back. "It's about time we change to go on liberty, then."

She wasn't sure it would be a night she'd remember as "a good time," but she knew it would be interesting.

✦ ✦ ✦

Pennyroyal and Leary had bunks near one another in the stern. The accommodations block already swarmed with cadets changing into the clothes they would wear on liberty. A few cadets had sprung for gray 2nd class dress uniforms. Though only commissioned or warrant officers had a right to wear Grays, senior cadets were customarily allowed the privilege.

That wasn't an issue with Pennyroyal: she couldn't afford to buy *anything* unnecessary until she graduated and was commissioned as a midshipman. Midshipman's pay wasn't much, but it was something.

"Leary, where did you get those!" Pennyroyal said as she finished pulling on the clean utilities she would be wearing and got a good look at her friend—wearing Grays.

"Umm, they're from a hock shop on the Strip," Daniel said, touching his left lapel with two fingers. There was barely visible fading where rank tabs had been removed. "A mate of Janofsky's tailored them for me. Some of these senior spacers do better work than you could get on the ground."

"Right, but you were broke!" Pennyroyal said. "Where did you find the money?"

"I *was* broke," Daniel said. "But I found the money. I'll explain it later, but for now I want to catch Platt before he leaves his cabin."

Pennyroyal fell in beside Leary, though he was walking toward the pair of aft companionways instead of the set amidships with the rest of the cadets. She said, "But we're supposed to gather in the main boarding hold at 1730. At least that's what I heard."

"I had a different idea," Daniel said. "Don't worry, we'll get there."

They skipped up the companionway in a shuffle of echoes. Even with only two of them in the steel tube, their boot soles on the non-skid treads were multiplied into a whispering chorus as overwhelming as surf in a storm.

Most warrant officers bunked in curtained cabins ahead of the racks of the common spacers. The master-at-arms and his—hers, on the *Swiftsure*—four corporals were a deck above for their own safety and comfort.

The ship's police were responsible for enforcing the ship's discipline. Even the best masters-at-arms were corrupt to a degree: there *would* be gambling during a long voyage despite regulations; limiting it to a few rings which paid for the privilege was better for discipline than a rigid ban.

The *Swiftsure*'s police were at the far wrong end of the corruption scale, however. What Pennyroyal had seen since she and the rest of the cadets boarded made her even more sure that Vondrian, known to be wealthy, had been set up by the ship's corporals in collusion with locals.

She and Leary left the companionway and almost collided with a lieutenant whom Pennyroyal didn't know by name. She jumped to the side of the narrow corridor and snapped a rather better salute than Leary, ahead of her, managed.

"What in blazes are you two doing on this level?" the lieutenant demanded. His words weren't slurred, but the odor of gin enveloped them.

"Sir!" said Daniel, holding his salute. "Corporal Platt ordered us to attend him in his quarters, sir!"

"Platt?" the lieutenant said with a grimace. "Bloody hell."

He pushed past and into the companionway. He had not returned the salutes.

Leary apparently knew exactly where he was going. They were nearly at the sternward end of the corridor when he stopped at a door, not a curtain, and knocked on the panel.

"Cadets Leary and Pennyroyal reporting, Corporal," he called toward the ventilator.

For a moment there was no response; then Platt jerked the light steel panel open. He held a communicator attached by flex to the flat-plate display against the outer bulkhead. There was a scrambler box in the line.

Platt's scowl turned into a false smile. He took off his headphones and said, "I was on my way down in a few minutes, Leary. I just needed to take care of a few things for tonight."

"We came about tonight, Corporal," Daniel said. "Pennyroyal and I had the notion of just the two of us going with you. Instead of thirty or forty cadets chipping in for a cattle car or whatever you've got laid on, I thought I could spring for a taxi. All right?"

"Umm...?" said Platt. He hung the handset and earphones back beneath the display. He was a middle-aged man, balding from the forehead; not fat but soft looking. "Well, if you're willing to pay..."

"I don't mind spending my father's money on giving myself a good time," Daniel said. "There was no bloody point in sucking up to the Speaker if I wasn't going to get something out of it."

Pennyroyal felt her face stiffen. In the past Leary had spoken of his politically powerful father only when he was drunk and someone asked him a direct question. His answers then had been uniformly curt and hostile; she would have said that Daniel was more likely to become a priest than ever to make up with his father.

As for money, Daniel had seemed interested in it only when he wanted to buy a round of drinks for the table but didn't have it to spend. The notion that Daniel Leary would patch up a bitter quarrel in order to afford taxi fare was ludicrous—except that was clearly what he had just implied.

"All right, Leary," Platt said. He stepped into the corridor and latched the door behind him. "I'd heard your Hogg saying something like that. Your Old Man's pretty well heeled, ain't he?"

"I'll say he's well heeled," Daniel muttered as Platt led them along the corridor toward the down companionway. "Anyway, it's just too much money to walk away from."

Platt glanced at the cadets; glanced at Leary, anyway. "I'll tell you what we'll do then," the corporal said. "We'll go out through the forward hatch. That's for officers' use, but I can square it. That way we won't run into the rest of your cadets in the main hold, and there's a better class of hire cars waiting."

"Sounds great!" said Daniel. He pulled a hundred-florin coin out of his belt purse. That was even more of a surprise to Pennyroyal than seeing her friend in Grays. "Say, are they all right with Cinnabar money at this club you're taking us to?"

"They're all right with any kind of money at the Café Claudel," said Platt. "And the more, the merrier."

From the purr in the corporal's voice, the same was true of him.

✦ ✦ ✦

"What's the fare in Cinnabar florins, my good man?" Leary asked in an upper-class drawl as they pulled up under the porte-cochère.

The hire car was a limousine with room for eight in the cabin, though there were signs of age and wear. The leather upholstery was cracked, much of the gilt was gone from the brightwork, and the soft interior lighting was further dimmed by burned-out glowstrips.

Even so, it was the most impressive private vehicle Pennyroyal had ever ridden in. She wasn't sure that she could have found its equal on her homeworld of Touraine. If she had, it still wouldn't have been carrying the orphan daughter of a parish priest.

"Thirty Cinnabar florins, master!" chirped the driver through the sliding window into the cab.

"Bloody hell, Leary!" Pennyroyal said. "Ten'd be high! It's not but three miles from the harborfront!"

A pair of husky servants in white tunics and gold braid opened the car's double doors. They weren't carrying weapons.

"Here you go," Daniel said, handing a fifty-florin coin through the window. "If you're still around when I'm ready to leave, there may be another one for you—but I'm on a twenty-four-hour liberty and I don't expect to end it early."

Platt had gotten out of the vehicle and was waiting beside the house attendants. Pennyroyal got out with Daniel following her. The driver called, "I'll be right here in the VIP lot, master. You can count on me!"

"I dare say we can, for that kind of money," Pennyroyal muttered.

"My father always said 'Spend money to make money,'" Daniel said cheerfully. "Well, that was one of the things he said. Regardless, Corder Leary certainly made money."

Café Claudel must have originally been a country house, though Pennyroyal had gotten only a glimpse of the building as the limousine approached by a curving drive. The gardens facing the house seemed overgrown, though the late-evening light wasn't good enough for certainty.

Platt led the cadets up steps to the doorway where an attractive blonde woman wearing a morning coat and striped trousers waited. "Say, Dolly?" Platt said as they approached. "These two are with me. See that they're treated right, okay?"

"The Claudel treats all of its guests properly, Master Platt," the woman said with a professional smile. She was older than

Pennyroyal had thought from a distance.

"I need to talk to Kravitz," Platt said. "Is he—there he is."

He turned and said, "I need to chat with the manager, Leary. You two come in and have a good time, okay?"

A trim little man with a goatee had just entered the anteroom from the lobby. The corporal went off with him. The doorkeeper's eyes followed them, then returned to Pennyroyal and Leary.

"You'll find a bar to the left within," the blonde said. "There's gaming off the lobby to the right. Upstairs, if you're interested in no limit games…?"

She raised an eyebrow.

"No!" said Pennyroyal, more fiercely than she had intended.

"I might be later," Daniel said, "but just for now I'm hoping to find a drink."

"The Claudel's cellar is famous," the doorkeeper said, "and we have a wide range of off-planet spirits also. If your particular preference isn't available, our bartenders can suggest a near approximation, I'm sure."

Pennyroyal wondered what the staff would suggest if she asked for industrial ethanol, the working fluid used in the Power Room, cut with fruit juice. They could probably find a high-proof vodka with a similar kick—though at a much higher price. But that was another matter…

"And perhaps…" Daniel added, "a friend or two to show me the establishment's sights. Eh?"

The doorkeeper's smile was minuscule but real. "I think you'll be able to meet someone congenial in the lobby, sir," she said. "If not, a word to any staff member will bring a further selection. And there are rooms upstairs for whatever sort of discussions you'd like to have."

A group—two older men and a woman of their age, accompanied by three much younger women—arrived. Daniel and Pennyroyal stepped into the lobby to clear the anteroom.

Pennyroyal whispered to Daniel, "This place is *way* beyond my budget, Leary. Even if the drinks are cheap. Look at the clothes these people are wearing!"

"Give me your hand, Penny," Daniel said. "I'm pretty sure they aren't going to throw you out for hunching over a beer and looking miserable, but right now you're part of my protective coloration."

"Pardon?" said Pennyroyal. When she didn't move, Daniel

took her right wrist in his left hand and pulled it toward him, then gripped her right hand with his own. There were two large coins in his palm.

"Leary, I can't take this!" she whispered, closing her fingers over the coins. They were hundreds from the size.

"I'll get it back, Penny," Daniel said cheerfully. "Trust me on that."

Grimacing, Pennyroyal transferred the money—two gold-rimmed hundred-florin pieces, all right—to her purse. *What in blazes is going on?*

The lobby was a high room with a railed mezzanine; the three tall windows at the back were capped with arched fanlights. The zebra-striped bar, running the full depth of the room, was staffed by three female bartenders. Daniel walked up to the youngest-looking and took out another hundred-florin coin.

"Can you break this for me, my dear?" he said, holding it up between thumb and forefinger.

"Certainly, sir," the woman—close up, she was over thirty—said. "Do you care what form the change is in?"

"So long as I can spend it here, it doesn't matter," Daniel said with a laugh. "I don't expect to have any left when I leave."

Pennyroyal assumed the bar was made of extruded material. Daniel rapped it with his knuckles and said, "Natural wood, by the gods! Is it native to Foret, my dear?"

"I believe it is, sir," the bartender said, her eyes on the small stacks of coins and scrip she was arraying on the bar in front of herself. "But from the southern continent. Master Kravitz may have more details."

"Ale for my friend and myself just now," Daniel said, sweeping his eyes around the room. There were forty-odd people in the lobby, half of them at the bar. He glanced at the price list on the back wall between a pair of paintings—mythological, presumably, since the men and women had feathered wings. He slid a local note back to the bartender. As she turned to draw the beers, Daniel stuffed a similar note into the brandy snifter of tips for her station.

"Let's circulate, shall we, Penny?" Daniel said as they turned away. On the couches between the windows and to either side of the anteroom sat attractive women and men, not couples though mostly in pairs. He sipped his beer and added, "Not bad at all."

Without changing his mild expression, Daniel said, "I'm not

one to preach, Penny, but we might decide to leave here rather suddenly. I'll probably be nursing this—"

He tapped the rim of his earthenware stein with a fingernail; it rang softly.

"—a lot longer than you're used to seeing me do."

Pennyroyal grinned. "Well, don't do anything I wouldn't do, Leary," she said. "Unless it involves those women, in which case feel free."

Pennyroyal walked toward the gaming room. She didn't like beer well enough to have an opinion as to whether this was a good brew, but she hadn't needed Leary's warning to decide that she wasn't going to get drunk tonight.

She didn't have any idea what Leary was planning, but she was rather looking forward to it. And that meant being fully ready for action when the time came.

RCN forever!

✦ ✦ ✦

The gaming room was large enough not to be crowded by what Pennyroyal estimated as over two hundred people. The roulette table near the door was getting the most attention, but it held no interest for her. She kept moving toward the windows at the back, checking each table as she passed.

Everyone, even among the attendants, was better dressed than Pennyroyal. Nobody seemed to care, though. And at least her utilities were brand new, though after tonight they would be going into the regular rotation with her other two sets.

On a two-step dais in a back corner, a young man with a faraway expression plucked a harp. In the corner across from him was a 21 table with modest amounts showing and two empty chairs. The pair of windows reached down to the floor; they could be swung open.

Pennyroyal took a chair and turned one of Leary's hundreds into chips. The table limit turned out to be the equivalent of seven florins. She stayed at five, playing carefully but not cautiously. She was a moderately skillful player—astrogation was a great deal more complex than keeping track of the cards already showing on the table—and she was perfectly willing to lose the whole two hundred florins plus her own eighty-five while she waited for something to happen.

The others around the arc of the table were locals; their garments, viewed closely, showed signs of wear. Their haunted expressions were an even clearer hint that they were on the downslope of life. The dealer was young and sometimes fumbled when she took a card from the shoe; occasionally Pennyroyal caught a flash of contempt on her face.

At least in part because Pennyroyal was alert but unconcerned about the results, she began to win. She stuck to her limit so that the results came in five-florin increments, but by the time she'd taken her third beer from a server she had more than doubled her stacks of chips.

The only other thing of interest that happened was that the harpist picked out a song Pennyroyal recognized as "Sergeant Flynn," about an ancient military disaster. Her father had been a trooper with the Land Forces of the Republic before he returned home and joined the Church.

Parson Pennyroyal didn't drink often, but when he did he was apt to sing that one: "*Your head is scalped and battered, and your men are dead and scattered, Sergeant Flynn...*"

Pennyroyal didn't touch her beer after that played. She'd known from earliest childhood what it meant to go into action. Tonight she was going into action.

She kept an eye open for anything of interest in the room. Daniel passed through once with a pair of red-heads: one plump, the other willowy. Pennyroyal nodded to her fellow cadet, then smiled faintly and returned to her cards. Daniel was a bright, personable fellow, but the women he chose were as dim as they were lovely.

She didn't see Platt until shortly after she'd taken her third beer. The ship's corporal came from behind the dais where a wall concealed a passageway. Pennyroyal had noticed members of the house staff passing to and fro that way during the evening, so presumably it was the office.

The restrooms were on either side of the doorway to the lobby and bar. That had surprised Pennyroyal initially; then she realized that the location encouraged those who had entered the gaming room to remain here rather than to leave for any reason.

There was even a small bar between the back windows. Servers shuttled between it and the players, sometimes without being summoned. Regardless of its other virtues, the Café Claudel appeared to be skillfully run.

Daniel returned with a different pair of women—girls, rather;

this time they were brunette and both petite. Platt was standing near a poker table, but he showed no sign of wanting to sit at one of the empty chairs.

A man came in from the lobby, heading straight for Platt. Though he was in a business suit, Pennyroyal recognized Riddle, another ship's corporal from the *Swiftsure*. He rushed past Daniel as though he hadn't noticed the cadet. Pennyroyal had seen that when Riddle had scanned the room on entry, his eyes had paused briefly on Daniel.

The two corporals spoke. Riddle waved his arms in apparent agitation. Pennyroyal scooped her chips together and dumped them into the right bellows pocket of her trousers. That was a big advantage of wearing utilities instead of more stylish clothing.

The other players looked at her in various mixtures of concern and puzzlement. The dealer paused with a faint frown and said, "Mistress?"

Platt and Riddle were heading for Leary. Pennyroyal rose from her seat and reached her fellow cadet just as the corporals did.

"Tim says there's about to be a raid!" Platt said. "We've gotta get you two out of here through the manager's office. It turns out the place is over the line and your liberty is only good for Broceliande!"

"Hell and damnation!" Leary said. "If my father hears I've been arrested, I'll be back out in the wilderness!"

That didn't match with what Pennyroyal had heard of Corder Leary's hard-charging personality, but a great deal of what she had seen this night was contrary to what she had thought she knew. She didn't speak.

"This way," said Platt, leading them toward the passage concealed behind the harpist. "There's a tunnel from the office over to the next street."

The floor-length windows on either side of the bar swung inward. People in rust-red uniforms stepped in, carrying batons or in a few cases carbines. Their shoulder flashes read BROCELIANDE POLICE. More police appeared in the doorway to the lobby and on the mezzanine railing above the gaming room.

"Too late!" said Platt. "I'm afraid you cadets are for it now. Riddle and me are okay because we've got jurisdiction anywhere on the planet, but you two have broken bounds for liberty."

"But you brought us here, Corporal!" Leary said. He sounded desperate. "Surely there's *something* you can do?"

Pennyroyal felt her lips tighten. Listening to Leary beg disgusted her as well as being a surprise. Leary had broken more than his share of rules—and had several times been caught. In the past he'd always taken his punishment like an RCN officer.

"Riddle, you know the local cops," Platt said. "Can you do something for the kids?"

"Well, that's Commissioner Milhaud," Riddle said, nodding to the man who had just waddled in from the lobby. The police official's uniform showed almost more gold braid than there was russet fabric visible. "But a quick warning, that's one thing. To get them—" he looked at Daniel "—out now is going to cost a bundle. Five grand in florins, at least."

"Can either of you raise that kind of money?" Platt said. Despite his "either of you," he was looking straight at Daniel when he spoke.

"Well, I can," said Daniel. He reached into his purse and brought out a credit chip. Holding it between his left thumb and forefinger, he said, "This is a letter of credit good for up to twenty, if I can get to a real banking terminal."

This is a scam! Pennyroyal thought. *What are you doing, Leary?*

The words didn't come out of her mouth. Leary had warned her not to show surprise.

"All right, we're in business!" Platt said. "Riddle, you go talk to your buddy. I know Kravitz has a terminal in his office. I'll be out with the money in no time at all, and the cadets'll just leave through the tunnel like they was never here."

The *crack* from outside could have been lightning rather than an electromotive carbine. The lighter *crackcrackcrack* an instant later was certainly from a sub-machine gun. A slug ricocheted from stone with a high-pitched howl.

Pennyroyal remembered that when Vondrian had been shaken down two years earlier, a guard was supposed to have shot a policeman. There wasn't any need for that charade tonight, though.

The nearest police turned toward the windows they'd just entered by. Dozens of helmeted figures approached across the grounds beyond; they wore dark blue and carried sub-machine guns.

The initial raid had caused only grumbling reaction among the players; Pennyroyal was pretty sure that she'd heard the raddled blonde at her table mutter, "Oh, not again!" as police clambered in through the windows.

This was different, and the loudest reactions were from the

municipal police. One whispered a prayer and flung down his carbine as though it had been burning his hands.

Riddle had almost reached the gilded Commissioner Milhaud. A squad in blue entered the gaming room and surrounded them. The newcomers' helmets were stencilled FEDERAL POLICE in black, and their shoulder patches were low visibility.

One spoke, his voice booming through the public address system: "I'm Major Picard of the Federal Police. Those of you who are here for recreation have nothing to fear. We're arresting corrupt members of the Broceliande police force and their civilian accomplices."

Platt snarled a curse and sidled into the passage to the manager's office. Daniel was with him. Pennyroyal followed only a half-step beyond, though she wondered if the Federals now entering the room would have something to say about it. They didn't, but Pennyroyal sneezed from the ozone still clinging to the muzzle of a recently fired weapon.

The door to the right at the end of the short passage was marked MANAGER/PRIVATE. Platt pushed it open and stepped in.

"Why's the lights out?" he shouted. He found the switch plate; his hand was at it when the lights came on an instant later.

A small door in the room's back wall was open. Pennyroyal recognized the man on his back as Kravitz, the manager. The other man was sprawled face-down; his right hand had brought a gun halfway out of his pocket before he dropped. Two more men wearing distorting masks hunched before a banking terminal.

Platt turned to run. Leary grabbed him by the left arm. Platt's sleeve broke away and his right hand came up wearing a knuckleduster.

Pennyroyal caught the corporal's right wrist and was twisting it backward when Leary slammed Platt's head into the doorjamb. Platt slumped limply. The weapon clanged when Pennyroyal let go of his arm.

The kneeling men pulled off their masks. "I think that's got it," said Janofsky, the bosun's mate.

"Lock the door, will you, ma'am?" said Hogg, the other burglar. "Nobody's supposed to be coming in after you lot, but there's no point in taking chances."

Pennyroyal was trembling as she shot the two heavy bolts. The action had been too brief to burn up the adrenaline which was flooding her system.

Platt sounded as though he were snoring. He'd need medical help, and soon. Pennyroyal felt a twinge of concern, but not serious enough to say something on the subject.

Hogg drew his mask, a stocking of some shiny fabric, over Platt's head. "Thieves fall out, don't you think?" he said. "Pop it, Janofsky, and see how well we planned this."

"It'll work," said the bosun's mate. He touched a small control device. Six puffs of smoke spurted, three each from left and right of the terminal. The explosions sounded like a single sharp crackle.

There were tools on the floor. Janofsky put a drill stencilled Swiftsure/RCN in a bellows pocket of his tunic. He and Hogg wore ordinary spacer's slops.

"What—" said Pennyroyal.

The terminal's faceplate dropped two inches with a clang, then toppled forward. The manager's outflung hand muffled the second impact. Coins of many kinds spilled from broken chutes.

Hogg tossed an empty sack to Pennyroyal and handed another to Daniel. "You two pick up the spillage," he said, "and I'll open the storage cans."

The cadets began scooping handfuls of coins into their sacks. Janofsky was putting another tool in his left pocket, an imaging sensor like those Pennyroyal had seen being used to check welds.

Hogg had filled a bag from the containers at the back of the terminal. It was mostly scrip, but there were also rolls of coins. Pennyroyal had seen at least one bundle of Cinnabar hundreds.

"Time to go," Hogg said as he rose. Janofsky had already started out the door in the back.

Daniel waved Pennyroyal ahead with a grin. She wondered what happened next, but simply doing as directed had worked fine so far tonight.

Why change a winning plan?

+ + +

The tunnel was lighted by glowstrips in the ceiling at long intervals. All they did was show direction: the tunnel kinked twice in what Pennyroyal estimated at 200 yards. There was nothing in the passage except for a central drain, and even that was superfluous at present: the concrete walls were dry to a finger's touch.

There was suction as the door at the far end opened. A pair of Federal police waited outside the exit.

Janofsky passed through. Hogg stopped and set down his bag of loot; Pennyroyal jerked to a halt to keep from running into Daniel's servant.

Hogg fished scrip out of a tunic pocket. "I know you boys 'll be taken care of in the share-out," he said, "but this is a little something from me personally. I appreciate it, right?"

He handed money to each policeman, then picked up his bag and strode on. "Come back any time," a cop called after him. They grinned at Pennyroyal as she passed.

Janofsky was climbing into the back of high-roofed blue van stencilled FEDERAL POLICE in the same style of black lettering as the police helmets. *It's a riot wagon!* Pennyroyal thought.

And so it was; but on the bench to the right sat a man whose blue uniform was of higher quality than those of the Federal assault force. Pennyroyal wasn't up on Foret's police insignia, but she was pretty sure that the horsehead on his lapel made him a colonel. The woman beside him wore RCN utilities with SHORE POLICE brassards. Her subdued commander's pips implied that she was in charge of the whole contingent on Foret.

Two clerks sat on the opposite bench, each with a thick tray on his lap. One was dumping the contents of Hogg's bag carefully onto his tray.

"I'll take that," the other clerk said to Pennyroyal—and did so. The trays made small sounds as they sucked in coins and bills, counted them, and dropped them into storage compartments.

Leary closed the door behind him and passed his bag to the nearer clerk. His fellow said, "We may need those extra bins after all." He was breaking rolls and bundles of money so that they could feed individually.

The clerks didn't pay any attention to the cadets except to take their bags. The sorting trays whirred, clicked, and occasionally pinged.

The van drove off sedately. Hogg and Janofsky seated themselves below the clerks, so Pennyroyal took the place beside the RCN commander. That officer grinned at her and said, "Impressive work, Cadet."

Pennyroyal swallowed. "Thank you, ma'am," she said. "Ah, ma'am? If I can ask... What's going to happen to us now?"

The Commander smiled more broadly. "I suppose you'll report back aboard the *Swiftsure* at the end of your liberty," she said. "We'll let you out at the edge of the Strip; then you're on your own."

Pennyroyal swallowed. She said, "Thank you, ma'am."

The Commander leaned forward to look past Pennyroyal. "You're Leary?" she said. "You planned this?"

"Ma'am, it was my idea," Daniel said, "but the details and the grunt work was all handled by other people. Including yourself, ma'am, and Colonel Lebel."

The Commander chuckled and said, "You'll go far, Leary. If you're not hanged first."

The Federal colonel said something from her other side. The officers talked between themselves too quietly for Pennyroyal to overhear without making it obvious.

Turning to Leary on her other side, Pennyroyal said, "Daniel, how long have you been planning this?"

"Since Vondrian told us how he'd been robbed," Leary said. He grinned at the memory. "I didn't know quite how we were going to work it till I met Janofsky when we reported aboard. There's a lot of the *Swiftsure*'s cadre who've been spoiling for a chance to get back at Platt and Riddle. Hogg—"

He nodded toward his servant, who was talking with Janofsky.

"—was talking to people in Harbor Three and elsewhere on Cinnabar. He got names and introductions to members of the Shore Establishment here on Foret. They've been pissed about the games the ship's police have been playing, but they couldn't touch the crooks without help. I said we'd give them help."

Pennyroyal felt herself grinning. "Now I see why you made up with your father, Leary," she said. "That was, well, a surprise."

Daniel's answering smile was hard. "This chip was blank," he said, holding up what he'd claimed was a twenty-thousand-florin credit. "I haven't had any contact with Corder Leary since the afternoon I enrolled in the RCN Academy. Saying that I did was just to explain why I suddenly had money. The ship's warrant officers, the good ones, clubbed together and came up with enough florins to make a splash. They'll get a third of the take."

"A third," Pennyroyal repeated.

She hadn't added a follow-up question, but Leary answered without it. "The Federal police get a third. They've been looking for a way to clean up the Broceliande force anyway. And the rest goes to Commander Kilmartin there for her people."

"But you?" Pennyroyal said.

Leary laughed. "I did it for Vondrian and for the RCN," he said.

"Getting scum like Platt and Riddle out is worth more than money. I suspect they'll both go down for the burglary—somebody's got to be blamed. At any rate, Kilmartin'll make sure they're off the *Swiftsure* and out of the RCN."

Pennyroyal brought the remaining hundred out of her purse. "I've still got this," she said. "And a pocket full of chips that probably aren't worth anything. I don't guess the Café Claudel will reopen any time soon."

"Keep it," said Daniel. "Or better, the four of us can tie one on properly on the Strip before our liberty's over!"

Hogg, from the other side of the van, must have been listening. "*Bloody* good idea!" he said.

"I couldn't agree more," Pennyroyal said. She stretched, feeling relaxed for the first time since the evening had begun.

The Lost Fleet is a military science fiction/space opera series written by John G. Hemry under his Jack Campbell pen name. It is set one-hundred-plus years into an interstellar war between two different human cultures: the Alliance and the Syndics. The key protagonist is a hero and legend to the Alliance named John Geary. Multiple books have led to multiple spin-off series, Beyond The Frontier and The Lost Stars. However, our present story is a brand-new Lost Fleet story which Campbell describes as "the earliest story in the Lost Fleet, taking place about twelve years before the Syndicate Worlds attack on Grendel that began the war with the Alliance and created the legend of John 'Black Jack' Geary. The origin of his nickname has been shrouded in mystery. Until now."

SHORE PATROL
JACK CAMPBELL

Captain Anne Spruance commanded the Alliance heavy cruiser *Redoubt*, currently in orbit about a planet in Augeas Star System. Ensign John Geary, in charge of the hell-lance weapons division onboard the *Redoubt*, was currently standing at attention in Captain Spruance's stateroom.

If there was one thing Geary had learned during his so far brief career in the Alliance fleet, it was the importance of keeping the captain of whatever ship he was on happy. Unhappy captains had ways of expressing their unhappiness which made for very unhappy junior officers.

At the moment, Captain Spruance did not look happy or sound happy. "Ensign Geary, last night you were in command of the shore patrol detachment sent down to the planet. Last night you also ended up in the local jail, along with about forty members of the crew, including all four members of the shore patrol."

"Yes, Captain," Geary said.

Standing up from the seat at her desk, the captain leaned her face close to Geary's. "Just what was it you thought your job was as commander of the shore patrol?"

"To preserve order among members of the crew and other Alliance military personnel who are on leave or liberty status," Geary recited from fleet regulations.

"Really?" Captain Spruance turned back to her desk and tapped a virtual window. "Let's see what the local law enforcement authorities think you were doing last night. Riot. Assault. Battery. Resisting arrest. Refusal to comply with orders of local police Disrespect for local government. Improper public behavior. What the hell happened, Ensign Geary? I can't wait to hear your explanation."

+ + +

Sixteen hours earlier.

"Geary! Get out here!"

Twisting to get through the access shaft to the power supply for the number two hell lance battery, John Geary worked his way out and into the passageway where Lieutenant Sam "Suck Up" Booth waited impatiently. "What's the problem?"

"You've got shore patrol duty tonight," Booth said. "The shuttle leaves in half an hour."

"Shore patrol? Setlie's supposed to be doing that."

"Setlie can't. You're doing it. Get going." Booth shoved into Geary's hands an armband with "Shore Patrol" embossed on it in big letters before turning away and walking off of at a leisurely pace.

Geary stood and counted to five inside before turning to call into the access shaft. "Chief, I've been tapped for shore patrol."

"Good luck, sir," the reply came back in tones that suggested luck would be badly needed.

Getting back to the cramped stateroom he shared with three other junior officers and changing into his dress uniform took nearly fifteen minutes.

"Shore patrol members muster in dress uniform on the quarterdeck."

Geary breathed a sigh of relief as the announcement was made, realizing that he had forgotten to take care of that. Dashing out into the passageway again, he found Ensign Daria Rosen waiting.

"I heard you got stuck, so I had the watch pass the word for the shore patrol to muster," she told him. "That okay?"

"You're a life-saver," Geary replied. "What happened to Setlie?"

"He's skating again. Complained to Suck Up Sam that he had too much work to do, so to oblige his little protégé Sam shoved the work onto someone else."

"Figures. Thanks, Dar." Geary waved a farewell and raced to the quarterdeck where the four members of his shore patrol waited.

He braked abruptly as he saw the four sailors waiting in dress uniforms. The heavy cruiser *Redoubt* only had about three hundred crew members, so Geary knew them all at least in passing. He recognized Petty Officer Third Class Demore, who until a few weeks ago had been Petty Officer Second Class Demore before being busted down in rate on various charges, as well as Seaman Alvarez, who was three years into a four-year enlistment and seemed determined to prove that for some people the simplest tasks were too difficult. The other two sailors were Chadra and Riley, both of whom had apparently decided within hours of enlisting that they had made a mistake. Every supervisor either one had worked for had quickly decided they were right about that, but the two continued to use up oxygen, food, water, and space that would have been put to better use by just about any other living object.

Geary turned about, walking just outside the quarterdeck as he tapped his comm pad. "Lieutenant Booth," he said, trying to speak diplomatically and respectfully, "are you aware of the individuals assigned to shore patrol?"

Booth sounded annoyed at the question. "Don't you think I can do my job, *Ensign*?"

"Those four sailors are not good choices," Geary said.

"You'll have to talk to the executive officer about that. It's his idea. If the worst performers are on shore patrol, they'll have to do a decent job, and they won't be able to get into trouble. I'm not going to argue with the XO. Are you?"

"Yes," Geary said, aware that he was unlikely to get any positive result from the argument but not willing to give in without trying.

"Unfortunately for you, the XO is off the ship, and I'm not going to bother him about your problems. So get the job done!"

Mumbling curses aimed at the ancestors of Lieutenant Booth, Geary went back onto the quarterdeck, where the sympathetic chief petty officer on watch called him aside. "Sir, they haven't been issued shockers yet."

"Of course not," Geary said, wondering what else could go wrong. "How long until the last shuttle drops?"

"Ten minutes. If you're not back I'll hold it, but the pilot won't like it."

"Thanks, Chief. Have the duty gunner meet me at the armory."

The four members of the shore patrol stiffened to various interpretations of attention as Geary addressed them. "We're going to the armory to get shockers. I don't want any nonsense tonight. No screw ups. Come on."

At the reinforced hatch to the armory where individual weapons were stored, the duty gunner frowned at the issue order in *Redoubt*'s data base. "Sir? This calls for shockers with no charges."

"What?" Geary read through the brief order, then hit his comm pad again. "Lieutenant, the issue order for my shore patrol specifies shockers without charges."

"That's right," Booth replied, sounding even more peeved. "The XO doesn't trust that bunch with loaded shockers. You'll be fine. Nobody with a shocker pointed at them is going to want to find out if it's charged."

"How am I supposed to impose discipline without any means to impose discipline?" Geary demanded.

"Use your command presence! Do I have to tell you everything?"

Mentally vowing to "accidentally" shoot Lieutenant Booth if he ever got his hands on a charged shocker, Geary made it back to the quarterdeck with one minute to spare. He led the way onto the crowded shuttle after making sure every sailor in his group had their Shore Patrol armbands on. They had barely strapped in to their seats when the shuttle dropped away from the *Redoubt* and headed down from orbit for the city officially named Barcara but known to sailors throughout space as Barcrawl.

Virtual screens inside the shuttle lit up with the port briefing, alternating views of the natural wonders of the planet below with stern warnings. "Barcara is the second largest city on the primary world of the Augeas Star System. Augeas is part of the Callas Republic, not the Alliance. As representatives of the Alliance and the fleet, you will be expected to maintain the highest standards of personal behavior. While many of the citizens you encounter in Barcara will be extremely friendly, do not forget that even if the services they offer are legal in Barcara you can still be prosecuted within the Alliance for any actions which are illegal under Alliance law..."

Geary noticed none of the sailors were paying attention to the port briefing. All of the ones he could hear were discussing the sort of "natural wonders" that would be hanging out in the bars of Barcara.

As the shuttle dropped down through atmosphere to the landing field, Geary hauled out his comm pad and quickly reviewed the captain's standing orders for the shore patrol. *Maintain good order and discipline. Refrain from use of force unless absolutely necessary. Identify the bar where most of the sailors of* Redoubt *are on liberty and station half the shore patrol there while patrolling with the other half...*

There went his plan to keep all four sailors with him at all times so he could keep his eye on the shore patrol that were supposed to be keeping their eyes on everyone else.

After landing, Geary let the other passengers on the shuttle leave the field while he held back with his shore patrol. "Demore, I hear you've been to Barcara a lot."

"Yes, sir!" Demore agreed, grinning. "Four times! Barcrawl is a great liberty port. You see that exit over there? Once you go through, all you have to do is turn right and in no time you'll be in among the bars and the rave huts and the girls and the boys and whatever else you want!"

"Where do you end up if you go left at the dock exit?" Geary asked.

Demore's grin faded into puzzlement. "I dunno, sir. I've always turned right."

"Listen up," Geary told his four patrollers. "There are two rules for tonight. One, do what I tell you to do. Two, don't do anything I didn't tell you to do. Any questions?"

"What's our job?" Alvarez asked.

"To keep fights from breaking out, to make sure no one does anything stupid, and to make sure no local laws are broken."

"Oh. Sir, I don't think four of us are going to be able to handle that."

"There's five of us," Demore pointed out.

"Oh, yeah. Okay."

"Follow me," Geary ordered, leading his patrol toward the exit. At least they all looked like shore patrol with their dress uniforms, arm bands, and holstered shockers.

Just outside the exit, he found four local police officers waiting, one of them a woman with a chief's star on each collar, and whose no-nonsense look promised trouble for anyone making trouble. "Shore patrol," she said. "Where are the rest?"

"This is it," Geary said.

"What about the Marines?"

"Marines? What Marines?"

The chief eyed Geary as if suspicious that he was a troublemaker. "A unit of Alliance Marines has been working with Callas Republic ships. They're on liberty in Barcara tonight."

"Marines?" Geary repeated. "On liberty? Here?"

"That's right. In the same place as your sailors. I don't want any trouble!"

"Neither do I."

"And I don't want any trouble with the sailors from the two Callas Republic warships who are also on liberty here tonight! Keep your Marines and your sailors quiet!"

Geary rubbed his forehead, trying to imagine how this could get any worse. The chief's next words answered that unspoken question.

"And there's a squadron of aerospace pilots having some sort of celebration downtown. I want them kept under control, too. No street strafing!"

"Street strafing?"

"*No* street strafing! Give me your contact info!"

Geary heard Petty Officer Demore chuckle as they left the local police, turning right and walking toward the lights and raucous sounds coming from the Entertainment District. "Contact info. Like that'll do any good in there."

"Why wouldn't comms work in there?" Geary asked.

"Bar owners are always dropping off disposable jammers on the streets so anyone wanting to use comms has to go into one of the bars," Demore explained. "They also jam calls between bars, so anyone wanting to talk to anyone else has to go to the bar someone else is in to do it."

Geary checked his comm pad, seeing it already reporting degraded conditions. "We'll have to pass information face to face? Why do the authorities in Barcara allow that?"

"The way it was told me, sir, was that the more money the bar owners make because of doing stuff like that, the more money they have to pay off the authorities and the police. So it's sorta a win-win."

"This just keeps getting better and better," Geary grumbled. As his shore patrol walked past the border of Barcara's proper-sounding Entertainment District, Geary watched the last bar on his comm pad disappear to be replaced by an out-of-contact notice. "Where are our people going to be hanging out? Any ideas?"

"I heard meet up at the Brooklyn Bar," Chadra offered.

"There's a Brooklyn Bar here, too?" Riley asked in amazement.

"Every port's got a Brooklyn Bar," Demore said with the authority of years of service. "It's like the Forbidden Palace bar, and the Bolivar Bar, and the Jungle Bar. There's one in every port."

"The same people don't own them everywhere, do they?" Riley asked.

"Nah. I don't think so."

"You ever been to Brooklyn, Ensign Geary?"

Don't get too familiar with the enlisted. That was the advice officers like Lieutenant Booth gave. But at the moment Geary wasn't too impressed by the advice of Lieutenant Booth. And it wasn't like he was sharing private information. "My family left Old Earth a long time ago. I don't know the last time anyone I'm related to went back there, if anyone ever has."

"We could be the ship sent for the celebration, right?" Alvarez said. "That's only a few years away, isn't it?"

"Every ten years," Geary said. "So the next trip back to Old Earth will be two years from now. It's a long haul, but *Redoubt* won't be the ship chosen. It's always a battleship or a battle cruiser. If you want a chance at going, you'll have to transfer to one of them. And you have to do it before the ship is chosen, taking your chances that the one you go to will be the one that goes, because my mother said when she was in the fleet as soon as the ship got selected everybody wanted to transfer to it."

"How could I make that happen, sir?" Chadra asked, surprising Geary with the question. As far as he knew, it was the first time Chadra had expressed interest in anything related to his work. Then again, Seaman Chadra was in Ensign "Skater" Setlie's division, so maybe his lack of motivation wasn't entirely Chadra's fault.

"You have to do a good job," Geary said. "Our captain has to recommend you for the transfer."

"And then maybe I could get to Old Earth?" Chadra grinned. "I'm gonna try that."

"Yeah, sure," Seaman Riley scoffed, rolling her eyes.

"Don't start," Geary warned them both. He'd noticed that Chadra and Riley were staying as far away from each other as they could while still staying close to him. But as long as they didn't let personal dislike get in the way of their work, he wouldn't make a big deal of it.

Barcara's main drag was even more garish than he had expected, virtual neon signs and images filling the street above head level, the sidewalks next to the bars and rave huts filled with a wide variety of local men and women dressed in clothing that varied from suggestive to borderline obscene. "Hey, sailor!" one called as she caught Geary's eye. "Special deal tonight! Just for you!"

"No, thanks," Geary called back, trying to spot the sign for the Brooklyn Bar amid the other bright advertisements floating overhead.

"There it is!" Demore called out, pointing to a sign featuring a smiling sailor waving in welcome against a backdrop of archaic skyscrapers.

Inside, the Brooklyn Bar was crowded, chairs filled around closely packed tables and the bar elbow-to-elbow. Aside from a couple of big virtual pictures cycling through scenes that might or might not show the actual Brooklyn, the decoration was made up of bottles behind the bar and a scattering of plaques from various ships on one wall. "Real wait-staff?" Geary asked, startled to see the men and women weaving among the tables to deliver drinks.

"Yes, sir," Demore said, grinning as he looked around. "Real wait-staff can, uh, interact with the customers, you know?"

"Oh." He was supposed to post half his shore patrol here. Geary looked them over, trying to decide. Demore was not only the most senior among them, but also likely the most reliable, which was a pretty sad commentary on the other three. Alvarez was at least trying to look professional, and she was a fairly experienced sailor. "I need to post two of you in this bar to keep an eye on our sailors. That'll be you, Demore, and Alvarez. You'll be here on your own while I patrol with Chadra and Riley. Can I count on you?"

Demore smiled and nodded so quickly that Geary immediately distrusted him, but that still left him no other options. Alvarez brightened, though, as if being pleasantly startled by being given the responsibility.

"Stay here," Geary said, pointing to the end of the bar nearest the door and speaking loudly enough to be heard over the noise filling the place. "Keep an eye on everything. If you see trouble developing, try to call me. If you can't, send Alvarez to find me."

"What if a fight breaks out?" Alvarez asked.

"Find me." Geary led Chadra and Riley outside again, dodging come-ons for a variety of entertainments. Spotting a pair of local cops strolling by as if oblivious to the raucous offers, he hailed them. "Excuse me. Have you seen which bar the Marines are in?"

"Jungle Bar," one replied, looking Geary over. "Shore patrol? Don't go in there."

"Thanks for the advice." Chadra and Riley followed as Geary walked down the street, studying signs while weaving between packs of sailors who had obviously already consumed copious amounts of alcohol and other recreational substances. Finally spotting a bright display which showed lions, tigers, and elephants hoisting drinks under palm trees, he went to the door of the Jungle Bar. Looking inside, he could see the place was packed with Marines. "You two stay right with me," he told the sailors.

Eyes and heads swung to watch as Geary entered the bar, Chadra and Riley nervously staying so close that they kept treading on the backs of his feet. "Good evening," Geary said to the nearest Marines as he fought off the uncomfortable sensation of being a target on a firing range. "How are you Marines doing?"

Wary looks changed to smiles when it became obvious that Geary didn't intend trying to throw his weight around. "Just fine, sir. What can we do for you?"

"Where are your senior people in here?"

"Right this way, sir!" one Marine announced. Geary followed until they reached a small table with only two occupants, seated facing each other. One, a master sergeant, turned his stern visage toward Geary, while the other, a gunnery sergeant, watched with a polite but unyielding look on her face.

"Yes... sir?" the master sergeant asked.

"I'm in charge of the shore patrol for the *Redoubt*," Geary said.

"I guessed that, sir."

"I just wanted to make sure there weren't any problems tonight between my sailors and your Marines. I'd appreciate your advice on how to keep our people out of trouble."

"If we keep them away from each other there shouldn't be no trouble at all, sir," the master sergeant assured him, mollified by Geary's request for advice. A waitress brought by two full shot glasses, setting one down before the master sergeant and the other before the gunnery sergeant. "If you will excuse me a moment, sir." The two sergeants toasted each other before downing their shots. "Where are your people at, sir?"

"Most of them are in the Brooklyn Bar," Geary said.

"Hey!" the master sergeant yelled, producing instant silence in the crowded Jungle Bar. "Stay out of the Brooklyn Bar, you apes!

And nobody go looking for space squids to fight! You all got that?"

"Yes, Master Sergeant!" Marine voices chorused, followed by a babble as individual conversations resumed.

"I can't ask for better than that," Geary told the master sergeant.

"You could," the gunnery sergeant said, grinning. "You being an officer and all."

"Yeah, I may be an ensign, but I'm not that dumb. I appreciate your help. Let me know in the unlikely event that you need my assistance with anything."

"We'll do that, sir," the master sergeant said as two more full shots arrived at the table. "Thank you for the offer. If I might offer you some more advice?"

"Please do."

"There's a bunch of pilots at the Lux. I might've heard something about street strafing."

Street strafing. Unwilling to admit his ignorance, Geary nodded. "Where's that at?"

"Down the street that way. You'll probably hear them before you see them." The master sergeant spotted Seaman Chadra watching him, and sized up Chadra with a single look. "Straighten up, you boot! You're on duty!"

"Yes, sir!" Chadra replied, coming to such a rigid form of attention that he seemed in danger of falling over.

"Don't call me sir! I work for a living!" The master sergeant paused, turning his attention back to Geary. "No offense meant, sir."

"None taken," Geary said. He wondered how long enlisted had been making that joke about officers. Probably for as long as there had been enlisted and officers. "Thank you, Master Sergeant, Gunny." He nodded farewell to the two Marines before leading Chadra and Riley back out of the bar.

Once on the street, Chadra exhaled so loudly that Geary gave him a worried look. "Are you okay?"

"That sergeant!" Chadra said. "I was afraid to breathe!"

"Mr. Geary wasn't scared of him," Riley said, smiling proudly.

"You just have to treat people with the respect they deserve," Geary explained.

"What's that mean, sir?"

"It means... don't be a jerk. Even if you think you could get away with it. Let's find the Lux."

As the master sergeant had predicted, the whoops and shouts

carrying into the street advertised the location of the Lux before they reached it. Somebody was having a really good time.

They passed a group of Callas Republic sailors huddled together. "Shore patrol!" one of them shouted, and the entire group took off down the street.

"What do you suppose they were doing?" Riley wondered.

"Not our problem," Geary said. "They're not doing it any more."

Reaching the door to the Lux, where several citizens of Barcara were lounging as if awaiting any calls for their particular trades, Geary found his passage blocked by a local police officer. "No enlisted sailors in there," the cop said. "Officers only."

"They're on shore patrol," Geary said, trying to sound assertive but knowing he had no authority over local police.

The cop plainly also knew that Geary had no authority over her. "Officers only."

Geary looked at Chadra and Riley. "Can you two just stand there and do nothing until I get back?"

Riley nodded. "We're good at doing nothing."

"Right. I have to go inside. I'll be right back out. Don't. Do. Anything."

The police officer let Geary pass. Once inside, he found a large room with all the furniture pushed up against the walls. More than a dozen pilots were leaping from one piece of furniture to the next while several others cheered them on.

"Excuse me, Lieutenant," Geary asked the nearest one. "What's going on?"

"Touch and goes," the lieutenant replied, taking a drink from the bottle in his hand. "They drink a round, then they go around the edge of the room without touching the floor, then they remove some of the furniture and do it again. Repeat until a winner is declared or any survivors are incapable of continuing. Who are you? Shore patrol? Really?"

"Yes, sir," Geary said.

"You going to bust us, Ensign? Hey, the Shore Patrol's here!"

Another lieutenant came up, eyeing Geary as she grabbed the bottle from the male lieutenant and took a drink. "Where are you from?"

"The *Redoubt*," Geary said.

"Whoa! Deep spacer! You're not jump happy, are you?"

"No, I'm just trying to make sure things don't get out of hand tonight." On the heels of his words a crash announced the failure of one of the pilots to negotiate a safe landing on a piece of furniture.

"Have no fear," the male lieutenant assured Geary. "As you can see, we are professionals."

"Are you wearing an eject assist harness?" Geary asked, pointing to the device strapped to the pilot.

"He knows what an eject assist harness is!" the woman lieutenant commented. "You ever done any street strafing, ensign?"

"No. I don't even know what it is."

"Say someone wanted to try flying down a street at low altitude with an eject assist harness. That would be called street strafing."

"You guys do that?" Geary asked. "I thought those belts had limited maneuvering capability."

"That makes it a challenge," the male lieutenant advised cheerfully. "Or so I've heard. Never done it."

"Me, neither," the female lieutenant said. "I don't know anybody who has."

"Why do you have a phrase like street strafing for something no one ever does?" Geary asked.

"That is a very good question! Want a drink?"

"I'm on duty. Could you guys please not make things any worse out there? I've got three ships worth of sailors and a bunch of Marines all drinking heavily."

"Seriously? Why don't you give up now?"

"I'm stubborn," Geary said.

The lieutenants grinned at him. "We will take your request under advisement," the man said. "Good luck, Ensign!"

Outside again, Geary broke through a ring of locals offering "services" to Chadra and Riley, who were back to back and looking around in confusion. "Follow me," Geary said, worried about what Demore and Alvarez might be up to back at Brooklyn Bar.

Their path was blocked by a group of Callas sailors moving like a herd across the street. Once past that obstacle, Geary stopped again as Riley called out. "Sir? Is that Petty Officer Frink?"

Looking that way, Geary saw Frink weaving alone down the sidewalk. Ambling along behind him were several citizens of Barcara, reminding Geary of predators waiting for a wounded prey to collapse. As eager as he was to rush back to check on Demore and Alvarez, Geary couldn't let this situation pass. "Hey, Petty Officer Frink, why don't you come along with us?"

Frink glowered at Geary. "I don't haveta. On liberty."

"Actually, yeah, you do have to," Geary said. "We're heading back to the Brooklyn Bar."

"Come on, man," Chadra urged.

With Chadra on one side and Riley on the other, they got Frink back inside the Brooklyn Bar. "Park him with some friends who'll look after him," Geary ordered his two sailors. "Make sure they know I'll be expecting them to get Frink back to ship in one piece. They shouldn't have let him wander off on his own in his condition."

He went to the bar, looking for Demore and Alvarez.

Neither was in sight.

But another sailor was standing at the near end of the bar, wearing the shore patrol armband, the shocker belt and holster at her waist. "Yerevan? What are you doing? You're not on shore patrol duty."

Petty Officer Yerevan squinted at Geary, then opened her eyes wider as if trying to identify him. Grinning, she saluted. "Oh, hi, Ensign Geary!"

It didn't take the smell of alcohol on her breath to let Geary know this sailor was loaded. "Where are Demore and Alvarez?" he repeated.

"Demore? Uh, I got no idea. Alvarez. That I know. She had to go to the bathroom really bad, so she asked me to take over for a few, because she said Ensign Geary told her someone had to be here," Yerevan explained. "She was being real responsible!"

"You can't—"

"Don't you worry, sir! I am fully funckal—functional!" Yerevan's eyes went past Geary, gazing down the bar, and lit with sudden fury. Before he realized what was happening, she had pulled out the shocker and was leveling it. "Get away from my glass, you beer-stealing bitch!"

"No!" Geary grabbed the sailor's gun hand, wrestling it down. "*Alvarez!*"

Alvarez came running up, hastily sealing her uniform. "Everything okay, sir?"

"No. Everything is not okay. Put back on the shore patrol armband, take back the shocker, and then stay here until I say otherwise!"

"You gonna report me, sir?" Alvarez asked, looking downcast.

"I don't see what purpose that would serve," Geary said,

surprised to realize that Alvarez had been trying and simply hadn't done a very good job of it. Besides, if he reported Alvarez he'd also have to report Yerevan, who when not drunk was a decent sailor. "Just do your best from here on."

"Yes, sir!"

"Where's Petty Officer Demore?"

"He's at the other end of the bar. So's we can see everything that's going on," Alvarez said with a proud smile. "That was his idea."

"I bet it was." Geary headed along the crowded bar, finally spotting Demore at the far end.

Apparently tipped off that Geary was approaching, the petty officer spun about to face away from the bar. Demore stood at attention and saluted, a performance spoiled only by the bleariness in his eyes. "All is under control, sir!"

"Have you been drinking, Demore?"

The petty officer gaped at Geary with a wounded expression. "Drinking? Sir, drinking on duty would be a violation of fleet regulations." He looked around as if gravely concerned. "Sir, I have been observing the activity in this bar, and I have to tell you that many of the personnel from the *Redoubt* are drinking to excess."

"You've noticed that, huh?"

"Yes, sir. And so are some of the sailors from those Callas ships. I think we should keep a close eye on that."

"You do? Demore—" Geary broke off as a sudden burst of noise drew his attention. He saw sailors leaping to their feet and racing out the door of the bar. "What the hell is going on?"

"I do not know, sir," Demore said, pronouncing each word with exaggerated care. "I will investigate and—"

"No. You will stay here. Get back down to the other end of the bar with Alvarez so you can keep an eye on each other! And if I catch you with a drink in your hand you'll be busted back to seaman!"

Joining the tail end of the rush out of the bar, Geary found Chadra and Riley standing to one side, watching the stream of passing sailors as if vaguely aware that they probably ought to do something but unable to figure out just what that was. "Come on!"

They caught up with the rest of the sailors from the *Redoubt* at an open area intended for large gatherings. At the moment, the center of it was filled with Alliance sailors grappling with sailors in the uniforms of the Callas Republic. Geary heard yells and shouts that sounded oddly happy given the battle apparently under way. As he ran toward the central mass of struggling sailors, he encountered two sailors limping toward him as they supported each other. "Stop!" he yelled, then halted, staring. One of the sailors was Alliance, the other Callas, and they were grinning. "What's going on?"

The sailor from the *Redoubt*, Petty Officer Yamada, saluted with his free hand. "My left leg ain't working so well, sir, and his right leg is kinda messed up, so we figured together we had two good legs."

"Brilliant thinking," the Callas sailor agreed, also saluting Geary.

"What is this fight about?"

"Fight?" The sailors exchanged baffled looks. "There ain't no fight, sir," Yamada assured Geary. "These ex-cell-ent sailors are teaching us one of their tra-di-tion-al games."

"Rugby!" the Callas sailor added. "Nothing like it on any world under any star!"

"*That* is a game?" Geary demanded, pointing at the clawing mass of humanity.

"I know it don't look like much," the sailor from Callas apologized, "because we're all sort of tired, but sometimes it gets really wild, you know? Arms and legs and noses and heads getting broken right and left and all about! Great fun!"

Geary heard a sound like a stick snapping followed by a whoop of pain. "Somebody just broke an arm or leg."

"It's getting good, then! Let's get back in!" The two sailors began turning about while still supporting each other.

"No! Everyone—!"

"Hey, shore patrol!"

Geary turned at the hail, seeing several local police officers approaching.

The officers paused by Geary to eye the mass of sailors. "Riot or rugby?" one asked the others.

"Kinda hard to tell," another replied. "I think it's rugby this time, though."

The first officer turned to Geary. "Do you want to handle this?"

Geary looked at his available personnel, Chadra and Riley staring back at him with very worried expressions, remembered that their shockers had no charges, and shook his head as he watched another sailor being carried off the field. "Be my guest."

The officers pulled fist-sized spheres from their belts, tapped some settings, then tossed them into the mass of sailors. Geary caught the edges of the subsonics being put off by the spheres, vibrations that were unpleasant at this range and unbearable closer in. The swarm of sailors scattered into individuals and small groups racing past Geary and the police. From what he could hear of their conversations, most of them were headed back to the bar.

About a dozen bodies were left behind. "Any of them hurt bad?" a cop called as two others strolled among the fallen, protected from the vibrations by their vests.

"Nah. Looks like they're all just too drunk to stand on their own. Except for this one. Broken leg."

"Only one broken bone? They must have just started. We're going to take these guys in," the cop told Geary, making it clear that the statement was not negotiable.

"Fine," he said, looking around, "Chadra, Riley—" Geary looked around some more, but neither were anywhere in sight. They must have joined the stream of sailors back to the bar, thinking that Geary would also do so.

"Lose something?" the cop asked.

"Someone. Excuse me." Geary checked his comm pad in the vain hope that the locater function would be working, seeing that it was jammed, too. He ran back toward the bars, seeing that most of the sailors had already rushed inside the Brooklyn Bar as quickly as they had recently dashed out. "Where are Chadra and Riley?" he called to Demore and Alvarez.

"We have not seen them, sir!" Demore called back.

He'd lost half his shore patrol. Geary ran back out to the street just in time to duck as someone shot past just over his head, trailed by the rumble of an eject assist harness and excited whoops.

More pilots followed the first, caroming off the upper stories of the buildings as they tried to control their flight and racing unscathed through the virtual signs and advertisements filling the air above the street. Sailors boiled out of the bars to cheer the pilots on.

Geary struggled through the crowds, looking for his two missing sailors, and finally spotted what he thought was Chadra and Riley. The two were close together, apparently either making out or trying to strangle each other. "Hey!"

The two broke apart with panicked expressions, bobbed in place for a moment like frightened squirrels, then dashed inside the nearest bar.

Which happened to be the Jungle Bar where the Marines were forted up.

Geary was still several meters from the entrance to the bar when Chadra came flying out the door as if he had been launched by a catapult. A moment later Riley followed, her body tracing a similar arc before landing in the street near Chadra. Both sailors groaned, proving that neither was dead. "What happened?"

He received a couple of bewildered looks in reply. "We weren't doing anything!" Riley protested.

"You were supposed to stay with me. Why did you run when I called you?"

"We thought we were in trouble!"

"So you ran into a bar full of Marines?" Geary rubbed his mouth as he looked at the door to the Jungle Bar. No matter what Chadra and Riley had done earlier, there was no doubt that while members of the shore patrol they had been assaulted. Which meant he had to do something.

Chadra and Riley had gotten back on their feet, their expressions changing to alarm as Geary took a step toward the door of the Jungle Bar.

"Don't go in there, sir!" Riley called. "It's full of crazy rah-heads."

"I'll be fine," Geary assured her, aware of the many drunken sailors in the street watching him, clearly wondering how the officer would handle this. About all he could be sure of was that failing to do anything would destroy what little ability he still had to try to control things.

"But they said they'd kill the next space squid who came in there!"

Geary hesitated, remembering some of the stories he had heard about Marines on liberty, but also thinking of all the eyes on him, waiting to see if he would back down, or stand up for his sailors. "I've got a job to do. Wait out here this time." Taking a deep breath, he went into the bar. "Who did that?" he asked of the nearest Marines.

One of the Marines squinted at him, trying to focus. "Did what, sir?"

"Assaulted those two sailors."

"This young officer wants to know if anybody has seen any sailors in here," the Marine shouted to his comrades.

A loud chorus of "No, Sir!" echoed off the walls of the bar.

Geary exhaled slowly, trying to remain calm. He threaded his way to the table where the Master Sergeant and Gunnery Sergeant had been sitting.

Both were still there, face down on the table, its surface now littered with empty shot glasses. One was snoring.

A nearby Marine spoke mournfully, her eyes brimming with tears. "If only you'd seen it, sir. A mighty battle. A heroic struggle. Look at all the ordnance expended!" she added, pointing to the shot glasses. "Neither one would surrender. Both fought to the end, not yielding a centimeter. Heroic, I tell you, sir!"

"They're dead drunk," Geary said.

"Yes, sir. That's what I said, sir."

"Who's in charge in here now that they're both out?"

The Marine pondered the question, looking at her nearby comrades. "Corporal Windsock!" one cried.

"Corporal Windsock!" the cry went up.

A Marine corporal was shoved up to the table, saluting Geary with a grin as she wavered on her feet. "Corporal Wysocki, sir. What may I help you with, sir?"

"I need—" Geary's next words were cut off by an eruption of sound near the door.

"Save Mr. Geary!"

"We're coming, sir!"

Drunken sailors from the *Redoubt* began pouring into the bar, led by Geary's shore patrol, their sheer mass shoving aside startled Marines. "Space squids!" the Marines shouted, rallying and charging to reclaim the lost ground. Within moments the bar was full of individuals packed together, struggling to fight even though they were having trouble getting enough space to move their arms and legs.

"We're here for you, sir!" Seaman Alvarez cried as she somehow wriggled through the mess until she was close to Geary. "No rah-heads are going to get—"

A wave of bodies slammed into them. Geary lost sight of Alvarez as he fell. Forcing his way up again to a sitting position, he saw a Marine next to him on the floor choking Demore. "Stop!" Geary yelled, but the Marine either didn't hear over the noise or was too focused on his task to pay attention. Geary's fist bounced off the Marine's shoulder with no apparent effect.

His other hand, still on the floor, closed on a strip of leather. One end of the strip had a weight sewn inside.

Demore's face was going slack.

Swinging the weapon against the Marine's head, Geary heard a thunk. The Marine went limp. Geary pried his hands off of Demore's neck just before several more furiously entangled sailors and Marines fell on both of them.

✦ ✦ ✦

"I think it was about then that the police arrived," Geary told the captain.

"You think?" Captain Spruance asked.

"I was a little dazed, sir."

"So I understand. The ship's doctor diagnosed you with a borderline concussion." She leaned back in her chair, eyeing Geary. "You certainly put a lot of effort into failing in your duty."

"I was doing my best not to fail, Captain."

Captain Spruance dropped a dark leather object onto her desk, one end clunking from the weight sewn into it. "Does this look familiar?" She didn't wait for an answer. "The police report said it was among your possessions."

"It isn't mine, Captain! I… I picked that up, as I said, because Petty Officer Demore was being choked and—"

"Do you know what it is? They come with a variety of names, but this kind is usually called a blackjack. It's not yours?"

"No, Captain!"

"That's good, because it's illegal to possess a blackjack on an Alliance fleet ship." Spruance leaned back in her chair again as she looked at Geary. "What should I do with you, Ensign Blackjack? These charges normally call for some fairly serious punishments. But before you answer, it's only fair that I tell you a few things. Every sailor on liberty last night as well as your four shore patrol have been interviewed, and none of them can recall you doing anything even remotely contrary to regulations. Apparently, you were a paragon of proper behavior and an inspiring leader.

"The Marines involved in last night's incident say that you demonstrated great resolve in trying to prevent trouble," the captain continued. "The master sergeant was not yet awake when they were interviewed, but the gunnery sergeant insisted that it was good liberty and a by-the-book and per regulations good time was had by all. She had no explanation for the arrests of so many sailors and Marines, saying it was an overreaction on the part of the local police."

Spruance paused, tapping her desk again to bring up another document. "The aerospace pilots who were also involved in the events of last night all claim that no drinking and no street strafing took place. They credit you with offering a 'good example.' Based on these testimonials, if you and a good part of the crew hadn't been arrested, I'd probably be putting you in for a commendation."

Geary stared at the captain. "I... have no idea what to say."

"Maybe saying nothing else would be a good idea. The only real evidence I have against you is what you've just told me," Captain Spruance concluded. "And I'm not really allowed to use your own testimony against you unless I first warn you about that."

How had the captain made that mistake? Geary wondered.

Had it been deliberate?

Spruance shook her head. "You do realize last night was a no-win situation for you, right?"

"Yes, Captain, I did get that impression pretty quickly."

"But you appear to have done everything you could, anyway. You didn't give up just because the situation was hopeless from the start. And you tried to succeed in a manner that earned the collective silence of the sailors who could have tossed you out the airlock with their testimony if they'd wanted to. Even the Marines and pilots who could have helped hang you were willing to keep quiet. For whatever reason, they all respect you, and that's important. You did *something* right. So here's what I'm going to do, Ensign Blackjack. I'm going to forget that last night happened. Officially, there's not going to be any record. I'm also going to tell you that it would be a very good idea for you to not leave the ship again while we are orbiting this planet. I'm sure that you have plenty to do aboard ship."

"Yes, Captain," Geary said, unable to believe his luck. "Thank you, Captain."

"Get back to work."

Geary left the captain's stateroom, still dazed, to find Ensign Daria Rosen waiting, worried. "How bad is it?" she asked. "Court-martial?"

"No. I'm just confined to the ship for the rest of the port call. Nothing official, though. Nothing on the record."

Before she could reply, the captain stuck her head out of the hatch to her stateroom. "Hey, Ensign Blackjack, the supply officer's locater is off again. See if he's in the wardroom and tell him I need to see him right away."

"Yes, Captain!"

"Ensign Blackjack?" Daria asked, grinning. "It looks like you did pick up a nickname."

"I hope not," Geary said. "I'd hate to go through my life with a nickname like Blackjack following me around." In years to come, as Black Jack came to be part of his official identity, he would sometimes recall those words and wonder just how loudly his ancestors were laughing as he said them.

"I've got shore patrol duty tonight," Daria said. "Any advice?"

"Hide somewhere on the ship until we leave orbit."

"I'm serious! You ended up in jail and still came out on the captain's good side. What can I do?"

John Geary thought about it, finally shrugging. "Don't give up. And look after the crew and the others on liberty in Barcara as best you can. If you do, they might look after you when you need it."

"Uh huh," Daria said. "Got that. Anything else?"

He tried to remember everything that had happened last night. "One other thing. Don't be a jerk."

"Thanks, Black Jack!"

"Don't call me that!"

When On Basilisk Station *was published in 1993, it launched one of the longest running, most beloved space opera series of modern times, popularly known as the "Honorverse" in recognition of its most famous occupant, Honor Harrington. In our final story, David Weber writes an untold story set twenty years before the events of that opening book, about how Eloise Pritchart—the first president of the restored Republic under the (restored) old Constitution—became a member of the resistance to the Legislaturalists who had subverted and destroyed the old Constitution. Pritchart becomes a key politician in the People's Republic in later times, but here's how it all started for her.*

OUR SACRED HONOR
DAVID WEBER

"I wish you wouldn't read that, Eloise," Estelle Pritchart said. Her striking topaz eyes were more than a little worried as she ran the fingers of her right hand through her long, platinum hair. "If InSec realizes you're reading proscribed material they'll make your life—*our* lives—a living hell."

"Well, they aren't going to find out," her sister Eloise replied, looking up from the old-fashioned, bootleg hardcopy. "That's why things like this get passed around on something as archaic as paper, Stelle." She smiled more than a little crookedly. "InSec's street agents aren't really all that smart, you know. How smart do you *have* to be to break heads? And the people who run their surveillance systems count on their InfoSys backdoors and hacks, not hawkeyed agents reading paper over someone's shoulder. If it's not electronic, it doesn't count as far as they're concerned."

"That's not what you told me the other day," Estelle pointed out. She jabbed an index finger at her sister. "You told me they have audio and visual pickups hidden everywhere!"

"Which provide *electronic* data, not printed," Eloise riposted. "And what I said was that they had them hidden everywhere in public, which they do. That's not the same as saying they sort all that take effectively, or even try to. All those petabytes of audio and video are useful as hell after something *else* points them at a specific subject or group, but I doubt many of their investigations *start* there. Oh, they do catch an occasional activist malcontent by straining the data, but mostly they only pick up on people stupid enough to vent in public."

"And how is it you know that?" Estelle asked.

"Because I am a wise, insightful, perceptive, and observant individual," Eloise told her with a smile. "And I'm also twice your age, so I've been around the block a time or two."

Estelle rolled her eyes, although it was true enough. The two of them could almost have been taken for twins, but in a society with prolong that didn't mean what it might have in an earlier century. In fact, Eloise was almost fifty and Estelle was only twenty-three. There were times when the gap between their ages and their life experiences seemed even greater than the two T-decades which actually separated them, but physically it would have been difficult to estimate which of them was the older.

"You worry me sometimes," Estelle said much more seriously. "InSec and the MHP don't fool around with anybody they even think is a malcontent, and you know it! One of these days you're going to slip up. That's what I'm afraid of. And you're all I've got, Eloise. The only person in the world who I *know* loves me. Can't you just… leave well enough alone? If anything happens to you, it'll just kill me!"

"Nothing is going to happen to me." Eloise laid the hardcopy aside and crossed to enfold her sister in a tight hug. "I promised Mom I'd take care of you, and I will. I always have, haven't I?" She squeezed even tighter for a second, then stood back, her hands on her sister's shoulders and shook her gently. "This isn't the safest stuff I could possibly be reading," she conceded, twitching her head in the direction of the hardcopy, "but I'm staying well away from anybody like the Citizens Rights Union or any of the other lunatic, hard-line organizations. Besides, this one isn't even officially proscribed."

"Only because they haven't gotten around to it," Estelle muttered. "I've only taken a couple of peeks at it, and even I know that much! Agit-prop, that's what they'd call it, and you know it."

"You're probably right, but it was still there in the library's public files, without any warnings or censorship notices. And I printed it out on one of the library faxes using a general patron ID, so unless they had one of those cameras reading over my shoulder as the pages came out of the hopper, they don't have a clue that I have it."

"But *why* do you read this stuff?" Estelle demanded plaintively.

"It's not like it's going to make any difference, and it's all ancient history, anyway. You can't change things any more than I can, and if I can't change them, I'd rather not spend my time wishing I *could*."

"There's something to that," Eloise admitted after a moment. "But that's Mom's fault, too. She's the one who got me started reading this kind of stuff when I was about half as old as you are now. And I think sometimes that if more people had read it before the old Constitution was scrapped, it wouldn't have been."

Estelle's worried expression tightened at that, and Eloise shrugged.

"I'm not going to stand on any street corners—or even hide in any dark alleys—and tell anyone else anything of the sort, Stelle. I'm older than you are; I'm not *senile*. But it's true. That's another one of the things Mom taught me. I wish you'd had longer to know her."

"I do, too... even if you do scare me to death when you start talking about all those things she told you."

Eloise chuckled a bit sadly, but it was true. And, if she was going to be honest, the way their mother had died had quite a bit to do with her own dissatisfaction.

Gabrielle Pritchart had been from Haven's last pre-prolong generation. Oh, if she'd been fortunate enough to have been born into the family of one of the Legislaturalist dynasties or one of their uppercrust allies she could have had prolong, but the rot was already setting in by then. The infrastructure to support first-generation prolong had been expensive, and only the wealthy—or citizens of star nations whose governments had cared enough to invest to subsidize it as a public health service—had been able to afford it. The Legislaturalists hadn't. Of course the costs had come down steeply as the therapies matured and spread, but not quickly enough for Gabrielle's generation. By the time they'd come down to something the Legislaturalists were prepared to bear for the rest of the PRH's citizens (propelled in no small part by increasing unrest from below), Gabrielle had been too old for it. Which was particularly (and bitterly) ironic, given that the daughter she'd borne at only thirty had received the *second*-generation therapies as part of the Basic Living Stipend guarantees. And Estelle, who'd been born when Gabrielle was fifty-six, had actually received the third-generation treatments.

Still, Gabrielle would have been only in her eighties today, which was scarcely decrepit even for a pre-prolong individual, given modern medicine. Assuming all the benefits of modern medicine had still been available to all of the People's Republic's citizens. They hadn't been, but it didn't really matter, because she'd been only sixty-one, less than thirteen T-years older than Eloise was now, when she'd died. She wasn't one of the people the Legislaturalists' security forces had simply "disappeared," but if the agencies charged with maintaining Nouveau Paris's infrastructure had done their jobs, the high-speed transit tube wouldn't have malfunctioned and driven Gabrielle Pritchart and three hundred and twelve other citizens into the Bichet Tower station's braking buffer at just over one hundred and eighty kilometers per hour.

Four other mass transit accidents in that same calendar year had each produced at least fifty-four casualties, but Bichet had been the worst.

And no one had ever been held responsible for the "unforeseeable technical failures" which had led to all of them.

Estelle had been four T-years old at the time, and in truth, Eloise was the only mother she'd ever known.

But Gabrielle had been the daughter of university professors driven from their posts and hounded onto the BLS they'd despised for daring to speak out against ratifying the Constitution of 1795 PD. They'd made the mistake of believing the decades of steady rot actually might be reversed at the ballot box, and they'd fought passionately for the last remaining vestige of the old Republic. For which, the Legislaturalists had purged them from their positions and insured that they would never be employed again.

Their fate had made their daughter wise, but Gabrielle had inherited their stubborn belief in the value of the individual, as well, and she'd inculcated it in her own older daughter. She'd also been careful to teach Eloise to conceal her own interest in such forbidden topics as the hardcopy on the sadly worn apartment's rickety dinner table. Perhaps if she'd believed, understood, how bad things were truly going to become, she wouldn't have encouraged such risky beliefs, but Eloise didn't think so. Her mother had understood that the human spirit had to be nurtured just as surely as the human body, and as she'd told Eloise more than once, *someone* had to remember.

There were times when Eloise remembered those conversations and condemned herself for not being more... proactive in the cause of remembering. But she wasn't her mother, and by the time she'd been old enough to begin paying attention, the last frail edifices of the Republic of Michèle Péricard had toppled. And because they had, she couldn't blame Estelle for her anxiety. That same anxiety was an omnipresent part of her, as well. Nor did Estelle need to remind her that they were all each other had, and what Eloise might have been prepared to risk for herself, she was not prepared to risk for Estelle.

That was something she would never tell her sister. Never even hint to her. Estelle was her hostage to fortune, and Eloise would never—ever—let her suspect that it was fear for her which had prevented Eloise from doing what she might have done otherwise.

"I think Mom would have liked you a lot, Stelle," she said now. "I know I do."

"Gee, thanks," Estelle said dryly, and Eloise chuckled again.

"Hey, you're my sister. Of course I *love* you! But *liking* someone can actually be harder than loving them, you know."

"Did I ever mention that you have some really weird perspectives on life?" Estelle asked.

"From time to time," Eloise admitted.

"Good. I wouldn't want you to think I hadn't noticed."

"Oh, believe me! I don't think anything of the sort."

Estelle laughed, then looked at the time display on the aged but still functional (more or less) smart wall and sighed.

"I'd better be getting to bed," she said. "I'm opening for Jorge in the morning."

"You are?" Eloise couldn't keep an edge of concern out of her tone, and Estelle shrugged.

"Vivienne screened in sick."

"'Sick,'" Eloise repeated, and Estelle shrugged again. Both of them knew "sick" had nothing at all to do with germs or viruses in Vivienne's case.

"I know. I know!" Estelle said. "But we're lucky to have her anyway. And when she's not dusting or patching, she has a really sweet disposition. You know how much the customers like her when she's straight."

"*When* she's straight," Eloise agreed. "Which seems to be getting less and less frequent."

"There's not much we can do about that," Estelle sighed, and Eloise nodded grimly.

More and more of Estelle's contemporaries were completely disengaging from anything even remotely smacking of personal responsibility. Eloise had a better notion than most Dolists of the precarious state of the People's Republic's finances, but the irony was that even Haven's ramshackle industrial sector was incredibly productive by any pre-diaspora standard. The government was ever more strapped to support the BLS and associated programs by which the Legislaturalists had bought the Dolist Managers' connivance in the institutionalization of their own power, yet it was persistently unable to find its citizens the sort of productive employment star nations like the Star Kingdom of Manticore had found for theirs. And a big part of the reason they couldn't, in Eloise's opinion, was because of the huge disincentive the BLS provided. Havenite manufactured goods might be shoddy, and they might be far less durable than comparable goods in other star nations, but they were certainly cheap. Cheap enough that the BLS allowed non-Legislaturalist Havenites to buy plenty of bread and circuses without ever working a day in their lives.

So they didn't.

Eloise couldn't really blame them, much though she wanted to. They were educated—programmed—to be drones, serving no real function other than to provide the reliable voting bloc that routinely shored up the Legislaturalists' supposed legitimacy. That was how a façade democracy worked, and it wasn't surprising that people who realized they contributed nothing more than that to their society weren't exactly the most responsible people when it came to their own lives, either. The desire to contribute, if only to repay, was part of a healthy personality, and so was the desire to build a better life for oneself and one's children. But too many people had realized—or decided—they were never going to rise out of the ranks of the Dolists, however hard they labored. So why should people who didn't *need* to work, and who realized that trying to work was pointless, *desire* to work? Of course a lot of them took the easier path, collected their BLS, cast their votes obediently, binged on cheap entertainment, or drugs, or (increasingly) lives of petty crime and violence, and tried not to think about the other things they might have done with their lives.

All too often, they succeeded in the not-thinking part.

Eloise understood exactly how that worked. She'd *seen* it working around her for almost fifty T-years, and she knew her mother had been right to rail against it. People who lost the belief that what they did *mattered*—or had it taken away from them— tended to develop *un*healthy personalities. And when enough of a society's citizens had unhealthy personalities, it did, too. She'd seen ample proof of *that* around her, as well.

There were still citizens of the People's Republic who'd avoided that deadly cycle. In her darker moments, Eloise suspected their numbers were shrinking daily, but they were still there, and Jorge Blanchard—and Estelle—were cases in point.

Even in Nouveau Paris, there were niches for people willing to work. The problem was that working was unlikely to change anything in their lives. Even Estelle and Blanchard knew that. The upper classes—indeed, even most of what passed for the middle-class—were the private preserve of the Legislaturalists, the Dolist Managers, and their families and cronies. The best anyone else could hope for was something like Blanchard's diner, a friendly little place down near the Duquesne Tower tube station with real, live servers, good food, and clean silverware. Jorge was never going to become wealthy, but he could look back at his life and know he'd made a difference. That he'd *accomplished* something in a world which might have been specifically engineered to prevent people from doing anything of the sort.

Eloise approved of Jorge Blanchard.

But it looked like he was going to lose Vivienne Robillard. Estelle was right; when Vivienne was free of one recreational drug or another, she was exactly the sort of server someone like Jorge's Diner needed. Unfortunately, she was sliding down the same blackhole which had claimed all too many of Estelle's age-mates. More to the point, though…

"Honey, I don't like you opening the diner by yourself," Eloise said now. "That's a rough neighborhood."

"Rougher than The Terraces?" Estelle demanded, widening her eyes. "Puh-leez, Eloise! Give me a break!"

Eloise's lips twitched ever so slightly, but she also shook her head.

"Granted, The Terraces are no bed of roses. On the other hand, I don't exactly encourage you to go traipsing around *there* by yourself, either."

"No, you don't," Estelle said rather pointedly. Eloise looked at her, and the younger Pritchart grimaced. "I know you think I'm still a baby, but I'm really not, you know. I'm all grown up, and sooner or later you're going to have to trust me to start looking out for myself."

"You're a regular octogenarian, you are!" Eloise retorted.

"Well, I may be younger than you are, but I really have been paying attention. I'm not going to run around by myself someplace like The Terraces or the Eighth Floor."

"No, you damned well aren't," Eloise said firmly. "But"—she raised a forestalling hand before Estelle could react to her authoritative tone—"you're right, you aren't a child anymore. I still don't want you walking around by yourself in the wrong neighborhood, but if pressed, I will concede you've demonstrated a modicum of situational awareness in the past. Still doesn't make me any happier about your opening the diner by yourself, though."

"Richenda and Céline are headed down to the tubes tomorrow morning with me, and Jorge's going to join us at Fifty. And I promise I won't stir a single step home till you get there to ride the shafts with me." Estelle sighed again, theatrically. "There, satisfied?"

"Satisfied," Eloise conceded, although the truth was that she wasn't entirely. Richenda and Céline were levelheaded girls, but they were within four or five years of Estelle's age. She didn't entirely trust their sensitivity to possible threats, but there was a certain safety in numbers, even in Nouveau Paris.

"Then I'll see you in the morning before I leave," Estelle said, hugging her again and kissing her affectionately on the cheek before she headed off to her own bedroom.

Eloise watched her go, then opened the sliding doors and stepped out onto the apartment balcony. That balcony—and their apartment's exterior position and the view that came with it—had cost a *lot* of their joint BLS and quite a bit of sharp trading with the manager of this floor of Duquesne Tower. Eloise's version of Jorge's diner was the clientele she'd built up as a tutor. Her own mother had made sure she was actually *educated*, even if she'd had to do that by schooling her at home, rather than simply warehoused in one of the PRH's so-called schools. Along the way, Gabrielle had impressed Eloise with her responsibility to "pay it forward" in turn, and there were parents even now, even in Nouveau Paris, determined to see that *their* children really learned something. People like Floor Manager Aristide Cardot, who hoped his son might find the Legislaturalist patronage that could lift him higher in his own life.

A tutor's pay wasn't much more than Estelle earned working in the diner, but it was satisfying work, and it provided a handy cover for Eloise's forays into the historical sections of the library and the InfoSys.

You're a fine one to talk about Estelle wandering around alone, she thought now, gazing out over the glorious light tapestry of nighttime Nouveau Paris.

In the darkness, looking at the incredible strings of light that caparisoned the city's mighty towers, watching the glittering fireflies of air cars and air lorries, or looking down, down, down into the mighty canyons to the lighted sidewalks, or looking even higher than the air cars, to where the running lights of cargo or personnel shuttles made their way from orbit to the spaceport, it was almost—*almost*—possible to believe that what that city once had been it might someday be again. But it wasn't going to happen, she admitted sadly, and maybe that was the real reason she hadn't tried harder to inculcate her own love of history into Estelle. Maybe it was better for her sister to never yearn for what had been true so long ago.

It would be better if I *didn't,* she told herself. *Better if I didn't understand everything we've lost, didn't want it* back *so much. Maybe then I'd be more content, or something like that. And maybe I wouldn't be so tempted.*

She sighed, bracing both hands on the railing, leaning on it as she looked out into the breezy darkness from her two-hundredth floor vantage point. Some of the other towers were far taller than Duquesne, and Estelle was right about the dangerous quadrants in their own building. Even so, there were moments like this when Eloise just needed to drink in the beauty, the sense—the illusion—of freedom and possibility in the breeze sweeping across the balcony.

"*We hold these truths to be self-evident.*" The words first written over three thousand T-years ago ran through her mind. The words Michèle Péricard had lived by when she drafted the Constitution the Legislaturalists had ripped to shreds. "*That all men are created equal; that they are endowed by their Creator with inherent and inalienable rights; that among these are life, liberty, and the pursuit of happiness: that to secure these rights governments are instituted among men, deriving their just powers from the consent of the governed...*"

She didn't begin to understand all the charges their drafters had leveled against their king. Details got lost in thirty-two centuries, and history as a discipline was... discouraged in the People's Republic. For, she thought sourly, reasons which were self-evident. But she understood enough. She understood those words' protest against sham government, against tyranny, and against what amounted to despotism that completely ignored "the consent of the governed."

Estelle was right, the biography of Péricard on her dinner table *would* have been proscribed if Internal Security or the Mental Hygiene Police had realized everything that was buried in it. In fact, the grand declaration from whence those words sprang *had* been proscribed; what passed for the authorities in the People's Republic of Haven simply hadn't worried about what the man who'd written Péricard's definitive biography a century and a half before might have included in its appendices.

A familiar shiver went through her as she looked out over that sea of lights, that *ocean* of lights, and those words went through her. In her own pantheon, no one stood higher than Péricard, the woman whose dream had created the Republic of Haven, the Athens of the Haven Quadrant. Whose dream had been murdered as surely as Hypatia of Alexandria.

She wondered, sometimes, what would have happened if Estelle had never been born. She loved her sister more dearly than life itself, and the thought of a world without Estelle made her shy away like a frightened horse. Yet if Estelle hadn't been born, if she weren't Eloise's "hostage to fortune," what might she have done differently in her life?

A part of her yearned for the answer to that question, although she knew it never *could* be answered, really. Yet there was that part of her, the part that remembered the fierce, proud conclusion of that ancient declaration.

And for the support of this Declaration, they'd written, *with a firm reliance on the protection of divine Providence, we mutually pledge to each other our Lives, our Fortunes and our sacred Honor.*

That was what they'd pledged: everything they had. Everything they held most dear in all the world. And those words spoke to her even now. Spoke to that part of her that secretly admired the Citizens Rights Union. Too many of them were obviously terrorists for terrorism's sake, but not all of them were. And at least they had the courage to stand and fight. *That* was what that secret part of her admired, even envied. Maybe some of them didn't really understand what they were fighting for, and maybe some of them were fighting only for vengeance upon a system which had failed them, but at least they were *fighting.*

And at least they have clarity, she thought. *I suspect most of them have a pretty severe case of myopia, but what they* do see, *they see clearly enough to be willing to pay cash for it. And maybe if there were a few people in something like the CRU who weren't myopic, a few people who remembered what they stood for, who could remind the rest of them…*

She drew a deep breath, and those words flowed through her one last time. *Our lives, our fortunes and our sacred honor.* Maybe the men who'd written them down would have understood the CRU—and remembered Péricard and *her* constitution—whatever the cost. *Whoever* the cost. And if *they* could have…

She stepped on that dangerous thought firmly, drew a deep breath, then turned and went back inside and closed the doors behind her.

✦ ✦ ✦

"You really should think about upgrading, Eloise," Kevin Usher said. "You need more standoff capability."

"What I *don't* need is any attention from InSec or the cops," Eloise replied, standing back and wiping her forehead. Then she reached behind her head, holding the hair tie with her left hand while her right tugged on her sweat-damp ponytail to tighten the tie. "They don't take too kindly to Dolists 'packing heat,' Kevin!"

InSec, MHP, Urban Authority, and just about every single one of the People's Republic police forces—of which there were no-one-really-knew how many, at the end of the day—took dim views of weapons in general, but they saved their special attention for firearms. Probably because firearms—even old-fashioned chemical-powered ones—posed a much greater threat to what passed for the champions of law and order in the PRH than a simple club or even a vibro blade.

"I'm not talking about sticking a tribarrel in your hip pocket, for God's sake," Usher said in a disgusted tone. Then his expression softened as he waved both big, powerful hands at the workout room around them. "You're good with your hands, Eloise, and you're one of the few people I know who keep right on getting better. But the best rule of all for hand-to-hand is to keep the other bastard from ever getting his hands on you in the first place. One of the first things the Marines teach you is that the only time you use your hands is when you don't have a gun or a knife and both feet are nailed to the floor."

Eloise chuckled, although she knew he was perfectly serious.

And she trusted his judgment, too. She and Kevin had known one another for over five T-years, ever since he'd opened his dojo on Duquesne Tower's Floor Hundred Ten. It was a ninety-floor commute for her, but it was located in the same quadrant on Hundred Ten as the Pritcharts' apartment on Two Hundred, so it was only about a fifteen-minute walk from the nearest lift shaft trunk. And Kevin, an ex-Marine, had come highly recommended by one of her students' older sister.

Over the last half-decade, Eloise had recommended him to quite a few of her other acquaintances, as well. Not all of them. Kevin was just as good as the original recommendation had suggested. In fact, he was probably even better. He was less concerned about specific "schools" or pure forms than he was with what worked. He referred to his personal style as "street brawler steroids," and it damned well did work. And from Eloise's perspective, what made him especially good was that he understood that each student's style had to work for her, he suited his teaching to the size and strength of his student, and he obviously liked women... and kept those big, strong, highly skilled hands of his utterly impersonal when he worked with one of them.

The reason she hadn't recommended him to all of her acquaintances was that she strongly suspected—no, "suspect" was too weak a word, she admitted—that he was associated with the Citizens' Rights Union. He was about the farthest thing she could imagine from a fanatic, which sometimes made her wonder how he could support all of the CRU's actions. Blowing up Legislaturalists in their offices or Internal Security posts, or ambushing a squad of Mental Hygiene Police on a public slidewalk, was one thing. Eloise actually found herself tempted sometimes to stand up and cheer when something like that happened. But the pure terror attacks, like the one on a private school whose sole offense had been that it was patronized primarily by Legislaturalist families... those were something else. The official reports in the faxes said the bomb had killed three children and injured six, but rumors floating around the InfoSys said the casualties had been at least three times that much, and probably even higher.

Personally, Eloise didn't care whether the true number was three dead, or nine, or nine*teen*. They were *kids*, just like *her* students. So they were the kids of Legislaturalists, of the people responsible for the absence of opportunities available to *her* kids. So what? They hadn't chosen their parents, and the thought of someone killing kids—*anybody's* kids—just to make a political statement turned her stomach. So how did Kevin justify an association with people like that?

But that was between him and his own conscience. She didn't know what might have driven him into the CRU in the first place, and she wasn't going to condemn him for it. No, the reason she hadn't sent some of her friends to him for training was that she refused to put them into contact with a potential CRU recruiter. *Those* friends were bitter enough they were probably *looking* for someone who could recruit them, and Eloise wouldn't be the person who found them that someone.

Even if he had become one of her closest personal friends.

And even if she did sometimes wish…

"Kevin, I don't want to start right out killing somebody if that isn't what it takes," she countered now. It was a familiar argument.

"Two thirds of the time, all you'll have to do is show fight," came the equally familiar response. "The kind of scum who'd pick on a single woman tend to back off quick when that happens. But sometimes it comes down to kill or be killed, with no other option. I don't like that any more than you do, but it's still true. And it's also true that the more lethal the fight you're ready to show, the quicker somebody who *might* back off goes ahead and finds reverse. And let's be honest, Eloise, you're not a big woman. You don't have the physical size to intimidate the ones who might not be as fast to take the hint. Especially not if they equate 'threat' with 'weapon,' not training and attitude. You know—the really, really terminally stupid ones like Cal?"

"Kevin, you're terrible!" Eloise laughed. "Cal's been perfectly nice to me since I broke his finger."

"And he never would've jabbed it in your face that way if he wasn't twenty centimeters taller than you and really, really terminally stupid," Kevin retorted. "And, yeah, I know he was drunk and you'd just turned him down for the evening. But that's part of my point, Eloise. Someday you may run into someone else—someone with something in mind a hell of a lot worse than Cal could ever think of—who's too dusted, or glittered, or hazed, or just plain drunk to think about what a trained person your size could do to them." He shook his head. "And then there's the minor fact that you're one of the best-looking women I know. Hell, that I've *ever* known!" He shook his head again, his expression sober. "You draw the eye, and not just because of your coloring. That's why Cal hit on you in the first place. He was only getting a little… too happy, maybe, but your looks make you more of a target for predators than most, and you know it."

"Of course I do," she replied, and her tone was as sober as his expression. "I'm not going to hide who I am, though. And I won't let that kind of 'predator' dictate the way I live my life, either!"

"Shouldn't have to," he growled. "And I wish to hell you didn't have to worry about it. If the frigging police would just do their jobs—or if just *one* of our beloved city or provincial administrators would *make* them do their jobs—you might not have to, and I'd be out of work. But they don't, they won't, and I like you too damned much to let you become one more example of why the hell they should!"

Eloise blinked at the genuine anger, the rage, simmering just under the surface of that last sentence. His brown eyes were dark, burning with an inner fury, and a small, still corner of her understood in that moment just how terrifying Kevin Usher could truly be. She wondered who he'd "liked too much" and who'd become "one more example"? Perhaps that was why he could be part of the CRU despite its too-frequent excesses.

"And in support of my theory," he went on after a heartbeat, his tone much lighter as if he'd deliberately stepped back from the abyss of anger, "I should point out that even at his drunkest, Cal's never gotten all touchy-feeley with *me*!"

"The mind boggles," Eloise protested. "Not only that, but the stomach turns!" She raised both hands in a pushing away gesture and shuddered theatrically at the image that conjured up. "I can't say for certain, but I'm *pretty* sure Cal's about as hetero as they come, Kevin. And let's be fair here. You're not exactly the best example of eye candy he could find. You're what I believe the bad novelists call, um… *rugged* looking."

"Gee, thanks." He grimaced. "'Beat-up,' don't you mean?"

"Of course, but I like you far too much to ever actually *say* it," she assured him earnestly.

"You're so kind to me," he said. "But my *point*, as you understood perfectly well, is that unlike you, I'm ten centimeters taller than *he* is. The one thing even I can't teach you is height, and the sad truth is that just like physical size is often a deterrent all by itself, its *absence* is like blood in the water for some people."

She nodded more seriously. In fact, Kevin was understating their size differential. She stood barely a hundred and sixty centimeters and tipped the scale at a scant fifty-five kilos. Kevin, on the other hand, was almost a hundred and ninety-four centimeters tall and weighed well over twice as much as she, all of it bone and muscle. His biceps were as thick as her thighs and his shoulders were more than twice as broad as hers. Coupled with his scarred knuckles and the sort of "rugged" face that resulted from frequent applications of someone else's knuckles when he'd been growing up, he radiated the sort of elemental fearsomeness that could make *anyone* back down. In fact, he looked like the sort of fellow who routinely tore chance-met strangers into tiny pieces for stepping on his toe. Which he wasn't. In fact, she suspected that very few people even imagined how thoroughly at odds with the inward man that outward appearance truly was.

Except for the toughness of course. And not that she doubted for a moment that Kevin Usher could become anyone's worst nightmare if he chose to.

He just *wouldn't* choose to without a very good reason.

She thought.

"I hear what you're saying," she told him now. "But I try to see trouble before it sees me. It's a lot easier to avoid when you do. And—like I say, Kev—I don't want to start out in a lethal-force confrontation if I don't have to. That's why I carry the baton."

"And very useful it is," he conceded.

Eloise favored a standard, length-configurable police baton with enhanced inertia-loading. It collapsed to fifteen centimeters but could be extended to ninety in fifteen-centimeter increments, and its deactivated length was small enough to fit the cloth scabbard Dorothée Tremont, one of her student's parents, sewed into the left thigh of every pair of pants she bought. Dorothée removed the liner of her left hip pocket at the same time, so that she could access the baton instantly... and she practiced regularly to do just that. She hadn't needed Kevin to tell her speed of response was the first and most important single element of self-defense. Used properly, that baton was highly effective—as the police had demonstrated often enough by breaking heads with batons just like it—and she'd carried it since she was a girl. In fact, she'd given Estelle one just like it for her eleventh birthday.

"The only problem I have with it," Kevin continued, "is that people don't think of it as a *lethal* weapon. Some of them, especially if there's more than one—and you know what kind of gangers roam some of Duquesne's floors—may figure they can take the damage, or—better yet, that one of their *buddies* can take the damage—until they get it away from you. If they're right, I guarantee you they'll end up using it on *you* just as a setting-up exercise. Even if they're *wrong*, you could get hurt bad demonstrating that to them. And I don't want you getting hurt at all."

"So what would you recommend instead?" she half-sighed. "I know I'm not going to shut you up until you tell me."

"Nope," he agreed with a toothy, much more cheerful grin. "And, since you've been so kind—and so prudent—as to ask, here's what I had in mind."

He reached into his trouser pocket and produced a twelve-centimeter cylinder, about four centimeters in diameter, and Eloise's eyes darkened as she recognized the vibro blade hilt.

"I don't know, Kev..." she began.

"Hear me out, first," he said, holding it up.

She looked at him for a moment, then nodded, and he pressed the activation button. The "blade" itself was invisible, of course. In fact, it wasn't even generated until the user pressed the contoured button in the grip and brought it fully online. But the high-pitched, unmistakable whine all such blades were legally required to emit whenever activated was even louder than most. The three-centimeter pop-out quillons deployed the instant the blade came live, preventing the user's own hand from accidentally amputating itself by slipping down into the cutting plane. The blade was supposed to make that impossible by shutting down the instant the user's grip on the activation button loosened, but that didn't always happen the way it was supposed to.

"This is a Martinez Industries Model 7," he told her. "Out-of-the-box, it's configurable to fifteen or thirty centimeters, and it's officially rated as a Class Three weapon, which makes it carry-legal. More importantly, the instant somebody hears it, they know you're carrying something a lot more dangerous than just a baton. And no one but an idiot's going to grab *this* puppy to disarm you!"

"I imagine not," she said, staring at it. "And what did you mean about out-of-the-box?"

"I mean I've... tinkered with it a bit," he said. "Trick a Marine armorer taught me. You can boost its max length all the way to *ninety* centimeters for about twenty-five minutes. Burns out completely after that but it kicks ass while it lasts, and most people won't expect the extra length. Won't *see* it, either, unless they have a really close encounter with it. Makes a hell of a close-quarters weapon, Eloise."

"I'm sure it would," she said in a faintly appalled tone. "I wouldn't know how to go about using it, though."

"Oh, bullshit!" Kevin deactivated the blade and tossed the hilt to her. "You and I spar with that baton of yours for fifteen minutes every time you come over here. This thing's weight is almost identical to the baton's—one reason I picked it for you—and I've worked you with both hands for over four years now. You're trying to tell me you don't think you could swing this sucker *effectively*?"

"Well…"

"What I thought," he grunted as she turned the hilt in both hands, staring down at it. "Now, you listen to me for a minute, Eloise. I'm not saying you have to start right out in slice-and-dice mode. To be honest, I wouldn't be suggesting this to you if I figured there was any chance in hell that'd be your default setting! But the fact that you're a southpaw's going to surprise eighty, ninety percent of the people you might run into just to start with, and after four years with me, you're frigging well ambidextrous with that baton.

"So, the way I see it, let's say you do get into a confrontation you can't avoid. I know you, and you're not going to be the instigator, but it could still happen. So say it does. Now what do you do? Baton in left hand, extended and ready for business. If they back off, well and good. They don't back off, maybe the baton's all you need, in which case that's all you use. But in the meantime, the right hand's filled with that thing," he pointed at the vibro hilt in her hands, "and if you need it, it comes up ready for business in a heartbeat. Two or three of them, maybe you bring it up sooner, let 'em hear it sing while they… rethink their position. But, trust me, *two* arguments in favor of rethinking are a hell of a lot better than one."

✦ ✦ ✦

"I'm really getting worried about The Terraces and the Eighth Floor, Aristide," Eloise said quietly, later that month, as Alphonse Cardot closed his tablet and headed for his room. "And I don't like what I heard about that incident down on Hundred and Ten last night."

"I don't either," Floor Manager Aristide Cardot replied. His expression was grim, and Eloise knew he wouldn't have admitted anything of the sort to just anyone.

As the manager of Two Hundred, Aristide was effectively the mayor of a city of close to ten thousand. Over a million people lived in Duquesne Tower's hundred and thirty residential floors. The other seventy-five floors were taken up with engineering offices and equipment, power systems, water and waste disposal systems, and commercial space, including three major fabrication facilities, at least eighty shopping malls—eleven of them sprawling over at least a hundred square meters of floor space—and thousands of cubic meters housing the ever expanding sprawl of the PRH's innumerable bureaucratic entities.

Aristide was an essential cog in that enormous mechanism, but he was *only* a cog. All he could do was the best he could do, and Eloise felt remarkably secure on the Two Hundred. There wasn't much he could do about the services which depended upon outside sources, and interruptions in power and plumbing—even ventilation, occasionally—had become increasingly frequent, despite his best efforts. But both he and Commissioner Cesar Juneau, who commanded the Floor Two Hundred Police, took their responsibilities seriously. When services went down, Aristide moved heaven and earth to get them back up again. And if Juneau's patrolmen and patrolwomen expected occasional "gifts" from the tenants—and weren't above a little discreet shakedown if those gifts weren't forthcoming—they were nowhere near so blatant about selling "protection" as the force on Eighth Floor. And they took their public safety duties seriously. They had a remarkably short way with the sort of youth gangs who terrorized Eighth and The Terraces. And they weren't especially shy about delivering summary punishment tailored to fit the crime rather than relying on the overburdened and apathetic courts, either.

It was unfortunate that the attitude of the Eighth Floor force seemed to be spreading upward, but it had a long way to go before it hit Two Hundred.

"I guess what I hate most about it is that we have to go past the other floors to get home," she said. "Once I get above One Hundred I start relaxing, but those lower floors, especially Fifty and Eight…" She shook her head. "Every time I get into the lift car below Hundred, I worry about who I may end up sharing it with."

"Cesar and I are trying to keep an eye on it," Aristide told her, "but there's only so much we can do from up here. Rembert down on Hundred is trying to work with us on it, too, and we're trying to beef up the Lift Shaft Police patrols. But those are trans-floor. We don't have jurisdiction, once we get past the lift car door. Even if we did, every floor manager and commissioner's way too strapped for manpower to do anything like that, even if we pooled our resources. And I hate to say it, but the Duquesne LSP's in even worse shape than *we* are. We've requested more shaft cops and better monitoring systems for the lifts from the Department of Public Safety, too, of course." He rolled his eyes—something else he wouldn't have done with just anyone—and puffed his cheeks. "I've been assured we'll receive them as soon as possible. It's all a matter of priorities, they say."

And Duquesne Tower's priority is somewhere south of zero, Eloise filled in mentally.

"Well, at least I've got my 'little friend' with me," she said out loud, and Aristide waved both hands in an averting gesture.

"Don't talk to me about that!" he scolded with a smile. "I'm not supposed to know about it, and I'm just as happy that way."

"Oh, of course," Eloise agreed with a smile. "I can't imagine what I was thinking to bring up a subject like that! I apologize."

"And well you should," he admonished her. "However, speaking hypothetically, if I knew what you were talking about—which I don't, of course—I'd probably approve wholeheartedly."

"Yes, I think you probably would." She smiled again, thinking it was just as well for his peace of mind that he didn't know about Kevin's recent gift, and patted him on the arm. "And on that note, it's time I was going. I need to get groundside before Estelle starts home."

"Be well," Aristide said, escorting her to his apartment's door, and she nodded. *Be careful*, was what he really meant, but it probably would have been impolitic to point that out.

✦   ✦   ✦

Eloise rode the lift downward and muttered balefully as she checked her chrono. She *hated* leaving Estelle waiting for her at the diner, and she'd allowed plenty of time for the trip... she'd thought. But that was before the delay on Hundred-Fifty. She didn't know what had caused the holdup—not officially—but she suspected she wouldn't have liked the answer if she'd known it. The regular uniformed Shaft Police keeping the lifts shut down hadn't been answering any questions. In fact, they hadn't been saying *anything*, and that usually indicated that one of the federal police agencies—usually InSec or Mental Hygiene—was involved. Which, in turn, meant that some hapless "malcontent" or "anti-social provocateur" was being dragged from her apartment.

It was bad enough to be running late, but the suspicion that government thugs were hauling yet another citizen off, probably to disappear forever, had put her in a truly foul mood. At least whoever it was, she—or they; there was no reason there couldn't be more of them, and InSec, especially, preferred to arrest entire families "just in case"—wasn't one of the Pritcharts' neighbors. The raid was taking someplace between One-Fifty and One Hundred, judging from where the lifts were shut down, which meant it almost certainly wasn't someone Eloise knew personally.

And wasn't it a hell of a note when that was the closest thing to a bright side she could find?

She checked the time again as her current lift car slid to a halt. Unlike many of Nouveau Paris's newer towers, Duquesne used zonal "half-century" lifts, with dedicated shafts serving each fifty floors. Passengers had to change lifts at each boundary, but the system precluded the kind of wait times to which even a high-speed lift was subject if it served a tower's full three or four hundred— or, for that matter, *five* hundred, in the newer towers—floors. The problem was potentially even worse in those taller, newer towers, but most of them had been built with smart shafts, with multiple lift cars and bypass shunting sections. Each smart shaft could handle up to a dozen cars simultaneously, with the computers keeping track of them and moving them out of one another's way when necessary. It would have been nice if Duquesne had boasted the same technology, but it hadn't been available when the older tower was built. And, predictably, none of the bureaus and agencies theoretically responsible for maintaining and updating Duquesne had any interest in investing the funds to make it available here.

She'd already changed lifts twice since leaving the Cardot apartment, including the sixty-eight-minute delay on One-Fifty, and she'd have to change twice more before she reached ground level. Most of the trip didn't bother her, but the next change was on Floor Fifty, and that was something else. That was where The Terraces, with almost 200,000 square meters of floor space, had once been one of Duquesne Tower's crown jewels. Located at the transfer point of two of the residential floors' main banks of dedicated lift shafts, it had served almost 800,000 people. That had been a sufficient volume of customers to make it a highly profitable location even in the People's Republic of Haven.

Until fifteen or twenty T-years ago, at least.

Eloise could remember childhood trips to The Terraces. Trips when her mother had been laughing and happy, when they'd shared ice-cream cones while they dabbled their feet in one of the fountains. When there'd been shopkeepers and clerks who'd actually looked customers in the eye, smiled, greeted them courteously, sometimes even known them by name.

But then, probably inevitably, the endemic corruption had changed that. First the floor police force had begun charging higher and higher prices for "protection," and the independents had found themselves being forced out. As they'd begun going under, cronies of the local Dolist manager and fronts for his Legislaturalist friends had made them fire-sale offers for their shops. One by one, they'd vanished, merged into far larger stores which relied upon the fact that they had a captive market rather than the quality of the service and the goods they offered. The taxes—although, of course, they were officially only "service and handling charges"—on goods ordered from somewhere outside Duquesne meant that only the tower's wealthier residents could avoid The Terraces or one of the other smaller, less conveniently located, and more poorly stocked malls. And, of course, there were very few wealthy residents in Duquesne. People that adjective described could always find better places to live.

And so The Terraces had deteriorated, slowly at first, but with gathering momentum, into someplace shoppers avoided after hours and where prudent people—especially women and girls— never ventured alone, regardless of the time of day. A place where gangs—both youth gangs and those not so young—routinely robbed and beat customers, more often for fun than for profit, as far as Eloise could tell.

She and Estelle could have avoided The Terraces by using the Beta Bank of lifts, but that would have cost them a full hour of extra transit time between shafts… and that was if the slidewalks were up and running, which they often weren't. Still, if things got much worse at Fifty, they'd just have to bite the bullet and change their route, and wouldn't that suck?

And at that, she thought now, as the lift car stopped, *it's still better than the situation on Eighth. The only good thing about Eighth is that we go right past it, so unless somebody gets on as we go by...*

She stood with one hand in her left hip pocket and the other in the right jacket pocket as the lift car slid to a halt. There were six men and seven other women in the car with her, and perhaps two or three dozen people from other floors were changing shafts when the doors opened. She saw no sign of any of the competing gangs' colors, which made a nice change, but she didn't take her hands out of her pockets. At least one of the other women in her car had a hand in *her* pocket, too, Eloise noted, and wondered what sort of "little friend" the other might be carrying.

She moved smoothly, confidently across to the next bank of lifts, her eyes sweeping the concourse steadily and alertly. The best way to avoid trouble, as she'd pointed out to Kevin, was to see it before it saw her, and though her expression never so much as flickered, she drew a breath of relief as she made it to the appropriate shaft, stepped into the car, and started it downward once more.

Now all I have to do is get past Eighth, she told herself. *Piece of cake.*

✦ ✦ ✦

Eloise's eyes widened in shock as she stepped off the slidewalk outside the tube station in Subbasement One and saw the cordon of yellow holo flashers around Jorge's Diner. The diner's windows were smashed, its doors were jammed in the open position, drunkenly crooked on their tracks, and a uniformed floor cop in full riot gear stood in front of the door.

His eyes flitted to Eloise as she left the slidewalk and his right hand moved to the pulser holstered at his hip, but he didn't draw the weapon. The armorplast visor of his helmet was up, and he watched her with neither the interest she saw in most men's eyes nor the boredom or hostility she saw in too many cops' eyes.

"Help you, Citizen?" he asked gruffly as she came to a halt.

"My... my sister works here," she said. "I walk her home at the end of every shift. What... what happened?"

"Can't rightly say," he told her, taking his hand from his pulser, and she heard a note of sympathy in his voice. "We caught the call about an hour ago, I guess. Passer-by said there was some kind of riot going on. By the time we got here, the place was trashed. Found a guy we think is the owner from his ID back in the kitchen. He didn't look good, but medevac got here faster than usual, and I'm pretty sure he'll make it. He's in the clinic over off Broad and Vine. Know where it is?"

"Yeah," she said even as ice flowed through her veins. "It's four or five blocks from here. You say you found Jorge—I mean the owner?"

"Yep," the floor cop said, and her muscles tightened as his tone answered the question she'd been going to ask next. But she went ahead anyway, almost as if her vocal cords belonged to someone else.

"And my sister?"

"Nobody here but him. I'm sorry," the cop told her compassionately.

"And you don't have *any* idea what happened?" she asked desperately.

"Not any more than the original call," he said, "but I noticed that." He pointed, and her eyes followed the gesture to a shattered camera. "I happen to know that camera and the two between here and the Alpha Bank were up and running when I went on duty this morning. They aren't now. And there's new gang graffiti on the wall under the camera right outside the lifts. *That* wasn't there this morning, either."

"Did you recognize which gang's?" she heard herself ask.

"Not one of ours. Looks like the Hellhounds. They're from up—"

"Up on Fifty," she finished for him, her voice as grim as her topaz eyes. "The Terraces."

"That's what our gang warfare unit tells me, anyway," the cop agreed. "We didn't know there was any staff here besides the owner, so we didn't put out an AFB on her. I can do that now, if you'll give me a description."

"She looks like me," Eloise said bleakly. "She looks *exactly* like me."

Something flickered deep in the cop's eyes, and she remembered her discussion with Kevin.

"I'll put it on the full tower net," he promised her, reaching for the button of his com.

"Thank you," she said, but she knew as well as he did that an All-Floors Bulletin wouldn't do a damned bit of good if it had been the Hellhounds. No one on Fifty was going to risk her life by telling anybody anything about the Hellhounds. And even if someone had been willing to, the Fifty Floor Police would never go after a gang that powerful over something as trivial as a single missing young Dolist woman no one could *prove* was even anywhere in their hypothetical jurisdiction.

"All floors, be on the lookout—"

The cop broke off as Eloise turned toward the outbound slidewalk.

"Where you going?" he asked sharply, and she paused to look back at him.

"To find my sister." Her voice was flat, unyielding as steel. For a moment, she thought he might try to stop her. But then his lips thinned and he shook his head instead, his eyes dark.

"You be careful up there," he told her quietly. "You be *real* careful up there. Won't do your sister any good if you get yourself killed."

At least he hadn't said "get yourself killed, *too*," she reflected. Maybe he was an optimist.

"Oh, I'll be careful," she told him softly. "Thanks."

He nodded again as she turned once more for the slidewalk. Behind her, she heard him speaking into his com once more.

Not that it was going to do any good.

✦ ✦ ✦

She got off the lift at Fifty.

The handful of other passengers with whom she'd shared the car flowed around her as she stood motionless in the middle of the lift concourse. She didn't know any of them. She hadn't spoken to any of them as they rode up with her, and none of them had tried to speak to her. She didn't know what they'd seen in her eyes, but a couple had looked at her oddly, even warily. Now they all moved away from her more rapidly than usual, even for people changing lifts on Fifty.

She realized she didn't have the least idea what to do, how to begin. The thought of going to the floor cops didn't even occur to her, but what could one woman possibly hope to accomplish? It was insane, and she knew it, but that didn't matter. All she could think of was Estelle, and she made herself draw a deep breath, turned, and strode into The Terraces.

She took a hair tie from her pocket as she walked, reached back, and gathered her long, gleaming hair into the ponytail she wore during her workouts with Kevin. Then she drew her baton, holding it reversed against the inside of her left forearm, instantly ready yet effectively invisible. That, too, was something she practiced regularly, but the familiar weight, the familiar pressure against her forearm, was less reassuring today.

Kevin had often remarked on her "situational awareness," and he'd helped her devise exercises and contests to keep it honed. Now her eyes swept back and forth and her hearing seemed preternaturally sharp. Even the pores of her skin seemed to vibrate like tiny sensors, and her mind was a hollow, singing stillness. She didn't even think, not really. She just walked into the refuse-strewn wasteland which was all that remained of the vast, thriving mall her childhood memories recalled.

There were people about, even here. Most were dressed even more flashily—and cheaply—than the Dolist norm, and many of them wore colored scarfs which identified the floor gang to whom they paid protection. Whether or not to wear them, and when, was always a judgment call, that icy hollowness at her core reflected. When the gang front was fairly quiet, rivals tended to leave one another's "clients" in peace, lest they provoke retaliation against their own. When gangs went to war—which happened depressingly often—the scarves only served to better identify targets of opportunity.

Eloise and Estelle had always eschewed the bright colors and cheap costume jewelry the majority of Dolists favored. Now, a bubble seemed to form about her as she passed through that gaudier sea of color in her dark trousers, dark-blue jacket and long-sleeved white blouse, its tailored severity relieved only by touches of embroidery at collar and cuffs. The Terrace's denizens had the wary, well-honed instincts of any prey animal. They recognized the intruder and probably wondered what insanity had brought a single woman here all by herself.

She walked on, deeper into the dilapidated mall, and the bubble moved with her. Five minutes she walked. Ten.

"Honey," a voice said quietly. She turned her head and saw an older woman—or one who'd lived the sort of life that aged someone, at any rate. "Honey, was I you, I'd go home," the other woman said. She glanced around nervously. "Woman looks like you, doesn't come from around here, doesn't wear one of these," she touched the red-, black-, and yellow-checked ganger scarf around her own neck, "she doesn't make out well. Go home."

"I'm looking for someone," Eloise replied, her voice calm. Then the colors of that scarf registered. "Maybe you could tell me where to find her."

"I don't know nothing about any off-floor people," the other woman said more sharply. She started to step back, but Eloise's right hand fastened on her forearm. The woman's eyes widened at the power of that grip. She tried to jerk free, but she couldn't.

"I'm looking for the Hellhounds," Eloise said, twitching her head at that telltale scarf. "Where could I find them?"

"You're crazy," the woman whispered, shaking her head violently. "You're gonna get yourself killed!"

"Maybe," Eloise conceded emptily. "Where can I find them?"

The woman stared at her for perhaps ten seconds, licking her lips nervously. Then she drew a deep breath.

"Down that way." She twitched her head. "Hankies—it's a bar, belongs to the Hounds. Usually some of 'em hanging out there. But you don't want no part of those people! Trust me—you *don't*."

"As a matter of fact, I do," Eloise told her, and released her grip.

She started in the indicated direction. Her informant stared after her, then shook her head and moved rapidly in opposite way.

+ + +

Hankies was exactly the sort of bar Eloise usually avoided like the plague.

The flashing holo sign above the door showed a naked, improbably endowed woman holding a single strategically placed lacy handkerchief. It was as tasteless as it was flashy, and it needed maintenance. So did the rest of the bar, for that matter. Two thirds of the windowed wall looking out over the mall's promenade were sparkling clean; the center third was streaked and dirty. Clearly someone had replaced the original self-cleaning smart crystoplast with a cheaper substitute, and that central third was littered with the graffiti which wouldn't cling to the surviving self-cleaning panels.

The fire-breathing dog's head of the Hellhounds was prominent among them.

Her stride never paused. The doors slid open, a little haltingly, before her and admitted her to a dim, dark cave that smelled of stale beer, spilled drinks, and at least half a dozen of the more popular smoked and inhaled recreational drugs, all with a faint but unmistakable garnish of urine.

Somewhat to her surprise, it was deserted when she walked in. There wasn't even a bartender behind the streaked and grimy bar or keeping an eye on the self-service dispensers along one wall.

She started to turn on her heel, but she changed her mind. Instead, she crossed to a corner table, choosing one that would let her sit with solid walls on two sides, and pulled out a chair. She couldn't see the chair seat clearly in the poor lighting, which was probably a good thing, judging by the condition of the tabletop and the floor.

She sat, laying the baton in her lap, and leaned the back of her skull against the wall. Under her brain's icy calm a voice she recognized screamed that she had to be up, had to be out, had to be *looking* for Estelle. But that cold stillness knew better. Racing around, hunting blindly, would achieve nothing. She needed to know *where* to hunt.

Minutes trickled past while she sat there, forcing herself not to think. To simply *be* there, waiting. And then the doors opened again and a tallish, dark-haired young man in an especially gaudy, tasteless red, black, and yellow jacket sauntered arrogantly through them.

The newcomer glanced around casually, but he didn't notice Eloise as she sat motionless at her corner table. Instead, he crossed to the bar and leaned over it, looking both directions. Then he snorted harshly and smacked his palm on a glowing square set into the top of the bar. A bell clanged discordantly.

"Marcel!" he bellowed. "Damn it, Marcel! You're supposed to be watching the frigging bar!"

"Yeah, yeah, yeah," a much whinier voice replied from somewhere in the back. "Keep your shirt on, Hilaire! I was in the can. Only gone a minute!"

"The hell you were," Hilaire retorted. "In there watching porn again, you mean!"

"Well, what if I was?" Marcel demanded with defensive anger. "It's your shift, and you're a good five minutes late! Wouldn't have had to leave the bar to take a dump if *you'd* been here on time."

"I *wasn't* late—which you'd know if you'd been where the hell you were supposed to be when I walked in the door. I don't give a damn who your brother is, Marcel. Not anymore. You've been warned about this kind of crap a dozen times! Now you get your sorry ass over to Bernadette Street and you tell Gaspar why you weren't on the bar when I came in."

"Gaspar?" The self-righteous anger had vanished from Marcel's tone, replaced by something much more like panic.

"Yeah, Gaspar. And I'm gonna screen him to tell him you're coming," Hilaire said, thumping Marcel's suddenly deflated chest with an index finger. "So was I you, I wouldn't waste any frigging time getting there. He's gonna have enough to say to you without adding that to it—understood?"

"Under… understood," Marcel muttered.

He stood irresolute a moment longer, then headed for the door, his dejected shamble the antithesis of Hilaire's arrogant saunter.

Hilaire watched him go with a satisfied air before he started around behind the bar. Then he paused in mid-stride as he caught sight of Eloise from the corner of one eye and changed course toward her.

Eloise watched him come and wondered what to say. She was a tutor, not a cop or a trained interrogator. She wasn't even an ex-Marine like Kevin! What did *she* know about—?

The question broke off as something glittered in the bar's dank dimness, and her breathing seemed to stop. The rearing silver unicorn wasn't huge—barely four centimeters from the tip of its tiny spiral horn to its rear hoofs, and it hung from a leather thong, not the delicate silver chain which had supported it the last time she saw it—but she recognized it instantly. It had once belonged to her mother, and to her mother's mother, and to *her*… before she gave it to Estelle on her sixth birthday.

It was Estelle's only true treasure, worn under her clothing to avoid the acquisitive eyes of the thieves who were all too common in Duquesne Tower.

She straightened in her chair, and Hilaire stopped suddenly, his eyes widening as if in surprised recognition when he got a good look at her for the first time. He stood for a moment, then shook his head and continued until he reached the table behind which she sat.

"Help you, cutie?" he drawled.

"I think you can." Eloise was astounded by her own calm, conversational tone. "I'm looking for someone."

Her grip shifted slightly on the baton in her lap, her thumb resting lightly, almost hungrily, on the extender button.

"Now, who might that be?" Hilaire asked mockingly, left hand reaching deliberately to toy with the unicorn and be certain she'd seen it.

"I think you know who," Eloise said softly, and her knee slammed into the underside of the small, cheap plastic table.

Eloise was not an enormous woman, but she was an extraordinarily *fit* one and the table was light. Kevin Usher would have been proud of the way her knee hit it, and it rocketed upward. It was far too light to actually hurt or even inconvenience Hilaire in any way, of course, but he leapt at least a meter straight backward, away from the sheer, unexpected violence of its movement.

And as he leapt, Eloise Pritchart came to her feet.

Her thumb tapped the button three times, the baton flicked out to sixty centimeters, and she lashed it across his left kneecap like a whip. The enhanced inertia-loading at its tip boosted the impact energy by a factor of almost two and the sharp *"Crack!"* of contact disappeared into Hilaire's scream as the kneecap shattered like glass. He tumbled backward, hands reaching instinctively for the source of his agony, and as he hunched forward, the baton struck again, rising to slash vertically downward. It slammed directly into his left shoulder joint with vicious, premeditated precision, fracturing both the scapula and the head of his humerus, and this time his scream was a shriek.

He hit the floor, trying to curl into an agonized fetal knot, but before he could complete the move that dreadful baton whipped back down once more, exploding across his *right* knee joint as the leg drew defensively up toward his abdomen.

He screamed in fresh agony, and his right hand scrabbled toward a pocket, only to meet that hammering baton yet again. He slammed back onto his spine again, reeling away from the pain of a wrist reduced to gravel, and then Eloise's knee slammed down on his chest, something cold and hard pressed the front of his throat, and he froze as he heard the sudden, shrill, terrifying whine of an activated vibro blade.

His eyes were huge, filled with pain and terror, and she pressed the vibro blade's hilt against his throat. Then she squeezed the button, bringing the actual blade up, letting him hear it whine as it sliced into the floor beside him, and her eyes could have frozen a star's heart.

"You know exactly who," she told him, her voice even colder than her eyes. "Now tell me where she is."

"I... I..."

"I'll ask you once more," she said softly. "Then I take off your right hand. Then I'll ask again… before I take off your *left* hand. And after that—well, you get the picture."

"How… how do I know you won't kill me anyway?"

"You don't."

+ + +

I should've killed him anyway, Eloise thought as she made her way quietly down the alley. *And if he's sent me on a wild goose chase, or if… if she's not all right when I find her, I damned well* will *go back and kill him!*

She reached the service door and paused. She wore the outsized jacket she'd taken from Hilaire before she'd locked him in the strong room which housed Hankies' liquor supply. She'd drawn its hood up over her head on her way here and she left it there, hiding her face and hair from any cameras that might be monitoring the alley as she leaned her forehead against the door for a moment.

She blinked her eyes furiously while her right hand touched the hard shape of the unicorn under her blouse. She stayed that way for a handful of seconds before she inhaled deeply and pressed the button under the speaker beside the door. Several seconds passed, then—

"Yeah?" a voice growled from the speaker.

"Hilaire sent me," she replied. "From Hankies."

"Oh, yeah? And why'd he do that?"

"He said if I showed you a good time, you'd show *me* one," she said.

"Did, did he?" The man behind the voice chuckled. "Well, chickie, we're always up for a good time around here. Aren't we boys?"

She heard more laughter and several voices announcing ribald agreement. Then a buzzer sounded and the door slid open.

She stepped through it, left hand at her side, right hand in the pocket of Hilaire's jacket. It gave access to a very short entry hall, and she raised her left arm and used her forearm to sweep the hood from her head. Then she stepped through into the room beyond.

There were eight men in it. One wore only a pair of none-too-clean briefs and three were naked to the waist. The rest were in various states of undress, and all of them leered at her. But only for a moment. Just long enough for her appearance to register.

It was interesting, a tiny part of her noted. She could actually tell which of them were the quickest. The recognition didn't come to all of them instantly. It flowed from the fastest on his mental feet to the slowest like some visible wave. The entire process couldn't have taken more than a handful of heartbeats, but it seemed much longer as she watched. There were more than she'd anticipated. Hilaire had told her there'd be only three or four of them, and that same calm corner of her mind wondered if he'd deliberately lied or truly hadn't expected the others.

She should be terrified. She knew that as she faced them, but she wasn't. All she felt was… cold. Very cold.

"I'm here for my sister," she told them.

"Your sister?" The man who'd answered her knock over the speaker was taller and looked as if he were probably older than the others, although none of them could have been any older than Estelle, and he glanced quickly at his companions before he looked back at her. "What makes you think she's here?"

He kept his hands easily by his sides, but the fingers flicked outward and the other seven began sidling away from him and from one another, spreading out as widely as the room would allow.

"Hilaire was very forthcoming," she replied, baton hidden against her forearm, the hilt of the vibro blade resting lightly in her right palm. They were going to get in each other's ways if—when— this turned ugly, that calm inner voice told her. That was good. "He said this is where you brought her."

"Did, did he?" The leader's tone was light, almost caressing, but his eyes were calculating. "He tell you we showed *her* a good time?"

"No, he told me you dragged her in here, and you beat her, and you raped her." Her voice was still level, but it was no longer calm, and her eyes locked with his, clearly ignoring anyone else in the room. "I'm here to take her home."

"Well, now, that's gonna be just a little hard," he told her, and his lips twisted in a sneer. "See, she's not here anymore. We already sent her 'home.'"

His head flicked toward the red-painted hatch of a refuse disposal shaft. The kind that fed trash into the fusion-powered incinerators that served Duquesne Tower.

"Wasn't any fun anymore, so we didn't see any reason to keep her around," he told her, his tone no longer light, and an icicle pierced her heart as his eyes glittered viciously at her.

"Let's see if *you* last longer," he said.

He started toward her unhurriedly, confidently, and the world disappeared.

Later, in the nightmares, she would remember her own primal scream, the fury and the hatred and the grief and the devastating loss. She would remember the sudden alarm in his eyes, the way he stopped in his tracks. And she would remember the baton licking out from her left hand like a viper's tongue, the vibro blade coming out of her pocket, screaming to life with a fury and hatred of its own as she sent it to its full, illegal length. And she would remember stepping into them like the angel of death herself.

She remembered very little after that. Not in any detail. Not until she caught the last of them halfway out the door. In the end, he'd turned to run, but the vibro blade swept effortlessly through his right thigh and he smashed to the floor, screaming, clutching at the blood-fountaining stump with both hands.

"*Please!*" he screamed. "Oh, Christ, please! *Please!*"

She paused, glaring down at him, realizing her stolen jacket was sodden with other people's blood, feeling it hot and stinking like molten copper, oozing down her face, dripping from her hands. She drew a deep, shuddery breath, glanced over her shoulder, and wondered with a sort of lunatic calm why she wasn't gibbering in horror.

There wasn't a single intact body.

She noted a pair of pulsers lying on the floor, one of them still clutched in the fingers of a detached hand, but she had no memory of seeing the weapons or the hand before. In fact, she realized, she didn't remember actually *seeing* any of the Hellhounds from the instant the vibro blade came live. But now she did. She saw the severed limbs lying in bits and pieces in thick lakes of blood. Saw a head lying on the floor, staring at her with wide, disbelieving eyes. Another head, split vertically from crown to clavicle. A torso sliced cleanly in half, spilling organs and blood and a sewer stench.

She saw *everything*, and the vision engraved itself forever upon her memory in the flickering instant before her eyes swung back to the ganger in front of her.

"*Please,*" he whimpered his voice weaker as the blood continued to pour from his thigh.

"You're no fun anymore," she heard her own voice say calmly, conversationally. "No reason to keep you around any longer."

"*No, pl—!*" he screamed, and then Kevin's gift silenced him forever.

+ + +

"Do you know what time it—?"

Kevin Usher stopped dead as he opened his door and the doorbell stopped buzzing.

Eloise Pritchart stood there, her dark slacks streaked with something far darker, the cuffs of her white blouse black and stiff, her face still smeared with streaks of dried blood her mopping hands had missed. There was more blood in her hair, under her fingernails, and the nightmare heart of hell was in her eyes.

"Eloise?" he said very, very softly.

"Kevin," she replied, and his jaw clenched. He'd never heard that flat, cold deadness from her.

He moved wordlessly aside and she stepped past him so the door could close behind her. She looked around his living room as if she'd never seen it before, but he didn't think she was really seeing it now, either. She simply stood there, hands by her sides, her expression empty.

He touched her shoulder, and she let him steer her as if she were a mannequin as he seated her in one of his well-worn armchairs.

"Eloise?" he said again, and she blinked. Then, slowly, those desecrated eyes focused upon him.

"She's gone, Kev." The words were no longer dead, and his heart flinched from the endless ocean of pain that filled them, instead. "She's gone," she said again. "Just... *gone*. I'll never see her again. Never hug her. Never—"

Her voice broke, her shoulders quivered, and she buried her face in her hands. She jackknifed forward in the armchair, and he went to his knees beside her, wrapping his arms about her, as the sobs tore loose at last and ripped the heart right out of her.

+ + +

"Here," Usher said an eternity later as he handed her the coffee cup.

She accepted it with a wan smile and sipped, then coughed on the stiff jolt of whiskey he'd stirred into it. She managed to avoid spraying any of it across him, then took another, deeper swallow and leaned back in her chair.

"Christ, I'm sorry," he said, sinking into a facing chair. "I'm *so* sorry, Eloise."

"Wasn't anything you could've done." Her voice was hoarse

from weeping, but she shook her head firmly. "Wasn't anything anyone could've done. Except maybe the bastards who're *supposed* to keep things like this from happening."

"How'd you get all the way back to Two Hundred like that?" he asked in the tone of someone trying to deal with his own shock and pain, and gestured at the bloodstains.

"You think anyone wanted to get close to me looking like *this*?" There was very little humor in her harsh chuckle. "I walked clear back across The Terraces without anyone saying a word. Then caught the lift and came straight here. I doubt the shaft police will worry about the surveillance imagery at all, assuming the cameras even noticed it. Commissioner Juneau might have a few questions, but I don't expect any trouble from him or Aristide. They... they really liked Stelle, too, you know."

Her voice quivered, dropping almost to a whisper, on the last sentence, and she took another quick swallow of the whiskey-laced coffee.

"Jesus, Eloise." He shook his head, his eyes dark with grief of his own. "What're you going to do now? How can I help?"

"You can help me a lot, Kev." She looked him in the eye. "You already helped a lot. Without that vibro blade, I'd be dead, too, instead of them. But I need you to do something else for me, too."

"Anything," he told her flatly. "Name it."

"You might not want to be quite that quick about it," she cautioned him.

"Name it," he repeated in that same, unflinching voice, and she drew a deep breath, holding the coffee cup in both hands, gazing at him across it.

"A few weeks ago, I was reading a biography of Michèle Péricard," she said. "It made Stelle nervous, but it was one my mom recommended to me years ago. I've got it in my desk, if you'd like to read it. I think you'd like it. And it's got some interesting stuff in the appendices. Including the entire text of something called the Declaration of Independence."

"It does, does it?" He sat back in his own chair, his eyes narrowing in recognition that the seeming non sequitur was nothing of the sort.

"It does." She nodded. "I've been thinking about that a lot since then. Have you ever read it?"

"Never even heard of it," he admitted.

"Then you really need to read it," she said. "It's all nonsense, of course. Any Legislaturalist would tell you that. It talks about the consent of the governed, about unalienable rights, like the right to life, and liberty, and the pursuit of happiness. And it says that when a government *takes* those rights, when it governs *without* the consent of the governed, that it's the right—the *right*, Kevin, that comes from God, not some privilege governments can take away on a whim—of the people to *change* that government. The people who wrote that declaration launched a revolution over three thousand years ago, one that Michèle Péricard brought here, *right here* to Nouveau Paris. And the bastards who wrote the 'Constitution' we have today took every single one of those things away from us. They *took* them, Kevin, and they're never giving them back. *Never!*"

Tears glittered in her eyes, and her voice shook with her passion.

"My sister is dead because Michèle Péricard's Republic died before she was ever born. Stelle never had a chance, any more than you or me, to know what the Republic of Haven—the *Republic* of Haven; not the *People's* Republic of Haven—was supposed to be. And I never tried to do a thing about it for her because I was afraid of what would happen *to* her if I did try.

"But it didn't save her in the end, did it?" The tears broke loose, flowing down her cheeks, less tempestuous than her early sobs but glittering with the distilled essence of grief and loss. "I never took a stand, never tried to change things not just for Stelle, but for all the other Estelles, all the other sisters and daughters and brothers and sons. But the people who wrote that declaration... *they* took a stand. They *fought*. In the end they won, but they didn't know they were going to—that they even *could*—when they wrote it. All they knew—*all* they knew, Kevin—was what every one of them pledged to the nation they helped to build, to the future, to God, and to *each other*: 'our lives, our fortunes, and our sacred honor.' That's what they put on the table: every single thing they had. And now... now maybe it's time *I* did, too."

She drew another deep breath, her lips trembling.

"I never asked you about this, but I've always known, Kevin. I've known you're a hell of a lot more than just an ex-Marine who runs a dojo. I'm not going to ask you for any names, *but I want in.*"

Silence shimmered between them for a long, long time. Then, finally—

"Are you positive about that?" he asked her softly, not even pretending to misunderstand her. "I think I do want to read that declaration of yours, because it sounds like the folks who wrote it really understood. But are you sure *you* do? What you did today you did at least partly in self-defense but also in vengeance. Personal, white-hot, *hating* vengeance, Eloise. I'm not condemning you for a heartbeat for doing that," he continued as she started to stiffen. "God knows if I'd been able to get to the bastards who killed Estelle, I'd've done worse than you did. They'd have taken a *hell* of a lot longer dying, Eloise.

"But my point is that what... the people you're asking to join do, they *don't* do in a white-hot heat." He held her eyes very seriously. "Oh, some of them do. Some of them are *always* white hot, although I try to stay as far from people like that as I can, and *all* of us are as inspired by anger as we are by any actual sense of principle. But when it comes down to it, when somebody dies—if we do it right—it's cold and it's calculated. It may be hate that helps carry us, but it's a *cold* hate, Eloise. It's cold, and it's bitter, and it's its own kind of poison, and in time, it... leaves a mark. Are you sure you really want to add that to what you're already carrying around after today?"

"Yes," she said softly. "I couldn't save Estelle. I know that. But I can still give her something. I can give back the Republic of Haven in her name and the names of everyone else it's killed. I can drive a stake through the heart of this monster, and every time I hammer that stake a little deeper, I'll remember Estelle. I'll remember *my sister*, and I will *destroy* the People's Republic.

"I don't have any fortunes, Kevin. And I don't know how much of a life I have anymore. Right this minute, it doesn't feel like all that much or all that important. But I still have this. I have the right to choose, the right to say this is where it *stops*, the right to fight—and the right to by God *die*, if that's what it takes—for what I know is right. And that's exactly what I'm going to do."

"Just the same to you, Eloise," he said with a flickering smile, "I'd like for both of us to avoid the dying part. Can't exactly rebuild anything if we're not around when the rebuilding starts, can we?"

"No. And I didn't say I *wanted* to die. But if that's what it takes?" Her eyes bored into his, and her voice was soft. "If that's what it takes, then so be it."

"All right," he said after another long moment. "All right. What was that you said after lives and fortunes?"

"Honor. Our sacred honor," she replied, and he nodded.

"Our sacred honor, then," he repeated. "Yours and mine, Eloise. However long it takes."

He held out his hand.

She took it.

EDITOR BIOGRAPHY

BRYAN THOMAS SCHMIDT is a Hugo-nominated editor and author. His anthologies include *Shattered Shields* with Jennifer Brozek, *Mission: Tomorrow, Galactic Games, Little Green Men-Attack!* With Robin Wayne Bailey, *Joe Ledger: Unstoppable* with Jonathan Maberry, *Monster Hunter Files* with Larry Correia, *Infinite Stars*, and *Predator: If It Bleeds*. His debut novel, *The Worker Prince*, achieved Honorable Mention on Barnes and Noble's Year's Best SF of 2011. It was followed by two sequels in the Saga of Davi Rhii space opera trilogy. His short fiction includes stories in anthologies for *The X-Files*, *Predator*, Larry Correia's *Monster Hunter International*, Joe Ledger, and Decipher's *WARS*. He also edited *The Martian* by Andy Weir, among other novels. His work has been published by St. Martin's, Titan Books, Baen Books, and more. He lives in Ottawa, KS. Find him online as BryanThomasS at both Twitter and Facebook or via his website and blog at www.bryanthomasschmidt.net.

AUTHOR BIOGRAPHIES

ROBERT SILVERBERG is rightly considered by many as one of the greatest living science fiction writers. His career stretches back to the pulps and his output is amazing by any standards. He's authored numerous novels, short stories, and nonfiction books in various genres and categories. He's also a frequent guest at Cons and a regular columnist for Asimov's. His major works include *Dying Inside, The Book of Skulls, The Alien Years, The World Inside, Nightfall* with Isaac Asimov, *Son of Man, A Time of Changes*, and the seven Majipoor Cycle books. His first Majipoor trilogy, *Lord Valentine's Castle, Majipoor Chronicles*, and *Valentine Pontifex*, were reissued by ROC Books in May 2012, September 2012, and January 2013. *Tales of Majipoor*, a new collection bringing together all the short Majipoor tales, followed in May 2013.

ORSON SCOTT CARD is the *New York Times* bestselling and award-winning author of the novels *Ender's Game, Ender's Shadow*, and *Speaker for the Dead*, which are widely read by adults and younger readers, and are increasingly used in schools. His most recent series, the young adult Pathfinder series (*Pathfinder, Ruins, Visitors*) and the fantasy Mithermages series (*Lost Gate, Gate Thief*) are taking readers in new directions. Besides these and other science fiction novels, Card writes contemporary fantasy (*Magic Street, Enchantment, Lost Boys*), biblical novels (*Stone Tables, Rachel and Leah*), the American frontier fantasy series, The Tales of Alvin Maker (beginning with *Seventh Son*), poetry (*An Open Book*), and many plays and scripts. His latest novel, *Children of The Fleet*, in an all new series Fleet School, releases from TOR in Fall 2017.

Card currently lives in Greensboro, North Carolina, with his wife, Kristine Allen Card, where his primary activities are writing a review column for the local *Rhinoceros Times* and feeding birds, squirrels, chipmunks, possums, and raccoons on the patio.

The author of multiple *New York Times* bestsellers, **BRIAN HERBERT** has won several literary honors including the New York Times Notable Book Award, and has been nominated for the highest awards in science fiction. *Dreamer of Dune*, his moving biography of Frank Herbert, was a Hugo Award finalist. Brian's acclaimed novels include *Sidney's Comet*; *Sudanna Sudanna*; *The Race for God*; the Timeweb trilogy; *The Stolen Gospels*; and *Man of Two Worlds* (written with his father, Frank Herbert), as well as the epic fantasy, *Ocean*, and *The Little Green Book of Chairman Rahma*, in addition to the Hellhole trilogy and thirteen Dune series novels co-authored with Kevin J. Anderson.

In addition to his writing projects, Brian is also president of the company holding all of the Dune-series copyrights. In that capacity he recently signed a film deal with Legendary Pictures, and will serve as an Executive Producer and Creative Adviser on future motion picture and television projects.

KEVIN J. ANDERSON is the author of 140 novels, fifty-five of which have appeared on national or international bestseller lists; he has over twenty-three million books in print in thirty languages. Anderson has co-authored fourteen books in the Dune series with Brian Herbert; he and Herbert have also written an original SF trilogy, Hellhole. Anderson's popular epic space opera series, The Saga of Seven Suns, as well as its sequel trilogy, The Saga of Shadows, are among his most ambitious works. He has also written a sweeping fantasy trilogy, Terra Incognita, accompanied by two rock CDs (which he wrote and produced). He has written two steampunk novels, *Clockwork Angels* and *Clockwork Lives*, with legendary Rush drummer and lyricist Neil Peart. He also created the popular humorous horror series featuring Dan Shamble, Zombie P.I., and has written eight high-tech thrillers with Colonel Doug Beason. He holds a physics/astronomy degree and is now the publisher of Colorado-based WordFire Press.

New York Times bestselling author **WILLIAM C. DIETZ** has published more than fifty novels—some of which have been translated into German, French, Russian, Korean, and Japanese. Dietz also wrote the script for the *Legion of the Damned* game (for iOS) based on his book of the same name—and co-wrote SONY's *Resistance: Burning Skies* game for the PS Vita.

He grew up in the Seattle area, spent time with the Navy and Marine Corps as a medic, graduated from the University of Washington, lived in Africa for half a year, and has traveled to six continents. He has been employed as a surgical technician, college instructor, news writer, television producer, and Director of Public Relations and Marketing for an international telephone company. He and his wife live near Gig Harbor, in Washington State—where they enjoy traveling, kayaking, and reading books. For more about William C. Dietz and his fiction please visit williamcdietz.com or find him on Facebook at: www.facebook.com/williamcdietz and Twitter as William C. Dietz @wcdietz.

Paul Myron Anthony Linebarger (**CORDWAINER SMITH**), 1913–1966, had a Ph.D. in Political Science from Johns Hopkins University and spoke six languages. He spent the better part of his childhood in China and also served there in the US Army Intelligence Service during World War II. His book *Psychological Warfare* is still well regarded in its field. He was a Professor of Asiatic Politics at Johns Hopkins for many years and a leading member of the America Foreign Policy Association as well as being an advisor to President John F. Kennedy.

He published his first science fiction story at age fifteen and wrote novels under two pseudonyms. His first Cordwainer Smith story, "Scanners Live in Vain," appeared in 1950 and made his reputation. His entire science fiction output fills only four books, but "The Game of Rat and Dragon" is considered one of his finest, a classic of the field.

LOIS McMASTER BUJOLD was born in 1949, the daughter of an engineering professor at Ohio State University, from whom she picked up her early interest in science fiction. She now lives in Minneapolis, and has two grown children. She began writing with the aim of professional publication in 1982. She wrote three novels in three years; in October of 1985, all three sold to Baen Books, launching her career. Bujold went on to write many other books for Baen, mostly featuring her popular character Miles Naismith Vorkosigan, his family, friends, and enemies. Her fantasy from

HarperCollins includes the award-winning Chalion series and the Sharing Knife series. More recently she has been exploring self-e-publishing with the novella-length tales of the sorcerer Penric in the World of the Five Gods.

Ten times nominated for the Hugo Award for Best Novel, she has won in that category four times, in addition to garnering another Hugo for best novella, three Nebula Awards, three Locus Awards, the Mythopoeic Award, two Sapphire Awards, the Minnesota Book Award, the Forry Award, and the Skylark Award. In 2007, she was given the Ohioana Career Award, and in 2008 was Writer Guest-of-Honor for the 66th World Science Fiction Convention. A complete list may be found here: http://www.sfadb.com/Lois_McMaster_Bujold. Her works have been translated into over twenty languages. More information on Bujold and her books is archived at www.dendarii.com and her blog at www.goodreads.com/author/show/16094.Lois_McMaster_Bujold/blog.

ELIZABETH MOON, a Texas native, is a Marine Corps veteran (Viet Nam era) with degrees in history (Rice University) and biology (University of Texas.) She has published twenty-seven novels in both science fiction and epic fantasy, including *Sheepfarmer's Daughter* (Compton Crook Award winner, first volume of The Deed of Paksenarrion), Hugo-nominated *Remnant Population*, and Nebula Award winner *The Speed of Dark*, as well as three short-fiction collections, including *Moon Flights* (2007) and *Deeds of Honor*, ebook and POD (2014). She received the Heinlein Award for body of work in 2007. Over forty short works have appeared in anthologies and magazines. Her latest novel is *Cold Welcome*, a return to the Vatta universe (April 2017) and she is nearing completion of its sequel, *Into the Fire*. This story fits between *Victory Conditions* (Vatta's War 5) and *Cold Welcome* (Vatta's Peace 1). Moon lives in Central Texas with her husband, and spends nonwriting time cooking, knitting socks, photographing native plants and animals, and singing in a choir.

DAVE BARA was born at the dawn of the space age and grew up watching the Gemini and Apollo space programs on television, dreaming of becoming an astronaut one day. This soon led him to an interest in science fiction on TV, in film, and in books. Dave's writing is influenced by the many classic SF novels he has read over the years from SF authors like Isaac Asimov, Arthur C. Clarke, and Frank Herbert, among many others.

CATHERINE ASARO is an author of science fiction, fantasy, and thrillers, and has written over twenty-five novels, as well as short stories and nonfiction. Her acclaimed Ruby Dynasty series combines adventure, hard science, math, romance, and fast-paced action. Among her numerous distinctions, she has won the Nebula and Analog Reader's Choice awards. Her most recent books are the novels *Undercity* (Baen/Simon & Schuster) and *Lightning Strike, Book I* (Spectrum). A collection of several of her Ruby Dynasty short stories is available in the limited release anthology titled *Aurora in Four Voices* (ISFiC Press). All her novels are available in audio form. Her book *The Bronze Skies* (a Skolian Empire/Major Bhaajan book) will be released from Baen in 2017.

Catherine earned her doctorate in theoretical chemical physics from Harvard. She has coached numerous math teams and currently directs the Chesapeake Math Program, and she is known for her advocacy in bringing girls and women into STEM fields. Her students have won top honors in many competitions, including the USA Mathematical Olympiad and the USA Mathematical Talent Search. An invited speaker at various institutions, including the National Academy of Sciences, Harvard, Georgetown, NASA, the New Zealand Context Writer's program, and the US Naval Academy, she is a member of SIGMA, a think tank of speculative writers that advises the government on future trends affecting national security. She also appears as a speaker and vocalist at cons, clubs, and other venues in the US and abroad, including as the Guest of Honor at the Denmark and New Zealand National Science Fiction Conventions. You can chat with her at www.facebook.com/Catherine.Asaro, twitter.com/Catherine_Asaro, and Google+.

NNEDI OKORAFOR's books include *Lagoon* (a British Science Fiction Association Award finalist for Best Novel), *Who Fears Death* (a World Fantasy Award winner for Best Novel), *Kabu Kabu* (a Publisher's Weekly Best Book for Fall 2013), *Akata Witch* (an Amazon.com Best Book of the Year), *Zahrah the Windseeker* (winner of the Wole Soyinka Prize for African Literature), and *The Shadow Speaker* (a CBS Parallax Award winner). Her adult novel *The Book of Phoenix* (prequel to *Who Fears Death*) was released in May 2015; the *New*

York Times called it a "triumph." Her novella *Binti* was released in late September 2015 and won both the Hugo Award and the Nebula and her young adult novel *Akata Witch 2: Breaking Kola* released in 2016. Nnedi holds a Ph.D. in literature/creative writing and is an associate professor at the University at Buffalo, New York (SUNY). She splits her time between Buffalo and Chicago with her daughter Anyaugo and family. Learn more about Nnedi at Nnedi.com.

JERRY EUGENE POURNELLE is an American science fiction writer, essayist, and journalist and also a polymath, with degrees in statistics, systems engineering, psychology, and political science. He started writing non-science fiction work under the pseudonym of Wade Curtis or J.E. Pournelle. His stories always display a strong military theme and depict the progress of the people as dependent upon the advancement in technology. Usually certain complicated social issues, arising from the technology, are dealt with through politically incorrect ways. He is also popular for the various "laws" that he published in his books, the most famous being his Iron Law of Bureaucracy.

As a journalist, he earned recognition in the computer industry for his monthly columns in *Byte* magazine, the industry's first and the longest-running monthly column, running for a period of over twenty years. After the termination of his contract he moved the column to his own website.

He attained great fame and recognition for the books he co-wrote with Larry Niven. Their 1985 novel *Footfall* reached the No. 1 spot on the *New York Times* Best Seller List and *Lucifer's Hammer* (1977) reached No. 2 on the same list. Another of their novels, *The Mote in God's Eye*, was a huge success as was the sequel *The Gripping Hand*. Pournelle won the John W. Campbell Award for Best New Writer in 1973. In 1992, his book *Fallen Angels* got him the Prometheus Award and he became the co-recipient of the Heinlein Society Award with author-friend Larry Niven in 2005. He is a fellow of the American Association for the Advancement of Science, the British Interplanetary Society, the Royal Astronomical Society and the Operations Research Society of America. Other important works include *King David's Spaceship*.

LARRY NIVEN graduated Washburn University in Kansas in June 1962 with a B.A. in Mathematics with a Minor in Psychology. His first published story, "The Coldest Place," appeared in the December 1964 issue of *Worlds of If*. He went on to win Hugo Awards for "Neutron Star," 1966; *Ringworld*, 1970; "Inconstant Moon," 1971; "The Hole Man," 1974; and "The Borderland of Sol," 1975. And a Nebula for Best Novel: *Ringworld*, in 1970.

His latest novels include collaborations: *Inferno II: Escape From Hell* with Jerry Pournelle, *The Bowl Of Heaven* with Gregory Benford, *The Moon Maze Game* with Steven Barnes, *Shipstar* with Gregory Benford. And forthcoming: *The Seascape Tattoo* with Steven Barnes.

JEAN JOHNSON currently has twenty-five books published, including two collections, and a plethora of short stories, with more on the way. Her specialty lies in epic multi-novel series, but she does enjoy writing for anthologies.

Currently, Jean lives and works in the Pacific Northwest, sharing her home with a cranky cat, cousins, and her computer. She hopes you'll enjoy her portion of the *Infinite Stars* menu, and if you'd like to chat with her, she can be found at www.JeanJohnson. net, on Twitter @JeanJAuthor, on Facebook at Fans of Author Jean Johnson, or at JeanJAuthor.Tumblr.com. (The usual disclaimer: the publisher, et al, are not affilliated with nor responsible for any of these websites. Travel the internet with common sense safety in mind, please.)

LEIGH BRACKETT (1915–1978), a screenwriter and author, spent most of her career deeply involved in the writing of fantasy and science fiction, for which she perhaps remains best known. Her screenplays include *The Vampire's Ghost* (1945) and *The Long Goodbye* (1973); and Howard Hawks's *The Big Sleep* (1946) and *Rio Bravo* (1958), and also the first draft for *Star Wars: Episode V—The Empire Strikes Back* (1980), for which she posthumously received a 1981 Hugo Award. None of her television work is in the fields of the fantastic.

In 1940 Brackett began publishing stories of genre interest with "Martian Quest" for *Astounding*, beginning her period of greatest activity in the science fiction magazines. Her work appeared mostly in Planet Stories, Thrilling Wonder Stories, and others that offered space for what rapidly became her speciality: swashbuckling but literate planetary romances, usually set on a Mars not dissimilar to Edgar Rice Burroughs's pioneering creation of a romantic venue out of the speculations of Percival Lowell and others about the possibility of canals—and hence civilizations, presumably ancient—on that planet. Brackett used something like Burroughs's Mars in much of her work, though there is only an occasional geographical or "historical" continuity linking her various venues. The most memorable result were her series of Eric John Stark stories.

By the 1950s, Brackett began concentrating more on interstellar space operas, including The Starmen and *Alpha Centauri—or Die!* But these pale beside Brackett's best single pure-science fiction work, *The Long Tomorrow* (1955), a slow, impressively warm and detailed epic of two boys and their finally successful attempts to find Bartorstown, where people are secretly re-establishing science and technology in a technophobic, controlled world. After 1955, Brackett generally preferred to work in films and television. She was inducted into the Science Fiction Hall of Fame in 2014.

EDMOND HAMILTON (1904–1977) was a married to Leigh Brackett from 1946 until his death. With E.E. "Doc" Smith and Jack Williamson, he was one of the prime movers in the creation and popularization of classic space opera as it first appeared in Pulp magazines from about 1928. His first story, "The Monster-God of Mamurth" for *Weird Tales* in August 1926, vulgarized the florid weird-science world of Abraham Merritt and only hinted at the exploits to come. This story and others were collected in his first book, *The Horror on the Asteroid & Other Tales of Planetary Horror* in 1936. But his true significance came with the publication of "Crashing Suns" (August–September 1928 *Weird Tales*), one of the founding texts of the kind of space opera with which he soon became identified: a Universe-spanning tale, often featuring in early years an Earthman and his comrades (not necessarily human) who discover a cosmic threat to the home galaxy and successfully—either alone, or with the aid of a space armada, or both—combat the aliens responsible for the threat. Though not technically part of the series, "Crashing Suns" is closely linked to the six Tales of the Interstellar Patrol stories, which followed over the next two years. Others of his works contributing to the creation of the form include "The Metal Giants" (December 1926 *Weird Tales*), "The Comet Doom" (January 1928 *Amazing*), and "The Universe Wreckers" (May–July 1930 *Amazing*).

Hamilton also occupied much of his time in the early 1940s with the Captain Future series, published 1940–1950 by Standard

Magazines in *Captain Future* (1940–1944) and afterwards in *Startling Stories* (1945–1946 and 1950–1951). The original idea for Captain Future had come from Mort Weisinger, a senior editor with the Standard Magazines group. Later, in 1941, Weisinger shifted over to DC Comics and took many of his top writers with him, including Hamilton, who worked for some time in the mid-1940s as a staff writer on *Superman*, along with Henry Kuttner and others.

His novels include *The Monsters of Juntonheim: A Complete Book-Length Novel of Amazing Adventure* (January 1941); *City at World's End* (1951); *The Star of Life* (1959) and *The Valley of Creation* (1964). It is for these novels that he is now mainly remembered. The best of them is probably *The Haunted Stars* (1960), in which well-characterized humans face a shattering mystery on the moon.

JODY LYNN NYE lists her main career activity as "spoiling cats." She lives near Chicago with her current cat, Jeremy, and her husband, Bill. She has published more than forty-five books, including collaborations with Anne McCaffrey and Robert Asprin, and over 150 short stories. Her latest books are *Rhythm of the Imperium* (Baen), *Moon Beam* (with Travis S. Taylor (Baen), and *Myth-Fits* (Ace). She also teaches the annual DragonCon Two-Day Writers Workshop.

LINDA NAGATA is a Nebula and Locus-award-winning writer, best known for her high-tech science fiction, including The Red trilogy, a series of near-future military thrillers. The first book in the trilogy, *First Light*, was a Nebula and John W. Campbell Memorial-award finalist and named as a *Publishers Weekly* Best Book of 2015. Book 3, *Going Dark*, was a runner-up for the Campbell Memorial award. Her newest novel is the very near-future thriller, *The Last Good Man*. Linda has lived most of her life in Hawaii, where she's been a writer, a mom, a programmer of database-driven websites, and lately, an independent publisher. She lives with her husband in their long-time home on the island of Maui.

ALASTAIR REYNOLDS was born in Barry, South Wales, in 1966. Early on in life he discovered a fascination for space and the future, two strands which led him first to a career in astronomy, and more recently his profession as a writer. He has been publishing short fiction for more than a quarter of a century, and recently saw the appearance of his massive retrospective collection, *Beyond the Aquila Rift* from Subterranean Press and Orion. He is currently finishing his fifteenth solo novel, which takes place in the same universe as "Night Passage". A committed European, he has lived in England, Wales, Scotland, and the Netherlands, and is married into an extended family with roots in France, Spain, and Germany.

POUL WILLIAM ANDERSON was born in Pennsylvania to Scandinavian parents and the family lived for a time in Denmark before moving back to the United States after the outbreak of the Second World War. They settled in Minnesota where Anderson received a degree in Physics from the University of Minnesota.

He began writing while still an undergraduate and saw his first story published in 1947. He was active throughout the second half of the twentieth century, producing such classic works as the Dominic Flandry books, *The High Crusade* and his Galactic Patrol stories. He won multiple Hugo and Nebula Awards and served as President of Science Fiction and Fantasy Writers of America as well as being a founding member of the Society for a Creative Anachronism. In 1988 he was honored as a SFWA Grandmaster. He died in 2001.

New York Times bestselling author **A.C. CRISPIN** (1950–2013) wrote prolifically in many different tie-in universes, and was a master at filling in the histories of beloved TV and movie characters. She began publishing in 1983 with the *Star Trek* novel *Yesterday's Son*, written in her spare time while working for the US Census Bureau. Shortly thereafter, Tor Books commissioned her to write what is perhaps still her most widely read work, the 1984 novelization of the television miniseries, *V*, which sold more than a million copies.

For *Star Wars*, Crispin wrote the bestselling Han Solo Trilogy: *The Paradise Snare*, *The Hutt Gambit*, and *Rebel Dawn*, which tell the story of Han Solo from his early years right up to the moment he walks into the cantina in *Star Wars: A New Hope*. She wrote three other bestselling *Star Trek* novels: *Time for Yesterday*, *The Eyes of the Beholders*, and *Sarek*. Her final tie-in novel was the massive *Pirates of the Caribbean: The Price of Freedom*, which was published in 2011. She was named a Grandmaster by the International Association of Media Tie-In Writers in 2013.

Her major original science fiction undertaking was the

StarBridge series. These books, written solo or in collaboration, centered around a school for young diplomats, translators, and explorers, both alien and human, located on an asteroid far from Earth. Series titles are: *StarBridge*, *Silent Dances*, *Shadow World*, *Serpent's Gift*, *Silent Songs*, *Voices of Chaos*, and *Ancestor's World*.

Crispin was a fierce advocate for writers. She and author Victoria Strauss created and co-chaired SFWA's "scam watchdog" committee, Writer Beware, in 1998.

BENNETT R. COLES served fifteen years as an officer in the Royal Canadian Navy. He thought his career was pretty cool, but that it would be even cooler if it was in SPACE! Lacking the budget to launch his own space navy, he started writing. The Virtues of War trilogy is the result. Coles draws inspiration both from his own time in uniform and from the great authors of military science fiction over the years. Both as an author with Titan Books and as the publisher at Promontory Press, Coles loves the fact that he can pursue his passion for a living. He makes his home in Victoria, Canada, with his wife and two sons.

ANNE McCAFFREY's first novel was written in Latin class and might have brought her instant fame, as well as an A, if she had written it in that ancient language. Much chastened by teacher and father, she turned to the stage and became a character actress, appearing in the first successful summer music circus in Lambertsville, NJ. She studied voice for nine years and, during that time, became intensely interested in the stage direction of opera and operetta, ending that phase of her experience with the direction of the American premiere of Carl Orff's *Ludus De Nato infante Mirificus* in which she also played a witch.

Her working career included Liberty Music Shops and Helena Rubinstein (1947–1952). She married in 1950 and has three children: Alec Anthony, b. 1952, Todd, b. 1956, and Georgeanne, b. 1959.

Anne McCaffrey's first story was published by Sam Moskowitz in *Science Fiction + Magazine* and her first novel was published by Ballantine Books in 1967. By the time the three children of her marriage were comfortably in school most of the day, she had already achieved enough success with short stories to devote full time to writing. Her first novel, *Restoree*, was written as a protest against the absurd and unrealistic portrayals of women in s-f novels in the '50s and early '60s. It is, however, in the handling of broader themes and the worlds of her imagination, particularly the two series The Ship Who Sang (which later became the Brainship series) and the fourteen novels about the Dragonriders of Pern that Ms. McCaffrey's talents as a storyteller are best displayed.

DR. CHARLES E. GANNON's award-winning Caine Riordan/Terran Republic hard science fiction novels have, as of this writing, all been Nebula finalists and national bestsellers. His epic fantasy series, The Broken World, is forthcoming from Baen Books. He also collaborates with Eric Flint in the NYT and WSJ bestselling Ring of Fire alternate history series. His other novels and short fiction straddle the divide between hard SF and technothrillers, and much of this work includes collaborations in the Starfire, Honorverse, Man-Kzin, and War World universes. He also worked extensively in game design and writing, as well as being a scriptwriter and producer in New York City, where his clients included the United Nations, the World Health Organization, and PBS.

A Distinguished Professor of English and Fulbright Senior Specialist, Gannon's *Rumors of War and Infernal Machines* won the 2006 American Library Association Choice Award for Outstanding Book. He is a recipient of five Fulbright Fellowships/Grants and has been a subject matter expert both for national media venues such as NPR and the Discovery Channel, as well as for various intelligence and defense agencies, including the Pentagon, Air Force, Army, Marines, Navy, NATO, DARPA, NRO, DHS, NASA, and several other organizations with which he signed NDAs.

DAVID DRAKE (born 1945) sold his first story (a fantasy) at age twenty. His undergraduate majors at the University of Iowa were history (with honors) and Latin (B.A., 1967). He uses his training in both subjects extensively in his fiction.

David entered Duke Law School in 1967 and graduated five years later (J.D., 1972). The delay was caused by his being drafted into the US Army. He served in 1970 as an enlisted interrogator with the 11th Armored Cavalry Regiment, the Blackhorse, in Vietnam and Cambodia. He has used his legal and particularly his military experiences extensively in his fiction also.

David practiced law for eight years; drove a city bus for one year; and has been a full-time freelance writer since 1981. He reads and travels extensively. His website, david-drake.com, will tell you a great deal more as well as permit you to contact him.

JACK CAMPBELL (John G. Hemry) writes the *New York Times* bestselling Lost Fleet and Lost Stars series, and the "steampunk meets high fantasy" Pillars of Reality series. His most recent books are *Vanguard*, the first book in *The Genesis Fleet*, and *Daughter of Dragons*. John's works have been published in twelve languages. His short fiction includes a wide variety of works covering time travel, alternate history, space opera, military SF, fantasy, and humor. May 2017 will see his critically-acclaimed Lost Fleet series come to comics for the first time. *The Lost Fleet: Corsair*—written by Jack Campbell and illustrated by Andre Siregar and Sebastian Cheng—is an all-new comic book from the universe of the best-selling sci-fi novel series. John has also written a fair amount of nonfiction, including articles on real declassified Cold War plans for US military bases on the moon, and "Liberating the Future: Women in the Early Legion" (of Superheroes) in Sequart's *Teenagers From the Future*.

John is a retired US Navy officer, who served in a wide variety of jobs including surface warfare (the ship drivers of the Navy), amphibious warfare, anti-terrorism, and intelligence. Being a sailor, he has been known to tell stories about Events Which Really Happened (but cannot be verified by any independent sources). This experience has served him well in writing fiction. He lives in Maryland with his indomitable wife "S" and three great kids (all three on the autism spectrum).

A lifetime military history buff, *New York Times* bestselling author **DAVID WEBER** has carried his interest in history into his fiction. In the Honor Harrington series, multiple volumes published by Baen Books, the spirit of both C.S. Forester's Horatio Hornblower and history's Admiral Nelson are evident. Weber's other space opera epic, Safehold, from TOR Books is in multiple volumes as well. He has written an epic fantasy, *Oath of Swords*, and many other science fiction books, including collaborations in the *1632 Ring of Fire* universe with Eric Flint, collaborations with John Ringo, Timothy Zahn, Steve White, and many more. He lives in Greenville, South Carolina, with multiple dogs, cats, children, and his lovely wife Sharon and a huge collection of Honor Harrington artwork.

For more fantastic fiction, author events, exclusive
excerpts, competitions, limited editions and more

VISIT OUR WEBSITE
titanbooks.com

LIKE US ON FACEBOOK
facebook.com/titanbooks

FOLLOW US ON TWITTER
@TitanBooks

EMAIL US
readerfeedback@titanemail.com